Assassin's Price

Tor Books by L. E. Modesitt, Jr.

Assassin's Price

The Eleventh Book of the
Imager Portfolio

L. E. MODESITT, JR.

TOR

A TOM DOHERTY ASSOCIATES BOOK
NEW YORK

ASSASSIN'S PRICE

Copyright © 2017 by L. E. Modesitt, Jr.

A Tor Book
Published by Tom Doherty Associates
175 Fifth Avenue
New York, NY 10010

www.tor-forge.com

Tor® is a registered trademark of Macmillan Publishing Group, LLC.

The Library of Congress Cataloging-in-Publication Data
is available upon request.

ISBN 978-0-7653-9047-9 (hardcover)
ISBN 978-0-7653-9049-3 (ebook)

Our books may be purchased in bulk for promotional, educational, or business use. Please contact your local bookseller or the Macmillan Corporate and Premium Sales Department at 1-800-221-7945, extension 5442, or by email at MacmillanSpecialMarkets@macmillan.com.

First Edition: July 2017

Printed in the United States of America

0 9 8 7 6 5 4 3 2 1

For Dennis,
proof that good things can indeed come from F&SF,
and to those who share that love

CHARACTERS

REGIAL FAMILY

LORIEN D'REX   Rex of Solidar

CHELIA'D'LORIEN   Lorien's wife, sister of High Holder Ryel

CHARYN D'LORIEN   Eldest son of Lorien

BHAYRN D'LORIEN   Second son of Lorien

ALORYANA D'LORIEN   Daughter of Lorien

HIGH HOLDERS

AISHFORD D'ALTE   Nordeau

BASALYT D'ALTE   Bartolan, High Councilor

CALKORAN D'ALTE   Vaestora

CAEMRYN D'ALTE   Yapres

DELCOEUR D'ALTE   L'Excelsis

FHAEDYRK D'ALTE   Dyrkholm, High Councilor

KHUNTHAN D'ALTE   Eshtora, High Councilor

LAEVORYN D'ALTE   L'Excelsis

MOERYN D'ALTE   Khelgror

MEINYT D'ALTE   Alkyra

NACRYON D'ALTE   Mantes

OLEFSYRT D'ALTE   Noira

OSKARYN D'ALTE   Cloisonyt, High Councilor

PAELLYT D'ALTE   Sommeil

REGIAL D'ALTE   Montagne Minor son of Ryentar

RUELYR D'ALTE   Ruile

RYEL D'ALTE   Head, High Holder's Council, Rivages

DORYANA D'RYEL   Wife of Ryel

SOUVEN D'ALTE   Dueraan
STAENDEN D'ALTE   Tacqueville
ZAERLYN D'ALTE   Rivages, brother of Alyna

IMAGERS

ALASTAR   Maitre D'Image
ALYNA   Maitre D'Image, wife of Alastar
AKORYT   Maitre D'Structure
BELSIOR   Maitre D'Structure
GAELLEN   Maitre D'Structure, healer
KHAELIS   Maitre D'Structure
SHAELYT   Maitre D'Structure
TIRANYA   Maitre D'Structure
ARTHOS   Maitre D'Aspect
CHARLINA   Maitre D'Aspect
CLAEYND   Maitre D'Aspect
DAVOUR   Maitre D'Aspect
DYLERT   Maitre D'Aspect
HOWAL   Maitre D'Aspect
JAIMS   Maitre D'Aspect
KAYLET   Maitre D'Aspect, assistant stablemaster
LHENDYR   Maitre D'Aspect
LYSTARA   Maitre D'Aspect, daughter of Alastar and Alyna
MALYNA   Maitre D'Aspect, niece of Alyna
NARRYN   Maitre D'Aspect
ORLANA   Maitre D'Aspect
PETROS   Maitre D'Aspect, stablemaster
THELIA   Maitre D'Aspect, Collegium bookkeeper
YULLA   Maitre D'Aspect
WARRYK   Maitre D'Aspect
ARION   Maitre D'Esprit, Maitre of Westisle Collegium
SELIORA   Maitre D'Structure, Westisle, wife of Arion
LYNZIA   Maitre D'Aspect, Westisle
TAUREK   Maitre D'Structure, Estisle
CELIENA   Maitre D'Aspect, Estisle

FACTORS

CUIPRYN D'FACTORIUS   Brass/copper

DUURMYN D'FACTORIUS   Livestock, stockyards

ELTHYRD D'FACTORIUS   Timber, lumber, Chief, Factors' Council, L'Excelsis

ESTAFEN D'FACTORIUS   Banque D'Excelsis, ironworks

GOERYND D'FACTORIUS   Pumps, plows, implements,

HARLL D'FACTORIUS   Brick and stone, Factor's Council, Montaigne

HISARIO D'FACTORIUS   Shipping, Factors' Council, Liantiago

JHALIOST D'FACTORIUS   Salt, coal, Factors' Council, Khelghor

JHULET D'FACTORIUS   Grain and maize

KARL D'FACTORIUS   Iron, smelting

KATHILA D'FACTORIA   Spices, scents, and oils

MAARTYN D'FACTORIUS   Brick and stone

LYTHORYN D'FACTORIUS   Mining, custom minting

ROBLEN D'FACTORIUS   Woolens and cloth

PAERSYT D'FACTORIUS   Custom forging

THALMYN D'FACTORIUS   Fishing, Factors' Council, Tilbora

WALLTYL D'FACTORIUS   Coaches, carriages, wagons

WEEZYR D'FACTORIUS   Banque D'Aluse

OTHERS

VAELLN D'CORPS   Marshal of the Armies

MAUREK D'CORPS   Vice Marshal

TYNAN D'NAVIA   Sea Marshal

CHAALT D'CORPS   Commander, Chief of Staff,

LUERRYN D'CORPS   Subcommander

AEVIDYR D'SOLIDAR   Minister of Administration

ALUCAR D'SOLIDAR   Minister of Finance

SANAFRYT D'SOLIDAR   Minister of Justice

LYTARRL D'ANOMEN   Chorister, Anomen D'Excelsis, brother of Elthyrd

SAERLET D'ANOMEN   Chorister, Anomen D'Rex

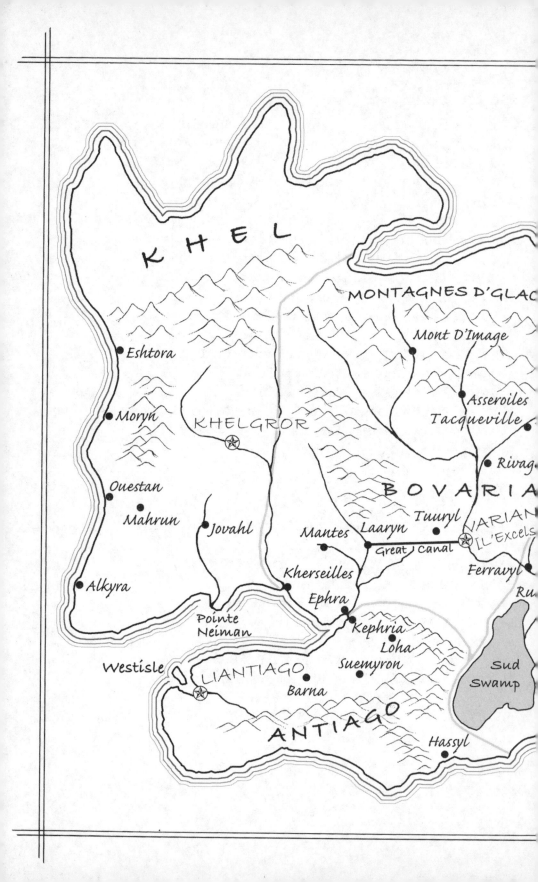

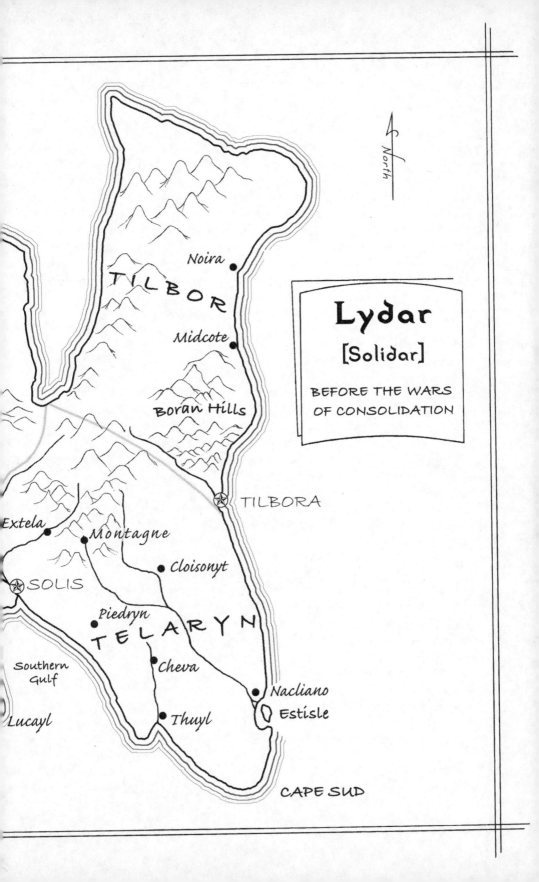

North

Lydar
[Solidar]

BEFORE THE WARS
OF CONSOLIDATION

TILBOR

Noira

Midcote

Boran Hills

⊛ TILBORA

Extela

Montagne

Cloisonyt

⊛ SOLIS

Piedryn

T E L A R Y N

Southern
Gulf

Cheva

Nacliano

Estisle

Lucayl

Thuyl

CAPE SUD

Assassin's Price

PRELUDE

At a quint before eighth glass, a chill early autumn wind blew through the covered courtyard. Two men stood at one end, one young and wearing a tailored greenish gray woolen jacket and matching trousers with black boots, the other gray-haired and wearing the black and green uniform of the chateau guards.

The younger man looked disgustedly at the man-shaped targets ten yards away, then turned. "Half the time, the Namer-damned pistol doesn't fire straight!" Charyn glared at Guard Captain Churwyl. "If I'm more than five paces away, it's unreliable. I've even brought a carpenter's vise out here and tried it."

"Lord Charyn, that's why I suggested . . ."

"I don't want to use a blade. If I'm ever attacked, it will be at close quarters, and I likely won't be anywhere near a sabre or any sort of blade. I need a weapon that fits inside a jacket and that can fire several shots."

The guard captain was silent.

"Isn't there anyone in L'Excelsis who can craft an accurate pistol?"

"You've tried all of those who now make pistols."

"Who now make them? Is there someone else who did or could?"

"It's said . . . only said . . . that Factor Paersyt used to make the best pistols."

"Used to? Is he dead?"

"No, sir. He doesn't do that now."

"How will that help?"

"It's the best answer I can offer, sir. You've tried pistols from every factor in L'Excelsis who makes them. You've found none of them satisfactory."

"Then we'll go to see Factorius Paersyt. Now."

"Now, sir? The factor may not—"

"Now! I'll meet you outside the stables in half a quint. We'll worry about what he may or may not wish later."

"Yes, sir."

Charyn ignored the Guard Captain's thinly veiled consternation and walked swiftly back to the chateau. Less than a third of a quint later, he was striding into the stable yard, wearing a riding jacket of the same greenish gray as his trousers. His riding gloves were gray, and he wore a gray visor cap without insignia.

Churwyl was waiting, with two mounts and two chateau guards.

"Where is Paersyt's factorage?" asked Charyn.

"On the West River Road, north of the barge piers, sir."

"Thank you." Charyn mounted the chestnut stallion.

Once the four riders were on the ring road that circled the Chateau D'Rex, heading south toward the Avenue D'Commercia, Charyn turned to Churwyl, who rode on his left. "What else do you know about Factorius Paersyt?"

"He is said to forge devices for all manner of other factors."

"A toolmaker of sorts, then?"

"More than that, it is said, but I do not know more than I have told you."

"Why do you know about him?"

"Upon occasion, those in the chateau have had need of his services. He created the locks for the strongrooms when the old ones failed. I also believe he created the framework in the kitchen that allows the roasting of many fowl at once."

"That seems rather a descent from making pistols."

Churwyl did not reply as Charyn turned the stallion onto the Avenue D'Commercia.

"Don't you think so, Churwyl?" pressed Charyn.

"I believe more people need special locks and other items on a day-to-day basis than pistols, sir."

"He must be quite clever if he can give up pistol making and do better." Charyn knew what he'd paid for the pistols with which he was displeased. He also wondered if he'd embarked on a fool's errand just out of anger and frustration. But just what was he supposed to do? His father didn't like him hovering around and asking too many questions. His father's ministers were afraid to tell him anything without his father's approval. His father had expressed displeasure when he'd mentioned talking to any of the Army High Command officers, and he'd read most of the readable and applicable books in the chateau library, and a good portion of the archives. And he had to admit it irked him that Churwyl could apparently aim either a rifle or a pistol at anything at any distance and seemingly hit whatever it was with no discernible difficulty.

"I suppose he must be, sir."

Despite the heavy riding jacket and the leather riding gloves, Charyn was definitely feeling chilled when he guided his mount onto the West River Road and headed south, not that he should have been surprised, given the steamy trails created by his mount's breathing.

"That's it up ahead, sir. The brown stone building on the left, with the one pier out into the river and the smoke from the chimney."

At first, Charyn found himself looking at the barge piers, farther south, which protruded from the river walls, and seemed anchored to them, but then he shifted his glance to the factorage, although he could barely see the smoke rising from the main factorage chimney, especially since the faint grayish haze was immediately blown toward the river once it was a yard or so above the top of the chimney. He rode almost to the door, dismounted, and then handed the stallion's reins to the nearest guard. Churwyl hurriedly dismounted and followed the heir.

Charyn knocked on the solid and aged oak door. No one answered. So he took the big brass knocker and slammed it as hard as he could against the knocker plate—twice . . . and then a third time. He stood back and waited, his breath steaming in the cold air. He was about to hammer the knocker a third time when the door opened.

A wiry gray-haired man, wearing stained brown leathers, looked at Charyn, then to the guard captain. "Given the insignia and the number of chateau guards . . . and your age . . . you must be Lord Charyn. Now that you've interrupted everything, you might as well come in. You, too, Guard Captain, but for your own safety, please don't touch anything."

Charyn had to admire the factor for his immediate understanding of the situation, and his calmness. "Thank you."

Churwyl stepped forward. "If you don't mind, Factorius?"

"Perfectly all right, Guard Captain." Paersyt stepped back, leaving the door open.

Churwyl stepped through the doorway and into the factorage, surveying the interior, then gestured.

Charyn followed, closing the door behind himself. The factorage was larger than it had appeared on the outside, and there were several forges spaced against the side wall, all in what amounted to a huge stone-floored hearth. One had an enormous bellows attached to it, although that forge fire appeared to be cold. Another was clearly hot, and boiling something, because Charyn could see wisps of steam.

"If I might ask why you are here, Lord Charyn?" The factor's voice remained calm.

"I heard that you forged the best pistols in Solidar."

"That is kind of you to say, but I don't manufacture pistols anymore, and I don't intend to again. Doing so was a mistake."

"Might I ask why?"

"It's time-consuming. You don't get paid what that work is worth, and the better it is, the more likely someone is going to get killed. It also ended up taking far more time than I'd ever intended." Paersyt smiled politely. "There are several factors who produce excellent pistols. What's wrong with their work?"

"None of them are accurate."

The balding factor laughed. "Lord Charyn, with your resources, if you can't find a pistol that is accurate, the problem is most likely with you and not the pistol. Most likely you're pulling the trigger and not squeezing it. Or you may not see as well at a distance."

"Then you won't make me a pistol?"

"So that you can get as upset with me as with the others?" Paersyt shook his head. "Whether I agree to make a pistol for you or not, you won't be satisfied, and I'd rather work on more productive efforts."

For a moment, Charyn was taken aback, but he had to admit that the factor was likely right about making Charyn dissatisfied. Even so, it took an effort for him not to lash out. Instead, he forced himself to nod. "What might those be?"

"I make the parts for mining engines."

"Mining engines?" Charyn hadn't the faintest idea what an engine was, let alone a mining engine.

"They power the pumps that lift the water out of the mines." The factor shook his head. "Come. I'll show you a drawing of one."

"You don't have one here?" asked Charyn as he followed the factor to the drawing board set before the window, but slanted so that whoever drew had his back to the light.

"They're rather large. I'm working on a way to make them smaller. You can see here a drawing of the pump and the engine."

Charyn looked at the drawing, but it didn't make much sense to him. "That's . . . different from making pistols."

"In some ways. I've always worked to fine tolerances." The factor pointed to the midsized forge. Set over the white-hot coals was a sealed kettle of some sort. From the top of the kettle a metal tube ran to a cylinder, hung by a thin rod from an iron pot holder. Thin streams of steam issued from the sides of the cylinder as it rotated.

Charyn studied the cylinder and realized that the rod was not turning with the cylinder. He also could not see any steam escaping from the cylinder except from the small conical nozzles at each side. He looked to Paersyt. "The steam makes it turn, doesn't it?"

"That's the whole point."

"Just to turn a cylinder?"

"No. Others figured that out some time ago. I'm using that cylinder to test the seals. Too much steam escapes in the present mining engines." The factor pointed to a small assembly sitting on a smooth and spotless workbench. "Look at the second model here. The steam pushes this piston back and forth, and the rod attached to the piston turns the crankshaft that turns the wheel. It could turn something else, anything from a large turning bench or to power a loom, in place of a waterwheel."

"The waterwheels do fine, and the water is free. Wood, charcoal, coal . . . they all cost money."

"There are many places where the land is too flat for that. Also a larger version could do other things."

"Such as?"

"Gelhorn uses a treadmill with an ox to operate a ferry. The treadmill turns a shaft attached to a paddlewheel. A larger version of this could do the same thing."

"If you could even afford to build one," Charyn pointed out. "If an ox works, why build this . . . steampusher?"

"Oxen get tired. You have to feed them. You could also use the engine—I prefer to call it an engine—to move a flatboat upstream, or make it go faster downstream."

"How much faster?" asked Charyn, intrigued.

1

"Good morning, sir," offered the duty guard to Charyn as the heir approached the door to the rex's official study.

"Good morning, Maertyl." With a smile, Charyn held up a hand. "Not until the glass chimes."

Maertyl raised his eyebrows.

"He doesn't like it if I'm early." *Or late.* As soon as the first chime of eight sounded, Charyn nodded.

Maertyl turned and rapped on the door. "Lord Charyn, sir."

Lorien's response to the guard was inaudible to Charyn, but Charyn had no doubt it was short and perfunctory.

"Thank you," murmured Charyn as he opened the study door and stepped inside. He closed it quickly and walked toward his father.

"Waiting until the last moment, again, I see," growled Lorien.

"You did say, 'as the chimes strike,' sir." Charyn smiled pleasantly as he took the middle chair of the three facing the goldenwood desk.

The rex's study was dark and gloomy, with the only real light coming from the two oil lamps in the bronze sconces on the wall behind the goldenwood desk. The light did not carry except faintly to the large oblong conference table at the west end of the study, where, occasionally, the rex met with either the High Council or the Factors' Council of Solidar, if not, occasionally, both of the councils. The wind continued its low moan outside the chateau. From where he sat behind the desk, Lorien lifted the sealed envelope that rested on the desk, likely delivered earlier that morning by a guard or a courier. "This just came. It can wait . . . for a bit." He set the envelope down. "I received the accounts on your Chaeryll lands. Minister Alucar says that over the past three years, you've done well in managing it. He doesn't know how."

"I went up there and talked to the tenants, sir. They suggested I let them try potatoes. Alucar had limited them to maize or wheat corn. I did. Because everyone else around there is growing wheat corn, potatoes brought more."

"How much more?" Lorien's question was almost a formality, as if he didn't really care, but felt obligated to ask.

"Around two parts in ten more." That was conservative. In two out of the three years since Charyn had been gifted the lands, the increased return had been more like four out of ten parts. He'd not only collected the rents personally, but kept track of the harvests. Some of the extra return might have just come from his closer oversight, but he had no way to know. He'd only put half of rents into the strongbox that was his in the family strongroom, since Alucar kept ledgers on each property. Even so, he'd had to use considerable ingenuity to keep a rather significant amount of golds hidden, and that was worrisome. At the same time, he didn't like the idea of being totally beholden to his sire, not when Lorien might live another twenty years . . . or at least ten.

"That's good, but don't start to think like a factor." Lorien coughed hoarsely, covering his mouth with a large kerchief. "Half of those that grow things spend more time at their exchange or whatever they call it than in doing what they should. Speculating on what price wheat will have three months from now? Or maize or flour? Ha! Not even the Nameless knows that. And the High Holders are worse in their own way, always moaning about how the weather makes it hard to pay their tariffs."

Charyn nodded, then watched as his father, with hands that had come to tremble more and more over the last months, opened the envelope. Just from the silver-gray sealing wax even Charyn could tell that it had to have come from High Holder Ryel.

Lorien, without so much as another glance at his son, murmured, "Yet another trial," and offered a heavy sigh as he began to read. Several more sighs followed.

Knowing that his father would only snap at him if he asked the nature of this particular trial, Charyn kept a pleasant expression on his face as he waited.

Finally, Lorien looked up. "The absolute gall of the man." He glared toward the window to his right.

Charyn wondered why he bothered, since neither of them could see it, frosted as it was on the inside, even behind the heavy hangings. Although the sun had come out, it wasn't that warm, even if winter was almost a month away, by the calendar, anyway.

"You read it," said Lorien, handing the letter across the desk to his son.

Charyn took it and began to read.

8 Erntyn 408 A.L.

Your Grace—

I trust that this missive finds you and all your family in continued good health as we approach Year-Turn, and I offer my best and heartfelt wishes for prosperity in the coming year.

    You had asked that I request another year's extension of my current term as head of the High Council. As you well know, I have already served in that capacity for a full six years. During that time, I have seldom left L'Excelsis and then only for the briefest of periods because of personal travails, notably the early and untimely death of my only son Baryel from the red flux. These past years have been a time of change and of great stress for all, and in consideration of the difficulties we have faced, especially at your suggestion a year ago last Erntyn, I requested from the other councilors a year's extension of my term as head of the Council, because I did not wish to be considered for another five-year term. They were gracious enough to grant that extension.

What were they going to do? thought Charyn. Deny it when both the rex and the Maitre of the Collegium wanted him to stay?

Much of my family has scarcely seen me for the past six years, and this has placed a great burden on my lady in dealing with Baryel's children and all the duties of administering the holding. I trust you can understand my desire to return to Rivages.

Charyn had forgotten that Baryel's wife had died after the birth of her daughter Iryella, and that Baryel's death left the High Holder and his wife as guardians of the holding's heirs.

Also to be considered is the fact that another extension of my term would be seen as very much against past practice and tradition, and might well generate unrest among those High Holders who have already expressed great concerns about the changes that you and the Collegium Imago have implemented and continue to pursue . . .

Charyn knew what Ryel wasn't saying—that the High Holder had no desire to be associated with the additional changes, and that if he stayed he would be forever marked as a tool of the rex and the Collegium. But then, isn't Father already a tool of the Collegium? Why should he alone suffer that burden?

. . . and for these reasons, I would suggest that it would be best for all concerned that you allow the High Council to choose another head of the Council for the next four years, either from the remaining members or from other qualified High Holders.

If not before, Doryana and I look forward to seeing you at the Year-Turn Ball, as do, I am certain, all the other members of the High Council.

Charyn lowered the missive.

"Well?" asked Lorien in a tone that was barely less than a bark.

"He doesn't want to preside over another increase in tariffs and over any more limits on the powers of the High Holders. He also likely does truly want to leave L'Excelsis."

"So he can plot from the relative safety of Rivages? That's what he wants. That's what he's always wanted. He doesn't want to tell all those High Holders who complain every time the weather turns bad that the weather's always bad part of the time, and that they still need to pay their tariffs."

"You don't think that he worries about his grandson?"

"The only worries he has about those children is how he'll use them to gain power. Karyel is fourteen, and Iryella is eleven or twelve . . . something like that. If it weren't for your mother, he'd have been making overtures to marry her to you."

"Why not Bhayrn? He's closer in age."

"Because Bhayrn won't be rex. Ryel's always been after power. He was behind pushing my late and unlamented brother to lead the High Holder revolt because he could influence Ryentar."

Charyn wasn't about to let his father rage on about his ungrateful brother . . . or more about Ryel, who was, unfortunately, his mother's scheming brother. At times, it was hard to reconcile the warm and seemingly kindly Uncle Ryel who had once presented him with new-minted golds on special occasions when he had been barely old enough to remember those events. "You haven't told me if you and Maitre Alastar talked this over and if the Maitre had anything to say about Uncle Ryel leaving the High Council."

"No, I haven't. As you could see, if you even thought, I just received the message early this morning."

Charyn again had to suppress his desire to snap back. "I have a thought . . . just a thought, sir."

"Spit it out."

"His missive emphasizes that he doesn't want to be Chief Councilor any longer. He also says that it would be a bad idea for him to continue in that post and that he would like to see his family more, doesn't it?"

"He just wants to go off and plot."

"But that's not what he wrote. You can act in terms of what he wrote, rather than what he may have in mind. What if you agree that his time as Chief Councilor should come to an end—"

"Absolutely not!"

"Sir . . . might I finish before you make a judgment? There's more that you might find to your liking."

"I doubt it, but go ahead."

"You agree that his time as High Councilor should come to an end, but . . . but in order for there to be continuity and a smooth transition, he should serve the next year as just a councilor, and that he and the other councilors should choose the new Chief Councilor from the current councilors. That way, he would be free to occasionally travel to Rivages and see his family . . . but his options for plotting would be limited and much more likely to be discovered while you still have him under some measure of scrutiny. That way, you also can portray yourself as somewhat sympathetic to his concerns."

"I don't know . . ."

"Why don't you talk that over with Maitre Alastar? Tell him it came up in a family discussion."

"Why not say you thought it up?"

"Because it's better that it be seen as . . . less specific. Either Mother, me, Bhayrn, or even Aloryana could have suggested it. If you do it that way, rather than suggesting it was your idea or mine, the Maitre is more likely to consider whether it is a good idea or not on the idea itself, rather than whether you came up with it or I did." Charyn smiled self-deprecatingly. "He might think it a bad idea, but how he answers might suggest other possibilities."

"Hmmmm . . ."

Charyn had the feeling that was about as much of a comment as he was going to get on that, and he eased the missive back onto his father's desk. "When do you meet with the Solidaran Factors' Council?"

"Not until the eighteenth of the month. That's when I meet with both the High Council and the Factors' Council. That meeting will be little more than a formality. The meeting in Ianus will be where everyone tells me what's wrong and what I should do that they don't wish to pay for. That's soon enough. Too soon."

"Are the factor councilors still opposed to the High Council's proposal to forbid excessive interest rates?"

"No one has told me. Since factors will do anything for gold, and hate to pay even an extra copper for anything, I imagine they are."

Charyn nodded. "What about the expansion of the regial post roads?"

"I almost wish that Maitre Arion hadn't disciplined the imagers in Westisle by making them build roads."

"Weren't the roads to Liantiago in terrible shape? Didn't they need rebuilding?"

"They did, but now the factors around Estisle want better roads, and the imagers building the new branch of the Collegium there aren't established enough to do that yet. The High Holders away from L'Excelsis and Liantiago are complaining that they can't get goods and crops to markets quickly, and that they're suffering from an unfair situation."

That made sense to Charyn, because in the years immediately after the failed High Holder revolt, the Collegium Imago in L'Excelsis had improved and widened the post road all the way to Kephria, as well as sections of the river road from the capital to Solis and the roads north from L'Excelsis to Rivages. "I thought the stone roads in old Telaryn were still in good condition."

"They are. Most don't lead to the larger cities or ports."

"Aren't the regional governors supposed to supervise post roads?"

"They claim I don't give them enough golds for all the work that needs to be done." Lorien shook his head. "There probably isn't after what they pocket."

"Maybe . . ." Charyn immediately broke off his words, then added smoothly, "Perhaps, as you replace each regional governor, you should make it clear that certain roads need to be repaired and improved, and that such repairs will determine in part how long they serve."

"They'd just steal more until I caught them."

Charyn was afraid that was true as well, but wanted to keep his father talking, in hopes of learning something he didn't know. "What about an additional tariff on the banques . . . the exchanges . . . ?"

"A plague on the banques and exchanges—they're what led to the revolt. Trading crops and debts and everything instead of producing. Speculation! Bah!"

Charyn nodded, but did not move. He'd learned early that patience was a necessity in dealing with his father . . . and most people.

Close to a glass later, he left the study, nodding again to Maertyl as he did.

He was headed toward his own chambers before his other appointments when he passed Aloryana's door, just slightly ajar.

"Oh, no! Noooo!"

Charyn was struck by the distress in Aloryana's voice, and since her sitting room door was indeed ajar, he knocked and pushed it open. "Are you all right?" Aloryana was straightening up as he stopped in the doorway.

"Oh . . . it's you. Thank the Nameless it wasn't Father. Or Mother!" Aloryana's eyes did not meet Charyn's.

"Oh?" Charyn could see that Aloryana held something silver in her hand. He thought he saw bluish gems as well. "Did you drop something?"

"Oh . . . nothing."

"It didn't sound like nothing." Charyn waited.

"It's just a hair clasp."

"Is it broken? Maybe I can fix it."

"Thank you, Charyn. I'll take care of it." Aloryana immediately turned away and hurried into her bedchamber, closing the door behind her, and leaving Charyn standing alone in the sitting room.

Charyn couldn't help wondering what she had broken that she didn't want him to know about. Finally, he stepped back into the corridor and gently closed the door to the main corridor. He thought he heard sobbing, but he was far from certain.

Charyn was waiting in the receiving parlor of the Chateau D'Rex on Meredi morning when the footman appeared and announced, "Ferrand D'Delcoeur-Alte has arrived, sir."

"Please show him in." Charyn rose and waited.

Ferrand appeared. He was perhaps several digits taller than Charyn, with the blond hair, gray eyes, and narrow face that ran in that branch of the family. Unlike Charyn, he had unblemished skin and a weak pointed chin. He wore a dark green riding jacket and trousers, with gray boots that were polished, but not enough to disguise the fact that they were well-worn. He inclined his head as he entered the parlor and stopped.

"How are you, cousin?" asked Charyn.

"I'm near-destitute, and I'd have few enjoyments at all, if it weren't for you."

"Let's not talk about that," replied Charyn cheerfully, lowering his voice and adding, "Not here." Then he said, his voice louder, "The weather's not the best, but I need to get out of the chateau. I'd hoped you'd join me on a ride through the hunting park. You could take the gelding you've ridden before."

"I suppose I could manage that." Ferrand grinned. "Especially since your invitation was to go riding."

"I do try not to surprise people. Not my friends, anyway." Charyn gestured. "Shall we go?" He turned and headed for the north center door to the chateau, the one that opened onto the rear courtyard, at the back of which were the regial stables.

Neither young man spoke beyond pleasantries until they were mounted and riding away from the chateau across the ring road to the west and through the old wrought-iron gates in the stone wall that bordered the western edge of the ring road and out into what remained of the hunting park that dated back to before the times of old Bovaria. Two guards with rifles followed at a distance, far enough back that quiet conversation could not be overheard.

Charyn guided his chestnut onto the graveled northern path that headed toward the bare-limbed woods that were not so well tended as they might have been, then turned in the saddle toward Ferrand, riding on his left. "How is your family these days?"

"The same as it always is."

That mean that Ferrand's father was spending too much, his mother drinking too much, and his sisters worrying about who would even consider a match with them.

"Sorry to hear it," replied Charyn in a voice meant to be both sympathetic and dry.

"What about yours?"

"As you said, the same always. Father worries about both the High Holders and the factors. They always want him to spend more than he gathers in tariffs. That never changes. Aloryana's excited that she can attend the Year-Turn Ball for the first time."

"She's only fourteen . . ."

"She can attend. They're not announcing she's eligible. Bhayrn's sixteen, and he's going. Not that he wants to. I'm just afraid I'll have sore feet by the time it's over. You're coming, aren't you? As an heir, you can." Charyn knew Ferrand understood that, but he wanted to emphasize that he'd like to have Ferrand there.

"Mother wants to come. Father could care less."

"Then escort her yourself, and claim your father's ill. That's certainly permitted. Everyone will understand. Your father might even be relieved."

Ferrand nodded. "He might, at that."

"Think about it."

"I will."

Charyn paused, then asked, "Does your family sell crops from the lands through the exchange, or directly to produce factors?"

"I don't know. I've never asked. Mother and Farouk handle that. I've never heard her mention anything about that one way or the other. What about your family?"

"Various factors, I think," replied Charyn offhandedly. "I was just wondering about that. About whether it might be time to change."

"I can't help you there, Charyn. You know more than I do about it. Then, it seems like I can't help you much with anything."

"Actually . . . you can. I was going to bring it up anyway. I have a favor to ask . . . and one that might allow you to pocket a few golds." Charyn managed to look sheepish.

"Oh? You're looking for a woman?"

Charyn smiled and shook his head. Another woman was the last thing he needed, especially given what his mother had said and done. "No. You remember the problem with the pistols? All the trouble I had?"

"I remember. You couldn't find one that would shoot straight."

"Well . . . I got that problem solved. But what am I going to do with five perfectly good pistols? I can't use that many. And if I tried to sell them, even through Norstan . . . word would get out. I thought . . . they're very good pistols, perhaps the best."

"But why even sell them? They're beautiful! You're the heir . . ."

"Exactly. I'm the heir, and I live on my father's sufferance. I'd rather have a few golds that he doesn't know about than three extra pistols. They're easily worth ten golds each, probably more." *Especially since I paid around twenty each.* "Even half of that . . ." Charyn smiled apologetically, knowing that Ferrand could likely get ten for each and would pocket five . . . and would do so, given the parlous state of his family's finances. "I'd expect you to keep some, of course, for doing me the favor."

"I couldn't."

"You can and you will. I'm the one asking for the favor. You said you couldn't help. Well, you can. But please keep it quiet. You understand?" It wouldn't hurt even if Ferrand did let it slip. In fact, that would work in Charyn's favor in another way.

"If you insist . . ."

"I insist." Charyn gestured. "If we ride quietly around the back of the next hill there, and then take the north path, we just might be able to see some of the red deer."

Charyn rode out from the chateau stables on the first Jeudi of Finitas a quint before seventh glass. The morning sky was gray, but the clouds were featureless and high, and there were only scattered gusts of light winds. With him were two guards, each wearing one of the nondescript brown leather coats that he had procured and personally paid for. He wore the gray-green woolen riding jacket and trousers, good garments but not that distinguishable from those worn by wealthy factors. The three took the ring road to L'Avenue D'Commercia straight to the Sud Bridge over the River Aluse.

Although he had only met Factorius Elthyrd a handful of times, and only in passing when Elthyrd came to the chateau to discuss matters involving the comparatively recently formed Factors' Council of Solidar, Charyn doubted that the factor, especially in his position as head of the Solidaran Council, would refuse to see him. Whether Elthyrd would acquiesce to what Charyn would ask was another question, although Charyn thought what he had in mind was not all that unreasonable—except to his own sire, which was another reason for the timing of his departure, since Lorien was anything but an early riser.

When they reached the Sud Bridge and began to ride across, Charyn looked north, upstream toward Imagisle. He'd heard stories about how Maitre Alastar had once turned the river to solid ice in putting down the army rebellion against his father, although his parents had said almost nothing about it, and he probably wouldn't have believed that story—except that six years earlier he'd personally seen three imagers kill almost two companies of rebel brownshirts who were attacking the Chateau D'Rex. They had been invisible until after they'd slaughtered almost all of the rebels, and none of them had looked that fatigued. As for what they'd later done to the rebel army . . . no one wanted to say much except that only a few hundred rebels survived—out of almost ten thousand.

Charyn couldn't see why anyone with any common sense would oppose the imagers. It made much more sense to be on their side, and it made even more sense not to be involved at all where the imagers might have to act. Too many powerful men—High Holders, senior army officers, and even his own grandfather—had died in one way or another when they'd crossed the Collegium.

Once on the other side of the river, he headed south on the East River Road. Less than a fraction of a quint later, he reined up in front of the expansive timber factorage with long piers. Several men were at work unloading a flatboat, but Charyn could see that Elthyrd wasn't on the piers. He dismounted and tied his horse to the bronze hitching post. "Just wait here."

"Yes, sir," replied Yarselt, the older of the two guards.

Charyn had barely stepped into the factorage when Elthyrd walked toward him, a concerned expression on his face.

"Lord Charyn . . . I must say your presence is rather unexpected."

"It's almost as unexpected to me as to you. I've come to ask for a small favor. I do hope it's a small one." Charyn smiled. "No, I'm not asking for special timber at a ridiculously low price . . . or at any price."

"Then might I ask why you have favored us with your presence?"

"Knowledge. In particular, information about how the commodity exchange works. If possible, I'd like to prevail upon you to give me a tour . . . as the nephew of a friend, not as Lord Charyn."

Elthyrd shook his head and laughed.

Charyn couldn't tell how much of the laughter was amusement and how much, if any, might be relief. He waited for the factor to speak.

"Do you really think that knowledge will prove helpful?"

"It might. As I recall, certain High Holders who were instrumental in the failed revolt did not understand the basics of the exchanges . . ." Charyn shrugged. "I doubt I know as much as they did."

"That you ask suggests otherwise. So does your presence a glass before the exchange opens." Elthyrd tilted his head. "I presume that you would like me to offer this . . . visit . . . this morning?"

"If it would not inconvenience you." Charyn offered a sheepish grin. "Or not inconvenience you excessively."

"The inconvenience is minor—today. I'm just as glad you picked today. We have a quint or so before we need to leave. I'd suggest we take my coach. There isn't much space around the exchange building, and it's usually crowded first thing in the day, particularly after harvest and early in the month . . . although it would have been far too crowded on Lundi, because it was the first day of the month."

"I did bring guards."

"There's a footman's stand. It will accommodate two, but that might be obvious with their uniforms."

"They're wearing brown coats that don't show their uniforms and plain visor caps, like mine."

"You weren't prepared to take a refusal, were you?"

"I was prepared for that. The coats and caps were necessary if you agreed."

Elthyrd nodded. "After I give word to ready the coach, I could go over a few matters about the exchange."

"That would be most helpful."

"If you would excuse me for a moment?" Elthyrd did not wait for Charyn's approval before turning and hurrying toward an archway to the right, which appeared to lead into a long corridor.

While he waited, Charyn took in the modest low-ceilinged entry hall that barely seemed big enough for the two small table desks, on both of which were neat stacks of papers. Neither was occupied at the moment. Behind and to the left of the second table desk was an open door, which likely led into Elthyrd's study, Charyn suspected.

Elthyrd returned shortly. "The coach will be here before long." He handed Charyn a pin shaped like a silver sheaf of grain. "Fasten that to your jacket where it can be seen. It's a visitor's pin."

Charyn saw a similar pin on Elthyrd's jacket, except the factor's pin was gold, with a small diamond stone set at the base of the sheaf. He fastened it to the narrow left lapel of his jacket.

"What do you know about the exchange?"

"Very little, except that it's where trades of large quantities of commodities are conducted. I've assumed that those trades set the basic price for those goods, and that the more hands through which goods pass after that, the greater the markup of the price."

"That's accurate, but a great oversimplification. Only the largest trades in this part of Solidar take place through the exchange, and not necessarily all of those, but that will be clearer once you see the exchange. You know that trading glasses are limited?"

"I hadn't thought about that," Charyn admitted.

"Trading only takes place Lundi through Vendrei, and only from eighth glass to the second glass of the afternoon." Elthyrd cleared his throat. "That doesn't mean other trades don't take place, but those are direct between buyer and seller . . ."

Charyn listened.

The older factor went on, for less than half a quint, when he looked up. "I hear the coach. We should go."

That was fine with Charyn. He wasn't certain he'd really understood some of what Elthyrd had said. He just hoped seeing the exchange would help his comprehension. He followed Elthyrd back outside, where the breeze had picked up, and motioned to Yarselt. "Tie your mounts here. You two will have to ride on the rear footboard."

"Too bad I don't have a rear dickey box," said Elthyrd with a smile, "But I'm just a factor."

Once Charyn and Elthyrd were seated, Charyn glanced back.

"We're fine, sir," Yarselt said.

"It's a fairly short ride," added the factor.

Charyn knew that, since the exchange was located east of the East River Road some two blocks north of L'Avenue D'Artisans.

As the carriage began to move, Elthyrd continued his explanation. "You might not have known from the outside, but the exchange building is divided into sections for purposes of trading. The north end is for metals and minerals—"

"Iron, tin, copper, coal?"

"And zinc, sulfur, and even salt," continued Elthyrd. "The middle section is for things that grow—crops, other food-stocks, and timber. The south end deals with the rest—most of that is livestock, or livestock products—leather, wool."

"What about silver or jewels?"

"Those aren't commodities. Individual factors handle those. That's enough for now."

Before long, the carriage came to a halt after pulling into a stone-paved turnout on the east side of the road, then creeping forward behind another carriage.

Once the two alighted, Elthyrd cleared his throat. "No one will remark on one bodyguard. That's allowed. Two . . . on the other hand."

"Yarselt, you'll accompany me. Varyst, you stay with the carriage"

"Yes, sir."

Charyn studied the exchange building as if he'd never seen it before long yellow brick structure with limestone quoins at all the corner limestone door and window frames. There were three double doors equally across the front—all oak, and not brass-bound—presum provide direct access to each of the trading areas.

Elthyrd headed toward the middle door. "The crops and timber section is the most active, and that will give you a better understanding more quickly." He smiled. "It's also closer."

Two guards stood at the entrance. Neither looked for more than an instant at Elthyrd, but one did look harder at Charyn, nodding as he saw the silver pin.

Once inside, Elthyrd led the way to a trading area.

Charyn didn't know what to expect, but what he saw made sense. What amounted to stalls were set up on each side of the hall. There was a railing on three sides of each stall, with the back side being the wall, with three men inside the stall, one at a table desk with several open ledgers before him, and one standing between two slates mounted on frames, another at the side close to the railing.

"Let's see how wheat corn is doing." Elthyrd's words were not a suggestion.

Charyn nodded and walked beside the factor. Yarselt followed closely.

Elthyrd walked to the corner of the railed enclosure, away from the handful of men at the center of the railing, and beckoned Charyn to move closer before he spoke. "The minimum trade for wheat corn is a single lot of a hundred bushels. Almost every trade will be much larger than that, but they have to be made in hundred-bushel lots. If you look at the slate, you can see that someone is offering ten lots of good wheat corn at twelve coppers a bushel."

Charyn nodded. *A hundred twenty golds for the ten lots.* "Is that size trade large or small, or about where most take place?"

"Crops aren't my field," replied Elthyrd dryly, "but ten lots is on the small side."

As Charyn watched, several of the men standing at the bar gestured. Abruptly, the trader looked to one man, who nodded, and then back to another and called out, "Done, at eleven and nine."

The young man beside the slate immediately chalked up, "10LT/11.9 10/5/08." The man at the table desk made entries in two of the ledgers.

"Next contract, fifty lots, prime, asking twelve and one . . ."

More than six hundred golds. Charyn glanced the length of the hall. While it wasn't that long, there were scores of traders, some moving from one commodity slate to the next.

Beside the first slate was a second one, which listed months and had numbers next to the months. Charyn murmured to Elthyrd, "And the board on the side?"

"Those are the latest prices for sale or delivery of a bushel on the first of the month."

"So you can buy a lot of wheat for delivery next Maris for that price?"

"I wouldn't, but you could."

Already another corn contract was being offered, Charyn realized. Close to a thousand golds changing hands in a fraction of a quint. Another thought struck him. "I don't see flour . . ."

"It's not a commodity."

"Why not?"

"I can't tell you that. I'm not a grain factor. I have enough trouble knowing all I need to know about all the woods."

"Do you have any thoughts on that, sir?"

"It's probably because flour gets bought in smaller lots. Wheat corn gets bought in larger lots by millers. There's no commodities market for finished wood planks for that reason."

"Because the buyers of large lots are only large factors like you?" Charyn thought for a moment. "Are there that many wood factors?"

"Not here in L'Excelsis. I'm one of the larger factors, but certainly not the largest even in Solidar, but factors from all across Solidar and even from other lands have agents here with standing or special instructions for certain kinds and qualities of wood. That wouldn't be possible if the River Aluse weren't navigable for most of its length . . ."

"Every tree is different. How can you price wood?"

"Logs are graded by type of wood and quality. The standard lot is generally five hundred board yards. That's a calculation, because you don't know exactly how many usable board yards you'll get, but the higher the quality . . ."

Charyn listened intently. He had thought he was reasonably intelligent, but he could tell it would take time for him to truly understand how the exchange worked . . . but he did have an idea. When Elthyrd finished, Charyn cleared his throat. "Who can trade on the exchange? Just factors? Or can High Holders?"

Elthyrd smiled indulgently. "We're not particularly selective in that respect. Anyone who can post the bond and who is endorsed by another member can trade."

"What is the bond? Thousands of golds?"

The factor shook his head. "There are two classes—merchant and factor. Merchant traders must post a five-hundred-gold bond, in physical golds held by the exchange. Factor traders must post a thousand-gold bond."

Charyn frowned. "But . . . I just saw trades of over a thousand golds in a few moments."

"The bond is proof of some assets. You still have to deposit or transfer golds upon a sale. Failure to settle accounts by a glass after the exchange closes results in immediate suspension. Failure to settle within two weeks results in permanent suspension. For a merchant or a factor who needs the exchange, that could destroy his business."

"Or cost so much that it might as well?"

"So far, no one who has been suspended has retained their factorage or lands."

For a moment, Charyn was taken aback. Finally, he asked, "Can anyone really apply to trade?"

"Under those conditions, yes."

Charyn swallowed, then said, "I fear I'm going to ask for another favor."

"Oh?" Elthyrd's words were skeptical.

"I'd like to set up a merchant account under a family name I can use. Would that be possible?"

The factor frowned.

Charyn waited.

"I think I'd like to know more."

"That's exactly why," Charyn replied. "I've already seen enough to know that I know little, and that it would take time to learn more. I cannot ask you or anyone else to accompany me here day after day. But . . . if it were known that I am the son of a distant High Holder trying to determine whether using the exchange would be beneficial . . ."

"Let me think about that while I show you more."

"As you think best, Factorius."

"Do you have any other questions?"

"What about iron? Does the exchange trade iron?"

"No. Karl and Vaschet's ironworks are the only ones in the whole midsection of Solidar producing pigs or plate. All you can do is try to get the best deal from either."

"I thought the Banque D'Excelsis . . . that's your son . . ."

"He owns the ironworks." Elthyrd snorted. "Between the Banque and the arbitraging and bills of exchange for foreign traders, he'll work himself to death, and that's without spending enough time on the ironworks."

"Does he like running the ironworks?"

"I have my doubts, but he's never said."

"He can't sell it?"

"To whom? It's worth a lot, but the margins are low, and no factor likes low-margin businesses, and none of the local High Holders either want it or could afford it. It's a lot of work for not that much profit—and that's when things are going well."

Interesting. "What about rope and hemp? Don't you factor that?"

"My younger son Therard has been running that. He's doing quite well."

"I don't imagine rope or hemp are traded on the exchange."

"That's good for our purposes." Elthyrd turned. "We might as well look at the timber contracts."

Charyn again followed, trying to take in everything around him.

Almost a glass later, Elthyrd drew Charyn aside under one of the high windows. "You realize that trading on the exchanges is risky, especially without experience. Traders have been known to lose ten thousand golds in a day. It's not an advisable form of gambling."

"Gambling has never held any attraction for me." That was absolutely true.

"What name would you wish to use?"

"Suyrien." Charyn spelled it out.

"From where?"

"I have a small property east of Talyon. It's called Chaeryll."

"How small?"

"Some five hundred hectares. Part of it is an old hunting lodge, but I have rents from over three hundred hectares."

"More than a mille on side isn't what most would consider small."

"It's small for a High Holder."

"So . . . you want the exchange membership under Suyrien D'Chaeryll?"

"If you would." Charyn paused. "This isn't something I planned for today. I don't usually carry five hundred golds."

"Most people don't." Elthyrd's tone was wry. "I'll set it up, since the sponsor has to submit the papers anyway. Then when you're ready, I'll take you over and you can present the golds yourself."

"Thank you."

"One other thing. You can also deposit additional golds in your account there. That way you can draw on what you have without touching the bond. Or you can transfer funds to someone elsewhere in Solidar through another exchange. I'd recommend depositing more before you trade . . . if you intend to."

"I have no immediate intentions, but I do appreciate the advice." *In short, don't trade without funds on account.* "I'll have the golds to you within the next few days, along with additional golds." He smiled. "For security and peace of mind." Especially his own security, since he could stop worrying about hiding all of his personal golds. *And Father would never think about an account with the exchange.*

Elthyrd smiled in return.

Charyn thought he detected a slight sense of relief. He doubted he was mistaken.

4

The rattling of rain on the chateau windows woke Charyn, and the dark gray light seeping past the heavy green hangings suggested that it was after dawn, but before sunrise. He rolled onto his back, looking up at the ceiling, then taking in the ornate gilded cornice in the corner of the bedchamber closest to the door to the sitting room. After a moment, he sat up. He wouldn't have slept that much longer anyway.

Then he glanced at the dark-haired woman lying on the other side of the bed. Her eyes were closed but he knew she wasn't sleeping. *Should you?* He shook his head. There were things he wanted to do before his father woke and started the daily round of demands . . . and he would have time . . . later. "Time to get up, Palenya . . ."

She did not budge.

"Possums do a better job," he said dryly.

She opened her eyes and turned her head. "You knew I was awake."

Charyn nodded.

"You could have . . ."

"We both have matters to attend to, and I'm hungry." At her glance, he added, "For food. Breakfast."

Palenya offered a pout that was excessive, followed by a smile that was more like a grin, showing that she knew the pout had been excessive.

Charyn had half-expected it, and she had known he expected it. He grinned. "You just don't want to tune the clavecin before you give Aloryana her lessons." Charyn knew that Aloryana wasn't the problem. His sister seldom was. The problem was that Palenya felt that the clavecin always needed tuning, because she wanted the sound to be perfect. Palenya would not have admitted that, but Charyn knew it. His mother did as well, but given that the instrument did sound better when frequently tuned, often necessary because Bhayrn was so ham-fisted with his playing, no one was about to say anything.

Palenya threw off the covers and sat up.

Charyn couldn't help but admire what he saw, even as he grinned. "You're doing your best to distract me."

"Isn't that what I'm here for?"

"You're very distracting, but if you don't put on some clothes, you're going to be very cold, very quickly." Charyn stood, moving toward the open armoire. "Especially if I lock away . . ."

"All right." Another smile followed.

Charyn enjoyed watching her dress. He still did, more than half a year after his mother had introduced Palenya into his life. He also enjoyed watching and listening as she played the clavecin, although he'd made a point of appearing only politely interested whenever she played for others, especially for regial events.

As Palenya quickly brushed her hair, Charyn asked, "Will you be playing this afternoon?"

"Lady Chelia has requested that I play occasional music while she entertains the wives of some of the senior army officers."

"Very light music, I presume."

"Almost all will be popular folk tunes arranged by Shastayl the younger. Some adaptations by Rajhym, perhaps the 'Pavane in a Minor Key' by Farray."

"Except for the Farray . . ." Charyn offered a theatrical wince.

"You'd prefer the works of Covaelyt?"

"After what you've taught me . . . yes."

"You are a very naughty young man to expect them to appreciate works four hundred years old."

"If I can appreciate Covaelyt as a young man—"

Palenya stepped toward him and laid a long and slender finger across his lips. "We can discuss composers later. I must eat . . . if I'm to tune the clavecin and then work with your sister. I will have to retune it later if your brother appears for his lessons."

Charyn nodded. He hardly needed a reminder that Bhayrn didn't have the lightest touch on the keyboard.

Once Palenya had left, heading for her own small room in the lowest full level of the chateau, and breakfast in the staff room off the kitchen, Charyn quickly washed up and dressed, then made his way to the family breakfast chamber.

Aloryana was the only one there.

"Good morning," offered Charyn as he seated himself.

"I'm glad it's morning. I had trouble getting to sleep last night."

"It didn't start storming until early this morning," replied Charyn.

"Outside, you mean," countered his sister snidely.

"Inside, it was quiet. I went to sleep early."

"To bed, anyway. At least she's nice."

"She's a good musician and a good teacher, you said."

"She is, and she's nice. But . . ." Aloryana shook her head. "There's no point in talking about it."

There wasn't, but Charyn couldn't even say that, because that would have made him seem callous and uncaring.

"Talking about what?" asked Bhayrn as he entered, yawning.

"Music," said Aloryana. "People have different tastes in music and musicians." Her voice was innocent.

Chelia, entering just behind Bhayrn, let her eyes fix on Aloryana for just an instant, suggesting displeasure.

Aloryana smiled. "Good morning, Mother."

"Good morning, Aloryana. I'm been thinking. Given how well you are playing, I think the chateau clavecinist should embark on teaching you some more advanced pieces. I'll talk to her after breakfast."

Aloryana stiffened, and Charyn concealed a smile.

Bhayrn failed to hide a smile, and Chelia turned. "Your playing has not been adequate. You think volume is technique. Perhaps a four-hand duet with Aloryana would inspire you."

Charyn concentrated on taking a sip of tea from the large mug.

"I'd like that, I think," said Aloryana.

Bhayrn stiffened.

"Then I'll talk to Palenya about arranging it." Chelia lifted her mug of tea, as if to signify that the matter had been decided, before turning to Charyn. "What are your plans for the day?"

"I'd thought to look into some matters in L'Excelsis, but they can wait, at least until the rain lets up." He'd planned to visit Factor Walltyl to talk over what it would take to build the racing cart he had in mind, but that could wait, at least until the downpour outside ended—or even a week or so. It wasn't as though he needed a cart, but it would be fun to take Palenya, or Aloryana, through the hunting park at a good clip. He also needed to make some quiet arrangements to get himself and his golds to Elthyrd, but he thought that might better be accomplished on Mardi. He didn't want to convey impatience. "I need some more arms practice also. The sabre I can do inside with Guard Captain Churwyl or one of the senior guards. The pistol, not until the weather lets up. Even the covered courtyard gets wet in this weather."

"Why can't I learn to handle a sabre?" asked Aloryana.

"We've been through this before," said Chelia. "You know what your father thinks of that."

"I know," sighed Aloryana. "Weapons are for men. I still don't see why. The Pharsi women of Khel carried weapons and fought."

"And Khel fell to the first Rex Regis," declared Bhayrn.

"Your father has made his decision," replied Chelia, turning back to Charyn. "And after arms practice? That won't take all that long."

"I also thought I'd spend some time, when he's free, with Minister Sanafryt. I've been working with him on getting a better understanding of the legal implications of the Codex Legis."

"How have you been doing that?" asked Bhayrn.

"He shows me the petitions Father receives. I give him my impression. Sometimes I even write a draft response, and then he tells me what's wrong with it." Charyn looked to his mother. "I asked Father first if I could study with Alucar and Sanafryt. I thought it wouldn't hurt to understand the finances and the law." Charyn had not told his father how he was studying, and didn't intend to.

"That's not a bad idea." Chelia nodded, then turned to Bhayrn. "If you don't like clavecin lessons . . ."

"I'll practice clavecin, whatever the piece is," Bhayrn said quickly.

Again, Charyn concealed a smile. Bhayrn had never been fond of scholastic studies, especially those that required writing and calculating.

Once he finished eating, Charyn made his way to the duty room for the chateau guards, where he asked Churwyl if one of his men was free to spar with him.

"How much of a workout do you want, Lord Charyn?"

"A good workout that will test my modest skills, but not result in too many bruises." Those bruises would have been wounds had they been using blades, even blunted ones. In any event, none of the guards would have dared to spar with him except with wooden wands, nor would Churwyl have allowed it, given that Charyn was, at best, adequate with a sabre.

"I'll have Murdynt meet you in the stable, then. I presume that's satisfactory."

"That will be fine."

Murdynt was a shade taller than Charyn, a touch faster, and two quints of trying to keep the guard from bruising him up too much was more than enough for Charyn, enough so that he had to return to his quarters to wash up and change clothes before making his way down to the main floor south corridor to Minister Sanafryt's study. Sanafryt was seated at the wide table desk with a stack of documents, likely petitions, on one side, the Codex Legis on the other. The minister's study wasn't all that large, no more than five yards by four, with several bookcases against the wall and a small table desk that Charyn had arranged to be added for his studies—set in the corner farthest from Sanafryt. The study was dim, with only the oil lamp on the minister's desk lit.

"Good morning, Minister," offered Charyn politely.

"Read this petition and tell me what you think," said Sanafryt mildly, lifting several sheets from the corner of the desk.

Charyn took the petition and withdrew to the table desk in the corner, where a second copy of the Codex Legis rested. He used a striker to light the oil lamp and began to read.

> . . . aggrieved party being Elmyranda D'Alte, Lady of Aishford, by violation of the Codex Legis revisions of 403 A.L. wherein the provisions of locus dominatus were revised . . .

Boring as the language was, Charyn forced himself to read through the two long pages of the petition. Then he leafed through the Codex Legis to the sections referred and read them before standing and returning to where the Minister sat at his large table desk.

"What is the petition about?"

"Locus dominatus."

"What about it?" Sanafryt's voice remained even.

"It's the old Tellan term referring to the legal right of High Holders to all justicing on their lands. The Codex Legis invalidated that. This petition by High Holder Aishford's wife is claiming that Aishford is violating the revised Codex by imprisoning her in her rooms for just less than the one-month maximum under low justice and then reimprisoning her for another thirty-four days?"

"Exactly."

"How did she even manage to write the petition?"

"It was sent under the seal of her brother, High Holder Fauxyn. She must have escaped to his lands. How would you address this, Lord Charyn?"

"Aishford is within the scope of the law as it's written, isn't he?"

"Is he?"

Charyn thought so, but the way Sanafryt had asked gave him pause.

"Read that section again, all of it . . . and then the general provisions at the end. Then come back and tell me what you think."

Charyn bridled at Sanafryt's condescending tone, but he held his tongue and didn't speak for a moment.

"You asked for me to teach you," Sanafryt said. "If you intend to get angry every time I suggest you do something, then perhaps we should not proceed. You look for a quick answer. Quick answers in law can get one in difficulty, even a rex."

Charyn inclined his head. "I apologize, Minister Sanafryt. I will go back over that section." He could feel Sanafryt's eyes on his back as he retreated to the table desk in the corner, where a second copy of the Codex Legis rested. *Why is he so Namer-damned prickly with me? I am the heir, after all.*

He had to force himself to read through all the clauses and conditions dealing with "Justicia Seconda," word by word, trying to discover what he had missed. He could find nothing that would change his initial opinion. With an almost inaudible sigh, he turned to the general provisions, some ten pages of them, and began to read.

Almost a quint passed before he located what had to be what Sanafryt had alluded to . . . and he realized that he should have listened more carefully to the minister's last words about the general provisions. He looked over the "evasion" section carefully, concentrating on the key phrases . . .

. . . notwithstanding the specific language of any provision set forth in this Codex, any attempt to exercise rights and privileges herein revoked or limited by any means, including non-continuous exercise of such, using other terms of law or language to evade the limitations imposed on High Holders . . . shall be deemed a breach of the Codex and shall subject the violator to the same punishments as would befall him . . .

Charyn nodded. That had to be it. He stood and walked back to Sanafryt. "Minister . . . would it be the evasion section of the general provisions?"

Sanafryt smiled. "It would be. Do you understand why that section was necessary?"

"I do."

"Good." Sanafryt reached for another petition. "See what you can make of this one."

Charyn took the second petition, much longer than the first. He wasn't so sure that he didn't envy Bhayrn. At that moment, sitting at a clavecin with Palenya instructing him would have been far more pleasant, not that he could ever be the musician she was, although he did pride himself on being somewhat better than Aloryana.

He had just finished reading through the convoluted language of the petition for the second time when there was a rap on the study door, opened by a guard. "Ah . . . Lord Charyn . . . the rex . . ."

"I'm on my way." Charyn stood. "Another sort of duty calls, Minister Sanafryt."

"Before you go, what was the purpose of that petition?"

"To have the rex affirm some water rights, but I couldn't tell from the way it was written whether the rights had lapsed or had never been exercised and were preempted by the neighboring landholder."

"They were preempted, but there's a specific wording that indicates that. Most junior advocates wouldn't know that wording, either. If you remind me whenever you next appear, I'll show you."

"I would appreciate that." Charyn inclined his head, then stepped out of the study.

He went up the grand staircase quickly, but without exerting himself, and then made his way to his father's private study.

The duty guard—Sturdyn—opened the door as he approached and announced, "Lord Charyn."

The door closed before Charyn was more than two steps inside the dimly lit study.

Lorien waited behind the desk while Charyn seated himself. The entire time the fingers of his slightly gnarled right hand were tapping impatiently on the top of the goldenwood desk.

"You requested my presence, sir?"

"Where were you?"

"Studying with Minister Sanafryt, as you agreed I should do from time to time."

"Hmmph."

Charyn took that to mean that while his father would have liked to have found fault, he couldn't, not on that count, at least.

"I understand that you've been frequenting the factors' exchange." Lorien looked hard at Charyn. "Why?"

"Only a few times." Charyn wasn't about to admit it had only been once. So far. "I wanted to find out for myself how and why they work."

"I doubt that is necessary. Norstan knows more about the exchanges than you'll ever have time to learn."

"That's very likely true," replied Charyn. *For the moment.* "Because trade and commerce are becoming more and more important in Solidar, I'd like to know enough so that I understand what you and your ministers are talking about . . . whenever you do let me listen to such matters."

"You'll have plenty of time. I'm not dead yet, Charyn. I'm not even close to it," snapped Lorien.

"No, sir, but you have told me how complicated the matters you must consider happen to be, and that I shouldn't expect to learn them easily or in a short time. That is why I am trying to learn as much as I can now."

"You like to use my own words to your own ends, don't you?"

Charyn managed to smile pleasantly. "I've tried to follow your advice, sir."

"When it suits your purpose."

"I've never gone against you." *Around you, but never against you.*

"You've got traits from your mother's family." Lorien shook his head. "What did you learn at the exchange?"

"The thing that struck me the most was how many golds change hands daily."

"That's more than some High Holders know." Lorien paused. "At least, you learned something. That's all I wanted to know."

There was something about the way his father had said those words that struck Charyn. "You've never said much about the exchanges before . . ."

"You want to know why I am now? Why I question you about it? Because I don't believe in coincidences. That's why."

Coincidences? Charyn had no problem showing confusion.

"It's a good thing you don't understand," Lorien said. "I just received a dispatch from the regional minister of finance in Solis. The factors' exchange in Solis was burned to the ground over a week ago." He snorted. "More than a week to let me know. I told Alucar to roast his regional finance minister for that delay, terrible weather or not. I'm supposed to be the first to know, not the last."

"How . . . how did it happen?"

"Someone set explosives and used oils. How else?"

"Why would anyone do something like that?" asked Charyn, hoping to learn more.

"Alucar tells me that the High Holders around Solis have been complaining that the factors have been using the exchanges to keep the price of grain and agricultural produce low. When the prices in Solis start to rise, growers from other areas start bringing in grains, especially wheat."

"But how do growers elsewhere know this?"

"Apparently, the Factors' Council of Solidar helped establish a system of sending price information over the regial post roads. Over my post roads, no less." Lorien shook his head. "At least they're paying for the privilege, unlike the High Holders who want the information without paying for it."

"But to blow up the exchange in Solis? Who would do that . . . and why? They don't store grain there, anyway."

"That's a good question, for once. It's likely some hothead High Holder, but it might be a smaller factor who can't afford to use the exchanges . . . or someone who has a grudge against factors."

"What will you do?"

"What can I do? I don't know enough to do anything. If it's a small factor and I blame the High Holders, then the High Council will have more support against me. If it's a High Holder and I blame an unhappy factor, I'll have both councils angry." Lorien glared at Charyn, as if his son might have had something to do with it.

At least, that was what the look implied.

"It's more of the same," Lorien went on. "The factors complain about the high-handedness of the High Holders, and the High Holders complain about the greed of the factors. Each group thinks it pays too much in tariffs and that the other pays too little. They all want more without paying for it, and then they blame me. And this explosion, it's only going to make things worse."

"I can see that, sir."

"You only think you can," replied Lorien. "You can go."

"Thank you, sir." Charyn rose, inclining his head, then made his way from the study. *You couldn't have picked a worse time to visit the exchange, but how could you have possibly known?*

He was still thinking over the fact that someone had destroyed the Solis exchange as he descended the grand staircase and he began to hear the clavecin being played in the music room. The notes stopped abruptly. After several moments of quiet, the same melody was played again, not quite as precisely, but accurately.

Charyn nodded. The second player had to be Aloryana. Bhayrn would have rushed the tempo.

He continued to make his way to his own chambers, where he sat down at the desk in his sitting room, which doubled as his study.

After this morning, should you really do this?

He smiled wryly. The explosion at the exchange emphasized just how uncertain matters were and why he needed to continue with his plans.

After a short time of thought, he began to write.

Vaelln D'Corps
Marshal of the Army

Marshal Vaelln—
Rather belatedly, it has come to my attention that I know far too little about the structure and the operations of the Army and the Navy. I would like to remedy this gap in my understanding and obtain greater familiarity in a timely fashion, hopefully long before I will need such knowledge. In obtaining such basic knowledge, I would not wish in the slightest to intrude upon your time, but trust that you could arrange a series of briefings at your headquarters with various more junior officers who could enlighten me . . .

Charyn paused for several moments before dipping the pen in the inkwell and resuming, forcing himself to write deliberately and precisely.

On Mardi, Charyn was up early. He had a long day ahead of him. As he prepared to leave his quarters for what would pass for breakfast—bread and cheese or something taken in the kitchen—his eyes dropped to the missive on his desk, the reply from Marshal Vaelln, confirming a series of briefings beginning at ninth glass. He immediately picked it up and slipped it into his jacket, then headed down to the kitchen.

He'd barely stepped through the side door when Hassala, the head cook, appeared. "Lord Charyn . . . we could serve you in the breakfast—"

"I have a great deal to do today, and I might have to leave the chateau early." Charyn offered his most winning smile. "Just a small wedge of cheese and a part of a loaf and a little lager to wash it down."

"Yes, Your Lordship." The tone of the cook's acquiescence implied a definite concern for propriety.

"If anyone asks, tell them I insisted." Charyn strongly doubted that anyone would ask, since what he had requested was hardly extravagant or improper . . . just not conventional. And it was much earlier than any of his family usually breakfasted. But what he was about to do had to be done early.

"Yes, sir. Be just a moment, sir."

Before long Charyn was chewing on fresh-baked bread, along with small wedges of white cheese. He finished the last of the mug of lager less than half a quint after entering the kitchen. Then he turned to Hassala, who was trying to hide a frown of disapproval. "Thank you. I do appreciate it."

When Charyn left the kitchen, he stopped outside the door he had not fully closed and paused for several moments, nodding to himself as he caught Hassala's words to one of the serving maids. "Don't know where he's headed . . . think any of us dare ask?"

So much the better. He took the side corridor before making his way up the narrow south circular staircase to the study that was his immediate destination, reaching it a good two quints before seventh glass.

Knowing that Norstan was always slightly late most mornings, Charyn didn't have to hurry in using his keys to enter the seneschal's study. He also didn't light the oil lamp on the table desk, nor the one in the polished brass wall sconce. A smaller key unlocked the ledger case, from which he pulled the two ledgers that might be necessary, setting them on the desk. Then he seated himself behind the desk and waited.

At roughly half a quint past the glass, the narrow door opened, and a broad-shouldered and burly figure stepped into the study, shrugged off a brown woolen jacket and reached for the green-trimmed black coat hung on the wall peg beside the door. He had one arm in one sleeve when he noticed that someone was sitting in his chair.

"What are you . . ." The newcomer broke off as he recognized the sandy-haired young man behind the desk. "Lord Charyn . . . you gave me a turn there."

"I meant to." Charyn smiled. "Go ahead and light the lamps. We need more than a little illumination here. Then take a seat."

The seneschal finished donning his coat, but lit both lamps before sitting in front of the desk. "Might I ask . . . ?"

"I think I'll start by doing the asking." Charyn smiled coolly. "I've been following the ledgers for a while. Charging the accounts fifteen coppers for a bushel of potatoes? Isn't that a bit much, Norstan? They were only running eighteen a bushel five years ago when all the crops failed from the droughts and floods. From what the ledgers show, you've pocketed more than ten golds from the potatoes alone in the past year."

"Your Lordship . . ."

"Spare me either reasons or excuses. Seneschals are supposed to profit a bit. Everyone expects that, even my father. I do think, if it came to his attention, that he would find the amount by which you are profiting, shall we say, a bit excessive."

"I've served your father faithfully and loyally, sir."

"You have served him faithfully, and you've been loyal. Given what you've pocketed, it would be a disgrace if you hadn't. Oh . . . you've been careful, but on your official stipend, I don't see how you could have bought that rich bottomland north of Lake Shaelyt that your tenants farm for you." For all his casual mannerisms, Charyn continued to watch the seneschal.

"You don't understand. It's not just the prices, but the quality . . ."

"I understand that some palms have to be greased occasionally, but . . ." Charyn frowned. "We haven't talked about flour. The miller can buy wheat for less than twelve coppers a bushel, mill it, and sell a barrel of flour that cost him less than thirty coppers in wheat for six silvers. He profits handsomely. So why do the ledgers show we're paying nine silvers? Sometimes ten?"

"The millers are charging more than a mere six silvers," protested the seneschal.

"I've looked at the prices paid for wheat over the past four months. It's never been more than twelve coppers. I've also had someone check the prices for barrels of flour. The highest has been seven silvers, and that was early in Agostos before the harvests came in. I could see five coppers or even a silver a barrel. You do have your expenses, but three silvers over the millers' prices?" Charyn shook his head. "You can take a small cut, Norstan. So long as you don't get greedy, we'll get along just fine. There is one favor I expect in return."

The seneschal looked fatalistically at Charyn.

"I need to know everyone who meets with my father . . . Everyone."

"I only know those who come to the regial study . . ."

"Those are the only ones I care about." That wasn't entirely true, but that was all Norstan needed to know.

The seneschal's brow knit.

"You're to tell me what you know about each one. Do you understand?"

"Ah . . . yes, sir."

Charyn could see a certain despair. "I'm not plotting against my father. In fact, I'm trying to keep him—and me—from being cheated too much since this is likely to be my inheritance in the future, and I'd like it to be healthy. I also want to make certain he's not being plotted against. I've also taken steps to see that, if anything happens to me, what I've discovered goes to both my father and Maitre Alastar. You might recall . . ."

Norstan nodded glumly.

"Norstan. You know your position. You do it well. I'd like you to keep doing it. You'd like to keep doing it. My father would like you to keep doing it—unless he found out how much you've been taking. This way is best for everyone." Charyn smiled warmly. "Just give me a daily listing of his meetings. Anything else we'll talk about."

"I already provide him with a copy of the next day's meetings each evening."

"That will be fine, with the names of those with whom he also met added to the next day's schedule."

Norstan nodded, less than enthusiastically.

Charyn's next stop was at the music room. He'd planned to step inside and perhaps practice a little, but he could hear Palenya playing, since no one else in the chateau played that well, and it was too early for visitors.

He was still standing there, listening, when Bhayrn appeared.

"Do you actually like what she's playing?" asked the younger brother in a low voice. "Or is it just because she's the one playing?" A sly smile appeared on Bhayrn's face.

"I like her," murmured Charyn. "I also like the music."

"How can you like something you can't play? Don't tell me you can. You're not that much better than I am, and Aloryana's better than either of us, and she can't play that."

Charyn started to reply that he was still better than Aloryana, then paused before he finally said, "I still like what I can't play." Then he turned and slipped away, still listening as he made his way toward the study of Alucar, the Minister of Finance.

Alucar offered an amused smile as Charyn entered the small study. "After over a week away, you've decided to come to the accounts. The rest of your life must be exceedingly dull."

"Unlike yours. I heard about the explosion at the Solis exchange. Have you heard anything more?"

Alucar shook his head.

"Why did it happen, do you think?"

The Finance Minister shrugged. "I could guess, but it wouldn't be a good idea. The exchanges make trading more effective. When things become more effective, there are those who gain and those who lose. Sometimes . . . the losers try to remove what caused them to lose."

"The High Holders, you think?"

Alucar shook his head. "It could be them. It could be small holders who don't produce enough grain or goods to use the exchanges. It could be a smaller factor, or a High Holder who doesn't manage his lands well. Any of those . . . or perhaps someone else. I've asked for more information, but I doubt anything more will be discovered that hasn't already." He paused. "Is that why you're here?"

"No. I'd planned to come even before I heard about Solis. Hearing that, though, made me think that I might find life even more difficult, or worse, if I don't learn more about what you do." That was true enough, but not the only reason for Charyn's efforts to learn more about the regial accounts and tariff system . . . and where the golds came from and where they went. "What would you recommend that I study today?"

Alucar lifted a small volume, one he had been clearly prepared to present to Charyn. "It's the compilation of qualifications for regial tariff collectors, the actions they are permitted to take on their own, those that require approval of a regional justicer, those that require approval of the high justicer, and those that are forbidden under any authority."

Charyn took the volume. While small, it did seem to contain a large number of pages to cover what Alucar had just described.

"If you have questions, I'd appreciate it if you would refrain from asking them until you finish the section that you are studying. You will see why after you read a complete section."

The implication behind those words was clearly an implication that only a dullard or idiot would not see. "Thank you, Minister."

Alucar just nodded and returned to reading the sheet before him, most likely an appeal, a writ of forfeiture, or a request for appointment as a tariff collector.

Charyn seated himself at the small table desk in the corner, again one he had personally carried in, and opened the volume, beginning to read.

> . . . in the year 393 A.L., following the reorganization of the collection of tariffs for all Solidar, as set forth under the *Codex Legis*, as revised by his grace and sovereign Rex Regis, Lorien, the following procedures, requirements, and associated definitions are hereby set forth . . .

Charyn took a long slow and quiet deep breath and forced himself to continue reading. It will be useful. In time, and in the meantime, he could discover information of a more immediately applicable nature.

When Alucar left the chamber, "for just a moment," some two quints later, Charyn went to the shelf that contained the ledger with the tariff records for the previous year—407 A.L.—and slipped the second volume out, carrying it to the desk where he was working. He did not immediately open it, but continued studying the small volume containing tariff procedures, knowing that when Alucar returned, he would have some questions about what Charyn was reading. He'd barely reseated himself when the minister returned.

"What is the principal requirement for a tariff collector?" asked Alucar, almost idly.

"That he be of good character and be without debts or other forms of indebtedness."

"Do you think that sufficient?"

"No, Minister. There have been men who appeared to meet that criterion who still abused their position."

"That is why there are tariff inspectors." Without saying more, Alucar returned his attention to the papers before him.

While Charyn had hoped to look through the ledger he had removed from the shelf for high holders and factors delinquent or late in paying tariffs, and for those who received large amounts from the regial coffers for work or supplies provided, it was clear that Alucar was watching him relatively closely, and the last thing he needed at the moment was for the minister to say anything to his father.

So he kept reading for a while, then looked up and said, "There is a sample of a tariff ledger page here, sir, with the notation preceded by a double star. There isn't any explanation of that notation."

"The double star indicates that the tariff was paid, but that the factor appealed the amount."

"How could I find out the reason for the appeal?"

"If you were me, you would look at the appeals ledger," replied Alucar dryly, as if Charyn should have known that fact.

Charyn didn't recall Alucar mentioning the appeals ledger, although the minister had gone over the possible grounds for appeal of a tariff. "Where is that kept?"

"On the second shelf of the corner bookcase. You're not ready to look into that yet."

Charyn continued through the small volume, and was more than halfway through when Alucar cleared his throat.

"I'm going to close the study, Lord Charyn. I need to go down to go over some matters with the clerks. It would be best if you came back later."

"I could stay."

"I'm sure you could, but I'd prefer that you not remain in the study alone. That might give the wrong appearance, possibly even to your father."

Charyn understood exactly what Alucar was not saying directly. "Can I leave the procedures book on the table desk?"

"That would be fine."

Charyn rose, and as Alucar turned, stepped toward the door and deftly replaced the volume he had earlier removed. "Thank you for helping me learn what you do and what you oversee."

"You should know that. I'm glad you're interested, for whatever reasons. As I mentioned before, and, as I will continue to remind you, I would caution you that any information you discover in the records should remain between you, me, and your father."

"I understand that, sir."

"Good."

Charyn did note that, as always, Alucar double-locked the door, first using the chateau door lock, and then with a heavy and unusual padlock that secured the heavy door by going through two heavy iron hasps. Charyn wasn't sure that even his father had the key to the second lock, and he certainly wasn't going to ask.

As he headed for the grand staircase, he could hear someone playing the clavecin, but it wasn't Palenya. He paused and listened. The heavy fingers on the keys meant it had to be Bhayrn.

He made his way up to his chambers, where he slid the bolt on the outer door and then proceeded to open the rear of the seemingly solid square pedestal that held a large, heavy, and admittedly less than attractive bronze oil lamp, one that emitted a great deal of light when lit, but one so heavy that no one questioned the overlarge pedestal on which it stood. It took Charyn some time, comparatively, perhaps half a quint, to remove one of the small chests hidden within. It took even longer to count the necessary golds, and then to place the few extras in the remaining chest.

Next, he had to place the chest in the sturdy leather satchel, and then he had to reassemble the pedestal and replace the lamp. Only then did he unlock the door and lift the satchel, heading down the narrow circular staircase, rather than the grand staircase, so that he would encounter no chateau functionary who might offer to carry the satchel.

He made his way to the rear courtyard, where the ostler was still readying the smaller coach. Yarselt and another guard stood waiting.

"Be just a few moments, Lord Charyn," called the ostler.

"Thank you."

Charyn forced himself to look bored. He doubted that his father would even notice his departure, but what mattered was getting away from the chateau and to Elthyrd's factorage. He hadn't sent a message to the factor because that was just another opportunity for what he was doing to be discovered, and he definitely didn't want that at the moment. Once he had things set up the way he wanted—or as close to that as possible—then he could always beg forgiveness from his father, since, at that point, the last thing Lorien should want was a revelation that he had attempted to forbid his own son from learning more about factoring and exchanges. *You just hope he's that reasonable.*

Nothing untoward happened, and in less than half a quint, the coach left the courtyard, with two guards, Yarselt sitting beside the driver, and Varyst in the rear dickey box. Both carried rifles, if unobtrusively. Charyn had a pistol, as usual, inside his jacket.

After the coach came to a halt outside Elthyrd's factorage, Charyn had only taken a few steps toward the entry when Elthyrd emerged, carrying a leather folder. "I thought you might be here today. Perhaps a little earlier."

"I was engaged with Minister Alucar. That took somewhat longer than I'd planned. I hope, again, that I'm not discommoding you unduly."

"I would that a few others were as solicitous, Lord Charyn." Elthyrd smiled wryly. "Since you're not interested, I presume, in trading today, we can add you to the merchant members of the exchange, if we hurry. The accountants and the bursar will be there until close to fourth glass."

"As you see, I do have a coach today. That should save some time."

Elthyrd raised his eyebrows.

"It's a smaller coach with no emblems or insignia, similar to many. I thought it unwise to transport golds on horseback."

"Then we should go."

When they were seated inside and the coach began to move, Elthyrd said, "Do you still plan to observe more than trade?"

"Until I know more, I plan only to observe. I had thought to investigate the possibilities of selling on the exchange, but I should have time, since it will be months before I have that much to sell."

"Your sire . . ."

"He's very wary of the exchanges. He prefers that I be most cautious." *And that's quite an understatement.*

"That does not surprise me." Elthyrd's words were droll, almost dry.

"I take it you have heard about the exchange in Solis," offered Charyn cautiously.

"Yesterday. Can you tell me anything?"

"No. I only know that explosives and oils were used. Who might have wanted to do such a thing?"

"Almost anyone who doesn't benefit from the exchange," suggested Elthyrd.

"That includes anyone except fairly large factors, doesn't it?"

"Even certain large factors might benefit from the closure of the exchange, but . . ." The timber factor left his sentence suggestively incomplete.

"The High Holders have the most to gain," suggested Charyn, "but that's so obvious that I have to wonder why a High Holder would risk doing something like that."

"I've thought that as well. Time may tell." Elthyrd laughed softly. "Then it may not."

Shortly, the coach stopped in the turnout. Charyn motioned for the factor to precede him, then lifted the heavy satchel out. "Yarselt, you'll accompany us."

"Yes, sir."

"The bursar's study is at the north end of the building," offered Elthyrd.

When they reached the northern door, Charyn noted that there were no guards. "The guards are only during trading glasses?"

"And for a glass after, while accounts are settled."

Inside the building, Elthyrd led Charyn and Yarselt to a black door in the middle of the inside north wall, which he opened.

Charyn turned to Yarselt. "You can wait here."

"Yes, sir."

Charyn then entered, closed the door, and followed Elthyrd, who had walked over to a table desk, behind which stood a stocky man in a mud-brown jacket.

"Bursar Thalyr, I had mentioned to you that I might be sponsoring the son of, shall we say a very wealthy individual. Bursar Thalyr, might I present Suyrien D'Chaeryll?" As he spoke, Elthyrd extracted a sheaf of papers from the leather folder he still carried and set them on the smooth black surface of the table desk.

Charyn noted that Thalyr had a pin on the lapel of his brown jacket—a silver sheaf surrounded by a circle. *That must be the pin used by those who work in the exchange.* "I'm pleased to meet you, Bursar Thalyr."

The bursar nodded, almost noncommittally.

Charyn set the small heavy chest on the table as well. "I understand the bond is five hundred golds . . . and that I can also deposit additional golds to my name in case I do decide to place trades at some time in the future."

"That is correct, High Holder—"

Charyn held up a hand. "Suyrien will do. At this point, I'm only the heir, although through inheritance I do have some lands of my own."

"Some five hundred hectares," added Elthyrd.

The bursar looked startled.

Charyn opened the chest. "If I've counted correctly, there are two thousand five hundred golds there."

Thalyr just looked at the chest of golds.

"My family is a somewhat old-fashioned," Charyn said. *That's definitely true.*

"You only want a merchant's account?" Thalyr frowned.

"That will be sufficient for now. This is a new venture for us, and the family would frown on any immediate excesses."

"Ah . . . yes . . . Suyrien." After a momentary pause, Thalyr went on, "We will need to fill out the necessary forms for a proper registration of membership."

Counting the golds and filling out the forms took close to a quint, and Charyn was surprised to discover that not a great deal of personal information was required. Apparently, large amounts of golds on deposit made detailed information superfluous.

When all the forms were completed and signed, Thalyr affixed the exchange seal to several of them, including both a small card and a certificate, both of which he presented to Charyn, along with a gold sheaf pin—without a diamond at the base. "You might wish to keep the card with you until the staff recognizes you by sight, Factor Suyrien."

"Thank you for the advice . . . and for your kindness in dealing with me later in the day than is customary." Charyn inclined his head slightly.

"You're most welcome, sir. We hope to see you often."

Charyn said little more until he and Elthyrd were in the coach returning to the factorage. "He was a little stunned by the golds."

"Usually, memberships are paid with bills of account drawn on other exchanges or banques."

"For some obvious reasons . . ."

"I have this feeling that your sire wants to keep his distance from this venture of yours." Elthyrd paused. "You're managing the lands, yourself, aren't you?"

"Listening to the tenants and overseeing would be a better description," Charyn admitted. "I have managed to improve the yield and return."

"Thoughtful oversight does have that effect."

Charyn had the feeling that Elthyrd's words applied to more than the lands of Chaeryll, but he merely nodded. He was more than relieved to have accomplished several purposes through gaining a merchant status at the exchange.

Now all he had to do was keep his father from finding out too soon. Eventually, such discovery was inevitable, but, as in anything, the timing mattered.

6

On Meredi morning, the narrow covered courtyard was still damp and more than a little chill, as well as gloomy, with little light entering through the high slits in the wall, unsurprisingly, given the high gray clouds that had hung over L'Excelsis for days, or so it seemed to Charyn as he walked away from the man-shaped targets fastened to the bales of hay stacked against the wall.

He turned quickly, but forced himself to keep his hand steady as he squeezed the trigger. He fired a second time, then lowered the short-barreled pistol, and studied the targets. *Not perfect, but enough to stop a man.*

He reloaded the small double-shot pistol, then walked farther away, before turning and firing again, twice. He winced at the second shot, knowing that he'd jerked at the trigger, rather than squeezing it. The first shot had struck what would have been the chest of a man. The second had barely clipped the outline of an arm. He had to admit that Paersyt had been right, much as it galled him. How such a small thing . . .

He shook his head, then looked up as Guard Captain Churwyl entered the courtyard and walked toward him.

"Good morning, sir."

"The same to you, Churwyl."

"You've gotten much better, I can see."

"Practice, and a little more technique. Maybe better understanding of the pistol." That was as far as Charyn was about to go in admitting his own shortcomings.

"Every weapon is different, even those made by the same gunsmith."

"Is there anything I need to know?"

"No, sir. I was just making my morning inspection, and I heard the shots. Thought it might be you, but I wanted to make sure."

"I appreciate your thoughtfulness." Charyn paused. "Do the guards keep a log of anyone visiting the chateau?"

"Yes, sir. But only people who enter the chateau to see the rex or the ministers. We don't make a big thing of it, and we don't ask for names."

"So if Marshal Vaelln brought another officer . . . and you couldn't find out, you'd just write out 'Marshal Vaelln and a commander,' something like that?"

Churwyl smiled. "Most times we do find out, but if we don't, then that would be the entry."

"I might like to look at the book sometime."

"That shouldn't be a problem, but ask for me. The rex is the only one who can ask for it from any guard."

"I appreciate that."

Once Churwyl turned and left, Charyn reloaded the pistol and moved to within five yards of the targets. He turned quickly and tried to fire immediately, without jerking at the trigger. Both shots did hit the targets, but barely.

You need to practice that more.

He reloaded once more and tried again.

Later . . . at a quint past seventh glass, Charyn knocked on the door to Norstan's study, then opened the door and stepped inside. "Good morning."

"Good morning, Lord Charyn." Norstan rose from behind the table desk, deliberately and not quite immediately.

"If you would, I'd like to see yesterday's appointments."

"Of course." The seneschal lifted a single sheet of paper from the side of the desk and handed it to Charyn.

Charyn scanned the listing of names: Saerlet D'Anomen, Delcoeur D'Alte, Alucar, Sanafryt, and Aevidyr, and Maitre Alastar. The last four made sense—the ministers of finance, justice, and administration and the Maitre of the Collegium. So, in a sad way, did Delcoeur, who was likely hinting for funds of some sort, from his cousin the rex. "What was the purpose of Chorister Saerlet's visit?"

"He did not say, but I would imagine he wants golds to refurbish the Anomen D'Rex." Norstan's lips quirked in obvious distaste. "The rex had mentioned something of the sort when he granted the appointment."

Charyn nodded, thinking, *It was completely rebuilt and refurbished less than twenty years ago, after it was gutted by Antiagon fire.* "And High Holder Delcoeur?"

"He sent a personal missive to the rex. The rex told me to inform the High Holder he had two quints at second glass yesterday."

"Did he meet with anyone not on his appointment list—besides you or members of the family?"

"No, sir."

"Thank you, Norstan. I'll see you later."

"Yes, sir."

Charyn was fairly certain Norstan was telling the truth, but he could easily check with Churwyl—and the entry logbook—if necessary. By comparing the log to the appointment listing, he could also find out a few other things.

Little more than a quint later, Charyn, Yarselt, and three other chateau guards were headed north on the ring road in the direction of army headquarters. Although it was barely seventh glass, there were already wagons and carts on the ring road, despite the overcast sky and the chill wind out of the northwest. Even so, no one seemed to pay much attention to the five riders, despite the fact that four were wearing the winter uniforms of the Chateau Guard. *Because no one expects you to be riding this early,* wondered Charyn, *or because no one really cares about the rex and his family anymore?*

Three quints later, the five slowed their mounts as they approached the gates to army headquarters.

An undercaptain rode forward to meet them. "Lord Charyn, welcome. I'm Undercaptain Raavyrn. If you would follow me."

The two gate guards presented arms as Charyn and the undercaptain rode past.

"Have you been posted here long?" Charyn asked.

"This is my first tour here, sir. I'm with the recruit training company."

Charyn looked more closely at the undercaptain, realizing that the officer was a good ten years older than Charyn himself, an indication that he had come up through the ranks, and relatively quickly. "Where were you posted before?"

"In Westisle, sir."

"It's a bit colder here."

"Yes, sir. I'd prefer it that way." After a moment, Raavyrn pointed. "The headquarters building is the large one on the left. It looks partly like an old chateau. That's because it once was, back in the time of the first Rex Regis."

When they neared the headquarters building, Charyn could see the lighter-colored stones and masonry in the walls, but he wondered for several moments why the replacement stones and bricks were two different colors. Then he recalled that on two occasions, rebel officers had planted explosives in the building in attempt to kill loyal senior officers, first almost twenty years before in the unrest that had led to his father becoming rex, and then again just six years previous at the beginning of the High Holder Revolt.

"Your men can wait inside until you leave the building to tour the post," offered Raavyrn when the group had reined up outside the front of the building.

"Yarselt will accompany me everywhere," Charyn replied pleasantly. "The others will appreciate not waiting out in the chill."

"Yes, sir."

Charyn dismounted, handing the reins of his chestnut to one of the guards. Yarselt also dismounted, but tied his mount to the hitching rail, as did the undercaptain, who then led the way up the steps and into the headquarters building. Charyn glanced back and motioned for the remaining four guards to tie their mounts and follow.

Once inside, past a pair of guards posted just inside, Raavyrn turned to the left through the central hall and down a wide corridor. He stopped outside an open door. "The marshal's study, sir."

A slender officer stepped out. "Lord Charyn."

Charyn would have recognized the sandy-haired and green-eyed Vaelln, even without the uniform of a marshal, from the times he had observed him visiting the Chateau D'Rex. "Marshal Vaelln. You're kind to meet me. I did not wish to impose on your time because of my lack of knowledge."

"I just wanted to welcome you to headquarters." Vaelln gestured to the study.

Charyn turned to Yarselt and said in a low voice, "You can wait here."

The guard nodded and stepped to the side.

Charyn let the marshal lead him into the study. The door closed behind them, and Charyn took in the two other officers who stood waiting.

"I'd like to introduce you to Vice-Marshal Maurek . . . and to Subcommander Luerryn, who will escort you around headquarters and brief you as he does." Vaelln gestured to each man as he spoke his name.

Maurek was black-haired, almost angular, with a sharp nose, and deep-set green eyes. Luerryn was a stocky man, with thinning brown hair and a weathered face that suggested he had more than earned his rank.

"I'm pleased to meet you both. I appreciate your taking the time."

Both men nodded.

Vaelln gestured to the circular conference table. "I thought Vice-Marshal Maurek and I would give you a brief overview of the army and navy, then answer any questions you might have. After that, Subcommander Luerryn will give you a complete tour of headquarters with even more detailed information."

"That sounds exactly like what I was looking for, Marshal." As he settled into the chair that Vaelln had pointed out, Charyn just hoped he could remember everything that he heard.

"I'll detail the aspects of the navy, and Vice-Marshal Maurek will go over the army . . ." Vaelln squared himself in his chair and continued. "At present, the navy has forty ships of the line, and fifty-four other warships of various classes, including the twenty-two war sloops used to combat coastal piracy . . ."

All told, Vaelln and Maurek each spoke for about a quint.

Then Vaelln smiled and asked, "Do you have any questions?"

"I have a few," admitted Charyn, "possibly not nearly so many as I should have. I've heard that there might be a problem with Jariolan and Ferran privateers boarding more merchant ships. How serious is that?"

Vaelln nodded. "The Jariolans in particular pose a problem. Not only do they have more ships of the line than do we, but the Oligarch has commissioned over a hundred privateers."

"For what? We aren't at war with them."

"They're empowering them to board ships to seek out Jariolan deserters." Vaelln's tone turned dryly ironic. "They always find some, even when there aren't any. That's how they're supplementing the crews for their warships. That's not surprising, given that they have sixty ships of the line."

"Isn't anyone doing anything about it?"

"Your father sent an envoy to Jariolt last summer. The Oligarch insisted that they have the right to seek out deserters. They were very firm about that. If we attempt to stop them by force, that will mean war."

"What about the Ferrans?"

"Since Ferrum borders Jariola and has some thirty ships of the line, as well as a large army, the Jariolans don't touch Ferran ships. Everyone else's ships are fair game. Any merchant ships that resist are attacked, and the survivors taken prisoner and pressed into service. Those who object are thrown overboard."

Charyn hadn't heard about the privateers impressing merchant sailors . . . and even killing them. "What are we doing?"

"We're somewhat limited, Lord Charyn. Your father has provided more funds for warships, but we're only able to build three new ships a year, four at times. We only had twenty-some ships of the line at the time of the revolt. That means we can keep the privateers well away from Solidar—most of the time—but our merchanters engaged in the spice trade with the lands of Otelyrn are largely at the mercy of the privateers. That's why some of them have built special ships—clippers—that can outrun almost any privateer."

"The privateers don't build faster ships?"

"The clippers are built narrower and lighter. Naval guns and shells are heavy. Boarding crews require more space."

"If they already have sixty ships, and we can only build four a year . . ."

"You can see the problem."

Charyn asked several more questions, including several about the location of army posts, and the rationale for those locations, before deciding that he'd asked enough to show interest, and hopefully not to have revealed the depth of his ignorance. "Thank you. You've given me a great deal to think about. Once I have, I may have additional questions." He turned to Subcommander Luerryn. "Then it's likely that the subcommander will provide even more information." Realizing that the officers were all looking to him, he rose. "Again, I must thank you."

"It was our pleasure, Lord Charyn," returned Vaelln.

Charyn got the impression that the marshal honestly felt that way. *But does he feel that way, or does he just want you to feel that way?*

For the next three glasses, Subcommander Luerryn and Alastar rode through every lane in headquarters and even out to the area where cannon were tested and ranged. Luerryn explained everything so clearly that Charyn had almost no questions.

When they finally rode back and reined up outside the headquarters building, Charyn turned in the saddle. "I have to thank you for all the time you've spent with me, Subcommander, and for everything you've tried to impart to me. I just hope I can remember it half as well as you presented it."

"You've been very attentive, Lord Charyn."

Far more attentive than expected. That was the feeling Charyn got from both Luerryn's words and his expression.

"If you were in my boots," said Charyn casually, "what would be the most important things for me to know?"

"In your boots, sir?" The subcommander shook his head. "I wouldn't even pretend to imagine that."

"Then . . . what would you say makes the difference between an adequate marshal and a good marshal?"

"A good marshal knows what every field-grade officer can do and what duties they're best suited to. He also knows who to trust with what."

"What about military skills?"

"In a good army, officers shouldn't be promoted to field grade without those skills. Marshal Vaelln's army and navy are good."

"Some of the army wasn't so good at the time of the revolt," suggested Charyn.

"Begging your pardon, Your Lordship . . . the army and its officers all had good military skills. That wasn't the question. The question was of loyalty and trust." Luerryn smiled pleasantly.

"Were the imagers as effective as people say?"

"Without the imagers, sir, you and I would be long dead."

"You were there? At the last battle?"

"I had command of a battalion of mounted infantry. We were outnumbered at least four to one, and we had only eight cannon . . ."

Charyn listened to the subcommander's summary of the battle, trying not to frown when Luerryn described what he said was the turning point.

". . . the rebels had drawn most of our reserves into the center, and then they charged our southern flank. We couldn't disengage quick enough, but Maitre Alastar threw all the imagers into the flank. They managed to blunt the attack—until the rebel imagers threw a huge ball of that yellow-green Antiagon Fire. It looked like it was going to swallow our whole left side . . . until two of the imagers charged it. How they did it, I don't know. One moment, we were about to be burned to cinders, and the next there was this brilliant lance of yellow-green so bright that none of us could see . . . and there was an explosion, nearly ripped me from the saddle. When I could see again, snow and ice was falling and that whole half of the rebel force was gone. All that was left was ice, just ice. It must have stretched a half a mille on a side. Nothing else. No horses, no bodies, no weapons, nothing . . . just ice . . ." Luerryn shook himself. "You don't forget something like that. The imagers lost about a third of their number, but they turned, and Maitre Alastar led them straight through the remaining fighting to the pretender's force. Some say he killed the pretender himself. I couldn't say. Then they rode back. I never saw anything like that before. Never want to see anything like it again." Abruptly, the pleasant smile returned. "I'd say you'd rather not, either."

"I'll take your word. I saw three imagers destroy two companies right in front of the chateau."

"You were watching, sir?"

"I wasn't supposed to, but I wanted to see what happened."

Luerryn nodded, but did not say more for several moments, then asked, "Is there anything else you'd like to know?"

There was, but not anything he wanted to ask. "No, thank you. All of you have given me a great deal to consider."

As he rode back toward the Chateau D'Rex, Charyn's thoughts drifted back to the subcommander's description of the last battle of the revolt. *Half an army or more destroyed in an instant . . . yellow-green fire and then nothing but ice?* He'd never actually heard the battle described by someone who had been there before . . . but to hear it that way, from a stolid career officer who had clearly come up through the ranks . . . that gave him even more to think about.

The clouds had finally begun to disperse by the time Charyn reined up in the chateau courtyard, but the light from the white sun didn't seem to add much warmth to the late afternoon as he walked through the sunlit center of the courtyard and into the shadows to the center rear door to the chateau. The guard by the door inclined his head as Charyn passed.

Once inside, he could hear someone playing the clavecin, and, wincing, realized that what he heard was Bhayrn. He made his way to the door of the music room, but stopped outside, waiting until Bhayrn stopped playing . . . or Palenya stopped him—because Bhayrn never practiced unless he had to.

The comparative silence, followed by a brief passage of far more nuanced notes, confirmed that belief.

With the next silence, after Bhayrn's largely unsuccessful attempts to emulate Palenya, Charyn opened the door and stepped inside. Bhayrn looked up from the clavecin hopefully, but his face fell as he saw Charyn.

"No, I'm not about to rescue you. You need to stop pounding the keys, as I'm certain Musician Palenya has already told you."

Bhayrn looked away, glowering.

Charyn turned to Palenya. "I need to talk to you when you're finished, but please do not cut short your instructional with Bhayrn. His playing needs all the help he can get. I'll be in my sitting room."

Bhayrn looked up and glared at Charyn, who offered a pleasant smile in return.

Then he turned and left the music room, closing the door quietly, and headed for the kitchen, where he made certain arrangements.

By the time Palenya arrived almost a glass later, the late afternoon tea and refreshments were waiting, and he gestured to the empty chair across the small table from him. "I've been waiting for you."

"You didn't have to do this."

"No. But I thought you would like, if not need, some refreshments and company after spending more than a glass with Bhayrn."

"He dislikes playing."

"But he fears displeasing Mother even more."

"That's wise of him."

"Especially since you're very skilled, and Mother knows it."

"There are other clavecinists who are just as skilled."

"I don't know of any others," bantered Charyn.

"You haven't looked. Here in L'Excelsis, there are many without positions."

"Positions for musicians are limited, I know."

"Especially for women. Your mother met with half a score."

She did? That did surprise Charyn.

"You know I'm only here at your mother's pleasure and for yours."

Charyn didn't like to think about that. "You make it sound . . ." He wasn't quite sure what to say that wouldn't be even worse.

"You see?" Palenya's voice was gentle. "This is the best I could ever do."

"You play so well, and you know so much. You've taught me more than I could have imagined. About music," he added quickly.

"About both," she added. "It's not an accident that I'm five years older than you, and widowed. Where else could the third daughter of a musician go that wouldn't be even worse? One who can't have children and wants to remain a musician?"

That was another thing Charyn didn't want to think about . . . but he did understand. "You'll always have a place."

"Don't make promises. What your family has granted me is more than I could have hoped . . . and Aloryana is still young."

Meaning that I don't yet control my destiny or yours and that there may be some years you can remain as her teacher. "I can certainly plan."

"Sometimes, what we plan works out. Sometimes . . ." Palenya shrugged.

Charyn lifted the pot and poured the tea. Then he edged the platter toward her plate. "The almond biscuits are quite good."

Palenya smiled. "I'm sure they are."

7

Charyn slept slightly later than usual on Jeudi morning, as he sometimes did when Palenya spent the night with him, then hurried through breakfast, and spent some time in the covered courtyard practicing with his pistols, after which he met briefly with Norstan. The only addition to Meredi's appointments list was Marshal Vaelln, who had met with his father late in the day, most likely when Charyn had been with Palenya. That meeting suggested that something more might have come up with the Jariolans.

He was just returning to his quarters to ready himself to leave the chateau when the guard usually posted outside his father's study hurried toward him. "Lord Charyn! Your sire requests your presence."

Now what? It was seldom a good thing when he was summoned. He turned and followed the guard back to the study.

"Lord Charyn, Your Grace."

That form of address was definitely not good.

Charyn stepped into the study, and the guard quickly closed the door.

"Young man. Get! Over! Here!"

Charyn took measured steps and sat down in the middle chair of the three facing the goldenwood desk. "You summoned me, sir?"

"Yesterday, you met with Marshal Vaelln and his staff. I won't have you going behind my back! I won't. You will not do anything like that again! Is that understood?"

"Sir," replied Charyn calmly, although he didn't feel as calm as his voice was, "my intent was not to go behind your back. I requested a briefing on the army and the navy. I even suggested that a junior officer was most appropriate to convey the basic information that I did not know—"

"That makes me seem incompetent in your education! I will not have it."

"Sir, how am I supposed to learn things? You've spent a lifetime learning. You weren't that much older than I am now when you became rex. You're going to live longer than your father did, and that means I have to learn things while you're still rex."

"By going behind my back?"

"I have asked you. Your answer is always the same. 'You'll have time.' I ask if I can attend meetings. You say no. You tell me a few words about a problem, but half the time, when I ask more, you tell me I know enough."

"That's enough, Charyn. You will not go around me again. If you *ever* talk to senior officers again . . ."

"Sir, I said nothing about what you or I thought. I only listened and asked questions. Not leading questions, either. Just factual questions. About the kind of basics you know and think I should know and that I don't. The marshal welcomed me. He talked for less than a quint. Then a subcommander gave me a complete tour of the headquarters post. I have a much better idea of what is there now. I asked nothing about any direction you may have given, and they asked nothing about you."

"Were they ever critical of me?"

"No, sir. Never. They even said that you were building warships as fast as possible to deal with the Jariolan privateers and warships."

"Not fast enough for the factors. They want me to spend more golds than any rex ever had just to build ships. What else did Vaelln say?"

"He said you'd sent an envoy—"

"Young High Holder Meinyt. Stronger than his father. That didn't do any good. The Oligarch told him that Jariola had the right to seek out deserters, by force if necessary. He even sent a very polite communiqué that implied the same thing. It's somewhere here. The only way to stop that is to fight. The last thing we can afford is a war. I can't even get the High Holders and the factors to pay enough tariffs to fund what needs to be done in Solidar."

"If the Jariolan merchants can build and arm ships, why don't our factors arm their own ships?"

"There are a few who do. There's a family in Westisle that does, and another out of Nacliano or Estisle, I forget which. Most don't. It costs golds, for the cannon, for the shells and powder, and for men trained to use them. The High Holders don't trade that much outside Solidar, and they don't want to pay higher tariffs to help the factors. The factors don't want to spend the golds themselves. They want me to, but they don't want to pay higher tariffs to provide the golds so that I can build more ships. Greedy bastards."

"What has the Factors' Council said?"

"That I should increase tariffs slowly, because most factors will be angry if I do so more quickly." Lorien snorted. "Slow increases means slow building of ships, and any increase means angry High Holders."

"What about tariffing goods landed in our ports?"

"The factors claim that higher tariffs will just increase smuggling. Unless I build more war sloops to patrol our own coasts. There's no easy answer to any of this, Charyn. There never was and there never will be . . ."

For the next half glass, Charyn mostly listened, slipping in an occasional question, all designed to let his father reveal more.

Abruptly, there was a knock on the study door. "Maitre Alastar, Your Grace."

"You may greet the Maitre, Charyn, then depart."

"Yes, sir." Charyn immediately stood and moved away from the desk and the chairs before it.

"Have the Maitre come in."

Charyn inclined his head to the broad-shouldered imager as Alastar entered the study, although he couldn't help but notice that the Maitre's once-silver-gray hair was more streaked with white than even the last time he had seen him several months ago. "Maitre."

"Lord Charyn."

"It's good to see you. I was just leaving."

"I wish you a pleasant day."

Charyn slipped out of the study and down the grand staircase, heading toward the music room. With luck, his father wouldn't even recall just how angry he'd been at Charyn. He frowned as he thought about the Maitre's appearance. Alastar didn't usually come to the chateau two days in three unless there was a problem.

"Message for the rex!" one of the guards called, loud enough that the words carried from the entry hall.

For a moment, Charyn paused. Messengers usually weren't that loud.

He had thought about going to the exchange, but decided against it immediately because he wanted to be around when Maitre Alastar departed. Instead, he made his way into the music room, but it was vacant. He looked at the clavecin, then sat down before it, and began to play, trying to recall the shortest of the Covaelyt pieces he'd learned to the limits of his ability in order to impress Palenya. He had achieved less success with several others of Covaelyt's works, but he still worked on them, if occasionally. It took him three attempts to get the short piece right . . . or mostly right, despite the fact that it was likely the easiest of those he practiced. When he rose and turned, he found Palenya standing just inside the door.

"Was the last one . . . acceptable?" he asked.

"Somewhat better than acceptable."

He smiled sardonically. He hadn't expected much praise from her. About music, Palenya was usually very honest and direct in her assessments.

"You could be better if you practiced more."

"I do practice. You know that. Even with more practice, I'd never be the best."

"Do you have to be the best at everything? Aren't there some things that you could be good at because you enjoy them?"

Charyn smiled, honestly. "That's why I still play. I do like it. I doubt I would were it not for what you've taught me."

"Flattery, yet."

"Flattery," he admitted, "with truth behind it."

She raised her eyebrows.

At that moment, Charyn heard the slamming of a door, and there was only one person who was allowed to slam doors in the Chateau D'Rex. The slammed door also meant that Maitre Alastar had already left the chateau—and that something in that message had very much upset his father. "Please excuse me." He eased around Palenya and hurried to the grand staircase and started up it, trying to be both quick and not too noisy.

He'd only taken a few steps when he caught sight of his father heading in the direction of his mother's sitting room. *Something in the message has him upset. Much more upset than usual.*

While he didn't dare linger outside the door, he could walk past, toward the playroom that hadn't been used in years, slowly . . . and trying to catch a sense of what had disturbed his father.

". . . can't just refuse . . ."

". . . know there's nothing . . . wouldn't stoop to . . ."

". . . veiled threat . . ."

Charyn wished he could have heard more, but he didn't dare linger as he turned and made his way to his own sitting room, where he left the door open before sitting down at his desk. There was only one person he knew of that might elicit that reaction . . . but . . . *that's still a guess.*

Even after his father returned to his own study, Charyn couldn't exactly drop in on his mother.

He still wondered.

After several moments, he took out a sheet of his personal stationery, uncapped the inkwell, and began to write. A quint later, he signed the letter and sealed it, then slipped it inside his jacket and headed down to the main level, where he walked to the main front entry where the two guards were posted.

"Were you two here when that message arrived?"

"Yes, sir."

"Who was the messenger?"

"He didn't say, sir. He wore maroon livery."

Charyn forced himself to nod. "Thank you."

He turned to make his way to the courtyard when he noticed Aloryana sitting alone in the receiving parlor, wearing riding clothes. Curious, he stepped inside. "What are you doing here?"

"I just felt like it. I was going to go riding with Bhayrn, but he was so beastly about it that I decided not to. I heard you talking to the guards. Why did you want to know about a message?"

Charyn debated evading the question, but then considered that she might know something he didn't. "I have the feeling that there is some-thing happening that we don't know. Today and on Lundi, Maitre Alastar came to see Father. Two visits in just a few days. I don't think that's hap-pened in months. Then a message came a while ago. The messenger wore the livery of the High Council. After Father read it, he started slamming doors. I could hear him talking to Mother. Not what they said, but he was loud and angry."

"Then he will be quiet at dinner tonight," replied Aloryana. "He gets that way when he's been angry and upset."

"Do you have any ideas?"

"He doesn't like Uncle Ryel." Aloryana offered an ironic smile. "Neither does Mother."

That was an understatement, to say the least. It was all too obvious to both of them, since their mother would almost never mention Ryel's name, even though he was Chelia's brother, and she was never visible on the few occasions when the High Council came to the chateau to meet with the rex. "But this was more than that."

"Mother hasn't said anything," replied Aloryana. "Do you think the High Holders are getting difficult? More difficult. Father always finds them difficult."

"That's possible. But Maitre Alastar didn't seem all that disturbed," said Charyn. "He never does. Not that I've seen."

"I think Father is wary of him."

"I'd be wary, too. Of any imager, but especially of the Maitre."

"Do you think people are wary of the women who are imagers?"

Charyn smiled. "If they aren't, they should be. Maitre Alyna—she's his wife . . ."

"I know who she is."

"She's said to be as powerful an imager as he is. She might be stronger now that he's getting older. She's the Senior Imager. That's the second-highest post at the Collegium, and—"

"I know that, too. What else?"

"She killed a lot of people in the High Holder revolt, and the head of the High Council worries more about her than Maitre Alastar."

"How do you know that?"

"I just do."

"Charyn, I hate it when you start sounding so superior." Aloryana stopped as shouts echoed through the lower floor of the chateau, most likely coming from the door to the rear courtyard.

Charyn immediately turned, stepped out into the hall, and headed toward the rear past the foot of the grand staircase, where he saw Bhayrn, looking pale, several guards, and Churwyl.

"What happened?" Charyn demanded, then, looking at Bharyn more closely, "Are you all right?"

"I'm fine. My horse isn't."

Charyn looked back to the guard captain.

"Someone shot Lord Bhayrn's mount. Then they shot one of the guards dead, and then the other's mount."

"Who did it?"

"We don't know. The surviving guard and Lord Bhayrn took the re-maining mount back from the hunting park. I've sent guards to see what they can find."

"They won't find much," predicted Charyn, turning to Bharyn and asking, "Did you see anyone?"

"Of course not. One moment I was riding looking for the red deer, and the next I was scrambling to keep from being crushed."

"The other guard saw a man in a brown cloak, but he was out of sight before the guard could recover his rifle."

Recover? Then Charyn realized that the guard had likely lost it when his mount went down. "Bhayrn. You and the guard and Captain Churwyl need to tell Father what happened. Now!"

"You're not—"

"Now! You think this was an accident or happenstance?"

Charyn watched as the three headed up the grand staircase. He had no desire to be present in their father's study. He'd hear enough later.

That possibility occurred sooner than he believed would happen, since less than a quint after Bhayrn had trudged up the grand staircase, Charyn and Aloryana had been summoned and were climbing the same steps and making their way to Lorien's study. When Charyn and his sister entered the study, they discovered that Chelia, Bhayrn, and their father were all waiting.

No one was seated, and Lorien was pacing back and forth beside the widows near his desk. He looked up. "Close the door."

Charyn was already in the process of doing so.

"Now that you're all here." He shook his head. "First the mess with the High Council and High Holder Ryel . . . and now this." Lorien glared at Bhayrn, then Charyn, before glancing briefly at Chelia.

"You didn't tell us about the High Council and High Holder Ryel," said Charyn mildly.

"It's none—" Lorien stopped as Chelia looked hard at him. "I suppose it is, since one of you got shot at."

"Ryel sent me a message this afternoon, insisting that he had to step down as head of the High Council not only because he has served long enough, but because of what he said were significant threats against him and his family. He claims not to know the source, but he doubts that it is from any High Holder. He didn't say why he believed that."

Since no one else spoke, Charyn did. "Do you believe him, sir?"

"I don't trust him. I've never trusted him." Lorien paused. "But . . . yes, I'm inclined to believe him. At least about this."

"Why?" asked Chelia. "Why now?"

"Because we've reached an accommodation with the High Holders. They've lost two revolts in twenty years, and I haven't proposed any significant increases in tariffs. What would be the point for any of the High Holders to threaten Ryel now?"

Chelia's expression conveyed reservations, if not doubt. "Could that be a concealment for the reasons behind the attack on Bhayrn?"

"The attack wasn't on Bhayrn," replied Lorien. "Whoever was shooting was good enough to bring down two horses and kill a guard in four shots. If they'd meant to have killed Bhayrn, they would have. The guard was killed to make that point."

"You haven't received any threats," Chelia pointed out.

"We will, before long." Lorien glanced toward the hangings that covered the window to his right. "It's easier to shoot at someone before they're warned."

"So what are we supposed to do?" asked Bhayrn.

"For one thing, no one is to go riding until we know more," declared Lorien. "No one. I've already instructed Churwyl to double the guards around the chateau and to engage in regular patrols of the hunting park. I've already sent summonses to Maitre Alastar, High Holder Ryel, and Factor Elthyrd to meet here with me at the first glass of the afternoon tomorrow."

"So early?" murmured Bhayrn.

Lorien whirled. "No comments from you. You're fortunate to be alive."

"You said they weren't aiming at me."

"They could have missed your mount and hit you, you know? Even the best marksmen occasionally miss." Lorien snorted. "That's all. Remember, no riding." He turned to face Chelia, as if to indicate that the three siblings were to leave.

Bhayrn did not quite bolt for the study door.

Charyn walked beside Aloryana, then motioned for her to precede him. He did let Maertyl, the duty guard, close the study door.

"What do you think they want from Father?" Aloryana asked quietly as they walked toward the central upper hall, well behind Bhayrn.

"I suspect he'll find out before long."

"Why are they doing it?"

"The last two revolts proved that the imagers can defeat both armies and small groups of attackers. It's much harder to deal with snipers and people who stay hidden."

"But . . . won't what they want reveal who they are?"

"You'd think so," replied Charyn, "but things aren't always what we think." After what had happened, that was definitely so, and another reason why he'd need to burn the letter he'd penned.

8

Although Charyn had thought to ride to the exchange on Vendrei morning, after what had happened to Bhayrn the afternoon before, he decided that discretion was to be preferred over senseless valor, and he took the small and elegant, but nondescript, coach, accompanied by Yarselt and another guard, both wearing the plain brown coats. He also left early so that his father was not up or awake enough to forbid his departure. There was little point in meeting with Norstan, either, since Charyn already knew who had visited his father.

His early departure meant that he needed to visit Elthyrd first, and possibly even Paersyt, before the exchange opened.

As he rode south on the Avenue D'Commercia, Charyn still wondered about the shooting in the hunting park. As his father had pointed out, the only way that made sense was if it happened to be a threat or a warning—but what kind of threat or warning? The only people who might threaten both Ryel and his father would be unhappy factors and merchants. What would be the purpose of such threats? Killing either man—or both—wouldn't solve the problems the factors faced, not immediately, assuming that was even the motivation. Nor would burning an exchange building, he realized, really do much besides express anger and create more anger in those who had to pay for its replacement.

He'd debated not doing what he had in mind, but his father had only explicitly forbidden riding. Besides, he doubted there would be any more attempts or threats until after his father received some sort of explicit threat. If he didn't . . .

Charyn shook his head. In that case, he and his family could spend years in the chateau waiting for something else to occur. *But that's not likely to happen.*

As seemed to be usual at Elthyrd's factorage, men were loading and unloading flatboats under a clear sky that should have indicated a day warmer than it was. Not seeing Elthyrd outside, Charyn entered the factorage, where a young square-faced clerk looked up from the farther table desk. His eyes took in the exchange pin on Charyn's jacket. "Sir?"

"Suyrien D'Chaeryll to see Factor Elthyrd."

"Ah . . ."

"I'll see him." Elthyrd appeared in the doorway of his study.

Charyn stepped around the table desks and joined Elthyrd in the study, closing the door behind himself.

"Are you here because of the summons your father issued?" asked Elthyrd, gesturing to the chairs in front of the desk.

"The first reason I came was to offer my thanks for your support of my membership in the exchange. Since I'll be going there shortly, it seemed that I should stop and offer thanks."

"The second reason being something your father wishes?"

"I'm not here because of anything my father has done," replied Charyn as he seated himself. "If I'm to be truthful, he'd prefer that I not associate with factors at all, except in the strict course of business."

"He has conveyed a certain distance."

Charyn merely nodded. Much as he agreed with Elthyrd, commenting was unnecessary and unwise.

"Do you have any idea why he requested my presence?"

"He only said that he had requested your presence. My sire doesn't divulge to me, or likely anyone, what he plans to say to you or others with whom he meets. I do know that he received a missive yesterday that greatly upset him and that someone took a shot at my brother yesterday."

"Someone shot your brother?"

"Shot at him. They hit a guard and the mounts."

"Shot at your brother . . ." Elthyrd repeated, almost musingly.

"I doubt that my sire would be pleased that I informed you, but you would be even less pleased had I not. We have no idea who did it, but whether that has any bearing on what he will discuss with you, I have no idea. Usually, I never find out anything he does not wish to reveal, and there is little he wishes to reveal."

"Even to you?"

"He tells me he has no intention of dying any time soon, and I have plenty of time to learn."

"I appreciate the information, but will not reveal that I knew previously."

"Thank you. The other matter about which I came to see you was something entirely different. The other day I got a briefing from Marshal Vaelln. He was telling me that the Jariolan privateers are taking a great toll on Solidaran shipping, particularly near Jariola and Ferrum. I also gained the impression that some of those privateers are heading into the southern ocean. That might well affect those trading with the lands of Otelyrn, particularly those in the spice trade."

"Ha! It already is. All you have to do when you're at the exchange is check the future price of pepper."

"I take it that the price is up considerably. Do you know if the Jariolan warships and privateers are taking more than supposed deserters?"

"I doubt it could be otherwise. Some factors claim they are. Some have lost ships. They're the most vocal of all those who want more warships built."

The way Elthyrd had phrased his response suggested something to Charyn, and he tried to phrase his next question carefully. "Is that why the Factors' Council is concerned about the pace of adding warships?"

"We've been telling your sire for two years that he's adding ships too slowly. There's no secret about that."

Except to me. "And the High Holders have been protesting that building more ships more quickly will require higher tariffs and will result in more unhappy High Holders and more unrest?"

"He hasn't told you that?" Elthyrd looked surprised.

"No . . . but it makes sense." Charyn smiled, sheepishly, he hoped. "I probably shouldn't be talking to you about this."

"Probably not, but you can see why some merchants and factors aren't terribly pleased with the situation."

Or Father. "It doesn't seem as though anything will make everyone happy."

"At the moment, no one's happy," Elthyrd pointed out. "The burning of the exchange in Solis didn't help matters."

"That's a very good observation." Charyn paused. "I will have to leave before long. Is there anything else you think I should know?"

"The way you're playing your plaques could be dangerous."

"I'm trying not to play at all, but if I don't learn more than I have, I may not be in the game at all when it comes my turn to play."

Elthyrd nodded. "It's good to know you don't consider yourself a player. I can see that is what you wish. Others may not be so charitable."

"There is that risk, and I appreciate your pointing it out." Charyn rose. "Again, I do wish to offer my thanks."

"You're more than welcome."

The slightly amused smile that accompanied Elthyrd's words concerned Charyn, because the factor's expression suggested Charyn was missing something.

Once he had left the timber factorage, Charyn directed the coach north to the Sud Bridge and back across the river, and then south to Paersyt's factorage. When Charyn entered the factorage, with Yarselt at his back, the factor looked up from the workbench.

"It's been a few days, Lord Charyn."

"I must apologize, but my time is not always my own. I am still very interested in the possibilities of your engine."

"You seem to be one of the few. Almost no one else is interested, except for a few factors who have deep mines."

"Why not? You've said that they could move flatboats and maybe even ships. There have to be places where that would be useful."

"The engines cost too much."

"What if you made them the way they do rifles?" asked Charyn. "Wouldn't that be cheaper?"

"How could I do that? I don't have the golds to buy or make the equipment . . . or the space or the turning benches. I'd need a complete manufactory."

"Could you, if you did?"

"Anything can be done with enough golds . . . and time. It would take time. And thousands of golds."

"Is anyone else trying it?"

"I don't know of anyone. Most people think I'm a fool for what I've spent already for only a few mines."

"They think you more the fool for trying to make something that doesn't exist and that very few people would want when you could make other things right now that would bring in more golds?"

"Golds aren't everything, but without them you can't do much of anything." Paersyt offered a harsh sound somewhere between a grunt and a snort. "I want to make something that will change everything, and that takes even more golds."

"How would your engine change things besides making boats go faster or against the current?"

"All sorts of ways. Looms wouldn't have to be built near the rivers. Ships wouldn't have to wait for the wind or tide . . ."

Charyn listened as Paersyt came up with a listing of improbable possibilities, then asked, "You really think all those are possible?"

"They're possible if people want to pay for them."

"You've given me some things to think about," Charyn finally said.

Paersyt offered a skeptical look.

"I do mean that, but, at the moment, what I can do is limited. What you need will take thousands of golds. While I have some golds, I don't have that many. There may be other possibilities. It will take a little time to look into them." *Time and persuasion.*

"At least you're honest about it."

"I try." *When circumstances allow.*

After leaving Paersyt, Charyn then directed the coach to the exchange. There, once again, Yarselt followed directly behind him as he made his way to the center door.

One of the guards stepped forward. "Sir . . . do you have a card as well . . . as your pin?"

Although the guard's tone was very polite, Charyn had to force himself to reply calmly. "I do." He was just glad he'd been told of the possibility. "Bursar Thalyr said I might need it." He eased the card from his jacket.

The guard studied it for a moment and handed it back. "Thank you, Factor Suyrien."

"You're welcome." Charyn managed a pleasant smile and a nod. Behind, he heard the few words said by the one guard to the other.

". . . another young one . . . lose a fortune . . ."

While there were certainly more ways to lose fortunes than to gain them, particularly in trading on the exchange, Charyn had no intention of buying or selling anything until he knew a great deal more. He did want to learn if he could get a better price for his own crops at the exchange. But that meant paying for transport to L'Excelsis, unless the buyer was closer to Talyon, although transport costs shouldn't be that high, given that Chaeryll wasn't that far from the River Aluse. *Shouldn't doesn't mean that's the way it is.* That meant more things he needed to look into.

After Elthyrd's words about pepper, Charyn made his way toward the stalls that handled spices. One look at the slates that held the prices, especially the futures' prices, and the number of traders or agents—agents wore brass sheaf pin with a blue stone—told Charyn that the Jariolan privateers, or some other causes, if not both, were definitely having an effect.

Charyn recalled that because Solidar didn't have that much tin, that was another commodity that came from the northern continents, and he walked to the north end of the exchange building. Only one of the metals' stalls seemed to have many traders or agents around, and that was, as he had suspected, the one handling tin and copper. Copper prices were down, which puzzled him. Was that because there wasn't enough tin to make bronze . . . or for some other reason?

He stood back and to one side, watching and listening.

". . . third ship this month carrying tin . . . sent to the bottom . . ."

". . . want tin . . . best use . . . Jariolan bottom . . ."

". . . copper down . . . can't make bronze without tin . . ."

". . . Ferrans shipping our copper to Abierto Isles . . . Diamond ships the only copper haulers not laid up . . ."

". . . always have been armed . . ."

". . . Abiertans . . . clip a dead man's coppers . . ."

". . . Ferrans . . . just take 'em before he's even cold . . ."

For more than two glasses, Charyn walked from stall to stall, checking back on several, including potatoes, wheat corn, tin, copper, and maize. He also listened intently, then left knowing that he would arrive back at the chateau when his father would be meeting with Ryel, Elthyrd, and Maitre Alastar.

When Charyn returned to the Chateau D'Rex, he got out of the carriage in the rear courtyard, removed the exchange pin from his coat, then entered the chateau through the main rear door, and made his way up the grand staircase, only to find his mother at the top, clearly waiting for him.

"I presume you have a moment, Charyn."

"Always."

Chelia turned and led the way to her sitting room.

Charyn did close the door when he followed her. He sat in the straight-backed chair that he picked up and placed opposite his mother, who had seated herself in the pale blue velvet armchair that was her favorite. "You are concerned about something?"

"Where were you this morning . . . and for most of the day? Your departure and return were tactfully and exquisitely timed to avoid your father's observation. You also did not directly violate his order about riding."

"I had to see Factorius Elthyrd and Factorius Paersyt. Then I visited the exchange."

Surprisingly, Chelia did not frown. "Why the exchange?"

"Because I believe what happens there tells more about what occurs across Solidar than all those scattered reports Father receives."

"You know your father would not believe that, don't you?"

"That's why I've told him little of it."

"I thought the exchange was limited to its members."

"Members or their guests. Factor Elthyrd has been most helpful in that regard."

"What has he asked of you in return?"

"Thus far . . . nothing."

"There will be a price, you know?"

"I'm quite certain of that, but since I've asked very little of him, except an introduction to the bursar of the exchange, under the land name at Chaeryll, I can refuse any unreasonable price, and even Father has not found the factor to be unreasonable."

"Or not excessively so." Chelia paused. "Under the land name?"

"I'm known at the exchange as Factor Suyrien or Suyrien D'Chaeryll. Since Elthyrd and Paersyt are likely the only factors who know me by sight, a single bodyguard in a nondescript coat seems adequate, and that is permitted as a matter of course."

"That does surprise me. That is more like . . . other relations, but wise." Chelia went on, "Over the past two months, you've taken a great interest in matters about which you have shown little interest in the past."

"You would like to know why?"

"It might be interesting. It might even be helpful."

Charyn fingered his chin, as if contemplating how to best address her interest. "It occurred to me that Father is still a young man. He has kept telling me that I have much more time to learn all that he was forced to learn quickly. I realized that others might regard the matter in a similar fashion, and that, over time, if I were not beginning to learn, and equally, being seen to learn and to take an interest in matters of import to those ruled, this would not reflect favorably upon either Father or me." He paused. "Also, truth be told, riding, hunting, and most other pastimes seem to have lost their overriding interest."

"Yet you still practice the clavecin, although there is no charge laid upon you to do so."

"Palenya has kindled a certain interest in my learning more about music."

"You must admit that this change occurred rather suddenly. What spurred it?"

Charyn smiled sheepishly. About that, there was no reason to dissemble. "My lack of marksmanship with pistols. I went to visit the factor who made the best pistols, only to find out that he no longer crafted them, but I saw what he was trying to build." He shrugged. "Somehow, the perfect pistol no longer seemed that important. And then I wondered why such a talented factor would abandon something that paid so well . . . and, from that, one thing led to another."

"That seems too unrealistic to be anything but the truth, especially since I've been able to verify certain aspects, even if you doubtless omitted what you feel I should not hear." Chelia's voice turned drier. "How long can we expect this unexpected transformation to last?"

"I still enjoy riding, and other pastimes, as you termed them, but not to the exclusion of newer interests that I feel will lead to a greater understanding of the challenges that Father faces and that in time I also may face."

"So nicely stated."

"I would hope so," replied Charyn.

Chelia offered an amused smile. "What is your immediate goal?"

"A reputation for seriousness and intelligence."

"Beyond that?"

"Power and wealth of the kind that won't diminish or encroach upon Father."

"Working with factors?"

"That's the only possible avenue. Working with High Holders would be seen as disloyal . . . and would be."

"At least, you've thought this out to some degree." After another pause, she said, "That's all I need to know. Don't leave the chateau. After your father finishes with Maitre Alastar and Guard Captain Churwyl, he wants to meet with all the family."

"Do you know what happened in the meeting with . . . the others?"

"Not at the moment. Your father will tell me when we have a moment."

Which meant that even then she wasn't about to tell him. Charyn nodded.

After leaving his mother, he made his way to his own chambers, where he stood before the sitting room window, looking south across the gardens where, in the late fall day, the only green came from the various evergreens and pondering over what his father might be discussing with Maitre Alastar.

It wasn't until after fourth glass that the regial family gathered in Lorien's study, seated around the oblong conference table, with Lorien at the head, and Chelia to his right. Charyn sat to his father's left, across from his mother, with Bhayrn beside him, and Aloryana next to her mother.

Lorien surveyed the other four in the study, starting with Celia and ending with Charyn, who had the feeling that his father's gaze lingered on him just slightly longer, then cleared his throat once more before speaking. "All that Guard Captain Churwyl and his men have been able to find out about the shooter is that he did wear a brown cloak. It was caught on a bush. There were no other signs." After a moment, he held up a single sheet. "This message was handed to Guard Captain Churwyl just after midday today and before I was to meet with High Holder Ryel, Factor Elthyrd, and Maitre Alastar. The man who delivered the missive was clad in the usual brown and black uniform of a public messenger. He likely was not one. The guard captain asked for the sender. The messenger said he'd been paid three silvers to deliver it by a well-dressed man in front of the Civic Patrol headquarters. I'd like each of you to read it. Say nothing until you all have finished reading it." Lorien handed the single sheet to Charyn, adding, "Your mother has already read it."

The first thing that struck Charyn was how much his father's hand shook as he handed the document over. The second was the clarity of the hand that had penned the words . . . and the brevity of the message.

> *What happened yesterday was a warning. It was also a promise.*
> *Unless Rex Lorien immediately announces and begins to implement*
> *stronger steps to halt the attacks on and the destruction of*
> *Solidaran ships and crews, and other threats to the healthy commerce*
> *of Solidar, the next attack will fall on someone more significant or*
> *more beloved.*

There was no signature.

Charyn passed the sheet to Bhayrn. Bhayrn frowned, then handed it to Aloryana, whose eyes widened as she read. She in turn handed the sheet to Chelia, who returned it to Lorien.

"I'd like your thoughts in turn, beginning with you, Charyn."

"Whoever wrote this wants you to believe it's from a merchant or factor. It could be, but it doesn't mean that it is."

Chelia looked at Charyn. "You have some contacts among the factors. Have they said anything?"

"I understand that the price of spices, especially pepper, is much higher. So is tin. The price of copper is down. Several factors, possibly more than that, have lost ships to Jariolan privateers—"

"Factor Elthyrd's been complaining about that for months," said Lorien dourly. "That's nothing new."

The fact that it's been going on for months without you doing anything might be why some factors are upset. Charyn wasn't about to voice that thought.

"Dear . . . do you think some factors might be upset . . . even angry?" Chelia's words were spoken pleasantly.

"They don't want to pay the tariffs to build more ships. Neither do the High Holders."

"So one group wants more warships, and one doesn't?" asked Bhayrn.

"And no one wants to pay for them," snapped Lorien.

"Has anyone else received a threat?" asked Aloryana.

"High Holder Ryel has. He didn't share the actual message, just that he and his entire family have been threatened if the High Council doesn't support stronger measures against the Jariolans." Lorien turned to Charyn. "You've met with Elthyrd. Did he say anything else?"

"No, sir."

"What about the toolmaker . . . Palsyt, is it?"

"Paersyt, sir. He builds things. He's never even talked about trade or ships."

Lorien shook his head. "If that's all . . ." He stopped as Chelia shot a glance at him.

"What are you going to do?" asked Chelia. "The last time . . ."

"I know. The first thing is to appear to do something. I can announce that the Jariolan piracy is unacceptable and that our warships will be ordered to attack any privateers preying on our ships . . . and that we will build more warships than we had previously planned, beginning immediately. We have enough golds in reserve to build one additional ship, possibly two. I'll also announce that significant additional shipbuilding cannot take place without a tariff increase, and that we will discuss that at the next meeting of the Factors' Council and the High Council. That won't set well with High Holder Oskaryn. He's violently opposed to any increase in tariffs."

"We're supposed to be shot at because he won't pay a few more golds every year?" asked Bhayrn.

"Quite a number of High Holders feel that way," said Chelia mildly.

"There's no point in talking about that now." Lorien went on, "I also asked Maitre Alastar to see if he and the imagers could assist in discovering who is behind this threat. That's why he stayed a bit longer. I've already talked to Churwyl about bringing on more guards. He has been suggesting we could use more. We can have some of them patrol the hunting park more often. Once they're in place, we'll see about riding there again. In the meantime, we also won't be going to services at the anomen. Service times are too well known."

That was fine with Charyn. Services were tedious.

"Isn't there anything . . . else?" asked Chelia.

"Besides what I've suggested, what you do have in mind?"

"You could impose a higher import tariff on Jariolan ships and cargoes until the piracy stops."

"That won't exactly please the factors," replied Lorien. "I could send a missive to Elthyrd suggesting that as another possibility for raising the golds for more ships, especially in view of the fact that so many factors oppose increased tariffs on their factorages." He paused. "There's not much more to be said right now."

"What about the Year-Turn Ball?" asked Aloryana. "Are you going to cancel it? You aren't, are you?"

"Why would I do that? Especially now?"

Bhayrn's frown was obvious.

"The High Council is invited, and the members of the Solidaran Factors' Council." At Bhayrn's expression of surprise, Lorien added, "I added the factors to make a point to the High Holders, and it won't hurt to require all of them to come here, especially since we won't be the ones exposed."

Charyn managed not to nod, but he did notice the faintest hint of a smile cross his mother's lips.

Lorien stood. "I'll see you all at dinner."

9

After breakfast on Samedi, Charyn was debating how to spend the day most productively, since the exchange was not open, and since neither Alucar nor Sanafryt worked on Samedi, and certainly not Aevidyr, not that Charyn had approached the Minister of Administration all that often. He was spared an immediate decision when he abruptly realized, with a sinking feeling, that he had never destroyed the letter he'd written to Ferrand on Jeudi, a letter he'd never given to the chateau messenger because of the attack on Bhayrn and his guards.

He went into his sleeping chamber and opened the armoire that held his jackets, looking until he found the greenish gray jacket he had been wearing. The letter was still there. He carried it into the sitting room and eased it onto the few coals still with a reddish hue, then watched as the flames slowly appeared and began to consume the paper. When he'd written the letter, what he'd put down would have been innocent enough, but after what had happened to Bhayrn, the words could have been taken in entirely the wrong way, particularly the phrase about the way things were going, other avenues appeared more productive than worrying about how to be accurate with pistols.

I'll need to be even more careful about anything put to pen now.

At that instant, there was a knock on the door.

"Yes?" Charyn glanced at the hearth, but the letter was only partly consumed and still recognizably a letter.

"Come see me when you have a moment."

There was no mistaking his mother's voice. If the letter had still not been burning and obvious, he just would have opened the door, given that he was alone and unoccupied, Palenya having left before breakfast.

Instead, he said, "I'll be there shortly."

Charyn waited a few moments, stirred the ashes with the poker, and then made his way to her sitting room.

"You didn't have to hurry."

"I was already dressed. I was just thinking." He offered a wry smile as he seated himself on the settee. "Not that I had any great insights."

"I've talked to your father about some of your recent activities. Initially, he was less than pleased."

"I imagine that is more than a slight understatement," replied Charyn sardonically.

"However . . ." Chelia drew out the word in a way that emphasized her refusal to comment on his observation. "He does concede that your use of the land name in gaining access to the exchange is prudent, and that it would be unwise not to allow you to continue to frequent the exchange and to gain whatever information you are able that might prove useful."

He's not about to admit that to me. But even an indirect concession was better than none. "I will let him know of anything I discover that could affect him or us."

"I thought you would."

"Have you any plans for today?"

"I was thinking about that."   .

"You might consider spending some time with Aloryana."

"Because she's effectively restricted to the chateau?"

"She's also worried."

"The words in the threat? Beloved?"

"How would you take them?"

"Most likely the way she is—that you, or Aloryana could also be a target, and that whoever is behind the threat wanted to make that clear."

"What does that tell you?"

"That whoever is behind the threats knows something about the family . . . or knows someone who does. I'd suspect the latter."

"Your reason for that suspicion?" asked Chelia.

"No one in the family is close to any factors. Father and I are the only ones with any real contact at all, and I've never mentioned family at all, except for very general statements about Father. Given Father, I doubt he's said anything at all."

Chelia nodded once more.

When she said nothing more, Charyn smiled. "I'll see what I can do about cheering up Aloryana."

"Thank you."

Charyn rose, inclined his head, then turned and left the sitting room, sensing her eyes on his back.

After first going to the music room, and seeing no one there, Charyn found Palenya in the small study that was hers, formerly a small storage space that barely accommodated a narrow table and chair. "I have a favor to ask."

She immediately stood. "You don't have to ask."

"I much prefer to ask. I'd like you to help me learn the part of the duet you were teaching Bhayrn to play with Aloryana, and then work with both of us. Starting right now, if you would."

"You worry about her?"

Charyn nodded. He wasn't about to admit he wouldn't have known if his mother hadn't brought it up. Also, Samedi was a good day, since he had far more free time.

"That would be better. She'll never understand how it should feel by playing it with your brother."

Understated as Palenya's words were, Charyn saw no point in admitting that directly. "It's another way of showing concern." He smiled wryly. "At least, I hope it is."

"She enjoys playing. So do you. If she did not . . . then it might be different." Palenya went to the music cabinet, opened it, and took out a bound sheaf of paper. She returned, placed it on the music rack of the clavecin, and looked to Charyn. "Go ahead. Let's see how well you can do."

Charyn seated himself at the bench, looked at the score, then began to play, ready to listen to whatever corrections or observations Palenya might have.

She said nothing until several moments after he finished, then asked, "You never played this music before?"

"I've heard it often over the past week," Charyn replied. *More than I wanted to . . . particularly played the way Bhayrn did.*

"Not that often. You've been away from the chateau too much to have heard it very many times."

"It seemed often." He kept his tone light and waited for her comments.

"You played all the right notes."

"Meaning that my tempos, fingering, and interpretation leave something to be desired? And I need to work on improving them all?"

"If you want to play it the way Farray composed it," replied Palenya, with an amused smile.

"Then, let's go over it, and you can tell me what to do differently."

"The first four measures are meant to be tentative . . . curious. See the markings above?"

"I thought that was meant to be . . ." Charyn shook his head and played the first four measures.

"Better . . . but linger a touch after the third beat . . ."

After a glass following Palenya's tutoring, Charyn was perspiring, even though the music room was cool, almost cold, as was most of the chateau, at least those chambers where there were no fires in the hearths. He blotted his forehead with his sleeve, then looked up to see Aloryana standing just inside the music room door.

"I thought I was going to play that with Bhayrn," Aloryana said.

"I decided I wanted to, also," Charyn said. "You can still play it with Bhayrn, if you want. We've never played a duet before, and I didn't know when we might get the chance again."

"That's true. We . . . I'd like that."

Charyn wondered what Aloryana had been about to say, but he wasn't about to ask with Palenya present. "Bhayrn didn't seem pleased to play the duet, and I wanted to do something more than ride with you or play plaques. We can play plaques later, after we practice with Musician Palenya." He turned to Palenya. "Would you mind letting us play it, and then taking us through it?"

"If you both would like that."

Aloryana eased onto the bench beside Charyn.

"Just play through it," Palenya added, "I'd like to listen before I make any corrections or suggestions."

After Charyn and Aloryana had practiced for close to an hour, Palenya said, "I think that's enough. You're both tired. You're making mistakes because you are."

"How are we doing?" asked Aloryana.

"How do you think you're doing?" replied the musician.

"Better. It's much easier to play with Charyn."

"You've answered your own question."

"Can we do this again tomorrow?" asked Aloryana, looking first to Charyn and then Palenya.

"If Musician Palenya is willing."

"In the morning would be better," offered Palenya.

"Ninth glass?" suggested Charyn, knowing that Palenya was not obligated to work on Solayi, and also not wanting to get up too early.

Palenya nodded, offering Charyn a knowing smile when Aloryana looked away.

As he stood, Charyn said to his sister, "I did promise you a game or two of plaques."

"I'd like that. I'll see you in the parlor."

When Aloryana hurried away, Charyn turned to Palenya. "Thank you."

She shook her head. "Thanks are not necessary. Would that all lessons were that enjoyable."

"Later?"

"Of course."

Aloryana was waiting, standing by the plaques table, when Charyn finally walked into the family parlor. "I thought you'd be here sooner."

"I needed to take care of a few things. I'd been sitting at the clavecin for more than two glasses." Charyn smiled and gestured to the table.

As they sat down across from each other, Aloryana asked, "Why do you always call her 'Musician Palenya' when I'm around?"

"I call her that whenever anyone is around. She is a musician, and a good one, and she should be recognized for it. High Holders are given their title. So are factors. So are you. You're now Lady Aloryana . . ."

"I am?"

"Now that Father allows you to attend balls."

"I'm not old enough to be a lady."

"No one would dream of saying otherwise."

"It might be nice to be a lady for a little while."

"You'll always be a lady."

"You don't know that," replied Aloryana.

"You're the daughter of the rex. That means you'll always be Lady Aloryana, no matter whom you marry . . . or even if you don't." Charyn noticed that Aloryana looked ready to dispute what he'd said.

Instead, she said, "It's your turn to deal. I'm glad you don't try to deal off the bottom the way Bhayrn does. That's why I don't mind losing when he does."

Somehow, that didn't surprise Charyn, either that Bhayrn cheated or that Aloryana knew it and dismissed it. But it saddened him, in a way.

He picked up the plaques and shuffled them.

10

So far as Charyn was concerned, Solayi was no different from Samedi, except that he didn't have another talk with his mother . . . and he and Aloryana practiced the Farray clavecin duet for a solid glass. Charyn had no doubts that they sounded far better than Aloryana and Bhayrn had, and he found he enjoyed it for more than just making Aloryana happy.

Even so, he was up early on Lundi morning, and after spending a few moments with Norstan, he headed out for the exchange.

Once again, when he and Yarselt reached the exchange, he had to show the card to the guard. He had the feeling that would happen until every guard recognized him. He smiled politely and made his way to the wheat corn stall, but the price hadn't changed that much, down a copper, and there were only two men there, talking to the stall manager.

". . . might change . . . flood in east Piedryn . . . standing water . . . cut next year's winter wheat crop . . ."

Charyn looked to the futures board, but didn't see any difference in prices five or six months out. Still looking as though he were studying the boards, he kept listening.

". . . not much difference, unless there's a dry spring . . ."

As the three continued to discuss next year's wheat corn crops, Charyn moved to the maize board, where there was also little activity, in fact, none. The next stall that had any activity was one he hadn't even considered—sugar. Several factors or agents were bidding on lots. Charyn thought the lots had to be hundred-stone, but that was a guess on his part, and he didn't want to ask. He also looked to the futures board, and the price in Fevier was a good four coppers higher than in Ianus, which was two coppers above the price of the last lot sold.

Why? Even as he asked himself the question, he realized the answer. Most sugar came from lands in Otelyrn . . . and was part of the trade being disrupted by Jariolan privateers.

As he watched, he couldn't help but overhear part of a different conversation.

". . . someone took a shot at the rex's younger boy . . ."

Charyn tried not to react to being lumped with Bhayrn as a "boy."

". . . too bad it wasn't the rex . . . new council keeps telling him . . ."

". . . another ship lost . . . Namer-damned sowshit so far as sugar and spices . . . got word on Samedi . . ."

". . . not the problem . . . High Holders . . . snotty council of theirs . . ."

". . . doesn't stand up to them . . ."

". . . imagers . . . not doing much . . ."

". . . least they did something once . . ."

The three agents who were talking abruptly turned and walked north toward the metals stalls.

Charyn did not follow but moved to the spices stall. Pepper didn't seem to be any higher on present quotes, from what he recalled, but the Maris price was definitely higher. He made a slow tour of the stalls of interest, noting that tin was also markedly higher, then left the exchange. It was definitely going to take time to learn enough to feel comfortable about knowing what transpired at the exchange and what it all meant— although even he thought he understood the basics.

When he returned to the chateau, it was close to second glass. He'd considered stopping to see Elthyrd, but he decided against that, since he doubted he could learn that much more, given the comparatively short time that had passed since he last met with the factor. More important, Elthyrd might question him, and he really didn't want to put the factor off by not answering the kind of questions Elthyrd might ask. And he certainly didn't have any answers for Paersyt, although he had some ideas.

He had no more than stepped into the rear foyer of the chateau than Vaetor, the senior footman, walked toward him.

"Lord Charyn, Lady Chelia would like to see you in the receiving parlor."

"At my earliest convenience?"

"Yes, sir."

"Then I will attend her."

Charyn made one quick stop before making his way to the receiving parlor.

His mother was sitting in the corner armchair, apparently reading a letter. She set the letter aside, but did not motion for him to sit down. "Good. You're here. I have some news for you."

"Good news, I hope."

"It's certainly not bad news. We're going to host a guest for a time, at least through the Year-Turn Ball," Chelia announced. "I've already told Aloryana and Bhayrn, but you left the chateau early."

"We haven't hosted a guest in months. Who is it, some High Holder from Tacqueville or Asseroiles or Laaryn—or from some other Nameless-forsaken place—whom Father wants to replace Uncle Ryel?"

"Nothing that ground-shaking. Her name is Malyna D'Zaerlyn. She's the youngest daughter of High Holder Zaerlyn."

"I've never heard of him."

"His holding is near Rivages. He also owns a massive ceramics facility somewhere, and some coal mines, I think. He's one of the few High Holders who have always supported your father. Indirectly, but support is support. He does not maintain a house in L'Excelsis, and has visited here only twice in his life. He asked for the favor of allowing his daughter to attend the Year-Turn Ball. He was worried about having her stay with High Holders whose interests he does not share. Your father agreed to allow her to stay with us. Since Aloryana can't go out that much, not at present, I didn't think it would hurt for her to have feminine company closer to her own age."

"And another woman of the proper standing as a model?"

"I understand she is quite her own woman, even at nineteen."

"You're not matchmaking, I hope?"

"From what I've heard, Charyn, she is anything but your type."

Ugly, overweight, and loud, no doubt. "I see."

"You don't, but you will."

Charyn had no doubts about that. He just hoped that the experience wasn't exceedingly painful or tedious.

"She will arrive tomorrow. She will need a gown for the ball. I doubt that anything she has will be adequate or in style."

"Uncle Ryel is from Rivages, and I understand style has never been a problem for him and his family."

"High Holder Zaerlyn is, shall we say, a bit more retiring. I much prefer that." Chelia's voice was cool.

"Uncle Ryel has always been reserved and polite at previous Year-Turn Balls. I have never met him at any other time. Not in recent years. Once he gave me shiny golds."

"That's because he can't stand ones that are worn or soiled. They remind him of his earlier years."

"Why?"

"It's not something I wish to discuss."

"Why not, might I ask?"

"Because you would not believe me, and you would believe him. That is how persuasive and charming he can be. The only people who can hold him in check are Maitre Alastar and Maitre Alyna. I believe he fears her more than him." Chelia smiled. "I know, whatever you come to think of Malyna, you will be on your best behavior."

"That, you can count on." *Even if it comes close to killing me.*

"I know." After a pause, Chelia added, "That's all."

Charyn inclined his head, then turned and left the receiving parlor.

Since he could hear no one playing the clavecin, he headed toward the music room. At least practicing his part of the Farray duet would take his mind off the questions that swirled through his thoughts, such as just who was High Holder Zaerlyn and why hadn't Charyn ever heard of the High Holder if he had been so supportive? And why had his mother been so dismissive of the idea of matchmaking? Or was Malyna actually good-looking, but his parents preferred that he not be interested in her?

Or . . . He shook his head. He just didn't know enough, especially about Zaerlyn and his daughter. But then, no one ever knew much about most High Holder's daughters. They were there to be married and to produce heirs . . . and to be as decorative and as pleasant as possible. *Aloryana has no idea how much more fortunate she is.*

The music room was indeed empty, and Charyn closed the doors. He didn't know the duet nearly as well as he would have liked, and he preferred to make his mistakes muted by the solid doors.

Again on Mardi morning, Charyn was up early, first meeting with Norstan, and then heading out in the plain carriage, first to see Elthyrd, and then to visit the exchange again. After that, he'd see.

When the carriage rolled to a halt outside Elthyrd's factorage, Charyn hurried out, followed by Yarselt. Although Charyn didn't expect to see the factor on the piers, he paused to look . . . and in fact saw the older man walking swiftly toward him. He moved to meet the factor, then waited for Elthyrd to take the last few steps.

"How is your family?" asked Elthyrd.

"They're fine. How is yours?"

"The same as always. I wasn't certain I'd be seeing you, after all that happened last week."

"As long as I dress more like a factor and take a plain carriage . . ." Charyn shrugged. "Most people don't know what I look like, and those that do aren't likely to shoot at me. That's what I hope, anyway."

"Especially if you use the land name."

"That helps."

"I imagine you'd like to know my feelings about the threat . . . and anything I might know."

"If you'd care to give them. I'm not the one to press."

Elthyrd chuckled ironically. "There is a certain implication behind your words."

"They're absolutely truthful."

"So is the implication, but I appreciate the relative directness. First, I have no idea who made the threat. Second, if I had to guess, I'd say that it had to come from a large factor or a High Holder heavily invested in shipping. Third, whoever it is likely used intermediaries. Fourth, whoever it is has little faith in the High Council and the Solidaran Factors' Council reaching an agreement that will allow the rex to increase tariffs enough to allow the building of a significantly larger number of warships."

"From what I've heard and overheard, no one wants higher tariffs, and only some factors feel the need for more warships to protect Solidaran ships and trade. Or is my information incorrect . . . or incomplete?"

"That you're asking reveals a certain . . . openness. In fact . . . what you're suggesting is close to the current situation. Most factors feel that they have been overtariffed for years, if not decades, and all too many High Holders feel that higher tariffs will ruin them."

"Is that feeling justified by any facts?" asked Charyn.

"There are a number of High Holders who continue to manage their lands in a fashion that will not allow the most effective use of those lands. They are reluctant to change their ways, and any measurable increase in tariffs will see them facing ruin if they do not change."

"What sort of change would increased tariffs require?"

"The problem is not just one of increased tariffs. Over the past ten years, and even longer, certain parts of Solidar, especially the lands to the west of L'Excelsis in old Bovaria, parts of Piedryn, and much of old Tilbor have suffered excessively bad weather, several early and late frosts, floods and excessive rains in midsummer, droughts at other times. This has happened year after year. Those High Holders who have changed what and when they planted have prospered. Those who did not are struggling, and many are near ruin. Higher tariffs will likely push many of them into ruin or into relinquishing their rights and position as High Holders, if not both."

Charyn had certainly heard his father's complaints about High Holders whining over the weather, but those words hadn't been put the way Elthyrd did—which, unhappily, made more sense. "I've heard about the weather for years."

"I'm certain you have. That's not the entire problem. Now that the factors have become more prosperous, more and more small holders are selling their produce to them or even in some cases on the exchanges. They're producing more, and that keeps prices lower. Not a great deal, but enough—"

"That it makes it even harder on the High Holders who aren't managing their lands as well as they could."

Elthyrd nodded.

"What about the factors? Wouldn't a tariff that built more warships help them?"

"Over time, it would. But it would help those in shipping and the spice trade far more than the others."

Charyn nodded. "I can see that." He wasn't sure he did, but it seemed wise to agree. "I appreciate your thoughts. Do you think your son—the one who owns the Banque D'Excelsis—would mind talking to me about these and other matters?"

Elthyrd laughed, not softly, but not heartily. "At least he'd know you weren't asking for golds."

"When it seems appropriate, I'd appreciate it if you'd mention that I might like to see him sometime. Does he look like you?"

"Not much. He's got a square-cut black beard, and all his hair, unlike his father. I'm sure he'd like to see you."

Charyn understood what hadn't been said, as well. "Thank you. I won't take any more of your time, but I do appreciate your sharing your knowledge and experience."

Elthyrd merely nodded.

In turn, Charyn inclined his head, then turned, and made his way back to the carriage, where he told the driver, "Now to Delcoeur D'Alte's."

As he climbed into the carriage, Charyn considered what Elthyrd had said . . . and what he had not, even as he studied the surroundings he passed.

The L'Excelsis dwelling of Delcoeur D'Alte was on the east side of the River Aluse, but northeast of the Nord Bridge. Charyn studied the river, and then Imagisle, as the carriage carried him north along the East River Road and past the "new" bridge that linked the isle to the eastern side of the city, by far the larger and more populous section. While he could see the upper levels of the imagers' anomen, and one taller gray stone building, for the most part, he could only glimpse parts of other buildings, given the trees that appeared to edge most of the isle. The gray stone river walls, and especially the grayish blue waters split by the northern pointed end of those ramparts that split the waters of the river into two, almost like the prow of a ship, gave the isle the look of a massive vessel heading upstream.

He still wondered how the first imagers had managed such impressive stoneworks that looked so recently constructed after four centuries, but then, they'd rebuilt the Chateau D'Rex at the same time, and its walls still looked almost new, and the stone was impervious to the sharpest blade.

The single guard at the gate to High Holder Delcoeur's "town" dwelling looked to be more like Bhayrn's age. Wearing frayed tan livery trimmed in green, he had to struggle to open the gate that squeaked noisily as he tugged it wide enough to let the carriage enter, and then when he closed it.

Ferrand was standing on the narrow portico by the time Charyn left the carriage and climbed the three steps to the entry terrace. "I thought I might hear from you sooner . . . but here you are."

"I wrote you a letter, but then some things happened, and I couldn't send it. So I decided it would be better just to drop in and hope you were here."

"I'm not going many places. Not now." Ferrand glanced back at the ancient bronze doors of the main entrance, then nodded in the direction of his father's study.

"I'm sorry to hear that. I'd hoped that selling the pistols might help a bit. You know that even my personal inheritance is managed by Alucar. That doesn't leave me much in the way of golds to spend."

"I understand not having much to spend. You do have something to look forward to."

"Is it that bad?"

Ferrand lowered his voice. "Worse. He came back from the Banque D'Aluse yesterday in a foul mood." He gestured. "We can go to the front parlor. No one will bother us there."

Charyn understood that message as well. He followed his cousin, noticing that there was no footman standing inside the entry doors.

Once in the parlor, Ferrand gestured to the armchairs, waited until Charyn took the one from where he could watch both Ferrand and the archway off the entry hall, then seated himself in the other. "So what happened to bring you here?"

"Someone took a shot at Bhayrn and brought down his horse. The shooter also killed a guard."

"I did wonder why you came by carriage. You usually ride."

"Father doesn't want any of us riding until the matter is resolved."

"Do you know why?"

"It's something to do with tariffs. And warships. Again." Charyn offered a sigh. "It is tiresome. I do hope you will come to the Year-Turn Ball."

"I talked to Mother about it. Father just might agree. We'll see. It would be nice to see a few people."

Without incurring an obligation you can't repay. Charyn nodded.

"Is there anything else of interest?"

"We're having a guest. It's rather strange. Malyna D'Zaerlyn. That's her name. I believe she may arrive at the chateau this afternoon."

"Zaerlyn . . . Zaerlyn. Oh . . . the . . . ceramics High Holder. They only go back a few generations. They bought the title. That was when matters like that were easier. Come-latelies. I've never heard of her, though. She must be the youngest daughter. I knew there was one. Not that anyone would pay much attention to that family, anyway."

"I gather that's not surprising. They don't have any presence in L'Excelsis. They never have had."

"Then why are you guesting her?"

"Zaerlyn's been helpful to Father in some fashion, and he asked if she could stay at the chateau in order to attend the Year-Turn Ball. Father agreed."

"Matchmaking, yet. They've decided your time has come. She'll only be the first." Ferrand paused. "How old is she?"

"Nineteen. Mother says she's not my type."

"She said that?"

"She did."

"She knows you too well, Charyn. By telling you that you couldn't possibly get along with this girl, she's playing to your contrary nature."

"I'd thought that. Perhaps I should make over her. Or perhaps you should . . . if you come to the ball. She might even have a handsome dowry."

"She'll have to be very good-looking . . . and not too strong-willed. A little spirit, but only a little." Ferrand smiled wanly. "A little spirit in a woman goes a long way. Aunt Asarya proved that." He paused, then closed his mouth without saying more.

"No one in my family talks much about Grandmother." Charyn knew that his father's feelings for his mother were anything but warm, and his own mother had never mentioned Asarya. Ever. Not in his hearing. Charyn himself had no recollection of her.

"Father detested her."

"Why?"

"Because of her dowry. Why else?"

Charyn had heard that before. He'd even looked into the records. His grandmother's dowry hadn't been that much, but it likely made a good excuse for Delcoeur's inability to pay for his extravagances. "Then you should look for a High Holder's daughter with a healthy dowry."

"I'm not sure I'd want to pay that price." Ferrand shrugged. "There doesn't seem to be any other choice, not that I'll have much say in the matter."

After another glass of conversation, Charyn excused himself and directed the coach back south along the East River Road.

It was well after ninth glass when he entered the exchange, again having to show his card. He did wonder just how long it would be before he was recognized enough that he didn't have to present the card. The exchange was slightly more crowded than it had been on Lundi, which surprised him, after Elthyrd's comments about Lundi being a busy day. He noted that the futures price of pepper had dropped, if only slightly, and wheat was holding, but then, oak futures were up, and there were several agents gathered at that stall.

He positioned himself behind a rotund clerk who was jotting down figures and did his best to listen.

". . . saw you at the Yellow Rose, Burchyrd . . . don't think she was your sister . . ."

". . . couldn't have . . . you were losing at Tydaal's . . ."

". . . not me . . . always do my losing at Alamara's . . ."

". . . think Haaslm's cousin's right?"

". . . got to build more ships sometime . . ."

". . . price'll drop, and your man'll lose a bright thousand . . ."

The conversation returned to even more personal matters, and after a time, Charyn eased away. While he doubted his memory was perfect, he wasn't seeing much change in other prices, except in goods from Otelyrn, and after another glass, he left the exchange, emerging into a cold wind very much at odds with the bright sunlight.

Snow tonight . . . or just cold rain? He didn't see any clouds, even two quints later when the carriage turned onto the ring road and then climbed the gentle slope of the rear lane to the back courtyard of the chateau, a courtyard largely empty except for two kitchen sculls trudging out to the renderer's collection yard.

Once the carriage stopped, Charyn strode across the paving stones to the rear entrance and then inside. Bhayrn lounged against the archway wall at the back of the small rear entry foyer. He straightened slowly as Charyn crossed the foyer.

"Good afternoon," offered Charyn cheerfully.

"It's afternoon. Not a particularly good one. Why do you get to go out and I don't?"

"Because I'm doing things that Father agrees I should continue doing."

"Such as?"

"You'll have to take that up with Father."

"That's not an answer."

Charyn started to step around his younger brother.

"You're not making things easier for me, either, by playing that duet with Aloryana."

"You're the one making it hard on yourself. All you have to do is practice more and listen to what Musician Palenya tells you."

"She's just a musician."

"She knows more about music than either one of us will ever know. If you want to get better at anything, listen to those who know more than you do."

"You should talk. You only listen to her because she's—"

"Enough." Even though Bhayrn was likely partly right with what he had been about to say, Charyn had no intention of admitting it to his younger brother. "She doesn't have a choice. You have a problem with me, it's with me. Don't take it out on people who can't defend themselves."

"Aren't you the champion."

I wish I were. "No. I'm no champion. We both know that. Neither are you."

For a moment, Bhayrn looked vaguely surprised. "She's here."

"Who's here?"

"Malyna D'Zaerlyn. She's even pretty. She arrived in a plain carriage. No livery on the driver, but two guards."

"Where is she now?"

"Mother and Aloryana are getting her settled in the guest chambers at the west end of the north wing. Well away from your chambers."

"Or yours."

"She's too old for me."

"Three years is nothing. Besides, you can learn from older women."

"Like you have?"

"I have. I'm not ashamed of it."

"That's just because they wanted to protect you. I'll be fortunate if a serving girl even looks at me."

That may be, but part of that is you. "Time will tell."

"Platitudes don't make you any wiser, Brother."

"No. But sometimes they're right."

"And sometimes they're not." Bhayrn turned and walked toward the grand staircase.

At the sound of lighter footsteps, Charyn turned to see Aloryana and another girl—or rather a young woman—dressed in a conservative green dress and matching jacket. Aloryana was talking as they approached.

". . . receiving parlor is to the right beyond the grand staircase . . . and there's a study on this side . . . kept closed most of the time . . ."

Charyn studied Malyna closely, hopefully without being unduly obvious about it, as she approached. She was almost petite, but a trace too trimly muscular for that, and perhaps a little more than half a head shorter than he was. Her skin was a light almost unnoticeable honeyed brown. Her nose was modest but straight, and her hair was light brown. Her chin was slightly square. Her black eyes fixed on him. She stopped a yard or so away and offered the slightest of curtseys, saying, "Lord Charyn," and lowering her eyes.

"You must be Malyna," he said.

"I am, and I appreciate your father's kindness, and that of your entire family."

"Please just call me Charyn."

"Except in public, I will, if that is your wish."

"It is."

"Charyn," interjected Aloryana, "I still have to show Malyna the rest of the main level and introduce her to Musician Palenya and some of the rest of the staff."

"Of course." Charyn stepped back. "Until later."

"You can flirt with her at dinner," declared Aloryana.

That took Charyn slightly off-guard, but he managed an indulgent smile, before turning and heading up to find Minister Sanafryt . . . and possibly access to some of the records. Still, as he climbed the grand staircase, he was puzzled. He'd expected almost anything but what he'd seen.

Malyna was attractive, perhaps not a raving beauty, but far more attractive than the majority of High Holders' daughters he'd seen over the years. Her voice had been firm, reservedly warm, and her initial gaze had been direct, but hadn't lingered or been flirtatious. What he'd seen looked to be very much his type.

So had Ferrand been right, that his mother had said all that to pique his interest? Except she had always been direct, if softly so, and any sort of contrary game-playing statements had been nonexistent in her relations with any of them. Including Father.

Charyn was still puzzled when he entered the family parlor before dinner. The only ones there were Aloryana and Malyna. Both looked from where they shared the settee.

"How was your trip from Rivages?" asked Charyn.

"I imagine all trips from Rivages are long," replied Malyna, "but since I've only made the journey once, my experience might not be usual."

"In a way, I envy you. I've never traveled that far."

"There's nothing to envy."

"Do you have any brothers and sisters?"

"I do, but I'm much the youngest. All the others have left the holding."

"Even your brothers?" asked Aloryana.

"Oh, yes. They're in charge of various things. One is working to improve the coal mines. Another is learning how the ceramics manufactory works . . ."

When Malyna finished the listing of her siblings, Charyn asked, "And what about you? What part of the family efforts are you involved in?"

"I was brought up just like my sister . . . and other younger daughters. I play the clavecin, adequately. I know mathematics, and Father insisted that I learn something about surveying and how to keep holding ledgers."

"Don't try to discover everything about Malyna all at once," interjected Chelia as she entered the salon. "You'll have more than a few meals with her. Besides, your father and Bhayrn are about to join us, and it is time for dinner. I'm sure your father will have a few things to ask our guest as well."

"I just might," added Lorien as he stepped into the salon. "Welcome to the chateau. I hope the guest quarters are to your satisfaction and that Aloryana and Chelia have made sure you know where everything is."

Malyna stood immediately, and she inclined her head. "You're most kind, Your Grace."

"No formal titles here," Lorien replied.

"The three of us call him 'sir,'" said Charyn drolly. "Mother calls him whatever she wishes."

"Yes, sir," replied Malyna.

"Shall we?" said Chelia, gesturing toward the family dining room.

Charyn found that the seating had been changed so that he still sat on his father's right, with his mother at the other end, but Aloryana was seated beside him, while Bhayrn sat on his mother's right, and Malyna on Lorien's right, which meant that Charyn was seated right across from Malyna.

Chelia looked to her daughter.

Aloryana immediately spoke. "For the grace from above, for the bounty of the earth below, for Your justice, and for Your manifold and great mercies, we offer our thanks and gratitude, both now and ever more, in the spirit of that which cannot be named or imaged."

Only after Aloryana had finished did the servers appear with the pitchers of red or white wine. Then came the platters with wine-marinated and braised veal cutlets, and served with a wine reduction, along with sliced and roasted small golden potatoes and beans with slivered buttered almonds, and two baskets of freshly baked bread.

Lorien lifted his goblet. "To our guest."

After the toast, no one lifted a utensil until Lorien did, not that the rex tarried in the slightest, immediately, if precisely, slicing off a portion of the cutlet before him.

Bhayrn immediately looked at Malyna. "Why did you decide you wanted to come to the Year-Turn Ball? I mean, it's mostly for older High Holders and heirs. Well . . . and some unmarried daughters."

"And the older couples are . . . less stimulating, and the heirs and their parents are looking at the marriageable daughters as a horse buyer might examine a prize filly. Wasn't that what you're suggesting?"

Malyna's tone was warm, pleasant, and so understated that it was a moment before the import of what she said struck Charyn . . . and he almost choked on a morsel of potato, but managed not to reveal his surprise. He did need a swallow of wine to clear his throat.

Bhayrn flushed, but Aloryana grinned, if only momentarily.

In that instant of silence, Malyna continued, "I thought I might never have another chance, and there is always the possibility that it might be exciting. After all, with all of you, and the High Council and now the members of the Solidaran Factors' Council all attending, when would a young woman from Rivages ever have more than one chance in a lifetime to see all of those people in one ballroom?"

Charyn was impressed by Malyna's ability to skewer Bhayrn, seemingly guilelessly, and then sound like the perfect High Holder's daughter, certainly quickly enough that any reply to her first words would be awkward.

"You see," said Aloryana immediately. "It's not just me, Bhayrn."

"Balls can lose their charm over time," said Chelia, gently, "but few women forget those whose charm is remembered."

"Some men remember them as well," added Lorien surprisingly. "In time, you might even remember one that favorably." He looked to Malyna. "Aren't you related to High Holder Calkoran?"

"He's my uncle through marriage. His sister is married to my father."

"There have never been any alliances with the Ryel holding, have there?"

"No, sir."

"Just as well." Lorien helped himself to another cutlet.

"You play the clavecin?" asked Chelia, although the question was scarcely that.

"I do play."

"Then we must hear you some evening, once you are rested, and you can hear Aloryana . . . and her brothers, if they feel so inclined."

"Charyn's been learning a duet to play with me," Aloryana announced. "We could play that." She looked to her older brother.

"If Musician Palenya feels that we play it adequately."

"She's already said that," affirmed Aloryana.

"Then we'll play," agreed Charyn with a smile.

Given the interest both his parents took in keeping the conversation away from political or other sensitive subjects, Charyn mostly listened for the rest of dinner, adding a few words or phrases here and there.

When he left the family dining room, after watching Aloryana draw Malyna away, Charyn made his way to the grand staircase, thinking how his father had been so courteous—and that was unusual, especially since Malyna was merely the youngest daughter of a High Holder. *High Holder Zaerlyn must have done more than just support Father indirectly. Much, much more.*

But what? It was another reminder to Charyn that there were all too many things he didn't know.

12

On Meredi, Charyn was awake early, hardly surprising since he'd gone to bed far sooner than was his usual custom, not that he ever made a habit of remaining up as late as his father. As he dressed, he looked outside. It wasn't raining, but the morning was gray, and a low wind moaned outside the chateau.

When he made his way to the family breakfast room, the only one there was his mother.

"Good morning," he offered cheerfully.

"Good morning, Charyn."

"I take it that Aloryana kept Malyna up late last night. I thought I heard them talking." Charyn eased himself into the chair across from Chelia.

"Aloryana wanted to know what it's like to grow up as a High Holder's daughter. She thinks she'd have more freedom." Chelia's tone was dry.

Charyn frowned. "But you're a High Holder's daughter. I've heard about your growing up."

"For girls, mothers don't count. Just like fathers often don't count for sons. You've had the opportunity to talk to Ferrand. Why do you think your father tolerates him? There's been no one like that for Aloryana."

"What if Malyna has had a freer upbringing?"

"She hasn't. That family has always required more from its offspring. They're raised with the education of High Holders and the expectations of factors."

"Is that another reason why you were willing to guest her?"

"Among several." Chelia took a sip of tea and then a bite of cheesed eggs.

"Why did you say that she's not my type? She's attractive. She seems to be both witty and intelligent."

"She is both witty and intelligent, and very strong-willed. I don't believe that she is your type, but I'd prefer that you discover that for yourself."

"You're not going to offer any hints?"

"You'd take them all the wrong way. And I'm not saying that to pique your interest. She is the kind that could easily break your heart . . . or worse. That wouldn't be good for you . . . or for Solidar."

"I could insist."

"Isn't that a little premature?" Chelia smiled. "She's been here less than a day. Get to know her first." She paused. "And don't try to separate her from Aloryana. That would be most unfair."

If you're matchmaking, it's definitely in a most peculiar way. "You almost sound like you would prefer she weren't here."

"Sometimes, what's best for any of us isn't necessarily what I'd prefer. What are your plans for the day?"

By that question, Charyn knew that the subject of Malyna was closed for the moment, at least in terms of Malyna's possible relationship to either himself or Aloryana. "I haven't decided. I'll likely go to the exchange, first. Later . . . Aloryana mentioned that we should practice the duet together." Charyn shrugged.

Chelia nodded. "I'll mention the practicing to Aloryana. That will give Malyna a respite. Or Malyna might want to listen or even meet Palenya."

Charyn took a sip of the tea the server presented, and then addressed his breakfast. Cheesed eggs weren't his favorite, but the berry preserves on warm bread more than made up for the eggs.

His mother was still sipping her tea when he left, but no one else had joined them.

His first stop was in Norstan's study.

The seneschal tried to conceal a sigh as he saw Charyn enter the small chamber. "Good morning, Lord Charyn." He extended the copy of the appointments list.

"Good morning, Norstan." Charyn scanned the list, noting that Minister Aevidyr was listed for first glass of the previous afternoon. "Was the meeting with Aevidyr a long one?"

"It was scheduled for a glass."

"How many times did the rex meet with the guard captain?" Charyn asked even though Churwyl wasn't listed.

"I don't know. Guard Captain Churwyl never requests a meeting with the rex from me."

Charyn nodded, then folded the list carefully and tucked it into the inside pocket of his jacket. "Thank you."

His next stop was to the guard duty room, where he hoped to find Guard Captain Churwyl. Churwyl wasn't there. A good quint later, Charyn

caught up to the guard captain at the door to the stables in the rear courtyard.

"Good morning, Lord Charyn."

"Good morning, Guard Captain. How are things going?"

"For now, there's nothing amiss." Churwyl's words were almost dole-
ful, as if he doubted that matters would remain quiet.

"Have you had any success in getting more guards?"

"We've always had plenty who wanted to be guards. The problem
has been finding those who want to be guards for the right reasons."

A low roll of thunder rumbled out of the north. Charyn wondered
how long it might be before the rain began, most likely freezing. "Those
who have some interest and pride in being guards and who see the task
of protecting the rex as a worthy duty?"

"Something like that, sir."

"More like honor and pride in being a guard and wanting to do the
task well enough to keep getting paid?" Charyn laughed softly. "You don't
have to answer that. Were you here when the High Holder's daughter
arrived?"

Churwyl looked relieved and then puzzled for an instant. "Yes, sir."

"I understand she came alone."

"No, sir. Not with a chaperone, but she has two of her father's men,
trained like guards, it seems to me."

"Oh? They stayed?"

"Yes, sir. Her father sent a message saying they could stand outside
watches. Not inside the chateau, of course."

"How well are they trained?"

Churwyl laughed. "I'd have them in a moment. They can handle sabres and rifles, and they've some considerable training in unarmed fighting. I can see why the High Holder felt safe in sending her with them."
After a moment, he added, "They have to be his best."

"Sending them with her suggests he values her highly."

"He should. She's a real beauty, sir."

"She is attractive."

After a pause, the guard captain asked, "Will you be needing the carriage and guards today, sir?"

"I will, in about a glass. Just a driver and one guard. I'll be going to
the exchange."

"Yes, sir."

As he walked away, Charyn couldn't help but feel a certain puzzlement. He knew that some High Holders kept armed guards, but the number allowed was limited under the last revision to the Codex Legis to a company or less. Keeping guards was a luxury, and that suggested that High Holder Zaerlyn was indeed well off. That kind of wealth could certainly sustain a dwelling in L'Excelsis . . . but then, if Ferrand thought the High Holder was a come-lately, perhaps Zaerlyn didn't see any point in spending the money. Yet . . . if he had, perhaps the family would be more accepted.

Charyn shrugged. Even after years of listening to his mother and talking with Ferrand, he didn't pretend to understand everything about why High Holders did what they did. With factors, it was much simpler. Regardless of what they professed, most of them wanted golds and the power that golds provided. A few, like Paersyt, wanted golds to build or create things, but even most of those factors wanted what they built to lead to golds and power.

By eighth glass Charyn was once more at the exchange, and in less than a glass after that he had left, heading back to the Chateau D'Rex, having seen nothing in the way of price changes that might have signified something. Nor had he overheard anything that piqued his interest.

When he reentered the main foyer, he did not hear anyone playing the clavecin. So he made his way to the music room, which was empty. He closed the door, then seated himself at the clavecin and began to play . . . rather to practice his part of the duet. The last thing he wanted to do was to play badly with a High Holder's daughter listening. *Especially that one.* He also wanted to finish any practicing before any of the councilors coming to the meeting might overhear.

He didn't know exactly how long he'd been practicing when he paused after misfingering a tricky passage.

"It's easier if you actually play it the way Farray wrote it, with the ritard before the last bars of the arpeggio."

He recognized Palenya's voice without even having to turn or think. Immediately standing, he gestured to the clavecin. "Perhaps I could do better if I heard it played correctly."

Without a word, she seated herself on the bench and played the section—faultlessly from what he could tell. Then she stood. "Now you should try it."

More than two quints passed before Charyn managed to play the section to Palenya's approval. Then he stood and stretched. "You're a hard taskmistress."

"You said you wanted to play it right."

Charyn offered a wry smile. "I did say that."

Palenya said quietly, "If you practiced as much as most clavecinists, you could be a decent musician, even good."

"But not great."

"There are few great musicians."

Just as there are few great rexes or High Holders. "I might as well try to be good at what I've been raised to do."

"I'm sure you will." Palenya offered an enigmatic smile, then said, "It's just before first glass. Aloryana will be here shortly. The two of you can go through the duet first. Then I'll work with her."

She had barely finished speaking when the door to the music room opened, and Aloryana, Malyna, and Chelia all entered.

"Oh . . . you're here," said Aloryana, her voice sounding disappointed.

"I was practicing the duet. Musician Palenya was instructing me. I thought we could practice it together first."

"While you and your brother are practicing," Chelia said cheerfully, "I'm going to talk with Malyna." She looked at Aloryana. "I've scarcely had a word with her. Then I'll have a word with you, and Malyna can play the clavecin by herself . . . if she wishes."

"I haven't played much recently," said Malyna, "but perhaps Musician Palenya might be able to offer me a few reminders."

"Splendid," declared Chelia.

Charyn managed not to frown. He'd never heard his mother use that word in that fashion.

"I would hope we could hear you all play on Solayi afternoon." Chelia looked to Malyna, and the two left the music room together.

"We might as well begin," suggested Charyn.

"If we must . . ." Aloryana looked ready to pout, but then sat down on the bench beside her brother.

"You can't have every moment of her time," murmured Charyn almost under his breath.

"You're just jealous," whispered Aloryana in return.

"We need to practice," returned Charyn in his normal voice, looking to Palenya, who had not bothered to disguise her amusement. He grinned in return, then positioned his hands. "You begin, remember," he said to Aloryana.

"I know," replied Aloryana, her voice falsely sweet.

Two quints later, Charyn left the music room. Since his mother was still talking with Malyna, and her sitting room door was closed, and since his father was meeting with the High Council and the Factors' Council, Charyn walked to Sanafryt's study.

The Minister of Justice looked up, then handed Charyn a sheaf of papers. "You might as well read these petitions. When you finish reading them, we'll talk."

Charyn nodded and took the papers to the table desk that had become his.

All three petitions were about tariffs. All were from factors, and from the amount of golds involved, the factors involved were likely at least as well off as many High Holders. Charyn read each petition twice before turning. "Minister Sanafryt?"

"You're read them all?"

"I have."

"What is the issue with Factorius Druesyl?"

Druesyl's petition had been the third one he had read. Charyn cleared his throat. "He's claiming that the judgment against him is not legal because a ship is the same as a factorage. Since the Jariolan privateers sunk the ship and seized the cargo, he states that this year's tariff levy was based in part on assets he no longer possesses, and he paid according to what assets he actually has. He's also complaining that a penalty of five hundred golds on top of what he did not pay is excessive."

"What does the law say?" asked Sanafryt.

"That buildings and other assets lost or destroyed will be deducted from the tariff rolls in the year following the destruction."

"Why might that be?"

Charyn didn't know, and didn't want to admit it. So he said nothing and waited for the minister to say something.

"Precedent, based on experience," declared Sanafryt. "Too many factors in the past suffered factorages that burned 'accidently.' Rather than tear down an old facility, they somehow discovered that such factorages just happened to catch fire. Such fires were timed so that the new facility was not completed until after tariff assessments in the next year. It was a way to lower tariffs for an extra year."

"I don't think losing a ship and its cargo is exactly a scheme to reduce tariffs," said Charyn.

"Nor do I, but the law is the law. Once a rex starts making exceptions, the petitions for exception will multiply like coneys in a harvest field."

"What about the penalty?"

"The same is true of penalties as well. The penalties are there to discourage such creative bookkeeping."

"How many petitions are like this in a year?"

"A score or so at present, but there were more than a hundred just from High Holders before the revolt. That happened because your father hesitated in denying the first ones immediately, and that delay encouraged more petitions of all sorts."

"But these three are from factors."

"That's because they haven't seen what happens when laws are flouted the way they were before the failed High Holders' revolt."

Charyn nodded. It was likely to be a very long afternoon . . . and after he left the minister's study, he doubted that he'd learn what happened at the council meeting his father had held with the factors and High Holders, not any time soon.

13

Over the next few days, Charyn didn't see much of Malyna or Aloryana, except at dinner, and under his parents' eyes, it was difficult to find out much more about the very polite but quietly enigmatic young woman, especially since it seemed as though his sister wanted to spend every possible moment with the High Holder's daughter. He did keep up his own routine, working with both Minister Alucar and Minister Sanafryt, almost always after visiting the exchange where he checked prices, listened, and asked occasional questions of the men who handled the bids and prices at various stalls—always when no other factors or agents were present.

He couldn't say that he was anywhere near knowledgeable enough to trade on the exchange, but he was beginning to get some understanding and some feel, especially when he looked at the futures slates. He hadn't understood why the prices of timber went up in Ianus and especially Fevier and Maris, until he heard two agents talking about when they thought the River Aluse would freeze over north of Rivages . . . and when the ice would break and how the price of straight pine had gone up in the year when the river remained frozen solid well into Avryl.

He also wondered when would be a good time to meet with Factor Estafen about his plans, but he couldn't do that, not until he at least provided certain information to his father . . . and at a time when all was relatively calm.

He also practiced his part of the duet when no one was in the music room, as well as other pieces that he knew he did well, or well enough that only Palenya would find fault with them. But then, he doubted he'd ever play well enough to avoid having her suggest improvements.

On Samedi morning, since the exchange was closed, and since neither Sanafryt nor Alucar was available, and since he was awake early, he ate and made his way to the music room, where he played for close to a glass before Palenya entered.

"You've practiced more in the past two weeks than in the previous two months. It shows. You might even become good if you keep it up."

"You're so encouraging," he said dryly, looking up from the keyboard.

"You've never liked false praise . . . in anything. Including your grooming."

Charyn tried not to flush. He still remembered her gentle praise about his wispy mustache—and the fact that he'd shaved it off as soon as he could.

Palenya lowered her voice. "You have said that you prefer honesty."

"Gentle honesty." Charyn tried to look sheepish.

Palenya offered a wry smile.

"What do you think about Malyna D'Zaerlyn?"

"What should I think?" replied Palenya. "Other than it appears she is here for you to observe and see if she might be a suitable match?"

"I don't think so. She's very polite, but somehow she's not like any High Holder's daughter I've ever met."

"I'm encountered a few," said Palenya. "She is kinder than most, in little ways. When she plays, she makes no mistakes, except a few with naturals or ritards. Her fingering is good. She does not play the most difficult pieces, it is true. What she plays, she plays well . . . although . . . she has not played that much recently, I would think. She is not a natural musician, but her technique is sound."

"You're saying that no one but a High Holder's daughter could play that way."

"No one else would pay to train someone without great natural talent so well." Palenya paused. "She plays like Heldryk, if not in as accomplished a fashion."

"Heldryk?"

"He was a great clavecinist. I heard him once when I was very young. No one could understand why he left L'Excelsis to live in Rivages."

Charyn nodded. "That would follow. Malyna's father's holding is in Rivages."

"He must be wealthy indeed, if Heldryk was his musician." Palenya glanced from Charyn to the door of the music room.

"Are you expecting Aloryana or Bhayrn?"

"Lord Bhayrn, and then I have to prepare to play for an afternoon affair for Lady Chelia."

"Wives of High Holders?"

"That I was not told, only that a glass of background music would be required while her guests take refreshments."

Charyn nodded. While his father remained aloof from the High Holders, his mother never had, and still occasionally entertained friends and acquaintances from her younger days, if quietly, and always in the afternoons. "Then it shouldn't be unpleasant."

"No. The choice of music is mine, and there are even a few who offer compliments when they leave. I don't hear them, but your mother is kind enough to repeat them to me."

"I won't keep you." Charyn rose from the bench. He really didn't want to be in the music room when his brother appeared.

Palenya smiled knowingly as he left.

After departing the music room and hoping he might encounter Malyna somewhere—and failing—he finally found Churwyl on the front steps of the Chateau D'Rex. "How are Malyna's guards working out?"

"If they're any indication of his personal guards, I'd hire any of them. One of them broke up a fight in the rear courtyard—two teamsters—so quick that it almost didn't happen."

"How did he manage that?"

"I don't know, but both of them were very subdued when they finished unloading and were ready to leave. I asked Kaylet—that's his name—and he just said that the two had had a misunderstanding. Both of them kept looking at him when they left."

"He must have hurt them badly and quickly."

"Just hard enough to make it clear that he wouldn't tolerate any fighting. I think he used the butt of his rifle like a truncheon, but it was so fast no one else saw anything at all."

"You think they're former army rankers?"

Churwyl shook his head. "They're too sharp and disciplined for that."

Too disciplined for army rankers? Charyn didn't disguise his puzzlement.

"They're more like junior officers who came up through the ranks, but they're both too young for that."

"Do you think High Holder Zaerlyn has a force to put at Father's disposal?" That might well explain his father's willingness to guest Malyna.

"I couldn't say, Lord Charyn. Neither of his guards will say much except that they're here to make sure Malyna is safe."

"As they should. Has there been any sign of other . . . possible assailants?"

"No, sir."

"That's good." *And even more worrisome in other respects.*

While Charyn did not exactly prowl through the chateau, he certainly made an effort to find a time when he could approach Malyna. That took until second glass of the afternoon, when he discovered that she was alone in the upstairs parlor.

He paused in the doorway. "Good afternoon."

"Good afternoon, Charyn."

"I haven't seen much of you, except at dinner." He eased into the parlor, standing beside an armchair.

"Aloryana has kept me busy."

"She been very glad of someone she can relate to, especially someone not her brother."

"You're hard on yourself. She's fond of you both."

"When you were her age, were you close to your brothers?"

"Not by then. They were trying to prove themselves to Father. I suppose all children do as they grow up. Or they rebel." Malyna offered a pleasant smile.

"And you? Rebel or pleaser?"

"A little of both. I always wanted to be myself, but I never wanted to displease. What about you?"

"The rebel came first. Then . . . not so long ago . . . I realized I needed to know more before I could do either. So I guess I'm still learning, not knowing exactly where it will all turn out. You play the clavecin well, Palenya says. Was that a way of pleasing?"

"Proving. I play adequately, but not truly well."

"Was Musician Heldryk your teacher?"

"How did you know that?" Malyna looked surprised.

"Palenya said your playing reminded her of him. She mentioned that he had left L'Excelsis years ago, when she was young, and gone to Rivages. So . . ." Charyn shrugged. "I thought that might be possible."

Malyna laughed softly. "What else have you deduced?"

"That there's more to you than being merely the youngest daughter of a High Holder. I just haven't figured out what."

"Isn't that true of all of us? Aren't you more than the eldest son of the rex? Don't you have interests that he does not?"

"I'm trying to find out about you," Charyn replied lightly. "You're making it difficult."

"There's not that much to find out. I've led a very sheltered life. Haven't you, compared to even the sons of High Holders?"

"That's necessary."

"Why do you go to the exchange? Do you trade there, or just observe? Aren't you the first one in your family to do that?"

Charyn managed not to frown. Who had told her that? "Right now, I'm just observing. I don't exactly have golds to lose."

"And?"

"I'm the first one, but part of that is that the exchange didn't even exist, I don't think, when my father was my age. The change in prices can show things that people won't always tell the rex . . . or his son."

"What are some of those things?" Malyna's voice showed more than casual interest.

"The future prices of spices are rising. That shows that traders are losing ships on the way to or from Otelyrn . . . well . . . it shows that spices are getting to be in short supply, and the most likely reason is because fewer ships are returning, either because fewer traders are taking that risk or because the Jariolan privateers are seizing cargoes and sinking ships."

"That's good to know. Can you give me another example?"

"Timber prices are higher for the next three months. I listened and heard that was because the northern reaches of the River Aluse have already frozen over, and the timber flatboats can't come downstream . . ." Charyn paused, then added, "Sometimes, the prices rise or fall, and no one knows . . . or they're not saying."

"But there has to be a reason, doesn't there?"

"There does. From what I've observed, most traders and agents keep that information to themselves, but the changes in prices show that something is happening. I still have a lot to learn." Even as he spoke the last words, Charyn wondered why he'd admitted that.

"A tutor I had said that people die inside some if they don't keep learning. What do you think about that?"

"I wouldn't argue against him or you."

"What should a ruler do if what he learns changes his views so that he doesn't believe in his own laws?"

"It's easy to say he should change the laws, but it might be better to decide what the effect of the change would be and whether the change would work the way he thought it might." Charyn was thinking about the petitions he'd read earlier in the week.

"You look like you've considered that."

"I've been studying with Minister Sanafryt and Minister Alucar."

After the slightest hesitation, Malyna said, "I'm afraid I'll sound ignorant, but what ministers are they?"

"Sanafryt is the Minister of Justice, and Alucar the Minister of Finance."

"How many ministers does your father have?"

"Just three, plus the Marshal of the Army. Vaelln counts as a minister."

"Then who is the other minister?"

"Aevidyr. He's the Minister of Administration. That's for roads and ports and other things. Why are you interested in all that?"

"Why shouldn't I be?"

Charyn felt off-balance. In fact, he'd been off-balance most of the time they'd been talking. "Most young women aren't, but it's clear you aren't most young women."

"Do you tell all High Holders' daughters that?" The words were gently humorous.

"I've never said that to any of them. None of them are like you." He laughed. "I've been trying to find out more about you, and you keep throwing questions back at me."

"Isn't that what well-bred High Holders' daughters are supposed to do . . . to encourage men to talk about themselves?"

Charyn shook his head, ruefully, then laughed again. "You'd know far better than I. You weren't really brought up that way, were you?"

"Until I was thirteen, and my father realized it wouldn't do any good. After that, I was allowed to pursue studies in history and other subjects."

"What subjects?"

"History and mathematics, including geometry. That helps with surveying and planning buildings or refurbishing rooms."

"There you are!" Aloryana swept into the parlor, then looked at Charyn. "Mother has something for Malyna and me to do."

"Then you both should go." Charyn turned from his sister back to Malyna. "I enjoyed talking with you."

"And I you." Malyna stood, with a grace that was both athletic and feminine, Charyn realized.

He watched as the two left, well aware that he'd found out almost nothing about Malyna, despite all his questions . . . and he still hadn't had a chance to talk to his father, not alone, about what had happened with the High Council.

14

Shortly before third glass on Solayi afternoon, Charyn joined Aloryana, Bhayrn, Malyna, and Palenya in the anteroom adjoining the music room. Aloryana wore a plain blue dress, while Malyna wore a teal dress that looked familiar to Charyn, although he could not have said why. Charyn and Bhayrn wore dark green trousers and matching jackets.

Palenya looked over the four, then said, "Your mother has requested that Aloryana play first, then Bhayrn, Malyna, and finally the duet with Charyn and Aloryana. Once everyone is seated, you will enter and sit in the chairs before the window. Aloryana will sit in the chair closest to the east wall, with Bhayrn next. Charyn will sit closest to the audience."

Charyn glanced through the open archway into the music room. Four upholstered but armless green chairs were set in a row in front of the window, while the clavecin was in its usual place, roughly a yard from the goldenwood-paneled east wall, and positioned an equal distance from the outside wall and the corridor wall. Charyn was surprised to see two rows of armless green chairs set in a gentle arc centered on the clavecin, with a good three yards separating the nearest chair from the instrument.

An audience for a family recital? He wasn't certain whether playing before an unexpected audience bothered him more . . . or the fact that he'd not been told anything about it. He pushed away that thought as he waited.

After less than half a quint, the hall doors to the music room opened, and Lorien and Chelia led a number of others toward the chairs. Charyn immediately recognized the three ministers and Marshal Vaelln. He presumed that the women who accompanied them were their wives. Lorien and Chelia took seats roughly in the middle of the front row.

Once they were seated, Palenya nudged Aloryana, who led the four who would play into the music room and toward the chairs set before the window. Charyn brought up the rear.

Aloryana did not sit, but paused before her chair and then proceeded to the clavecin.

As the other three seated themselves, Charyn covertly studied the audience. All had pleasant expressions, not particularly intent, but without any trace of overt boredom, unsurprisingly, given the setting and the fact that the performers were primarily from the regial family. Charyn could feel a cold draft from the windows behind him and was glad his jacket was relatively warm.

Aloryana took the bench, positioned her hands, and began to play.

Charyn had to admit that, after a shaky opening bar or so of the Serkuyn prelude, Aloryana settled down and played better than he had heard before, especially the second piece, an étude by Devor. After she finished, all ten of the listeners applauded politely.

Bhayrn followed with a dark and brooding Devor nocturne, which he played far too bombastically. At least, Charyn thought so. The polite applause was slightly less than that for Aloryana.

When Malyna took her place at the clavecin, Charyn's eyes were on her, and her alone. She was so poised that he had trouble believing she was only nineteen. She played two pieces that Charyn had never heard, the first one seemed to be a scherzo, and the second a nocturne that sounded like it might have been written by Covaelyt. Neither the scherzo nor the nocturne sounded that easy to Charyn, since he wondered if he could have even gotten through either without major misfingerings. The applause was, Charyn judged, slightly greater for Malyna than for either Aloryana or Bhayrn.

At the end of that applause, Malyna stood, moved back from the clavecin, curtseyed to Lorien, smiling warmly, and then returned to her chair, beside Charyn.

As he stood to take his place at the clavecin with Aloryana, he murmured to Malyna, "You were superb."

"Thank you," she returned in a low voice.

Did she blush, just slightly? That disconcerted him enough that he hesitated, drawing a quick glance from Aloryana, but he recovered quickly and smoothly, reaching the bench at the same time as his sister. They seated themselves almost simultaneously.

Aloryana was even better in playing the Farray duet than she had been in playing her first pieces, and Charyn felt that he played better than he had before. *You hope.*

The applause was again modest, but increased when the two others joined them for a bow, or curtsey in the case of Malyna and Aloryana.

Then Lorien rose. "We have refreshments in the anteroom."

As the ministers and their wives moved toward the archway, Charyn turned to Aloryana. "You played that well."

"So did you," she replied cheerfully. "Wasn't Malyna wonderful?"

"I thought so."

"For her playing," returned his sister.

"That's what I meant."

The four performers eased into the anteroom after the audience, where one sideboard held red and white wine, and the other held an array of delicacies on small platters, including small circles of pâté on individual circular cuts of toast, miniature apple tarts, almond wafers, and an array of cheeses.

Aloryana stayed close to Malyna, while Charyn found himself face-to-face with Marshal Vaelln and his wife.

"You're a man of many talents, Lord Charyn," offered the marshal.

"A man of modest talents," demurred Charyn. "The talented ones are Malyna D'Zaerlyn and my sister."

"I'm surprised a young woman that talented on the clavecin and that attractive isn't already spoken for," Vaelln added. "Or is she?"

"Not by me," replied Charyn lightly. "I only met her a week ago."

"Don't wait too long," suggested Vaelln.

"You make it sound like an army maneuver, dear," offered the marshal's wife.

"All relations between people are maneuvers," returned the marshal.

"Speaking of maneuvers," said Charyn, "have there been any other shootings or events such as the one that occurred here at the chateau?"

"Not that I know of," replied Vaelln, "but this isn't the place to discuss such matters."

"Of course," replied Charyn. "I do appreciate your coming, and your kind words about my playing. If you will excuse me . . ." He smiled warmly and eased away toward where Malyna and Aloryana were talking with his father and mother.

"I very much enjoyed what you played," said Lorien to Malyna. "I don't believe I've heard either before. What were they?"

"The first piece is called 'Variations on a Scherzo.' It was composed by Heldryk D'Musica. The second was 'Nocturne on a Stormy Night' by Covaelyt."

Charyn nodded to himself as he slipped closer.

"You played excellently," added Lorien, looking directly at Malyna.

"I played as well as I ever have, but I fear it was far from excellent."

"You are too modest, my dear," said Chelia. "You play very well."

"I played better because I worked with Musician Palenya this week.

She is an excellent teacher and a fine musician. You're fortunate to have her."

"So we are," declared Lorien. "You must have had a good teacher as well. Fine as Palenya is, she could not accomplish miracles in a mere week."

"I was favored to learn from a great musician as well."

"Who might that have been?" asked Chelia.

"Heldryk," replied Malyna.

"The one who composed the first piece you played?"

Malyna nodded. "Yes, sir."

"Did he teach you that piece?"

"He did. It was a while ago. I've always liked it."

"Very cheerful. I like that. Too much gloom around here lately. You must have some of the red wine." Lorien motioned to one of the servers. "A red wine for the young lady."

Malyna accepted the wine with a nod, and Charyn took the other goblet on the server's tray.

Chelia looked to Charyn. "You played better than I've ever heard."

"I couldn't let Aloryana down." *And she deserved better than Bhayrn's ham-fisting the keys.*

"You both looked like you were enjoying it," added Chelia.

"I hope Aloryana was. I was." Charyn realized that he had enjoyed it, more than he'd expected.

"She'll remember it," said Malyna. "I wish one of my older brothers had played a duet with me."

"They didn't?" asked Chelia.

"I'm much the youngest. By the time I was Aloryana's age, we were all in different places. You two are fortunate."

At that moment, Minister Sanafryt appeared, clearly directing himself toward Charyn. "You've obviously been studying clavecin in addition to law. Well as you played, Lord Charyn, I fear your future lies more in law. A ruler who is known to be as accomplished as you clearly are on the clavecin runs the risk of being thought frivolous."

"Whereas such a comparatively frivolous accomplishment in a woman is lauded?" asked Malyna gently. "Even when it is difficult enough that there are few truly great clavecinists?"

Charyn could see his mother block a smile, even as she quickly said, "Charyn will just have to keep his accomplishments within the walls of the chateau, I fear. That will allow us, at least, to enjoy his playing."

"He does play well," added Malyna.

Charyn kept a smile from his face at Sanafryt's momentarily confused expression.

"I'm so glad you came and enjoyed the recital," Lorien said cheerfully.

"I wouldn't have missed it," replied the minister, "and Clorynda was especially pleased that you included us."

"We will see her at the Year-Turn Ball, will we not?" asked Chelia.

"Indeed you will." With a nod and a smile, Sanafryt retreated.

"Minister Sanafryt is a good minister, and he knows the law well," Lorien observed, "but he's well-meaning, if sometimes pompous. Not that pomp is unknown elsewhere in the chateau." The rex actually smiled.

Charyn barely managed not to choke on his wine. He thought he glimpsed a glint in Malyna's eyes, but he wasn't certain.

Lorien and Chelia moved away, easing toward Minister Alucar and his wife, when Bhayrn strode up, his goblet almost empty.

"Aren't you looking smug."

"Pleased. Not smug. I'm happy that it's over. I think we all did well."

"That's because of Palenya," declared Aloryana.

"That's why I think Palenya should have been here at the reception," Charyn said.

Before Aloryana or Malyna could say anything, Bhayrn replied, "Chateau workers are never at receptions, except to serve. That's the way it's done. Everyone has their place."

"Is because it's always been done that way a good reason to continue?" asked Malyna.

"You'll continue in the path all High Holders' daughters do, just as Aloryana will, or I will. Second sons don't have much choice, either." Bhayrn snorted, then turned, and walked toward the sideboard with the wine.

Charyn looked at Malyna. "For what it's worth, you asked two very good questions. I liked the first one as well."

"I'm hungry," said Aloryana. "There won't be dinner after this." She took Malyna's arm and dragged her toward the sideboard with the delicacies.

Charyn couldn't help smiling as he watched. *And at least we don't have to go to anomen services.*

15

On Mardi morning, the wind was bitter, and strong enough to whip the light snow that had begun to fall sometime before dawn across the paving stones of the West River Road when Charyn stepped out of the carriage in front of the narrow gray stone building with shiny black bars covering the windows and a stone plaque with the letters stating BANQUE D'EXCELSIS positioned above the brass-bound heavy oak door. Both wood and brass gleamed. Charyn looked to the guard and driver who accompanied him. "I won't be that long." *One way or the other.* "Just wait here."

"Sir . . . ?"

"You're guarding the outside. There are guards inside. I should be quite secure." He turned and walked to the heavy door, which moved easily as he opened it, and stepped into the banque.

Neither of the two banque guards, each with a sabre at his side, gave him more than a passing glance as he crossed the gray marble floor of the small entry foyer and made his way into the single large chamber that lay beyond the square arch at the inside end of the foyer.

At the back of the chamber was a long counter graced by a bronze railing fastened to a bronze plate, with bronze bars connecting the plate and railing. At three places, there were openings in the bronze bars. A man wearing a green jacket sat behind each tell. A single customer stood before the tell on the right, watching as the teller counted out silvers.

According to what Elthyrd had told Charyn, Estafen had a dark black beard, square-cut. Although Elthyrd had indicated he would tell his son that Charyn might come to the banque, Charyn wasn't counting on that.

Yet, even before Charyn finished surveying the south wall of the chamber, Estafen was on his feet from where he had been seated behind a table desk set in a corner from where he could observe all who entered the banque. He walked toward Charyn with a pleasant smile. "Greetings, sir. My sire said that you might be coming. If you wouldn't mind coming this way?"

"Not at all," replied Charyn, smiling warmly. He was conscious of the fact that Estafen had said absolutely nothing that would reveal Charyn's identity to anyone who did not already know him. And, so far, in his limited dealings with Elthyrd, the head of the Factors' Council of Solidar had been direct and forthright about what he promised . . . although Charyn had the definite impression that the older factor was cautious about what he promised.

Estafen led the way to a very small study, one with just a circular table and two chairs, a single bookcase, and two file chests on narrow tables. He closed the door behind Charyn, then gestured to the table and chairs, waiting to seat himself just after Charyn did.

"It's not often that we're graced by so . . . regial a personage."

"I'm not that yet, Factorius."

"Might I ask . . . ?"

"Why I'm here? You might. I've been talking to your sire over the past weeks. He mentioned something about the ironworks." Charyn knew that it had slipped the minds of most that Estafen had obtained the ironworks when the heir of Factor Vaschet defaulted on his loans to the Banque D'Excelsis.

Estafen raised his eyebrows. "Oh? I hope you didn't misunderstand. We're more than current on our tariffs."

"I have no doubt of that. I'm not a tariff collector for my father. Your sire said little except that he felt you were working long glasses." Charyn offered an understanding smile. "Handling a banque and an ironworks take much effort, and both are time-consuming. Now that Factorius Karl has procured flatboats . . ." He shrugged.

"Good parents always worry about their offspring."

"That your sire does scarcely surprises me. He's very impressive."

Estafen laughed. "Impressive. He'd hate being described like that, but it fits."

"It does." Charyn kept a pleasant expression, but did not volunteer more.

"I don't believe you've explained why you might be here," said Estafen cautiously.

"I have not. It's a delicate matter, but not in the fashion of most delicate matters you must handle. My sire is still a young man for a rex. I don't fancy being an ornament or trying to get in his way under the guise of being of assistance. Knowing what you do of him, I trust you understand." What Charyn didn't say was that Estafen had likely faced a similar situation in regard to his own father.

"I believe I understand."

"It has occurred to me, especially after the unpleasantness of last week, that my family and I have little in common with the factors of Solidar. From what I've observed at the exchange in just the past few weeks, factors are becoming more powerful. That's as a group. Some individual factors, I am certain, are worth more than many High Holders, but the strength of factors lies in their numbers. Not necessarily in individual wealth." Charyn looked directly at Estafen. "Or do you think I am mistaken?"

"I cannot dispute what you say."

Charyn could see that Estafen would not be drawn out. He couldn't blame the banking factor. "Also, many of the regial lands are not managed, if I can be honest about it, in as practical a fashion as might be. This might pose difficulties in the future. I had thought that a change in regial practices might be in order. If I began such a change on my own, as I have with my own personal lands, and do not involve my sire . . ." Charyn paused and offered a small shrug.

Estafen frowned. "Go on . . . if you would."

"By the time I become rex, I would have the experience to better understand and talk with factors. My efforts would also be affected by both the laws and nature in the same way as theirs."

"Ah . . . I'm not quite certain I understand."

"I was thinking of persuading you to allow me to make an offer on the ironworks."

"What if I do not wish to sell?"

"Then you have every reason to reject my offer. I think I have a proposition you might find . . . interesting."

"I'm skeptical, but tell me more."

"Once the imagers quashed the High Holders' revolt, the profits of the ironworks also dropped, did they not?"

"You obviously already know the answer, Lord Charyn."

"I prefer the title of Factor Suyrien. I actually hold lands. The land name I use is Suyrien D'Chaeryll. I'm also a member of the exchange under that name. Your father assisted in that."

Estafen offered an amused smile, then shook his head. "If anyone knew . . ."

"It's to your advantage and that of most factors that they don't. You're interested in the highest return on your investment, I assume?"

"The highest reasonably safe return, yes."

"Of what? An investment of six thousand golds?"

"More like eight."

Charyn suspected it was closer to seven, but did not comment. "My proposition will address that and accomplish my own end—that of eventually owning and operating an ironworks profitably."

"Why, might I ask?"

"To begin with, in time, I'd like to use the ironworks to produce certain . . . machines that will improve factoring. I'd also like to prove that the heir of a rex isn't merely an empty-headed figure lolling or playing around or trying to increase his worth through higher tariffs." Charyn smiled. "I made this visit to raise the possibility. I'd like you to think over the gradual transfer of the ironworks to me personally. During that period, I would work under my factoring name as an assistant to you part-time at the ironworks. You would receive regular payments, and keep all the profits. If there are losses, provided the ironworks continues to operate as it currently does, you will not bear them."

"What might people say?"

"Why should they say anything? I absolutely do not want it known that I might become owner of the ironworks. I think it would be best if others are led to believe that you accommodated a wealthy factor who prefers to remain nameless in allowing his heir to learn just how much effort it takes to operate an ironworks."

"There will still be rumors."

"Aren't there always?" After the slightest pause, Charyn added, "Right now, this is just a proposal. I'd like you to think about it, and then perhaps we could talk again after Year-Turn." He held up a hand. "I am asking that you not tell me your decision now."

"My thoughts may not change."

"They may not. Or they might. I think it's only fair to ask you to consider it." Charyn grinned. "You might even figure out a way to make it more advantageous to you and the banque."

"You do give a man pause . . . Factor Suyrien."

"I hope so." Charyn stood, knowing that Estafen would not take that initiative. "A prosperous Year-Turn."

Estafen rose quickly. "The same to you."

As he made his way outside to the carriage, Charyn was particularly careful as he stepped out of the banque, but no one seemed even to notice him, and the ride to the exchange was quick, perhaps because the wind and snow, which had almost stopped, had kept many people off the roads. At the exchange, there were few traders, factors, and agents, almost as if no one really expected much to change. He heard little of interest, not even of a gossipy nature, and less than a glass later he returned to his coach and headed back to the Chateau D'Rex. While on the way, he removed the exchange pin from his coat.

He had just stepped into the chateau and finished handing his coat to Vaetor when Norstan appeared.

"The rex would like to see you immediately."

"Thank you."

Charyn made his way up the stairs at a good pace, but not hurrying, and Maertyl, as the duty guard outside the study, immediately announced him and opened the door, closing it quickly once Charyn was inside.

Charyn walked to the desk where his father was seated, but did not sit down until Lorien motioned for him to do so.

"I understand you went out this morning." Lorien's tone was curt. "Despite the snow."

"Yes, sir. I did. The snow was light. It's since stopped."

"Into the heart of L'Excelsis, no less. What if someone had shot you?"

"That would have been unlikely, sir. I took the unmarked carriage. Very few in L'Excelsis know who I am by appearance, and my guards wore brown jackets. For the present, I can ride largely unnoticed. I would like to do so while I can, so as to have a better idea of not only the city but other nearby areas. Before long, I grant you, that will not be possible."

"For what purpose?"

"Sir . . . are you like your sire . . . or grandsire? Have any of the best rulers of Solidar merely copied their predecessors? I cannot be you. I'd be a poor imitation, because an imitation can be at best a copy. For me to succeed you successfully, when the time comes, and I do hope it is not soon, and for many other reasons—"

"Give me one," snapped Lorien.

"I don't judge people well immediately. I think I judge them better each time I meet them. The more experience I have, and the more people I meet, the better I'll be."

"What else?"

"Solidar is changing. Not all those changes are easily seen from within the Chateau D'Rex, and the more I see outside the more I can learn and inform you."

For a moment, Lorien did not respond. Finally, he said, "At least you've thought it out. What were you doing in L'Excelsis?"

"I met with Factor Estafen. He owns the Banque D'Excelsis. I understand that the ironworks that former factor Vaschet built might be for sale. His son didn't handle them well. He defaulted on the loans to the Banque D'Excelsis."

"Good! Vaschet got what he deserved." Lorien frowned. "The Civic Patrol never did find out who shot him, did they?"

"No, sir. That was just before Murranyt took his stipend."

"He left L'Excelsis rather hastily, too, as I recall."

"I wouldn't know, sir." Charyn smiled apologetically.

"You always have a reason for bringing up something. What is it this time? About the ironworks, I presume?"

"Yes, sir. I thought about working out an arrangement to buy the ironworks."

"Why on Terahnar would you even think of that?"

"To improve our financial position. To make clear our alignment with the factors . . . and to learn that which I cannot otherwise."

"What? Are you out of your mind?"

"I hope not. We obtain most of our revenues from lands. Yields are falling. An ironworks would—"

"Only lose thousands of golds?" Lorien's scorn was more than palpable.

"I think not, sir. Might I explain?"

"You might as well." The resignation in Lorien's voice suggested the explanation was likely to be in vain.

"There are several reasons. First, I think we can make some golds over time. Anything more we can make will be of benefit. Second, if we have an ironworks, it will be seen that we know something about manufacturing and factoring . . ." Charyn went on to explain, including the point about accomplishing the purchase gradually and without notice. When he finished he waited for his father to reply.

"I have grave doubts. Still . . . over the past several months, you've shown yourself much more interested in matters. I'm inclined to oppose the idea, but I'm not going to say no yet. I'm also not going to say yes." Lorien cleared his throat. "On another matter, have you been watching the surroundings on all these trips you've been making through L'Excelsis?"

"Yes, sir."

"Have you seen anyone who followed you? Have your guards?"

"Not so far. Have there been any more threats?"

"No. That worries me."

"You announced that you would be building more warships, didn't you? Isn't that what they demanded?"

"It is. I've even had Alucar draft the shipbuilding order and send it to

Solis, as well as make arrangements for the necessary disbursements." Lorien scowled. "I don't like it, and it won't keep those hothead factors happy for long. Then what do I do? Spend from the tariff reserves to start building another? Vaelln tells me that we can't build more than two or possibly three additional ships this year. There isn't the space in the ship-yards, and there aren't enough shipfitters. He should know. He spent years as the Sea Marshal."

"What about doing what the Jariolans are doing? Commissioning privateers to prey on Jariolan ships?"

"That's likely to get us into an all-out war, and our warships are out-numbered almost two to one, if we're talking ships of the line. I told you before I don't want to start a war there's no way to win and no way to pay for."

"I suppose you've told the Factors' Council that, then."

"I've told them about the problem with building and commissioning more warships quickly."

Charyn managed not to frown, as he tried to think why his father hadn't mentioned the problem with commissioning privateers. "You didn't mention the possibility of war if you commissioned privateers because they'd blame you for not having built more warships earlier, even though no one would pay the tariffs necessary to build them?"

"Exactly! They'd ignore the fact they opposed more tariffs and just blame me, and then whoever is behind that threat would make another attempt."

"Has there been any success in discovering who might be behind it?"

"Hardly. All it takes is a handful of well-trained shooters and less than a hundred golds. Almost any large factor in Solidar could manage that. I've taken a few other steps, but the less anyone knows about them, even you, the better."

"What about your regional governors? Can't they help? Doesn't each have an army battalion at his disposal?"

"He does. Just what good does that do when neither they nor I know who is behind the attacks."

Charyn wasn't about to raise the point that the governors should know something and should be informing his father more, not while there was still the possibility of his father approving the purchase of the ironworks. "I can see that, sir. Is there anything else you can do to give the impression to the factor hotheads that you're doing all you can?"

"There's not very much else I can do, and that's the problem."

"Are you getting any suggestions from either Chief Factor Elthyrd or High Holder Ryel?"

"Ryel's not sent me anything. He's almost begged me to let him off the Council, and I'm tempted to let him go. I'm not the one who'd as soon see him dead. Well, not as much as your mother would. She wouldn't even go to the memorial service for Baryel. But I'm not about to tell Ryel anything until the Year-Turn Ball . . ."

"And Elthyrd?"

"He doesn't have any ideas beyond those he's already offered."

"Did anything happen at the meeting you had with both councils?"

"Nothing except half of them weren't there. I knew they wouldn't be, this close to Year-Turn. Everyone agreed that something should be done. No one could agree on anything, and there weren't enough factors there to insist on specifics. I told you nothing would happen until the Ianus meeting . . ."

Charyn continued to ask questions and listen carefully, since the times when his father was willing to talk, especially in detail, were few . . . and the more he talked the better a chance Charyn had to accomplish what he had in mind.

16

The next several days proceeded largely uneventfully. Charyn had breakfast at the same time as his mother, checked the previous day's appointments list with Norstan, although no names were added, suggesting nothing untoward, then proceeded to the exchange. Upon his return, he studied with Sanafryt on Meredi and Alucar on Jeudi. He practiced on the clavecin in the late afternoon, had dinner with the family and Malyna, who never seemed to be free from either Aloryana or Chelia, if not both, and spent the later evening and night with Palenya.

On Vendrei, the wind picked up, and the day got colder with each passing glass. By the time Charyn returned to the Chateau D'Rex in early afternoon, his breath steamed in the frigid air of the courtyard as he crossed the paving stones to the rear entry.

He was well inside and halfway up the grand staircase when Vaetor hurried down to meet him.

"The rex?"

"Yes, sir. He said he wanted to see you as soon as you returned."

"I'm heading there now."

Before he reached the study door, Charyn pulled a handkerchief from his jacket pocket and blotted his nose, slightly runny from the bitter cold outside.

The study guard announced, "Lord Charyn," then opened the door.

Lorien, sitting at the goldenwood desk, motioned Charyn to the chairs before the desk and picked up a single sheet of paper or parchment from a stack. "It's about time you were here."

"I came straight to the study, sir." Charyn sat down in the middle chair.

"You talked about the factors and how you thought buying an ironworks would help! What do you think of this?" Lorien thrust the single sheet at Charyn with a motion so violent that several scraps of sealing wax broke loose from the paper and dropped to the carpet.

Charyn took the sheet, his eyes going to the words that seemed to stand out.

. . . regret to inform you that the silos of the main granary at the Tuuryl estate were set on fire on the night of Mardi, the twenty-fourth of Finitas. Several silos exploded and were partly or totally destroyed. The perpetrators were not detected. Anything that was not burned was ruined. Nothing could be saved. Attached is the sheet that was knifed to the landwarden's door . . .

"All the granaries on the estate?"

"The smaller and older silos in the other granary were spared, but they weren't close to being filled."

"What was the landwarden doing? Isn't it his job to keep the crops and livestock safe?"

"That's why he's about to become the former landwarden. The idiot couldn't even see who did it? Setting fire or explosives to all those silos had to take time."

"What does the other sheet say?" asked Charyn.

Lorien snorted. "It says that so long as the factors take losses from the rex's inability to deal with the piracy and sinkings of Solidaran ships, his own losses will continue."

"That's blackmail."

"Tell me something I don't know."

"Explosives . . ." mused Charyn. "Do you think there's any connection to the granaries and the destruction of the factors' exchange in Solis?"

"What connection could there be?"

"I don't know. They both deal with grain. I just wondered. How much grain did they destroy?" Charyn handed the sheet from the Tuuryl land-warden back to his father.

"There were twenty silos there . . . Alucar told me we have two hundred and forty storing wheat. That's all across Solidar. They aren't all full, right now, of course. I should have sold more, but Alucar cautioned me against that. Now I can get nothing from those silos."

Charyn calculated. If the silos were the size of those at Chaeryll, each one would hold about five thousand bushels of wheat. "A hundred thousand bushels at twelve coppers a bushel . . ." He swallowed. "That's . . . around twelve thousand golds . . . we lost. That's the cost of three ships of the line."

Lorien frowned. "How did you know that?"

"The current price at the exchange is twelve coppers a bushel, and the average silo on our lands holds five thousand bushels. The rest is just mathematics."

"Maybe you should have been a factor. All that calculating in knowing what we lost doesn't help in determining what to do about it." Lorien turned toward the window.

Charyn could see through the small section of panes that were not covered by hangings that a light snow had begun to fall.

"Those factors will pay for this," Lorien went on. "I can't let them get away with it."

"We have to find out who they are before we can do anything to them."

"If the Factors' Council doesn't find out, then I'll raise tariffs on all factors, and I'll build their Namer-damned ships . . . and repay our losses out of the tariffs. They either bring whoever did it forward, or they'll all pay."

"That might make more of them angry."

"What am I supposed to do? Let them get away with it? If I do, then I'll just have more trouble in the future."

"Why don't you just ask the Factors' Council exactly how you can build ships as fast as they want? You've told me that it's not a matter of golds, but of dockyards and shipfitters. That way you don't have to be the one talking about golds and tariffs."

Lorien opened his mouth, then closed it. After a moment, he said, "They'll say that with enough golds anything can be done."

"Tell them they're right, and then ask how they'd propose to get those golds. If they talk about your having golds, tell them that the unknown factors just burned more than the cost of three ships, and then ask how destroying your grain and attacking your family is going to build ships."

"They don't care. They're not thinking. They'll just throw it back at me." Lorien snorted again. "They want me to pay for it all."

"Maybe you should start another ship or two."

"Why? The more I do without making them pay, the more they'll want me to do. That's what led to your grandfather's death. I can't give in. I'm going to have to raise tariffs, and I'm going to have to announce it immediately, and the reasons why. Doing nothing won't deal with the problem."

"That will mean more attacks," predicted Charyn.

"I'll also announce that if the attacks continue, tariffs will go up again. The arrogant bastards will pay. They will."

"You might be better off announcing that any factor found to be behind the attacks will forfeit all his property."

"I'll do that as well, but the rest of them have to understand that they can't keep silent when they know who's behind the attacks."

"Only a few likely know," Charyn pointed out.

"It doesn't matter! It's the principle of the thing. They want everyone else to pay for their protection, and they're attacking me and my family because they're not willing to contribute their share."

Charyn could see that there was no point in discussing that aspect of the matter, not at the moment. "Then you'll bring it up at the next joint meeting of the Factors' Council and the High Council?"

"When else? I could yell and send messages, and no one would read them until after Year-Turn. But they'll hear then, by the Nameless. That they will."

For the next half glass, Charyn mostly listened, easing out of the study when Alucar arrived to discuss the latest results of the past year's tariff collections, since some tariffs always arrived late.

17

Given the continuing wind and cold, by Solayi afternoon Charyn was more than happy to accept his mother's invitation to her salon to play whist. His father and Bhayrn didn't like whist, and that meant Charyn found himself sitting at the plaques table, covered in the traditional dark blue felt, across from his mother, who was his partner, with Malyna to his left, and Aloryana to his right. He hoped he didn't make any truly stupid mistakes, since he doubted he'd played in almost a year, and since his mother played at least occasionally with some of her acquaintances, as did Aloryana, if even less occasionally.

"Thank you for joining us, Charyn." Chelia smiled warmly at her son.

"It's my pleasure." At least, he hoped it would be, and that he could learn more about the mysterious Malyna.

Chelia fanned the deck across the table, facedown, then turned over a single plaque—the knight of crowns. Charyn had always wondered why the term "knight" persisted, since there hadn't been any since the time of the Naedarans. In turn, Malyna turned over a chorister of sprites, Charyn a seven of crowns, and Aloryana a three of eagles.

With that, Chelia flipped over the four plaques, inserted them in the deck, and handed it to Malyna, who shuffled the plaques twice, expertly, and returned the deck to Chelia, who cut it, and then dealt.

After Chelia dealt the last plaque to herself, Charyn picked up his hand, fanned the fifteen plaques, then arranged them by suits, but not in hierarchical order, which would have been crowns, sprites, eagles, stags, and serpents. That would have given too much away, at least to Malyna and probably even to Aloryana. Ideally, he should have played with the plaques left in the order he'd picked the hand off the felt, since a truly expert player could tell much about the content of his hand after several tricks had been played, but he wasn't comfortable with that, knowing that he would likely make a stupid mistake if he didn't at least have his plaques ordered by suit and card rank.

He studied the plaques. Just four honors, the knight and chorister of sprites, the rex of eagles, and the knight of serpents. His longest suit was sprites, with five. Not an awful hand, but hardly exemplary.

Since Chelia had dealt, Malyna had the opening bid. Smiling pleasantly, she said, "One." That meant she and Aloryana had to take eight tricks, the basic book of seven and one more.

Charyn looked at his hand again. He had two sure tricks, possibly three at the outside. "Pass."

"Two," added Aloryana.

"Powerful bid, there," offered Charyn.

"I didn't see you bidding," returned Aloryana sweetly.

"Pass," said Chelia, raising an eyebrow at Charyn.

No more sardonic comments for a bit. Charyn smiled pleasantly.

Malyna led the six of serpents, establishing serpents as trumps.

Charyn didn't have that much choice. He played his singleton knight, and Aloryana dropped the seven of serpents, while Chelia played the three. With that, Charyn gathered the trick, turned the plaques facedown, and led the four of stags, which Aloryana covered with the knight. Chelia trumped that with the four of serpents, suggesting she was short of trumps, since whist required either following suit or trumping, unless the player had no plaques left in the suit that had been led. Malyna overtrumped with the five of serpents, suggesting she had at least five trumps, possibly six.

"You think that's high enough?" asked Charyn cheerfully.

"We'll see, won't we?" she replied with a grin, then led the two of serpents, on which Charyn dropped the two of eagles.

For an instant, Aloryana looked dismayed before playing the eight of serpents. Chelia took the trick with the rex of serpents, then led back the ten of eagles, in response to Charyn's discard. That also suggested that Chelia had no more serpents in her hand.

Malyna hesitated, then dropped the six of eagles, which Charyn covered with the rex, hoping his counts were correct. They were, because Aloryana did not trump, which she certainly would have if she could, but instead played the four of eagles. Charyn returned with the three of eagles, which Aloryana covered with the knight, and Chelia dropped the five, while Malyna dropped the six of sprites, meaning she was out of eagles. The next trick Aloryana led the two of crowns, which Chelia covered with the seven, and Malyna took with the chorister. All Charyn could do was drop an eight.

Malyna then led the chorister of stags, on which Charyn dropped his lowest remaining stag, the eight, followed by Aloryana's seven, and Chelia's two. Still in the lead, Malyna offered the rex of stags and took that trick. Then she led the three of stags, but Chelia took the trick with the nine. The next trick went to Malyna when she trumped Chelia's chorister of eagles.

In the end, Malyna made her bid exactly.

"Nicely done," said Charyn.

"Very well done," added Chelia. "You kept us from using our good sprites until the end, when it was too late."

"I was fortunate in where the plaques lay." Malyna handed the plaques from the tricks she and Aloryana had taken to Charyn.

"Fortune doesn't help much, if you can't play to it," replied Charyn, combining the plaques he had with the ones from Malyna before shuffling the deck twice and presenting it to Malyna.

She cut the deck and then began to deal. "I really haven't played that much whist recently. It almost seems like fewer people play it these days. Or perhaps that's just where I've been. We're a little isolated that way."

"It was always that way in Rivages," replied Chelia. "I didn't get much of an opportunity to play whist until I came to L'Excelsis. If you lived here, dear, I'm sure you'd have more than a few who would enjoy having you."

"Let's hope you still feel that way after the game."

"I doubt your play will be any less expert."

Chelia took the next bid with three, after Charyn passed and then didn't raise. When she and Charyn ended up taking twelve tricks, he was personally discomfited because only the bid tricks counted toward the eleven points that made a game, although Chelia merely smiled as she said, "You can count knights as sure tricks when your partner opens with three."

"I'd forgotten. I've likely played even less in the last year than Malyna has." As he took the cards from Aloryana, cut them and began to deal, he turned to Malyna. "Just what have you been doing to keep yourself busy up in Rivages?" *Besides waiting for your father to find you a husband.*

"I've found a tutor in advanced mathematics, and I've also learned the basics of handling a sabre. My father taught me basic knifework, but he didn't see much point in teaching me longer blades, since a woman can conceal a knife but not a blade."

"And he let you practice with a sabre?" Charyn wished he hadn't asked the question as soon as the words were out.

"I would have been dying of boredom if I just sat and waited for the important things in life to happen. Besides, why shouldn't a woman know the basics of using a blade to defend herself? It's not as though any of us are going to become . . . marauders . . . or brigands." Malyna added smoothly, "We're living in uncertain times."

"And I suppose you can handle a rifle, too?" Charyn kept his words light.

"I know how one works. I'd prefer not to use one or even practice with something almost half as tall as I am."

Charyn noticed that while Chelia's eyes widened at the words about the sabre, she had seemed totally unmoved by the mention of the knife. "Has some of that time you've spent with Aloryana been spent adding that to her skills?"

"Yes, since she asked."

"Would you consider sparring with me . . . using light wands, of course?" asked Charyn.

"I'm likely not anywhere near your match."

"Then, if that is so, you'll get better. If you're underplaying your skill," Charyn replied pleasantly, "I will."

"I wouldn't mind practicing—just with wands—if you wouldn't mind." Malyna looked to Chelia. "If it wouldn't be too . . . untoward?"

"With padded jackets and no strikes below the waist," replied Chelia. "That is, if you two will do so using the interior gallery on the lower level. The guards and others shouldn't see that. And Aloryana and I will be present to satisfy all proprieties."

"Tomorrow, perhaps, since it appears it will continue cold and unpleasant outside?"

"Late morning," said Chelia. Her words were not a suggestion. "Your father will be receiving Marshal Vaelln and his vice-marshal and their wives at second glass for refreshments, and all of you are invited. He decided that on short notice."

Charyn wasn't certain which surprised him more, that he was to give Malyna practice or a lesson or that his father had agreed to an informal reception. Or that Malyna had accepted his suggestion, one made almost, but not quite, in jest.

In response to Charyn's unspoken question, Chelia went on. "I did suggest the reception, since most of us cannot go anywhere, and since the vice-marshal's wife has never been here, unlike the other wives of senior army officers, and it is likely that he may succeed Marshal Vaelln. You might pick up your plaques, Charyn. We are playing whist."

Charyn finished dealing and picked up his hand. The plaques in it were even worse than the last hand . . . and he had the feeling that it was going to be a longer afternoon than he had thought, especially given the look Chelia had offered after her last words . . . and the fact that both Malyna and his mother were better players than he was.

18

Charyn woke up alone—and early, even for him—on Solayi morning, his thoughts still circling around all the questions he had about Malyna. There was no doubt that she was the daughter of High Holder Zaerlyn, but what High Holder raised daughters like her? She knew surveying and higher mathematics. She played the clavecin better than he did . . . and better than either Bhayrn or Aloryana. She'd been taught by a composer and master musician, one that Palenya clearly respected. She had turned out to be at least as good at whist as his mother, and possibly better, all the time demurring that she'd been fortunate.

Then there were the questions of the weapons. What High Holder's daughter was good with a dagger and carried one all the time? He'd never heard of one. As for one who had even lifted a sabre in practice . . . that seemed even more unlikely. Was Malyna one of those women who weren't really women? Had his mother and Malyna set up the sparring business to make that clear to him?

He washed up and dressed in plain greens, similar to those worn by the chateau guards, then went down to breakfast, where he discovered that someone had eaten earlier because the serving girl was clearing away several platters.

"Who ate early?" he asked.

"Lady Chelia and Lady Malyna."

Charyn nodded and sat down. His mother was an early riser, and apparently so was Malyna. Aloryana was not, in taking after their father. But if Malyna was an early riser, why hadn't she breakfasted with his mother before? *Because she's humoring Aloryana? But why to that extent?*

As soon as the mug of tea arrived, he took a swallow, still thinking. Almost a glass later, he was just finishing the slightly overcooked cheesed eggs that he had lingered over when Bhayrn appeared.

His brother grinned. "I understand you're going to be teaching blades—or wands—to our guest."

"I wish I'd never agreed to it," Charyn admitted, although it hadn't exactly been agreement since he'd brought it up in the first place. *The more fool you.* "If she's even halfway good with the wands, that will make the point that Aloryana could also learn blades, at least enough to defend herself."

"Then she probably is that good," replied Bhayrn, "and Aloryana put her up to it. You know she's always thought it wasn't fair that she couldn't ride without a chaperone or learn bladework."

"Why would Mother even agree to it?"

"I don't know, but she always has her reasons."

Charyn nodded. *That . . .* he did know. He also recalled that when Aloryana had asked why she couldn't learn bladework—even with wooden wands—Chelia had always declared that their father had said that women shouldn't learn to use weapons. *Had she wanted to learn bladework?*

Why? That was another question he should have thought about . . . and found a way to ask.

"Malyna might be better than you think," added Bhayrn.

"Why do you say that?"

"She gave the impression that she could barely play the clavecin, and she was far better than any of us. I also heard that she protested she hadn't played plaques in a long time, and she was good at that."

Charyn wasn't about to admit that a similar thought had crossed his mind. "Well, it's only supposed to be for exercise."

"I'm looking forward to it." Bhayrn grinned.

"It was only supposed to be—"

"The four of you. I know. But Mother said I could come."

Why? "I suppose one more family member won't matter, so long as it's not Father."

"Even I know he shouldn't find out until later. Besides, I think Aloryana's right."

That also surprised Charyn, and that bothered him, for more than a few reasons.

After finishing his eggs, and taking a last swallow from his third mug of tea, Charyn returned to his chambers where he dug out the padded practice jacket that he hadn't worn in several years. It had been loose on him. Now it was tighter, but not enough to hamper his movements.

At half a quint before ninth glass he took the jacket and the three wooden wands he had and headed down the spiral staircase off the south corridor down two flights to the lower level and the inside gallery.

Aloryana was lighting the oil lamps in the wall sconces. Malyna and Chelia stood several paces from the door, talking quietly. Charyn glanced around for Bhayrn before realizing he was lighting the lamps on the south wall.

Charyn walked toward Malyna. "Are you ready for this practice session?"

"As soon as you put on your jacket," she replied with a smile.

Charyn noted she already wore a padded jacket.

"One of Bhayrn's older ones," Chelia explained. "I had the ones you two outgrew saved."

Charyn slipped on his own jacket and was about to offer the wands to Malyna, when he saw she already had one. "Would you prefer any of these?"

"No, thank you. This one suits me."

In less than a fraction of a quint, Charyn found himself facing Malyna, roughly in the middle of the gallery, an empty space a good eight yards wide and close to twenty long. The air was chill, but not cold enough that his breath was steaming.

Charyn tried a standard opening, which Malyna slipped with ease, seeming not even to have done so before resuming her guard/defense position. Charyn tried another move, an angled cut that was supposed to end up with a straight thrust, except that Malyna sidestepped it even before he got to the thrust and knocked his wand down before retreating to her guard position.

In return, he just held guard position, waiting to see what sort of attack she might make.

For several moments, neither moved.

Finally, Malyna started what Charyn thought was a feint to one side, so that he did not shift his weight, but merely his wand. In turn, she brought hers up hard, knocking his own wand up and aside, and he had to jump back in order to avoid being struck.

She's faster than you are. Charyn didn't like that idea at all. *But you're taller and stronger. Use your height and reach.*

As they continued, Charyn realized something else. Malyna made no unnecessary moves, but when she did, those moves were swift, sometimes blindingly fast, and always left him off-balance or twisting and jumping back to avoid getting struck. Yet somehow, her wand never actually touched him, although several times it was close. After less than a third of a quint, Charyn was sweating profusely, despite the chill air of the gallery, and he'd never managed to even come close to touching her.

After another third of a quint, he was soaked and close to exhausted, still never having touched Malyna.

He took several steps back and lowered his wand.

Malyna lowered hers.

Charyn then said, "There's an old saying about discretion being the better part of valor." He managed a wry smile, difficult as it was. "You're far better than any of the guards I've practiced against. I have my doubts that you've just practiced a little . . . and if that's just a little for those who taught you, I'd very much want them on my side." What he wasn't about to say was that if Malyna had wanted she could have left him bruised all over. He did wonder why she hadn't struck him once or twice, but then realized that, by not striking him and by not letting him strike her, she'd been even more impressive in an understated way, possibly, he hoped, not quite so obvious to those who watched.

"Thank you," replied Malyna, "but I am far less accomplished than those who have taught me."

"Might I ask whom?"

"My uncle, I must admit, picked those who worked with me. He's much more adept with weapons than my father."

Before Charyn could say another word, Chelia spoke up. "You and Malyna, especially you, Charyn, need to wash up and prepare for the reception."

Although Charyn was about to protest that almost three glasses offered more than enough time to wash up and change everything he had worn, which would be necessary, given that he was soaked through in his own sweat, he realized that his mother was commanding, not requesting. "When would you suggest we be in the main salon?"

"At a quint before third glass."

As Malyna turned, Charyn moved to her side and said quietly, "I do appreciate your kindness in sparing me the embarrassment I deserved. Thank you."

For the first time since she had arrived at the chateau, Malyna showed an expression of surprise, if but for an instant before replying in an even softer voice. "I did bring up the matter of blades. Shall we call it even?"

"You're more than fair." Charyn inclined his head.

As Chelia, Malyna, and Aloryana left, Charyn noticed that Bhayrn remained and moved closer.

"She's better than any of the guards," said Bhayrn. "You're fortunate—"

"I know. We won't talk of it more. Anywhere."

"Why—"

"Just ask yourself why our mother permitted it and then didn't want any more said."

Bhayrn opened his mouth and then closed it.

"There's much more to Lady Malyna than meets the eye, and Mother's trying to convey that without saying anything. I think it's best we don't say anything more or interfere until we know more, don't you?"

"Oh . . ."

"Exactly."

Bhayrn frowned.

"Unless you have a better idea," added Charyn.

His younger brother shook his head.

"I need to wash and change," said Charyn dryly.

"That might be advisable."

As he climbed up the circular staircase to the third level, Charyn continued to ponder Malyna. She was clearly the well-educated and highly intelligent daughter of a High Holder, but she was more than that, and his mother had known that from the beginning. That bothered him more than he wanted to admit. As the heir and eldest son, shouldn't he have been privy to some of whatever was being kept from him? Yet . . . his father never wanted to confide anything, and his mother had been giving hints from the beginning.

It's clear that Mother's making the point that Malyna's not for you . . . but what a waste of brains, beauty, and skills. He couldn't help the next thought. *With all that, who could she marry whom she wouldn't be superior to?*

He was still figuratively shaking his head after he'd dressed in formal greens and was approaching the main salon a few moments before the time specified by Chelia.

Malyna and Aloryana were already there, Aloryana in a blue silk tea dress and Malyna in a shimmering silver-gray dress and a black jacket. Chelia appeared momentarily, with Bhayrn in tow, looking less than perfectly happy.

If Charyn had read his mother's lips correctly, she had said something to the effect of "Not another word."

Bhayrn nodded.

"You may all go in," said Chelia warmly, as if whatever harsh words she had uttered to her younger son had vanished without ever having been spoken.

Charyn opened the salon door, then stepped back and gestured for Malyna and Aloryana to enter. The fact that Vaetor was not there to serve as doorman underscored that the reception was personal and informal, although the senior officers and their wives would be escorted from the main entry hall.

Since their guests were not there and since it was an informal reception, Charyn made his way to the sideboard and procured two goblets of Saanfal, then returned and handed Malyna one.

"Thank you."

"You're a most unusual woman," Charyn said quietly, after lifting his goblet slightly in an unspoken toast.

"Do you say that to every woman?" Malyna's voice was light, but not cold.

"I don't recall saying those words to any woman before, but I believe the question is about you."

"Yes, I am in fact the youngest daughter of Zaerlyn D'Alte. I was taught mathematics and surveying and clavecin and other skills not usually considered proper for girls and young women. That is a family tradition. As I said earlier today, I have had some additional education from my uncle, at my request, and my father was willing to let me gain those skills."

"Including rather impressive skills with a wand, and, I suspect, a full-fledged sabre."

Malyna nodded. "Your point being?"

"That you're impressive. I've never heard of a High Holder's daughter being educated so broadly."

"Have you asked?" She smiled gently, glancing toward the salon door, where Marshal Vaelln and his wife had entered.

"I'd never thought to ask anyone about whether they were good with a sabre."

"Because men should be . . . and women shouldn't even consider it?"

"It's not . . . usual."

"You mean, not traditional? My female cousins all have been trained with weapons. That was always the Pharsi tradition."

"You . . ."

"My mother is the sister of High Holder Calkoran, and there are others with a Pharsi background in my family. You can probably find the most important name in the chateau archives, near the beginning of the reign of the first Rex Regis. She was the first Pharsi in the Zaerlyn line."

"If I knew what name to look for," he replied with a grin.

"Vaelora." Malyna turned as Chelia approached.

"Malyna," began Chelia, "you never had the time to talk with Sephia D'Vaelln last week, and I thought you two should have the chance."

"Until later." Malyna nodded to Charyn, then turned back to Chelia.

At that moment, Vice-Marshal Maurek walked toward Charyn. "Greetings on this cold and miserable day, Lord Charyn."

"Your presence makes the day more pleasant. I do hope that the drive here was not too chill."

"A little discomfort, that was all, and Amalie has never seen the Chateau D'Rex. For that matter, I've seen little except the entry, the grand staircase, and your father's study."

Looking over Maurek's shoulder, Charyn could see Amalie D'Maurek was seated in the corner and talking with Chelia and Aloryana, while Bhayrn and his father stood talking with the marshal. "Then it's well past time that you did."

Maurek cleared his throat, and spoke in a lower voice. "The young woman?"

"Malyna D'Zaerlyn. She's the youngest daughter of Zaerlyn D'Alte. She'll be with us until after the Year-Turn Ball, as a favor to her sire for his support."

"I see."

Charyn laughed—softly. "It's not like that. She's not either my type or Bhayrn's. It truly is a favor . . . although she is most pleasant to look at and converse with, and she is most accomplished."

"That appears regrettable."

"Regrettable, indeed." After the slightest pause, Charyn went on. "Has the army encountered any unpleasantnesses of the type that occurred here earlier this month?"

"The army has not seen any hostilities or uprisings in Solidar. The navy has. In fact, Marshal Vaelln has likely just told your sire that two of our ships have engaged and sunk Jariolan privateers, near the Abierto Isles. Unfortunately, they did so after the two had sunk one of our merchanters. A smaller Jariolan ship was nearby, but immediately fled."

"The Abierto Isles? That's not exactly close."

"No, but Marshal Vaelln has studied the matter, and that is one place where the privateers tend to prey on our ships. So he sent a flotilla there. It appears that he was wise to do so."

"You know that the rex has ordered more ships to be built this coming year."

"Marshal Vaelln has told me that. Several more ships would be help-ful."

"Only several more? The factors would prefer a much greater number."

"That might be, but who would crew them, and how would the navy pay the sailors, unless the rex raises tariffs?"

Charyn hadn't fully considered the pay issue. "How many men does it take to crew a ship of the line?"

"That depends on the class of ship. First-raters are large two-deckers with forty guns. Marshal Vaelln said the newest first-rater—that's the *Deucalon*—will carry forty-eight. With full gun crews, you'd need close to four hundred men, I think. For the exact crew size, you should ask him. A third-rater, more like a frigate, would have a single gun deck, but more than two hundred men."

"And, of course, there are all the provisions, gear, and supplies necessary?"

"You should talk to the marshal or Sea Marshal Tynan."

"Talking to the Sea Marshal might take some doing."

Maurek smiled. "It is warmer in Solis this time of year."

Belatedly, Charyn realized that the vice-marshal was empty-handed. "My manners are abysmal. You need a goblet. Saanfal is an excellent white, and if you prefer red, the southern Montagne is quite good."

"The red . . ."

"Excellent!" Charyn turned toward the sideboard. In moments, he returned with the goblet that he handed to Maurek.

"Thank you."

"I have another question. The army supplies the battalions that are at the disposal of each regional governor, as I understand it. Is it always the same battalion for each region?"

"Oh, no. That's prime duty. A battalion only serves a year in a regional capacity. Also, it wouldn't be good for any regional governor to see that battalion as their personal force. The majors are selected carefully as well."

"Couldn't they be used against these rebels?"

"They could . . . if we knew who the rebels are and where they're located."

The same problem Father mentioned. Charyn nodded. "I understand you served as the field commander during the revolt . . ."

"No, sir. Marshal Wilkorn was in command personally. I was second-in-command. Until the end, when he died leading the last charge to break the remaining rebels."

"Do you think any rebel factors will form an army?"

"They'd be foolish to do so. Once they formed up, the army and the imagers could destroy them. This cowardly business of firing granaries and threatening the rex only works so long as they stay in hiding."

"But if there are a lot of them . . . ?"

"That's a problem, but not as big a problem as an armed revolt." Maurek smiled pleasantly.

"Well, well," interrupted Lorien as he approached. "You haven't offered Marshal Maurek any solid refreshments . . ."

From those words, and Lorien's presence, Charyn had no doubts that he would discover little more from either Malyna or Maurek for the rest of the reception. "I must apologize again, Marshal. Shall we indulge ourselves?" He smiled warmly.

19

Right after an early breakfast on Lundi, and meeting with Norstan to arrange for a copy of the list of attendees for the Year-Turn Ball, Charyn was back in the archives. Since Malyna had suggested that Vaelora, whoever she was, had appeared early in the time of the first Rex Regis, he just began at the beginning, methodically going through the papers in each file chest. Even so, he almost overlooked the first sheet with her name, one appointing an envoy to Khel, suggesting that it occurred even before Lord Bhayar had completed the unification of Solidar and declared himself Rex Regis. But there were two identical sheets, except one named Vaelora Chayardr as envoy, and the other named Commander Quaeryt Rytersyn as envoy, and described him as the foremost field commander. He kept looking, and then found an entire sheaf of documents signed and sealed by Vaelora Chayardr as Minister of Administration.

Her ancestor was the Minister of Administration for Rex Regis. Just who was she to be an envoy and a minister? So far as Charyn knew, there had never been a woman minister in Solidar—except for this Vaelora.

Eventually, he found out in a document written to the Minister of Administration, beseeching Vaelora, as not only the Minister of Administration for Bovaria but as the sister of the rex, to allow the widow of a High Holder to administer the lands of her dead husband, as the rex had allowed in the case of Tyrena D'Ryel.

But other than those documents, and a few others Vaelora had signed and sealed as minister, he could find nothing for pages and pages, until he found a notice by Rex Clayar, proclaiming a day of mourning for Lady Vaelora and her husband the Maitre Quaeryt.

Charyn stopped. The first Maitre had been a commander? The "foremost field commander" of the rex? In charge of several battalions? He shook his head and continued looking.

There were no other mentions of Vaelora in that chest, nor in the next. It was as though she had been quickly forgotten.

The sister of Rex Regis married to a Maitre of the Collegium, most likely the first Maitre. And she had been an ancestor of Malyna? A second thought struck him.

If Vaelora had been Pharsi, then Rex Regis had been as well. *The first Rex Regis was Pharsi?*

As he closed the file chest and brushed away the dust, he frowned. Malyna couldn't have made that all up. She wasn't the kind to do that anyway. That much, he did know.

Does she have aspirations to be a minister someday? He shook his head. *She's more practical than that.*

While the time he'd spent searching the archives had answered his question, he still wondered why Malyna had essentially intrigued him into looking in the first place. *Because you wouldn't have believed her . . . or you'd have doubted her?* That just might have been the reason. He had the feeling that she didn't like to be questioned or doubted.

He straightened and made his way from the archives to the main level of the chateau, where he reclaimed a heavy winter coat before heading out to the courtyard and the undecorated coach. The air in the rear courtyard was chill, but the wind had died away, although the sky was covered by high clouds thick enough to block the sun. There were still small drifts of snow against the walls in a few places.

"Good morning, sir," offered Yarselt as Charyn approached the waiting coach.

"We'll just be going to the exchange this morning. I may be there somewhat longer, though."

"Yes, sir."

As the coach left the chateau, Charyn watched as the driver went from the ring road and then turned onto the Avenue D'Rex Ryen heading toward the West River Road. No one seemed to be paying any attention to the coach, and there were few wagons, carriages, or riders anywhere. Even the sidewalks had only scattered people, all walking quickly.

When Charyn reached the exchange and stepped out of the coach, he did note more carriages around the building than he had seen on his latest visits. Belatedly, he remembered to replace the exchange pin on his coat, but the guard barely looked at him as he entered, followed by Yarselt.

His first stop was at the grain stall, where he noted that the Avryl price of wheat was up a copper a bushel, as was the Mayas price. *If the Mayas price goes to fifteen a bushel, it might pay to sell the regial grain through the exchange . . .* Then again, arranging to do it without revealing who he was might be tricky.

As he was calculating the possibilities, he couldn't help overhearing the words that passed between an agent and the exchange man.

". . . young fellow there?"

". . . asked myself . . . Factor Suyrien D'Chaeryll . . . here often in the last month . . . some sort of heir . . . lots of land, though . . . always has a bodyguard, too . . ."

". . . looking at the futures' prices intent-like . . ."

". . . may be thinking of selling . . ."

". . . too soon for that . . . ground froze early east of here, even in Piedryn . . ."

Charyn had to wonder about their words. The reports from the land-wardens hadn't indicated anything like that . . . or were the two trying to get a reaction? He turned, smiled pleasantly, and headed for the timber stalls.

There, oak prices were up, and at the metals stalls, copper prices, present and future, continued to remain low, while at the spice stalls, he noted that pepper futures were high months out, as were those of most other spices.

Yet, he noticed that by the time he'd been there a glass, many agents and factors were leaving, although there had been far more than the week before. He headed back to the grain stall and was fortunate to find the exchange stall orderman alone.

"Yes, sir?"

"You know I'm fairly new. I just wondered. Will there be a flurry of orders and contracts near the end of the week?"

"There usually are. Traders closing out their books, taking profits and losses in whatever way makes their ledgers look good. Sometimes Jeudi's the busiest, sometime Vendrei. It all depends. With this weather . . . might not be the best to wait till Vendrei. That's if you've a mind to trade, sir."

"Thank you."

"My pleasure, sir."

Charyn nodded and turned, making his way from the exchange out to find his coach, thankful that it was neither snowing nor blowing.

Again, on the return to the chateau, he watched the avenue and the ring road closely, but he saw no sign that anyone was paying any attention to the coach.

As soon as he stepped out of the coach in the rear courtyard, he turned to Yarselt. "Did anyone follow us?"

"No, sir."

Charyn looked around the courtyard, but, outside of the driver, who was easing the coach toward the coach house, they were the only ones out in the courtyard. "Thank you for keeping an eye out."

"My pleasure, sir."

Charyn doubted it was pleasure, but he merely nodded in acknowledgment before turning and walking to the steps up to the chateau door. Just as Charyn entered the smaller rear foyer of the chateau, Aloryana appeared out of the side corridor.

"Have you seen Malyna?"

"No. I just came inside. Why?"

"I can't find her anywhere. You didn't see her outside?"

Charyn shook his head, then removed his coat.

"I don't see where she could have gone . . ."

"I haven't gone anywhere," replied Malyna, emerging from the lower west corridor. "I just wanted to be alone for a few moments."

Charyn could certainly understand that, given how close Aloryana had been to Malyna, and he had a hard time concealing a smile.

"I just came from there," said Aloryana, exasperation coloring her voice. "I looked in every chamber."

"What can I say?" replied Malyna. "Except that I didn't mean to upset you. I was just exploring a little."

Charyn looked closely at Malyna. He wasn't certain, but he thought her face was slightly red, as if she'd been out in the cold. Yet he hadn't seen her outside, and she certainly hadn't been in the courtyard. He and Yarselt had been the only ones there. And there was no outside exit from the west corridor except through the rear foyer . . . or through a window. He had to hold back a smile at the thought that Malyna might have tried to climb out a window to gain a few moments of freedom from Aloryana, however unlikely that might have been.

"Excuse us, Charyn," said Aloryana, "we need to go."

As she turned, motioning for Malyna to accompany her, Charyn grinned at the High Holder's daughter. In return, he received a humorous smile.

After debating whether he should spend the early afternoon with either Minister Alucar or Sanafryt, he decided instead to pay a visit to Aevidyr, the Minister of Administration, despite the fact that Aevidyr's curmudgeonly manner and the dullness of his post had made him a distant third in Charyn's desire to learn more about the governance of Solidar. Now, at least, he had something which he could discuss with the graying and curt minister.

Aevidyr's study was on the main level, off a short corridor under the grand staircase.

Charyn eased open the door and waited for the minister to recognize him.

"What is it now, Charyn?" Aevidyr's voice was gravelly, rumblingly grating to Charyn's ears. "Come in and close the door."

Charyn did.

"What is it?" repeated Aevidyr. "Now that you've succeeded in interrupting me?"

"I had a question, Minister Aevidyr. I was reading the early archives, and I came across a name of the first Minister of Administration . . ."

"Oh? And who might that have been?"

"Vaelora Chayardr."

Aevidyr nodded. "What else did you find out about her?"

"She was the sister of Rex Regis and the wife of a Collegium Maitre."

"She was the wife of the first Maitre of the Collegium Imago. He was the imager who created the Collegium."

"Was she a good minister?"

"I have no way of knowing. Most likely she was." Aevidyr paused, then asked, "Why would I say that?"

"If she had been bad, I imagine there would have been stories or records . . . somewhere."

Aevidyr shook his head. "Had she been terrible, there would have been no records at all. She was the rex's sister. Any unfavorable mentions or documents that showed her as incapable would certainly have been destroyed. There are also no citations or notes on how great she was. There are just clear procedures and good records dating from within a few months after the defeat of Rex Kharst."

Charyn frowned. "I could only find a few in the archives."

"That's because the most important ones are here in my files. Those in the archives are largely duplicates or about matters no longer relevant, things like procedures for land transfers immediately following the conquest." His voice seemed less grating, or maybe Charyn was getting used to it.

"Why do you keep the older ones?"

"Hasn't Sanafryt instructed you on the importance of precedent? When there are no specific provisions in the Codex Legis, precedent becomes important. If a practice has been in place for centuries, that grants it a certain status in law, for better or worse."

"So that is why my father had to make changes in the Codex Legis?"

"Precisely. There were certain aspects of precedent in the tariffs that required a specific . . . correction."

"What else do the older documents tell you about Minister Vaelora?"

"She was very careful and very precise. I don't know that I would have liked her, but I think I would have respected her. I have the feeling that the first Rex Regis felt the same way."

Charyn frowned, not wanting to voice his question.

"There aren't any proclamations or 'clarifications' to the initial Codex Legis. I consulted with Sanafryt on that. She and her husband apparently drafted the Codex Legis. Since the three lived a number of years after the establishment of Solidar, the fact that there were no changes during that period suggests that the three were in agreement and that there were few problems."

"Did she have any children?"

"I have no idea. There might be records at the Collegium. Why do you ask?"

"Her name came up, and I wondered."

"Once she left the chateau and entered the Collegium, there are few mentions of her. Almost none, as I recall."

"Thank you."

Aevidyr nodded, and Charyn left the study, closing the door quietly, still wondering why the sister of the rex would marry an imager. Certainly, imager men did marry women who were not imagers. They had to, because there had always been fewer women imagers. *But why would she have allowed it? Or had Rex Regis insisted on it to keep some control over the first Maitre?* Charyn doubted whether he'd ever know that.

As he headed up the grand staircase, he could hear someone playing the clavecin, pounding out the notes, then stopping almost immediately. That could only be Bhayrn. He had not quite reached the top of the stairs, when Vaetor hurried from the northwest corridor.

"Lord Charyn, sir . . ."

"The rex, I assume, requests my presence?"

"Yes, sir."

Charyn repressed a sigh. *What now?* Instead, he smiled pleasantly. "Thank you. I'm on my way."

He had barely entered the study and closed the door when Lorien looked up.

"Where were you this time?"

"Learning a few things from Minister Aevidyr."

"You're not keeping my ministers from their work with all this . . . are you?"

"No, sir. They set me a problem or a legal petition or a question and leave me to work it out. Later they explain where I was right, and where I was wrong, and there's usually something I missed."

"What was Aevidyr explaining?"

"How what is in the records, and what is not, still reveals aspects of administration. What to look for that should be there and is not. Those sorts of things."

"You're still not going to be rex any time soon."

"I have absolutely no desire to be rex any time soon." So far, the more Charyn had seen and learned, just in the past few months, made him wonder if he even wanted to be rex.

"Well . . . I'll add to your learning. You worried about the factors sitting on their hands and not doing anything, There's some good news. Finally, some of those shipping weasels are showing some spine. It's about time." Lorien gestured to the chairs.

"They're supporting you?" asked Charyn as he seated himself.

"Not from a factor. Direct support from them would be too much to expect," replied Lorien sarcastically. "There's a High Holder in Nacliano who owns all the Diamond ships. One of his ships used its guns and sank two Jariolan privateers."

That doesn't exactly mean much as far as the factors are concerned. Charyn wasn't about to say anything like that. "Yesterday, Vice-Marshal Maurek told me that two navy warships sank two other privateers and chased off a Jariolan frigate." Maurek hadn't said the ship type, but if it was smaller than the Solidaran ships and near the Abierto Isles, it likely had to be a frigate.

"That's a start. A few more weeks like that . . . and maybe the factors will see."

"They should have seen before this, sir."

"All they care about is golds. Their golds. We've talked about this before." Lorien barked a laugh. "Namer-damned shame that a High Holder can see what those gold-grubbing merchants can't."

"It does seem strange."

"Life can be strange. Since you're here, tell me anything you've learned from all your visits to the exchange."

"The factors don't think matters are going to change with shipping to Otelyrn. The present prices of pepper and other spices are higher, and the prices for pepper even six months out are higher."

"I said they were greedy bastards. Go on."

Charyn smiled pleasantly before clearing his throat. He was going to be in the study for at least a glass, unless someone else interrupted.

20

The snow hurled itself out of the northeast, falling so fast and furiously that, in less than a glass, by late afternoon on Meredi, the steep white stone steps of the Chateau D'Rex were covered knee-deep, and none could tell where stone ended and snow began. The gardens were simply lost under the snow. Since it was the thirty-second of Finitas, winter had not even begun, at least according to the calendar.

Chill radiated from the upper-level window from where Charyn looked down at the snow-covered drive and the curtain of falling white that blocked any further view of the expansive lands to the south of the Chateau D'Rex and beyond the ring road. He turned toward Aloryana, still seated at the small plaques table, who, at times, looked much older than her fourteen years. "If this continues, Father may have to cancel the Year-Turn Ball." He kept even the hint of a smile from his lips as he waited for a response.

"These storms pass, Brother dear. It is only Meredi. Besides, what's a little snow?" Aloryana's voice was even and measured. "I'm quite certain that there will be a ball and that we will be there."

Charyn doubted his sister felt that calm. The Year-Turn Ball would be the first their father had permitted her to attend.

"Besides," Aloryana went on, "Father has agreed that Malyna should have this one chance to attend a Year-Turn Ball."

"The weather doesn't much care what commitments a rex may make," replied Charyn dryly. "Where is Malyna, by the way?"

"Talking to Mother. Mother said it would be a while. She told me, almost ordered me, to come play plaques with you and keep you busy."

"As if I could go anywhere in this storm? I can't even study with any of the ministers. They stayed home."

"Anyway," Aloryana continued inexorably, "if the snow gets too deep, surely the imagers could remove mere snow on the main boulevards."

"Father would never ask them. You know that."

"He wouldn't have to. The Maitre and his wife are coming. They always do. They'd have to clear their own path."

"You want to see them, don't you?" Charyn let the hangings fall back across the window to block the chill. He turned and moved toward the table. "Or have them see you."

"I've seen them before, at the Year-Turn Balls."

Only from the corridor when they came up the grand staircase. Charyn didn't voice that thought, but asked dryly, "You're not impressed by the successor of your distant cousin?"

"We're not related to the Maitre in any fashion. He came from nothing, and he's from Westisle."

"You're right. Most Maitres have come from nothing, and we're not related to him. You might like to know, however, that we are not only descended from the first Rex Regis, but we're also distant cousins of the first Maitre's wife, who was the sister of that Rex Regis."

"You're making that up. Another story." Aloryana sounded annoyed.

"Actually, I'm not. Her name was Vaelora, and she was the sister of the first Rex Regis, and she married the first Maitre of the Collegium. And Vaelora was an ancestor of Malyna."

"You're telling stories."

"Ask Malyna, if you don't believe me. She only hinted that I should look into an ancestor of hers named Vaelora."

"How did you find that out?"

"Reading the chateau archives can tell you all sorts of interesting facts. Sometimes, they're even useful."

"I will ask Malyna." Aloryana frowned. "Useful for what else?"

"Preparing for the people I'll meet at the ball and elsewhere, especially some of the High Holders."

"What difference would that make? Father never lets you meet with any of the High Council or the Factors' Council."

"I've met with some of them." *Just not in their formal meetings.* "And I have met a number of times with Factor Elthyrd."

"Not any on the High Council, except Uncle Ryel, and he doesn't count. You know Mother—"

"I know," Charyn replied quickly, forestalling what his much younger sister would surely say. He'd heard more than enough from their mother about the dangers of exaggerating, especially in uneasy times, and particularly for him as the heir. He paused for just a moment. "I have met more than a few factors. Factor Walltyl—"

"That's because you had him build that racing chase."

". . . Factor Roblen . . ."

"Those fine woolen jackets."

"Factor Elthyrd . . ."

"The wood for the chase," countered Aloryana.

"It doesn't matter." Charyn wasn't about to mention exactly how he had gotten Elthyrd to sponsor his membership to the exchange. "I've met them, and I've dealt with them. That means more to them than just standing around at a ball and offering pleasantries." Not that Charyn hadn't learned a great deal at balls, but learning and gaining trust weren't the same things. He stepped back toward the table. "Do you want to play another round?"

"We might as well. It's more than a glass until dinner. Malyna is still talking with Mother. I'd rather play with you than with Bhayrn. He still tries to palm the plaques."

Charyn sat down opposite Aloryana. "That's stupid. When you have golds, you don't have to cheat. All you can do is make people distrust you." He pointed to the deck. "It's your turn to deal first."

Slightly more than a glass later, Charyn and Aloryana joined Bhayrn, their mother, and Malyna in the salon that adjoined the family dining room. Chelia sat in the smaller of the two armchairs. The larger one, vacant, was always reserved for their father. Malyna sat in one of the straight-backed chairs.

"The snow's stopped," announced Bhayrn.

"For now," said Charyn mildly. "The clouds are still low. It might snow more tonight."

"Let us hope not." Chelia looked to Aloryana. "I just read your copybook."

Charyn could see his sister stiffen, but she merely nodded and waited.

"Your writing and grammar are excellent . . . when your words can be deciphered. Your hand leaves a great deal to be desired. You will rewrite today's assignment. Without any assistance from Malyna. I expect it on my desk by seventh glass tomorrow morning." Chelia turned to Bhayrn.

Charyn's brother's smile vanished.

"Your calculations were erroneous in several places. Some of that was doubtless due to your failure to keep your figures neat. When you cannot even read your own numbers, how can you expect to calculate accurately?"

"Others will be doing—"

"Nonsense! You're the younger son. If you're fortunate, you'll get a

High Holding that you will have to run, and if you can't do calculations accurately, your children will be lucky to live as well as the poorest of factors. You're far too old to be making the mistakes you are."

Charyn was just glad he hadn't had to do lessons for more than five years, but then learning under the various ministers had been tedious more often than not.

At that moment, Lorien stepped into the salon. "Good evening, everyone. Shall we dine?"

All the others rose, and Aloryana led the way into the dining room, followed by Bhayrn. Charyn and Malyna entered just in front of Lorien and took their places across the table from each other, waiting for Lorien to seat himself before they sat.

Chelia looked to Malyna. "You should say the gratitude."

The young woman nodded, then said, "For the grace from the Nameless, for the bounty of the earth, for justice, and for all manifold and great mercies, we offer our thanks and gratitude, both now and ever more, in the spirit of that which cannot be named or imaged."

Charyn managed not to show any surprise at a gratitude that barely mentioned the Nameless.

Only after Malyna had finished did the servers appear with the pitchers of red or white wine. Then came the platters of doves poached in brandy and then roasted, accompanied by laced potatoes, and sliced and baked autumn squash, with dark bread.

When the servers retired, Lorien addressed the first dove breast on his plate—as did Charyn, knowing that the time to eat was before his father began to ask questions.

"One good thing about the storm," finally mumbled Lorien. "I didn't have to meet with the Maitre or High Holder Ryel."

Charyn could see his father's right hand trembling as the older man set the knife on the side of the wide platter with a faint clank. Charyn could also see that his mother noticed as well, especially by the quick glance she shot his way.

"Is the Council still complaining about your equalizing the tariffs on exchanges of goods?" asked Chelia.

"What else is new? I compromised on phasing in the tariff on exchanges right after that abortive revolt because times were bad, and I didn't want more rebellious High Holders. I told them that the tariffs would be equal by this coming year. They agreed. Each year the tariff on exchanges went up by one part in five. Now that many had bad crops this past year . . ." The rex shook his head and then brushed a limp lock of gray hair away from his forehead with the back of his left hand. Then he cleared his throat. "It's just another way for those arrogant High Holders to avoid tariffs."

Malyna's pleasant expression did not change, and she took the smallest sip of the white wine in her goblet. Aloryana offered Charyn a knowing look.

Charyn almost laughed. His sister already had known what their father would say.

"Factors have to pay tariffs on what they sell." Lorien coughed several times. "These holders who have become factors as well in their desire for more golds wanted to avoid that by not selling, but by exchanging what they produce or grow with what other High Holders produce or grow. They claimed that the Codex only required tariffs on actual sales. That was one of the reasons for the revolt, because Maitre Alastar had suggested that the High Holders were cheating me on their tariffs. And those bastards were. Every one of them." He paused and looked to Malyna. "Your father is not one of them. I wish more were like him."

"So do I, sir," replied Malyna. "He has to tread carefully."

"Would to the Nameless he didn't," added Lorien. "The rest of them aren't worth the blades to slaughter them."

Bhayrn rolled his eyes, not surprisingly, since he, Charyn, and Aloryana had heard similar words all too often.

"That was why you changed the Codex after the revolt," Charyn said quietly, words he'd used more than a few times before.

"I did indeed."

"As you should have," added Chelia warmly.

"Thank you, my dear."

"What will you do?" asked Aloryana.

"The change is already in the Codex. I'm not going to change it again. They knew what was coming. High Holder Ryel will try to persuade me . . ."

Charyn also didn't miss the sharp glance his mother bestowed on his father.

". . . and I can't afford to let him."

"What about the Collegium?" asked Chelia.

"The Maitre's always supported you, hasn't he?" Aloryana added almost simultaneously.

"As long . . . as I do what he thinks is right."

Chelia looked at her husband, but did not speak.

"Do you disagree with him that much, sir?" asked Malyna.

"We're not that different in what we think is best," replied Lorien. "We get there different ways."

Charyn kept his amusement to himself. Those words were about as much as his father would admit that he sometimes overreacted before listening to Chelia—or the Maitre.

"Being rex isn't what you think it is, Aloryana." Lorien's voice was resigned, almost dull. "It's not like in the old days, in the time of the first Rex Regis. Back then, a rex had power, real power. He had almost a hundred thousand soldiers, and even the imagers jumped to do his will. Back then the factors collected tariffs for the rex, and no one questioned what the tariffs were. Now . . ." Lorien shook his head.

"Your father hasn't mentioned that most of those who were rex in those days died young and violently. Rex Regis was the exception." Chelia's voice was pleasant. "Even in the time of your grandfather, there was a great deal of violence. You might recall that your father and I were almost burned alive in the Anomen D'Rex. The Maitre and his imagers saved us."

"Had to," mumbled Lorien. "Didn't have much choice."

Chelia glanced at her husband once more.

"I'll give him credit for knowing that, and for seeing what that bastard Chesyrk was up to." Lorien's words were not quite grudging as he went on. "Later on, he did put his own life at risk in putting down the revolt, and he got the High Holders back in line."

"All of you know that," said Chelia brightly, "and it's a gloomy day to talk about such matters."

"Are you going to cancel the ball?" asked Bhayrn hopefully.

Aloryana turned and offered a mock glare, almost as if it were expected, Charyn thought.

"Don't you think about anything else?" muttered Bhayrn.

"Just because you don't want to dance with the wives and daughters of High Holders isn't any reason to penalize the rest of us," said Charyn, his voice light. "And Malyna's only going to have this one chance to attend, most likely."

"There's no reason to cancel it," declared Lorien stoutly. "Why should I? Those who want to come can find a way. If they don't care enough or don't want to brave the weather, so much the better. Nothing worse than a fair-weather factor or High Holder."

"Except perhaps a scheming, fair-weather High Holder," added Chelia. "Or one who has to be constantly reminded he lives on sufferance."

Charyn knew exactly whom she meant . . . and why. His mother might forgive, occasionally, very occasionally, but she *never* forgot. He smiled pleasantly and took a small sip of the white wine, content to listen as much as possible, rather than to talk. He still had more than a little preparation to complete before the ball.

21

Although the snow stopped late on Meredi evening, even by Vendrei morning only the main avenues were passable, but Charyn definitely wanted to see what the trading at the exchange was like, since as the thirty-fourth day of Finitas, Vendrei was the last trading day of the year. He was assuming that there would be more going on than he'd seen in the past week because agents and traders had to balance out their ledger in some fashion. At least, he thought they did. In any event, it should be instructive in some fashion or another.

Because the snow had limited travel and those seeking to see his father, Charyn only spent a few moments with Norstan, but he did obtain a copy of the list of those attending the Year-Turn Ball, which he took to his chambers and slipped into a drawer. He'd need to study the list later in the day, something he'd put off longer than he should have. Then he donned a heavy winter coat and made his way to the rear courtyard and the waiting coach. The air was chill, and Charyn could see patches of ice in the lower places between some of the paving stones. His breath was like smoke, and he was more than glad that the coach had been warmed somewhat by heated bricks. Their heat wouldn't last, and the return ride would be much colder.

Should you go at all?

He pushed aside the question. Year-end trading happened only once a year, and who knew when he'd get another chance?

The trip to the exchange took more than a glass because the passable parts of the avenues and streets were narrowed by the snow pushed or shoveled to the sides. When he arrived, he was glad that he'd worn heavy boots because he had to walk through snow that was knee-deep in a few places before he got to the cleared walks leading to the main doors. *At least, the wind isn't blowing.*

Again, the exchange guards barely looked at Charyn's exchange pin, but he had no idea whether that was because they recognized him or because they were already too cold to care.

As he walked toward the grains stalls, Charyn couldn't help but notice a number of agents at almost every stall, but only a comparative handful of individuals wearing the pins of factors or full factors. He saw a few faces he'd seen before, not that he knew their names, but he didn't see Elthyrd.

He stood to the side of the stall to watch the wheat trading, where it appeared that the chalked futures prices were changing, both up and down in a matter of moments, especially for grain to be delivered in Mayas. *Because of the early and cold weather in Finitas?* He listened but didn't hear any talk. Those present all seemed intent on the chalked prices, as someone offered a contract or bid on it.

In time, he moved to the spice trading, where pepper prices were changing, if not so quickly . . . and not fluctuating, but slowly rising, as if no one believed that pepper would be easier to get. Seeing that there was little talk there, Charyn made a slow circuit of the entire exchange.

When he finished, he realized that he'd seen far fewer factors than he'd thought initially, and it appeared as though most of the trading and bidding was by traders and agents. *To balance ledgers? Or to shift losses or gains into the current year or the next one?* Those were only guesses on Charyn's part, something he needed to talk over with Elthyrd or someone else with similar experience.

When he left the exchange, slightly more than a glass later, he found it was no warmer outside, but no colder either. The coach ride back to the Chateau D'Rex was as cold as he'd feared. He entered the rear foyer and hurried up the grand staircase, half-listening to someone playing the clavecin, either Palenya or Malyna, since there were no mistakes and no halting, and half-wondering if he'd be summoned once more to his father's study, but no one seemed to be seeking him, and he reached his sitting room without encountering anyone.

He immediately slid the latch bar into place, took off his heavy coat and hung it up, then retrieved the invitation list and laid it on the otherwise bare desk. Next he took out his personal journal, a pen, and an inkwell.

One of his own weaknesses, Charyn knew, was that he had trouble linking names to faces unless he'd met someone several times or unless he'd read their name and found out some information about them. Like it or not, he also needed to dance with as many of the eligible young women who would be trotted out by their parents. Not because he was looking to be married, but because he definitely wanted to know which of the young women would not appeal to him under any circumstances.

He looked at the pages set out on his table desk, then walked to the window, pulled back the heavy hangings, and looked out through the partly frosted window. Except for the drive to the chateau and the ring road, snow seemed to cover everything else, and a chill radiated from the window, despite the weak white early afternoon sunlight. There was even frost on the windowsill below the pane.

After several moments, he stepped back, leaving the window hangings slightly open, trying to get a bit more light into the sitting room. Finally, he returned to the desk and stared at the first page of the attendance list. In time, he began to read the names, and to enter the names of possibly eligible daughters of High Holders, along with the names of each daughter's parents. *More like a copybook penmanship chore.*

Was that because he doubted that any other of the High Holders' daughters would be as intelligent and as attractive as Malyna?

Probably.

He knew Malyna wasn't interested in him in the slightest, not in any romantic way, and with his mother clearly opposed to his seeking to even get closer to Malyna, there wasn't a Namer's chance with the Nameless that he could even raise the issue. And he didn't want to . . . not if Malyna wasn't interested.

At the same time, he also didn't want to become indifferent and become involved with a young woman who simply saw him as a means to wealth and power. *As if there's as much power in being rex as anyone thinks.* From what his mother had said, and from what he'd overheard, his grandmother had been that kind of woman, and it had contributed to his grandsire's unfortunate and early death.

With a long deep breath, he forced his concentration back to the list, knowing he'd make a fool of himself—or come off as frivolous and unconcerned—if he didn't remember a good share of the names of those who might prove of interest. And when he finished going over the shorter list he was creating, then he'd have to go back over the notes he'd taken from the last Year-Turn Ball to see what young women were returning . . . and which he wished to avoid . . . and why.

He kept writing and concentrating, knowing that he should have started on the task far earlier.

Far earlier.

22

At just a few moments before half past seventh glass on Samedi evening, Charyn positioned himself on the far side of the grand staircase, beside one of the gilded urns, from where he could watch those entering the grand ballroom without being noticed . . . and, equally important, hear the herald announce them.

The first two couples were younger, and did not bring daughters. Nor did the next three, all of whom were older. Then came a High Holder pair of middling age, escorting a daughter Charyn was certain he had not seen before. He listened intently.

"High Holder Kastyl, Lady Kastyl, and Faerlyna D'Kastyl . . ."

Faerlyna . . . brown-haired, blue gown trimmed in peach . . . father Kastyl . . . Charyn concentrated on retaining that for an instant before turning his attention to the next young woman accompanying her parents.

"High Holder Nacryon, Lady Nacryon, Cynthalya D'Nacryon . . ."

For the next quint, he took in names and tried to fix details in his mind.

"High Holder Baeltyn, Lady Baeltyn, Shaelyna D'Baeltyn . . ."

"High Holder Fhernon, Lady Fhernon, and Ferron D'Fhernon-Alte . . ."

For a moment, Charyn was surprised that Fhernon even had an heir, but then he hadn't been paying attention to the senior heirs. He'd just been concentrating on the daughters.

"High Holder Shendael and Alyncya D'Shendael-Alte . . ."

Alyncya . . . father widowed . . . and she's the heir . . . interesting . . .

"Lady Delcoeur and Ferrand D'Delcoeur-Alte . . ."

Charyn nodded. That made sense. No one would ignore Ferrand the way they would shun his father—because of High Holder Delcoeur's considerable debts, although more than a few would suspect Ferrand of dowry hunting. Charyn needed to make a point of talking to Ferrand. Ferrand had enough problems without being shunned by his cousin.

Charyn wished he could have observed longer, but he needed to be in the sitting room not that much later than his siblings—and Malyna— and definitely before their parents arrived.

Still, Charyn was likely half a quint late when he stepped into the small sitting room that adjoined the grand ballroom, since he was expected to be there two quints before the glass. He wasn't looking forward to the next quint or so. While the Year-Turn Ball began officially at half past seventh glass, Charyn knew that his father and the High Councilors had an understanding that the councilors were not expected until eighth glass. Since the rex and his family could not appear until just before the High Councilors arrived, and since Lorien insisted that his offspring all appear in the sitting room at two quints before the glass . . . that meant two quints spent with Aloryana and Bhayrn . . . and Malyna. Aloryana alone would have been fine, and he certainly wouldn't have minded the time with Malyna, but with the other two there, especially given Bhayrn's clear dislike of the entire ball, having three siblings in a small room, even with an outsider, was likely not a recipe for harmony.

"You're late," snapped Bhayrn, from where he stood beside the sideboard that would hold refreshments—but did not at the moment. He looked sourly at his older brother.

"Only a few moments." Charyn hadn't even brought the small bound volume he continually updated, just in case his memory failed him, because his siblings would note if he referred to it, and so most likely would Malyna, and that would counter the very impression he worked so hard to cultivate. He smiled ironically as he closed the door from the private corridor. The small orchestra was not playing in the ballroom, but Palenya was at the clavecin, offering occasional music, not dance music, since the dancing to the orchestra would not begin until after the five High Councilors were announced and the rex received the Maitre and his wife.

Aloryana already sat on one of the straight-backed chairs, adjusting her position every few moments, in between glances at the doorway from the small sitting room to the grand ballroom. She wore a high-necked ball gown of pale blue, trimmed in a darker blue, with that trim edged in the thinnest line of white lace. The lace was minimal, not to give the impression of avoiding ostentation, but because too much white would make his sister's fair skin look pasty. Her hair was swept back and held in place by silver clasps adorned by dark blue sapphires.

Charyn frowned. Something about the silver clasps and the sapphires looked familiar. Had one of the clasps been what Aloryana had dropped and been so upset about, as if she had broken it, but hadn't wanted to tell him? Or something similar?

Malyna sat beside Aloryana, also wearing a high-necked gown, but of a deep teal that fringed on the regial colors, suggesting a relationship to the regial line, a color, he realized, that she had every right to wear, but one that might cause a certain amount of comment.

Bhayrn was attired in manner similar to Charyn. Both wore close-fitting jackets of regial green, trimmed in silver, with pale green shirts and black cravats, black trousers, with black belts and silver buckles, and highly polished black dress boots.

Charyn smiled. "It will all be over in less than three glasses."

"Three long and tedious glasses," countered Bhayrn.

"I'd prefer that you not make it be over before it even begins," said Aloryana.

"I'm looking forward to it," Charyn declared.

"That's because every High Holder with an attractive daughter will be pushing her at you," said Bhayrn. "All the others will be looking at me."

Only until Father finds a suitable bride for me. Then your turn will come. Charyn didn't bother saying that. Bhayrn wasn't in the mood to hear it. "There just might be some shier beauties. They're often the best." He glanced at Malyna.

"Shyness is often perceived erroneously," she replied.

"Sometimes, brothers are awful," said Aloryana to Malyna.

The two young women shared a smile.

"Your turn will come as well," prophesied Charyn. "When you're older."

"It might not."

"Oh?" said Charyn. "You're the daughter of the rex. You don't think High Holders and their sons won't be interested?"

For a long moment, Aloryana was silent before saying quietly, "It might not work that way."

"You've been telling us you'd be here, even before Father decided," pointed out Bhayrn.

"That's different. I *knew* I'd be here tonight."

"How?" asked Bhayrn, scornfully.

"I knew. I just did."

Charyn concealed a frown. When Aloryana said something that way, she was almost never wrong. *But then, how could she not be at the Year-Turn Ball once she was of age to attend, if only to make the High Holders aware that she was a functioning family member and would be a suitable wife for someone in years to come? Yet* even when the snow had been pouring down, she'd been absolutely convinced . . . *She was just wagering on Father's stubbornness.* Still . . .

"Likely tale," scoffed Bhayrn.

Charyn noticed a momentary expression of concern cross Malyna's face, one quickly replaced by a faint smile.

He settled into a chair he positioned so that he could talk to, or at least look directly at, the other three, knowing that while the first of the High Holders—and their daughters—had only begun to dribble into the grand ballroom, others were doubtless ascending the grand staircase, while the coaches of the Maitre and High Councilors would not arrive until roughly a half quint before the glass. He could hear an occasional voice or two through the closed door to the ballroom during lulls in the music.

"Who will you dance with first?" Bhayrn asked Charyn, almost half-heartedly.

"Aloryana. The first dance begins with the rex and his lady and the rest of the regial family."

"That's not much of a choice."

"That includes Malyna," Aloryana said sweetly. "She's a distant relative, but a relative."

Bhayrn said nothing for a moment, then finally said, "No one told me that."

"Her gown should have told you that," added Aloryana. "She couldn't wear that color or appear with us unless she's related."

"No one tells me anything," snapped Bhayrn. He turned to Charyn. "Did you know?"

"She's a descendant of the sister of the first Rex Regis," Charyn replied. "It's in the archives. Anyway, after the first dance, it's up to you. You can dance or not. Father won't care that much. Mother will. You know the rules. You can't dance with the same partner two dances in a row, and no more than two dances with any—"

"I know!" snapped Bhayrn.

"I wasn't sure you were listening this morning . . ."

"Will you dance every dance, Charyn?" asked Aloryana sweetly.

"That will depend on my feet and my boots."

"What's the point?" asked Bhayrn with a snort. "Meaningless chatter for half a quint at most with someone you'll see for the same fraction of a quint twice or three times a year for the next twenty."

"Won't there be some friends there?" asked Malyna.

"There might be," replied Charyn, "if they're the eldest unmarried son of a High Holder. Ferrand is here, I know."

"Hunting for a rich dowry," sneered Bhayrn.

"He's still my friend," declared Charyn, looking to Malyna and adding, "You might see a few people you know."

"That would be nice." Malyna's tone was pleasant.

At perhaps half a quint before the glass, the side door from the corridor opened, and Lorien and Chelia entered. The rex wore a jacket and trousers similar to those of his sons, except for the addition of a gold-edged deep green formal sash. Chelia wore a high-necked teal gown with long tapered sleeves.

Charyn immediately stood. Bhayrn turned. Aloryana and Malyna rose swiftly, but later than Charyn.

"It's time to enter," announced Lorien.

"Charyn, you escort Aloryana, and Bhayrn will escort Malyna," announced Chelia.

The fact that Bhayrn would escort Malyna, with the color of her gown, would indicate that the regial family accepted her familial link.

That was a slight departure from the usual order of precedence, when Chayrn, as the heir, would have escorted his mother, although, being of age, he was officially first in the line of succession, rather than requiring a regency.

Bhayrn extended his arm to Malyna, then opened the door to the ballroom, and the two stepped out. Immediately, the players began the "Processional of the Rex."

Charyn moved beside Aloryana and offered his arm.

She took it. Once they were inside the ballroom, she said, "It's different being here, rather than watching."

"It's always different when you're part of something."

"I'll always remember this."

"You'll have more than enough balls to remember."

"This one . . . will be . . . special."

Charyn wondered at the pause, but only said, "It is your first. There's something special about that."

Ahead of them, Bhayrn and Malyna took a position before and on the right side of the dais on which the players were seated. Charyn guided Aloryana to an equidistant position on the left. That positioned him beside his mother when Lorien, as rex, took his position in the center.

Chelia asked quietly without looking at Charyn, "In addition to listing possible partners, have you also picked out the order in which you'll ask them to dance?"

Charyn wasn't surprised. "No, and I may not be able to dance with all of them."

"I'd keep your journals a bit more private."

"You've read them?"

"I was tempted, but, outside of the first page, which was last year's ball, I haven't. I trust you've applied the same diligence to others beyond the young ladies."

"More to the others. I don't have the easiest natural skills with people."

"You underestimate yourself, but that's scarcely the greatest fault."

In the pause that followed, Charyn studied those in the ballroom, picking out the three ministers and their wives, as well as Marshal Vaelln and his wife.

Lorien gestured, and a brief fanfare filled the ballroom.

"Maitre D'Image Alastar, Maitre D'Image Alyna," announced the chateau herald.

Charyn let his eyes take in the pair who effectively ruled the Collegium Imago as they approached the rex and the rest of the regial party. Maitre Alastar remained a striking and broad-shouldered figure, although his once-silver-gray hair was now streaked with white. His carriage was erect, his steps strong. Beside him walked Maitre Alyna, a good head shorter than her husband. While she was trim, she was too muscular to be petite, and there was something about her, to Charyn's eyes, that was formidable, especially when her eyes passed across him just before she and the Maitre paused before the rex. There was also something disconcertingly familiar about Maitre Alyna, something he had not noticed at previous balls.

Both inclined their heads slightly, and Lorien replied with an equal nod. Then the two maitres turned and proceeded past Chelia and Charyn, where they took a position a yard or so to Aloryana's right.

Chelia did not look once in the direction of either maitre as she murmured in a low voice, "I will remind you once more. You are to limit your attentions beyond the dance floor as we discussed. That is why matters are as they are."

"I understand perfectly," he replied with a smile. "Your arrangements are perfectly satisfactory. More than that, in fact, and I appreciate the care you have taken."

"Thank you. I learned more than I wished from your uncle. We will not discuss the matter more."

Charyn nodded and concentrated on watching and listening as the first councilor entered the ballroom.

"High Councilor Basalyt D'Alte and Lady Basalyt."

As were most of the High Councilors, Basalyt was older, allowing him to spend much of the year in L'Excelsis, while his heir handled the estates and any factorages, but he moved gracefully with perfect posture as he and Lady Basalyt entered the ballroom and made their way to one side, since none of the councilors would join the rex. That would have signified a formal meeting, which balls were not.

"High Councilor Khunthan D'Alte . . ."

"High Councilor Fhaedyrk D'Alte and Lady Fhaedyrk . . ."

"High Councilor Oskaryn D'Alte . . ."

"High Councilor Ryel D'Alte and Lady Ryel . . ."

Charyn studied the Chief Councilor, the uncle he only met briefly and in passing, if upon a number of occasions, whose once-blond hair had silvered and thinned noticeably over the past few years, as he and Doryana made their way among the High Holders who had already arrived.

After several moments, the orchestra began to play, and Charyn turned to his sister, bowed, and then took her hand.

When they began to dance, Charyn smiled and said, "I know it's not very exciting to have your first dance in public with your brother, but we both know it's a matter of form."

"You dance well, and I don't have to pretend with you," Aloryana replied. "I won't be thrilled to dance with some of those approved by Father. You get to choose, if with certain considerations, I'm sure. You'll be quite busy."

"Father would be very disappointed otherwise," Charyn replied, "don't you think?"

"Doesn't it bother you?"

"It's a small price to pay." *There are others far greater.*

"The first of many."

"I thought you'd be happier tonight."

"So did I."

"Why aren't you?" asked Charyn, trying to express the concern he felt.

"I don't know."

Charyn thought she did, that she'd thought the ball would somehow be special, but that it had turned out to be simply larger than their everyday life, with more elegant clothes and more people. He didn't press. "Enjoy what you can, and learn all you can."

"You make everything sound so cold."

"You know I'm far from cold."

"That's what I don't understand."

"It's to be kept from being used. Almost everyone wants to use us for some purpose. Like it or not, you can't forget it."

"So you'll do them one better?" asked Aloryana softly.

"No. I just don't wish to be anyone's tool." *Especially Father's.*

As the music died away, Charyn guided his sister back to the dais, where Bhayrn was waiting. Charyn had no doubt that one of their parents had strongly "suggested" Bhayrn request the dance from Aloryana.

In turn, he moved swiftly but gracefully to Malyna. "Might I have the next dance?"

"You might."

As Charyn took her hand, and they began to dance, he offered an amused smile, then said, "I think this will be the most private conversation we've had since you came to the chateau."

"I've never avoided you."

"But we've never been in the same room alone. Well, once, but only for a few moments."

Malyna raised her well-formed eyebrows and gave a quick look around the dance floor. "This is alone?"

"Sometimes there might be more privacy in a crowd. Anyway, as you must know from my earlier comments, I did some looking through the archives, and I found Vaelora. Not only was she Rex Regis's sister, but she was the first Minister of Administration for him, and she married the first Maitre of the Collegium. So that confirms that we're related, if rather distantly."

"You were rather persistent." Her smile was one of amusement. "I didn't know that she'd also been a minister. I doubt there have been any others since."

"I wouldn't doubt that, either. In fact, I'm inclined not to doubt anything you say in all seriousness."

"That could be dangerous, too."

"I said 'in all seriousness.'" Charyn smiled. "You've never said when you will be returning to Rivages."

"Your father and the weather will have a great deal to say in that regard. At present, with the snow as it is, I fear I will be in L'Excelsis for some time, either here at the chateau . . . or elsewhere."

"If you must remain, I trust you will remain at the chateau."

"As we both know, that is not my decision to make."

"That may be, but you make the chateau a much more pleasant place by your presence."

"You're too kind."

"You should know me better than that." When Malyna did not reply, he asked, "What, if I might ask, do you and Aloryana talk about?"

"Mostly about what High Holder girls do. You must know that she feels hemmed in, almost kept."

"She's said as much. But isn't everyone?"

"It's different to be walled in by privilege rather than by poverty."

"I wouldn't argue that, but to some degree, everyone is limited by their situation."

"You seem able to escape many of those limits."

"For the moment, yes. I don't see my father escaping them, not without severe and adverse consequences."

"Such as those that befell your grandsire?"

"I'd prefer not to get into that position."

"What if the conflict between the rest of the world and your position were to place you in that situation?"

Charyn laughed softly. "That's a good question. I'm glad I don't have to answer it at the moment."

"You may in the future."

"Why do you think so?"

"Times are changing. If we cannot change the times, then it may be that the only way to survive and prosper is to change ourselves."

"That doesn't sound like the thought of a High Holder's daughter."

Malyna laughed. "It's not. I cribbed it from my uncle. He's not a High Holder. My father would likely dispute the thought."

As the music ended, Charyn guided Malyna to the dais, where, surprisingly, Maitre Alastar waited.

"If I might borrow the young woman, Charyn?"

"Of course." Charyn stepped back, wondering. Had his mother requested that the Maitre ask Malyna to dance?

Rather than waste time on speculation about it, Charyn moved away from the dais and his family toward the nearest young woman whose name he knew, stopping short of her father, inclining his head, and asking, "High Holder Nacryon, might I ask your daughter for the next dance?"

Nacryon nodded. "You might."

Charyn turned to the oval-faced blonde with gray eyes. "Mistress Cynthalya, might I have the pleasure of the next dance?"

"You might, Lord Charyn."

As the music began, he took her hand and eased her away from her parents. "You look lovely this evening."

Cynthalya raised both eyebrows.

Charyn grinned once they had moved farther away from her father and were separated by other dancers. "More than lovely . . . ravishing. That's what I would have said if your father had not been so interested in my words. The green gown sets off your eyes."

"You must say something like that to every woman."

"Oh, no. I do say in what manner each looks lovely, but that's not a lie, and it's also so that I don't cause hurt feelings and comparisons between young ladies and the parents of the young ladies, but once we've danced away . . . then I can express myself more freely."

"What if she's already married?"

"Then, I congratulate her on her husband's good fortune and lament the fact that I can't possibly do anything untoward."

Cynthalya offered only a faint smile.

"They know I'm exaggerating slightly, but it does no harm, just as most men like to be told that that they dance well, even when they can barely avoid planting their feet on their partner's shoes."

"You do far better than that, Lord Charyn."

"You see? I'm a good dancer, but not outstanding, and you're not exaggerating in your compliment . . . and I try hard not to do that as well." As he moved, he glanced back toward the dais, where he saw that Maitre Alastar was indeed dancing with Malyna, and his father was dancing with Maitre Alyna. He nodded and listened.

"Do you feel you have to charm all the young ladies?"

"I'd rather do that than bore them, but I'd rather listen to what you can tell me about yourself, since all that I know is what I see and that your father is High Holder Nacryon . . . and that your hold is near Mantes."

"Since you insist . . ." Her smile was polite, but not especially warm. "I am the youngest of four. I have two older brothers and an older sister . . ."

Charyn listened, prompting with an occasional question.

At the end of the dance, he escorted her back to her parents, then made his way to High Holder Ryel, whose eyes obviously narrowed at his approach.

"Good evening, Uncle."

"Good evening. Will we be formal?"

"Not excessively so. How are you faring?"

"I'd be far happier if your father would let me relinquish the position as head of the High Council."

"He's mentioned that. Why do you feel it's time to step down?"

"I've served long enough. Now I'm getting threats from factors."

"From factors?"

"Who else could it be? Especially with the mentions of protecting trade and keeping tariffs low for factors. Almost no High Holders are in shipping. Then that business about the exchange in Solis is being laid at the feet of High Holders. Why would any High Holder bother with destroying a building whose function is easily moved?" Ryel's expression of disgust faded, replaced by a warm smile. "He hasn't mentioned what he intends to do, has he?"

"He's told me that you've been threatened and would prefer not to remain. He hasn't told me or even hinted what his decision will be."

"Does he keep everything that close?"

"At least that close." *Except to Mother.* But Charyn wasn't about to mention that.

"Your sister is quite beautiful. So is the other young lady. Is she someone . . . special?"

"I suppose she is, but not in the way you think. She's a distant relative, the youngest daughter of High Holder Zaerlyn. Malyna D'Zaerlyn."

"She must be his youngest. I don't recall her."

"She is. Her father requested that we guest her so that she could attend the Year-Turn Ball."

"Rather unusual for your father to grant such a request, I would think. He's never done that for anyone before."

"Repaying a favor, I believe. What favor I have no idea." Charyn knew he probably shouldn't have said that, but he wanted to get a reaction.

"I can't imagine what favor a porcelain-factoring High Holder might offer to the rex."

"Neither can I." Charyn inclined his head. "How is your family?"

"As well as can be expected, Doryana brought the children here for winter. She doesn't have as much to do with the lands in winter."

Children? Then Charyn realized his uncle was talking about his grandchildren, whom he seemed to regard as his children, which, Charyn supposed, they were in a way, since their parents were both dead. "It's good to see you again. I need to fulfill my responsibilities to the young ladies."

Ryel only nodded in return.

As Charyn headed toward the nearest unoccupied young lady, Shaelyna D'Baeltyn, he had the feeling that the ball was the last place that his uncle wanted to be. Charyn couldn't blame him, given that neither of his parents cared for Ryel. What Charyn didn't understand was why, if they both disliked him so much, his father was reluctant to let Ryel leave the High Council.

After the dance with Shaelyna, who was polite, poised, and not terribly interested or interesting, Charyn approached High Holder Basalyt, who looked stern and bored.

"Good evening, High Holder."

For a moment, Basalyt looked annoyed, but then smiled. "Lord Charyn, you surprised me."

"I just wanted to greet you personally. I have neither messages nor an agenda . . . except to exchange a few words, tell you that I appreciate the effort you and your wife made to come in this weather, especially since it is somewhat more chill . . ."

"Than Bartolan? It is indeed, but it's also more pleasant in L'Excelsis, or at our dwelling outside L'Excelsis, in the summer."

After passing a few pleasantries, Charyn then made his way to High Holder Fhaedyrk and his wife, who were merely observing the dancers.

"Lord Charyn? Making the rounds, are you?" Fhaedyrk smiled broadly. So did his wife, a large and big-boned woman who looked not to carry any excess weight.

"I didn't think it would hurt to see if you were enjoying the evening, or at least not being tortured by the tedium of a ritual event."

"It's good to see the young people enjoying themselves."

"Might I ask, Lord Charyn," interjected Lady Fhaedyrk, "who the dark-haired young woman escorted by your brother might be? Her gown . . ."

"Suggests a familial tie? It does. She is the youngest daughter of High Holder Zaerlyn, who is a very distant relative descended from the sister of the first Rex Regis. Her father asked if she could guest here in order to attend the Year-Turn Ball."

"And there's more than that?"

"Unhappily, no," replied Charyn with a laugh.

"Such a pity . . ." offered Lady Fhaedyrk. "She's lovely."

"She's also very intelligent," returned Charyn.

"There's something about Zaerlyn . . ." mused Fhaedyrk, "but I can't recall what it is." He shook his head. "It will likely come to me in the middle of the night. That's what comes with age. Enjoy your youth, Lord Charyn. It vanishes all too soon."

"You sound so gloomy, dear," said Lady Fhaedyrk. "It doesn't disappear that quickly."

After several more exchanges of not-quite-banalities, Charyn slipped away and made his way to the next young lady he recognized.

"You look lovely this evening, Mistress Alyncya," offered Charyn as he inclined his head. "Might I have this dance?" Charyn looked to High Holder Shendael, who nodded, and then to Alyncya.

"You might, Lord Charyn."

As the music swelled and he guided her away from her father, he said, "I think I prefer you in the peach, rather than the crimson." And he did, because it seemed to bring out her sandy brown hair and hazel eyes.

For the briefest of moments, Alyncya's countenance showed surprise. "I'm surprised you remembered. How did you manage that? Please don't tell me that a single dance of less than half a quint remained in your memory for an entire year."

"Then I won't. Not completely. I studied the invitation list and the replies," he answered truthfully. *More intently that anyone could possibly guess.* "When I saw your name, I did remember what you wore." *With a little help.*

"I do appreciate the effort, Lord Charyn, but why do you bother? None of us would dare refuse." Alyncya's words were warmly humorous.

Charyn had to admit that he liked both the honest appraisal in her eyes and the warm firmness of her voice. He kept his tone light as he replied. "Because I'd prefer not to be considered regially imperious . . . or not so beyond the circumstances of my birth, about which I can do nothing."

"You could turn a woman's head with such diligence."

"But have I turned yours?" Charyn laughed easily.

"How could you not?" she returned almost playfully.

He almost grinned at the way she had turned his own words back at him. "You are a dangerous woman, Mistress Alyncya."

"Scarcely that, just a High Holder's unwed daughter trying to hold to her wits when every word must count for everything and commit one to nothing."

"While seeming to promise everything?"

"Of course. How could it be otherwise?"

How indeed? "Is that not life?"

"I doubt it could be otherwise for one destined to inhabit the Chateau D'Rex."

"Is it that different in a High Hold?"

"There are always distinctions between positions and places. I am not one to judge whether those distinctions are truly differences."

"Are any of us without great experience able to make such judgments?"

"We all make judgments. Whether they're wise . . ." Her hazel eyes met his for an instant.

He almost lost track of the music and the dance, and it seemed like forever before he managed a reply: "I wouldn't claim wisdom at my age." Almost immediately, he regretted the words. *How did that happen?*

She laughed gently. "I think I liked that better than anything you've said."

"I didn't," he admitted. "It was far too pompous."

"Very pompous, but spoken without calculation."

"You're suggesting that every word I speak is calculated?" Again, he tried to keep his tone light and humorous.

"Perhaps not every single word . . ." There was definitely a hint of humor in her words.

As the music came to an end and he guided her back to her parents, Charyn was feeling slightly unsettled. Still, as he released her hand, he inclined his head. "I enjoyed the dance. Thank you."

"As did I, Lord Charyn."

Charyn forced himself not to look back.

He wasn't up to another dance like that, not immediately, and he made his way to Chief Factor Elthyrd, whom he had not seen enter the ballroom and who stood alone, although another man, possibly Factor Harll, had just walked toward one of the sideboards where refreshments were being served.

"Good evening," offered Charyn.

"Cold, but good. Most seem in good spirits, except for Basalyt. He looked annoyed that you spoke to him."

"He could have been surprised."

"Likely surprised and annoyed. He's not your father's greatest admirer."

"Are any of the High Councilors?"

Elthyrd laughed.

"I'd thought that Oskaryn D'Alte was the High Councilor who admired my sire the least. He's the one who's always declaring that tariffs are too high, sometimes more vociferously than any factor."

"As a factor, I've found that those who concentrate on keeping tariffs low rather than increasing their income usually lose both."

"That is a very good point."

"I'm glad you think so." Elthyrd's words verged on the sardonic. "Some factors have not always appreciated my observations."

"They should have, but then, some factors likely admire neither you nor my father."

"Some of us respect him for what he's trying to do."

"But not enough of you to keep others from strongly opposing him."

"That's true, but I've done what I can, and so have most of those on the Solidaran Factors' Council." After the slightest pause, Elthyrd added, "There might be one whom I doubt is very insistent, but I'm not about to say who that might be. I could be wrong. Now . . . I understand you met with Estafen . . ."

Charyn understood that Elthyrd had said what he would, but he wondered which factor was the one who was not all that supportive of either Elthyrd or Lorien. "I did. I hope we can work out something . . . but it has to be handled carefully."

"I do understand that. By the way, you've created an awareness of Factor Suyrien. Are you going to do any trading?"

"Only when I have something to trade."

"It's probably better that way."

As the dance music faded away, Charyn excused himself and looked for a young woman who seemed to need a partner. He did not know the next young woman whom he approached, mahogany-haired, slender, and almost as tall as he was, not that he was anything more than of average height for a man. Nor did he recognize the High Holder. He bowed. "Might I ask the young lady for the next dance?"

"You might. Her name is Rhyella."

It took Charyn a moment to match names. "Thank you, High Holder Hallryn." He turned, "Might I, Mistress Rhyella?"

Rhyella nodded, flushing slightly.

Charyn took her hand. "This is your first time to a Year-Turn Ball, isn't it?"

"It is. It's the first large Ball I've ever attended. There aren't any in Tuuryl."

"Did you just come for the ball?"

For a moment, Rhyella did not answer. Finally, she said, "We came with my younger brother. We wanted to see him off. He's going to be an imager. Except he already is."

"That must have been hard." *As might well be the fact that your father accepted the invitation as a way to show off a marriageable daughter.*

"It might be for the best. I have two older brothers, and Rynhahl is far from the largest of High Holdings."

Charyn decided not to ask more about her brother, not given that too many High Holder families regarded having an imager offspring as unfortunate. "How are you finding L'Excelsis?"

"For some reason it seems colder than Tuuryl. They say it's not."

"You've arrived during one of the coldest periods I've known. It's not usually this cold, especially before winter begins . . . although tomorrow . . ."

"That's good to know."

Despite her initial embarrassment, and as tall as she was, Rhyella was light on her feet and danced exceedingly well. That was obvious from the first moments, enough so that Charyn didn't hesitate to say, "You dance very well, in fact better than anyone with whom I've danced this evening." That also was true.

Rhyella blushed slightly once more. "Thank you."

As the end of that dance neared, Charyn kept the conversation light and casual before returning the shy Rhyella to her parents. As he made his way toward the dais where the players were taking a slightly longer pause than usual, he saw young Ferron D'Alte returning Aloryana to where Bhayrn stood beside their father, who was talking to Maitre Alastar. Charyn did not see their mother, although Maitre Alyna was standing back slightly.

Charyn smiled and walked toward the group, stopping before Alyna. "Might I have this dance, Maitre?"

"Of course, Lord Charyn." Her smile was pleasant.

While he waited for the music to resume, he asked, "How do you find the ball? Different each year . . . or much the same?"

"The form is always the same, as you well know. Beyond that . . . I think most will see what they wish to see. That makes it different for each who attends."

"And for you?"

"This is the first time you've honored me. Why now?"

"You've always seemed unapproachable." *And formidable.*

"Do I seem that different now?"

"No," he admitted, "but I might as well get used to it." *Before I have to.*

"I'm almost old enough to be your mother."

"She is also formidable, if in a different way."

"Then I'm in good company." She extended a hand as the music began.

Charyn took it, well aware of the covert glances that followed them around the floor. He was surprised. Maitre Alyna danced well enough, but not outstandingly, and somehow he had expected that she would.

"You dance well," she observed. "I don't match your standards. I hadn't danced for years until we began to attend the Year-Turn Balls. Dancing isn't part of the instructionals at the Collegium. You never did say why you asked me to dance this year."

"It's the first year I dared to." That was a complete truth, and he laughed softly.

She smiled warmly. "You've decided to make your own alliances, then."

Charyn managed not to stiffen at her perceptiveness. "Everyone must at some time . . . if they're to chart their own course."

"Even your sister? Does she have that choice?"

"She won't have the same choices I do."

"Few will," replied Alyna dryly.

"Will your daughter have the choices you did?" Charyn countered, his voice light, worrying that he might have misspoken, but he thought he'd heard that she and the Maitre had a daughter.

"She's already had more. All girls at the Collegium do."

"Can she choose whom to marry?"

"We've done our best to guide her."

"Just guide her?"

"Laying down prohibitions for a strong imager is unwise, especially if she happens to be one's daughter."

After a moment, Charyn laughed. "You're far wiser than I, Maitre."

"Wisdom is the result of avoiding and surviving mistakes, Lord Charyn."

"How would you suggest I avoid mistakes, then?"

"Study the mistakes of others." She offered a smile that contained a hint of mischief. "That way, at the least, you'll be able to make different mistakes."

"Unlike the High Holders, who always seem to make the same ones?"

"So it's said."

"Are there many at the Collegium who come from a High Holder background?"

"Four at the moment . . . no, five. We received another from a High Holder background on Meredi."

"Is that a considerable number for High Holders?"

"It's the most in several years. Having a child who is an imager is not considered an emblem of honor by many High Holders, although some have risen to considerable distinction. Maitre D'Esprit Arion heads the Westisle Collegium, and his older brother is High Holder Calkoran."

Charyn had to struggle for an instant, until he remembered that his father and Malyna had both mentioned Calkoran . . . and that Malyna's mother was Calkoran's sister. "That's a Pharsi lineage, isn't it?"

"It is. Pharsi families tend to have more imagers. They also tend to respect imagers more."

"More than position and power?" asked Charyn.

"I know few who do not respect power."

"And honor?"

"Pharsi families tend to respect both."

"While other High Holders honor power alone. That is clear. Beyond those who honor power, are you aware of more than a few who have even considered a concept of honor?"

"There are some," she replied, "just as there have been some in the Chateau D'Rex who have held honor above power."

"And what of past Maitres?" asked Charyn, emphasizing the word "past" just slightly.

"Quaeryt and Elsior were both highly honorable. Others have been less so. That lack of honor contributed to the decline of the Collegium."

"Because power exercised without honor leaves a successor in a weaker position?" suggested Charyn.

"Over time, honor requires power, and power requires honor."

Charyn could see that, especially if honor was not held as a virtue by others. But there wasn't much point in pursuing that any further. "You've been here in the Chateau D'Rex a number of times. I never have been to the Collegium. I would very much like to see it . . . but only if Maitre Alastar and you would find that acceptable."

"I'm certain that would be to our advantage as well as yours, assuming that the rex would also agree. Have you asked him?"

"I had thought to see if it would be acceptable to you before approaching him."

Alyna nodded. "If he agrees, you are welcome. Just give us a few glasses' notice."

Charyn didn't ask whether Maitre Alastar would agree; Alyna's tone indicated that he would. *But then, she is the Senior Imager as well as his wife. Who else would know without even asking?*

As the music died away and the dance came to an end, Charyn guided Maitre Alyna back to where Maitre Alastar stood. Then he inclined his head to Alyna. "Thank you for the dance and for your counsel." He looked to Alastar. "I thank you for your kindness in allowing me the dance."

The tall Maitre offered an expression between a smile and a grin. "Lord Charyn, I have nothing to do with allowing Alyna anything. Her choices have always been hers, and I've been the better for that. She also has excellent judgment and advice."

"Then I must thank you both." Charyn inclined his head, then turned. While he would have preferred to skip the next dance and take several swallows of strong red wine, doing so would have revealed to anyone who had been watching him the strain of that last dance.

So he spied another young lady and made his way toward her. He did not recognize her or her father, but he bowed politely. "You look lovely this evening, mistress," offered Charyn, bowing slightly and turning to her father. "Might I have this dance, sir?"

"If Diasyra wishes to," replied the High Holder.

The young woman's name was enough to jog Charyn's memory.

"I'd be honored, Lord Charyn." Her voice was slightly shaky.

"It would be my pleasure." He turned back slightly. "Thank you, High Holder Taulyn." Then he guided Diasyra out away from her parents. "Is this your first ball, Diasyra?"

"It is."

Since the invitation and reply lists did not list ages, Charyn had to go by name and appearance in asking for a dance, but it was quite clear by the reaction of both daughter and father that the quite lovely Diasyra was likely only a few years older than Charyn's own sister and very much unsure of herself. "I'm certain that in a few years, when you've attended more balls, you'll find them much less strange. You may have slightly sorer feet from having too many boots tromp on your toes, and you will doubtless hear compliments that cannot possibly be true."

"That may be." Her voice remained tentative, but polite.

Charyn could see that, for a girl at her first ball, she danced well, and better than many more experienced, but he did not say that, knowing that she would take it as insincere. *Which would be ironic, because it wouldn't be.* "Do you have a place here in L'Excelsis, or did you come all the way from Nordeau for the ball?"

"Father maintains a modest dwelling several milles north of here, on the west side of the Aluse. We often spend part of the summer there. It's cooler."

"Do you ride much?"

"I love riding, especially early in the day. That's when everything is cool and fresh . . ."

Charyn listened, asking a question or two, and found himself enjoying the dance, simply because Diasyra was being herself, as if, young as she was, she knew that the dance would lead nowhere and that she had no worries. *In time, she could make the right man very happy.*

After leaving Diasyra, Charyn made his way to Ferrand, holding a goblet of red wine and standing not all that far from the sideboard.

"How are you faring?" asked Charyn.

"Less fortunate than you, I fear. I've not been rebuffed outright, but I've received a few glances that could have frozen the Aluse."

"From the fathers of daughters?"

"Who else?" Ferrand took a sip from his goblet. "I must say that Malyna D'Zaerlyn is quite attractive."

"You should ask her to dance. She'll be very pleasant, and her father isn't here to glare at you."

"She wouldn't even think of me as a match."

"Enjoy the dance. Besides, if others see you dancing with her . . ."

"You calculate everything, don't you?"

"Not everything. Far from everything."

"Everything you can."

"Hardly." Charyn wasn't about to admit that he'd learned young that his initial feelings were not always to be trusted, and sometimes they still weren't. Calculation helped . . . sometimes. "Oh . . . and you could ask Aloryana to dance."

"More calculation."

"No. Aloryana can only dance with a handful of men. As a cousin, you're one of them. She'll appreciate not dancing with immediate family or graybeards. But ask Malyna first."

"But . . ."

"Go ask her. Just be charming. You can even tell her I suggested it."

"I just might." Ferrand handed his goblet to a server, nodded to Charyn, and departed.

Charyn's next partner was Faerlyna, the daughter of High Holder Kastyl. She was reserved, almost stiff, as if she feared him, although he did his best to be charming, and she did seem a trace less stiff when they parted.

He then passed a few words with two of the other High Councilors, High Holder Khunthan, who was genial, and High Holder Oskaryn, who was cool and almost dismissive.

Before long, he lost track of just how many young ladies with whom he danced. And, as required, he danced the last dance with Aloryana, then led the way to the adjoining sitting room, escorting Malyna, followed by Bhayrn and Aloryana, and their parents. He very much wanted a glass of wine, possibly more than one, but that would have to wait.

"You must have danced with every eligible woman in the ballroom," declared Bhayrn.

"And a few others," replied Charyn lightly.

"Such as Maitre Alyna," declared Bhayrn. "Why on Terahnar did you ask her?"

"Very few asked her to dance," replied Charyn. "I thought she might like the chance. She was quite interesting."

"She could turn you into ashes at a glance," said Bhayrn. "Or maybe something even worse."

"Not if I didn't give her cause."

"How many did you favor with a second dance?" asked Aloryana.

"None." Charyn had thought about asking Alyncya a second time, but if she had been the only one with whom he had taken a second turn that would have made a statement he wasn't about to have made public. "I was fair. I only danced once with each one, except you. I did notice you dancing with Ferron D'Alte . . . and Ferrand."

A quick expression of surprise flitted across Aloryana's face. "I don't see how you had time to notice anything else."

"Did you find Ferron interesting?"

"He was nice enough, but he was really interested in Malyna."

Charyn looked to Malyna.

"He was charming and very polite," she replied.

"Does Ferron dance well?"

"Passably well," replied Aloryana when Malyna just smiled. "You dance better. So does Ferrand, and so does Maitre Alastar, except he's old enough to be a grandfather. He said he has a daughter not much older than I am. That's hard to believe."

"Why? Maitre Alyna is much younger than he is," replied Charyn.

"Why would she marry someone that much older?" interjected Bhayrn. "She's still good-looking, and there are always more men imagers than women."

A faintly amused smile crossed Malyna's face, but vanished almost instantly as Chelia and Lorien entered the chamber.

Charyn would have liked to have asked his father whether he had spoken to Ryel about staying on the High Council, but he knew inquiring about that would have to wait.

Aloryana turned a withering glance on Bhayrn. "Maitre Alyna obviously didn't want to marry a weakling. The only imager stronger than she is happened to be Maitre Alastar."

"That attitude will limit your choices," said Bhayrn snidely.

"I think that is quite enough," declared Chelia firmly. "Once the High Holders leave, there will be refreshments for us in the family parlor. There will be no unpleasant comments."

That meant another glass of largely insignificant conversation, Charyn knew. He smiled politely. "I could use a glass of wine."

"So could we all," replied Chelia, "except Aloryana. A half glass will suffice for you, dear, but we will wait to leave here until most have left."

"Did the ball meet your expectations?" asked Charyn, turning to Malyna.

"It did, but it was different. Not that many people seemed to be enjoying themselves."

"You danced with Maitre Alastar," said Bhayrn bluntly.

"He asked me. I wasn't about to turn him down. He was very nice. It's some— . . . I mean, it's hard to believe that he's killed so many men and turned rivers to ice."

"I met a subcommander when I got a tour of army headquarters," said Charyn. "He said he was there when the Maitre and the other imagers destroyed most of the High Holders' army. He said the ice stretched half a mille in every direction." Even as he spoke, Charyn wondered what Malyna had almost said.

"The Maitre did something like that all by himself," said Chelia, "when he saved your father and me in the first uprising."

"I didn't know that," said Malyna.

"It wasn't our greatest moment," declared Lorien dryly. "I'd prefer not to discuss it." He turned to Aloryana. "Did you enjoy the ball?"

"I did, Father. Thank you so much for letting me be here."

Charyn was surprised at the clear appreciation and the hint of emotion in his sister's voice.

"Thank you, dear." Lorien looked directly at Bhayrn. "What about the rest of you? Or was it just a trial to be endured?" His eyes focused on Bhayrn.

"No, sir. There were some nice girls—"

"Young women," corrected Chelia.

". . . and I did have a chance to talk to Pietyr, since I haven't been able to go anywhere lately."

"And you, Charyn?"

"Very pleasing, very rewarding, and enjoyable."

"Rewarding? An interesting choice of words." Lorien looked to Malyna. "And you . . . how did you find it?"

"It will be an experience I'll never forget," replied Malyna. "I appreciate your allowing me to be here."

"We're all very glad you're here." Chelia looked to Lorien.

"I think we can go down to the family parlor now," said Lorien.

Bhayrn immediately headed for the door to the side corridor, without so much as a glance back at the others.

"Don't be in such a hurry," cautioned Chelia.

Bhayrn slowed down, although he reached the top of the grand staircase just before everyone else. Aloryana, Charyn, and Malyna were next, with Charyn in the middle on the wide steps, followed by Chelia and Lorien. At the base of the staircase, Bhayrn paused, then turned left toward the family parlor. When he reached the main level, Charyn gestured for Aloryana to go ahead, then Malyna.

At that instant, abruptly, one of the chateau guards at the foot of the grand staircase turned, pulled out a pistol, and fired almost point-blank at Lorien. Even before the rex started to topple, the other guard had out a pistol, and both guards began to fire at the rest of the family—except the bullets sprayed away from Charyn, Aloryana, and Malyna.

Then one of the guards looked startled, dropped his pistol, and clutched at his chest, as his legs crumpled under him.

The other one froze.

"Tie him up!" commanded Malyna. "Quickly! Now!"

No one moved for a moment.

"Charyn!" snapped Malyna. "Tie him up. I can't hold him much longer and protect the rest of you."

Protect the rest of you? Because he didn't have anything to tie the guard with, Charyn went for the pistol. He had to struggle to wrest the pistol from the guard, not because the man was struggling, but because the pistol felt as though it was fastened firmly to him. For a moment the guard tried to move, and the pistol came free, and the man stiffened again. Charyn thrust the pistol at Aloryana, then unbuckled his belt, pulled it free and wrapped it around the stiff guard, fastening it behind him.

"Drop him to the floor!" snapped Malyna.

"I can't. He's frozen in place."

"Oh! Now."

The immobile guard started to go sideways, and Charyn pushed him facedown. The man hit the stone floor with a dull sound, but did not move.

"Hold him down," said Malyna. "I have to let go of that shield."

Charyn scrambled into position, then glanced back at his father, who lay at the base of the grand staircase, with Chelia cradling his head in her lap. Only the slightest trace of blood had oozed from the wound in Lorien's forehead.

He's dead . . . he's dead. How could that have happened . . . so quick . . .

The guard beneath Charyn was no longer stiff, and shuddered. Charyn thought he was breathing.

Three other guards, rather Guard Captain Churwyl and two guards, arrived as Charyn knelt on the no longer stiff, but somehow still breathing chateau guard. Behind them, Charyn saw two other guards shielding Bharyn.

Charyn looked up. "He shot Father." He still wasn't certain he believed it had happened, but then his eyes flicked toward where his mother cradled his father.

"He shot at everyone," said Malyna. "Both guards were traitors."

Churwyl looked from the motionless guard that Malyna had apparently killed, somehow, and then bent to look at the one Charyn had restrained. "These aren't the men I assigned."

"We'll need to talk to the one Charyn's kneeling on," said Malyna, her voice a commanding tone Charyn had not heard before. "Can your men keep him safe and alive?"

Churwyl looked bewildered.

"Do as she says," declared Chelia.

"Now!" snapped Charyn.

"Yes, sir."

Blood covered the face of the surviving traitor guard as the two guards with Churwyl lifted him to his feet. He moaned slightly.

"We'll need to find out who hired or bribed him," Charyn said, after standing and stepping back, knowing he was repeating what Malyna said.

"Yes, sir."

When Charyn glanced back toward his parents, he saw that his mother had eased herself back slightly and positioned his father so that Lorien lay straight on his back, his sightless eyes looking upward. She slowly rose to her feet, then put her arms around Aloryana, who was sobbing silently.

Churwyl looked to Charyn, as if awaiting orders.

Abruptly, Charyn realized that *he* had to give those orders. *What orders?* It seemed like forever before he could finally speak. "Make certain that none of the more recently hired guards are anywhere inside the chateau. Anywhere. Do that immediately. Move my father"—he found himself pausing—"to the stately guest chamber at the top of the grand staircase and post a guard there immediately. We need to move to the family parlor." He tried to think of what else needed to be done. "Also . . . send a messenger to inform Maitre Alastar immediately of what has happened."

"Yes, sir."

"Once all that is taken care of, and you are confident that the Chateau is actually secure, report back."

"Yes, sir."

"I'll go with him," Chelia said.

Charyn knew exactly what she meant. "Do you—"

"No. I'd like to do that alone. You need to take care of the others."

"Are you—"

"Yes. I am."

Charyn nodded, although his eyes flicked to his father's countenance, a frozen expression there not even showing surprise.

How . . . How did it happen so quickly . . .

Charyn waited until more guards appeared and his mother followed his father back up the grand staircase before motioning Malyna and Aloryana toward the family parlor. Aloryana clutched Malyna's hand.

His thoughts continued to race as he walked behind them, but those thoughts were fragments tumbling over fragments. . . . *had to be planned . . . months in advance . . . Malyna . . . she was ready . . . yet caught off guard for a moment . . . her guards . . . no . . . couldn't be them . . . Father . . . Mother . . . had to know about Malyna . . . Churwyl . . . he involved? . . . unlikely, but . . . message to the High Council . . . not yet . . . Mother . . . so terrible for her . . . Ryel . . . could he be the one . . . or factors . . .*

Once the four of them were in the family parlor, with two chateau guards posted outside, and Malyna, Bhayrn, and Aloryana were seated, Charyn looked at Malyna. "Who are you, really? Besides an imager."

"I am Malyna D'Zaerlyn. My aunt is Maitre Alyna. She's my father's sister."

"But . . . but . . ." Bhayrn stuttered

"You were here to protect Aloryana, weren't you?" interjected Charyn. "And the two personal guards who accompanied you weren't from Rivages at all. They're imagers as well, aren't they?"

"Yes."

"Why couldn't you stop them from killing Father?" demanded Aloryana.

"I'm sorry, Aloryana. I couldn't act fast enough. Your Father made it clear I was to protect you, first, then Charyn and Bhayrn. He said that whoever had attacked wanted to use all of you to pressure him. He wouldn't allow any imager in the chateau except me. I'm not the best. I'm only a junior Maitre D'Aspect, but I'm the only one who could fit in here in the chateau close to you without being suspected in moments. Maitre Alastar had to argue to get your father to allow Kaylet and Dylert to pose as my guards, and he'd only allow them to serve as outside guards."

Charyn stood stock-still for a moment, realizing just how clever Malyna had been. She had never once lied . . . about anything. "Your uncle . . . you were talking about Maitre Alastar, weren't you?"

"He is my uncle, you know, since Alyna is my aunt."

Charyn could also see the brightness in Malyna's eyes, and realized that she was upset as well. Again . . . he had to think before he spoke. "You were in a difficult position. Mother knew, didn't she?"

Malyna nodded.

"You'll have to stay for a while, you know," Charyn said.

"I know."

Charyn hoped he didn't have to spell out why. The two false guards had been ordered to kill all of them.

"Anyone who wants a goblet of wine can have one. I certainly intend to have one. Just one, though."

Sipping it might give him a few moments to think through what he should have done and had not . . . and what else he needed to do, even as his thoughts went back to what had just happened . . .

After dealing with everything he could, Charyn went to bed alone. He did not sleep well. His dreams were troubled, although he could not remember the details when he woke to the moaning of the wind in the grayness before dawn on Solayi. He did remember the feelings that those dreams had created well enough that he had no desire to attempt to sleep longer. *Just a wonderful start to the first day of the year.* He pushed away the thought that matters couldn't get worse. Even he knew they could.

He was still struck by how quickly—and effectively—Malyna had reacted to the assassins the night before. She was three years younger than he was, and he doubted that he could have moved as quickly as she had, even if he'd had a pistol in hand.

But she's a trained imager maitre. That thought was sobering . . . and a reminder of why his mother had kept dropping hints that Malyna was not for him.

He washed and dressed quickly, then used the more private circular staircase to descend to the main level. He didn't reach the family breakfast room before Churwyl found him.

"Sir?" offered the guard captain, almost tentatively.

"What is it?" Charyn kept his voice level, although he had the feeling he had missed something . . . or that the guard captain had more bad news.

"The man you captured . . ."

"Did he say anything?"

"He's dead."

"How did that happen?" Charyn had to force himself not to snap.

"He wouldn't say anything. I was trying to get him to talk, and he just . . . went into convulsions and died. Even though his hands were bound. He kept chewing on the lapel of his jacket."

"The uniform jacket was poisoned?"

"It would seem so. He also had a blade in his collar and some powder in his wallet. The powder killed a rat."

"He said nothing?"

"He just kept repeating that he didn't know anything, and he'd done what he had to do."

"What about the other guard?"

"He was provisioned the same way."

"Who makes the guard uniforms?"

"I've already sent someone. I'll let you know what I find out."

"Did the message to Maitre Alastar get delivered?"

"Yes, sir . . . well, to the duty maitre at the Collegium."

"Then I'm sure he'll get it. Is there anything else? Oh . . . what about Maitre Malyna's 'guards'?"

"She's a maitre, an imager maitre?"

"She is, young as she is, and she's the reason the rest of us are alive. She immobilized the one guard and killed the other before I could even take a single step." For some reason, Charyn decided not to mention the shields. "Father worked out something with Maitre Alastar. I think it was so that Maitre Malyna could protect Aloryana." *Why else was Malyna always so close to her?* "He never said anything about it to any of us." *Except possibly Mother.*

"But . . . the rex . . . I mean your father . . . he said she was a High Holder's daughter."

"She is. She's also an imager. Now . . . about her 'guards.' They're also both imagers. I'd like them moved to watch the doors, especially the rear courtyard door."

"They're . . . staying?"

"For now. We'll see about later." Charyn paused. There was something else . . . something about the chateau guards. "Oh . . . were the two traitors among the more recently hired guards?"

"Ah . . . not among the latest hired, but they were hired in Erntyn when Zakart and Blevyn took their stipends. They came highly recommended."

"By whom?"

"The former head of the Civic Patrol, Commander Murranyt. I talked to him myself."

Murranyt? What was there about Murranyt? There was something, but Charyn couldn't remember what it had been. It might have been something his father had said. He wished he'd started paying more attention earlier. "That doesn't say much about him. Can you find out where the commander might be? And why he might have had a reason to want us all dead?"

"I can see."

"Were there any other guards hired in the last few months, that is, until you were allowed to find more guards several weeks ago?"

"No, sir."

"For now, keep the newer guards out of the chateau proper."

"Yes, sir."

"Is there anything else I should know?"

"Right now, I can't think of anything, sir."

As Churwyl hurried off, Charyn realized that he should have sought out the guard captain immediately on waking and that he should have thanked Churwyl for seeking him out.

When he finally reached the breakfast room, he was the only family member there. Especially after talking with Churwyl, he didn't feel all that hungry. In the end, he managed to eat most of the cheesed eggs and a chunk of warm bread, and finish a mug of tea.

As he was leaving, he asked, "Has my mother been down?"

"No, sir. Her maid requested a tray for her. Werlya took it up to her a quint or so ago."

"Thank you."

Again using the private staircase, Charyn climbed up to the upper level and walked to the door to his mother's sitting room, where he rapped gently on the door. "It's Charyn. Might I come in?"

"If you're alone."

"I'm alone."

Charyn waited. After several moments, he could hear the lock bolt sliding back, and then his mother opened the door. Her eyes were bloodshot, but her cheeks were dry. She stepped back, and he entered the sitting room, and relocked the door. By then she had retreated to her armchair.

He took the chair facing her. "I heard you ordered a tray."

"Werlya insisted. I ate a little. The tea helped."

"I ate a little more than that. The tea helped me, too."

There was a silence.

"I'm sorry," Charyn said. "I had no idea . . ."

"Your father said he didn't need protection. He said the rest of us did." Chelia smiled wanly. "He kept saying that they were using all of you to put pressure on him, and there wasn't much point in killing him. I tried to persuade him otherwise."

"He could be very stubborn."

"It's been a family trait."

"I'm surprised that he allowed any imagers in the chateau."

"Maitre Alastar suggested that. He remembered what happened the last time. Your father wouldn't have that. He didn't want the chateau turned into a fortified prison. Maitre Alastar then offered Malyna to be inside and imagers to guard the outside. Your father agreed to that only because of Malyna's background. He wanted her to protect Aloryana. He thought she'd be the next target."

"I think we all were the next targets. Without Malyna . . ." Charyn shook his head. "I think she's upset that she couldn't stop them from shooting Father. She said something last night, that she wasn't the best for protecting us, that she was only a junior maitre."

"She said that?"

"While you were . . . with Father . . . she did."

"I'll have to talk to her. You should, too."

"I tried. Last night. I don't think she heard me. Not really."

"Then try again. You owe your life to her."

"I will . . . later." *Talking to you is more important right now.* "Can I do anything?"

"Not now. You will have to speak at the memorial service."

Charyn hadn't even thought about a memorial service.

"You will do it, but you'll do it with an imager escort to shield you. I won't lose a son as well."

"I will take care of it, as you suggest. I hate to bring this up, but did Father ever mention if he knew anything about who might be behind the shooting . . . at Bhayrn, I mean?"

Chelia shook her head. "He had no idea. If he did, he never mentioned it to me, except that it had to be greedy factors who were shipowners."

"I'm sorry."

"Don't be. You needed to know. You're the rex."

Now. Charyn wanted to shake his head. He definitely didn't feel like a ruler. "I can still be sorry. Can I do anything for you?"

"There isn't anything you can do. What do you intend to do about Malyna?"

"Keep her and the other two imagers who were posing as her guards here at the chateau for at least a while . . . if they're agreeable to it."

"You can't keep them here forever."

"I know. But it might give me a little time to think and to talk things over with Maitre Alastar . . . and others."

"Talk to them but never reveal your inclinations. Not until you decide."

Charyn nodded.

"You need to go. Talk to Malyna, and then get to the study and look over what's there. Don't forget to talk to Alucar and Sanafryt, especially. I can take care of myself."

"Eat a little more, if you can."

Chelia smiled wanly again. As he stepped back, he realized that he hadn't noticed before how much her blond hair was shot through with silver. Or was some of that from last night?

His next stop was at Malyna's door. When he rapped on it, there was no answer. He nodded to himself and made his way to Aloryana's door. He knocked more softly.

"Who is it?" The voice was Malyna's.

"Charyn. I need to talk to you."

"Just a moment."

When Malyna finally opened the door, she was wearing trousers, a blouse, and a jacket, all gray—imagers' grays.

He just looked for a moment.

"There's no point in hiding it now. Everyone in the chateau knows. Please speak quietly." She stepped back to allow him to enter and pointed to the closed door to the adjoining bedchamber. "Aloryana's sleeping. At last."

Charyn closed the door as quietly as he could, taking in the circles under Malyna's eyes. "It looks like you could use some sleep."

"I got some."

"You slept here last night?"

"She was very upset. For a number of reasons."

"I think everyone is, but she's the youngest."

"Will you be summoning Maitre Alastar?"

"I sent him a message. I didn't request his presence, but . . . I think he might come, anyway. If not, I'll request his presence."

"I need to talk to him. About imager matters. It's important."

"I'll make certain you can."

"Thank you."

"There is one other matter," Charyn said quietly. "Not a small one."

"Oh?"

"You saved my life. You saved Aloryana's life, and Bhayrn's, and my mother's. You captured . . . one of the assassins. You couldn't have done more. Not with the instructions my father gave. I didn't know. Obviously. Not until my mother told me this morning."

"It happened so quickly, but I should have . . ."

"The shot was behind you. You turned, immediately shielded all of us, and then killed one attacker and froze the other, all before I even knew what had happened."

"I couldn't hold three shields at once. That was why I had to kill the one. What about the other?"

"He had poison sewn or leached into the edge of his uniform where he could chew it. He died of convulsions while Churwyl was questioning him."

"Poison?"

"He had two separate poisons on him, and a sharp blade on the inside of his collar. So did the dead guard."

"It was planned, well in advance."

"It had to be. What I wish I knew was what else has already been planned. If it's agreeable to you . . . and to Maitre Alastar . . . I'd appreciate it if you and the other two imagers could remain here at the chateau for at least a time until I can sort matters out."

"That has to be Maitre Alastar's decision."

"I understand that. I thought you would like to know my wishes. I suspect Aloryana would feel safer as well."

Malyna nodded.

Charyn wasn't certain exactly what the nod meant. "You have your doubts?"

"I doubt that anything will be as it once was."

"Because a rex has never been attacked in the chateau, let alone assassinated?" From what he had overheard, Charyn had his doubts about his grandsire's death, but his father insisted that his own father had died of a seizure brought on by one of his frequent fits of rage.

"That might change things."

"I think it's because things have already changed. They have changed more than we know, I fear."

"Why do you say that?"

"My father knew little or nothing about the exchanges, and the vast sums of golds that can change hands there every day. He had no idea that the Jariolans were building so many warships and commissioning so many privateers until it was far too late. None of us have the slightest idea who is behind these attacks, but they were planned well enough that someone was able to place at least two assassins among the chateau guards months ago."

"Could there be others?"

"Those two were the only guards hired recently—except for a handful that Churwyl has been training, and, for now, they're restricted to postings outside the main chateau proper. I've asked him to position your imagers who are acting as guards inside where they can watch the entrances to the chateau." Charyn paused. "There could be others. Too many men can be bought if the price is high enough, and it's not likely that our enemies are short of golds."

"Do you think building more ships will stop them?"

An unfortunately good question. Charyn managed a wry smile. "I have my doubts, but it is possible that making a good effort might satisfy all but those whom nothing will satisfy. That might leave them without supporters . . . or far fewer supporters." *If your judgment is correct and if you can manage such an effort . . . and if you can get the higher tariffs necessary to pay for it . . . without setting off another revolt.*

"I shouldn't keep you."

Charyn inclined his head. "Thank you . . . again. I cannot tell you what we owe you."

"I wish I could have done more."

"You did more than anyone could have. For the moment . . . if you'd just stay with Aloryana."

"I'd thought to."

When he finished with Malyna, Charyn walked back along the north corridor to the study that had been his father's.

Sturdyn, one of the usual study guards, was waiting there. "Good morning, sir. Are you expecting anyone?"

"It is Solayi, but Maitre Alastar might call."

"Very good, sir."

"But I need to talk with Minister Alucar, and then Minister Sanafryt . . . or the other way around, whichever can see me sooner . . . and Norstan. Please get word to them. You may have to send a messenger, since it's Solayi." With every step he took, he was thinking of something else that needed to be done. *And likely missing as many things as you're thinking of.*

"Yes, sir."

Charyn crossed the study and looked down at the goldenwood desk and at the neat stacks of papers. Finally, he sat down behind the desk. He was halfway through the sheets in the first stack when Alucar arrived.

"Sir." Alucar paused. "My deepest condolences."

"Thank you." Charyn did not stand, but motioned Alucar to the chairs before the desk. "I'm sorry to summon you on a Solayi, but there is a great deal I do not know."

"I wouldn't have expected otherwise."

"Do you have any ideas about who might be behind such an outrageous attack?"

"Outside of a suspicion that it likely had to be someone wealthy who is losing much to the Jariolans, no, I don't. Were there any more threatening notes . . . or things like that?"

"Not that I'm aware." Charyn swept his hand above the stacks of paper. "Unless there's something here. I haven't had a chance to go through all of these."

"Some of them have been there a considerable time."

Charyn decided not to comment. "What are the most immediate problems you see facing me?"

"You know about the loss of the granaries in Tuuryl?"

"I do. At the current prices of wheat, I'd estimated the loss at around twelve thousand golds. How close is that?"

"Not all the silos were full. The estimate was ninety thousand bushels destroyed. The lost grain would have brought a little less than eleven thousand golds, but it will cost at least several hundred golds for repairs to the silos and for cleaning."

"What else?"

"If you do not increase tariffs for this present year you'll likely face a shortfall in revenues."

"How big a shortfall?"

"It might be as much as ten thousand golds."

Charyn thought for a moment. "Does that include building the two extra warships?"

"No, sir."

"How much is set aside in reserves?"

"Twenty thousand."

From there, the accounting got even more depressing, as Alucar ticked off the possible expenditures that had not been considered, such as additional supplies for the army if maneuvers or attacks against rebels were required, or the fitting-out costs for the additional ships, the requests for roadbuilding in Estisle and Nacliano . . .

By the time the Finance Minister finished and left for his home, since

Charyn didn't see the point of requiring him to stay on Solayi, Charyn could see why his father had so often not been in the best of moods . . . and why he didn't think that much of the complaints of the High Holders and the factors.

No sooner had Alucar left than Norstan hurried in.

"You wished to see me, sir?"

"I did. Have any arrangements been made for my father?"

"Yes, sir. Lady Chelia has told me what she wishes. The memorial service will be on Samedi in the Anomen D'Rex . . ."

Charyn listened as Norstan provided the details, then said, "Please let Guard Captain Churwyl know, if you haven't already."

"Yes, sir."

Charyn took a deep breath and just sat there for several moments.

After Norstan, and several more documents, the next arrival at the study door was Sanafryt.

"My condolences, sir. In the chateau . . . that's so hard to believe."

"I appreciate your coming in on Solayi." *Even if I did summon you.*

"Did Churwyl find out who it might have been?"

"The surviving assassin swallowed hidden poison before he revealed anything. Do you have any ideas?"

"Whoever it is has to have wealth and knowledge about the chateau." Sanafryt eased into the chair before the desk. "There are more than a score who could fit that description."

"They also have to have a certain amount of power," reflected Charyn. "The assassin committed suicide, and for someone to be able to command that . . ."

"They have to have great control over others," added the Justice Minister. "Certainly someone with great wealth and knowledge, but someone whom no one really pays that much attention to. Most likely a factor."

"Why do you think that?"

"Have they not been the ones who demanded that your father act? I could be missing something, but the High Holders have already lost twice, and the Collegium backed your father in both instances. Their tariffs will be equalized with those of the factors by the end of the year no matter what happens. Also, the wealthiest factors have more ways to use their golds without anyone knowing about how they are used."

Thinking about the exchange alone, Charyn nodded. "That's a good point."

"I'm certain you didn't request my presence to discuss the . . . unfortunate matter. How might I be of assistance?"

"What do I need to do involving the legal proprieties?"

"There has to be a proclamation of regial assumption and a statement of regial responsibility."

"Is that the same for each rex, or are there matters that need to be stated differently or changed?"

"It's largely symbolic . . ."

Meaning that there are some things that aren't. "How soon can I see a draft?"

"Not before tomorrow, sir. I'll need to check some of the precedents."

"What else?"

"You should likely have your own seal. I'll also draft messages to the High Council and the Factors' Council of Solidar asking for a postponement—"

"No." Charyn said the single word firmly. "The last thing Solidar needs is a postponement of the meeting on—" He had to struggle to recall the date. "—the eighteenth of Ianus. Nothing much got done at the last meeting. Putting off doing something will just make whoever is behind the assassination even angrier."

"Pardon me, Rex Charyn . . . but won't doing something just embolden them?"

"It depends on what we do. Not doing anything isn't helping Solidar, and it's not helping in collecting tariffs. Not doing anything might also result in losing another eleven thousand golds' worth of grain. If I do something, and then there's another attack, would that not strengthen my position?" *You think.*

"Perhaps . . . if you survive the attack."

"What do you suggest?"

"I can tell you what you can do under the Codex. I can tell you what not to do. I cannot tell you what action might be most successful because I agreed with the positions your father took, and those actions did not turn out for the best. No one ever imagined that someone disgruntled with the rex would attempt to assassinate his entire family. No one thought it was possible. People thought revolts and rebellions were possible. Now . . ." Sanafryt shrugged. "The world has changed. For the first time in history, those without ties of a sort to the rex have golds and resources enough to do something like what happened last night, without anyone knowing."

"You're saying that the High Holders have ties to the rex?" Charyn very much had his doubts about that.

"In the sense that they can be controlled. It might take time, but you could eliminate the High Holders by force. Their holds and their resources are known. They are still largely tied to their lands. They tend to be separated from each other physically, but they are linked by marriage and inheritances. At the very least, you could create such damages that it would take years for them to recover, and they know this." Sanafryt cleared his throat, swallowed, and went on. "The factors are linked by golds, but none know that much about each other. Alucar will tell you that he knows what each large factor is worth. He does not. He knows what they report, but unless we send tariff inspectors to look into the factorage, we only know what they report."

"That's true of everyone."

Sanafryt shook his head. "Everyone knows when a High Holder buys or builds a factorage . . . at least when he buys one near his holding. Because buying or operating factorages far from the hold requires trust, most High Holders refrain from that. Factors rely on golds. Word spreads on who pays and who does not. A High Holder can juggle things within his holding because he controls everything. A factor cannot. Only the golds matter. And so long as he meets his obligations, no one asks from where the golds come or for what they are used."

Charyn frowned.

"You have visited the exchange, I understand. Do most know from where the golds come when they sell there? The exchange knows, but so many golds change hands for so many contracts that over a time, no one remembers, and no one knows. There are records, but it would take days, perhaps years, to sort out what any one factor might have done."

Charyn definitely had not thought about that.

When Sanafryt finally left the study, dismissed to leave the chateau and to return to his dwelling, Charyn realized another thing. He had no idea if his father had said anything to his uncle about staying on the High Council. Later . . . possibly several days later, he would need to ask his mother whether she knew.

With a deep breath, he returned to the papers on the desk, concentrating as he went through each stack quickly. Even so, it took him more than two glasses before he finished sorting the papers into four stacks—those that he'd need to deal with in the next day or so, those he'd have to deal with at some point, those that contained information he needed to know, and those he had no idea why they'd even come to the desk of the rex. And none of the papers shed any light or even suggested any more than he already knew about who might have been behind the shooting . . . or why.

He was just about to take a second look at the more urgent stack, when Sturdyn rapped on the door.

"Guard Captain Churwyl, sir."

"Have him come in."

Churwyl entered.

Charyn thought the guard captain looked worried, as worried as he'd ever seen the man, although that was certainly understandable. "You look worried."

"Yes, sir. I've found out more about last night. You might recall that the assassins weren't the guards assigned to the staircase?"

Charyn nodded, waiting.

"Vaelsyk and Andomart were standing guard at the foot of the grand staircase. They were relieved at precisely tenth glass by Bolomyrt and Chastant—the two assassins. The two guards who were supposed to be the reliefs were missing. We found their bodies a glass ago, in the rendering yard. I think they were given sleeping draughts at the evening meal, because each had a single stab wound to the heart."

"Trained assassins," mused Charyn. "But they clearly knew they were going to die. Why would they accept that kind of job, even as assassins?"

"Someone made them an offer they could not refuse. Possibly offering immediate death if they refused, or their families were threatened. It could have been both, along with the payment of a great number of golds."

"What about former Commander Murranyt?"

"I sent a guard to Civic Patrol headquarters. He hasn't returned yet."

"What did Vaelsyk and Andomart have to say?"

"Bolomyrt told them that the assignments had been changed. It has happened when guards were ill or injured, and, well, guarding the stairs has usually been almost a ceremonial function."

"Should it have been considered such after the shootings and the burnings?"

"Burnings, sir?"

Father didn't tell him? "Twenty grain silos near Tuuryl were burned, and some exploded. That was over a week ago. There was another threatening missive left. Didn't you know about that?"

The stunned expression on Churwyl's face left little doubt of the answer.

"No, sir."

Charyn could also see that the events of the past day seemed to have aged Churwyl, who was not a young man, by any means. He said quietly, "Let all the guards know about that as well, and let me know when you hear more about Murranyt."

"Yes, sir."

After Churwyl left, Charyn just sat there for several moments. Why hadn't his father let Churwyl know about the granaries? Because he didn't want the guards to think matters were out of control? Because he didn't think it related to safety at the chateau?

Charyn had no idea, and doubted he'd ever know.

He knew he should probably be doing something besides react, and study papers, but he had no idea what that might be. *Order the army to protect the chateau?* That wouldn't have prevented the assassination and likely wouldn't prevent another attempt.

"Maitre Alastar is here, sir," announced Sturdyn.

"Have him come in." *Thank the Nameless.* Once more, Charyn felt awkward about using the chamber he always thought of as his father's study, perhaps because he'd always been ushered out when Maitre Alastar arrived. *But you're the rex now, like it or not. And you need to give an impression of being in control . . . or not being out of control.*

Unlike his father, he deliberately stood as the white-and-silver-haired Maitre crossed from the door to the chairs before the goldenwood desk.

"My deepest condolences on your loss, Rex Charyn." Alastar's voice was mellow, but sounded as though he meant what he said.

"I appreciate that, Maitre. Thank you for coming. Especially on a Solayi."

"It was the least I could do. Your father and I did not always see eye-to-eye, but he tried to do the best he could under very difficult circumstances. You do know, I hope, that the Collegium had offered more protection?"

"I didn't know until this morning. I also have to tell you that Malyna saved all the rest of us. She was able to shield us, immobilize one assassin, and kill the other, all at the same time. I don't know how she reacted so quickly." Charyn paused, then added quickly, "Before I forget or get distracted, she needs to see you before you leave the chateau. She said to tell you it was an important imager matter."

"I can do that." Alastar paused. "You didn't summon me."

"No, I didn't."

"Might I ask why?"

"It would have been terribly presumptuous," Charyn admitted.

"That hasn't stopped any of your predecessors," replied Alastar wryly. His voice turned warmer as he added, "I do appreciate the courtesy."

"Thank you."

"Before you say anything else . . . have you heard about High Holder Oskaryn?"

"The High Councilor? No. What happened?"

"He was shot and killed shortly after the end of the ball as he stepped out of his carriage under his own portico at his L'Excelsis dwelling. The shots came from a rifle, according to the Civic Patrol."

The Civic Patrol? So the Collegium had close ties with the Civic Patrol? *Or closer ties than the Chateau D'Rex does.* "Oskaryn was the High Councilor most opposed to building more warships to deal with the privateers and the Ferrans." Charyn didn't know much more except that Oskaryn had vehemently opposed higher tariffs for any reason. "But he was only one of five High Councilors, and none of them are all that fond of higher tariffs."

"Could it be exactly because he was the most outspoken?"

"I don't know. I've not meet with either the High Council or the Factors' Council. I'd rather not make a judgment until I do. That could be the reason, but there could be others."

"The Collegium would prefer that matters not deteriorate into another situation similar to the High Holders' revolt."

"So would I, Maitre. At the same time, it's hard to know what to do when my father already promised to build more ships and make greater efforts to protect Solidaran merchant shipping . . . and he was still assassinated. He'd taken steps to make certain everyone knew that."

Alastar nodded. "There were even reports in the newssheets."

Newssheets? After a long moment, Charyn said, "I have to confess my ignorance."

"For the past several years, *Veritum* has been printed twice weekly. There are reports on everything from the Civic Patrol to murders or drought or flooding. Last year a second newssheet was started. It's called *Tableta*, and it reports once a week more on factoring matters. Both of them reported on your father's effort to safeguard Solidaran ships. As I recall, *Veritum* suggested his acts were a good beginning. *Tableta* repeated what many factors believe, that tariffs were already too high, and that the rex needed to find another way to finance any shipbuilding, or even road building."

After a moment of silence, Charyn said, "I had thought to ask you about the possibility of allowing Maitre Malyna and the other two imagers to remain here at least for a few days, if not longer."

"How long did you have in mind?"

"At least until the meeting of the High Council and the Factors' Council on the eighteenth of Ianus."

"That might be possible. Do you think that the meeting will change matters?"

"I have hopes, but hopes are hard to bring to pass, and more easily dashed by those who do not see the value of aspirations."

"You're cynical for one so young."

"Not cynical enough for one raised in the Chateau D'Rex, I suspect. Would my outlook be different if I had been raised on Imagisle?"

"Different, I have no doubt, but imagers also tend to be skeptical, sometimes cynical."

"Also, as I mentioned to Maitre Alyna, I would still like to visit the Collegium."

"We'd welcome you at any time."

"It will have to be after Samedi. That's when the memorial service is scheduled. I trust you will be there. That brings up another problem. I can't very well hide, but appearing in the Anomen D'Rex . . ." Charyn looked to the Maitre.

"You feel you'd be inviting another attempt?"

"I understand the last memorial service required your efforts to save my parents."

"Alyna and I would be happy to stand behind you at the memorial service. That is close enough to shield you."

"I would appreciate that greatly."

"It's also to our self-interest. Solidar doesn't need to lose another rex any time soon."

Charyn decided he would have to think over the implications of Alastar's words. "Let me have someone summon Maitre Malyna. I'll step out, and you can talk to her here." Charyn smiled. "I won't eavesdrop. Neither will the guard."

"Thank you."

"Sturdyn!"

The door opened.

"Yes, sir?"

"Would you find Maitre Malyna, and convey her here. I'll be quite safe with Maitre Alastar."

"Yes, sir."

As the door closed, Alastar smiled. "You say that quite confidently."

"After what I saw last night, if you wished to harm me, there is no power on Terahnar that could save me. You also don't strike me as a man who would let harm come to me while you are sitting here."

"Do you think you're that good a judge of a man you scarcely know?"

Charyn smiled ruefully. "I'm likely a terrible judge of character. I have to judge people by their actions and hope I interpret the actions correctly."

"There is much to be said for that."

"And much to be cautious about, as well."

After a rap on the door, Sturdyn announced, "Maitre Malyna."

"Have her come in." Charyn stood. "Sturdyn and I will be down the corridor."

Malyna entered the study, glancing toward Alastar, who had also stood, and then Charyn.

Charyn gestured to the chairs. "I'll leave you two until you're finished. Just let me know." He had no worries about the papers on the desk. He doubted there was anything in them that Alastar didn't already know, except for the legal petitions, and he doubted any of them would concern the Maitre. He also doubted Alastar would look at a single one. He closed the study door as he left, then motioned for Sturdyn to accompany him.

He stopped some ten yards toward the grand staircase. He hated waiting, but he didn't want to be too far away.

Less than half a quint later, the study door opened, and Malyna stepped out.

"Are you done?"

"We are, Rex Charyn."

Charyn walked back, noticing that Malyna had immediately reentered the study. He closed the study door behind him, walked back to the side of the goldenwood desk, and turned to face the two maitres. He did not sit down. "You both look very concerned."

"I dislike adding to your problems, Charyn," said Alastar, "but I'm afraid I must."

"Now what?" Charyn tried to soften the words, but only partly succeeded, he feared.

"The imager problem Malyna mentioned? It is indeed a problem, but it's partly a regial problem, too."

Charyn found himself frowning. "Could you explain a bit more? You're being a bit cryptic."

"There's no way around it. Your sister Aloryana is an imager." Alastar smiled sadly.

Charyn just stood there. *Aloryana an imager?* How could that be? He remained silent, thoughts spinning, remembering . . . *the broken silver hair clasps . . . that she wore . . . unbroken.*

"She will need to come to Imagisle. That will take care of her safety, but . . ."

"How do you know she's an imager?" Charyn still wasn't sure he believed it.

"She told me," said Malyna. "Then she showed me."

"There's never been . . ." Charyn broke off his protest, then asked, "Was Vaelora an imager also?"

"Yes. It's not widely known, but she was. She also had farsight, and that's something your sister also has, apparently."

Charyn swallowed. "That was why she wanted to go to the ball. She knew it would be the only one she'd attend. She sounded so certain."

"We can make one accommodation that most entering imagers do not get," Alastar said. "That is, if your sister will agree to it."

"What is that?"

"She could live in the Maitre's house," said Malyna. "I lived there with Uncle Alastar and Aunt Alyna until last year. That was after I became a maitre. She'd have her own room, and she'd have company. Lystara is sixteen. It's not the chateau, but it's very spacious and comfortable."

"She has a great deal to learn about imaging," added Alastar. "If she doesn't, she could hurt herself, perhaps seriously."

"Does she have to leave . . . right now?"

"Soon . . ." said Alastar.

Then Charyn shook his head. "I suppose it doesn't matter as much as I thought. I wanted Malyna to stay to protect her . . ."

"She needs a few days to get ready," said Malyna.

"And the Collegium will need a few days as well," added Alastar. "I would prefer that she arrive on Mardi."

So soon? "Does she know . . . she must, I suppose, if she knew she wouldn't be attending other balls."

"I've told her," said Malyna. "Even though I'm not living at the Maitre's house, I'll still be able to see her every day. And I think she and Lystara will get along."

"They will indeed," declared Alastar.

The Maitre's tone left no doubts about *that* in Charyn's mind. "I'll need to tell her mother."

"It might be better . . . if the three of us told her," said Malyna. "You, Aloryana, and me."

"You're probably right about that," conceded Charyn.

"I think I should wait . . . until after you tell her," said Alastar. "Just in case."

"That's a good idea." Charyn turned to Malyna. "If you would get Aloryana and meet me . . . Mother should be in her sitting room."

"Aloryana is already there."

"Then we should join them." Charyn paused and looked to Alastar. "It might be easier if Malyna and I accompanied Aloryana to the Collegium. That way, we both could see it at the same time. If that would not pose a problem?"

"That might be for the best, in many ways."

"Now . . . we need to tell my mother." Charyn gestured toward the study door.

"I will come with you," said Alastar, "but I'll wait outside the sitting room, in the event my presence is required."

Charyn nodded, then led the way from the study and out into the north corridor.

Chelia looked up from her armchair as Malyna and Charyn entered the sitting room. "Everyone looks so serious. We are obviously going to have a great revelation. Is it, perchance, the fact that Aloryana is an imager?"

Charyn managed to keep his jaw in place, but barely. "Did she tell you?"

"No. There have been hints and suggestions . . . and I did hear Malyna explaining certain aspects of the Collegium, far more than necessary. I wondered, and then when Malyna was summoned to meet with Maitre Alastar . . ."

"You're not upset?" asked Aloryana. "You're really not?"

Chelia smiled. "Anything but. You will have choices and more freedom than I ever have had, but when you can visit me safely, I hope you will."

"Always!"

"No one else has been told," Charyn said, "except Maitre Alastar. It will take a day or so to make certain arrangements. She will leave for the Collegium on Mardi. If Aloryana is agreeable, she will stay at the Maitre's dwelling. She will have her own room. Maitre Alastar and Maitre Alyna have a sixteen-year-old daughter who is also an imager."

"I spent most of the last six years with them," said Malyna. "I came to the Collegium when I was about your age."

"You'll like their dwelling," said Chelia. "It's spacious, but very warm. So is Maitre Alyna."

Both Aloryana and Malyna looked puzzled.

"Your father and I spent the night there many years ago, before you were born. That was just after Maitre Alastar saved us from the Antiagon Fire at your grandsire's memorial service." Chelia looked hard at Charyn.

"Maitre Alastar and Maitre Alyna will be standing behind me at Father's memorial service."

"I'm very glad to hear that."

"You're really not upset?" asked Aloryana again.

"I am not. You will be far happier. At least you will have the chance to be far happier. Whether you are is up to you."

A broad smile appeared on Aloryana's face, more relief than happiness, Charyn suspected.

After leaving the sitting room and walking down the grand staircase with Maitre Alastar and then to the main entry to see the Maitre off, Charyn then made his way down to Norstan's study.

The seneschal bolted to his feet. "Sir . . . you could have summoned me."

"I was nearby, and it was quicker to find you myself. I understand that there are two newssheets being printed in L'Excelsis. They're called *Veritum* and *Tableta*. I want a copy of each, each time either comes out."

"Your father . . . ah . . ."

"That was his preference. Mine is different. I expect them on my desk the morning after each appears, if not sooner."

"Yes, sir."

"Are you aware of any other pamphlets or other materials being circulated?"

"Ah . . . those happen all the time, sir."

"I'd like to see them, all of them."

"Sir . . . some of them . . . they're awful."

"That may be, but ignoring them isn't going to make them go away."

"Yes, sir." Norstan's voice contained more than a little acceptance . . . and resignation.

Charyn then returned to the study, and resumed his more detailed study of the reorganized papers. He actually had almost a glass to himself before Churwyl returned and entered the study.

"What is it, Churwyl?"

"Commander Murranyt has left L'Excelsis, sir."

"When did he leave?"

"Last month, according to the neighbors. No one seems to know where he went. The Civic Patrol says they have no idea."

"Do you have any idea why he left, Churwyl?"

"No, sir."

"Did he seem nervous when you talked to him before?"

"No, sir."

"What did he say about the two men?"

"That he had found them reliable and dependable, but that they had left the Civic Patrol to work as private guards because they could get better pay."

"Who had they worked for?"

"Factor Goerynd. He makes pumps and other implements."

"Why were they more interested in working at the chateau?"

"They said it was because Goerynd was falling on hard times and had let them go. Some factors have been."

"Did you talk to Goerynd?"

"No, sir. I thought the recommendation of the commander was sufficient."

"Try to find out more, if you would."

"Yes, sir. Since it is Solayi, I may not be able to discover more until tomorrow."

"As soon as you can."

"Yes, sir."

After Churwyl left, Charyn took a deep breath. He knew he didn't know enough, but . . . was anyone looking into anything in any depth?

He looked at the papers and resumed reading. He needed to get through them all, just to know what he had to do immediately.

His eyes were burning, and his head was aching by the time he left the study for dinner.

The others were waiting in the family parlor.

Chelia glanced at him.

Charyn ignored the glance. "Has anyone here mentioned to anyone else the fact that Aloryana is an imager?"

The others exchanged glances. Bhayrn shook his head. Chelia frowned.

"I have not," said Malyna.

"Mother?"

"No."

"Good. I think it best that we not even speak of it anywhere that we can be overheard. Aloryana should continue the same schedule as she has until almost the glass she leaves for the Collegium."

"You think someone on the staff is untrustworthy?" asked Chelia.

"I don't know. It's more likely than not. I have no doubts that Aloryana will be safe so long as Maitre Malyna is near her, but I think it is wise to be cautious." Charyn looked to his sister. "Aloryana . . ." he said, "lead on."

Charyn followed the others into the family dining room. He did not sit at the head of the table but in the position where he had always seated himself, thinking that he should have asked others to be circumspect much earlier.

Chelia looked at him.

"I prefer to leave Father's position as it is until after the memorial service, call it a personal memorial." *A recognition that he died too soon and too young.* And a reminder of other sorts. "I'll say the gratitude tonight." He cleared his throat gently, then began, "For the grace from above, which we may not understand, for the bounty of the earth below, for Your justice, and for Your manifold and great mercies, we offer our thanks and gratitude, both now and ever more, in the spirit of that which cannot be named or imaged. We also give thanks for those who are not here, and for all that they have meant, and all that they have conveyed in thought, word, and deed."

Then Charyn waited until all the goblets were filled before lifting his glass. "To Father, for all that he did and for his love and kindness to us."

"To Father," repeated Bhayrn and Aloryana.

"To Lorien," said Malyna and Chelia.

Charyn could see the brightness in his mother's eyes, but she said nothing as she lowered her goblet.

When everyone was served, slices of roasted mutton in a brown sauce, with herbed mashed potatoes, and baked seasoned carrots, as well as hot dark bread, Charyn cut a bite of the mutton and ate it, just so that everyone else could begin eating. Then he took another sip of the Montagne red wine.

He was about to ask Malyna about the Collegium when Chelia glanced at Malyna and asked, "When did you know you were an imager?"

"I knew I was when I was eleven. I managed to keep it hidden until I was ready to leave for Imagisle. I'd heard from my father just how dangerous imaging was, and how imagers had to be very careful. I was *very* careful."

"Had you ever been in L'Excelsis before?" asked Charyn.

"No. Neither had my father. He also wanted to make certain I would be taken care of. He also wanted to meet Maitre Alastar."

"How is the Collegium different from a High Holding?" asked Chelia.

Malyna smiled. "From what I've seen, my upbringing was very demanding compared to other High Holdings. Most girls there didn't have to learn things like mathematics, geometry, surveying, or about how to groom and treat the common ailments of a horse . . . how to inspect a wagon or carriage to make certain it was sound . . . Even what crops are best grown in what kinds of land. They had to learn the clavecin, and whist, and the social graces, and how to read and write proper letters and invitations. We had to learn all that as well. So going to the Collegium wasn't hard. I just had to learn some new things, such as the limitations of imaging and the proper technique . . . what kinds of imaging are dangerous . . ."

Charyn listened intently as he ate, occasionally interjecting a question, knowing that his mother was trying not only to learn more about the Collegium, but to draw out Malyna in order to help prepare Aloryana.

That was more than fine with him. A quiet dinner with the conversation centered on Aloryana's future was best for all of them, even if the absence of his father felt all too unreal, as if he were just absent . . . and not dead.

Later that evening, he sipped a single brandy across the table in his sitting room from Palenya, thinking.

"You're quiet this evening," she observed.

"After the last day . . ." He shook his head. "What are you thinking?"

"About Lady Malyna. She's an imager, everyone says." Palenya looked down at her half-drunk goblet, almost as if she didn't want to look at Charyn.

"She is. She's a very accomplished imager for her age. She's a maitre."

"Is she really a High Holder's daughter?"

"Yes. That's why none of us suspected." Charyn wasn't about to say anything about Aloyana also being an imager. Not yet. He wanted his sister safely out of the Chateau D'Rex before that became known to anyone outside the family and, of course, Alastar and Malyna.

"It's all so strange. You are suddenly rex, and Lady Malyna is an imager, and two trusted guards turn on your father . . ."

"It's very strange," Charyn agreed.

"How do the people who wanted your father dead think this will help? I wouldn't want to do anything to help people like that."

"I won't always be able to do what I'd like, even if I did order it. Even if I am rex. That's one of the things that caused problems for my father. He couldn't build that many more warships, because there aren't enough shipyards and shipwrights. You can't build shipyards and train shipwrights in weeks or even months." Charyn shook his head. "I can't believe that's so hard for people to understand . . . but it is."

Palenya laughed softly. "People can be stupid when they don't understand things. They ask me if I will play Farray's third processional. It's magnificent. It's also a beastly piece of music that was written for a full orchestra. There isn't even a clavecin score. Well . . . there might be, but no good clavecinist would ever think of playing it. It would take tens of glasses of practice to learn it well enough not to make mistakes, and it wouldn't sound that good." She shook her head. "They say, 'You're a musician. You must know this.' No musician knows all the music in the world. One could spend life after life learning music and never learn it all. Yet they all blame you for not being able to play every piece that they wish to hear."

Charyn nodded. "I don't think I want to talk about it tonight." He massaged his forehead with his left hand, trying to work away some of the tightness.

"We don't have to. I just wanted you to know that even poor musicians must deal with stupid people."

Charyn took another sip of the brandy, but just a sip, knowing that too much would leave him with an even worse headache in the morning.

When Charyn woke up early on Lundi, his headache was gone . . . and so was Palenya. Had he said something in his sleep to upset her? Or had she not slept well? He climbed out of bed and went to the window, pulling aside the window hangings. He had to scrape the frost off the glass to see out into a gray morning where the sun had yet to rise. From what he could tell, the wind had stopped blowing, and the sky was cloudless. The chill off the glass suggested that it was even colder outside than it had been the night before.

He let the hangings fall back across the window, then turned and just stood there, thinking about all the things he had yet to do . . . and that didn't include whatever he hadn't thought of and should have.

He washed, shaved, and dressed, then made his way down to the breakfast room. As seemed to be usual, he was the only one there, and he ate quickly. After finishing, he walked to Norstan's study.

The seneschal bolted up from behind his desk. "Yes, sir?"

"Who has asked for an audience . . . or time with me?"

"I don't know that it's a request. Chorister Saerlet wishes to speak to you about the memorial service."

"I'll see him at eighth glass tomorrow."

"He had hoped . . ."

"At the moment, I'm not going out of the chateau to meet anyone. You can tell him that my father has been assassinated and all of us have been shot at, my brother twice. I'm more than happy to speak with him, but it will be here."

"Yes, sir."

"Anyone else?"

"No, sir. Not yet."

Charyn understood exactly what Norstan had not said. Once word spread that there was a new rex, after a time, there would be a flood of people wanting to meet with him, for various reasons, few of which were likely to be in Charyn's best interests . . . or in the best interests of Solidar as a whole.

After he left Norstan's small study, Charyn immediately went up the circular staircase to the rex's study, where he sat down and wrote out a missive to Marshal Vaelln. He managed to draft it with enough care that a second copy was not necessary. He read it over, slowly, twice.

Commander—

I would greatly appreciate your presence at the Chateau D'Rex on Jeudi, the fifth of Ianus at the first glass of the afternoon so that you can inform me of the immediate requirements of the Army and the Navy and so that we can discuss arrangements for the memorial service honoring Rex Lorien, which will take place at the Anomen R'Rex on Samedi, the seventh of Ianus, at the first glass of the afternoon.

Then he signed and sealed it before sending for Churwyl, only to be informed that the guard captain had not yet returned to the chateau after having left at seventh glass that morning. So Charyn walked to Alucar's study, where he knocked, but did not wait before entering.

"Good morning, Minister Alucar." Charyn did not seat himself.

"Am I still minister?" asked Alucar genially as he stood.

"If you wish. Until I decide otherwise."

"Then what can I do for you, Your Grace?"

"Tell me what you think I should do . . . or should not do . . . and why."

"Telling a rex what he cannot do is generally not a wise thing to do, sir."

"Failing to tell me what I should avoid doing, in your judgment, may be even less wise." Charyn tried to keep his voice level.

"Do not make any hasty decisions. You may know what you wish to do in various matters, but do not hurry at the moment, except where you truly have no choice. If others press you for a decision, tell them you are new to being rex, and a bad decision will harm you and them, because if a bad decision pressed on you by another harms you, you will in turn see that it harms the person who insisted on a hurried decision."

"That makes sense. What else?"

"Few things are as urgent as most people claim. The larger the amount of golds required for something, the less you should hurry in deciding whether it should be done."

"Does that include shipbuilding?" asked Charyn dryly.

"I believe that matter has been discussed for some time. I imagine you've had sufficient time to draw your own conclusions."

"Marshal Vaelln told my father that there were not enough shipyards or shipwrights to increase the number of warships being built by very much. What is your view on that?"

"The marshal is likely correct. That isn't the question you should ask. The question is what it will cost to create or expand a shipyard capable of producing the number of ships that will be required for the foreseeable future. You will need to choose between paying someone else to do that or doing it yourself."

Charyn frowned.

"At any one time," Alucar went on, "there will be only a little additional capacity in any goods produced because capacity costs golds. Factors—or shipwrights—don't want to pay for capacity that cannot be used. You don't want to pay extra guards, or extra cooks if there's no need for them. So it will always be expensive to build just a few more ships. Yet building an entire shipyard is very costly. Still . . . if one plans to build fifty ships in ten years, it may well be cheaper to build a shipyard and train your own workforce than to use the existing shipyards."

"Can you determine which might be better?"

Alucar laughed. "I can give you a good estimate . . . if you can tell me how many ships, of what kind and size, and how soon you want them. It will be better than a guess, and it will still likely cost more than I will calculate . . . and it will take time even to make that estimate."

Then why even make an estimate. Charyn didn't voice that question.

He might as well have because Alucar went on. "All estimates on anything are suspect, but they are better than deciding to do something merely because one feels it should be done. If the estimate is done correctly, it will give you more information and a better base for a decision."

"I hope to be meeting with Marshal Vaelln on Jeudi. After that, we will talk again about building ships. Is there anything else I should know?"

"There will likely be floods in the area of the barge piers on West River Road this spring, unless the river walls there are raised. They will be worse than the floods last year."

"Why is that?"

"Your predecessor chose not to have the river walls repaired and raised."

"Because there were not enough golds in the treasury?"

"He did not tell me. The river does not trouble itself with whether there are golds or not. If the walls are high enough and strong enough, it does not flood. If they are not, it does."

"I will keep that in mind." Charyn paused. "Isn't there a proposal on . . . my desk?"

"There is. Minister Aevidyr submitted it some time ago."

"I'll have to look at it in more depth. Thank you."

After he left Alucar, he made his way to find Malyna, who was in the music room, watching as Palenya instructed Aloryana. Charyn didn't even have to motion to Malyna, who quietly walked to join him.

Charyn guided Malyna outside the music room into the empty corridor, then said, keeping his voice low, "What time would be best to arrive at the Collegium?"

"I don't think anyone expects you to meet their convenience, sir."

"Perhaps not, but I'd prefer Aloryana's arrival to be less inconvenient, rather than more."

"A quint before noon would be best, I think. That way, Alyna won't have to cancel instructionals, and the Maitre should also be free."

"Can we drive the coach directly to the Maitre's dwelling?"

"You can. That was what the Maitre suggested. Would you prefer a Collegium coach?"

"I thought we'd take the plain coach from here, but have your imagers wear grays instead of Chateau Guard uniforms. They can use mounts from the stable. We'll take an extra guard, but they'll wear brown coats and ride the rear of the coach to Imagisle."

Malyna nodded.

"Can you make the necessary arrangements with your imagers and arrange it so that they won't tell anyone?"

"I can do that."

"Will you also tell Aloryana and my mother the arrangements?"

"Of course."

"Thank you. I do appreciate it." Charyn offered a warm and thankful smile. At least, he hoped it was. Then he headed back to the upper level of the chateau.

A nervous-looking Churwyl was waiting outside the study when Charyn returned and motioned for the guard captain to enter before him. Charyn walked to the desk and turned, but did not seat himself.

"What did you find out from Factor Goerynd?"

"Ah . . ."

"What is it?"

"Young Factor Goerdyl took over his father's factorage at the beginning of Finitas, upon the death of his father. He has no knowledge of either Bolomyrt or Chastant."

"Did they work for him at all?"

"He does not know. Apparently, the elder Goerynd engaged in . . . other activities . . ."

"Such as?"

"No one will say. There are rumors . . ."

"What sort of rumors?" Charyn tried to keep his voice level, despite his exasperation.

"He might have been involved with the assassins' guild."

"So . . . you took the word of someone who had been hired as an assassin?"

"No, sir. I took the word of the commander of the Civic Patrol. That seemed a good reference to me."

Charyn did not say anything for several moments. "I can see that it might seem that way. From now on, I'd like to know more about new guards. And try and find out more from the young Factor Goerdyl."

"Yes, sir."

"There's one other thing, Guard Captain." Charyn lifted the sealed message from the desk. "Please have this delivered to Marshal Vaelln."

"Yes, sir." Churwyl inclined his head, then turned and left the study.

Charyn could tell he was less than pleased.

Why was it that there was so much about which he knew nothing? Things he likely should have. He'd come to realize that there was too little he knew about, but he'd thought he'd have more time. Was there even an assassins' guild? Or was its existence only in shadowy rumors that could never be proven?

After pacing up and down in the study, he left in search of Palenya, although finding her was not difficult, since she was still in the music room, seated at the clavecin, but not playing.

"Why did you leave so early this morning?"

"I felt unwell, and unable to sleep. I didn't want to disturb you."

"How are you feeling now?"

"Better. I had tea in the kitchen."

"Do you know why you don't feel well?"

"Yes."

"Oh . . . the time of month."

"It's always just before."

Charyn nodded. "I'm sorry." He didn't know what else to say.

"Some things just are."

"Have you ever heard of an assassins' guild?"

Palenya offered a puzzled frown.

"Someone mentioned it. I just wondered."

"It was said that the great musician Heldryk fled L'Excelsis because . . . because he had become the lover of a wealthy factor's wife, and the man had declared that if he did not leave, he would set the assassins on Heldryk." Palenya shrugged. "I don't know if that is true. But that is what I heard."

"Did you ever hear anything else about assassins?"

"Besides that? No."

"How was your lesson with Aloryana?"

"She seemed happier."

"That's good." Charyn paused. "Why don't you go rest . . . No. I'll make it a regial command." He grinned. "Go rest."

Palenya smiled back. "I wouldn't disobey that command."

Charyn slipped out of the music room and headed up to the study. He needed to dig out Alucar's report or proposal to deal with river flooding . . . and try to read through more of the reports he'd stacked so neatly on the desk.

25

By seventh glass on Mardi morning, in addition to having a quick breakfast, Charyn had arranged for the plain coach to be ready at a quint before ninth glass and for Yarselt and one other guard to accompany it—wearing the nondescript coats they had used in accompanying him to the exchange. He'd also met with Norstan and Malyna, and made certain with his mother that Aloryana would be ready before ninth glass.

Then he settled into the study and dug out Aevidyr's proposal dealing with the river walls near the barge piers. After studying it, he could see why his father had deferred it, given the estimated cost of nearly four thousand golds, and that was for the bare minimum. He read an older proposal from the regional governor Voralch in Solis requesting eight thousand golds to rebuild roads in Solis, Nacliano, and Estisle, and then placed that in the pile of requests to be deferred for more thought.

Then came a legal petition by a Factorius Aquillyt from Ouestan dealing with the diversion of stream waters that left his mill without enough water flow to operate. The factor claimed that his family had established rights to the water prior to the rights of the upstream user, a High Holder Eskobyl, but the regional governor had denied his appeal on the grounds that High Holders always had seniority over others. Sanafryt's attached opinion noted that such seniority did not exist under the Codex, and had never been established in precedent in the lands that had once been Khel, but that the precedent had unfortunately been established in old Telaryn. Sanafryt's attachment did recommend a clarification through a change to the Codex Legis, but not what that clarification should be, although the use of the word "unfortunate" did hint that Sanafryt would favor a provision that stated that the seniority of water rights would always be based on the date of initial claims or usage, and not upon any other basis.

Another act that will anger someone, no matter what you do.

Charyn was still considering that when Sturdyn announced, "Chorister Saerlet is here, sir."

"Have him come in." Charyn stood and studied Saerlet as the chorister walked toward the desk.

The chorister was neither slender nor corpulent, but a round face suggested he was not particularly muscular, and his dark black hair glistened as if kept in place by oils or wax. His jacket, trousers, and shirt were all the same shade of dark gray, and around his jacket collar was the black and white chorister's scarf that did not quite reach his belt. He stopped short of the chairs before the desk and inclined his head, saying, "Rex Charyn." His voice was warm, but somehow just a trace sycophantic.

"Chorister Saerlet." Charyn smiled and gestured to the chairs, then seated himself behind the goldenwood desk.

"I am sorry to be here on such a less than pleasant matter as the memorial service of a rex who died far too young." Saerlet offered a sympathetic smile.

Charyn thought the expression was well-practiced, although that was a guess on his part. "His assassination was not something any of us expected."

"I thought we should discuss the memorial service, just so that you could review the normal order of the service, and decide if that is appropriate . . . or if you would like any changes, additions, or omissions." Another smile followed Saerlet's words. "It would, of course, have been somewhat easier if you had been able to come to the anomen where I could have shown you as well as told you."

Easier for you. "With your experience, Chorister Saerlet, I am most certain you will be able to accommodate any modest changes we may have." Charyn nodded. "Please go on."

"Yes, sir. We will be following the normal order of a memorial service . . ." Saerlet paused. "Except your mother has requested that the confession be omitted. This is not usual . . . but I assume . . ."

His mother had wanted the confession removed? Charyn certainly had no objections to that, but it was interesting that Saerlet had brought it up. "That would have been my father's wish as well. Go on."

"The other change is that she wished the hymn after the charge to the congregation to be 'In Vain a Crown of Gold,' rather than 'In the Footsteps of the Nameless.'"

The hymn change was definitely appropriate, although Charyn had no idea whether his father would have wanted that. "That's the way it will be."

"You, of course, will speak after that."

"There will be one other change. I don't know if my mother mentioned it. The regial party will be standing behind the pulpit from the beginning, and it will include Maitre Alastar and the Senior Imager of the Collegium."

"That is quite a departure."

"I assure you that it is quite necessary." As Charyn saw the confusion or reluctance on Saerlet's face, he added, "Given the continual physical attacks on the regial family."

"I would think, in the very anomen . . ."

"My father was nearly assassinated in that very anomen. You may find it sacred, Chorister, but it is very clear that others do not."

"I find it hard to believe . . ."

"There will be no discussion of that point," Charyn said firmly.

"I can see that."

"Are there any other matters you wish to discuss?"

"Once you are more settled into your duties, sir, perhaps we could talk at greater length."

"Perhaps we should," agreed Charyn amiably, rising from behind the desk. "We will see you a quint or so before first glass on Samedi."

"I look forward to hearing what you have to say."

So do I.

As soon as Saerlet had been gone long enough to be out of the chateau, Charyn left the study, then ducked back to his own rooms for a heavy jacket and gloves and made his way down to the main level to see if the unadorned coach was ready. From the rear doorway, he could see both imagers, in their grays and mounted, flanking the coach. Yarselt and Kynon stood waiting beside the coach, both in the brown coats that concealed their Chateau Guard uniforms and with plain brown visor caps.

At the sound of steps, Charyn turned to see Malyna and Aloryana walking from the foot of the grand staircase toward him.

He waited until the two were only a few yards away before speaking. "You said good-bye to Mother?"

"Upstairs." Aloryana's eyes were bright, but not bloodshot.

"Her clothes?" Charyn asked Malyna.

"Those she can wear at the Collegium are already packed in the case under the rear boot of the coach. Kaylet has kept watch over them."

"Thank you."

Charyn gestured toward the courtyard door. "We should go. There's no point in waiting."

The guard at the door opened it as Aloryana approached, and a frigid gust of wind swept over the three as they stepped out and down the stone steps to the courtyard. Featureless gray clouds covered what parts of the sky Charyn could see. Once in the coach, Malyna positioned herself and Aloryana on the rear-facing seat, leaving the front-facing seat to Charyn.

"So you can see behind us?" he asked.

The maitre nodded.

In moments, the coach eased forward and then headed down the stone-paved drive to the ring road. Before long, they were on the Avenue D'Rex Ryen, heading east.

"How do you feel?" Charyn asked.

"Excited . . . a little scared . . . a little sad." Aloryana turned to Malyna. "How did you feel?"

"Much like you do."

Sitting in the coach and looking at Malyna, Charyn was again struck by Malyna's composure and her youth. She was only three years older than Bhayrn, and yet, within instants of his father's shooting, she had killed one man, immobilized another, and shielded four others . . . and then apologized for being unable to immobilize the other assassin.

"Will I wear grays like yours?" asked Aloryana.

"All imagers wear gray, from the day they arrive." Malyna smiled. "The only time I haven't was at the chateau. I don't know of another time when imagers haven't worn grays."

Charyn glanced out of the coach as they passed the Anomen D'Rex, where on Samedi, he would have to speak about his father . . . and he still really hadn't thought about what he would say.

Before long, the coach was on the West River Road and turning onto the approach lane to the bridge over the western channel of the River Aluse, the bridge that led to Imagisle, all of which belonged to the Collegium Imago.

"Did you first come to the Collegium this way?" asked Aloryana.

"No. I came down the East River Road to the east bridge."

Charyn watched as the coach crossed the gray-blue waters of the river and then passed a stone sentry box at the eastern end. "A sentry post?"

"They were created at the time of the last High Holder revolt. The

High Holders' brownshirts were shooting at student imagers from hidden places."

"Did they kill any?"

"Yes. They did. They used poisoned bullets."

That was something Charyn hadn't heard. "Did the Collegium find out who was behind it?"

"Several High Holders were found to be quartering or supporting the brownshirts. Almost all of them died in some fashion or another."

That didn't surprise Charyn. He turned his attention to studying the grounds and buildings the coach passed. To the south, he could see an anomen, built of stone and brick unlike the other buildings, all of which seemed to be constructed of perfectly cut gray stone. All the streets or roads appeared to be paved with gray stone.

"The large building on the right," said Malyna as she pointed, "is the administration building. That's where the senior maitres have studies, and where most of the rooms used for instructionals are. There's a small library as well, and the archives. Aunt Alyna designed it, and she did most of the imaging to build it."

Charyn took a good look at the structure, which was a good two stories in height and looked to be almost a hundred yards long and perhaps thirty wide. *One woman imager did that?*

The coach turned up a stone-paved boulevard, its center a park-like expanse. On each side were neat dwellings, seemingly similar, if not identical, except for the colors of their doors and shutters, each constructed of gray brick or brick-sized cut stones, with a slate tile roof. The brass-bound and oiled oak doors were set in the middle of wide covered front porches.

"These are the cottages for married maitres. Unmarried maitres share cottages. I live with two other women."

The coach slowed and then came to a stop outside an imposing two-story dwelling with walls of gray granite. It extended a good forty yards across the front and was completely surrounded by a covered porch. Broad stone steps led up to the stone-tiled porch, supported by stone pillars. Wide windows graced both floors, and the brass-bound double front doors held small etched glass windows. The shutters and window trim were painted a luminous light greenish brown.

As Aloryana and Malyna got out of the coach, and Charyn followed, he could see Maitre Alastar and Maitre Alyna standing on the front porch, along with a third figure, a young woman also in imager grays who was almost as tall as Maitre Alastar.

"Welcome to the Collegium, Aloryana," offered Alyna warmly, adding as she nodded to the young woman beside her, "This is our daughter Lystara. Lystara, this is Aloryana, and the distinguished man beside her is Rex Charyn, who has brought his sister here and is making his first visit to Imagisle."

Lystara inclined her head. "Rex Charyn, welcome." Then she smiled at Aloryana. "I hope you like it here."

"I'm sure I will."

"All of you, please come in," said Alyna.

Malyna hung back slightly and looked to Charyn. "There's one thing I forgot to mention. Young as she is, Lystara is already a junior maitre. If she weren't so young, she might already be a Maitre D'Structure."

"She's more powerful than you are?" asked Charyn in a low voice.

"Not that much more, right now, but it's likely, if she works, that she could be a Maitre D'Esprit, or even a Maitre D'Image like Uncle Alastar and Aunt Alyna."

"Are there any imagers that aren't powerful?" Charyn tried to sound wry.

"Many. There are quite a few that can only image small objects."

Charyn looked toward the rear of the coach, where the two imagers were unstrapping the case that held the clothes and belongings Aloryana had chosen to bring, according to Malyna's instructions. Then he walked with Malyna up onto the porch and into the modest foyer.

As Charyn entered the Maitre's house, he was struck by the solidity of the structure, a solidity that reminded him of the Chateau D'Rex . . . except that the Maitre's house seemed more welcoming.

"Lystara will show you your room, Aloryana, and the rest of us will be in the parlor."

No sooner than had Charyn and Malyna entered the parlor with Alastar and Alyna than Alyna turned to Charyn. "Rex Charyn, if it is to your approval, it might be best if Alastar showed you the Collegium while Malyna, Lystara, and I help Aloryana get settled. Then you could return here and say your farewells." She smiled. "She's fortunate to have family close. Most imagers do not."

Knowing that Alyna's words were really not a suggestion, Charyn replied, "That would seem to be for the best." He turned to Alastar. "Shall we begin?"

Alastar nodded. "We'll walk. It's not that far, and if we get cold, there are plenty of places where we can duck inside and warm up."

As he followed the Maitre from the parlor into the foyer and out into the chill gray day, Charyn was glad he'd decided on a heavy coat and gloves.

Once they walked past the coach, Alastar gestured southward. "All of the cottages immediately facing the green and boulevard and the Maitre's dwelling were imaged into being by the very first imagers. Those on the lanes behind them were added later, as it became necessary. The large gray building ahead is the administration building."

"Malyna said that it was designed and largely imaged by your wife."

"That's true. She is far more accomplished in those matters." The Maitre pointed. "The low gray building—not that they're not all gray— is the surgery and infirmary, and the one to the south of it is the student dining hall, although maitres and single imagers can eat there as well."

Charyn nodded.

"The buildings west of the green area behind the administration building are the student quarters."

"How many students do you have?"

"At the moment, there are about a hundred and ninety here. Ten of them aren't imagers, but are the children of imagers. There are roughly a hundred imagers who aren't students, but only thirty who are maitres. Most of those are Maitres D'Aspect. That's the most junior maitre."

"Malyna said your daughter is a maitre."

"She is. That has proved to be a challenge. She's the youngest woman ever to become a maitre, and less than a handful of men have become maitres that young. Having that much ability that young is extremely dangerous."

"Then she's possibly even more capable than that?"

Alastar did not answer for several moments, then said, "Let us just say that with slightly more maturity she will be a Maitre D'Structure, as will Malyna."

"I take it that kind of ability is rare?"

"Maitres of Structure and higher are considered senior maitres. There are only thirteen in all of Solidar."

"You mentioned that there are almost two hundred students here. Are there others elsewhere?"

"There are about forty students at the branch of the Collegium in

Westisle. At least there were last month. There are perhaps ten in Estisle as well, but Maitre Taurek has only been there a little less than three years. It will be a while before he has created enough buildings and facilities for more students and imagers there."

When they reached the front of the administration building, Alastar said, "We'll come back here, and you can see how it's set up inside. I thought we'd go on to the stables, the forges, and the factorage from here, then circle back around the anomen and the student quarters."

"I defer to you, Maitre. All this is new to me."

By the time Charyn and Alastar finished the walking tour, close to three quints later, and entered the administration building, Charyn was shivering, despite the gloves and heavy coat.

"You look like you could use something hot. Tea?"

"Just being in a warm place will do, I think."

"We'll go to my study, and you can ask any questions the tour has brought up, as well as any others."

Once inside the building, Alastar and Charyn walked a short way southward along a wide corridor before turning in to a large anteroom, where several armless wooden chairs were set against the wall. An older man in gray sat at a table desk set outside the open door into what appeared to be a large study.

"Maercyl, Rex Charyn and I are not to be disturbed, unless the matter is extraordinarily urgent."

"Yes, Maitre."

Charyn didn't see any sign of surprise on the part of the older imager at the table desk.

Alastar gestured for Charyn to enter the study, then followed and closed the door. Rather than sit behind the desk, he took one of the chairs in front of the desk. Charyn took another, turning it slightly to face the Maitre.

"The side door there leads to the conference room where the senior imagers meet, usually once a week, unless something unforeseen comes up." Alastar paused. "Have you any questions?"

"A few. I'm not certain where to start, however."

"Anywhere you like."

"Are there really only four hundred imagers in all of Solidar?"

"There are probably a few more, but they're likely the ones who can only image a few small things. You should remember that, out of that four hundred, less than one in ten can do what Malyna did. There were only fifteen imagers involved in the battle that ended the High Holder revolt, and those fifteen were almost all of those who could protect themselves against bullets. There might be a few more today, but powerful imagers are very rare."

"Why did you offer protection to my father?"

"We felt that no one should get in the habit of shooting at rulers, or High Councilors, or factor councilors, for that matter. Also, we failed to make that offer during the revolt, and it cost us dearly."

"I wasn't aware that anyone had shot at the regial family."

"A threat was made, which we failed to recognize. You can ask your mother for details, if you wish."

And if she'll reveal what it was. "How strong an imager is Aloryana?"

"We don't know. She's had no training, and we have not yet tested her. The fact that she can image metals and re-form jewelry suggests she could be a maitre. How strong a maitre and how long it will take her to reach her full abilities are another question."

"Will she be safe here?"

"No one is absolutely safe anywhere. It's more than fair to say that she will be far safer here than in the Chateau D'Rex."

"You seem rather sure of that, Maitre."

"You don't think that those behind your father's assassination will just disappear, do you?" asked Alastar.

"No, Maitre, I don't. At the same time, the ease with which they killed my father suggests that there's very little that can be done to stop an assassin who does not mind dying to kill someone."

"At the Chateau D'Rex, that is true. Here on Imagisle there are thirty maitres, and she will be living with three."

Charyn couldn't dispute that.

"As for you, the repetition of such an occurrence might be made much more difficult. Do you have a personal secretary?"

For a moment, Charyn was taken off-guard. "A personal secretary? Someone to draft messages and the like? No. I'd never thought . . . You're not suggesting an imager in that position?"

"I am. At least for a time. There is a young imager maitre who has very strong shields, good reactions, pleasant manners, and a very good hand. He is also quite bright, and might well benefit from some time in the Chateau D'Rex."

"He'd also know everything that happens," replied Charyn dryly. "If he is truly to be my personal secretary."

"True, but would that be so bad at present? Your ministers already know. Are we any less interested in your welfare than they are?"

Charyn almost protested, but then held his tongue, considering that the Maitre just might be right on that account. "How do we arrange this?"

"Howal D'Ryter will arrive for an appointment to visit you about the position tomorrow or the next day. If you find him satisfactory, you offer him the position and quarters somewhere in the chateau, since he needs to be at your beck and call . . ."

Charyn listened as Alastar explained. Although he had some misgivings, he didn't want to make the same mistake that his father had.

It was well after third glass before Charyn was in the coach headed back to the Chateau D'Rex, accompanied by the two imagers and having said his good-bye to Aloryana, who seemed almost relieved to be at the Collegium.

How long has she known she was an imager?

Charyn had the feeling it had been months, if not longer.

Once he returned to the chateau, he immediately made his way to his mother's sitting room, entering and closing the door.

"How is she?" asked Chelia from her armchair, setting aside the history she had been reading.

"She seems to be fine. She has a room to herself, just one chamber, but it is quite spacious, almost the size of her sitting room, and the Maitres' daughter, Lystara, appears quite welcoming."

"The daughter, she is an imager?"

"According to Malyna, Lystara is already a junior maitre and is more powerful than Malyna."

"Good."

Charyn frowned.

"Aloryana will be safe, and she will find out quickly that she must work if she is to be successful."

Charyn nodded. After a long silence, he finally said, "I hate to ask this, but . . . did Father ever tell you if he talked to Ryel at the ball . . . and what he might have said about his request to leave the High Council?"

"He did talk to him. I asked him what he said. He told me we'd talk about it later. He didn't seem as though it had been either particularly pleasant or unpleasant."

That could mean anything. Charyn had been hoping, but there wasn't anything more to be said about it to his mother. "I'm also going to be taking on a personal secretary . . ."

Charyn settled into the chair across from his mother. He needed to explain . . . and to hear her reactions, and doing both would take some time.

26

The first thing Charyn did after breakfast on Meredi was to seek out Norstan, who was, as he should have been, in his small study. The seneschal stood the moment he saw Charyn. "Sir."

"Do I have any callers today?"

"None that you have approved. There are several who have requested an audience."

"Who are they?" asked Charyn cautiously.

"One is Hisario D'Factorius."

"The Factor Hisario? The shipping factor from Liantiago who is on the Solidaran Factors' Council?"

"The very same one, sir. Your sire refused to meet with him privately."

"Did he say why?"

"No, sir."

That was a stupid question. Father almost never explained himself to anyone outside the family. And seldom enough to family, Charyn knew all too well. "Let me think about that. Who else?"

"Argentyl. He claims to be a master silversmith, and head of the Metalworkers' Guild."

"Did he give a reason?"

"He claimed that he represented all the guilds in L'Excelsis."

"He just might," mused Charyn. "Grant him an appointment at eighth glass tomorrow morning."

"Yes, sir."

Charyn ignored the veiled disapproval in Norstan's voice. "And I might as well see Factor Hisario at ninth glass." After a pause, he added, "There is one other matter. A young man by the name of Howal D'Ryter will be calling on me. I'll see him whenever he arrives."

Norstan frowned slightly.

"He comes highly recommended, and I find I may need his talents."

"I have not seen any such commendations."

"I don't believe you have, Norstan, but I'll see him in any case."

"Yes, sir. There is one other matter, sir."

Charyn nodded.

"A rather large number of missives addressed to you have arrived. I took the liberty of placing them on the desk in your study. The ones addressed to Lady Chelia went to her study."

"Messages of condolence, most likely."

"I could not say, sir."

"Thank you."

"One other matter, Norstan. I haven't seen any newssheets, either *Tableta* or *Veritum*."

"Yes, sir. I'll look into it."

After leaving Norstan's study, Charyn saw Vaetor in the entry hall.

"Has Minister Alucar arrived yet?"

"I don't believe he has."

"Please check and see if he has. If he's here, I'd like to see him in the study. If not, I'd like to see him when he arrives."

"Yes, sir."

Charyn used the grand staircase to get to the study, where he continued his efforts to sort through the stacks of papers by putting the unopened envelopes in a new pile, and then opening each and reading it quickly. He had been right. All of the more than twenty were in fact missives of sympathy and condolence.

Less than a quint later, Alucar arrived, and Charyn motioned for him to take one of the chairs.

"I had thought you might need my services earlier, sir," offered the minister as he seated himself.

"I probably did, except it's taken a while to sort through various matters. On Solayi, you asked if there had been more threatening missives. So far there have not been. Now . . . we had also discussed tariffs . . . and possible shortfalls. You only offered general figures. I assume you calculated what tariff increases would be required for the projects you and Aevidyr proposed . . . and for increasing the numbers of warships to be built?"

"Your sire forbade me to present any figures."

"So you did the calculations and kept them until he asked for them . . . if he did?"

"There are rough figures," Alucar said carefully.

"Good . . . I need to know what building ten more warships a year would cost, plus all roads and river walls you two feel are absolutely necessary and anything else. Then figure out what that would require in tariffs. That is, how much of an increase would be necessary."

"You're not going to . . . after everything . . . in a single year, Your Grace?"

"No. I'm not." That wasn't quite true. "But I need to know what they all are likely to cost. Ignoring the costs isn't going to make the problems go away. At least, it hasn't so far. And if I'm going to appear even half-way intelligent when I meet with both councils, I need to know just what we're talking about."

"Do you want the total increase?"

"I want to know what the increase will be for each ship. How much will the first extra ship of the line cost each High Holder, and whatever it's likely to cost the average factor. How much will the river walls here in L'Excelsis cost, the improved roads and streets in Estisle and Nacliano. Then you can do a total."

"The numbers will only be estimates."

"I know that. Everything will cost more than the estimates, but we have to start somewhere."

"This will take several days . . ."

"I'll need the best figures you and your clerks can work out by Lundi the sixteenth." Charyn paused. "It also might help to be able to present those figures in terms of how much the increase would be in terms of coppers on the golds of their existing tariffs."

Alucar nodded. "For some, such a comparison will be more useful, especially for the factors."

"And add any other figures you think might prove useful."

"Numbers can be useful, but they can also be useful to those who oppose you."

Charyn smiled. "They already have their numbers."

Alucar actually smiled in return. "I'll see what we can do." He inclined his head. "By your leave?"

"Go do your best."

No sooner than Alucar had left, Bhayrn strode into the study.

"You're quite the portrait of the studious and hardworking rex. With all your concerns, I thought you might have forgotten that you have a brother . . . since I haven't seen you in days."

Because you sleep late and avoid me the rest of the time. Charyn wasn't about to say that. "There have been a few matters to deal with."

"I have a very minor one. Now that you are rex, might I be able to go riding again?"

"If you want to die well before your time, I'd recommend going riding immediately."

"They've already killed Father. What else can they do?"

"Kill you and kill me." Charyn shook his head. "Have you already forgotten? Both the assassins were shooting at all of us. If Maitre Malyna hadn't shielded us, we'd likely both be dead."

"You're rex now. Don't coddle the bastards. Send the army after them and shoot them all down."

"Shoot whom? You tell me who hired the men who killed Father, and I'll be happy to oblige you."

"All the factors, of course."

Is he serious? "There are thousands of them. Where do you suggest I begin?"

"With the ones who shot at me and killed Father." Abruptly, Bhayrn laughed. "I love it when you get so serious you don't see I'm twisting your thumbs."

Charyn decided to say nothing and see what his brother would come up with next.

"Father agreed to build more ships. You aren't going to change that decision, are you?"

"Father agreed to build one or two more ships. There aren't enough golds to build more than that this year."

"So what's the problem? You aren't going to change what he said, are you?"

"That might not be the wisest course."

"You haven't gotten any more of those messages, have you?"

"That means nothing. It's only been four days."

"You still have two imagers here."

"They're barely sufficient to protect the chateau, and I can't very well send one of them to protect you so that you can ride as you please."

"You go where you want."

"In a closed coach . . . and with guards. The only place I've been since Father was killed was to take Aloryana to Imagisle."

"How long am I supposed to be walled up in the chateau?"

"I'm not walling you up. If you want to ride around and take the chance of getting yourself killed, go ahead. Personally, I'd suggest not trying that, at least not until after Father's memorial service. Possibly until after I meet with the High Council and the Factors' Council of Solidar."

"You're some help."

"I've persuaded the Maitre of the Collegium to keep providing imagers to help stop more assassins. I'm doing my best to figure out how to get us out of this mess. If you have some specific suggestions, I'll listen. If not, I need to get back to unscrambling everything." Charyn looked levelly at his younger brother.

After several moments, Bhayrn finally said, "I'll think about it." Then he turned and left the study.

For the next glass, Charyn went through the petitions, jotting down a few notes on each and putting those on top of each petition, so that he could go over each quickly with Sanafryt. He was about to send for the Minister of Justice when someone knocked on the study door.

"Yes?"

"Howal D'Ryter to see you, as you requested, sir." The voice was that of Norstan.

Charyn smiled. Did Norstan think he was looking for a successor to the seneschal?

You'll need to make it clear that you're not. "Have him come in."

The door opened, and the imager walked in, wearing gray trousers, a white shirt, and a black jacket. Howal was of middling height, possibly a digit or two shorter than Charyn himself, and likely a few years older. He was muscular, but not stocky, and his light brown hair was short and neatly trimmed, unsurprisingly, given that seemed the requirement for male imagers. His eyes were pale green and met Charyn's, even as he inclined his head. "Your Grace." He straightened and handed a sealed missive to Charyn.

Charyn took it, then used the letter knife to cut under the seal and open the envelope. Two single sheets were inside. The first simply read:

Charyn,
Howal seems very nice. Be kind to him.

The signature was "Ryana," which was what Bhayrn had called Aloryana for years, until she had forcefully insisted he stop.

The second sheet, from Alastar, was a more standard communication, stating that Howal should be a good fit as a personal secretary, as well as for other duties, "as previously discussed," and giving a physical description. The description matched the young man in front of Charyn.

"Before we begin," said Charyn as he set the letter from Alastar on the desk, "might you be able to provide a small and quiet demonstration of those other abilities?"

"Of course, sir. I believe you must have dropped this, sir," added Howal, as a duplicate of the letter knife appeared from nowhere in the imager's other hand, except that the duplicate was a miniature less than a third the size of the one on the desk. Howal reversed the knife and extended it to Charyn hilt-first.

Charyn reached for it, except his fingers hit an invisible barrier just short of the missive.

"Very impressive, and neatly done," murmured Charyn, adding in a louder voice, "Thank you." Since the barrier seemed to have vanished, he took the second letter knife and set it on the desk beside the first, and then took Alastar's letter and slipped it and Aloryana's note back into the envelope. "As for addressing me, 'sir' will do," replied Charyn, gesturing toward the chairs in front of the desk and seating himself. He waited until Howal was settled before continuing. "I know your current location and occupation, but what I don't know is where you grew up and similar matters."

"Yes, sir. I grew up in Ferravyl. My father is a factor who builds lamps of all types. He was the first to build a lantern that could be used safely in the mines. He even developed wicks for different kinds of oils." Howal offered a crooked smile. "I did not have those talents, but I loved numbers and writing. So I drafted bills of sale from an early age. I wrote his letters and proposals, and I kept the ledgers . . . until I came to L'Excelsis, of course."

"You were fairly young, weren't you?"

"Eleven, sir."

Charyn gestured to the stacks of papers. "I'm going to need some help with these. If I gave you general directions for how I wanted to deal with each, could you provide a rough draft?"

"I believe so, sir."

"Excellent. Now, there is one other matter. You will need to remain fairly close to me, at least for a time, in order to have a better idea of how I approach things. We will arrange for quarters for you here in the chateau. You'll eat with the senior staff, such as Norstan and Churwyl, but, upon occasion, you also may be required to dine with the family."

Howal nodded.

"I think that the next thing should be to introduce you to my mother, and, of course, my bother Bhayrn, and then to Norstan, the chateau seneschal."

"As you see fit, sir. I did leave some clothes and gear with my mount."

"You can get them after we make the introductions." Charyn stood. "We'd best get started."

Surprisingly, Charyn did not find his mother in her sitting room, but in the music room, playing by herself. For several moments he listened at the doorway, as she finished the piece, something that was familiar, but that he could not name. He'd forgotten how often she had once played.

When she finished and looked up, he and Howal walked to the clavecin, where she had stood, but not moved away from the instrument.

"Mother, I'd like to introduce you to Howal D'Ryter," said Charyn, lowering his voice to add, "Maitre Howal, although you're the only person who knows that." He nodded to Chelia. "Howal will be serving as my personal secretary for a time."

"I'm very glad to meet you, and that you are here at this difficult time," replied Chelia. "I hope you will be able to help Charyn through the difficulties ahead."

"I will do my best, Lady Chelia." Howal bowed, just slightly.

"I'm certain you will. Those who come with your recommendations have always done well. Welcome to the Chateau D'Rex."

"Thank you. I'll do my best to live up to those recommendations."

"Have you seen Bhayrn in the last glass or so?" asked Charyn.

"I believe he's in the receiving parlor, waiting for Amascarl," replied Chelia.

"Thank you," said Charyn. "We'll start tracking him down there."

Bhayrn was indeed in the receiving parlor, pacing back and forth. A momentary expression of surprise crossed his face as Charyn and Howal appeared.

"Bhayrn, this is Howal D'Ryter. He will be acting as my personal secretary to help me get through the papers and everything for a time."

"I don't believe you mentioned a personal secretary," said Bhayrn before turning to Howal and saying, "I'm glad to meet you. My brother will need all the assistance he can muster in the months ahead."

"I am here to help in any way I can." Howal inclined his head.

"I'm sure you'll be of great assistance." Bhayrn smiled pleasantly, then turned to Charyn. "You don't plan on using the plaques room, do you?

Amascarl is bringing two friends so that I can improve my whist game. It appears I'll need to do something for a while."

"The plaques room is yours, except when Mother has her group."

"I checked with her already."

"Good," replied Charyn pleasantly. "I need to introduce Howal to Norstan and Churwyl." As he led Howal back out into the main entry foyer, he added, "Churwyl is the guard captain, and Norstan is the seneschal."

"Norstan and Churwyl," repeated Howal quietly.

Charyn found Norstan leaving the kitchens.

"Norstan, this is Howal D'Ryter. He's the man who will be helping me as a private secretary for at least a time so that I can deal with all the petitions and other papers that have piled up on my desk. Howal, this is Norstan. He is the chateau seneschal and the man who does his best, in spite of all of our efforts to the contrary, to make things run smoothly within the chateau."

"I'm pleased to meet you, Norstan," offered Howal.

"I'm glad that Rex Charyn could find a capable personal secretary. I trust you'll find the chateau to your liking."

"I think it will be a challenging position," returned Howal pleasantly, "and I look forward to working here."

"Norstan," said Charyn, "I'll need a few words with you after I introduce Howal to Guard Captain Churwyl."

"I'll be in my study, sir."

"Good."

Churwyl was in the alcove off the main entry foyer that held the duty desk for the chateau guards. As he saw Charyn approaching, he stepped out. "Sir."

"Guard Captain, this is Howal D'Ryter. He's my new personal secretary, and he'll have quarters here in the chateau. I've found that I'll be needing to do a great deal of work with petitions and other written materials. Howal, Guard Captain Churwyl has been in command of the chateau guards for the last ten years."

"I'm honored to meet you, Guard Captain," offered Howal, inclining his head politely and smiling cordially.

"Pleased to meet you, Secretary Howal."

"If you would pass the word, Churwyl."

"You can count on me to take care of that, sir."

As they left the duty desk, Charyn looked to Howal. "You'll need to get your gear. Just bring it to the study and wait, if I'm not there. I have a few matters to take care of." Then Charyn escorted Howal to the court-yard entry, and explained matters to the guard there before hurrying back to Norstan's study.

Norstan bolted up as Charyn entered. "Sir."

"I can tell you're concerned about Howal."

"Sir . . . is it wise . . ."

"Howal comes with the best recommendations any young man could possibly have. I wouldn't have it any other way. You've seen those stacks of papers in the study, haven't you?"

"Yes, sir."

"I've read through most of them, but almost all of them require some kind of written reply or opinion or decision. That's one of the many reasons why I decided I needed a personal secretary."

"Your sire . . ."

"We're very different, Norstan. You should know that by now. I do want to make one thing clear. I am *not* bringing in Howal to replace you. He has no knowledge of all the things you do. He does write well, and he writes quickly, and I am going to need that ability in dealing with the High Council and the Factors' Council of Solidar. I will also need that ability in dealing with the stack of unanswered petitions on the desk. He will not be here forever, but only so long as I need his services. I prevailed upon his present employer to lend him to me, but his future is else-where."

"Yes, sir."

Charyn thought he sensed relief in the seneschal's reply, but his ability to read mixed emotions had never been good, if better than that of his father. "Now, I want him quartered in the guest chamber two doors west of my chambers."

"The smaller ones, you mean?"

"That's right."

"I'll have the maids ready them immediately."

"Don't disrupt everything. Howal and I are going to be occupied going over papers, most likely ones pertaining to Minister Sanafryt, for a time this afternoon."

Norstan nodded. "By third glass, then?"

"That would be fine."

"We'll see to it, sir."

Charyn was back in his study before Howal returned. He smiled wryly as he observed a copy of a newssheet on the corner of his desk. He picked it up and discovered it was *Veritum*. He also found that the headline of the lead story read "Rex Lorien Killed." He kept reading.

> . . . Rex Lorien was shot inside the Chateau D'Rex just after the traditional Year-Turn Ball ended. Those close to the Chateau indicate the assassins wore the uniforms of Chateau Guards . . . Rumors running through L'Excelsis suggest the assassinations were the work of factors dissatisfied with the failure of Rex Lorien to deal with the ongoing plundering of Solidar merchant ships by Jariolan privateers . . .

Charyn continued to read, noting key phrases.

> . . . both assassins are dead. One died immediately, the other shortly thereafter. The causes of their deaths have not been revealed, but one was reported killed during the attack, and the other died shortly thereafter . . . first year that the members of the Factors' Council of Solidar were invited to a gala that has previously been limited to High Holders and the Maitre of the Collegium Imago . . .
>
> . . . the regial family included a distant relative, Malyna D'Zaerlyn, the youngest daughter of High Holder Zaerlyn, who was observed dancing with both Lord Charyn and Lord Bhayrn. Others close to the Chateau have suggested she is also Maitre Malyna, a junior master imager . . . and just what was she doing at the Ball, given that she is also the niece of the Collegium Maitre . . .

So all L'Excelsis knows that now . . . or will before very long.

> . . . Lord Charyn is now rex . . . remains to be seen how he will deal with the High Council and the tariff questions that bedeviled his sire . . .

How indeed?

Charyn scanned the rest of the newssheet and, finding nothing else of immediate interest, set it down, noting that his fingers were black in places. *Inferior ink.*

At that moment, Howal returned to the study, carrying a single bag that looked like a soldier's kit.

"Just put it beside the conference table. You can use one end for your desk. You'll have to move things on the few times when the councils meet here, but that's not very often." Charyn stood. "We'll walk down to Minister Sanafryt's study so that you know where it is, and then I'll show you where Minister Alucar's study is, and then Minister Aevidyr's."

Howal nodded.

When they reached the door to Sanafryt's study, Charyn opened it. When Sanafryt looked up from his desk, Charyn said, "This is Howal D'Ryter. He's my new personal secretary. Would you come up to the study in about a quint?"

Sanafryt nodded.

After that Charyn directed Howal to the studies of the other two ministers, introducing Howal, but not requesting them to see him later, before returning to the rex's study, where he gestured Howal to a chair before the desk and then sat down.

"I really am going to need your writing skills."

"That would be best, I think, for both of us."

"You won't be bored, or at least with little to do, and I'll be able to get more done."

"Might I ask why your sire did not have a personal secretary?"

"He had his ministers draft things, and then he rewrote them." *Sometimes.* "He didn't want anyone besides them, and himself, knowing what was in the various proposals. That included me. That's why I've spent much of the past four days reading through all these papers."

"You're not concerned that I might read them and pass on the information?"

"The one to whom you might pass such information probably ought to know most of it in any event. I'd appreciate it if that is as far as anything you might report goes." Charyn picked up the petition on the top of the papers he needed to discuss with Sanafryt. "While we wait for Sanafryt, you can read this."

Howal had finished reading when Sanafryt entered the study.

"You requested my presence."

"I did. I read through your opinion on the petition from Factorius Aquillyt in Ouestan. I gather that you feel that the best solution to the problem is to draft a change to the *Codex Legis?*"

"That might or might not be the best solution, sir. It is the only solution that will preclude more petitions such as Aquillyt's."

"Have there been others like his?"

"Not recently, but it is likely there will be more."

"Why?"

"Because the factors are becoming more and more prosperous, and they are going to be less and less willing to defer to the High Holders. They will have the time and the golds to offer more petitions."

"And if I side with the High Holders, that will generate more opposition from the factors?"

Sanafryt nodded.

"And if I side with the factors, that will generate even more petitions, and each will anger the High Holders?"

"That is how I would view it, Your Grace."

"Then I'd like you to draft the language to change the Codex Legis in a fashion to declare that the seniority, if that is the right term, of rights to streams or other surface waters is based solely on the initial time of use and appropriation, and that such rights follow the land. Those rights must be inseparable from the land—and cannot be transferred without the land. Should the land be split, the water rights are split in proportion to the size of each portion. Also, as of the date of the change, all water rights reside with the land."

"Do you want to tie the water rights absolutely to the land, sir?"

"Of course. Otherwise, we'll have High Holders and factors holding on to the water rights and charging the later landowners to use the water. That will create even more problems."

"Might I ask why you wish to address this in that fashion?"

"Because every other way I can think of will create more problems. Do you disagree?"

"I fear I do, sir. What you propose will anger both factors and High Holders."

"That's true. You just told me that this is the first petition on this in some time, but that there will be many more if I don't do something. I'd rather have all of them angry about something that hasn't happened, because most of them, except for High Holder Eskobyl, haven't actually lost any golds or rights so far, and Eskobyl hasn't lost anything, anyway. He's just trying to grab something that isn't truly his. They'll get over something that hasn't hurt them a lot sooner than over something that has." *You hope.*

"I'm not aware that High Holders ever get over anything, sir."

"You're likely right, but I'm far more worried about the factors. Now, let's talk about the next petition, the one about the High Justicer's judgment that High Holder Vrenean violated the limitations on low justice by imposing recurring times of confinement . . ."

Just from the momentary expression on Sanafryt's face, Charyn knew the remainder of the afternoon would be long . . . very long. But he wanted to deal with all the petitions as quickly as possible, for quite a number of reasons.

It was three quints past fourth glass when Sanafryt left the study, looking less than perfectly pleased.

Once the study door closed, Charyn looked to Howal. "In the future, I'll be telling you to write out the sort of thing I told Sanafryt. Will that be a problem?"

"No, sir. You were quite clear."

Charyn had the feeling that Howal might not have agreed with some of his decisions, but Charyn had to follow his feelings and what he had learned, knowing he was still going to make mistakes.

"Pick up your kit. Your quarters should be ready. You'll be two doors from me." Charyn stood, then headed out the study door.

Howal followed.

Once Charyn had Howal in his chambers, he realized that he was more than a little hungry. He also hadn't told Palenya about either Aloryana or Howal. So he ordered tea and refreshments up to his sitting room, and then went to find Palenya. She was in the music room, practicing on the clavecin.

She stopped as he entered, looking at him, but not speaking. She did not rise as he walked to the clavecin.

"I thought you'd like to join me for tea and refreshments in half a quint in the sitting room."

"I will be there."

"I look forward to it."

After he left the music room, he wondered at her coolness, and hoped that she didn't think the tea was so that he could tell her something unpleasant. All he had wanted to do was have something to eat with someone pleasant.

The tea and refreshments—which included biscuits, cheese, and apples—arrived just before Palenya did. He stood and gestured to the table, then seated himself, watching as she gracefully eased into the chair across from him. For a moment he just looked at her, taking in her brown eyes and smooth dark brown hair. "Thank you for coming."

"How could I not?" Her words were warmly ironic.

"I still appreciate your presence." He poured the tea for both of them, then took a biscuit and ate it, following the last bite with a swallow of tea. He was hungry.

Palenya followed his example, except she only took a sip of the tea.

"Are you feeling better?"

"Much better than on Lundi." She paused, then said, "Aloryana left in a coach yesterday morning. She didn't return. Will she be gone long?" Palenya's eyes fixed on Charyn.

"For the rest of her life, except when she visits."

"You married her off? She's only fourteen!"

Charyn shook his head. "It turned out that she's an imager. She's gone to Imagisle to learn how to handle that ability."

"I knew something was bothering her."

"I think Aloryana knew that for a while. When she found out that Malyna was an imager maitre, she told her."

"Your mother was pleased, but sad, wasn't she?"

"She was, I think. How did you know that?"

"I'm a woman."

Charyn frowned, thinking, before finally saying, "She did say that Aloryana would have more choices as an imager."

"You doubt that? Look at Maitre Malyna. She is more powerful than almost all men, and she can choose whether to marry and whom to marry. Does any woman besides an imager have that power and freedom?"

Charyn smiled wryly. "I think you'd like to be an imager."

"Any woman in Solidar would. If any even dared to think about it. The rest of us don't have that choice. Aloryana was lucky."

"Most imagers aren't from highborn families," Charyn pointed out.

"Even those who come from highborn families are better off as imagers. No one here even knew that Malyna had become an imager. Obviously, no one cared. Did you not ask others about her?"

Charyn nodded. Even Ferrand hadn't known Malyna's name. He'd known a great deal about High Holder Zaerlyn and the family, but only that there had been a much younger daughter.

"Well?" asked Palenya, an amused expression on her face. "What did they say?"

"No one even knew her name, only that High Holder Zaerlyn had a much younger daughter."

"And *she* came from a powerful family. Those girls who become imagers from poorer families are even more fortunate. They live better than any but the wealthiest. They can decide whether to marry or not . . . and whom. They are respected because they are powerful. They live where they are safe and do not have to bow to any man."

"I don't make you bow."

"You do not, but your position does."

Charyn winced.

For several long moments, Palenya did not speak. Finally, she said, "Now that Aloryana is gone, when will I be departing?"

"Do you want to leave? Have I been cruel or . . . otherwise?"

"I am not your future. We both know that."

"You may not be my future, but that does not mean you do not have a future here at the chateau."

"Once you decide to marry, I will not be your mistress. That would not be fair to her or to me."

"I haven't even considered being married."

"You should. Choose carefully. Otherwise all of us will suffer."

"I may have to make that choice. I'm in no hurry to do so, and I'm certainly not about to push you out, either now or then."

"It would be awkward if I stayed."

"I also understand that, but we're nowhere close to that right now, and I still need your support and insight."

"You don't ask that often."

"I should ask more." He took another biscuit and ate it, then said, "I now have a personal secretary to help me with all the papers and petitions. His name is Howal."

"Was he the one in the black jacket?"

"He was wearing that today."

"How do you know you can trust him?"

Charyn smiled wryly. "Because he's been found trustworthy by those who have my survival and interests at heart."

Palenya raised both eyebrows.

"There are a few. Not many, I know." He took another swallow of tea. "Will you play the Farray duet with me? I know I'm not nearly as good as you, but I do like the piece."

"I'd like that. You could be good enough to become a musician. I told you that before."

"But I'd only be good, not great."

"Is it so bad to be only good?"

Charyn had to laugh at her look of gentle amusement. "No. It's better to be great, but . . . I suppose I'd like to be better than good at something."

"No one will ever call a rex good. No matter how many good things he does. Not until he is safely dead."

"You're right about that." Charyn smiled.

"You are rex now. Is there some ceremony . . . ?"

Charyn shook his head. "That would be a form of Naming."

"But there will be a memorial service . . ."

"That is to recognize who my father was, not the power of his position."

Slowly, Palenya nodded. "I had not thought of it in that way."

Looking at Palenya, Charyn felt that she was not as wary as she'd been when she had entered the sitting room. He hoped he was right.

27

The family parlor seemed almost empty when Charyn met his brother and mother there just before dinner.

"I haven't seen that much of you today," observed Chelia, "except to introduce that young man who is your personal secretary."

"As if you needed one," murmured Bhayrn.

"That happens when you have to do things you don't know enough about." Charyn ignored Bhayrn's words and tried to keep his tone light as he gestured toward the dining room. Once they were seated at the table, he said again the gratitude that he had offered for the last several nights, ending with a slightly different variation on the conclusion. "We also give thanks for those who are not here, but elsewhere, either in L'Excelsis or beyond, and for all that they have meant, and all that they have conveyed in thought, word, and deed."

"Thank you," murmured Chelia.

The meal was modest, just roasted fowl, with garlic-roasted potatoes, and a vegetable ragout, accompanied by wine, a Montagne white from a regial vineyard there.

"You could have asked for a red wine as well," said Bhayrn, "or dark lager. You know how I feel about white wine."

"I didn't think about it," replied Charyn. "I left the menu up to Hassala." *As Father usually did.*

"You're rex now. Do we have to follow his rules?"

"For the moment, yes."

"Why?"

"I could say, 'Because I'm rex,' but the truth is that I've got a few other things on my mind besides the choice of dinner wines." *Father didn't exactly go out of his way to prepare me for being rex.* Except, out of deference to his mother, he wasn't about to say that out loud. Instead, he took a swallow of the wine. "It is a rather good white, though."

Bhayrn frowned, opened his mouth, and then shut it without speaking.

"It seems rather quiet without Aloryana and Malyna," said Chelia.

"It is," agreed Charyn.

"She seemed almost happy to leave," said Bhayrn.

"That's understandable, I think," replied Charyn, "especially right now. We're almost prisoners of the factors, or whoever it is, and after the ball Aloryana realized that wouldn't change, no matter what."

"You mean that we'll always be walled in?" Bhayrn sounded almost outraged.

"That's not what I meant. Aloryana would have to marry someone Mother and I approve of, and she'd always be limited by whatever her husband wanted."

"That's a life without worry," countered Bhayrn. "Her husband would be the one concerned with providing for her."

"Would you be happy if you had to rely on a woman providing for you, Bhayrn?" asked Chelia quietly.

"That won't happen. That's not the way things are."

"No, they're not," said Chelia. "But should they be that way?"

"Why shouldn't they be?"

"Maitre Malyna saved your life," Chelia pointed out. "She was able to do that because the imagers train boys and girls in the same way. Isn't your sister as bright as you are? Doesn't she ride as well?"

And she plays the clavecin far better, thought Charyn.

"Just because imagers do that doesn't mean anyone else will," returned Bhayrn. "The Collegium has been around since the consolidation, and I don't see anyone following their examples. With women or anything else."

In the momentary silence that followed, Charyn took another swallow of wine. He'd always been aware of the Collegium. How could he not have been, considering that the imagers had saved his father and mother and put down two rebellions against them? *But how much do the imagers really affect most people?*

"You're looking rather thoughtful, Charyn," offered Chelia.

"I was thinking that most people have little to do with the imagers, and know less about their abilities and customs. For most people in Solidar, the Collegium is just a name, and a place that takes care of the problem of imagers. The only people who are concerned about imagers are the High Holders, and there are only a few thousand of them."

"We're concerned," declared Bhayrn.

"Because we deal with the imagers and the Collegium Maitre more than anyone else," agreed Charyn.

"There's another reason no one pays much attention," said Chelia. "There are far fewer women imagers than men. There always have been.

So there aren't as many women imagers in positions of power, even at the Collegium."

"How do you know that?"

"I have talked with Maitre Alyna a few times over the years."

"She's powerful, isn't she?"

"Very much so," replied Chelia. "She's the first woman to be the Senior Imager in centuries."

"There hasn't been a Maitre of the Collegium who was a woman, has there?" asked Charyn.

"Not that I've heard," said Chelia. "Any woman that powerful might not wish to be Maitre."

"Why not?" asked Bhayrn.

"She'd likely have to use even more imaging and power than past Maitres have used, and she'd have to be almost a tyrant in order to get anything done."

Charyn could see that. He could also see the puzzled expression on Bhayrn's face, as if his brother didn't have the faintest idea what their mother had meant. "Would you defer to Aloryana if she became Maitre?" *Or would you cheat to win the way you did when you played plaques with her?*

"If I knew the whole Collegium was behind her."

Charyn had his doubts, but he wasn't about to bring them up at the moment. Instead, he looked to his mother. "I think I might have to do some entertaining in the future. It might be helpful."

"It probably would be, dear," replied Chelia. "We should talk about it when you feel the time is right."

Meaning not before the memorial service. Charyn nodded again.

28

Howal was waiting outside the study door at just before seventh glass on Jeudi morning when Charyn arrived.

"Good morning, sir."

"Good morning, Howal. I hope you slept well and that you're finding your way around the chateau without much problem." Charyn opened the study door, but left it open for Howal to follow him inside.

"I think I've managed. I did take some time last evening to walk all the corridors on all levels just to get my bearings." Howal closed the door and followed Charyn to the desk, but remained standing, as did Charyn.

"I'll be seeing a master silversmith named Argentyl at eighth glass. I'd like you to remain in the study when he arrives, but at the conference table, where you will take notes on anything of import he may say or reveal in any other way."

"Yes, sir."

"In the meantime, gather your paper and pen and sit down across from me. I'll give you instructions on letters to draft. It may take several drafts at first, until we understand each other better." While Howal gathered his supplies from the end of the conference table, Charyn settled behind the desk and began to open the latest missives that Norstan had left on the corner of the desk, reading each quickly before starting another pile of condolences that would require a response of some sort. Then he waited until Howal was seated and ready before beginning. "We'll go through several of these letters of condolence, and I'll give you a reply. Then I'll need you to draft responses, and we'll go over them. After that, if it seems that I'm been clear enough and you understand me well enough, you can draft a response to each, and then I'll go over each of those with you later." Charyn smiled wryly. "There's already a stack of these, and there will likely be more."

If Howal could do most of the work on the responses to the condolences and letters of sympathy, that would leave him more time to deal with other matters. Ignoring the condolences could only generate ill will, largely among the High Holders and wealthier factors, who were the only ones to write, at least so far.

He picked up the top letter. "This one is from my uncle, High Holder Delcoeur." *Who wrote immediately because he hopes I'll favor him more than Father did.* "My dear Uncle Delcoeur. Your immediate thoughtfulness and concern are both greatly appreciated, as is the timeliness of your sympathy and condolence. In these troubled and troubling times, it is good to know those who are indeed true in their support and concern, and for this, we all thank you . . ."

When Charyn finished, he looked to Howal, who was still writing. He waited until the imager finished.

"The next one is to Factor Elthyrd. He's the head of the Solidaran Factors' Council, but he's been personally quite helpful and supportive to me. Factor Elthyrd. Your letter of sympathy was among the first to arrive and the first read. If I have not already conveyed my appreciation of all that you have done, I would do so now, as well as extend my deepest appreciation for your thoughtful and kind words about my father . . ."

By the time that Argentyl arrived at eighth glass, Howal was seated at the end of the conference table, busy drafting replies to the condolences.

Charyn had just put down the copy of *Tableta* that he had only finished moments before, and which had a smaller story on the assassination than the one in *Veritum* . . . but which had asked what Rex Lorien had done to cause two assassins to kill him in a near suicidal attack. *What about angering every factor in shipping?*

As the door opened and a smallish, black-haired man entered, Charyn stood. "Welcome to the chateau, Craftmaster Argentyl."

"Thank you, Your Grace." The master silversmith glanced at Howal and then back at Charyn.

"Howal is my trusted personal secretary. He'll find out whatever we talk about in any event." Charyn gestured to the chairs in front of the desk and then seated himself.

Argentyl took the middle chair of the three.

"Why did you ask to see me, Craftmaster?"

"I thought it couldn't do any harm and might help."

"With what?"

"I'll come to the point, Your Grace." The silversmith cleared his throat. "Your father had something to do with creating a Council of Factors for all of Solidar. You meet with that council, regular-like, I hear."

"My father did. I haven't yet, but I will."

"We—that's those of us who are craftmasters—thought that was a good idea for the guilds as well, here in L'Excelsis and the nearby towns. We've been meeting for near-on three years."

Why haven't you heard about this? Charyn just nodded for Argentyl to continue.

"It seemed to me that you might like to know what the craftmasters think and what they do for L'Excelsis, and what might make things better for everyone, things that apply to the guilds, that is."

"Are you the senior member of this council, or were you asked to approach me?" Charyn was curious. "Or is there a specific matter of interest to the guilds?"

"For the present, I am the head of the Craftmasters' Council. That's just here in L'Excelsis, Your Grace."

"And your reason for wanting to see me?"

"To keep standards of quality, Your Grace."

"You're going to have to explain more than that, Argentyl."

"All of the guilds have standards. In metalworking, the guild doesn't allow metals to be plated. Otherwise, a piece that's silver-plated copper could be sold as sterling. That'd be fraud, sir. The problem is that the factors are bringing in imported metalwork. Lots of it doesn't meet our standards. The same is true of cloth, and of other goods. The Factors' Council here in L'Excelsis is ignoring the Artificer's Standard. Each guild sets standards for work and working conditions. We've petitioned the L'Excelsis council, but they've declared that our standards only apply to what we make, not what artificers in other cities or lands make."

"They're bringing in inferior goods and selling them for less, then?"

"It's happening more and more, and not just in L'Excelsis."

"Have you brought this matter to the attention of Minister Aevidyr?"

Argentyl looked down for a moment, then squared his shoulders. "His clerks said that the matter was one for the Factors' Council, not the rex. They would not grant me an appointment."

Charyn nodded. "Then what do you think I could do?"

"You make the laws, Your Grace. If the Artificer's Standard is applied to all Solidar, the factors could import whatever they wish, so long as it meets the requirements. If it does not meet the requirements, then it must be sold at the guild price."

Charyn frowned. "If it *does not* meet the requirements?"

"Yes, Your Grace. We do not believe outsiders can produce goods as well as we can. If they can, and they can do so for less, then that is justified and our loss."

"Just who would set the standard for all Solidar?"

"The guild craftmasters of the largest cities—L'Excelsis, Solis, Liantiago, Tilbora, and Ouestan. Then it would be the law of the land."

"If it becomes a law, then there must also be penalties."

"Yes, Your Grace. We would not set them. We would only set the standards. You would determine the penalties."

Charyn fingered his chin. "I'm going to have to think about this."

"We do not expect an immediate decision, Your Grace, but all crafters are facing problems like this. I found a set of silver bowls. The mark on them indicated they were sterling. They were sterling washed over copper. That is fraud. The Factors' Council dismissed my petition."

"I can see where this might be a problem." Charyn nodded. "I will consider your request." He stood. "Where might I send any missives dealing with this problem?"

The craftmaster hurried to his feet. "To me, Argentyl. My shop is one block north of the corner of where Fedre crosses Quierca, on the south side."

Charyn glanced to Howal. "If you'd write that down."

"Yes, sir."

Charyn returned his attention to Argentyl. "I will let you know what I decide. It will not be that soon. I had not expected to become rex this early in my life or in the way it happened. There is much to do."

"Thank you, Your Grace." Argentyl bowed. "Thank you for seeing a humble crafter."

Once the silversmith had left the study, Charyn looked to Howal. "Do you know anything that might shed some light on this?"

"No, sir. I know the Collegium doesn't allow anyone to image anything crafters make, except for use on Imagisle. That's unless it's something that no one else crafts."

"That's what they do at their factorage?"

Howal nodded.

"Sturdyn." Charyn raised his voice. "I'd like to see Norstan."

"Yes, sir."

In less than half a quint, Norstan was in the study, trying not to look worried. That was a guess on Charyn's part, but Norstan was showing the signs of being ill at ease.

"Norstan . . . I met with Argentyl a little while ago. Just how did he manage to come to your attention? He never got past Aevidyr's clerks."

"Ah . . . he's married to my wife's cousin, sir. I told her that I could only ask you if he'd meet with you."

"You didn't think I'd agree, did you?"

"No, sir."

"You were right to ask me, but I might not be so quick to agree to your next suggestion."

"Yes, sir."

"If the cousin asks anything, you can say that what he suggested involves a great number of people and a great deal of work. For that reason, I'm not likely to make a quick decision."

"Yes, sir."

"That's all. I just needed to know."

Charyn thought Norstan was relieved, but he wasn't certain . . . as he often wasn't.

After the seneschal had departed, Charyn looked back to Howal. "I'm not used to being rex. I should have asked Norstan how Argentyl came to his attention when he first mentioned the craftmaster."

"I think it must take some time to learn that. I've heard that Maitre Alastar asks those kinds of questions, but he's been Collegium Maitre for almost twenty years."

You're going to have to learn faster than that.

Promptly at ninth glass, Sturdyn announced, "Factor Hisario."

Charyn debated whether he should stand, then did so as the gray-haired and angular shipping factor entered the study. He still worried about seeing a member of the Solidaran Factors' Council privately, but the more he knew before the meeting of the combined councils the better. The factor glanced at Howal and then back to Charyn, who gestured toward the chairs in front of the desk.

Hisario stopped short of the chairs and inclined his head. "Rex Charyn, I offer my sympathy and condolences for the death of your father. We did not agree on much, but I would not have wished such a death on anyone . . . or upon his family."

"Thank you. I appreciate your words." Charyn motioned toward the chairs and seated himself. Smiling pleasantly, he waited for Hisario to speak.

Finally, the factor began. "I do not know what you know about the situation facing the factors of Solidar, especially those of us engaged in shipping spices, copper, and tin." He looked to Charyn.

"I know that the prices of pepper have been rising, and the future prices are even higher. I understand that copper prices remain low because ships bringing tin to Solidar have been . . . hampered."

"Sent to the bottom of the Northern Ocean is more like it. The zinc, too, but the tin is what we need most. The Ferrans and the Jariolan privateers sink our ships, and then they use their own merchanters to ship the tin we would have bought to the Abierto Isles. We have to pay twice as much when the Abiertans ship it to Eshtora . . . if we can even get it. To boot, we have to ship it from there to Solis, and then take it upriver to Ferravyl."

"I take it you've lost ships?"

"Two so far. Can't sail to Jariola or Ferrum now, and it's not much better going south and west to Otelyrn. The privateers are everywhere."

"I understand the navy has dispatched warships to deal with the privateers."

"I've got no problem with the navy. They do right well . . . but there aren't enough warships. The privateers just wait until the warships aren't around."

"I understand some factors are arming their ships," said Charyn.

"That's costly, Rex Charyn. Cannon, shells, and powder are expensive. You have to build magazines. That costs golds and takes space from cargo. You need more crew, and that's more in provisions. All that slows a vessel, and then you can't outsail the bastards."

"If your ships are faster, then . . ." Charyn offered a puzzled expression.

"We have to port, sooner or later. They just wait near a port out of sight or at one end of the straits, or somewhere that we can't maneuver. That pretty much keeps us from trading with either Jariola or Ferrum."

"And most of the privateers have sailed south around Otelyrn?"

"That's right."

Charyn frowned. "How do our warships compare to the Jariolan ships?"

"When your warships are around, there's never a problem. They're not always around. That's the problem. Trying not to argue, sir, but you don't have enough ships to protect your shippers."

"It might be difficult to build enough ships to protect everyone all the time."

"More ships would help, sir."

"Before his death, my father decided to build more ships than he had planned. That effort will continue. How many will depend on what it costs. I have the Finance Minister looking into that."

"You're not thinking of raising tariffs, are you?" Hisario's eyes narrowed.

"I'm not about to commit to anything more than my father announced until I know what it will cost. The same is true of tariffs. It would be foolish for me to announce that I am building ships Solidar cannot build or cannot afford. It would also be foolish for me to announce changes in tariffs until I know what the needs might be and what meeting those needs might require in tariffs. It would be especially foolish to do either before meeting with the two councils. But, at the same time, you are telling me that it would be foolish for me to do nothing. Isn't that what you're saying, Factor Hisario?"

"That's what it comes down to."

"Do you know who might be behind the assassination of my father?" Charyn hoped the direct question, hopefully out of nowhere, might reveal something.

"No, Your Grace. I don't."

"The only message we received indicated that my father and the family would be in danger until more was done to protect the merchant ships of Solidar. That would tend to suggest a factor or someone in shipping."

"Factors are not the only ones in shipping."

"That's true, but most of those in trade are factors." Charyn shook his head. "No one seems to know anything about it. My father found that hard to believe, and I'm beginning to feel the same way. In days, if not sooner, prices on the exchange reflect what has happened in the Northern Ocean. Factors know who is selling what and why. Golds change hands on whispers of what one factor or another has done . . . and yet not a one of you has the slightest idea who might be hiring men to burn regial granaries and assassinate the rex."

"Burn regial granaries? I had not heard that."

"Fire and explosions destroyed twenty regial silos filled with grain in the fourth week of Finitas."

"Where was that?" asked Hisario.

"At the regial estate in Tuuryl. The loss of grain and the damage to the silos amounted to more than twelve thousand golds. That's roughly the cost of two warships of the line."

"How do you know it was done on purpose?"

"There was a very explicit message pinned to the landwarden's door with a knife." Charyn wasn't certain about the knife, but it had to have been affixed to the door with something, and he thought it had been a knife. "It said that until the rex did more to stop the factors' losses caused by the rex's inability to deal with the piracy and sinkings of Solidaran ships, the rex's losses would continue."

"That doesn't mean . . ." Hisario's words died away as he looked at Charyn.

"If it waddles like a goose, swims like a goose, and hisses like a goose, the odds are that it just might be a goose, Factor Hisario." Charyn paused, then went on. "Even so, my father made arrangements to immediately build two more warships and announced those plans. And then he was still assassinated." Charyn offered a cool smile. "What, exactly, would you suggest that I do? That is physically possible."

"Build more warships. Seek an agreement with the oligarchs. Whatever it takes."

"I cannot build ships any faster than we are. There isn't more space in the shipyards, and I doubt there are that many shipwrights who are not already quite busy."

"Your Grace, I cannot afford to lose more ships. Neither can most in the shipping trade."

"Factor Hisario, I understand that. Why can you not understand that I cannot build more ships without more golds, more shipwrights, and more shipyards?"

"I beg of you . . . please do something."

"I have been rex for five days." *And Father couldn't find a way out in years.* "I will think on it. I would request that you do so as well. We will discuss the matter and any thoughts we each may have at the meeting on the eighteenth of Ianus." Charyn stood. There was little point in continuing any discussion. He didn't have any other ideas, and it was clear that Hisario didn't either.

"I thank Your Grace for hearing me out." Hisario's words were even, not flat, but not showing any warmth either.

"And I appreciate your directness and honesty." *If not your single-minded pigheadedness.*

After Hisario left the study, Charyn looked to Howal. "You heard everything. What are your thoughts?"

"They have a problem, sir."

"That means I have one, because what they want costs more than I can raise without increasing tariffs, which everyone opposes."

Howal gave a polite nod.

Charyn realized, at that moment, and belatedly, that he should have asked Hisario what he thought about the destruction of the exchange in Solis. *Another thing you should have done.*

At half a quint before the first glass of the afternoon, Sturdyn announced, "Marshal Vaelln."

"Come on in!" called Charyn, standing.

The slender and sandy-haired marshal entered by himself. That surprised Charyn, because it had appeared to him that Vaelln had seldom visited his father without other officers present.

"Good afternoon, sir," said Vaelln, inclining his head politely. He barely even looked at Howal as Charyn gestured for him to sit down.

"I hope the ride here wasn't too cold."

"I've ridden in worse." Vaelln smiled ironically. "In better, too." He seated himself in the middle chair. "Where would you like me to begin?"

"With the memorial service, if you would."

"We had thought to follow the plan for past memorial services. An army honor guard would escort the regial family coach from the Chateau D'Rex to the anomen, and then back to the chateau after the service."

Charyn nodded. "There will be two coaches. The first will be the official coach. It will contain two army officers. The second coach will be plain and will follow the first. The regial party will be in the second."

"You fear another attack?"

"There have been two so far. I'd rather not see a third succeed."

"I cannot find fault with that."

"You are not to tell anyone of the coach plan. No one. Not the vice-marshal. Not your wife. No one."

"I understand. I will not. Even so, you do understand that we can only do so much in protecting you and your family. Attacks by cannon or by Antiagon Fire of the sort that was directed at your father at the memorial service for your grandsire is not something the army can do much about."

Charyn decided not to mention that the Antiagon Fire had been used by disloyal army officers. Besides, Vaelln's basic point was accurate. "I am very aware of that." *Especially after the attack on Father.* "That is why I will be the only member of the regial family at the service, and I will be accompanied personally by both Maitre Alastar and Maitre Alyna. That is also between the two of us. Do you understand?"

"Yes, sir."

"I will have Alucar ready a cask of coppers and silvers—and two golds—but I would appreciate it if you would pick out a strong and worthy ranker to scatter the coins at the end of the service." Left unsaid was the fact that the ranker got to pocket a few of those coins. That was also a tradition.

"I have someone in mind, a senior squad leader who has served well and faithfully for twenty years."

"Good." Charyn paused. "There is one other matter, that of the Jariolan and Ferran privateers. Earlier today, I had a visit from Factor Hisario. He expressed great concerns about the problems created by the Jariolans and Ferrans. He has already lost two ships to the privateers. How effective have the navy warships been in dealing with the privateers . . . and the Jariolan and Ferran warships?"

"At least as effective as anyone could reasonably expect, and at times, more than that. I have reason to believe that our warships built in the last five years are superior to both the best of the Jariolan and Ferran ships. Of the same class, that is. As an indication, in the first two weeks of Finitas, I received reports detailing the sinking of six privateers in Feuillyt. Four were destroyed in Erntyn."

"Ten privateer ships in two months. You have forty ships of the line, as I recall. Is that correct?"

"That's right. Forty ships of the line, soon to be forty-one, and fifty-four other warships, including twenty-two war sloops."

"Are the fifty-four other warships capable of dealing with the privateers?"

"With most of them," admitted Vaelln.

"So you have ninety-five ships able to deal with the privateers, and you can only sink ten in two months?"

"It's not as simple as it sounds, Your Grace. There's a problem of discovering who is a privateer. They look like any other merchanter from a distance. That's until they attack a ship. They often fly the ensigns of another land, such as the Abierto Isles, and they often change the name and the outward appearance of the ship. We'd have to stop and board such a ship to discover if it even had guns . . . and having guns doesn't make a ship a privateer. Then there is the fact that the Northern Ocean is vast, and we must patrol our own coasts, the waters around the Abierto Isles, and, as we can, the waters off Ferrum and Jariola. Under these conditions, we are spread thin. There's no way we can send enough ships to patrol all the waters off Otelyrn."

"Isn't there anything else that can be done?"

"We've suggested that we escort trading ships from our ports to Ferran or Jariolan ports, convoy them, if you will. The factors claim that costs them too much and that such a plan would slow them down because warships are slower than the fast traders and clippers, and because they would have to wait for such convoys to be gathered together. It would also allow other traders to profit by knowing what ships are headed where and when they are going."

"What about positioning ships off Ferran and Jariolan ports? Factor Hisario claimed that the problem was in waters near the ports where they had less room to maneuver."

"I doubt that the Jariolan Oligarch would take kindly to even a small Solidaran fleet off their coasts, and they do have more warships than we do."

Charyn nodded . . . and realized he was nodding a great deal. Was that a mannerism for avoiding actually answering?

"If the Ferrans agreed with the Jariolans," continued Vaelln, "and they well might, that would put us at a greater disadvantage. Together, they have more than twice the number of ships of the line as we do."

"What would you suggest, then?"

"Continue doing what we are doing. The Ferrans and the Jariolans cannot object that much if we destroy ships caught attacking or raiding our ships. It may still come to war, but if you keep building ships, and we keep destroying those that attack our ships, the longer before it does, the better."

"If I survive long enough to continue doing that," replied Charyn sardonically.

"Maitre Alastar cannot help you?"

"I wouldn't be alive now without his assistance. One of his imagers kept the rest of the regial family from being killed along with Father." While the details of what happened would spread, had already begun to spread with the story in *Veritum*, Charyn saw no reason to hasten that. "The problem is that the surviving assassin killed himself almost immediately. There is nothing to point to whoever is behind it—only the previous messages saying that the attacks will continue until the factors' losses are addressed by the actions of the rex."

"I can see that presents a certain difficulty, sir. It is not one where the army can be of much assistance, and where the navy's assistance will take time to accomplish what is necessary."

That's not telling me anything I don't know. After a brief moment, Charyn said, "It might be helpful for me to know a great deal more about where your ships are deployed, the rationale for that deployment, and the results in each area of deployment." He wasn't sure knowing all that would help, but it might, and not knowing it could well hurt him when he had to deal with the two councils in less than two weeks. Especially since he had no idea what his father had told his uncle.

When Vaelln left the study, more than a glass later, after providing the information Charyn had asked for—in great and depressing detail—Charyn realized that he had not given any real thought to what he was going to say at the memorial service.

Without saying a word, he walked to the window and pulled back the hanging so that he could look out on the cold afternoon, cold enough that dirty snow still lined the ring road and was piled up beside the stone way that led from the rear courtyard down to the ring road. Chill radiated off the glass.

What can you say that would be accurate and favorable without being sentimental? Father hated sentimentality.

He took a deep breath and sat down at the desk. Then he took out a fresh sheet of paper and a pen.

29

On Vendrei morning, the latest edition of *Veritum* was on Charyn's desk when he arrived. That was a mixed blessing. It meant that Charyn had another source of information, but, unfortunately, the newssheet also contained a small story speculating on whether Charyn would marry Malyna, even though she was an imager, wondering why else she had been at the Year-Turn Ball as part of the regial family.

By midafternoon, after meeting with all three ministers in the morning, Charyn was still struggling with what he would say at the memorial service, while Howal continued to draft—and then re-draft in final form after Charyn's corrections—replies to the three score or more letters of sympathy and condolence.

One of the problems Charyn faced was that his father had hated sentimentality and despised hypocrisy and empty flattery. The other was that no one, even the High Council, could understand how hard his father had worked just to hold Solidar together . . . and his just saying that would be ignored or dismissed, if not both.

But do most people even remember what is said at a memorial service?

He smiled sardonically.

For some reason, his thoughts drifted to Malyna, and the fact that she was descended from Vaelora, who had married the first Maitre. *But who had the first Maitre really been? Had he been anything like all the legends?* He pushed aside those thoughts. He needed to concentrate on his remarks. *Except . . .*

If he talked to his mother, she might have some thoughts.

He abruptly stood from where he had been sitting at the desk and looked over to Howal. "I'm going to talk to Mother. I won't be long."

"Yes, sir. Would you like me—"

"If I'm not safe on the upper corridor of the chateau . . ." Charyn shook his head, then smiled sadly and left the study.

He found his mother where she usually was, especially in recent days—in her sitting room.

"I'm surprised to see you here now." She smiled warmly.

"I'm having trouble finding the words for the memorial. It's hard to put feelings into words that don't sound maudlin or overblown. I don't want to do either, and Father wouldn't have wanted that, either."

"You're right." After a moment, she said, "You could say just that as a beginning."

"I just might."

"I don't think that's all that's on your mind."

"No . . . it's not. I was thinking about Malyna . . . and the fact that we're both descended from the father of the first Rex Regis, but she's also descended from the first Maitre. There aren't many imagers who could claim that today, just her."

"And her aunt, Maitre Alyna."

"I hadn't thought about that. I should have. How real do you think first Maitre was?" Charyn asked.

"I'm quite sure he was real, dear," replied Chelia, "but that's not what you meant, was it?"

"No. I've been through a great portion of the chateau archives, and he's seldom even mentioned. Yet all the legends suggest this giant, this titan of an imager. He must have had great abilities, but those that are attributed to him by legend are greater than could possibly be wielded by even a score of maitres with the power of Maitre Alastar."

"Legends can exaggerate. They usually do. What exactly is your point besides that?"

Charyn tried not to flush. "The oldest records I can find show that the first Maitre and the founder of the Collegium was Quaeryt Rytersyn. In old Ryntaran, that means 'the questioner of every man.' We know Vaelora existed, and she was the sister of the first Rex Regis, but doesn't it seem odd that the questioner of every man was married to Valor?"

"As I recall, dear, Rytersyn was the surname given to Ryntaran or-phans, and in those days children of imagers were often likely to be orphans. As my tutor once told me, latter-born daughters were often named after desirable characteristics. Again, what is your point?"

After that quiet rebuke, Charyn found he had to concentrate before continuing. "This . . . legendary founder of the Collegium was not only an imager, in addition to that, he was the foremost field commander of Rex Regis. That suggests he had a great deal to do with the destruction of the armies of the Rex of Bovaria."

"All the histories are clear on the destruction of the Bovarian armies," Chelia pointed out. "Aren't the archives as well?"

"They say that they were obliterated under a wall of ice that killed tens of thousands, and covered the western shore of the River Aluse for milles. Even Maitre Alastar never came close to that."

"Why does all that disturb you?" asked Chelia. "Because it shows what power imagers might be able to raise?"

"They can't do that now."

"They can do enough, Charyn. They can do enough. Maitre Alastar turned a shore of the River Aluse to solid ice. It was a stretch almost half a mille long and a quarter mille wide. He created ice that covered all of the Aluse from the west bank to Imagisle. In an instant, he used that ice to kill an entire regiment. One imager protected your father and me. We were encircled by ice. I saw all that with my own eyes. Once the ice melted, the imagers buried almost two thousand men. They had to. There were no survivors."

"You saw that? You only said that he saved you."

"Your father asked that we not tell you until you were older. You're older, old enough that it is dangerous for you not to understand what power they have. Little more than two handfuls of them destroyed all the cannon of the High Holder rebels and almost four regiments of mutinous army troopers and officers. It took less than two glasses."

"Then . . . why . . . ?"

"Your father asked the same question. The rex and the Collegium must always side with each other. I hope you can figure out why by yourself, because taking my word won't be enough . . . and shouldn't be."

The cool way in which his mother uttered those last words chilled Charyn, more than a little. Then she smiled, more warmly. "I did find what else you discovered very interesting, and I really liked hearing the way you put it. That ability will help you now, especially." Her smile faded, sadly.

Charyn knew exactly what that meant, but there was no point in dwelling on it. "I do hope so. I appreciated what you had to say as well." And he did.

He still had to finish composing his remarks for the memorial service.

30

Slightly after midday on Samedi Charyn studied himself in the mirror in his bedchamber, taking in the formal regial greens and the black-trimmed mourning sash that he wore. He picked up the single sheet of notes for what he would say at the memorial service, folded it, and slipped it into the inside pocket of his jacket. Then he turned and made his way out to the sitting room.

"You look very somberly formal," observed Bhayrn from where he stood by the window, where he had pulled the hangings back just enough to look out across the entrance to the Chateau D'Rex and the snow-covered formal gardens beyond.

"Thank you."

"I still think I should be going with you."

"Strictly speaking, you should. There's one problem, however. You're my heir. Effectively, my only heir. That's why I thought it wiser that you not accompany me."

Bhayrn looked surprised, then nodded. "I hadn't thought of that."

"I'd like you to spend some time with Howal while I'm gone. Anything you can tell him about yourself or about the chateau would be helpful, and it will make things easier for me."

"I can do that . . . but Mother . . ."

"Actually, it might be best if the two of you talked with him." Charyn had already told Howal that would likely be what happened, but he wanted Bhayrn to initiate the discussion. "I'm going down to the receiving parlor. It won't be long before Maitre Alastar and Maitre Alyna arrive."

The two left the sitting room, and Bhayrn walked toward Chelia's sitting room, while Charyn headed down the grand staircase and made his way to the receiving parlor.

Maitre Alastar and Maitre Alyna arrived at the Chateau D'Rex at two quints past noon, and Charyn met them in the parlor. Both wore imager grays, but Alyna also wore a black-trimmed green mourning scarf across her shoulders.

"Greetings," offered Charyn. "I deeply appreciate your accompany-ing me."

"We would have attended the memorial in any case," said Alastar, "and it is in the best interests of the Collegium that Solidar not lose another rex."

"I also appreciate your lending me Howal. He has proved to be an outstanding personal secretary, and that has made the last week far less difficult than it might have been. I've asked Bhayrn and my mother to spend the time while I'm gone briefing him on matters I may have over-looked."

"I take it that you've received no more messages," said Alastar.

"No. I doubted that there would be until after the memorial service."

"Your words suggest that you expect such a message," replied Alyna.

"I'd be surprised if I didn't. Anyone who has gone to the lengths they have isn't likely to stop now. Do you think otherwise?"

"I'd like to hope otherwise," said Alastar, "but I fear you're right."

"What I don't understand is how anyone thinks that the rex can do the impossible."

"I might have an idea what you mean," said Alastar, "but a little more explanation might make your question clearer."

"I've been looking into the shipbuilding, building warships, that is, and there's no way to build very many more much faster. If I built a large shipyard, then over the next ten or fifteen years I could build quite a few more ships, but there's really no way to do that now." Charyn laughed nervously. "And that's not even counting the fact that the regial treasury doesn't have the golds to build that kind of shipyard or that many ships. If I can figure that out in a few days, surely someone who deals with ships all the time must know that, shouldn't they?"

"Just because they should," returned Alyna, "doesn't mean they do. The High Holders should have known that attacking the Collegium and Imagisle was a very bad idea. Those that did seemed surprised at what happened. They should have known better . . . but they didn't."

"That might be because . . . well . . . it's something else I've been thinking about—" Charyn stopped abruptly as he saw Marshal Vaelln approaching the open doors of the receiving parlor.

"Your escort company is ready, Rex Charyn," declared Vaelln when he stopped just inside the doors. "I trust you don't mind, sir, but you felt strongly about the possibility of someone attacking the regial coach. I'd prefer not to risk officers' lives either. So I brought two figures dressed in formal greens. My men are strapping them in place. I didn't tell any-one until the last thing this morning."

Alyna raised her eyebrows.

"We'll be in the coach following the regial coach," Charyn explained.

The two maitres exchanged a quick glance, but said nothing.

"We might as well leave," Charyn said, nodding to Vaelln.

With all the arrangements, it was almost a quint later before Charyn, Alastar, and Alyna were seated in the plain coach as it started out of the rear courtyard behind the regial coach.

"I know it's not been long," said Charyn, looking across at the two imagers who sat on the backward-facing seats, "but how is Aloryana doing?"

Alyna smiled. "It's been good for both her and Lystara. Lystara was always the younger one with Malyna. Now she gets to explain, and Alo-ryana is very quick. She's also very sweet."

"What about her . . . imaging?"

"It's too early to tell, but she's learning the basics quickly, and she's very interested in personal shields, which we're encouraging . . . for obvious reasons."

"Could she become a maitre?"

"She has the ability. If she continues to work as hard as she has been, she likely will be, but not for several years. Lystara and Malyna were among the youngest maitres in a very long time, and they became mai-tres less than a year ago."

Charyn frowned. "I thought Lystara was only sixteen."

"She's the youngest ever, I've discovered," admitted Alastar. "It's wor-ried us greatly. Frankly, we're hoping that Aloryana will be helpful in that regard."

That confused Charyn even more, and his face must have showed it, because Alyna immediately replied.

"Lystara is the one teaching Aloryana. Teaching educates the teacher to limitations and concerns more than it does the one learning. By mak-ing Lystara responsible for Aloryana . . . and with the understanding that Aloryana is the sister of the rex . . . that requires Lystara to be more cautious."

"I'm glad Aloryana is providing a benefit as well. Does she seem happy?"

"Yes." The single word came from both maitres simultaneously.

"Good."

The coach was silent for a time that seemed almost endless to Charyn before he finally said, "Oh . . . just before we left the parlor, I was about to mention something that occurred to me the other day. I'd like your thoughts on the matter. After thinking over everything that's happened, and how quickly Malyna acted, and then what happened when you saved my parents years ago, it dawned on me that most people, even most High Holders, have little knowledge of imagers and even less contact with them. That might be why some of those High Holders were in fact surprised by what the Collegium could do."

"That has been a problem," Alastar said. "It's one of the reasons why we're in the process of establishing a branch of the Collegium at Estisle, and why we're having imagers do more and do so more obviously. Part of that difficulty is that there are so few imagers."

"If less than two thousand High Holders cannot understand what imagers can do," added Alyna, "the problem becomes even larger when we consider the thousands of factors and the tens of thousands of others who have little contact with imagers—except to believe that we're the offspring of the Namer."

"As you pointed out in the chateau," Alastar continued, "people often don't even fully consider the implications of what they know. It has to be worse when they're demanding you or the Collegium act on something they know nothing about."

"My father was always talking about that," said Charyn. "He kept saying that too many High Holders didn't understand."

"High Holders are no different from other people," replied Alastar. "Often people don't want to understand."

"Someone certainly doesn't want to understand that I can't build all the warships they want, and if Marshal Vaelln is right, even that probably wouldn't be enough to stop all the losses unless we go to war with Jariola."

"You're not . . ." began Alyna.

"No," replied Charyn. "Right now, we'd lose a naval war, and we don't have a big enough army or enough ships to carry the soldiers to Jariola. But that's the problem. Nothing I can do immediately is going to satisfy either the factors or the High Holders. And if I do nothing, I'm concerned that the attacks on regial properties and the regial family will continue. I'm just glad Aloryana is on Imagisle." Charyn thought about saying more, but decided against it as the coach turned off the Avenue D'Rex Ryen and began to slow as it neared the entrance to the Anomen D'Rex.

"You do have your hands full," said Alastar.

And then some.

Charyn nodded to Alyna as Yarselt opened the coach door. The Maitre D'Image positioned the mourning scarf over her brown hair, hair that showed a few streaks of gray, quickly adjusted the scarf, and stepped out of the coach, followed by Alastar and then Charyn.

Two soldiers in dress green uniforms formed up before the two imagers, and another two fell in behind Charyn. Then the soldiers began the march up the paved walk to the entry, a walk guarded on both sides by troopers in dress uniforms.

A horn fanfare blared across the chill afternoon. For an instant, Charyn wondered why, before realizing that it was announcing his arrival.

Once inside the anomen, the troopers took a narrow side corridor that led to a door that accessed the sacristy dais. They stepped back as Alastar led the way, opening the small door. Alyna eased behind Charyn, and the three moved through the door. Alyna eased the door closed, and joined Alastar and Charyn in position against the wall and even with the pulpit.

Moments after the chime of the anomen's bell died away, Chorister Saerlet stepped forward, standing silently for several moments before offering the invocation.

"We are gathered here together this afternoon in the spirit of the Nameless, in affirmation of the quest for goodness and mercy in all that we do, and in celebration of the life of Lorien D'Rex and in memory of his service to the land of Solidar."

The opening hymn was traditional—"The Glory of the Nameless." Charyn sang softly, not really wanting his less than adequate voice to be heard. He did not hear Alastar singing, and Alyna was singing as softly as Charyn was.

Next, Saerlet skipped the confession, as requested by Chelia, and delivered the charge. "Life is a gift from the Nameless, for from the glory of the Nameless do we come . . ." Another hymn followed his words, not a traditional one, but the one Chelia had insisted upon—"In Vain a Crown of Gold."

> *"All words of praise will die as spoken*
> *As night precedes the dawn unwoken . . .*
> *To claim in vain a crown of gold,*
> *Belies the truth the Nameless told . . ."*

Only a fraction of the congregation knew the words, much less the melody, and Charyn was among them. *Why did Mother want that hymn?* Sometime, he'd ask her, when it wouldn't be too painful.

Then Saerlet announced, "Now we will hear from Rex Charyn . . ."

For a moment, Charyn didn't move, caught by surprise, even after Saerlet's statement. Then he eased out his notes and stepped forward to the pulpit, where he laid out that single sheet, and looked out across the anomen, largely filled, although most of those in the back of the anomen were most likely working men and women who doubtless had only come in hopes of obtaining some of the coins they knew would be scattered. The forward third of the anomen was reserved, of course, for those of position, but besides those in front, the three ministers and their wives, and Marshal Vaelln, Charyn could only make out Factor Elthyrd and his son Estafen, and High Holder Delcoeur and Ferrand. The only High Councilor he could see was High Holder Fhaedyrk.

Charyn glanced down, noticing for the first time an envelope set on the side of the flat area that held his single sheet of notes. The outside read "Rex Charyn."

He forced his attention back to the anomen and those who waited for him to speak. Finally, he began.

"It is difficult to talk about someone who has just died. It's all too easy to slip into simple phrases about someone you respected and loved. Or to exalt them beyond belief or to become overly sentimental. My father, Rex Lorien, would have wanted none of that. Even as his son, I found him almost an enigma, a man who was devoted to his family and his land, but who refused to show how much he cared. He believed in being fair, and he changed the laws in many instances to make them more fair, yet those were the changes that created upheaval and discontent. He hated to take advice, yet he could tell what was good advice and what wasn't, and he usually took the good advice, much as it galled him. He disliked people who saw a problem and refused to address it, but he did his best to remain civil in dealing with them. He was also honest and direct in saying what he believed. As with all of us, he was not always right, and he was sometimes grudging in accepting when he was not right, but I never saw him fail to accept what was right when the time came . . . in the end, I can only say that he was a far better rex and a far better man than even he believed himself to be. Would that any of us will be able to have that said of us when our time comes."

After Charyn finished, he picked up his notes and the envelope and stepped back.

Saerlet moved to the pulpit. "At this time, we wear gray and green, gray for the uncertainties of life, and green for its triumph, manifested every year in the coming of spring. So is it that, like nature, we come from the grayness of winter and uncertainty into life which unfolds in uncertainty, alternating between gray and green, and in the end return to the life and glory of the Nameless. In that spirit, let us offer thanks for the spirit and the life of Lorien, as both a rex and as a man. Let us remember him as a child, a youth, a man, a husband, and a father, not merely as a ruler or a name, but as a living breathing person whose acts and spirit touched many. Let us set aside the gloom of mourning, and from this day forth, recall the fullness of Rex Lorien's life and all that he has left with us."

With those words, Alyna and the women in the anomen let the mourning scarves slip from their hair.

Then came the traditional closing hymn—"For the Glory."

> "For the glory, for the life,
>   for the beauty and the strife,
>   for all that is and ever shall be,
>   all together, through forever,
>   in eternal Nameless glory . . ."

When the closing hymn ended and Saerlet had delivered the benediction and sending forth, those attending—at least those in the rear of the anomen—hurried out onto the paved area before the church, where Vaelln's picked man would scatter the coins.

Then Alastar looked to Charyn and said, "That may have been one of the best and most accurate statements I've ever heard about your father. You did well."

"Very well," murmured Alyna.

And so far no one has shot at me or exploded Antiagon Fire around us. At that moment he recalled the envelope he still held and immediately broke the unstamped black wax seal. The note inside the envelope was short.

> *If you fail to protect your factors, you will suffer the same fate as*
> *your father.*

Charyn handed the sheet to Alastar. "The envelope was set on the pulpit, just to the side. I didn't see it until just before I was to make my remarks. Someone seems very set on protecting the factors."

"Someone with considerable resources," replied Alastar after scanning it, showing it to Alyna, and then returning the sheet.

Charyn eased the single sheet back into the envelope.

"I'll get Chorister Saerlet," said Alyna. "He might have seen someone. You two move back into the corridor."

Alyna didn't have to go far, because she returned with the chorister in moments, almost as soon as Charyn and Alastar were standing in the corridor beyond the door.

Charyn couldn't help but notice that Saerlet looked annoyed.

"Is something amiss, Rex Charyn?"

"You might say so." Charyn lifted the envelope that held the threat. "This envelope holds a threatening note. It was set on the flat of the pulpit," said Charyn. "How did it get there?"

Saerlet glanced from the envelope to Charyn. "I wouldn't know, Your Grace. It wasn't there when I went over everything."

"When was that?" asked Alastar.

"A quint before the service, Maitre. It might have been a bit earlier. There were some men, they said they were factors, but I don't think they were, even if they were dressed like they were . . . You know how sometimes people just don't fit in their clothes."

"What about the men?" asked Alyna.

"Oh, they were trying to get into the factors' section and my assistant felt they didn't belong there. They left in a huff."

"Distraction," said Alastar. "Would you recognize any of them? Not that we'll likely ever see them again."

"I . . . I don't think so, Maitre."

"If you learn more, I'd like to know. Immediately." Charyn looked hard at the chorister.

"So would we," added Alyna in a firm voice.

Charyn could see the chorister shrink into his robes. "I will. I certainly will."

"Good," said Charyn.

The same four escort troopers were waiting, if slightly farther down the corridor.

"Sir, Maitres, it'd be best if we waited a bit. Chassart's still flinging coins."

"We can wait," said Charyn.

"You were right about the threats continuing," observed Alastar, "not that I doubted it for a moment."

Charyn paused, thinking, then said, "I'm going to be meeting with both the High Council and the Factors' Council of Solidar on the eighteenth, the first glass of the afternoon. I'd very much like you to be there. Would you consider that?"

Alastar laughed softly. "For the very fact that you asked, I'd be happy to be there."

"Thank you."

It was almost a quint later before the three of them were in the plain coach headed back to the Chateau D'Rex.

Charyn was still thinking about his impulsive invitation. *Is it really a good idea to include the Collegium Maitre?* Charyn almost shook his head. It might be a very bad idea, but his father had tried to keep the imagers out of things until he'd had no choice, and that hadn't avoided battles and bloodshed. Maybe bringing them in now would be better. He didn't see how it could be worse.

But *if it is* . . . He tried not to shudder.

31

Once Charyn was back at the chateau and had thanked Alastar and Alyna profusely and seen them off in the plain gray imager coach, he made
his way up the grand staircase and to his mother's sitting room.

The three seated there all immediately stopped talking and looked at
Charyn, Howal especially.

"I'm back. No one attacked me, or even tried. They did leave me a
note." He withdrew the envelope from his jacket. "You might want to
read it. Maitre Alastar and Maitre Alyna were with me. They've already
read it." He handed the envelope to his mother.

She extracted the single sheet, read it, and handed both envelope and
note to Bhayrn without speaking.

Bhayrn read it and looked to Charyn.

"Howal can read it. He needs to know as much as anyone."

After Howal read the words, he slipped the note back into the envelope, then returned both to Charyn.

"Does anyone have any thoughts about the note?" Charyn looked to
his mother.

"No . . . except that they seem rather single-minded."

"What do you mean by that?" asked Bharyn.

Charyn was glad his brother had asked the question, because he'd
wanted to, except he'd thought it was a stupid question to ask.

"Both the High Holders and factors have more than just problems
with the Jariolan privateers," replied Chelia. "Many of the High Holders
have not changed their planting and harvesting for centuries. Your brother
has, and it's increased the harvest and golds on his personal lands by a
third, and he's only twenty-two. Your father instructed the landwardens
to look into doing the same . . ."

Charyn hadn't known that, but somehow that seemed so like his
father.

". . . He's had enough sense to learn about the exchanges. Most High
Holders know nothing. Only a comparatively small number of factors

avail themselves of the exchanges. There are problems everywhere, but whoever killed your father persists in focusing on just one thing."

"Factors do that," replied Bhayrn. "All they care about is golds, and what costs them golds."

"That's true," said Charyn, settling into the straight-backed chair across from his mother, "but the High Holders aren't much better."

"I can't imagine a High Holder demanding that the rex protect the factors. They'd sooner die. Any of them," countered Bhayrn.

"What do you think, Howal?" asked Charyn, knowing that he wasn't going to get much more of import from his brother.

"I cannot speak to what the factors or the High Holders think or may do, sir, but the fashion in which the note was written was interesting."

"In what way?"

"It was written in standard merchant hand—"

"I told you!" exclaimed Bhayrn.

"If you would let Howal finish," said Charyn firmly. "Go ahead."

"Standard merchant hand is used by anyone in trade. That person could be a clerk, a factor, or a High Holder who has factorages. Clerks are trained to copy the letters in exactly the same way, against a copybook that has precise renderings of the letters. Any deviation from the letters is severely punished. That was how I was taught as a boy. It is almost impossible to determine who wrote something in standard merchant hand."

"Could you still write that?" asked Charyn. "Is it a skill that one never loses? So that a man who once learned it could still do it?"

"I could," replied Howal. "I can't speak for others."

"That means it could be anyone involved in merchanting or trade," concluded Chelia. "Or anyone who has clerks. Is that not right?" She looked to Howal, not to either of her sons.

"Yes, Lady Chelia."

"It still makes it more likely that it's a factor," declared Bhayrn.

"More likely, but that doesn't rule out many others. For all we know, the writer could be an army officer or senior squad leader who was trained as a clerk or someone who is neither and who is a skilled forger imitating standard merchant hand," Charyn pointed out. "What it does mean is that whoever is sending these notes not only has resources, but is very clever." *As if that hadn't been obvious from the start.* "And that they're familiar with the standard merchant hand, which is something I'd never even heard of before Howal mentioned it. I'd be willing to wager that more than a few High Holders have never heard of it, either, especially those not in factoring or trade."

"I said it had to be factors," insisted Bhayrn.

"So you did," replied Chelia, "but it could be others."

"Thank you," Charyn said to Howal. "I never would have known."

Chelia nodded to Howal, then turned back to Charyn. "Did you hear anything about Aloryana?"

"I did. I asked the maitres how she was doing. Maitre Alyna assured me that she was doing well and that she was getting along very well with Lystara."

"Lystara?" asked Bhayrn.

"Their daughter. She's sixteen and already a maitre. Maitre Malyna said that Lystara was even a stronger imager than Malyna herself and that Lystara is the youngest person ever to be a maitre."

"That's not surprising, given her parents," said Chelia. "What else did they say?"

"Lystara is teaching Aloryana the basics of imaging. Maitre Alyna said that it appeared Aloryana has the talent to be a maitre, but that it will take several years of dedication and hard work."

"Good," said Chelia.

Charyn suspected that meant his mother was glad that Aloryana would have to work hard for several years.

"She can concentrate on imaging and being who she is," added Chelia, "and not worry about who she'll have to marry."

"So that all sorts of less desirable types can try to persuade her to marry them for whatever inheritance she has?" said Bhayrn sarcastically.

"She has no inheritance, Bhayrn," said Chelia, "except what your brother chooses to give her."

"Can imagers even inherit?" asked Charyn. "I'll need to ask Sanafryt about that."

"I know that factors make a practice of disinheriting sons who are imagers," said Howal. "Especially firstborn sons."

"Do they have to?" asked Charyn.

"I don't know that, sir. I just know what I said, coming from a factor's family, you know."

Charyn almost asked if Howal had been a firstborn son, then realized that might suggest to Bhayrn who Howal really was . . . and he didn't want to do that, not because he distrusted his brother, but because Bhayrn often talked before he thought . . . and having outsiders know that Howal was an imager would make it even harder for the imager to protect Charyn and Bhayrn. *And after that warning note . . . you'd be even more vulnerable.*

"Factors only care about golds and who gets them."

"Bhayrn," said Chelia coolly, "that refrain is getting tiresome, true as it may be. We all know that."

Charyn thought he saw a trace of a smile appear at the corner of Howal's mouth and then instantly vanish.

Bhayrn appeared about to say something when Chelia added, "That's quite enough." Once more she looked to Charyn. "How did the memorial go . . . and whom did you see there?"

"I did see Factor Elthyrd, and of course Marshal Vaelln and Minister Aevidyr, Minister Alucar, and Minister Sanafryt . . . and their wives. Ferrand and his father." Charyn wasn't about to mention Estafen, although he had appreciated Estafen's presence, because that would reveal more than he wanted even his family to know.

"Not Lady Delcoeur?"

"I didn't see her."

"Not surprising. She's never liked memorial services."

"I was glad Ferrand came. Oh, the only other High Councilor that I saw was High Holder Fhaedyrk. There might have been others, but I wasn't in the best position to see everyone who might have been there."

"Did Saerlet omit the confession?"

"He did, and the hymn after the charge was the one you requested, 'In Vain a Crown of Gold.'"

Chelia nodded. "Could you tell what the reaction was to what you said?"

"They were all attentive." *What else could they be?* "Outside of the envelope, there was no sign of any trouble."

"I'm very glad of that, dear." Chelia smiled. "I think Bhayrn and I must have inundated poor Howal with more than he ever wanted to know about the chateau. I'm quite ready for some quiet, and I imagine you are as well."

Charyn got the message and stood. "We'll leave you until later." He nodded to Howal, although he knew that the gesture was quite unnecessary, since the imager had stood when Charyn had done so. "Are you coming, Bhayrn?"

Belatedly, his brother rose, and the three left the sitting room. Charyn was the last, and he smiled warmly at his mother before he closed the door.

32

Charyn walked down the grand staircase. He usually took the circular staircase when he was going to breakfast, but for some reason he found himself walking down the center of the polished marble risers, his boots echoing with each step, an echo that seemed deeper and more ominous. Why that would be he had no idea. Nor did he have any idea why his breath steamed so much in the chill air. Had the chateau staff failed to keep the fires burning?

As he neared the bottom, he noticed that neither of the two guards posted there moved, almost as if they were statues. He could see his breath, but not theirs. He tried to slow his steps, but it was as if his legs would not obey, carrying him downward until he was on the last riser, and then on the polished white stone of the main level, even with the pair of guards.

The guard on the right turned, unbelievably swiftly.

Charyn gaped, because the man had no face, even as he raised a pistol that Charyn had not seen and aimed it right at Charyn's forehead.

Charyn tried to throw himself to the side, but his entire body felt as though it were encased in freezing molasses, so gelid that he was unable to move quickly. He could see the bullet as if it crept across the freezing air toward him as he struggled against whatever held him captive. He could not look away . . .

"No!"

The sound of his own voice shouting hoarsely echoed everywhere.

"NO, no, noooooo . . ."

Abruptly, he could move—except he was back in his bedchamber, sitting bolt upright in his bed, with Palenya looking at him.

"It's all right . . ."

Even her words seemed to echo in his ears. ". . . all right . . . all right . . . all right . . ."

"You had a nightmare. You're all right," she repeated.

Even in the cold air of the bedchamber, Charyn realized that he was sweating.

"Do you want to tell me?" asked Palenya.

For a moment, Charyn couldn't speak, because his throat was so dry. Finally, he managed to moisten his lips. "I was walking down the grand staircase . . . One of the guards at the bottom shot me. I couldn't move in time. I could see the bullet coming, and I still couldn't move in time. And the guard was faceless." He couldn't help shuddering. "It seemed so real. I didn't even think it was a dream."

"It was only a dream."

"Only a dream?"

"You're here. You weren't shot. There are only guards at the bottom of the grand staircase when there's a ball." Palenya paused. "In the dream, were you alone?"

"Yes."

"That's another thing. You'd never be walking down the grand staircase alone at a ball."

"Maybe it means I will be . . . someday."

"I can't imagine you walking down from a ball all alone."

"I couldn't move, even when I saw him aim the pistol at me."

Palenya put her arms around him. "It was a dream. How could you not have a dream about what happened? What happened was terrible, and you were right there. You told me that they fired at you as well."

"They did."

"The guard was faceless because you don't know who the man who hired the assassin is."

"Palenya . . ." Charyn spoke carefully. "My grandsire was probably killed. My father has just been assassinated. When those things have happened, dreams might be more than just dreams." What he didn't say was that he did have some Pharsi blood . . . and that Aloryana had foreseen some things that had come to pass.

He tried not to shudder.

In some fashion that Charyn did not quite understand, the days after his father's memorial service flew by. In the evenings, he was careful to spend them with Palenya. That way, he wasn't alone. And he made certain, every morning, that he took the circular staircase down to breakfast, even though he had no more nightmares.

Still . . . somehow before he knew it, it was almost noon on Jeudi, the twelfth of Ianus, less than a week before the joint meeting with both the High Council and the Factors' Council of Solidar . . . and he still didn't have the figures he had requested from Alucar. And it didn't help that both *Veritum* and *Tableta* had contained stories in every edition reporting on the latest merchant ships either attacked and escaping or those attacked, plundered, and sunk. One story—only one—had mentioned that a navy frigate had sunk two privateers and saved three Solidaran ships. Charyn had read that in *Veritum* even before Vaelln's dispatch arrived with the details of the navy's success.

Charyn looked up from the petition before him—this one, as Sanafryt had predicted, another one dealing with the conflict of water rights between a small holder and a High Holder. "Howal, would you ask Sturdyn to have someone summon Minister Sanafryt for me."

"Yes, sir."

While he waited, his thoughts went back to a thought he'd kept having, ever since he'd ridden in the coach with the two maitres. *Shouldn't you make a formal request that Alastar attend the joint meeting of the two councils next week?* Whether anyone liked it or not, the Collegium was a powerful force, and Maitre Alastar might just keep tempers in check, or at least the overt expression of those tempers. *You did ask him, and he said yes.* But a formal request . . . He decided to think more on that and returned to the petition.

By the time Sanafryt entered the study, Charyn had finished reading the petition, and was reading another protesting the levying of tariffs on land flooded and unable to be planted and harvested.

"You asked for me, sir?"

"I did. How are you coming on that draft on the language clarifying the seniority of water rights?"

"I should have it ready before the meeting next week."

Charyn sighed. "I'm not bringing it up at the meeting, and I'd like whatever you have now."

"Your Grace . . ."

"Now, Sanafryt. If it's not in final form, you can tell me what you don't like, what you need to change, or anything else that isn't to your satisfaction, but I need it now."

"In a quint, sir?"

"A quint."

As Sanafryt left, Charyn was convinced that Sanafryt had scarcely done anything on the water rights language. That wasn't surprising, given the increasing number of petitions that had begun to arrive, as various claimants reopened old issues or brought up those that they hadn't dared to bring up before, all with the hope that the new rex would see matters differently from his predecessor.

But the whole idea was to preempt some of those petitions, not to react to them.

"Do you have to read all those petitions, sir?" asked Howal.

"You mean, could I just have Minister Sanafryt read them, draft a determination of law or fact, and sign whatever he put in front of me? Yes, I could, but I'd have less and less of an idea of what people are upset about, and what should be changed and what shouldn't." *And you know too little of that already.*

More like two quints later, Sanafryt returned. He handed two sheets of paper to Charyn, who took them and began to read.

Whereas water and access thereto is a valuable commodity, the following provisions with regard to all forms of surface water shall apply and shall supersede any and all pervious and existing legal determinations, petitions, and findings, and shall constitute the law of the land henceforth:

1. The term "surface waters" includes all flowing waters of a continuing nature, including those that are intermittent and/or seasonal as well as all lakes, ponds, and other permanent bodies of standing water, whether such bodies be natural or created by artifice . . .

Charyn slowly read through the entire two pages of the document, then looked up. "This seems to do what I requested. What will be the problems after I sign and publish such a change?"

"There will be few problems immediately. Most will not even consider the changes. The next time there is a drought, however, you will be attacked and vilified by every factor or High Holder who finds he cannot use water he thought he could. High Holders will likely do as they please, and the factors will appeal to you to do something."

"There's no provision here to make people obey the law."

"How would you suggest that be done, sir?"

"What would you recommend, Sanafryt? You're the advocate."

"The usual remedy is financial, sir. A significant fine and damages to be paid to the offended party."

"Add a one-part-in-twenty addition to their annual tariffs for failure to pay the fine and to restore access to the water. Forfeiture of the lands to the rex for a second offense."

"That will not be popular."

"Most likely not, but they all seem to be moved by golds and little else. Besides, all they have to do is obey the law. Those who would be affected are not tenant holders or laborers, but men who should know better."

Sanafryt nodded. "I can have another draft in the morning."

"Good." Before Sanafryt could turn away, Charyn spoke again. "I have another question of legality. Can imagers inherit goods and property, or receive gifts of property?"

"Sir? Are you thinking of the Lady Aloryana?"

"I was, but it raises a larger question. I understand that factors go to certain lengths to disinherit sons who turn out to be imagers, especially firstborn sons. Is this based on custom, or is there something somewhere in the law?"

"I don't recall anything exactly like that, but I'd like to look into it further."

"I'd appreciate it. Thank you."

Once Sanafryt left the study, Charyn went back to thinking about the problems with tariffs based on lands and buildings and property, especially when they were based on ships that had been sunk or lands that had been flooded. Yet, if he changed tariffs to those based solely on revenues and income, how could he ever know whether they were accurate. Import tariffs were one thing, because the goods came on ships. *Except those that are smuggled when the import duties are too high.*

Charyn was still considering whether to read another petition when Sturdyn announced, "Minister Alucar, Your Grace."

"Have him come in."

Alucar hurried in. "I'm sorry to interrupt you, sir. I just received a dispatch from the regional minister of finance in Solis. He reported that he has been unable to determine who was behind the burning of the factors' exchange. His dispatch was in reply to my inquiry at your father's behest."

More like Father's orders. "Did he say anything new?"

"No, sir."

"What do you think?"

"I still believe it could be anyone from a High Holder to a small factor who felt he had been hurt by the exchange."

"Have you received any word from other regional finance ministers about difficulties between factors and High Holders?"

"Nothing like this. At times, in all regions, the factors complain about the high-handedness of the High Holders, and the High Holders complain about the greed of the factors. Each group thinks it pays too much in tariffs and that the other pays too little."

"What about petitions against High Holders by factors?" Charyn almost added, "Or the other way around," but didn't when he realized that there wouldn't be any because the High Holders tended to do what they pleased and that forced the factors into bringing petitions against them.

"I wouldn't know, sir. You'd have to talk to Sanafryt."

"There have been a few. There are some on the desk here. I just wondered if you knew anything about them."

"No, sir. Do you want me to convey anything else to Regional Finance Minister Khalyarn?"

"Not at the moment. Now . . . what about those figures and cost estimates for building ships and a shipyard?"

"I'm almost finished. I should have them by tomorrow."

Another thought struck Charyn. "How much of what is spent on things like the army, the navy, ships, roads, tariff inspectors, regional governors, all those—how much comes from the estates and how much from tariffs?"

"Roughly nineteen parts in twenty come from tariffs, one part in twenty from the estates. That's not exact, but it's close."

"Only one part in twenty?"

"Most of the revenues from the lands go back into maintaining them and paying for all of the expenses of the regial household here in L'Excelsis."

"None of the tariffs have ever been are used for that, I understand."

"No, sir."

"How much are all the lands and estates worth?"

"I have no idea, sir. They're worth what others might pay, but since none have been sold recently . . ." Alucar shrugged. "There are fewer properties with each rex. Your father gave away the great holding in Montagne to his brother. You have the lands at Chaeryll. Those are not entailed."

Meaning that Charyn could give them to anyone he liked without difficulty, not that he had any immediate ideas along those lines.

"And my late uncle promptly joined in with the rebels." Charyn had never understood why his father had not reclaimed the lands but let his uncle Ryentar's young son retain the lands and the title of High Holder, even if the boy had only happened to be four at the time of the revolt. "And another thing . . . how many golds could I draw without imperiling anything?"

Alucar frowned.

"I have an investment for the future in mind. Just let me know."

"Yes, sir."

"That's all."

Alucar inclined his head and left.

Charyn sat there for several moments. He decided he'd go through the Codex Legis himself . . . later that night. For the moment . . .

He turned to Howal. "I think I need to take a walk. How about you?"

"I'd like that as well. Are you planning on going far?"

"Just around the chateau and the courtyard. I don't want to offer myself as an easy target."

"You think that anyone will shoot at you even before you've done anything?"

"No. But I don't feel like giving them the opportunity." *Especially not after that dream.* Charyn stood and stretched. The remaining petitions could wait for a quint or two. And he still had to decide whether to request Maitre Alastar's presence at the joint meeting of councils, something that wasn't likely to set well with any of the councilors.

On Vendrei morning, Charyn was in Norstan's study almost as soon as the seneschal appeared, a good quint before seventh glass.

"Are there any more requests for appointments?"

"Yes, sir. Quite a few."

"Start out with the ones you think I should see."

"There's a local factor, Cuipryn. He wants to talk to you."

"Did he say why?"

"Something about problems with tin or the right kind of copper."

"Is this because of another relative of yours, Norstan?" Charyn tried to keep his tone jesting.

"No, sir. He said it was something you ought to know as rex. I can't say why, sir, but I think you should see him, if only for a moment."

"Who else?"

"Factor Paersyt. He said you'd been talking to him . . . and Yarselt said you'd been to his factorage. I asked Yarselt to see if it was true because he was the one who always accompanied you when you left the chateau."

"I do need to see Paersyt. I should have done so earlier. A quint past eighth glass on Lundi for Cuipryn, and a quint before ninth glass for Paersyt. Who else?"

"Chorister Saerlet . . . he said you had indicated you were agreeable to a meeting."

Charyn shook his head. "No. I said I'd let him know. Tell him that I'm swamped in getting ready to meet with both councils and that it will be several weeks before I can discuss matters." The last thing he wanted was to hear Saerlet weaseling for more golds. "Who else?"

"Factor Weezyr."

Charyn managed not to hide a frown. "Did he say why?"

"No, sir. He just said it might be mutually beneficial."

"First glass on Lundi afternoon."

"Then there's Refaal D'Anomen."

"He's the new chorister for the Anomen D'Excelsis. I don't want to meet with him until after I meet with Saerlet." Charyn didn't want to deal with either chorister, not until he had a better idea of the regial finances.

"He was most insistent . . . something about the state of his anomen."

"Tell him I'm quite busy, but if he wants me to address something, he can write me immediately or see me later."

By the time Charyn finished with Norstan, and received the latest edition of *Veritum*, which he had accepted without looking at, it was after seventh glass when he made his way to the duty alcove to find Churwyl.

The guard captain looked surprised to see Charyn. "Sir? Is anything amiss?"

"Not that I know of. How are you coming with the training of the new guards?"

"It's coming, sir. It's always slow at first, and we've adjusted duty schedules so that the new guards are always paired with experienced partners. When do you think we could begin using them for chateau duties?"

"Not for a while yet. What about Murranyt? Have you discovered any more about what happened to him?"

"No one seems to know, sir."

"What about Factor Goerdyl? Did you find out any more from him?"

"He didn't seem to know much of anything at all about the . . . more shady side of his father's life."

"Or he took it over and doesn't want to admit it. Try again. See what you can find out. See if others in the family know anything."

"Yes, sir."

Charyn had the feeling that the guard captain's voice might have carried a trace of resignation, as if it he knew he wouldn't find out any more. Charyn didn't care. Surely, *someone* had to know something. "Thank you." He managed a pleasant smile before heading for the grand staircase.

As he made his way up to the study, thinking about his brief meeting with Churwyl reminded Charyn of something he'd meant to do, but had let slip. As soon as he entered the study, he walked over to the conference table, where Howal was working on yet another reply to a letter of condolence, most likely from a High Holder located well away from L'Excelsis who, in the future, just might want a favor or a meeting with the new rex.

He kept his voice low as he spoke. "Can you get a message to the Maitre, perhaps through the two imager guards?"

Howal nodded, glancing toward the door.

"I'd like to know anything he can tell me about the former Civic Patrol commander—Murranyt. There was something about him, but my father never told me exactly what." Charyn knew his father had said something, but he really didn't want to admit he hadn't paid enough attention, at least not enough that he remembered. "Also, does he know if a deceased factor named Goerynd had anything to do with assassins?"

"I can do that. It might take a day or two." Howal wrote the two names on a small sheet of paper.

"Thank you. Now, I'd like you to take down an official request to Maitre Alastar, one that will be sent by chateau courier." Charyn smiled at Howal's momentary expression of surprise and continued. "Draft a polite request for him to attend the joint meeting of the High Council and the Factors' Council of Solidar next Meredi, the eighteenth of Ianus, here at the chateau at the first glass of the afternoon. Write that while we talked about this and he agreed, the request is a formal confirmation, since decisions made or announced as a result of the meeting will affect all of Solidar, including the Collegium, and that it would appear beneficial to the Collegium if he attended all such meetings from here on."

Howal was silent for several moments before replying, "Is that all, sir?"

"For the request, yes."

Howal returned to the conference table, where he seated himself to begin drafting the request.

As soon as Charyn sat down, he immediately began to read *Veritum*, hoping that there were no more stories or articles about him or the various shipping problems. That was a vain hope, because there was a short story about the fact that the new rex would be meeting with both councils on the forthcoming Meredi, and it was likely that a bitter discussion would occur over building warships and the tariffs to pay them. The writer suggested that, surely, the wealthy regial family didn't need to impose higher tariffs, particularly on hardworking factors, when it appeared that the rex didn't do that much anyway . . . and that the factors had also suffered other reverses, such as the burning of the exchange in Solis the previous month.

Why is the newssheet mentioning that? Still wondering about that, Charyn read the rest of the newssheet with some trepidation, but that was the only story that affected him, even indirectly.

Before long, Alucar arrived, carrying a small sheaf of papers, which he set on the edge of the desk as he seated himself across from Charyn.

"What can you tell me about building a shipyard so that the navy isn't at the mercy of the existing shipbuilders?"

"It's not a simple matter, Your Grace. The best location for a regial shipyard dedicated to building warships remains Solis. There the daily wage of a master shipwright runs between one and two silvers. That is higher than the wages in Westisle, Nacliano, Estisle, or Tilbora, but there are other aspects to consider. The best wood for shipbuilding is the live oak that grows in the forests around the Sud Swamp. The timber can be floated down the Sud River to the Aluse and from there to Solis. The next best is Midcote oak, but there are few shipwrights in either Tilbora or Midcote. Most of them build for the coastal trade or for fishing—"

"What does all that have to do with what it will cost to build a regial shipyard?"

"Your greatest costs are timber and men, not the shipyard itself. There are vacant properties along the bay at Solis. They can be had for a reasonable amount. You can get the shipwrights by paying slightly more than a silver a day, just by guaranteeing them work year around. In Midcote and Tilbora, the winters are long and cold, and for at least a third of a year, you cannot build ships. In other areas besides Solis, you would have to ship the timbers a great distance at a much higher cost or to use inferior wood . . ."

Charyn forced himself to listen as Alucar laid out all the reasons for building a regial shipyard in Solis. When the minister finished, he asked, "How much will all this cost?"

"Ten thousand golds this year, fifteen thousand next year, and five thousand a year thereafter. That does not include the actual costs of each vessel nor of its fitting out."

Charyn tried not to swallow. "How much of that can we raise without increasing tariffs?"

"That depends on what you decide not to spend, Your Grace. Currently, if matters go as in the past, and if you build the two extra warships announced by your sire, and you use all the reserves, you will have at most five thousand golds to spare."

"How accurate have your predictions been in past years?"

"If there is no widespread drought or flooding, they have been very accurate. Floods and droughts change everything."

"Do you have detailed figures on what you just told me?"

"Yes, sir." Alucar lifted the papers and handed them to Charyn. "I believe those cover everything I have told you."

"Thank you."

After Alucar had left the study, Charyn stood and turned to Howal. "Let's take a walk down to see Minister Sanafryt. I need to get out of the study, at least for a few moments."

Howal grinned as he stood. "As you wish, sir."

"Getting a little tired on variations of the same letter?"

The imager only smiled.

The two walked from the north corridor to the grand staircase. Charyn glanced down the shimmering stone structure. There were no guards at the bottom, not that there ever were, except at balls or grand occasions. He descended carefully, then made his way eastward along the south corridor.

When he knocked and immediately opened the study door, Sanafryt rose from behind his desk. "I would have been glad—"

"I needed to move about." Charyn nodded for Howal to close the door, but he remained standing. "I asked you yesterday about imagers being able to inherit. Last night, I went through the Codex Legis. I couldn't find anything that prohibited it. In fact, the only section on inheritance dealt with High Holders and the restrictions on entailment. There was nothing about inheritance for anyone else, not even the rex. Did I miss something?"

Sanafryt shook his head. "There isn't anything else. There likely wouldn't be under the circumstances."

"Why not?"

"Vaelora and Quaeryt are supposed to have drafted the basic codex for the first Rex Regis. You may recall he was also a scholar . . ."

"He was?" *Why was so much about the first Maitre so hidden?*

"He was. With Vaelora being the younger sister of the rex and being married to an imager, I somehow doubt that the rex would have made it impossible for him to gift anything to her."

"So I could gift Aloryana . . ."

"It's not that simple. There is the matter of precedent. A number of justicing determinations have found that property owners do have the right to disinherit sons who are imagers. Part of the reasoning behind that lies in the fact that Imagisle is exempt from tariffs, both through precedent and a decree from the first Rex Regis, which has never been revoked, and since imagers do not pay tariffs, they should not have property that would otherwise be subject to tariffs . . ."

"That sounds like stretching logic."

"It may have been, but that decision was rendered three centuries ago, and upheld a number of times since. There has been no problem when regial lands have been gifted, because only the rex and his immediate family are exempt from tariffs. So, if Aloryana were not an imager, no one would say anything."

"They won't anyway, assuming I did so."

"The High Holders and factors might. You know how they feel about tariffs."

"Does everything in Solidar these days turn upon tariffs?"

Sanafryt offered an ironic smile in return.

Charyn laughed. "Of course it does."

Sanafryt nodded. "Is there anything else?"

"The water-rights addition to the Codex?"

"Taemylt is writing out a fair copy right now. It should be ready within the glass. Once you sign it, the clerks will make copies and send one to the High Justicer, each High Councilor, and each regional governor."

"I can give them to the High Councilors on Meredi, but make additional copies so that I can give them to the members of the Factors' Council of Solidar as well."

"That we will, Your Grace."

"Thank you." Charyn nodded, then turned.

Howal had already opened the door. After the two left the study, Howal closed the door and hurried to catch up to Charyn.

"He's not happy about that," said Charyn as he and Howal walked toward the grand staircase.

"I've heard it said that advocates seldom are happy with changes in the laws, and that when they are, it is a cause for worry."

"I wonder who said that. The man who recommended you, perhaps?"

"It just might be, sir."

"Well . . . back to the rest of what lies waiting in the study." Charyn started up the grand staircase.

35

Charyn did not so much sleep late on Samedi morning as lie in bed thinking until well past sixth glass when he finally turned over and looked at Palenya. "Later today, I want you to begin to teach me a new clavecin piece."

"Will you have time?" She offered a humorous smile.

"It's Samedi. None of the ministers are here. Besides, you said I should practice, and I'd like something new to add to what I know. And you want to feel that you're earning your pay as a musician."

"Then I'd better leave and get ready."

"I said later. Besides, I told Hassala to send up breakfast for both of us at a quint before seven."

"I don't know if this is such a good idea . . ."

"It's a very good idea, and the sitting room is far warmer than the senior staff room this early in the day. You can also take your time."

"You *are* insistent."

"No . . . I just want your company."

Shortly thereafter, breakfast arrived, carried on two large trays.

As Charyn settled into one of the chairs at the sitting room table, he looked to Palenya. "You also get to eat sooner this way."

"Are you trying to bribe me to stay?"

"Am I succeeding?" Charyn poured tea from the teapot kept warm by a small candle, first for Palenya and then for himself.

Palenya laughed warmly. "You're succeeding in flattering me."

"That's a start. Don't let your breakfast get cold." He looked down at the browned ham strips, the cheese and mushroom omelet, and the warm loaf of dark bread—and the sweet berry preserves that accompanied it.

"I wouldn't get this downstairs."

"That's why you're getting it here. I'm going to enjoy it much more with your company, and I hope you enjoy it more with mine."

Almost a glass later, Palenya left, insisting that it would be a challenge to find music suitable for him to play, especially something challenging, but not impossible. After washing, shaving, and dressing, Charyn made his way to the study, where Howal was already at the conference table, writing.

The imager looked up. "I'm just finishing the last of the replies to the sympathy and condolence letters."

"Until we get some more from places like Estora and Noira that likely haven't even heard about the assassination. There probably won't be that many of those."

"What would you like me to do once I finish the letters?"

"We'll start on the simpler petitions. We'll draft a response and have Sanafryt review it for law and precedent. It's likely to be faster that way." *And you can get more of them off the desk . . . and probably make more factors and High Holders unhappier even sooner.*

A little more than a glass later, as Charyn was working on petitions with Howal and still half-thinking about how to present matters to High Council and Factors' Council, Maertyl rapped on the study door.

"Your Grace, there's a messenger here from Maitre Alastar. He says he can only deliver the message to you."

Charyn gestured to Howal. "Have him come in."

"Yes, sir."

As the messenger in imager grays entered, Charyn again looked to Howal, who nodded.

"Your Grace, I have three missives, two are to be delivered to you. The other is from Imager Aloryana to Lady Chelia. Maitre Alastar said that no immediate response is required."

"Thank you. I'll take them so that you can report that you delivered them to my hands."

The messenger stepped forward and handed three sealed envelopes to Charyn, who inclined his head. The messenger then stepped back, turned, and departed.

"We'll take this one to my mother immediately," Charyn said.

His mother was not in her sitting room, surprisingly. Charyn finally found her leaving the kitchen.

"You just got a letter from Aloryana." He handed Chelia the still-sealed letter.

"We'll all go to the receiving parlor."

Once the three were in the parlor, and seated, Charyn said, "You read it. Then you can tell us however much you want to."

"I'm sure there's nothing . . ."

"That might be, but the letter is to you."

As Chelia extracted two sheets, written on both sides, she smiled. "Apparently, she does have a great deal to say."

Charyn watched his mother's face as she read, but he could see no signs of worry, and several brief smiles.

When she finished and had replaced the letter in the envelope, she faced Charyn. "She is definitely pleased to be with the Maitre and Maitre Alyna. Lystara is like an older sister, if a quietly demanding one. Alyna says she is already an imager second, whatever that means, and both maitres have told her she's likely to become a third within the next year." Chelia looked to Howal.

"If she makes third at her age, she's almost certain to be a maitre. That's if she works at it."

"What else?" asked Charyn.

"She's getting tutored in mathematics by Maitre Alyna, who makes geometry interesting and inspiring. She has to run two milles every morning that the weather permits. All the imagers whose health permits have to do that. They also have exercises she has to do. She says she needs to get stronger in order to be a better imager."

"Imaging can take great physical strength," added Howal in a low voice that barely carried.

"Oh . . . the food at the Maitre's dwelling is quite good. The food in the dining hall where she eats her midday meal is filling and not much more." After a moment, Chelia said, "You can read it later, if you wish, dear."

"Thank you, but it is her letter to you."

Not until Charyn and Howal had returned to the study did Charyn open the first missive from Maitre Alastar. The key sections were comparatively short and succinct.

Although there was never any absolute proof, events strongly suggested that Commander Murranyt poisoned his predecessor with the assistance of the former, and late, High Holder Laevoryn. Murranyt also avoided looking into various crimes, including arson and murder, perpetrated by the brownshirts housed on Laevoryn's L'Excelsis estate.

He took a stipend from his position as Commander of the Civic Patrol less than a year after the High Holder revolt and lived quietly in L'Excelsis for some *time after that before departing. I am having others look into when he left the city and where he may have gone, although it may be difficult to ascertain much about either.*

I am also looking into Factor Goerynd and his son. As soon as I know more, I will be in touch.

Charyn handed the letter to Howal for him to read, then opened the second. It was far shorter.

As Maitre of the Collegium Imago, I appreciate your desire to include the Collegium in the meeting on Meredi, 18 Ianus, and will be present.

The Collegium also appreciates your determination to include it on a continuing basis in meetings of the councils.

With a relieved smile, Charyn let out the breath he hadn't even realized that he had been holding. He took the first letter as Howal returned it, and handed him the second.

When he had the second one back, he replaced both in their envelopes, which he laid on the desk. He fingered his chin, thinking. *Should you talk to Churwyl about this?*

Finally, he shook his head. There really wasn't much point in doing that until and unless Alastar discovered information that changed what Churwyl had told Charyn himself.

By the first glass of the afternoon, Charyn had dealt with more than enough petitions and other correspondence. He stood up and looked at Howal.

"I think you should take off the rest of the day and Solayi. There's not that much for you to do here, and I'm not going anywhere. I promise not to leave the chateau. I also suspect I'm going to need your presence a great deal in the week ahead."

"Sir . . ."

Charyn walked over to where the imager stood by the conference table and lowered his voice to a murmur. "You can check with the Maitre, and if he disagrees, you can return immediately. I'd rather not take complete advantage of you."

"Under those circumstances . . . I thank you."

Charyn smiled. "Now . . . go."

"Yes, sir."

After Howal tidied up the papers on the table, and departed, Charyn headed for the music room, where he hoped to find Palenya—and did.

"I've found something that should challenge you," she said with a smile, one that was not quite mischievous. "It's also by Farray."

"I don't know that I want to be challenged immediately. Could we play the Farray duet first?"

"We can . . . Yes, I'd like that." She eased onto the clavecin bench beside him.

Charyn had to concentrate, and yet, at the same time, feel the music. He managed both, although he wasn't quite certain how, but he found himself smiling when he lifted his fingers off the keyboard at the end of the duet.

"You're ready for the other Farray piece," Palenya said, slipping off the clavecin bench and walking to the sideboard that held the sheets of music. As she walked back to the clavecin, she continued, "This is a short nocturne. Most are longer, but it has a hint of syncopation, and Farray himself said it represented nostalgia lit by passion." She placed the music before Charyn.

"What is it called?"

"Farray didn't name the nocturnes. It's just Nocturne Number Three."

Charyn looked at the music once . . . and then again. "Are you sure I can play this?"

"No. You can't play it, but you're good enough to learn to play it. The opening bars are the key." She sat down beside him. "Try to think of a summer evening when both moons are full." Her fingers almost caressed the keys as she played the passage.

Charyn could immediately feel why she liked the nocturne.

"Now . . . you try it."

He stopped after two bars and shook his head.

"Why did you stop?" Her words were gentle.

"It . . . didn't feel right . . . didn't sound . . . together."

"That's good."

"Good?"

"Good that you could sense it immediately."

Charyn wasn't so sure.

More than a glass later, he still wasn't sure, despite Palenya's insistence that he was doing well on a difficult piece. "I thought I asked for something challenging, not impossible."

"It's not impossible. It's just very difficult, but it's something you can do . . . if you want to work on it."

While her words weren't said in a challenging way, Charyn felt that giving up would disappoint her . . . and, for some reason, he found he didn't want to do that.

He smiled ruefully. "Would you play that last part again?"

When Charyn finally left the music room, sometime after third glass, he discovered that he felt better, and more cheerful, than he had any time since finishing breakfast, even if the only parts of the nocturne he felt he had played well were the opening bars and perhaps a third of the first page of the music.

36

When he left Norstan and headed for the study on Lundi morning, Charyn was still feeling cheerful, perhaps because there were no letters or dispatches waiting for him, and Norstan had no additional requests for meetings. It might also have been because he'd had a very quiet Solayi, with a morning spent with Palenya, and time to actually work on learning the Farray nocturne, and although he could see that it would take a great deal of effort to learn to play it smoothly and accurately, he'd still enjoyed the practice.

Because it's something where you can hear the results . . . unlike matters of petitions, tariffs, and council? He checked his wallet again, making certain he had the golds he needed, then stepped into the study.

As seemed to be Howal's wont—*or sense of duty*—the imager was already at the conference table.

"Did you enjoy your time off, Howal?"

"I worried some, sir, but I did. I came back last night."

Charyn nodded. "In a bit, a Factor Cuipryn will be here. Norstan thought I should see him. I'd appreciate your keeping an eye on him, closely, until we know more."

"I can do that."

"After that, we'll be seeing a toolmaking factor I've known for a time. His name is Paersyt. He's developed a steam device, an engine that might be able to be used for many things. Just listen carefully. This afternoon, Factor Weezyr will be here. He owns the Banque D'Aluse." Charyn picked up the three sealed envelopes on the corner of the desk. "I'd wager these are more condolences."

"That's a wager I wouldn't take."

Charyn smiled wryly and slit open the first envelope before sitting down, then the second and third. He read each quickly. He'd been right. "You can work on these, Howal, while I read a few more petitions." He wasn't looking forward to those, either, but the sooner he went through them, the sooner he'd be done. *Until more arrive.*

"Factor Cuipryn, sir," announced Sturdyn, shortly after eighth glass.

"Send him in." Charyn stood and waited.

The man who entered the study wore a brown jacket and trousers of good quality, but with a certain wear. His sparse brown hair was shot with gray, and his face bore definite worry lines.

Charyn offered a pleasant smile and motioned to the chairs in front of the desk. "Please sit down."

"Your Grace . . ."

"You can sit." Charyn seated himself, then waited for the factor to do the same before asking, "Why did you wish to see me?"

The graying factor glanced down for a moment before replying. "Factor Elthyrd. He said that you might grant me an audience. He said you wouldn't grudge me even if you didn't agree to see me."

"Just what might be the matter that concerns you?"

"I'm a copper factor and a coppersmith, Your Grace. It's getting harder and harder to get tin or zinc. That's not good. If I want to keep my factorage working, I may have to use copper ores that have more arsenic . . . or even add it."

"Arsenic?"

"Yes, Your Grace. The metal from the arsenic ores takes more work-hardening, and you've got to be real careful in casting. The fumes, you know. More than a few apprentices have burned their eyes, even lost their sight. Not mine, mind you. I've been careful, but it'd be much better with tin, or zinc."

For a moment, Charyn did not reply, thinking. "Which ore is more costly?"

"They're all costly these days. It takes more work with the arsenic, and more can go wrong."

"What do you expect from me?"

"I expect nothing, Your Grace. I can only tell you what I know."

"What if what it takes to get you tin and zinc will raise your tariffs? Building scores more ships does not come cheaply. Then what?"

"I cannot say that would be good for me. I might have to let one of my apprentices go."

"I think you've made your point about arsenic, Factor Cuipryn. Is there anything else?"

"No, Your Grace."

"Have you shared these concerns with others?"

A puzzled expression crossed the older man's face. "A few other factors. The problem with the Jariolan pirates affects us all."

Charyn stood. "I thank you for telling me all this. I will think about it before I decide."

The copper factor stood and bowed deeply, then backed away for several steps, before turning and leaving the study.

Charyn turned to Howal. "What do you think?"

"He said what he said to someone else, and they persuaded him to try to say that to you."

"Another form of trying to persuade me to do what I don't have the golds to do," said Charyn dryly.

A quint before ninth glass, Paersyt stepped into the study, his gray hair slicked back. He wore a deep maroon coat, rather than the stained and worn leathers that Charyn had seen before.

The toolmaker bowed, then straightened, as if he were not certain what to do next.

"I'm sorry you had to request a meeting. I've been meaning to get back to you, but," Charyn gestured vaguely around the study, "as you must know, my life has been rather upended. Please sit down."

Paersyt did so.

"I still am very interested in your steam . . . engine . . . and what it might be able to do. Have you had any others interested in it?"

"No. No one thinks it will make golds for them."

Charyn nodded. "If you obtained limited funds for now, could you keep working on it?"

"I could. For models, not to build a large working engine, one that could move a small flatboat."

Charyn nodded, then reached into his wallet and extracted the golds, leaning forward and setting them on the desk before the toolmaker. "Here are ten golds. Keep working on it."

"Your Grace . . . I never asked . . ." Paersyt made no move.

"I know you didn't, but there's a chance you can develop something very workable." Charyn couldn't have said why he felt that way, but he did. There was just something about Paersyt. "Use them carefully. Just let me know when you have made some progress."

"Yes, Your Grace. I will."

Charyn stood. "I look forward to seeing what you can do."

Once Paersyt had left the study, Charyn looked to Howal, who had not quite concealed his puzzlement. "I'd like to see what he does with ten golds before I spend a thousand times that." Charyn didn't explain further, but said, "Let me see those last letters."

Between the two of them, they finished the last of the responses to the letters of condolence and drafted four petition replies for Sanafryt to review by the time, just before first glass, when Sturdyn announced, "Factor Weezyr."

Charyn had pictured Weezyr as a dark-haired, narrow-shouldered figure with deep-set eyes and hunched shoulders. The reality was rather different. The banking factor was tall, with broad shoulders, perfectly brushed blond hair, and cheerful green eyes. As he entered the study, his immediate smile was warm and welcoming.

"Your Grace, I do so much appreciate your seeing me."

Charyn gestured toward the chairs and immediately reseated himself. "What might be the reason you wished to see me?"

"I had an idea that might be of benefit to Solidar," said the factor as he sat down.

"Go on."

"Well . . . as you must know . . . anyone can mint coins . . . so long as they meet the standards set forth in the Codex Legis."

"Since you're bringing the matter up, do you think that's a problem?"

"It is for the banques and the exchanges. We have one man who spends much of his time weighing and water-checking golds and silvers. We have to go as much by weight as anything. People complain if we won't accept full value for coins that have been clipped or shaved. Have you ever thought of a regial mint? Or having a banque mint coins for you?"

Charyn hadn't thought of either. "What would be the advantage?"

"Every regial coin would be accepted at stamped value, unless obviously clipped."

"That would be to your advantage," said Charyn. "Why might it be to mine? If the regial coins are the best, people would hoard them and use others in trade. If others' coins are better, then they'll use the regial coins, and everyone will say that the rex is trying to cheat them."

"In time, you might forbid other coins for trade."

"This is something I'm going to have to think about, Factor Weezyr." Charyn wasn't going to think too hard. To make regial coins the only coin of the land would require changes in law. Not only that, but he'd have to build the mint and obtain the raw gold. In the end, the cost of those changes would fall on the factors and High Holders . . . with both of whom he already had enough trouble. *Perhaps in the future . . .*

After ushering Weezyr out, Charyn decided he'd much rather see coppersmiths and toolmakers than ever deal with Weezyr again. *That doesn't mean you won't have to.*

He looked at the remaining petitions and took a deep breath.

37

By ninth glass on Mardi morning, Charyn was still poring over the figures that Alucar had supplied him, not to mention the latest figures on the golds in the regial treasury and what could be expected over the coming year. At about a quint past the glass, there was a rap on the study door.

"Undercaptain Baaltaar with an urgent dispatch from the marshal," announced Sturdyn.

Charyn looked to Howal, who immediately set down his pen and nodded.

"Have him come in."

The study door opened, and the officer entered, a man who looked even younger than Charyn, wearing duty greens, with his visor cap under one arm and a sealed envelope in his right hand. He walked to the desk, inclined his head, set the envelope down and said, "A dispatch from Marshal Vaelln."

"Thank you, Undercaptain. Does the dispatch require an immediate reply?"

"No, sir."

"Then you may go."

"Thank you, sir." The officer inclined his head once more, then turned and departed.

Charyn picked up the envelope and slit it open, without breaking the green wax seal. He began to read.

> Your Grace—
>
> We have just received word of a naval encounter off the east coast of Jariola that occurred on the twenty-third of Finitas. The incident took place between two of our third-rate ships and one first-rate ship and a five-ship flotilla of Jariolan warships, each roughly equal to a second-rate ship of the line. The Jariolan ships were in the process of preparing to attack three Solidaran merchant vessels. They refused to lay off, and one attacked our leading third-rater.

In the ensuing battle, we lost the third-rater, but sank three of
the Jariolan vessels and damaged the others. The surviving
Jariolans withdrew, presumably to Jariolt. The merchanters
proceeded, apparently unharmed. They indicated that their
destination was the Abierto Isles.

This is the first encounter involving the loss of more than a
single Jariolan warship at one time, and I thought you should
be apprised of it . . .

Charyn reread the dispatch. The words didn't change. He doubted that
the Jariolans would feel anything but outraged that their attempted piracy
had turned out the way it had.

*Is this enough to lead to war . . . or will there be just threats of war? Or will nothing
be said while they redouble their attacks on our ships?*

It didn't matter that such an attack amounted to piracy. The Oligarch
wasn't going to be pleased, and that likely meant an increase in attacks
on Solidaran merchanters. And then whoever had killed his father and
sent the latest note would strike again. Charyn also had no doubts that
what was in the dispatch would be in the next edition of *Veritum* . . . and,
if not, in the next one of *Tableta*.

"Howal, you should read this." Charyn held up the single sheet, then
waited for the imager to take it. "When you finish, I'd like to hear what
you think."

Howal stood and crossed the room. After receiving the dispatch, he
remained before the desk and read it. He cleared his throat before handing the sheet back to Charyn. "I am not a military person, sir. I would
think that the Jariolans would not be pleased. They lost three warships
to a smaller force near their own shores."

Charyn nodded. "If they retaliate by attacking more of our merchanters, there will be even more cries that the rex needs to do something.
It's likely that they may already have responded. That happened almost
four weeks ago."

"Four weeks, sir?"

"Word reached me more slowly than I would have liked, but the ship
carrying the message may have had adverse winds. Under the best conditions, for a warship under full sail, it would have taken the news almost two weeks to reach Kephria, and another five days for a courier
from Kephria to reach L'Excelsis."

"Wouldn't the ship go to Westisle?"

"It likely would, but a fast sloop or schooner from there would reach Kephria faster than a courier." He'd learned that from Vaelln, something he wouldn't have known months earlier.

He'd have to tell the members of both councils what had happened with the Jariolans, although he wouldn't be surprised if some of them found out before the meeting tomorrow, but whether any who did would reveal that knowledge was unlikely, because it would indicate they had a spy in army headquarters . . . or a relative, although most officers closely related to High Holders were supposed to be posted away from L'Excelsis. *It only takes one.*

He still had no way of knowing whether his father had released his uncle Ryel from his duty as head of the High Council or demanded that Ryel remain. Although it was likely Ryel would appear at the meeting in any event, it would be good to know. *But would it?* Charyn frowned. Since he didn't know, and since his father was known to have kept his decisions to himself, even if Ryel had heard a decision, Ryel might well think Charyn didn't know . . . but . . .

Charyn shook his head. He'd just have to act as if he'd never heard anything and as if he'd expected Ryel to remain as the chief of the council. If he acted any other way, that would lead others to expect he knew more than he did, when he already was aware that he knew far less than he should.

38

The first thing Charyn did upon reaching his study on Meredi morning was to read *Veritum*. While he was relieved that the contents of Vaelln's dispatch hadn't appeared in the newssheet, the salient points of the lead story were bad enough.

> . . . word is that the new rex has received a threat similar to the one Rex Lorien received before his assassination . . . appeared immediately after he spoke at his father's memorial service at the Anomen D'Rex . . . likely that some ship-owners are tired of losing vessels to the so-called privateers . . . nothing more than pirates commissioned by the Jariolan Oligarch to destroy Solidar's trading . . . Rex Charyn might face worse than paper threats if he doesn't take a stronger stand . . .

How can you take a stronger stand . . . and with what?

Finally, he set aside the newssheet. For the rest of the morning, he and Howal dealt with the last of the petitions, all of which had requested special considerations in paying annual tariffs, and all of which he had denied, on the grounds that granting special treatment for certain losses of structures and vessels and not others amounted to regial favoritism.

By a quint before first glass, Charyn was nervous. *What if some of them don't come . . . or all of them?* He stood by the window and pulled back the hangings. While the day was gray and looked cold, there was no sign of snow—except in the dirty heaps remaining from the last storm. He let the hangings fall back into place and turned back to look at the empty conference table. Howal was on the main level and would escort the factors to the study.

Charyn had debated having the various council members ushered into the study before he joined them once all were present, but decided on following his father's example of allowing the factors to gather in the music room and the High Councilors in the receiving parlor and then having both groups enter the study beginning with the factors. Since the

Maitre was perceived as being more allied to the rex, Charyn had left instructions for Alastar to be immediately escorted to the study.

At just after a quint before the glass, Alastar entered the study. "Good afternoon, Charyn."

"Good afternoon, Maitre." Charyn did not sit down. He was too nervous to sit. "Did you see the story about the threat in *Veritum*?"

"I did. Alyna and I told no one."

"The only one who knew about the contents of the note were you, Alyna, my family, and Howal. I never mentioned what was actually in the note to anyone. Even Chorister Saerlet only heard that there was a threat, but not what it was."

"I assume you have kept all those notes under lock."

"Hidden lock," replied Charyn.

"Then the contents were revealed by whoever wrote the note. They were likely given to someone else, anonymously, and dispatched by public messenger."

"In merchant hand as well," suggested Charyn dryly.

"Someone wants everyone to know you've been threatened. Can you think why that might be, besides trying to put pressure on you by letting all the shipping factors know that someone is desperate enough or angry enough to try to kill two rexes if you don't stop the Jariolans?"

"That's the only reason I can come up with," Charyn admitted. "Do you have any thoughts on the matter?"

"Only that they're intelligent, well-informed, and scarcely short of golds."

"That only limits my enemy to a few thousand people."

"Less than that. Whoever it is either lives in L'Excelsis or has minions that do and has been diligent enough to learn a great deal about the chateau and how matters proceed within."

That was obvious, but Charyn knew quite a few people who fit that description, and doubtless there were others who did.

As the chimes struck the glass, there was a rap on the study door. "All the factors and High Holders are here, sir."

"Have Howal escort the factors here. Norstan should follow with the High Holders."

"Yes, sir," replied Sturdyn.

Alastar picked up one of the chairs set before the goldenwood desk and carried it toward the conference table. "I think it might be best if I took a chair slightly away from the table, to your left."

"I defer to your far greater experience and understanding, Maitre." Charyn moved to the head of the table, his back to the north windows as he stood behind the chair. "I'll be announcing that three navy warships sank three Jariolan second-rate ships of the line, and damaged two others. The Jariolans were attempting to board three Solidaran merchanters near Jariolt." He glanced at the table, where copies of his change to the water-rights section of the Codex Legis were set before each place.

"You don't sound that pleased." Alastar's tone was even.

"I fear it's a step toward greater hostilities, if not war. Even if Marshal Vaelln's ships are as successful in every encounter, our factors and those High Holders involved in shipping will continue to suffer losses for some time."

Elthyrd led the factors into the study. He was followed, in order, by Jhaliost, Thalmyn, Harll, and Hisario. The five took their places on the left side of the table, the side away from the west wall. Almost immediately, the four remaining High Holders entered. Ryel was the last, and he smiled warmly and then nodded to Charyn before taking a position behind the chair at the far end of the table. Basalyt took the position closest to Charyn on the right side of the table, with Fhaedyrk next, and then Khunthan.

"Welcome to the chateau," said Charyn, gesturing for everyone to sit. "I appreciate all of you coming." He seated himself. "Before we begin the matters proper of the meeting, I do have some information for all of you. Yesterday, I received a dispatch from Marshal Vaelln informing me that three of his warships intercepted a Jariolan flotilla attempting to board and sink three Solidaran merchanters . . ." After finishing the description of the event, he added, "Marshal Vaelln has every confidence that our newer warships are superior to Jariolan ships of the same class, but we are still outnumbered considerably by the Jariolans, and the Ferrans appear more than willing to attack our merchant shipping when they think they can get away with it." Charyn waited.

"Before we deal with the issue of trading, warships, and the like," said Fhaedyrk quietly, "from what is on the table before me, I can see that you are changing that section of the Codex Legis dealing with water rights. I do not believe you even consulted with the High Council on this matter."

"Copies of the change are before each of you." Charyn smiled pleasantly. "I had the Minister of Justice review both the previous provisions of the Codex as well as the legal precedents. The problem that arose is that the precedents differ in different parts of Solidar. The entire point of the Codex is to make laws the same everywhere in Solidar. The most sensible precedents were those based on water rights being tied to the ownership of the land and that the claims to water rights being established by the first date of productive use."

"High Holders have always had seniority in old Tilbor," declared Fhaedyrk.

"Seniority has always been based on first use in Khel," countered Jhaliost.

"That conflict is exactly why I have added the provisions to the Codex Legis. I thought it was necessary because it is clear that no regional governor would ever allow such an issue to reach the High Justicer. Only by a petition did I even hear about this," said Charyn. "Perhaps you think otherwise, but the point of law is to establish a certain degree of fairness. Would you claim it fair for a High Holder to take water used by a factor whose family has exercised the rights to that water for generations? Especially if that High Holder had never used that water productively before?"

"That has always been the custom in Tilbor."

"I understand that. That is why laws supersede custom. That is the principle established by the first Rex Regis, and my duty as rex is to follow that principle." Charyn could see that all the factors were looking at Fhaedyrk.

"I am surprised that you chose this . . . precedent . . . so soon."

"I could see that the matter wasn't going away, High Holder. The longer I waited to address it, the more conflicts that would have been likely to arise."

"You have only changed one type of conflict for another."

"That may be," replied Charyn, "but it will be more open and under the law, not custom, which seems often to be what people wish to believe."

Elthyrd gave the smallest of nods, as did Jhaliost, while High Holder Basalyt's face stiffened momentarily.

In the silence that followed, Charyn spoke again. "Both the High Council and the Solidaran Factors' Council have expressed concerns about the piratical acts of Jariolan privateers." Charyn looked down the table, looking directly at Ryel for a moment. "Dealing effectively with those privateers, and now, even Jariolan warships, will require building more ships of our own. According to the master ledgers of the Minister of Finance, construction of a ship of the line costs about four thousand golds, and another two thousand to ready it for battle. At present, the navy is building about four new ships a year, and my father committed to building two more in this coming year.

"That is the most we can build under current conditions. But . . . if we develop our own shipyard just for warships of the line, we could increase the number of ships being built each year to eight . . . and the cost of those ships would be less for each one, possibly even a thousand golds less."

"That sounds very impressive, but I cannot believe that can be done with the current level of tariffs," said Ryel calmly. "As you may know, the High Council is opposed to any additional increase in tariffs at this time . . . or in the foreseeable future. We have borne significant increases over the past five years, and the High Holders feel that such increases should be more than sufficient under prudent management."

Charyn decided not to mention the shortage of funds. *Not yet.* "What is the High Council's position on the destruction of Solidaran shipping by Jariolan privateers?"

"We find it barbaric and regrettable." Ryel paused. "At the same time, successful shipping factors make great profits. Such profits come with great risks. Building more and more warships beyond what is already planned in order to reduce those risks would require increased tariffs. Those tariffs would fall mainly on High Holders and factors who do not profit from sea trading. So the majority of factors and High Holders would be more heavily tariffed to increase the profits of a comparative few." His voice was smooth, even showing a sense of regret as he finished.

"Honored High Holder," began Hisario, irony dripping from his words, "all of Solidar benefits from trade, except perhaps some High Holders. Bronze and brass are essential. Making them requires tin or zinc. We have little of either in Solidar. You'd also like your cooks and vast kitchens to have spices, I'd wager. Your ladies and daughters would not like to do without the silks from Otelyrn. Nor would you get the best of teas from Stakanar. I could spend glasses listing all that comes from trade. If this piracy is not stopped, prices for everything will continue to increase—"

"And so will your profits," countered Khunthan.

"Not if my ships lie at the bottom of the oceans," retorted Hisario.

"Tariffs are high enough," muttered Jhaliost.

"Too high," added Factor Harll.

To those comments, both Thalmyn and Basalyt nodded.

Charyn noticed that neither Ryel nor Elthyrd showed any change of expression. "Why don't we look at the tariff situation," he suggested. "The tariff rolls show that there are close to sixteen hundred High Holders and almost thirty-six hundred factors who pay two hundred golds or more in tariffs each year. An additional ten golds in tariffs on those factors and those high holders would raise slightly more than fifty thousand golds, enough to build and equip eight more ships each year. In five years, we could be on an equal footing with either Jariola or Ferrum." That was oversimplifying, because not that many more ships could be built in the coming year, and those tariffs would have to go toward building the necessary shipyard, but overall it could work.

"That's absurd," declared Basalyt.

"Your mathematics and logic overlook a fundamental unfairness in the tariff system," said Ryel, his voice firm and without emotion. "Tariffs are based on property and assets. Trade and commerce based on reselling of what others produce do not require nearly the physical assets that land and manufacturing do. The cargo of a merchanter is far, far more valuable than the vessel. If you impose additional tariffs on all High Holders and factors, you are penalizing even more those whose income arises from land or mining, or the manufacture of various goods, in order to improve the protection of traders and shippers, who already pay effectively lower tariffs."

Charyn nodded, trying frantically to think of a reply to his uncle's calm statement. "Would any of you like to comment on this? You, perhaps, Factor Hisario?"

"That's cherry-picking, most honored High Councilor," retorted the shipping factor. "I get tariffed on my warehouses, my piers, and my ships. I pay tariffs for roads I seldom use, for an army and a navy that haven't been that much help so far, and doubtless for lots of other things that don't benefit me. That's likely true for all of us."

"Are you referring to High Holders as well?" asked Ryel.

"I'm talking about everyone who pays tariffs," replied Hisario.

For a moment, there was silence, but only for a moment.

"How much of our tariffs go to support you and your family and all your great estates?" asked Basalyt.

"I'm glad you asked that, High Holder. I actually went over those figures with the Finance Minister. The regial estates, including the Chateau D'Rex and the Anomen D'Rex, fully support themselves. One part in twenty of the golds from the estates are paid in lieu of tariffs and provide more in golds for shipbuilding, roads, and other Solidaran requirements than the tariffs of any ten High Holders."

"You have ten times the lands anyone else does."

"You wanted to know if your tariffs are supporting the regial family," Charyn pointed out. "They're not. In effect, the rex pays tariffs as well."

"How do we know?"

Charyn smiled. "I'd wager that I'd much rather have you look at the regial accounts than you'd wish my Finance Minister to look at your private accounts."

Fhaedyrk offered a fleeting and amused smile.

"You've said nothing, Maitre Alastar," offered Elthyrd. "What are your views on the matter?"

"You must decide whether your particular interests are more important than those of Solidar as a whole. If you all decide that your interests are greater than those of Solidar, then Rex Charyn will have to decide whether fighting another revolt is worth the time, effort, and golds."

"Those are hard words, Maitre," observed Ryel.

"They are," agreed the Maitre, "but when the rex needs golds to protect some of his subjects and others refuse to pay what they must under the Codex, then such failure amounts to revolt or rebellion. That has already occurred twice in the last twenty years. It's better said in the open than concealed behind ambiguous words . . . or pleasant ones that are deceitful."

"Not paying tariffs—" began Khunthan.

"Is a repudiation of the authority of the rex," interjected Alastar. "That is rebellion. You might call it civil or tariff disobedience, but it amounts to the same thing."

"That's absurd!" declared Basalyt loudly.

Alastar turned and fixed his eyes on the High Holder. "Is it? As I recall, several High Holds near yours were razed in the Wars of Consolidation for failing to obey the rex. When Jariolan ships attack Solidaran merchanters and warships, it might as well be called war."

Basalyt looked away from the Maitre, even as he said in a low voice, "We're supposed to give everything up for others?"

"I don't believe the rex asked for that," replied Alastar. "If I heard correctly, he wanted an average of ten golds a year more from each of you."

"For many High Holders," said Ryel, "that amounts to an increase of one part in twenty, and for some who are already struggling, it might be as much as one part in ten. You're asking much at a time when times are not the best."

"That is also not an insubstantial sum for many of the smaller factors," added Elthyrd.

"Any increase is too much," insisted Basalyt.

"Especially now," added Harll with a nod.

Charyn was mentally calculating. If two-thirds of the factors were smaller . . . and the smaller factors only paid five golds, he could make that work. "Perhaps five golds for the smaller factors, and ten for the larger factors and the High Holders."

"Too much," declared Jhaliost.

"Agreed," said Basalyt.

"Is ten golds worth waging a war over?" asked Alastar dryly. "Or five for a small factor?"

Elthyrd cleared his throat. "The factors might consider accepting that . . . if the rex does indeed build the additional ships and he agrees not to levy further additional tariffs for warships in the coming years. But . . . we need to establish who is a small factor."

"What would you suggest?" asked Charyn.

The factors exchanged glances. Then Jhaliost leaned toward Elthyrd and murmured something.

After a moment, Elthyrd nodded and said, "Any factor who pays less than fifty golds a year in tariffs would be a small factor, just for purposes of this additional tariff. And those who pay less than twenty-five golds in tariffs should only have an increase of one part in ten over what they now pay."

Ryel looked as though he might object, then nodded. No one else said anything.

"I would agree to that . . . with one provision," replied Charyn, "that, if Solidar is threatened, or faces extraordinary circumstances, I reserve the right to raise additional tariffs, but I would not do so before consulting the two councils."

"A man can't argue with those two points," conceded Elthyrd. "So long as we're consulted first."

"The High Council does not agree with the need for additional tariffs," declared Ryel, "but in the interests of preserving harmony, we will accept the tariffs under the conditions you just stated. We also understand that the tariffs will not be imposed or due until the normal time when tariffs are collected. The High Council will not agree until you have sent a formal declaration setting forth those conditions."

"I will send a declaration with those conditions to you and to Factor Elthyrd, with copies to the other councilors." Charyn paused momentarily. "I will also send a copy to the High Holder selected to take the place of the late High Holder Oskaryn, once he is named and you have informed me."

Ryel merely nodded.

"Are there any other matters any of you wish to bring before me?" Charyn looked down the table.

"Will you be making more changes to the Codex Legis?" asked Fhaedyrk.

"I have no others I am considering."

"That response is not particularly reassuring."

"I do not intend any others at this time. If other situations arise where precedents conflict or precedents and laws conflict, I may consider changes, but I know of nothing like that at present."

"That seems fair enough," interjected Ryel before Fhaedyrk could say more.

Charyn hadn't expected Ryel's words, but he appreciated them, even as he wondered why his uncle had effectively cut off any further discussion of the matter by the High Holders. From what his mother had said more than once, Ryel never did anything merely out of kindness, and there was always a reason behind every action.

"Are there any other matters you wish to bring before us, Rex Charyn?" asked Ryel formally.

"Not at this time, High Councilor. Seeing as I am new to these responsibilities, there may be other matters when we meet next month . . . on the eighteenth of Fevier." Charyn looked, in turn, to Elthyrd. "Have the factors anything else they wished addressed."

"No, Your Grace."

"Then . . . we will meet next month." Charyn gestured as he stood.

He remained standing at the head of the conference table as the councilors stood and departed, noting that Ryel did not look at him. Charyn had the feeling that his uncle had not been totally pleased with the way the meeting had turned out, even though Ryel had not been vociferous in his opposition to the tariffs.

Once the councilors had left and the study door was closed, Charyn turned to the Maitre. "What do you make of that?"

"You never mentioned that you had been threatened," said Alastar.

"It didn't seem wise to admit that. I can't say why."

"You were likely right. It might have seemed to some that you wanted to tariff them to save yourself."

"I greatly appreciated your presence."

Alastar smiled. "One might think that you had observed such meetings before."

Charyn shook his head. "I was worried. So much could have gone wrong. Your presence kept everyone calmer than it would have been."

"Sometimes my presence does. Sometimes it does not. It takes judgment to know when."

Charyn laughed ruefully. "I have to say that I was just hoping it would."

"You have their agreement on tariffs. You realize that neither your father nor your grandfather obtained such."

Charyn heard a flatness in Alastar's voice, and he paused a moment to consider just what the Maitre had said and the implications before he responded. "I doubt I would have obtained it without their efforts and your presence." *And the agreement doesn't mean my troubles are over, only that I can plan to build warships.*

"You don't sound elated, Charyn."

"I'm not. Building warships will take time. We'll lose more merchanters and warships in the meantime, and many factors and High Holders won't be happy." He offered a crooked smile. "But it is a start."

Alastar nodded.

"If you have a moment, I would think my mother would appreciate any news you might be able to give us about Aloryana."

"I can certainly spare a little time for that."

Charyn led the way out of the study, and they walked along the north corridor to Chelia's sitting room. When the two opened the door and entered, Howal eased out, but stationed himself in the corridor outside. Charyn closed the door.

"Maitre Alastar, how good of you to see me."

"Charyn thought you might like to hear about Aloryana."

Chelia pointed to the chair closest to her. "Please, do sit down. I know Aloryana's only been at the Collegium two weeks, but how is she doing?"

"She's doing quite well," replied Alastar as he seated himself. "She's well ahead of the other seconds and thirds in academic instructionals, except for mathematics and geometry, but Alyna and Lystara are tutoring her, and she's making excellent progress. She's beginning to grasp the basics of practical imaging, and she can already hold a weak shield for a fraction of a quint."

"Enough to protect herself?"

Alastar shook his head. "That will likely take a year or more, but most imagers don't get as far as she has until they've worked at it months, if not longer. Most never develop strong shields. Usually only maitres do, and it takes time . . ."

From where he sat on the settee, Charyn tried to listen, but his mind was elsewhere, still thinking about the meeting with the two councils. Everything he knew told him that matters shouldn't have gone that smoothly. Was that just because Alastar had been present? Or were they just agreeing because they expected him to be assassinated as well? Even before they had to pay the additional tariffs?

After Alastar had spent a quint with his mother, Charyn escorted him to the front entry, then headed back up the grand staircase with Howal, only to find Bhayrn standing at the top, glowering at him.

"Why didn't you tell me that Maitre Alastar was here and telling Mother about Aloryana?"

"I didn't know where you were."

"You could have sent someone to find me. She's my sister, too, you know."

You never seemed to care that much before. You didn't even want to play duets with her. Charyn kept those words to himself. "The Maitre didn't have that much time."

"Whereas I have all the time in the world, doing nothing, and you couldn't even spare a moment to have someone find me."

"I have had a few things to deal with, Bhayrn."

His brother snorted. "As if you ever cared."

"If I didn't care . . ." Charyn shook his head.

"Will I ever be able to go riding again?"

"It's only been three weeks—"

"More than a month! It was the twelfth of Finitas. A month of doing nothing but indoor exercise and too much clavecin practice. A month of—"

"You're absolutely right."

"It's so kind of you to grant that. How long?"

"Until we either stop getting threats or can discover who is making them and dealing with them."

"That could take years."

"If . . . if I don't know more in another month, you can do whatever you please."

"Is that a promise?"

"It is."

"I'll hold you to that." Bhayrn turned and walked toward Chelia's sitting room.

Charyn shook his head . . . again.

"Your Grace," offered Howal quietly, "if anything happens to both you and your brother, the only possible heir is High Holder Regial, and he is not of age."

"The way I feel right now, Howal, is that if the High Holders and factors of Solidar are self-centered and stupid enough to allow that to happen, they Namer-well deserve what befalls them."

"Does everyone else?"

Charyn paused, then sighed. "Probably not, but, outside of the Collegium, I don't see anyone terribly interested in what's best for Solidar."

"Does that matter?"

Charyn laughed ruefully. "I suspect I know who tutored you." He could just imagine Alastar offering such a question.

Howal only smiled, if faintly.

The two continued toward the study, but Charyn was thinking about Howal's observation about the young High Holder Regial, the only son of his father's unlamented late brother Ryentar. It seemed an unlikely fact for Howal to know and bring up. *Unless Maitre Alastar briefed him.* Charyn nodded.

Once in the study, Charyn sent for Alucar, since the Finance Minister needed to know what had happened.

Alucar arrived with a concerned expression, doubtless because he had to have known that Charyn had met with both councils. "Your Grace."

"Apparently, I've reached an agreement with both the councils on obtaining additional tariffs for additional warships and also building a regial shipyard."

For a moment, Alucar looked stunned. "Sir?"

"There are conditions. I can't collect the additional tariffs until the regular tariffs are due this fall, and there are two levels of levies . . ." Charyn went on to explain the details. When he finished, he said, "That was the best I could do under the circumstances, I think."

"That you got any agreement at all is remarkable." Alucar paused.

"I thought you would like to know so that you could work out estimates of when and from where the funding will come for next year's shipbuilding."

"That will be most helpful. I do foresee some difficulties . . ."

Charyn refrained from sighing. "I'm certain there are a number of aspects I did not anticipate."

"It will take time to find and purchase the land necessary, and the master shipwrights . . . and finding the necessary timber—"

"Use the exchanges, either the one here or the one in Solis."

"Ah . . . there is the matter of membership . . ."

"The head of the Factors' Council, Factor Elthyrd, is an exchange member. Or perhaps the head of the shipyard, when he is selected, could become a member in Solis. There might be other possibilities as well."

"I suppose that could be arranged."

"What else?"

"If you hire the best shipwrights, it will cost more, and those wanting to build merchanters will be angered . . ."

Charyn listened and commented for another quint before Alucar finished enumerating and describing other difficulties, all of which seemed both accurate—and surmountable. "I appreciate your thoughts. Let me know immediately if you have problems in dealing with any of those issues."

"Yes, Your Grace." Alucar inclined his head. "Thank you for letting me know."

"If you don't know, you can't do your job." Charyn stood, smiling pleasantly, and watched as the Finance Minister departed. Then he turned to Howal. "Now we need to draft a letter to both councils stating the agreement reached, as well as the conditions I agreed to." He had no doubts that there would be several drafts . . . and that Sanafryt might well suggest changes in the wording for reasons of law.

39

The comparative ease with which he had secured agreement for the additional shipbuilding tariffs was still worrying Charyn when he woke on Jeudi morning, far more than the minor word changes that Sanafryt had suggested for the letter to the two councils. All he'd heard for years was how difficult, how impossible, the High Holders were. *And how greedy and gold-grubbing the factors are.* Yet they'd agreed . . . and he still wasn't sure why.

Before he left his sitting rooms for breakfast, he went to the sitting room window, pulled back the hangings, and scratched away enough of the frost on the glass to peer out. Scattered snowflakes drifted down from the gray clouds, with only a hint of wind, and the windowpane was cold enough that frost began to re-form almost immediately. He let the hanging fall closed and headed for the family breakfast room.

Once there, he ate quickly, and then he made his way to Norstan's study.

"Good morning, sir," offered the seneschal.

"Good morning, Norstan. Are there any requests for appointments?"

"Only one, sir. That's Chorister Saerlet."

"Again?"

"Yes, sir."

"Tell him . . ." Charyn shook his head. "I'll see him at first glass of the afternoon. Did he say what he wanted?" *Besides golds to refurbish a perfectively good anomen.*

"No, sir. He just said he needed to see you."

"Send someone to tell him."

"Yes, sir."

"No one else?"

"No, sir."

Charyn thought there would have been more, even despite the cold and snow. People had always been clamoring for appointments with his father, not that Lorien had granted that many. Why did so few wish to meet with him? Were they waiting to see what he did first? Or was there some other reason? He looked hard at Norstan. "Are you absolutely sure?"

Norstan took a step back. "Yes, sir. I am, sir."

"I may not wish to see all who ask, but I need to know who requests to see me and why. Is that clear?"

"Yes, Your Grace."

Charyn's next stop was by the duty desk of the Chateau Guard, but Churwyl was not there, although the duty guard assured him that the guard captain was in the rear courtyard of the chateau conducting an inspection.

"Tell him I might be making an inspection of the grounds myself sometime later."

"Yes, sir."

Charyn half-wondered what had made him say that. *Because you feel so confined? Because you want to see for yourself how and where the chateau guards are posted?*

He was still pondering over that, as well as Meredi's meeting and the sudden lack of interest in meeting with him, when he entered his study, nodding to Howal. "Apparently, almost no one wants to meet with me."

"You haven't been rex all that long, sir."

"That may be." Charyn wasn't convinced. After thinking over what the duty guard had told him, Charyn said to Howal, "Get on a coat. We're going to walk around the outside of the chateau."

Howal frowned.

"The walk will do me good, and I've never really looked at who is posted where. I'll wear my green jacket and visor cap. I'll meet you at top of the grand staircase."

After returning to his room and donning the green riding jacket that was almost identical to the ones the guards used and the visor cap, Charyn walked to the top of the staircase, where Howal was already waiting. The two walked down to the main entry.

Churwyl hurried forward, his face red, mostly likely from the cold outside. "Sir?"

"Howal and I are going to walk about the chateau. I'll be close the whole time."

"Your Grace . . ."

"I haven't left the chateau in days." *It feels more like weeks.* "Have your men seen anyone suspicious?"

"No, sir." Churwyl's voice was resigned.

"Good. We won't be all that long." Charyn turned and nodded to Howal.

Once they were outside and walking down the white stone steps toward the front drive, Howal said quietly, "It might be best if we stayed close together."

"Thank you. I appreciate the reminder." Charyn recalled that Malyna had experienced some difficulty in holding shields across several people and eased closer to the imager.

"Do you think this is wise, sir?"

"Probably not, but I'd like to see who might be watching and what happens." Charyn glanced back over his shoulder. He wasn't surprised to see Churwyl and two more guards standing at the stop of the entry steps. As he watched, Churwyl motioned the guards back inside and turned.

As he walked down the drive, Charyn found the wind stronger than it had seemed, and in moments his eyes were watering from the chill. Halfway down, he turned north along the stone walk that divided the topiary gardens on the east side of the chateau, smiling as he recalled playing seek-and-find among the sculptured trees. Aloryana had complained, often, about being at a disadvantage in skirts. Charyn chuckled to himself, recalling that all the women imagers he'd seen, in grays, anyway, always seemed to wear trousers. *She won't have that excuse now.*

"Sir?"

"I was thinking about Aloryana." Charyn paused in the middle of the east garden, looking down at the ring road to the east where he could see only two horse-drawn wagons and a single carriage, the carriage headed north, and the wagons south. After a considerable time, he turned toward the chateau and studied it. There were no guards on the east side, but then, he supposed there didn't need to be, since there were no doors on the east side, and the first-level windows were barred.

Overhead, the clouds seemed to be darkening, but the snow did not seem to be falling. Wind had blown the few flakes that had fallen earlier into the garden, where they were piled around the base of the various sculpted trees. "It's colder than it looked." Charyn resumed walking toward the drive that ran from the ring road up to the rear courtyard, with its stables, coach houses, and barracks.

Howal said nothing.

Charyn glanced at the imager, who was looking everywhere, and immediately felt concerned. *You really shouldn't have done this.* When he reached the drive, he glanced toward the ring road, but saw no one and no wagons or carriages on the ring road near the drive. He started up the drive, noticing that the guards at the courtyard gates were watching him. As he and Howal passed the pair of sentries, one on each side of the stone pillars that supported the ironwork gates, he could see the sentries' eyes turning to follow him.

At that moment, he heard one crack and then another. From the corner of his eye he saw Howal stagger, and then a puff of snow or dust on the stone wall next to stable door. He glanced over his shoulder and down the drive. He saw no one there.

"Sir! Inside. Now!" Howal's words were a command.

Charyn didn't hesitate, but ran alongside the imager to the rear entrance and up the stone steps. Once inside, though, he stopped immediately and looked back at the courtyard, asking Howal, "Are you all right?"

"I'm fine. What about you?"

Charyn forced himself to concentrate on his own body. "I didn't feel anything hit me."

"Good. That was a rifle shot. Two shots."

"I heard. One of them hit the wall by the stable door."

"Which side?"

"The right side. The north side."

"Then the shots came from south of the drive." Howal frowned. "How high was it?"

"Just above the night lantern bracket."

"Rex Grace! Your Grace!" The words came from Churwyl as he sprinted through the courtyard gates and toward the rear steps. "Are you all right?"

"We're fine." Charyn stepped back. He discovered that his legs were shaking. He took a slow deep breath and waited until Churwyl stood in the rear entry hall. "What did you see? Did you find anyone?"

"I heard the shots, and I started running. I have guards searching. I didn't see anyone. It could be that whoever shot at you was hiding in the lower east garden. Or they could have fired from the alleyway across the ring road. My men are checking both places."

"Keep looking."

"Yes, Your Grace." Churwyl cleared his throat. "Your Grace . . . ah . . . do you think . . ."

"The shooting either means that someone wants to kill me regardless of what I do, or that they think whatever I'm doing isn't enough. And, unhappily, it means that I shouldn't walk where I can be seen."

"That might be . . . for the best, Your Grace." Churwyl glanced nervously at Howal and then toward the courtyard.

"Go," said Charyn. "See what you can discover. Then come and tell me what you find."

"Yes, sir." The guard captain backed away, then turned and hurried out the rear doorway.

"We might as well go up to the study." Charyn paused. "I suppose I ought to tell Mother that someone shot at me. It wouldn't do for her to hear from someone else." He turned and headed for the stairs, only to find Chelia coming down them.

"What was all that about?" Chelia looked at Charyn, then Howal.

"Howal and I went out to check the postings of the guards. Just as we entered the rear courtyard someone shot at us."

"At you, you mean."

"The shots were closer to Howal."

Chelia again looked at Howal and her son. "Of course, they thought you were a guard and he was you."

"I'm blond. His hair is brown."

"It's light enough to be mistaken for you, especially at a distance." Chelia looked to Howal. "I know he's the rex, but do remind him that people want him dead if he wants to take another walk."

"Yes, Lady Chelia."

She turned back to Charyn. "Did you see the shooter?"

"He was behind us. I took a quick look back, but didn't see anyone."

"I didn't either," added Howal.

"You're fortunate neither of you were hit."

"Howal might have been . . . except . . ." Charyn didn't finish the sentence.

Chelia looked to Howal. "I cannot tell you how much I appreciate your presence."

"I'm glad I've been able to help."

Charyn cleared his throat and waited for Chelia to look at him before he said, "I'd appreciate it if you told Bhayrn what just happened. When I suggested that going riding was a bad idea, he didn't take it well. If I tell him . . ."

Chelia nodded. "I will tell him."

"Thank you." Charyn offered a lopsided smile. "Since walks seem to be something to avoid for now, Howal and I will address various matters and papers."

"I think that's a very good idea."

Charyn nodded and then started up the grand staircase.

Once he was back in his study, he immediately walked to the window by the desk. He pulled back the hangings and looked out the window and down at the courtyard. He probably hadn't had the training in geometry that Howal had, based on what Maitre Alastar had said about Aloryana, but from what he recalled, the bullets could not have come from the ring road, not if anyone wanted to hit him. The drive downhill to the ring road was steep enough that the bullets would have struck the stone wall even higher than they had. Conceivably, the shooter could have fired from an upper-floor window in the building on the far side of the ring road . . . but the shooter would have to have had excellent eyesight and been an outstanding marksman. Then again, those who had shot Bhayrn's horse and the chateau guard must have had those skills. He felt that there was something . . . something he was missing.

More than one thing. Why hadn't he been shot at when he had been walking along the east side of the chateau and through the garden? He'd been far more exposed then. Or hadn't the sniper recognized him because of the guard jacket and cap . . . until the guards in the courtyard obviously deferred to him? Still . . .

He shook his head. "Howal . . . if you'd come here."

"Yes, sir."

"You were on my right, and we were just inside the gates when the sniper fired. The first bullet hit your shields, didn't it?"

"It did, but I think it might have been a little high. My shields extend a ways from my body."

"The second shot went over our heads and hit the wall just above the lamp bracket. That's even more to the right. I don't see how the shooter could have fired from across the ring road, unless he was in a building. Do you?"

Howal looked down at the courtyard and then to the east, clearly measuring with his eyes. "I'd have to agree with that."

"And given the angle from which the bullet came, he couldn't have been standing on the drive or north of it . . . Or even in a building across the ring road."

"You're saying he was standing in the garden. Not too far below the walk."

"That's what it seems like to me. But there was no one there when we walked by. At least, I didn't see anyone. Did you?"

"No, sir. I was looking carefully, too."

"That means that the shooter was waiting there, crouching down behind one of the topiaries. But why did he wait so long to shoot?"

"It might be because, if he shot when we were closer, he wouldn't have had as much time to get away."

"That's one possibility," said Charyn. "The other is that whoever it was . . . the guards thought he belonged there."

"You think it was another chateau guard?"

"That's what comes to mind, especially after what happened to my father. At this point, it could be any of a number of guards." Charyn let the window hangings fall back into place, darkening the room despite the fact that all three lamps were lit. He walked to the desk and sat down. "I didn't mean to start the morning this way. Well . . . let's see what *Tableta* has to say."

The newssheet didn't mention the meeting at the chateau, but there was a short story mentioning the naval engagement with the Jariolan warships near Jariolt. He'd barely finished reading *Tableta* when Churwyl arrived in the study.

"What did you find out?" asked Charyn, who did not motion for the guard captain to take a seat.

"Someone was in the lower corner of the garden, behind one of the trees. The tracks in the snow show that he stepped out to take the shots."

"How did he get in there?"

"He could have climbed over the wall along the ring wall. We found fresh bootprints there in the snow. It's old snow, and it's hard to tell even how big the boots were."

"Just how did he get there without your guards noticing him?"

"You can't see that corner from the posts at the courtyard gates or from the front entry."

"If he couldn't see the courtyard gates, how could he possibly have gotten a shot so close to me?"

"He hid out of sight. Once you walked past, he moved farther uphill in the garden to where he could see the gates. There are tracks to that point. Then he retreated the way he had come and climbed over the wall. He probably stayed behind the wall until a wagon or carriage came by and then ducked behind them to cover his escape across the ring road. He left the rifle behind."

"And no one saw him get away?"

"No, sir. I looked for someone when I heard the shots, but I never saw anyone, and I wanted to find out if anyone had been hit."

Charyn supposed he couldn't blame Churwyl for that. "Is the rifle one of ours?"

"No, sir. It doesn't have one of our numbers. I checked."

"Why?"

"After what happened to Rex Lorien . . . I wanted to make sure. The rifle is the same kind as ours. That's also why I checked. But it's not. It looks . . . well, it looks a little different . . . like the ones the brownshirts used in the revolt. There were a lot of those around at one time."

"Did you find anything else?"

"No, sir."

"And none of the guards saw anything?"

"No, sir."

Charyn felt like yelling at Churwyl. Instead, he took a deep breath. "That will be all. See if you can find anything else."

"Yes, sir."

As the guard captain left, Charyn wondered how many times he'd told Churwyl to find out more, not that Churwyl ever seemed able to do so.

"Sturdyn," Charyn called out, "have someone tell Minister Aevidyr that I need to see him."

While he waited for Aevidyr to appear, Charyn walked to the window, eased the hangings back, and looked down at the rear courtyard. It was empty, except for the two guards by the gates, just as if nothing had happened.

"Minister Aevidyr, Your Grace."

"Have him come in." Charyn turned and waited, then motioned for the older man to sit down before seating himself.

"You asked for me, sir?"

"I did. Please check with Minister Sanafryt to see if he has sent a letter to the regional governor of Khel with the change in the provisions of the Codex Legis dealing with the seniority of water rights. Sanafryt should have noted that the change supersedes and invalidates his decision on the petition by . . ." Charyn had to rummage through the papers on his desk to find the right one. ". . . Factorius Aquillyt from Ouestan against High Holder Eskobyl."

Aevidyr frowned. "Normally—"

"I just got shot at this morning. I'm not in the best mood. I'm not asking you to write anything. After we're done here, I just want you to find out if Sanafryt sent out the letter. If that would upset you, then just tell him that I need to see him."

Aevidyr stiffened. "I can do that, Your Grace."

"Good. Now, tell me about the regional governor of Khel . . . everything you know."

"Warheon is the second son of High Holder Khunthan . . ."

Charyn couldn't say that he was exactly surprised, but he kept listening.

". . . has been very effective at assuring that tariffs are collected on time and forwarded to L'Excelsis . . . has the best collections from factors . . . his wife is the youngest sister of High Holder Basalyt . . ."

"And I suppose his son is married to the sister of the previous High Councilor from Khel?"

"Ah . . . to the daughter of Draalan, the High Councilor before Khunthan's predecessor."

Charyn nodded.

When Aevidyr finished, Charyn simply said, "Thank you. If you'd tell Sanafryt I'd like to see him."

"Yes, Your Grace."

In less than half a quint, Sanafryt was in the study facing Charyn, who remained standing.

"Minister Aevidyr said that you wished to see me?"

"I wanted to know if you'd dispatched the water-rights change to the Codex Legis to the regional governors."

"The copying was finished yesterday. I'm working on the letter to Regional Governor Warheon."

"Good. Let me see it tomorrow, before you send it."

"Perhaps I should re-draft it for your signature."

"I take it that you weren't going to specifically tell Governor Warheon that the change in the law overrides his decision on Factorius Aquillyt's petition . . ."

"I hadn't thought it necessary . . ."

"Given the way High Holders think, it is. To make it perfectly clear, perhaps you should also draft a second letter that overturns his decision. And draft a letter to Factorius Aquillyt so that he knows as well."

"Do you plan to act as your own Minister of Justice, Your Grace?"

"Only if you make it necessary that I do so. I value your legal knowledge and understanding, but I do have this feeling that it should serve Solidar and not any one group. If you do not agree, of course, you are perfectly free to offer your resignation."

"I have only offered what I have felt was the best advice, Your Grace."

"I do understand, Sanafryt. Believe me, I do." What Charyn really wondered was whether Sanafryt was also receiving funds from elsewhere. "I'd like to see all those letters by first thing tomorrow. I know you can do that. Please don't disappoint me."

For the first time, Sanafryt looked worried, if but for a moment. "Yes, Your Grace."

"Thank you." Charyn offered what he hoped was a warm smile, but once Sanafryt had left the study and closed the door, he turned to Howal. "Did Sanafryt look worried?"

"More than worried, I would say, sir."

So it wasn't just your imagination.

Chorister Saerlet arrived promptly at the first glass of the afternoon. His round face looked more drawn than Charyn recalled, and his dark black hair was somewhat disarrayed, as if he'd walked through the wind and not bothered to comb or smooth it down.

"Good afternoon, Your Grace." Saerlet glanced toward Howal.

"Howal is my personal secretary. He's been an enormous help in assisting me in dealing with all the petitions and papers I found awaiting actions." Charyn motioned to the chairs and seated himself. "What brings you here today?"

"I wanted to know if the memorial service was to your satisfaction, and, of course, that of Lady Chelia."

"It was. You did exactly what she requested, and she was pleased that you did. My apologies for not sending you a missive confirming that. Things here have been . . . somewhat stressful."

"I'm most sorry to hear that. Is there anything I can do?"

"Not unless you might know who it is who keeps taking shots at the regial family."

"Oh . . . dear. I had not heard . . ."

"It just happened a little while ago. You wouldn't have heard. Someone fired several shots from the ring road, but he disappeared before anyone actually saw him. Somewhat like whoever left that missive for me in your anomen."

"There were so many people there, Your Grace. I never saw any of the congregants even approach the pulpit . . . but I told you that."

"You did. Did anyone else?"

"Ah . . . one of the ushers did."

"And?"

"He was approached by a man who handed him an envelope. The

man said it was a note of condolence for you. It was light enough that it could only be a letter. He didn't think anything of it."

"Does he remember what the man looked like?"

"No, Your Grace."

Something was gnawing at Charyn. It took him a moment to realize what it was. "Usually there aren't ushers in an anomen."

"That's true, but for something like this, we have members of the congregation act as ushers. So many people, you understand."

"Why did you wait so long to tell me?"

"I didn't know until last night. The usher read about threats against you in the newssheet, and he thought about the envelope and told me what happened. You'd told me there was a threat . . ."

Charyn nodded. Unfortunately, what Saerlet said made sense. It also revealed that whoever had been behind that threatening letter was very familiar with the procedures for memorial services at the Anomen D'Rex. "Thank you. I do appreciate your letting me know."

"I am very sorry, Your Grace. I just didn't know."

"Under the circumstances, I can understand that."

For a time after Saerlet left, Charyn just stood by the window, thinking. He had a feeling that it all made sense, except he couldn't figure out how.

At fourth glass, he went to the kitchen to arrange for dinner for two in his rooms. Then he went to find Palenya. As he'd hoped, she was in the music room, apparently sorting sheet music and arranging it in the special cabinet designed just for that purpose.

When she saw him, she set down the sheets she held and hurried toward him, stopping just short. "Are you all right? Hassala said someone shot at you."

"They almost hit Howal. Churwyl couldn't find the shooter. Neither could any of the guards."

"The guard captain couldn't find a fresh-baked loaf in the kitchen if it was pointed out to him with a pitchfork."

"You don't think much of him."

"None of kitchen help or the maids like him at all. They've told me he hires guards whose parents pay him for the privilege."

Charyn knew, if only from the way Hassala smiled when he asked for dinners for two, and from the fact that those meals were often better than what was served in the dining room, that Palenya was on good terms with Hassala and the others. "What else?"

"Isn't that enough?"

"It's more than enough, but I can't dismiss the entire senior staff all at once."

"The entire staff?"

"Not the cooks or kitchen help, or the ostlers, or you, but . . . well, you should know. The ones who are taking advantage of their position. Among the more senior people, that's almost everyone, except for you and Hassala, from what I can tell."

Palenya smiled faintly. "I'm not as good as you think. I'm taking advantage of you just by staying."

"And I'm taking advantage of your lack of opportunities, even more of you than you are of me. If you're going to be honest, you should see that." He looked directly into her eyes.

After a moment, she looked away.

Charyn smiled as warmly as he could. "It's been a long day. I'd really like to sit at the clavecin and play the duet with you . . . and then have you work with me on the nocturne. I'm tired of petitions, letters to obstinate regional governors, ministers who take forever to do things that Howal and I could do in less than a day . . . that is, if there were two of us. That doesn't even count the factors and High Holders." He shook his head. "No wonder Father was always in a bad mood."

"I can do that . . . if you'd really like to."

"I very much would . . . and I've arranged for dinner for the two of us."

She laughed gently. "It's not as though I could say no."

"You could, and I'd honor that, but I hope you won't."

"You mean that."

"I do."

"There are times when I might like to turn you down. Not today."

Charyn smiled and gestured toward the clavecin. "Shall we?"

40

By Vendrei morning, Charyn felt better. Spending the night with Pale-nya had definitely improved his mood, although just spending time and talking with her had helped the most. But one remark of hers still stuck with him, the fact that Churwyl was paid by the parents of the men he hired. That didn't surprise Charyn. It seemed as though half the senior staff, if not all, were trying to make golds off their positions. What bothered him were the differences between what Churwyl had said about hiring the traitor guards and the fact that he was being paid off. The guard captain had represented himself as looking for the best, but it was more likely that he'd just wanted to recruit more guards to fill his own wallet. Could he have been paid off for another purpose?

He was still pondering that when he sat down at the breakfast table across from his mother. He also realized that he and Howal had never finished the final version of the letters about tariffs to the two councils. "Good morning, Mother."

"You look a little pensive this morning."

"There's a lot to be thoughtful about."

Chelia lifted her mug and took a swallow of tea. "I think it's time for you to move into the regial quarters."

"I don't want to displace you."

"I appreciate the thought, dear, but remaining where you are would do great disservice to both of us."

"Because everyone will think I'm your tool? And that I'm not in control?" Charyn laughed softly. "No rex is really in control of Solidar."

"Are you just saying that to excuse yourself from acting?" Chelia's voice was level.

He shook his head. "I'll certainly do what I can and what I think best, and those who owe position and power to me will follow my direction unless they see a greater self-interest and feel that they can escape the consequences. That doesn't mean I can stop certain forces greater than any of us."

"Such as?" Chelia's tone of voice was between skeptical and sardonic.

"The imagers, for one. The growth of the power and wealth of the factors. The shortsightedness of both the factors and the High Holders. The continuing piracy of Jariola. That, I might stop in time, but certainly not immediately."

"That doesn't mean you can't direct those forces to some extent."

"I might have, a little, on Meredi when I did get both councils to agree on a small increase in tariffs, enough to create a shipyard and to build more warships."

"That's a start."

"What do you honestly think of Sanafryt?"

Chelia raised her eyebrows. "Why do you ask?"

"Because he was not happy when I insisted that he enforce a decision I made about water rights. I changed the Codex Legis so that all Solidar was under the same rules, and those were the ones that were the most fair. He tried to avoid telling Governor Warheon that the governor's decision against a factor had been overturned. That would have required the factor to file another petition to get the law enforced against the High Holder who had usurped his water rights."

"Sanafryt has always supported the High Holders. Your father knew that. He didn't often oppose Sanafryt's legal rulings because he knew that would cause more trouble. Sanafryt didn't go against what was specifically in the Codex."

"But he shaded things in favor of the High Holders wherever it wasn't obvious?"

"I don't know that. Your father seldom revealed names or specifics. I wouldn't be surprised, though."

"What about Alucar?"

"The most honest of the three ministers. He's the only one I'd trust out of my sight . . . or yours."

"And Aevidyr?"

"He toadies up to everyone who has golds or power, and then gets offended if any idea of his is in the least criticized. That's what your father said."

"Why did he keep them?"

"He said he doubted he could find better."

Charyn took a sip of the tea that had appeared before him without his really noticing it. He'd never heard any of this before.

As if she'd read his thoughts, Chelia added, "There was no point in telling you. Your father didn't want to, and he would have gotten furious if I had, and nothing would have changed."

"Does Bhayrn know what you've said?"

"No. He's more like your father."

He even sleeps late like Father. Charyn wasn't quite sure from where that vagrant thought had come. "Did he ever say much about Marshal Vaelln?"

"He thought he was honest, bright but not too bright, and loyal to the rex. He also listened to his better officers."

"What about Norstan?"

"I understand you know him well enough to deal with him."

Charyn didn't ask how she knew. His mother often had her ways. Instead, he said, "If I take the regial quarters . . ."

"I'll take the large guest suite. It has a lovely sitting room and good south light."

Charyn nodded.

"What do you intend to do about Palenya?"

"I've talked to her. She says she'll leave before . . . well . . . before allowing me to sleep with her if . . . there's anyone else."

"Idealistic, but not totally practical."

"I owe her—and you for allowing her to teach me—a great deal. I wouldn't feel right just throwing her out. I'd thought of buying her a dwelling suitable for her to teach and giving her a stipend of some sort."

"That would be fair. It might be best if the dwelling were not in L'Excelsis. People might be less likely to try to use her to get to you."

"Use her?" Charyn paused. "I suppose they would. Some people would use anyone if it furthered their interests a single digit." He stopped as the serving girl appeared with his breakfast—cheesed eggs with ham strips and a small loaf of dark bread. All steamed in the slightly chill air of the breakfast room. He took several bites of the eggs, cut the ham into smaller bits, then ate them. He had some of the bread with the cherry conserve before he spoke again. "Where would you suggest?"

"When I talked with her about becoming the chateau musician she mentioned that she'd always liked the old town of Nordeau."

"Do you know anyone there?"

"I still have a few acquaintances. Would you like for me to look into a suitable dwelling there . . . Elaerya might even know if there is a possibility for a talented musician and clavecinist."

"I'd appreciate that. I'm in no hurry, none at all, but sometimes these matters cannot be arranged at the last moment."

Chelia nodded. "I've always thought that preparation leads to good fortune. In all matters."

"Thank you."

"It is my pleasure."

Charyn understood. He wasn't totally happy, but he did understand, although he wasn't about to part with Palenya until he'd gotten to the bottom of the threats against him and ended that danger. *Assuming you can.* He smiled wryly to himself. If he couldn't, Palenya wouldn't be a problem at all. Not for him, anyway.

He finished his breakfast quickly, stopped by Norstan's study, and discovered, not totally to his surprise, that there were no requests for meetings.

"Are you most certain, Norstan?"

"Yes, sir." The seneschal didn't have the slightest hesitation, nor did he flinch from Charyn's hard glance.

Either Norstan was a better liar than Charyn thought, or there were no requests. He supposed the latter was possible, given how cold and windy it was, and that scattered snowflakes continued to fall intermittently.

The first thing he did upon reaching his study, after greeting Howal, was to read the copy of *Veritum* that lay waiting on his desk. All the article about the meeting said of interest was:

> . . . both the High Council and the Factors' Council of Solidar met with Rex Charyn on Meredi. Several of the factors said that the meeting was helpful, but refused to say more. None would discuss whether the rex indicated if tariffs would be raised . . .

Charyn could see why Elthyrd might be discreet, but the others? Or was it that they wanted any increase in tariffs to be laid at Charyn's feet? That was more likely than discretion, far more likely.

Charyn had only set down the newssheet when Sanafryt arrived, carrying several papers.

The Justice Minister handed them to Charyn. "Here is the letter to Governor Warheon with the explanation of the change in Codex Legis and how it affects the factor's petition that he denied. Whatever you approve, I'll use the same explanation language transmitting the change in the law to the other regional governors."

Charyn motioned Sanafryt to the chairs in front of his desk, then sat down and began to read. When he finished, he smiled pleasantly. "This is quite good, Sanafryt. You always write well, but this expresses what I had in mind quite accurately. I'll sign it, and Howal will make copies. I'll have him dispatch the letter and the sheet with the Codex changes to the governor. He'll make sure you get a copy for your records."

For an instant, Sanafryt looked surprised. Then he nodded. "Thank you, Your Grace. I'm glad you found my words to your liking."

Why had he been surprised? Because Father was always having things written and re-written? Or for some other reason? "I'm not much for rewriting if the words are clear and the point made accurately. You did both."

Sanafryt nodded in acknowledgment, almost as if he didn't know what to say.

Charyn stood. "It shouldn't be that long before you have copies."

The older man stood, inclined his head, and then left the study.

Howal moved toward the desk. "I can start on those now."

"Thank you." He thought about asking Howal his reaction to Sanafryt's surprise, then decided against it. He couldn't keep asking others what they thought about reactions, not in so many words . . . and not immediately after they left.

Less than a quint later, Maertyl rapped on the study door. "Two messages for you, sir. One is being delivered by an imager courier."

"Have the courier bring them both in." He paused. "Where did the other come from?"

"Public courier, sir. Left with the entry guards."

Charyn didn't like the sound of that.

Apparently, neither did Howal, who moved toward the desk and said in a low voice, "Let me take that one first."

Charyn nodded as the study door opened and the young man in imager grays entered.

"A message from Maitre Alastar, sir." He extended one envelope.

Charyn took it. "If you'd give the other to Howal, please."

"Yes, sir."

"Is an immediate reply requested?"

"No, sir."

"Thank you, and convey my respects and thanks to the Maitre."

Once the imager courier had left and the study door was closed, Charyn turned to Howal.

"It's light, and there's no powder in the envelope. It's not oily, either, and the paper's not discolored."

"I'll open it carefully." Charyn took the envelope. The name on the outside was simply "Rex Charyn." It had been written in standard merchant hand, and that alone suggested to Charyn that the words inside were likely to be yet another threat. He slit the envelope carefully, holding it well away from himself and in a fashion so that he did not break the flat black wax seal. Then he put the envelope on the desk and used his knife to ease the single sheet, folded in half, out of the envelope. The paper also appeared untainted, but he still used the knife to unfold the sheet.

The words were along the lines he expected . . . and in standard merchant hand.

> You were warned, again, yesterday. Promising to build a few more ships won't stop the losses suffered by factors. Higher tariffs will be wasted on your excesses, not on real improvements for Solidar.
>
> If you don't stop the Jariolan piracy and seizures, you won't be rex much longer. Especially if you increase tariffs.

Charyn set down the missive on the desk. The way it was written didn't give a clue as to whether the writer knew about what had happened in the councils' meeting. The promises to build more ships had been public for weeks. He stepped aside so that Howal could read the message as well, then waited before asking, "What do you think?"

"They aren't too happy with what you're doing, and they don't want higher tariffs."

"I doubt most of the factors and few of the High Holders are happy with what I'm doing. I'd like to see them do better." He managed not to take a deep breath as he opened the imager envelope. The letter was from the Maitre.

> Rex Charyn—
> I have made inquiries about Murranyt D'Patrol, the former Commander of the Civic Patrol of L'Excelsis. He asked for and received a stipend for his years of service to the Patrol. The effective date was 18 Fevier 404 A.L. He remained in

his own private dwelling in the east part of L'Excelsis until Ianus of 406 A.L., when the dwelling was sold to the current occupants by the Banque D'Aluse, on account of debts owed. According to neighbors, Murranyt said he was suffering from a lung flux caused by the cold weather in L'Excelsis and that he was moving to Kephria to live with his sister. None of his few former acquaintances or colleagues have seen him since early Fevier of 406 A.L.

As soon as he saw the date of Murranyt's disappearance, Charyn felt a tightness in his guts. He handed the sheet to Howal. "I'm going to my rooms for a moment. I'll be back as soon as possible."

As he left the study, he wanted to shake his head. He should have asked Palenya about Churwyl earlier. She was one of the few who'd likely be honest with him, and she was pleasant enough to the chateau staff that they talked to her.

He walked quickly to his rooms, and then to his bedchamber. There he eased his best pistol from its case in the second drawer of his armoire and slipped it inside his jacket pocket. Then he walked calmly back to the study, taking care to close the door gently, but firmly. He would have preferred to have slammed it.

"Are you all right, sir?"

"I think we need to find Guard Captain Churwyl and have a little talk with him. And I think you had best remain close to me."

"I would agree, sir."

Before leaving the study, Charyn slipped both messages into the desk drawer. He said nothing as they walked down the north corridor, but as they started down the grand staircase, Charyn thought he saw a guard hurry toward the rear entry out to the courtyard. Or was it Churwyl? He couldn't tell.

When they reached the duty desk, the older guard seated there bolted upright. "Your Grace, sir."

"I'm looking for Guard Captain Churwyl."

"You just missed him, Your Grace. He went to the armory to check on something. He was out there earlier."

"What was he doing there?"

"He didn't say. It was right after the imager courier came with that urgent message for you, sir. Captain Churwyl wanted to deliver it himself, but the imager insisted. You don't argue with imagers. He hurried off right after that. I can send someone for him."

"We'll find him."

The duty guard murmured something under his breath as Charyn and Howal left, but Charyn couldn't make out the words.

"Sir . . ." offered Howal.

"At this point, Howal, you, my mother, Palenya, and Hassala are about the only senior members of the entire staff I can trust. Oh, and Minister Alucar. Exactly who else can I trust to deal with Churwyl besides the two of us? And if we dither, he's likely to be gone."

The two rushed by the guard at the rear entry and down the stone steps to the paved courtyard. Charyn slowed down because there were patches of ice, and he didn't want to slip and fall, especially not at the moment.

The armory door was closed, but not locked. Howal moved forward and opened it, glancing around. "Stay behind me, sir."

Charyn didn't argue, but followed the imager.

Less than three yards away, Churwyl stood beside a keg. He turned toward Charyn, smiling. "You didn't have to come out here, sir. My men could have let me know you wanted to see me." Churwyl's breath steamed in the cold air.

"I'm sure they could." Charyn stepped past Howal and closer to the guard captain. *Not too close.* He could sense Howal easing up behind him. "It's better this way."

"What did you have in mind, Your Grace?"

"I was curious to know why you betrayed my father." Charyn thrust his hands into the pockets of his winter jacket.

"How could you even think that? I served him for years," protested Churwyl.

"It might have something to do with the fact that Commander Murranyt was already dead at the time you said you talked to him." Charyn shrugged. "Or that you were the one who poisoned the second traitorous guard. Had you expected him to be killed before he could be questioned? Or would you have killed them both if they'd tried to escape." That was more guess than verified knowledge. "There's also the fact that you had the bodies of the traitorous guards burned as soon as possible."

"You seem convinced that I had something to do with all these deaths." Churwyl was fiddling with something small in his hands, but in the dimness of the armory, Charyn couldn't make out what it was, only that it was too small to be a knife or pistol.

"The only question is whether you did it because you felt you were slighted in some fashion or because someone paid you an enormous sum to make the risk worthwhile."

"You're accusing me? You . . . who've done nothing worthwhile in your life?"

"This isn't about me. It's about who was behind my father's murder. You were behind the men who carried it out. The question is merely whether you did so of your own volition, or whether someone else made it worth your while. Given your lack of imagination, I doubt you could have planned it and carried it out on your own."

"My lack of imagination? You don't have enough imagination to see how the women around you have played you like a clavecin, let alone rule as even a second-rate rex. Not even a third-rate rex."

Charyn realized that Churwyl was playing for time, and that meant trouble. His finger stayed on the trigger of the pistol.

"Why didn't I betray him earlier is a better question. He was selfish and greedy—" Abruptly, Churwyl lunged at Charyn, something in his right hand glinting.

Charyn fired the pistol through the jacket. Churwyl staggered, tried to move toward Charyn, when Charyn fired the second shot into the other side of the guard captain's chest.

"Never thought . . ." A knife clattered to the stones.

"Who paid you off?" Charyn demanded. *Who didn't is a better question.*

"I . . . never knew . . . too many golds . . . to refuse . . . won't do you . . . good . . ." Churwyl fumbled with the small object in his left hand, and a flame flared from his fingers before he leaned back and dropped it on the top of the barrel. Then he shuddered. His legs gave out, and he dropped to the stone floor.

Flame flared from the barrel.

Then everything went black.

A cold darkness swathed Charyn, a darkness pierced by flames that somehow seared him, yet did not, while the cold crept up from toes and feet
he could feel, but somehow not move, no matter how hard he tried. Nor
could he move his fingers or his hands, or even turn his head.

Was there a voice somewhere, someone calling him?

He realized that he was flat on his back, lying on something very,
very, hard . . . and that his entire body ached. His eyes were blurry, but
he could make out a face, someone speaking.

"Charyn . . ."

The voice was definitely familiar

"Can you move your fingers?" That voice wasn't in the slightest
familiar.

Charyn tried, and this time his fingers did move. "Yes."

"Your hands and toes?"

Charyn nodded. As his vision cleared, he saw a man in a guard uniform half-kneeling beside him. It took him several moments before he
realized the guard was one of the two imagers who had been helping
guard the chateau, but he couldn't recall his name. Then he saw his mother
standing beside the guard, and her face was drawn. "I . . . think . . . I'm all
right . . . except . . . an awful lot . . . is sore . . ."

"Cross your arms," said the imager guard.

Charyn did so.

"Try to bring your knees up. Slowly."

He could do that as well.

"Let me help you sit up. If anything gives you a sharp pain, tell me
immediately."

Charyn could actually sit up without difficulty, although he was very
conscious that quite a number of assorted muscles were sore. He could
see that he was still in the armory . . . and that it didn't look all that
different. But then, the walls were solid stone. "How's Howal?"

"I'm in better shape that you are. You were in front of me. Even with
shields, you took more of the blast."

Charyn could see Howal standing on the far side of his mother. He could also see a blanket lying across a body. "Is that Churwyl under the blanket?"

"What's left of him," said the imager guard.

Charyn got up on his knees and then slowly stood. He looked at Howal, who appeared absolutely drained, his face pale.

"You look ready to drop."

"You both need something to eat, Howal especially," said the imager guard. "Holding those shields took everything he had."

"I wasn't planning on holding back an explosion, Dylert."

"You can explain later," said Chelia firmly. "The family breakfast room. You, too, Dylert. Or should it be Maitre Dylert?"

"I'm just a junior maitre, like Howal and Kaylet." Dylert brushed the dust and ashes off his uniform, except some of the ashes left gray streaks.

Three maitres here . . . and you still almost died? Charyn had no doubts that, without Howal's shields, he'd have been lying beside Churwyl. He walked carefully, very carefully, out of the armory and across the courtyard, under a clear sky, but his breath steamed, and the white sun offered little warmth.

He shivered, not totally because of the cold. *How could Churwyl do that?*

For all of the guard captain's hateful words . . . had Charyn himself been cruel . . . or condescending? *Enough for a man to blow himself up to get to you?*

In less than half a quint, Charyn and Howal were seated at the table in the breakfast room, along with Chelia. Howal was drinking lager, alternating that with mouthfuls of bread. While Charyn didn't care that much for lager, he was also drinking it, largely at the insistence of his mother.

Dylert appeared shortly. "I was sealing Churwyl's room. I want to search it to see if there's anything there that might tell us something."

Charyn realized that he should have thought of that.

Chelia looked across the table at Charyn. "Why did you have to go after Churwyl yourself?"

"Once it was obvious Churwyl was involved, who else could I trust besides Howal? Also, once Churwyl left, I doubted that he'd ever be found again. I knew Howal had shields, and I had a pistol. I knew I could be accurate at short range. I don't think anyone would have thought that he'd try to blow up the armory."

"He couldn't have done that," said Dylert. "There wasn't enough powder in the keg for that. If there had been, you and Howal wouldn't be here."

"If Howal hadn't shielded me, there was enough to make sure I wasn't here."

"That was what Churwyl was counting on," said Dylert. "I've been watching him. He calculates everything. He probably sold half the powder in the keg first."

"What on Terahnar were you thinking when you confronted him?" asked Chelia.

"That I needed answers and that every time I've waited, the answers came too late." That wasn't totally true, but it was the way Charyn felt. "When I saw him coming with the knife, I just shot him. I could say I wasn't sure that shields were proof against knives at close range, but I was just plain scared. So I shot him. Such a noble rex." Charyn laughed harshly, then stopped. His ribs ached just with a single laugh. He looked at Howal. "You heard what Churwyl said, didn't you?"

"He said he didn't know who bribed him. Or paid him off. He killed himself trying to kill you. That doesn't make sense."

"It does if his family or someone he cared about was threatened," said Chelia.

"I didn't think Churwyl had a family," replied Charyn, adding after a moment, "Anymore. Not since his wife died in an accident last year."

"It might not have been an accident," suggested Chelia. "He never cared much for her."

"But if his wife was dead . . . ?"

"He only had one daughter, but she had two sons. He was proud of them. They live somewhere north of L'Excelsis. He never said where."

"So whoever paid him also threatened his daughter and grandsons?"

"It's the only thing that makes sense," mused Dylert.

"All this assumes that he knew I knew," pointed out Charyn.

"A message comes from the Maitre," Howal said slowly. "The courier won't let Churwyl touch it and insists that it goes to you. Churwyl hears you coming. He already knew you were suspicious because of the way you questioned him after the attempted shooting in the courtyard."

"He had to be the one who fired the shots. No one else could have."

"He knew that, and when an urgent message came from the Maitre," continued Howal, "that likely made him think that he might be discovered. So he went to the armory where he set it up to kill you. He must have guessed I'm an imager, because the only thing that might break through shields would be a large explosion."

"He might have been trying to blow up the entire chateau," said Chelia.

Dylert shook his head. "There wasn't that much powder there, and the way the rifle cartridges are stored, an explosion wouldn't set them off."

Charyn took another swallow of the lager, bitter to his taste, but all lager tasted that way to him. Then he took his left hand and massaged his temples. "That still leaves me with more problems than solutions." *Such as which chateau guards I can trust, if any.* He looked at Dylert, "How would you like to be acting guard captain, Maitre Dylert?"

"I wouldn't, sir . . . but I'll act as such until Maitre Alastar arrives. My remaining here is between the two of you."

Chelia turned swiftly. "Is Maitre Alastar coming now?"

"Kaylet sent for him. He said the Maitre wouldn't be terribly pleased at a second assassination attempt in weeks. Kaylet would also appreciate talking to you, Your Grace," added Dylert.

"I think we should all go up to the study once you've had enough to eat, Howal," said Charyn.

Chelia rose immediately. "I'd like to speak with you, Charyn, and Maitre Alastar, but after you have dealt with the more pressing matters."

"I'll make sure of that," Charyn replied, appreciating his mother's withdrawal.

"Sir . . ." offered Dylert, "I think it might be best if I search Churwyl's quarters immediately. Even if they're sealed, given a little time . . ."

"Go ahead."

Less than a quint later, Howal and Charyn were in the study, waiting for Dylert.

Before long, Dylert walked through the study door carrying something wrapped in a worn blanket and a cloth pouch.

"What did you find?" asked Charyn.

"Almost nothing. No papers. His uniforms and personals. A spare pair of boots, smallclothes, and this pouch and the strongbox under this blanket. The pouch was beneath his mattress. It has ten golds in it. I'm guessing, from the weight, that the strongbox has coppers and silvers in it, but I wanted Howal to help me open it."

"You think it might have traps?" asked Howal, standing.

"I'd rather be careful after Churwyl's last attempt. That's why it's wrapped and shielded." Dylert carried the blanketed object to the conference table and set it on the end, then eased away the blanket, revealing a plain oak box with three iron bands around it. An iron bar, secured by a heavy lock, went through the hoops in the bands—except the lock was not closed.

"You didn't open it?" asked Charyn.

"Considering that the lock wasn't snapped shut, that was the last thing I wanted to do."

"Except for the bands, it's all wood," said Howal. "We could just image off one end and hold shields."

Dylert nodded. "You image, but shield yourself."

Howal nodded and moved toward the table. "Ready?"

"Any time."

After several moments, the end of the box closest to Howal and Charyn just vanished. Howal squinted at the opened end of strongbox. "There are coins in there, coppers, it looks like . . . and something else. It might be a knife."

"There's probably a spring under it," offered Dylert. "I'm going to image away the top."

The wooden top vanished, leaving the iron bands in place, and something flew from the box before hitting the invisible shields of the imagers and dropping to the floor. Both imagers waited.

Finally, Dylert bent and looked at the knife without touching it. "Needle blade. Smeared with something."

"Poison," said Howal, unnecessarily.

"Left for someone, possibly Bhayrn, to open," suggested Charyn. "Is there a note inside?"

Dylert moved closer to the box. "No, but the coppers are smeared, too."

"Can you destroy it?"

"There's too much metal there to do that easily. Be better just to burn it and let the heat destroy the poison." Dylert took a scrap of blanket he had either cut or imaged off and picked up the knife and dropped cloth and blade into the box, then carefully wrapped the blanket around the box. "I'll take care of this after we're done."

The two imagers took seats across the desk from Charyn, and Dylert took the cloth bag and eased the golds onto the wood. "They're new, all of them. The lettering is still clear, and they haven't been shaved or clipped."

Charyn picked up one and studied it. "That suggests someone who is very wealthy, most likely a factor with great holdings." He put the gold down and watched as Dylert returned the coins to the bag and handed it to him. "What can you tell me about Churwyl that I should have noticed and didn't?" Charyn addressed the question to Dylert, who sat in the chair nearest the window. Howal sat in the one nearest the door, leaving the one in the middle empty.

"I don't know what you've noticed, sir."

"I believe he was paid by families to hire their sons for guards. I have no way of proving that. He certainly lied to me about how he hired the traitors who killed my father. He's the one who shot at me and Howal . . ." Charyn paused and looked at Howal. "That's how he knew you were an imager. He wasn't trying to kill me at all, but when your shields deflected the bullet, he knew. He shot at you as a warning to me, just the way he was probably the one who shot Bhayrn's horse and the guard with Bhayrn. He wore that brown cloak over his uniform, shot the horses and guard then ducked under cover, leaving the cloak before emerging somewhere else." He paused. "That's what I know." *You should have seen it all earlier.*

Dylert nodded. "Some of the guards are very good. Most are adequate. A very few I would dismiss. Churwyl may have been corrupt, but, for the most part, the guards are good at their duties. I cannot speak to their trustworthiness."

"Are the ones you would dismiss the ones most recently hired?" asked Charyn.

Dylert shook his head. "I think a few have become lazy and complacent, but some are younger, some older. I believe he was taking a small part of every guard's pay, from what I overheard, but without looking at the pay records, I could not tell."

"We'll see if the Finance Minister can shed any light on this." He raised his voice. "I need to see Minister Alucar."

"Yes, sir."

Perhaps a third of a quint later, the study guard announced the minister. Charyn did not stand as the study door opened. He was both sore and irritated.

After Alucar entered the study, he looked quizzically at Howal and Dylert, who both had stood and moved to stand near the conference table, and then turned to Charyn. "Your Grace?"

"I don't know if you've heard about Churwyl . . ."

"Yes, Your Grace. I did. I cannot believe it. I mean . . . it happened, but it seemed so unlike Churwyl. He was always so organized."

"Who handles the pay for the chateau guards and staff? The actual records?" asked Charyn.

"Guard Captain Churwyl handled the pay ledgers for the guards, and Norstan handles the ledgers and pay for the rest of the chateau staff."

"Did you ever notice any discrepancies in the ledgers or accounts for the chateau guards?"

"No, sir. His ledgers were always in order."

"Thank you, Minister Alucar. That's all I needed to know for the present."

"Sir." Alucar inclined his head, turned, and departed.

Once the study door closed, Charyn said, "It looks more and more like someone got to Churwyl."

Howal and Dylert exchanged glances.

Picking up on their expressions, Charyn added, "Except there's more to it than that, isn't there?"

"He was an almost perfect marksman, wasn't he?" asked Dylert.

Charyn nodded.

Before he could say more, there was another rap on the door.

"Maitre Alastar, Your Grace."

Charyn didn't even have to tell the Maitre to enter, because Alastar was on his way into the study, and the other imager who had been serving as a chateau guard—Kaylet—was with him.

Charyn couldn't help but notice the worried expression on Alastar's face, and, strangely, how short the imager guard's fine brown hair was cut, or his narrow, but very-competent-looking face.

Alastar's first words were not quite a command. "Why don't we all sit down around the conference table?"

Charyn almost bridled, but managed to nod. He walked to the table, took the chair at the head, and seated himself. Dylert eased the blanket-wrapped trapped chest away and set it at the far end of the table.

Alastar sat to Charyn's right, with both Dylert and Kaylet to his right, and with Howal to Charyn's left. The Maitre spoke immediately. "Kaylet's filled me in on what happened in the courtyard. What else do I need to know?"

"Churwyl had to be behind most of what happened here at the chateau." Charyn went on to explain what he knew and surmised and what had happened leading up to Churwyl's setting off the explosion, then said, "We were about to discuss what else might be involved."

"Before we get into speculations," Alastar replied, "you should hear what Maitre Kaylet has to say. That might add more information on which any speculation might be better based."

Charyn certainly couldn't disagree with that and nodded to Kaylet.

"Yes, sir. I don't know if Maitre Alastar ever told you, but I've been the assistant stablemaster of the Collegium for the past two years . . ."

Charyn managed not to sigh. He had a feeling he knew the general nature of what Kaylet had to say.

". . . I couldn't help noticing some things. When oats were brought in, at least one barrel stayed in the factor's wagon, and it appeared silvers changed hands between your stablemaster and the teamster. I also saw silvers pass between the stablemaster and the farrier . . ." At the end, the imager said, "Some of those might have an innocent explanation, but there were too many instances in the short time I've been here to believe they all were. No one's teaching the stable boys to be ostlers, either. The stablemaster treats them like his personal servants, and they really don't know the best ways to groom a horse. One of them almost gave near-freezing water to an overheated courier mount. Another didn't refill the water buckets in the rear stable until I reminded him. A healthy horse needs to drink two of those buckets every day, and it's best to make sure they have water within the two glasses after they get fed . . ." Kaylet broke off his words. "Sir?"

"Thank you. I can't say I'm surprised. I've been discovering problems everywhere. You're telling me that the stablemaster is careless, if not incompetent, and that he's stealing as much as he can get away with. What about his assistant?"

"He drinks so much ale that he doesn't notice. One of the serving girls brings a pitcher to him three or four times a day. I don't know her name, and I felt it might be unwise to ask anyone who might know."

"How did he get along with Guard Captain Churwyl?"

"They avoided each other as much as they could. I don't think the guard captain cared much for the stablemaster. Most didn't."

"Is there anything else?" asked Charyn.

"Not about Stablemaster Keithell, sir."

"What about Guard Captain Churwyl?"

"He was very formal with both of us, sir. He always wanted to know where we were. In a quiet sort of way."

"Did he ever follow you?" asked Alastar.

"Not obviously. He did ask other guards where we were or what they thought about us. Some of them didn't like that. They told us."

"While you four are here, I think we need to talk to Stablemaster Keithell," said Charyn. "Immediately. I think he should be escorted here by two guards who you think are trustworthy, Maitre Dylert. If that is agreeable to Maitre Alastar." Charyn looked to the Collegium Maitre.

"Under the circumstances, I'd agree with Rex Charyn."

For that, Charyn was glad, because he was well aware that he had absolutely no power in the matter without Alastar's approval. "Thank you."

Dylert stood and made his way from the study. A half a quint later, he returned with two guards, one of whom was Yarselt, and Keithell.

Charyn surveyed the portly stablemaster, noting the fine quality of his leather vest and the linen of his shirt. He could also see perspiration on the man's wide forehead, even though the study was not all that warm. "Just stand right there, Keithell."

"Your Grace . . . I beg you . . ."

"For what? My forgiveness?"

"I'm a hardworking stablemaster, Your Grace. I attend the anomen faithfully and trust in the Nameless. I don't beat my wife and children."

"All of that may be true. It doesn't merit forgiveness for taking bribes from factors, for letting them take full payment for grain measures that are short. You may not beat your wife and children, but you beat the stable boys. You also don't teach them what they need to know, and the stable is not kept as it should be."

"Your Grace . . . you can't trust imagers. I've worked for the regial family my whole life. You'd put what they saw in a few days over what I've done in a lifetime?"

"Considering that those untrustworthy imagers have saved my life at least three times in the last month while you've been pocketing silvers from grain and produce factors and taking coins from your assistants . . . yes, I would put more trust in what they say."

"You could not expect any more from a stablemaster than I've given your family for many years, Your Grace . . . I beg you."

"Are you telling me to my face that you did not do any of these things?" Charyn's voice was hard.

"I do the best I can, Your Grace. A man must do what he must . . ."

"That is the only thing you've said with which I agree." Charyn shook his head. "Yarselt, take him out and lock him up in the guards' brig," said Charyn. "I'll decide on his punishment after I talk to the Minister of Justice." *And after you look into a few other details.*

Keithell said nothing as the two guards with Dylert seized then escorted the stablemaster from the study.

Charyn rose and went to the single small bookcase in the study, from which he extracted a single volume. He stood by the bookcase and began to leaf through the pages. It took him almost a third of a quint to find what he was seeking. He nodded and marked the page with the minia-ture letter knife Howal had created, then set the volume on the desk. "Sturdyn! I need Minister Sanafryt. Now!"

"Yes, sir!"

Charyn looked to Kaylet. "Do you know where the stablemaster keeps his ledgers?"

"No, sir."

"I imagine you can find them. Would you mind doing so?"

Kaylet looked to Alastar.

The Maitre nodded.

"I can do that, sir."

"And if you, Dylert, could find Churwyl's ledgers, with Maitre Ala-star's approval of course, I'd very much appreciate it."

"Now, sir?"

"If you would. I need to discuss a few matters with the Maitre. Howal, would you tell Lady Chelia that it's likely to be a while longer before Maitre Alastar will be there?"

"Yes, sir."

Charyn returned to the conference table and sat down, waiting until the three junior maitres had left and he and Alastar were alone. "You realize that it's a little unsettling to be in a room with four imagers who could destroy me in a moment if they desired."

Alastar smiled warmly. "You seem to be the first rex in generations who's worried about that."

"It could be because I'm the first to escape three assassination attempts, except I guess it's actually two and a warning. And I still have no idea who might be behind it all. It has to be someone who has great wealth and resources and no compunctions about killing anyone who might reveal who he is."

"Wealthy, brilliant, skilled, cunning, and ruthless, with great knowledge of the chateau and the regial family," offered Alastar almost blandly. "That's quite a combination."

Charyn knew he was missing something. "You have an idea?"

"There are only a few individuals like that in all of Solidar. You or your mother would know far better than I who they might be."

"Until I can figure this out, might I have the loan of Dylert, Kaylet, and Howal?"

"That might be for the best, but it wouldn't be wise for you to drag this out, if you can possibly discover who is behind it all."

"I understand that." Charyn frowned. "I think all the members of both councils should be apprised of Churwyl's attempt at assassinating me."

Alastar nodded. "How would you inform them?"

"I should write a letter informing them of what happened, and that Churwyl admitted, just before he set off the explosion, and in front of witnesses, that he had been paid to kill me, and that he had also been paid to arrange my father's assassination."

"Do you think that would be sufficient information for the council members?"

"Probably not," replied Charyn. "I could tell them that I am restructuring matters at the Chateau D'Rex and looking into the evidence and seeing where it may lead."

"That would seem a good first step."

"And what might be the second?" asked Charyn.

"It might be useful to mention that you reserve the right to call another meeting of the councils before the next scheduled meeting in Fevier."

"Depending on what I discover, I presume?"

"Or if you need to see how any of them react."

He's definitely hinting at something. But before he could pursue the thought, there was another knock on the study door.

"Minister Sanafryt, sir."

"Have him come in." Charyn remained seated.

"You summoned me, Your Grace?" Sanafryt looked uneasily around the study, his eyes going from the empty desk to the conference table, taking in the Collegium Maitre before returning to Charyn.

"What are the limits to the power of the rex with regard to those in regial service?"

"Your Grace?" Sanafryt appeared confused, for the very first time ever, at least when Charyn had been around.

"If a member of the regial staff commits an act of theft or appropriation of regial property, what punishments might I visit upon him under the Codex Legis?"

"That depends on the amount of the theft. Thefts of more than a gold can be punished by loss of a hand. More than a hundred golds, you could order an execution."

"What about the selling of favors, granting of regial privileges not approved by the rex?"

Sanafryt's lips tightened for a moment before he replied. "Dismissal and flogging, if the value of the favors cannot be quantified. If the value can be quantified, then in addition to dismissal and flogging, the same penalties as for theft or wrongful appropriation."

Charyn smiled pleasantly. "Thank you."

"Might I ask . . . ?"

"Keithell, the stablemaster. He appears to have done both. I'm getting very tired of people who have abused their position."

"Yes, sir. Is there anything more I can do?"

"No, thank you. Not at the moment."

When the study door closed, Alastar actually grinned. "That was a rather politely delivered warning without ostensibly being a warning at all. You didn't trust that he would answer truthfully, did you?"

"I thought he would, but without checking, how would I have known?"

Almost another quint passed before Dylert and Kaylet returned, along with Howal, who, Charyn suspected, had been waiting for them in the north corridor.

It took Charyn less than half that time to see that Churwyl had been guilty of great theft, as well as extorting part of the wages of those he had supervised by simply docking each guard a copper a week for "gear maintenance." In Keithell's case, the ledger numbers didn't really add up, and he had put in a weekly "adjustment" number to get the entries to balance. That also suggested that Norstan had either been sloppy or tacitly complicit.

When he finished his quick survey, Charyn looked up. "I'm going to need some help to get things straightened out here at the Chateau D'Rex. Maitre Alastar has kindly agreed that, if you three are willing, I may keep you here for a fairly short period to assist me."

The three looked to Alastar.

He nodded.

"Then we're willing," said Dylert.

"I'd like you to take over the Chateau Guard, to work with the guards, and determine who would be the best guard captain to succeed you, and who might be the best second. Kaylet, you may have the toughest task. From what you've said, everything handled by Keithell needs to be tightened up and improved."

"I'd like to do that, sir. I really would." He grinned. "Then I could match Petros's tales."

"Howal . . . Norstan has been sloppy at best, possibly worse than that. Do you want that challenge?"

"Yes, sir."

"Dylert, Kaylet, you can start right in with what needs to be done. Do you need me to say anything to anyone?"

The two exchanged glances, then grinned.

"No, sir," replied Kaylet. "I think word has gotten around."

"Then go."

Dylert quietly picked up the poisoned box.

As they left the study, Charyn looked over at Howal. "You and I will deal with Norstan tomorrow morning. While the Maitre and I are talking to Lady Chelia, I'd like you to write down any suggestions, any suggestions at all, for improving the functioning of the chateau."

A few moments later, Alastar and Charyn walked from the study along the north corridor.

"You've set yourself some ambitious tasks, Charyn," observed Alastar. "Especially so soon after becoming rex."

"The ones around the chateau are small compared to dealing with the factors."

"I wouldn't count out certain High Holders. They're just as opposed to higher tariffs as the factors are."

Charyn nodded. *That's all too true.*

When the two reached Chelia's sitting room, they found Charyn's mother having a serving maid stack books into piles.

"Go and take a rest, Delya," said Chelia. "We'll continue later."

The maid hurried out, inclining her head politely to both men and closing the door.

"Please do sit down. I apologize for the clutter, but I thought I might as well start to prepare for my move to my new rooms." Chelia's voice was sweet. "Did you have a good meeting?"

"Good? I don't think so," replied Charyn. "Largely successful, yes. Kei-thell's locked up, and Maitre Alastar has agreed to lend us Maitres Dylert, Kaylet, and Howal to clean up the way the guards, the stables, and the chateau have been run, while, of course, helping to keep us safe. That's while we figure out who might be behind all this. I can tell you all about that later. I believe you wanted to talk to us about something . . . Aloryana, perhaps?"

"That would be lovely, dear, Maitre." She seated herself in her cus-tomary armchair and brushed back a stray lock of blond and silver hair.

Charyn could tell that the conversation would be about Aloryana, and only about Aloryana.

42

While the conversation between Alastar and Chelia lasted less than a glass, Charyn spent most of the rest of the afternoon with Howal, discussing what might be necessary in dealing with both Norstan and the structure and duties of the rest of the chateau staff. After that, they finished up the final drafts of the tariff letters to the High Council and the Solidaran Factors' Council, a task that had been sidetracked by the morning's events. Howal then arranged for their dispatch.

Then Charyn wrote a second letter to each council member, detailing the events of that morning and adding that he might be required to call a meeting earlier than the next regularly scheduled meeting. After reviewing that draft and changing it, Howal went to work on individual letters to each councilor. They didn't finish until well after sixth glass.

Dinner was quiet. Even Bhayrn was subdued, possibly, Charyn thought, because Churwyl's treachery and the explosion in the armory emphasized just how dangerous matters remained.

After dinner, Charyn lingered outside the dining room, then asked his mother, "If you wouldn't mind, could we go up to your sitting room and talk over the matter of your moving to new rooms?"

"I don't see that there's all that much to talk about, but if that's what you wish, we certainly can."

Charyn looked to Bhayrn. "Do you want to join us?"

"If it's all the same to you, I'd rather not."

"Then I'll say good evening," replied Charyn.

"Good evening to you, and to you, Mother."

Charyn and Chelia made their way up the grand staircase and to the sitting room without talking.

Once Charyn had closed the sitting room door, Chelia seated herself in her armchair and smiled pleasantly. "I do hope you had something else in mind besides the moving of garments and furnishings."

Charyn took a straight-backed chair and moved it closer to the armchair before seating himself. "I had a rather interesting exchange with Maitre Alastar this afternoon. I asked if he had any ideas about who might have put Churwyl up to all that he did. He never answered me directly. From my few conversations with him, that seemed very uncharacteristic. Am I mistaken?"

"No, that kind of indirection is very uncharacteristic of him."

"I had the definite feeling that he was offering hints as to who made the threats and suborned Churwyl."

"What exactly did he say that made you think that?" asked Chelia.

"As I recall, he said that whoever it was had to be wealthy, brilliant, skilled, cunning, and ruthless, with great knowledge of the chateau and the regial family. Then he said that it was quite a combination that only a few individuals in Solidar possessed, and that you or I would know who that might be far better than he would."

Chelia said nothing for a moment that stretched out.

"Mother?"

"What else did he say?"

"Not much, except it wouldn't be wise for me to drag the matter out. It was almost as if he expected me to know who it is."

"He doesn't expect you to know, dear. He expects me to know."

"But why wouldn't he be more clear?"

"I'd judge that he has a very good idea, but that he has no proof. In some ways, the Maitre is bold, in others very cautious."

"Why would he be cautious about this?"

"Because if the person is who I think he meant, the Maitre would be accused of having concealed the other wrongs done by that person. He did that for the good of Solidar. He and your father agreed on that. Now, if the Maitre is the one to mention who it is, he cannot claim he did not know of the past evil that he concealed. Also, since your father was part of that concealment, it would weaken your position as well. The only way in which your position is not weakened is if you are seen to be the one who discovered the malefactor and dealt with him."

"Would anyone care?"

"The factors would. Some High Holders would. All would regard both the rex and the Collegium with even greater suspicion."

"As if I'm not dealing with enough of that now." Charyn paused. "Since you seem to know, who is it?"

"Who is the most powerful, wealthy, cunning, and untrustworthy person we know?"

Charyn swallowed. "But . . . he was threatened as well."

"Was he? Your father never saw any evidence. Did anyone else? Even if he received a written threat, he certainly wasn't above arranging that in order to misdirect everyone. He was the one who persuaded the High Council to oppose your father, and then for your father's brother to throw his lot in with the rebelling High Holders. We all knew it, but there was never any proof. Is there any proof right now of who is behind all the threats?"

"He'd do that to you? His own sister?"

"You have no idea what he has done . . . or what he would do."

Charyn just sat there for several moments. Finally, he said, "You're saying that he's so cunning that he's left nothing of physical proof and so ruthless that no one will say anything against him."

"If there's even anyone left alive who knows enough to be able to say anything."

"What does he gain by this? He's already the most powerful High Holder."

"Revenge . . . and more power."

Doesn't he already have enough power? Charyn dismissed that thought. His uncle would likely never feel that he had enough power. "With all the emphasis on the factors in the notes . . . that's where everyone is looking." Charyn shook his head. "But I can't say anything. Everyone would think I was the one to blame somehow and that I'm willing to sacrifice my own long-suffering uncle who has been trapped in L'Excelsis for the past six years heading a High Council he just wants to leave. That's why he agreed to the tariff increase . . . or allowed me to impose it without actually agreeing to it." He paused. "Or did he tell the others that, under the circumstances, I might not even live to actually impose it?"

"He wouldn't have said that. He would have said something that, only in context, would imply that, but something that, if repeated, would sound harmless or mean something else entirely."

"Like . . . this tariff will only be imposed if the current conditions persist?"

Chelia merely nodded.

"So . . . to save my life and Solidar as we know it, and most likely your life and Bhayrn's, I have to stop the most powerful High Holder without a shred of proof while imposing a tariff no one likes and proving I can actually rule?"

"You don't have to conquer three other lands the way the first Rex Regis did," Chelia pointed out dryly. "You don't have an armed rebellion, either."

"Yet. I have my doubts as to whether I can ever get all of these things straightened out." Charyn shook his head. "I don't know where we'd be if Malyna hadn't been there at the ball. Looking at all of this, I have to wonder why Father even allowed any imager inside the chateau."

"I told him that I'd leave and throw myself on the mercy of the Maitre if your father didn't at least protect Aloryana because she didn't deserve to be killed because of his stubbornness."

"Then you saved the rest of us."

"You're making a good effort to take advantage of that opportunity. You did manage to get your tariff increase without setting off a rebellion. That's a beginning."

At the moment, that beginning looked very insignificant to Charyn.

43

When Charyn entered his study at just before seventh glass on Samedi morning, after nodding to Maertyl, Howal was already at the conference table, making notes as he went through the seneschal's account ledger.

"Did you get the letters dispatched to the councilors?"

"Yes, sir."

"Thank you. Does Norstan's journal look as bad as I feared?"

Howal looked up. "He doesn't add all that well . . . and then he just makes up entries so that the numbers balance. It doesn't look like he's actually taking silvers so much as covering up mistakes. At times, they almost cancel out."

"I caught him taking bribes from factors and growers. If what you're finding holds, it would seem that Norstan's light is honest by his own candles. That is, he thinks he can't take silvers from the rex, but he can take them from those who sell to the rex. There aren't any hints that he accepts damaged goods or short measures, are there?"

"From the ledgers, it would seem that way."

"What about Keithell?"

"Whatever he was doing doesn't show in Norstan's ledgers. I didn't think it would from what Kaylet told me. Norstan just reports disbursements to those who supply the stables, and he shows the stablehands' pay on a weekly basis."

"Keithell was extorting coins from them right after they were paid, and accepting those of the factors in return for letting them short-measure the grains and hay. I'd call the taking of wages theft, and the accepting of short measures misappropriation, but I'd best check with Sanafryt before I decide on punishment. What about Churwyl? Have you gone through his ledger?"

"I did that last night. He was deducting a copper a week from each guard's pay, calling it an equipment maintenance fee. He also had two guards on the payroll who never existed. All in all, that amounted to more than four golds a month."

"That doesn't count whatever he collected from the guards who paid him to get their positions."

"No, sir. It also doesn't include whatever he was paid to kill your father and you. Or if someone else paid him for things."

"What I don't understand," mused Charyn, "was how Alucar didn't catch this. I don't think I'll summon him to come in on a Samedi, but I'd appreciate your not talking about it until after I talk to him on Lundi, not that you likely would."

"I understand, sir."

Charyn walked to the window, where he eased back the hangings and looked out. *Another gray winter day.* While there was a light dusting of snow everywhere, the flakes had stopped falling before Charyn had gotten up, and the high clouds suggested that much more was unlikely.

As he let the hangings fall back, he couldn't help thinking about the way his uncle had masterminded events, from almost before Charyn himself had been born, so that even those that knew he'd done what he'd done could find no proof, or not enough to convince those who needed to be convinced. *How do you find proof when there is none? When someone has been clever enough to leave none?*

Charyn shook his head. It wasn't as though he could charge his uncle with his crimes. Not without proof. If he could even connect Ryel with the threatening notes . . . He frowned, then nodded. *Perhaps . . . just perhaps.* He'd have to think that through.

He turned to Howal. "Do all of Norstan's ledger pages seem to have the same kinds of mistakes?"

"So far, sir. I've been through something like thirty pages."

"That's enough for Alucar, then." He paused. "Who handles the accounts at the Collegium?"

"Maitre Thelia. She's done it for years. Her mother is an important factor."

"What happens if someone does something wrong at the Collegium?"

"It depends. If it's minor, the Maitre handles it. If it's really serious, there's a hearing in front of three senior maitres picked by the Maitre."

"Who are the senior maitres?" Charyn recalled Alastar mentioning senior maitres, but not the details.

"You have to be at least a Maitre D'Structure to be a senior maitre. Then comes Maitre D'Esprit, and then Maitre D'Image."

Alastar hadn't mentioned the higher ranks. Of that, Charyn was sure. "And Maitre Alastar and Maitre Alyna are both Maitres D'IImage."

"Both he and Maitre Alyna are the only Maitres D'Image. They say it's the only time there have been two maitres that strong since the beginning of the Collegium. Most maitres of the Collegium have been Maitres D'Esprit. Maitre Arion is the only Maitre D'Esprit right now. He's in charge of the Westisle Collegium."

"Does anyone advise the Maitre? Formally, that is?" Charyn had no doubt that Maitre Alyna advised Alastar, whether he wanted advice or not.

"The senior maitres do. That's why they meet every Meredi. Maitres D'Aspect aren't allowed in their meetings."

"So he has almost a council of senior imagers?"

"They don't call it that."

Charyn nodded.

"Why did you want to know, sir?"

"Because I know too little about something as important and powerful as the Collegium." That wasn't the only reason. He hadn't really understood that the head of the Collegium in Westisle was also a powerful imager. He'd almost forgotten that there were imagers there. "Are there imagers elsewhere? Besides the few in Estisle?"

"Yes, sir. There's a small branch in Mont D'Glace where imagers who have lost their abilities because of their wrongdoing live."

"Mont D'Glace is sort of a prison, then?"

"More like a village of imagers who made bad choices, I hear, sir."

A prison by any other name.

"Howal . . . I have a question. Can you image paper? Good paper?"

The imager frowned quizzically. "Paper? Yes, sir. That's something most imagers learn to do early. All the paper used at the Collegium is imaged there." He offered an amused smile. "We can match the finest papers or parchment. It saves the Collegium. We use a lot of paper, I found out. Why, might I ask?"

"Your knowledge of paper might be helpful in uncovering who was behind my father's assassination. I don't know if your talents will be necessary, but I thought I'd ask." Charyn smiled pleasantly. "I think we should take a very careful tour of the chateau, chamber by chamber. I'd like you to keep your eyes open and to tell me if you see anything that strikes you as strange."

"Yes, sir."

Charyn had no real idea why he'd come up with the idea, but it couldn't hurt, and it just might lead to something. If it didn't, then that meant there were some things he didn't have to worry about. *You hope.*

44

Lundi morning found Charyn in his study, pacing back and forth, waiting for Sanafryt and Alucar to arrive at the chateau. The clouds that had covered the sky on Samedi and Solayi had passed, but an intense chill had descended upon L'Excelsis, a chill for which the feeble white light of the winter sun was no match.

Unsurprisingly to Charyn, Alucar was the first to arrive, half a quint past the glass.

"You wished to see me, Your Grace?"

"I did. As a result of the investigations I made after the unfortunate incident with Guard Captain Churwyl, I discovered that the fashion in which the business of the Chateau D'Rex was being conducted was far worse than I had thought." Charyn smiled coolly. "And I had not thought well of it before. In particular, the finances of the stables and the chateau itself have been haphazard and worse. Stablemaster Keithell has been locked up since Samedi. Churwyl, of course, is dead, and what happens to Norstan has not been determined. My question to you is whether you knew of this, and, if so, why you never brought it to my father's attention or to mine?"

"I will plead guilty to not bringing it to your immediate attention, Your Grace. I felt you had more pressing matters to deal with. As for your father, I brought the matter to his attention time and time again."

"Is there any proof of this?"

"There is indeed. If you wish you can accompany me back to my study where I can show you the file chest with all the documentation."

"That might be best. If it is as you say, and given your demeanor, I suspect it is, then everyone will know the truth."

Howal moved immediately to accompany Charyn, and the three made their way to the study of the Finance Minister.

Alucar walked immediately to the top file box in the second stack of boxes, unlocked it, and stepped back, moving to stand beside his desk. "Everything in the box deals with Norstan's accounts."

"Thank you." Charyn moved forward and began to read. The first sheet was a directive from his father addressed to Alucar. The substance was simple and direct:

> . . . I fully realize that you must continue to bring this matter up. Norstan's accounting is not up to your standards. There is no evidence that he is pocketing coins or extorting coins from the staff. He does what I wish. I do not intend to replace or reprimand him, and I regard this matter as closed unless you have absolute evidence of wrongdoing beyond carelessness . . .

Charyn blinked, then looked at the signature and seal. Both were his father's. He handed it to Howal, who read it as well.

Howal's eyes widened, but he handed the single sheet back to Charyn without speaking.

Next, Charyn read the previous paper, one from Alucar stating that, without auditing Norstan's records and those who reported to him, there was no way to tell if others were defrauding the rex or pocketing coins. For almost a glass, he stood there and read back through the papers. Finally, he closed the file box. "I can see you were in a difficult position."

"I did what I could, Your Grace. As you can see, your father was aware of the problem, but for his own reasons chose not to act on it. I heard rumors about the stablemaster, but no one would say anything to me, and without going through all of Norstan's records . . ."

"Why didn't you do anything about Keithell?"

"I did. Your father said Keithell had served him faithfully, and that I was not to slander a loyal servant. Without proof, I saw no point in proceeding. Norstan submitted bills of accounting that were inaccurate and poorly rendered. I was not allowed to examine his ledgers. Your father did so twice, at my insistence. The second time he was most unhappy. That was when he wrote that letter, also at my insistence." The Finance Minister offered a wryly bitter smile. "I feared that someday I would be charged with misfeasance on that account. Your father did not speak to me for two weeks."

Charyn could see how that might have been. "We will be talking to Norstan, and from here on, once we make the rules clear to all, you will have access to all account ledgers and records. You may wish to have a clerk review all those." Charyn was sure Alucar would prefer that, and his words were to give the minister that choice.

Alucar inclined his head. "Your Grace."

"My apologies for my suspicions, but I trust you understand that I have reason to be suspicious after the events of the last month."

"I do indeed, Your Grace. We will all be most grateful when you resolve these matters."

Charyn nodded. *At least he said "when" and not "if."* He did not say anything more until he and Howal returned to the study. Once there, he asked Howal, "What are your thoughts on the matter?"

"I would keep him as minister if you can."

"Now, it's time to see Norstan. Have someone summon him."

"Yes, sir."

While Howal talked to Sturdyn, Charyn walked to the window, eased the hangings back, and looked out. The sky remained clear, and the cold radiating off the glass of the windowpane seemed more intense than on any other day of the winter. *So far.*

Norstan arrived in less than half a quint. He stood in front of the desk, looking first at Charyn and then at Howal, both of whom remained standing. "Your Grace . . . ?"

"We've been looking through your ledger, Norstan. Things are not as they should be."

"Your Grace, you must know that I'm not the best with figures. Your father knew that, and so does Minister Alucar. That's no secret."

"I suspect that it's as much a matter of care as ability," Charyn said sardonically. "That is not why you are here. Not totally."

Norstan's face twisted into a momentary expression of puzzlement. "You had my ledger taken . . ."

"For another reason." Charyn decided not to explain. "You never looked into Stablemaster Keithell's accounts, did you?"

"I know little of horses and stables."

Charyn had his doubts about that. "Let us just be generous and say that you chose to know nothing of horses and stables. Keithell took great advantage of that. He also abused the stable boys and accepted short measures of grain and hay in return for coins from some factors and growers. And his assistant did little but drink ale."

"I knew nothing of that, Your Grace."

"It might be more accurate to say, again, that you chose to know nothing of that."

"I had nothing to do with Keithell."

"As seneschal, you were in charge of him, and you failed in keeping him in line."

"Your Grace . . ." The seneschal was almost pleading.

"For that reason, the new stablemaster will be required not only to keep his own ledger, separate from your account, but to submit that ledger to the Minister of Finance so that one of his clerks may keep track of what is purchased and from whom. In addition, if you wish to remain as seneschal, you will improve the accuracy of your ledgers, and your ledger and accounts will also be reviewed by the Finance Minister, as he determines necessary—under my guidance." Charyn paused. "Is that clear?"

"Yes, Your Grace. Whatever you wish." The relief in Norstan's voice was palpable.

"Minister Alucar, or one of his clerks, will direct you as to how he wishes your ledgers kept."

"Yes, Your Grace."

"And you will dismiss the assistant stablemaster. Today. If he is not gone today . . ." Charyn looked hard at Norstan.

"Yes, Your Grace."

Once Norstan had left the study, Charyn turned to Howal. "We'll have to talk to Dylert and Kaylet about setting up the ledgers the way Alucar wants them, but they've got enough to do at the moment. Have the letters to the Factors' Council and the High Council all been sent and received?"

"Yes, sir. All nine of them. We're holding the one for High Holder Oskaryn's replacement."

"We haven't looked into his death," mused Charyn. "He was shot, but it seems odd, because, if he was in the majority of the High Holders opposing increased tariffs, then he was on the side of whoever's been threatening me." Moreover, although Charyn wasn't saying it, assuming his uncle was behind the assassination, why would Oskaryn have been killed? That didn't make sense. *Unless Oskaryn knew too much or unless Ryel arranged his death to throw suspicion away from himself.*

"Could it just have been personal, sir, with someone taking advantage of the situation to confuse matters?"

"That's certainly possible, but . . . that seems awfully convenient. I just wonder what else there is that we don't know."

Less than half a glass later, Sturdyn rapped on the door. "A courier with an urgent message for you, sir."

Charyn nodded to Howal.

The courier was an army ranker, understandably, since the army staffed and ran the regial courier service, who stepped into the study, his face still red from wind and chill. "Your Grace, sir, an urgent dispatch from Regional Governor Voralch." He extended the small sealed dispatch pouch.

Howal took it and broke the seal, inspecting the pouch as he did, before taking the sealed envelope inside and handing it to Charyn, then handing the dispatch pouch back to the courier.

"Is an immediate reply requested?" asked Charyn.

"No, sir."

"You may go . . . but stop by the kitchen to get something warm before you leave."

"Yes, Your Grace. Thank you, Your Grace."

Charyn waited until the study door closed before slitting the envelope and taking out the two sheets of paper. He began to read.

> Your Grace—
>
> It distresses me to report that the former palace of the Lords of Telaryn, which has served as the residence and workplace of the regional governor, was consumed in a fire the night of Meredi, 18 Janus 409 A.L. The fire was deliberately set, using a mixture of explosives and volatile oils. Three guards were killed. That enabled the arsonists to infiltrate the palace grounds and set the explosives and oils. Four servants were killed in the blaze, and a number of others were injured.
>
> The only evidence found was the attached message. It was found in a bag knifed to the seat in the surviving coach and found on Jeudi morning.
>
> At present, I am quartered in the summer villa of High Holder Garleuch. Needless to say, this is a less than tenable situation, and I await your instructions on how to proceed in regard to obtaining a more permanent governor's residence.

The seal and signature were presumably those of Voralch.

Charyn studied the short message, once more written in standard merchant hand. Like the others, it was short.

> Rex Charyn—
> We can strike anywhere. If meaningful action to stop Jariolan piracy

without imposing more tariffs is not forthcoming, before long you
will face the same fate as your predecessor.

If the destruction of the ancient palace had been the work of Ryel,
the warning was certainly cleverly worded to throw suspicion elsewhere.
Except that the decision on the tariffs was not made until within a few glasses of the time when
the palace burned, and Solis was a four-day ride by the fastest of couriers. But then, Ryel
had to have known that, in the end, Charyn would have to raise tariffs.
Even if Charyn hadn't decided that, the term "meaningful action" was so
vague that anything Charyn did, or anything he did that Solidar could
afford, could be declared as too little and too late to be "meaningful."

Wordlessly, he handed both sheets to Howal, then waited for the
imager to read them.

Also without a word, Howal looked up after he finished.

"What do you think about the paper the threat was written on?"

Howal held the sheet up to the light of the nearest wall lamp. After
several moments, he said, "The finish, the sizing, if you will, on the paper
used for the threat is the kind used by factors. If you run your fingers over
the paper used by the regional governor, I'd wager that it feels smoother."

"Could you image either kind of paper so that the writer could not
tell the difference?"

"It might take a glass or so to get it right, but I could. Maitre Alastar
likely could in a fraction of a quint."

"What about the ink?"

"Oh . . . that's a common carbon black ink with a touch of iron gall.
You can find that in any factor's study. I wouldn't be surprised if there's
some here in the chateau. It'd be easy to image."

"And anyone with much knowledge would say that the paper and ink
likely came from a factor or merchant?"

"Be unlikely to come from a High Holder, and a crafter wouldn't have
much use for sized paper and ink."

"Would you image a copy of the threat note, one as perfect as possible? I'd like a copy, but I'd rather not have anyone else here at the chateau
see it."

"I can do that, sir."

"After you do that, we need to meet with Alucar and let him know
about the burning of the old palace. Then we'll discuss the best way to
improve the ledgers." Charyn knew that would take a while.

After that, he'd have to tell Aevidyr about Governor Voralch's veiled demand for a suitable dwelling, another drain on the treasury's already thin resources.

And he still needed to think out just how he could trap Ryel.

45

By Mardi morning, Charyn still had not figured out anything beyond his general plan for dealing with his uncle. After breakfast, he met with Norstan only to discover once more, not to his surprise, that there were no requests for meetings. *No one sees any point in meeting with you, not when most who might seek an advantage by meeting with you believe you'll be dead within weeks.*

Then Dylert and Kaylet each stopped by his study and reported on what they had discovered and were doing. Four guards were missing, and the assistant stablemaster had vanished before he could be dismissed.

Charyn doubted any of the five would ever return to the chateau.

Shortly after eighth glass, Maertyl rapped on the study door and announced, "Minister Aevidyr, sir."

"Have him come in."

After glancing at Howal, seated at the conference table, perusing lists of supplies purchased by Norstan, Charyn donned a pleasant smile, but remained seated behind the goldenwood desk. He gestured for Aevidyr to take one of the chairs in front of the desk, then waited.

"Your Grace, while you informed me about the loss of the old palace in Solis yesterday, I did not understand the extent of the loss until I received a dispatch from the governor this morning. Regional Governor Voralch has absolutely no suitable . . . situation . . . from which he can conduct the tasks of being regional governor."

"Could he not take a study in the navy headquarters in Solis?" Charyn knew that wasn't feasible, given that the navy compound was walled and guarded, but wanted to see Aevidyr's response.

"Your Grace, High Holders and factors cannot be expected to submit to waiting outside a guarded gate."

"I suppose that's true enough, although any tariffs he collects might be safer. His message to me said that he was ensconced in the summer villa of High Holder Garleuch. I cannot imagine it is that cramped a dwelling."

"It is a *summer* villa, Your Grace. It is midwinter."

"It doesn't even snow in Solis . . . almost never, anyway." Charyn shook his head. "Voralch wants an immediate replacement dwelling at his convenience and at my cost. There are two aspects to the problem, Aevidyr. First, Voralch needs a suitable domicile from which he can function as regional governor. Second, for reasons of history and politics, the old palace needs to be reconstructed. The first needs to be taken care of immediately. The second can wait."

"Governor Voralch knows that golds are scarce. He has proposed merely taking one part in ten of the tariffs he collects and applying them to the reconstruction."

"While having me purchase or lease a suitable domicile for him?"

"Ah . . . I believe that is what he has in mind."

"At present, his suggestions are not feasible."

"Your Grace . . . he is only looking out for your family heritage."

"Aevidyr . . . think about this. Both the factors and the High Holders are complaining about tariffs. I've just told them there aren't golds to build enough warships to protect their ships and cargoes. If I even hint about spending golds to rebuild a palace for a regional governor, I'll have undone everything . . . and I'll never work out anything with the councils. You are not to encourage this foolishness, either through commission or failing to tell Voralch that he is limited to five hundred golds for the purchase of a governor's domicile or a hundred to lease one for the next year."

"That sum . . ."

"Will easily purchase a handsome dwelling, and we both know it." Charyn tried not to show that he was losing patience with Aevidyr. "Draft a letter for your signature saying that he can have one of those two options, and to let you know which one he chooses. We'll have the navy vice-marshal in Solis provide the golds when he has a written agreement for purchase or lease. I'll add a few words below your signature and sign and seal the letter as well."

"That is . . . not customary."

"Perhaps not, but I want it clear that you're carrying out my wishes." Charyn smiled pleasantly. "That way, Governor Voralch can blame me, not you. After all, it is my decision."

"Yes, Your Grace."

"Good. I trust you'll have the letter ready by early this afternoon. And, if you would, have Alucar come see me."

"Yes, Your Grace."

Although Aevidyr's voice was pleasant enough, Charyn could tell that Aevidyr was anything but pleased. That alone suggested that the Minister of Administration might need to be replaced, and that his ledgers as well might need to be audited. *But do you want to do that right at the moment? With no idea of who might be a good and an honest replacement?* Charyn was well aware that by acting quickly when he didn't absolutely have to might cause him even more difficulties, especially since he didn't even know anyone remotely qualified to replace Aevidyr, at least not anyone who wasn't an imager.

He was still mulling that over when Alucar arrived.

"You requested my presence, sir?"

"I did. Please sit down. As I mentioned yesterday, Regional Governor Voralch needs a domicile and a place from which he can collect tariffs and handle his other duties. He also sent Aevidyr a letter suggesting that I rebuild the old palace."

"That would cost more than several warships."

"I know. I asked Aevidyr to draft a letter allowing Voralch five hundred golds to purchase another suitable dwelling or a hundred to lease one, but, in either case, to present documentation before we sent any authorization for the vice-marshal of the navy to release the funds." Seeing the expression on Alucar's face, Charyn stopped explaining and asked, "What did I miss or forget?"

"The old palace likely had much in the way of brick and stone, as well as metals that could be salvaged and sold. There might be more than a thousand golds of value there."

"I'll need to have him re-draft the letter, then, insisting that all valuable materials from the rubble be inventoried, including everything we can think of, and requesting an accounting of their salvage value before I can determine the amount he'll receive for a lease or purchase."

"Given Governor Voralch's tastes, perhaps you should only allow him a few golds for a temporary lease, and require him to purchase something within the next two seasons. Also, you might have Marshal Vaelln instruct the sea marshal to oversee the salvage and inventory. Some of the smaller and more valuable items are doubtless already in others' hands. Scavengers were likely there before the embers cooled, and I doubt that Voralch even considered that."

"I suspect some are already in Voralch's hands, and he'll doubtless claim that they were lost in the fire," said Charyn sourly, wondering if Voralch might already be an accomplice of Ryel. *Except it would be hard to arrange all those explosives and oils without it being noticed by the governor's palace staff. More likely, Voralch wouldn't have been a party to it simply because he wouldn't have wanted* to be discommoded. *And Ryel wouldn't have trusted anyone whom he couldn't control absolutely.*

He was beginning to see why his father had trusted no one and why he'd tried to keep everything he could to himself. *But that didn't work in the end, either.*

Managing a pleasant smile, Charyn said, "Thank you for the advice and observations. I'll make sure they're included in the final version of the letter." That likely meant another draft, but Howal could do that.

As soon as Alucar had left, Charyn turned to Howal. "Could you draft that letter to Marshal Vaelln?"

"How strongly do you want to convey your wishes?"

"Have the sea marshal exert all possible efforts to reclaim and account for any valuables, building materials, and other items of value . . . or words to that effect."

While Howal set to work drafting the letter, Charyn looked at the single new petition that had somehow found its way to his desk. *Because Sanafryt doesn't want to talk to you any more than absolutely necessary?*

The petition seemed straightforward enough. One Factor Barryl operated a gristmill just north of Piedryn. The same waterwheel that powered the mill also drove his looms, which were part of a factorage where cloth was woven and dyed. The problem was that, upstream of Barryl, one of High Holder Haebyn's tenants had begun to operate a large hog farm, and the runoff from the hogs made the water unusable for washing and dyeing the cloth. Barryl had pled his case before the regional justicer and been denied. Regional Governor Voralch had upheld the denial.

That didn't exactly surprise Charyn.

He sighed. He'd need to talk to Sanafryt, whether Sanafryt wanted to talk to him or not. So he had Maertyl send for the Justice Minister.

Sanafryt entered the study a half a quint later with a faint smile.

Charyn waited until the older man had seated himself before speaking. "I read the petition you had placed on my desk. How can Haebyn's tenant get away with fouling the stream to such an extent?"

"There's no prohibition against allowing waste into streams. It's never been a problem before," stated Sanafryt.

"So this High Holder Haebyn can turn the water filthy, and there's no law against it?"

"No, Your Grace, there is not. I would advise against writing one at present."

"Why?"

"Because there is no way to enforce such a law. Farmers all over Solidar do the very same thing. Many factorages do as well."

"That doesn't make it right."

"No, Your Grace, it does not, but laws must not only prohibit evil, but also be able to be enforced. If they cannot be enforced, then the idea of law itself becomes mocked and disregarded. It would take a veritable army to scour the countryside to make sure that such a law was obeyed. How would you pay for that?"

Charyn knew the answer to that question. He handed the petition to Sanafryt. "Write him a kind letter denying his appeal."

"Yes, Your Grace."

Charyn just sat there for a time after Sanafryt left, a short time. He still needed to come to a decision about Keithell. Finally, he said, "Howal, please send someone to find Dylert and tell him that I'd like to see him, but he's not to interrupt anything he's doing."

"Yes, sir."

Less than half a quint after Howal gave the word, Dylert was in the study. "Sir?"

"I've decided what to do about the stablemaster. Under the law, he could be executed for what he did. With everything that's been allowed around here . . ." Charyn shook his head. "He will be dismissed and flogged with an order to remain far from the chateau . . . on pain of execution. If you'd have someone bring him here, I'll tell him the sentence myself."

Dylert nodded. "That might be best."

Charyn wasn't sure whether Dylert thought Charyn's pronouncing the sentence was best, or that the sentence was the best possible under the circumstances. He didn't feel like asking.

Another quint passed before Dylert returned, along with Keithell and two guards.

Charyn stood and looked squarely at Keithell. "You have stolen from me and from the chateau. You have stolen so much that, under the law, you can be executed. Had you stolen even a fraction of what you took, you would lose your right hand. You have beaten and abused stable boys. You have not done the job for which you were responsible. Worst of all, you have had the temerity to insist you have been loyal. For all that, you owe me your life."

Keithell shuddered as if Charyn had struck him physically. "Please . . . Your Grace . . . if it please you, I have done much less than others . . ."

"Who besides Churwyl and the traitorous guards has done worse or stolen more?" asked Charyn evenly.

Keithell looked down.

"Name them."

Keithell only said, "Please . . . Your Grace."

"Churwyl is dead, and he would have died regardless. Still . . . as you point out, much laxness has been allowed. For that reason, you are to be flogged, with twenty lashes. You are dismissed . . . and if you are ever found within a mille of the chateau, for any reason, your life is forfeit." Charyn looked at Dylert. "Take him away. Have him flogged in the rear courtyard within the glass, in such fashion as you think most suitable. Announce his crimes first."

"Yes, sir."

Charyn could see the fear . . . and the anger in Keithell's eyes before the man was dragged out. *Perhaps you should have executed him.* A second thought struck him. Had someone else, besides Churwyl, done worse? And if so, why had Keithell not named them? Even greater fear of someone else? Or had his words about others just been an attempt not to be executed?

When the study door closed, Charyn looked to Howal. "Answer me honestly, Howal. Was I too lenient?"

Howal did not answer for a moment, then said, "You were too lenient on Keithell, but executing him for what he did would have been seen as too harsh by most in the chateau. He may try to cause trouble when he recovers from the flogging."

"In short, there was no good punishment."

"No, sir."

"Thank you." Charyn moved to the window overlooking the courtyard and pulled back the hangings. He stood there, thinking and waiting, for nearly two quints while much of the chateau staff assembled and two guards set up the flogging frame.

The flogging itself took less than a quint, and by the end, Keithell sagged against the ropes that bound him in place.

Charyn could see several of the stable boys watching intently, their faces seemingly impassive. He wondered what they might be thinking when they finally left the courtyard. He let the hangings drop, turning to look at Howal.

"How do imagers punish their wrongdoers?"

"For imager students, small mistakes merit extra work and confinement to Imagisle. For imagers or students, any more severe offense brought before the senior maitres requires blinding or death."

Charyn stiffened.

"Imagers cannot afford to have any imager seen as a wrongdoer," said Howal quietly. "Wrongdoers lose their ability to image and their freedom, or they lose their life."

"How often does that happen?"

"Not often. I've seen four blinded since I've been at the Collegium. The Maitre killed all the rebel imagers, I'm told, during the last battle of the High Holder revolt."

Charyn managed a nod. "I'm going down to the music room for a time."

"Perhaps I should accompany you until . . ."

"Until you get word from Kaylet and Dylert that they have matters under complete control? Especially after what just happened?" Charyn didn't mention that he was carrying the pistol he'd used on Churwyl all the time now. There just might be a time when Howal couldn't protect him.

"Yes, sir."

"That suggests that Dylert has discovered more about some guards than anyone knew, except Churwyl."

"One of the four guards who departed the chateau in less than a quint after the explosion was a cousin of Churwyl."

"Dylert mentioned that. Is Kaylet having the same sort of trouble?"

Howal shook his head. "Everyone in the stables and carriage houses is more than pleased that he's there. He'll likely need to be here longer than Dylert, though. It'll take time to teach some of them how things really should be done, and there's no one else there who can do that."

That sounds like we'll need a few experienced men from outside the chateau . . . or that Kaylet will be very, very busy.

For all of Howal's concerns, Charyn saw no one except Howal during his walk down the grand staircase and as he made his way to the music room.

Howal settled into a corner chair as Charyn walked toward Palenya, who was seated at the small secretary desk. It appeared that she had been copying music.

"I hope I'm not interrupting anything important."

She smiled faintly. "With Aloryana gone and Bhayrn less inclined to want any instruction, I have a great deal of time. I thought I'd use it productively and make copies of some of the music that is worn."

"I hope you'll make copies for yourself as well." Charyn immediately realized that his words could be misinterpreted. "No, you're not leaving. I just thought it would be a pity if you didn't take the opportunity to increase your personal music library while you have the opportunity." He paused. "I believe the Farray nocturne music is yours, and, if you have time, I would greatly appreciate having a copy of my own."

Palenya's smile widened. "I already made one for you."

"Then I would like to use it, with your instruction."

"Now?"

"Now. I need a break from . . . regial tasks."

"You watched . . . didn't you?"

"I had to. I ordered it."

"You may have been too merciful. The stablemaster was not as good a man as he might have been."

"That may be, but he was allowed to be that way." Charyn didn't want to explain more. He thought Palenya would understand. "The nocturne?"

Her smile was sad as she walked beside him toward the clavecin.

46

By Meredi morning, Charyn was again worrying about just how he could implement his vague plan to deal with Ryel . . . as well as who else might have been doing worse than Keithell that he might not even know about. Was he becoming as preoccupied as his father had been with who was loyal and who was not?

How can you not worry?

Again, Norstan had informed him that there were no requests for appointments with him. Was Norstan summarily refusing appointments? Or was his situation perceived as so precarious that no one even wanted to meet with him until they were certain he would remain as rex?

Both Dylert and Howal were in the study waiting when Charyn arrived, even though he was there well before seventh glass, a time when his father had barely roused himself.

"Since you're both here, I get the feeling that there are more changes needed in administering the chateau guards."

"There are some improvements that would be helpful," replied Dylert with a smile.

"Are we paying the chateau guards enough?" asked Charyn.

"The wages for a guard are higher than for an army ranker," replied Dylert. "They also get fed a meal a day, and their uniforms, and the single men get bunks, as well as breakfast in addition to the other meal. That's why people would pay Churwyl to get their sons placed in the Chateau Guard."

"If pay isn't the problem . . ."

"The problem isn't the base pay. It's that there's no real chance for advancement and increased pay. There were only four senior guards who made more than the basic pay."

"So loyalty and greater ability don't get rewarded?"

"Not exactly. Churwyl apparently gave 'bonuses' to guards he favored."

"I suppose those extra silvers came out of what he got from the maintenance fees and the wages of the two nonexistent guards?"

"It would appear that way. There weren't any ranks. No first-level guards, second-level guards. Guards didn't get pay increases for serving more years, either."

"So the longer a guard served, the more likely he was to feel unappreciated. Would you suggest restructuring the Chateau Guard more along the lines of the army?"

"Not exactly. More like a cross between the imagers and the army. I'm working out something for your approval. It should be ready tomorrow."

"I'd like to see what you come up with." Charyn hoped Dylert's plan wouldn't raise the pay costs too much, but it seemed like everything was turning out to cost more than he'd thought or planned. On the other hand, the old system had clearly failed. "One other matter. I'd like to know everyone who comes to the chateau, even if they meet with someone else besides me. There was supposed to be a logbook, but I suspect it may not have been all that accurate."

"The guards say there was, but there's no sign of it. I'm setting up a new one."

Charyn nodded. *Churwyl again? Or someone else?* Another thing he doubted he'd ever discover.

Once Dylert had left the study, Howal stood abruptly. "I'll be back in a few moments. Don't go anywhere."

"I'm not going any place." Charyn smiled wryly, as he picked up the copy of *Veritum* that was waiting for him on the corner of the desk. He immediately noticed the story entitled, "Mysterious Explosion at Chateau D'Rex," and began to read it, noting particular words.

. . . recently learned that Guard Commander Churwyl perished in an explosion within the Chateau armory last Vendrei. Word also indicates that Rex Charyn was injured slightly in the explosion, as was another functionary . . .

. . . no memorial services were conducted . . . appears that Churwyl may have been pocketing regial golds . . . no statements from the rex or the Chateau seneschal . . .

Charyn nodded. It could have been worse. He set aside the newssheet and turned his attention to Aevidyr's revised letter to Regional Governor Voralch. After reading about three lines, he sighed and shook his head. *For the Nameless's sake, this reads like Voralch is the rex, and I'm the regional governor.* He was about to call Howal over, before he remembered that Howal had left, probably to answer a call of nature, if the fidgeting Charyn had seen had been any indication.

At that moment, Sturdyn called out, "Guard Captain Dylert wants to see me, sir. Yarselt and Cauthyrn are replacing me while I'm gone."

"That's fine," answered Charyn, returning his attention to the letter, murmuring the words Aevidyr had written.

> . . . understand the difficult position in which the deficiencies of the regial treasury have placed you . . . rest assured that I will endeavor to rectify the situation . . .

Charyn snorted and lowered the letter just in time to see Cauthyrn open the door and walk into the study, followed by Yarselt. Both carried unsheathed sabres.

Without hesitation Charyn bolted to his feet and drew the pistol. Two armed guards entering the study when Howal wasn't there meant trouble. Yarselt took two steps toward the desk and paused, gesturing for Cauthyrn to move to the side.

Cauthyrn moved more toward the conference table, widening the distance between himself and Yarselt.

"Move closer!" snapped Yarselt. "He can't hit anything."

Charyn fired.

The shot took Yarselt in the middle of the chest. He staggered back, an expression of utter surprise on his face. Then his legs collapsed, and he went down in a heap, falling back and to the side.

Cauthyrn halted.

"You want to chance it?" asked Charyn.

Cauthyrn stood there, waiting, almost to see what Charyn might do.

Charyn wasn't about to do anything until he had to, not with a single shot left in the pistol. "Who paid you off?"

Cauthyrn grinned. "Wouldn't you like to know?" He took a step forward.

Charyn waited. He didn't want the guard too close, but he also wanted him closer. "Not particularly. I just thought you might want to gloat."

"Everyone with golds or power wants you dead."

At that moment Howal rushed through the study door, and Cauthyrn froze, unable to move.

Charyn continued to watch the open study door, in case someone else came in, but he could see that Cauthyrn was turning red, a red that darkened toward purple. Then Howal released the shields, and the guard toppled forward. From somewhere a length of rope appeared, and Charyn wondered if the imager had carried it, or imaged it into being. Regardless of where the rope had come from, in moments Howal had Cauthyrn securely tied up and lying on his back only a yard or so from the end of the conference table.

"How much was the bonus to kill Rex Charyn?" asked Howal.

Even lying on his back, Cauthyrn smirked. His face stiffened, as if he could not move. After several moments, his skin began to turn red . . . and even redder. Abruptly, the stiffness vanished, and the guard took a gasping breath.

"How much?" asked Howal.

Cauthyrn tightened his lips and then stiffened.

Charyn could see that Howal was using shields to suffocate the guard.

When Howal released the shields again, he said, "I can keep doing this until your lungs are bloody shreds, and you suffocate slowly in your own blood."

"You'll . . . kill . . . me . . . anyway . . ." gasped Cauthyrn.

"Very well," said Howal coldly, clamping the shields back in place.

After five more rounds of suffocation, Cauthyrn whispered, "Enough . . . a hundred golds."

"Who told you that?"

"Yarselt . . . said he'd split it with me."

"Who promised that to him?"

"He . . . didn't know . . . said the fellow was cloaked . . . gave him five golds . . . said he'd get the rest when the young rex was dead. Yarselt . . . gave me two."

Charyn heard boots running down the north corridor, and Howal turned immediately and stepped back from the trussed Cauthyrn.

The first face through the door was that of Dylert, followed by Sturdyn. Dylert's eyes immediately went from Yarselt's corpse to the pistol in Charyn's hand to Howal and the rope-bound guard. Dylert was breathing hard, but said, "You two managed, I see."

"Barely," replied Charyn. "Howal returned just in time. I had to kill Yarselt." Given that Charyn hadn't dared to try just wounding Yarselt, not with a two-shot pistol, besides which he'd been truly angry, given how he had trusted Yarselt. "He's been questioning Cauthyrn."

"Go ahead. I'd like to hear what else he has to say." Dylert turned to Sturdyn. "You're back on duty."

"Yes, sir." Sturdyn stepped back, closing the study door.

Howal looked down at Cauthyrn. "Who else is involved?"

"No one . . . didn't want . . . to split the golds . . . didn't know who to trust . . ." Cauthyrn coughed up a bloody foam.

"We need to sit him up," said Dylert, moving over and pulling Cauthyrn up into one of the chairs at the south end of the conference table. "You used shields to suffocate him?"

Howal nodded. "Thought we needed to know in a hurry."

"Why did you take the golds?" asked Charyn.

"Why not? You . . . won't . . . stay rex . . . long . . . might as well . . . another revolt . . . we'd get killed . . . anyway . . ."

"Who told you that?" pressed Charyn.

"Churwyl . . ."

"How would he know?"

"He . . . knew lots of things . . ." Cauthyrn offered another retching cough, and blood oozed from the corners of his mouth.

"Go on," ordered Charyn. "What else did he know?"

". . . knew you . . . playing at being a factor . . . knew your sister . . . no imager . . . just a way to get her away from . . . chateau . . ." Another retching cough followed the words, with more blood issuing from the guard's mouth.

"Where did Yarselt meet the man who gave him the golds?"

". . . never . . . said . . ."

"Did he say anything else about him?"

". . . thought he might . . . know who . . . wouldn't say . . ." Abruptly, Cauthyrn slumped forward, then toppled out of the chair onto the floor.

"Frig!" came the exclamation from Howal. "I didn't mean to be that hard on him."

"He might have weak lungs," said Dylert, turning over the crumpled figure.

As he did, Cauthyrn shuddered once and was still.

"He's dead. His heart's not beating." Dylert rose.

"I'm sorry," said Howal. "I didn't think I was that hard on him."

"He might have had consumption anyway," replied Dylert. "Or a weak heart."

"How did you know we had trouble?" asked Charyn.

"As soon as Sturdyn found me, I knew, because I hadn't asked for him. We both ran back up here. How did they get in?"

"They waited until Howal left to answer nature's call, and then told Sturdyn you'd asked for him and deputed Yarselt and Cauthyrn to stand in. I imagine whoever it was picked Yarselt because he'd often acted as my personal guard when I left the chateau. Whoever bought them off likely found out earlier about Yarselt from Churwyl. After Sturdyn was well out of hearing, they just walked in."

"Someone knows a great deal about you and the chateau," observed Dylert.

"I've already realized that. The real question is how many more traitors there will be," said Charyn, his tone somewhere between wry and bleak.

"There are always those who will betray, given a great enough reward and the chance that they can survive to benefit from their treachery," said Dylert. "The last few days have suggested to any in the chateau that survival after treachery is unlikely. Most would-be traitors prefer to live."

Unless someone has great power over them and those they love. "So my greatest worry now is from those outside the chateau?"

"That would be the greater worry."

Meaning that nowhere is totally safe . . . as if that hadn't just been emphasized. Another thought struck Charyn. "We need to search the bodies. Also their foot chests. I'm looking for the golds they were paid . . . and anything else that just might give a hint as to who paid Yarselt off."

Howal immediately began to search Yarselt, but he had no golds in his wallet or anywhere else.

Dylert found two golds in slots on the inside of Cauthyrn's belt. He studied them for a moment, then handed them to Charyn. "Those came from a private mint."

"How do you know that?"

"There's a mint mark. I don't know what it means, but I can find out for you."

Charyn handed one of the golds back to Dylert. "Please do. I wouldn't know where to begin." He paused, then moved to the bookcase, from where he extracted the cloth bag and brought it back to Dylert. "See if these have the same mint mark."

Dylert looked at all ten. "All of them are the same. They're all newly minted. It looks like that anyway."

There was something about that, but Charyn couldn't recall what it was. "That's more than coincidence. It might help to know where they were minted."

"I won't have an answer until tomorrow."

"Keep one of the golds to find out."

"Yes, sir."

Howal gestured to the two dead guards. "What about them?"

Charyn glanced toward Yarselt, on whose dead face remained an expression that might have been surprise. "Have the bodies burned. No service, no ceremony, no words." The coldness in his own voice even surprised Charyn . . . except he knew where that cold anger had come from. He'd never been cold or cruel to Yarselt, and he'd even trusted his life to Yarselt. *And someone had used that trust against you.*

A third of a quint later, Charyn and Howal were again alone in the study. Before he replaced the pistol in the inside pocket of his jacket, Charyn reloaded it. Then he replaced the bag with eleven golds in it in its hiding place.

Finally, he looked at Howal and picked up the letter to Governor Voralch. "We need to rewrite this letter."

Almost a glass later, after two revisions of the letter, and after allowing his anger to cool, Charyn summoned Aevidyr. The Minister of Administration appeared promptly and settled into the chair across the desk from Charyn.

"Your Grace?"

"I have read the letter you wrote to Governor Voralch." Charyn picked up the original version, glancing at it as he continued. "Telling him that you will endeavor to rectify the situation suggests that I am in error in not immediately opening the treasury to him to rebuild the palace whose comforts he enjoyed at my father's pleasure and at mine. It is *not* an error to refuse to spend golds that the treasury does not hold."

"I felt that being conciliatory and sympathetic would serve you better, Your Grace."

"Sympathetic is one thing. Suggesting your ruler is in error is very much another. Exactly how will that be helpful when it's apparent that more than a few factors and High Holders have doubts that I will long remain rex? I understand that arrogance just angers people unnecessarily, but your suggesting errors on my part and being excessively conciliatory will only convey the appearance of weakness." Charyn paused. "The wording in this letter conveys weakness."

"I am sorry that you see it that way, Your Grace."

"I do. I've rewritten it along the lines I had in mind. Now, you can read it and suggest any changes you believe would improve it. Without suggesting error or weakness." Charyn handed the reworded letter across to Aevidyr.

The Administration Minister read it slowly, then said, "I would have no problems signing this."

"Could you make it better without conveying arrogance or weakness?"

Charyn thought that, just for an instant, his words had surprised Aevidyr.

"I could try, sir."

"Then do so." After a moment, Charyn went on. "All this brings up another question. Just why do so many seem to think that I will not remain rex for long?"

"I can only surmise that those who feel that way believe that all the attacks on you and your family are based on a wider discontent than may be the case."

"Who are those who feel that way? You certainly have contacts among the High Holders and others?"

"I know of no one by name, but I would say that the majority of those who feel that way are located comparatively close to L'Excelsis, and, based on the burning of the old palace, possibly in Solis. You are not receiving petitions from the nearby areas of old Bovaria, but the petitions continue from elsewhere."

Yet another reason to suggest that your dear uncle is behind this. "Your reasoning makes an unfortunate sense, Minister Aevidyr."

"Thank you, Your Grace."

"I'm not flattering you. I'm commending you. If you can finish your revisions to the letter, I'd like to see it this afternoon so that I can add my few words and we can dispatch it to Governor Voralch."

"I will have it on your desk shortly."

"Thank you."

After Aevidyr left, Charyn stood and walked to the window and pulled back the hangings. Despite the fact that a moderate snow had been falling since dawn, the rear courtyard and the drive down to the ring road were both clear, something Charyn hadn't seen happen so quickly in years.

Some matters are improving. If only he could figure out how to implement the first part of his strategy to deal with Ryel.

47

Even when Charyn walked into the family parlor before dinner, he was still pondering the resentment that had been created among some of the regial staff over the years. While he likely had contributed to it in some fashion, he certainly hadn't developed or perpetuated the pay structure that had made some of the guards unhappy—and worse—nor had he been the one who had ignored the problems. What he worried about was what he didn't know and what other problems in the chateau might be exploited to his detriment and that of his mother and brother. He wasn't worried nearly so much about Aloryana now that she was an imager, since the imagers were more than capable of protecting her.

Bhayrn was already there, and he turned to Charyn and asked sardonically, "So what did you do to get Yarselt mad enough to try to kill you?"

"I told him that he'd have to guard you when you start riding out next month," replied Charyn dryly.

"Most humorous, elder brother."

"Someone offered him a hundred golds, and gave him five in advance."

"A hundred golds? That seems rather petty. I'd think a thousand would be more appropriate."

"It might be, but a guard will be lucky to see two or three golds perhaps once in his life, if ever."

"So much for loyalty," sneered Bhayrn.

"I don't think you can buy loyalty, but you can certainly buy disloyalty from those who only work for coin."

"Maybe you should be a philosopher."

"Rather than a rex? I don't think I have that choice at the moment."

"You never did," interjected Chelia as she entered the parlor. "Most choices are illusions." She gestured toward the family dining room. "Shall we eat?"

The dining room was cool, almost cold, despite the fire in the hearth at the far end, as the three seated themselves. A tacit acknowledgment to that chill and the season was the inclusion of hot mulled wine, along with carafes of both red and white wine. The dinner was a large roasted chicken, along with cheesed mashed potatoes and carrots casseroled in molasses.

Charyn nodded to Bhayrn. "You can do the gratitude."

"For whatever grace may come from above, whatever bounty there may be, for what passes for justice and mercy, we offer our thanks and gratitude, in the spirit of that which cannot be named."

"That is a rather cynical version of the grace," observed Chelia mildly.

"I'd prefer to say that it is more accurate," replied Bhayrn.

Charyn poured white wine for himself, then looked to his mother.

"The hot mulled, please. Today felt like the coldest of winter so far."

Charyn filled her mug, leaving her wine goblet empty, then served himself white wine before passing the platters. "You were saying that most choices are illusions."

"They are. Your choices are two. Be a good and effective rex or die. Abdicating is not a choice, but an illusion of choice. If you tried to leave, you would be a threat to whoever succeeded you. That would mean you would always be a threat to those who relied on the whims and wishes of your successor. Sooner or later, someone would assassinate you. Unless, of course, you became a nameless laborer someplace. You are not suited to that so you would likely also soon die. Your father's brother thought he had choices as well, and that he could be rex. His only real choice was the same one all younger brothers have, to accept estates and become a High Holder. He refused that choice. In doing so he threatened not only your father, but the Collegium and the factors. He died in the struggle. So did thousands of those who supported him." Chelia took a sip of the hot mulled wine.

"You make it sound like there are no meaningful choices," declared Bhayrn.

"There are meaningful choices. We three are alive today because your father went against his beliefs and allowed imagers into the chateau. I could have chosen not to marry your father and married someone lesser. There would have been less tragedy, but also less opportunity to be a part of something meaningful."

"Some of us have fewer meaningful choices." Bhayrn's words were tinged with bitterness.

"Everyone has some meaningful choices," returned Chelia. "The fewer you have, the more important they are."

"That's easy enough to say." Bhayrn took a healthy swallow of the red wine.

Charyn tried not to wince, both at how quickly Bhayrn was drinking his wine . . . and at the thought of that much cool red wine with fowl.

"You're right," Chelia agreed. "It's always easier to say something than to do it."

Bhayrn opened his mouth, as if he had been ready to dispute whatever his mother said, and then closed it.

"Although most apparent choices are illusions of choice, part of wisdom is understanding which choices are illusory and which are not. You cannot know when you will next face a meaningful choice."

"Because some choices that we think are just illusions of having a choice turn out to be meaningful and some choices that seem to be meaningful are not?" asked Charyn.

"That's something you'll have to decide for yourselves." Chelia took another sip of the mulled wine. "Do you think it will get colder by Samedi?"

"It's stopped snowing," said Charyn. "The skies are clearing, and that means it will be cold tonight."

"You've at least got someone to keep you warm," murmured Bhayrn.

"Except I can't keep her," replied Charyn. "Not for long."

"Why not? You're the mighty rex."

"If I kept her against her will, she'd soon be too cold to keep me warm. And she won't be my mistress once I decide to court anyone. Nor will she wish to remain here."

"You could still—"

"Bhayrn." Chelia's voice was as cold as the moaning wind that blew outside the Chateau. "Trying to keep anyone against her will soon destroys all her charms. It also will turn you into the sort of man few women could marry, let alone love."

Bhayrn's jaw set.

Charyn took another bite of chicken. The sooner they finished eating the better. The last thing he wanted to do was deal with Bhayrn . . . especially given that their uncle was most likely trying to kill both of them, and possibly their mother. And telling Bhayrn that, with Bhayrn's stubbornness and current contrariness, and Charyn's lack of hard proof, would only make matters worse.

48

When Charyn reached the family breakfast room on Jeudi, Chelia was already seated at the table, sipping tea and waiting for him. She had finished her breakfast.

"Have you recovered from yesterday, Charyn?"

"Perhaps from dinner, but not from so many people wanting to profit from my early death." He settled into the chair across from her.

"You already know that everyone seeks to profit from the rex in some fashion." Her words were dryly matter-of-fact. "I'm completely into my new quarters. Now you can move into the regial rooms."

"Thank you." Charyn was not in any hurry to move.

"I've already arranged for Delya to move your clothing. She'll begin at noon."

Charyn took a cautious sip of the mug of tea before replying. "You do want me moved."

"It's another indication of permanence. You need all the indications you can get. Speaking of which, you need to formally announce the spring season-turn ball and send out invitations to anyone you particularly wish to attend."

Charyn had totally forgotten about the timing of the next ball, not that it was a matter of pressing concern, especially in comparison to his other problems. By the calendar, spring began on the first of Maris, even though winter weather usually lingered into the middle of Maris. The season-turn balls were always held on the evening of the thirty-fifth of the month, which meant the Spring-Turn Ball was only six weeks and two days away.

"I would suggest inviting by name a number of eligible daughters of High Holders," Chelia continued. "That cannot but help your position. Since you kept notes for the past several balls, that certainly would not pose a problem."

"Would it be too improper to invite Maitre Malyna, as a gesture of thanks?"

Chelia frowned, momentarily, then offered what could only be described as a delighted smile. "I had not thought of that. It's an excellent idea, for a number of reasons. It will establish in an unorthodox fashion that you are your own man, and that you will make your own alliances. Now . . . if you will provide a list of the young ladies in the next day or so, I will take care of the invitations."

"In the next day or so," he agreed.

Charyn's breakfast arrived at that moment, as did Bhayrn.

"You're up early," offered Charyn.

"It's the only time I can see you unless I wait until dinner." Bhayrn seated himself beside his mother and beckoned to the serving girl. "Hot cider."

"I need to see to some matters, dears," said Chelia, smiling pleasantly and rising.

"Then we'll see you later," replied Charyn.

Bhayrn nodded.

"You had something in mind?" asked Charyn after taking several bites of egg and ham slices.

"I just wondered if you were going to do anything to put the factors in their place and stop all the attacks on us. Among other things, I'd like to ride some and visit friends."

"You can take the plain coach and a pair of guards if you want to visit," offered Charyn. "If the guards wear brown coats, no one will even notice." He shoveled in another mouthful of breakfast, followed by a swallow of tea.

"I'm supposed to sneak around L'Excelsis? A member of the regial family skulking like an overindebted High Holder? Like Cousin Ferrand and his father?"

"Well," said Charyn, drawing out the single word before continuing, "you could take the regial coach and run the risk of getting shot. Better yet, just ride out in regial green."

"Most humorous, elder brother. Most humorous."

"What do you want me to do? Execute every hundredth factor until someone confesses? Something like that would keep anyone from paying tariffs as well as start not just a revolt, but a war."

"It's better than doing nothing."

"No. Doing things that make matters worse are not better than doing nothing, although you might have noticed that I have been doing a few things, such as obtaining agreements for more tariffs to build warships, as well as restructuring the Chateau Guard, and the rest of the staff. I've also gotten more help from the Collegium." He paused and took another bite. "All that may not be as dramatic as mass executions, but it's likely to be more effective over time."

"Provided you don't get killed in the meantime by whoever it is that seems to want to destroy the entire regial family."

"I'm working on that."

"How?"

"That's something I'll be keeping to myself for the moment."

"Secret plans . . . how dramatic." Bhayrn snorted, then took a swallow of the hot cider that the server had put in front of him.

"Not dramatic, just prudent, given that all too many around the chateau have proved to have interests that did not include our well-being." Charyn concentrated on eating for a time.

"That's all you have to say?" Bhayrn finally asked.

"What else is there to say? We're short of golds and under attack by someone who apparently holds us personally responsible for the Jariolan piracy. I'm doing everything I can think of to deal with the problems. If you have any suggestions, I'd like to hear them."

"Just find out who's behind it and execute them."

"Excellent idea. The imagers and I have been working on that for almost a month. The only problem is that whoever it is seems to be able to set matters up that his agents either don't know who he is or they die before they can say anything." Charyn hastily swallowed the last sip of tea and rose. "It's time to see what other problems are about to beset me."

Before he made his way to the study, Charyn stopped by the duty desk, hoping to find Dylert. He did.

"You wish to see the logbook, sir?" asked the imager politely.

"If it's ready to be seen."

"There aren't many entries, just those from midday yesterday."

Charyn opened the log to the first page. Dylert was right. The handful of names were all tradespeople—a farrier and a grain factor to see Kaylet, a produce factor for Norstan, an imager courier with a message for Dylert.

"The message was a letter from my wife," Dylert explained. "She sent a list of trustworthy factors and suppliers, as well as a list of those to watch, and those to avoid." After glancing at Charyn and seeing his expression, the imager added, "She's the bookkeeper for the Collegium and comes from a prominent factoring family. She's also a maitre. I thought such information would be useful for Kaylet and whoever becomes stablemaster, as well as for the seneschal. I asked Howal to make copies for you and for Kaylet and Norstan. Oh . . . and the mint mark is that of Factor Lythoryn. His mines and his mint are just north of Asseroiles." He extended a small leather pouch. "Here's the gold, sir."

"Thank you." Charyn had never heard of Lythoryn. "Do you know if Lythoryn has the closest mint to either L'Excelsis or Rivages?"

"It's the closest mint that does silvers and golds. That's what Thelia wrote. Cuipryn here in L'Excelsis does most of the coppers."

"Thank you . . . and convey my thanks to her as well."

"I will, sir, when I can."

From the duty desk, Charyn went straight up the grand staircase to his study, doubting that he needed to check with Norstan about appointments after seeing Dylert's logbook.

Once inside his study, he picked up the weekly edition of *Tableta* and began to read the story entitled, "Mystery Explosion and Deaths at Chateau." The story was similar to the one that had appeared in *Veritum*, but had added one other detail:

> . . . six Chateau guards are missing . . . and two are believed to have died in an attempted attack on the new rex. The entire Guard structure is being changed . . . but the acting Guard Captain would only say that the changes will work better for the guards and that they were worked out under the direct orders of the rex . . .

Charyn also noted that Dylert's name did not appear in the story.

After he finished with the newssheet, he unlocked the hidden compartment in the low and wide bookcase against the wall behind the desk. Everyone would look for such a compartment in a desk, few in a bookcase. From there he extracted the threatening notes and the golds. First he examined the golds, those obtained both from Cauthyrn and from Churwyl, adding the gold he had received from Dylert. All not only had the same mint mark, but were still shiny, almost new. Asseroiles wasn't all that far from Rivages, where his uncle's holding was located. Except he's spent most of the past six years here in L'Excelsis. Still, the likelihood that a wealthy factor, whose coins came from everywhere, would have all the golds used to purportedly pay off assassins come from a mint in one location was a great deal less than for a High Holder. Yet another indication, but such a frail one. A second thought occurred to him. Ryel will never leave absolute or even partial proof of the kind to convince either a council or a High Justicer.

That meant the attacks and threats would continue until Ryel was stopped, or Charyn himself was dead. Stopping Ryel meant removing him in a way that seemed justified, or Charyn would likely be left with yet more unrest and quite possibly demands for his own head or the fragmentation of Solidar—which was what the High Holders had effectively supported for years.

He replaced the golds in the pouch and set it aside before laying out all of the threatening notes side by side. As Howal had said earlier, the hand on each note was identical to that on every other note. Even comparing them, letter by letter, Charyn couldn't see the slightest deviation.

"Howal . . . ?" Charyn gestured for the imager to join him, then waited until Howal could see all the notes before asking, "Does the paper look exactly the same?"

The imager bent and studied each sheet before finally straightening. "I don't see how they could be more alike."

"I'd like you to image several sheets of paper—without the writing. Can you do that?"

"It might take me a little while. How many sheets do you want?"

"Five, I think."

"Let me take one over to the table, if you would."

"You can take the one I got in the anomen." Charyn handed it to the imager. As Howal walked away, Charyn studied the text of the various messages.

The first message had been impersonal, referring to Rex Lorien in the third person. The other five all addressed either Charyn or his father as "you." *Why the change?* It took Charyn several moments to figure out that the sender wanted to make certain that the first message actually reached the rex. That also meant that, if Ryel were successful in killing Charyn, the next message would go to Bhayrn. Charyn could just imagine it.

> You have been warned. If you fail to act more decisively than the preceding rexes, you won't be ruler of Solidar any longer than your immediate predecessor.

That might not be the exact wording, but it would be close. And after Bhayrn was dead . . . Charyn swallowed. *Was that why Howal had been briefed to mention young High Holder Regial? Yet . . . why would Ryel want young Regial . . . Ryel's granddaughter Iryella! Was Ryel really that devious?*

Charyn smiled sardonically.

A quint later, Howal said, "I think I've got it, sir."

Charyn rose and walked across the study to the conference table.

Howal handed him a sheet of paper.

Charyn studied it closely, then felt it, and even smelled it. "It would take a paper mastercrafter to see the difference, if there even is any. Excellent."

"Five sheets, you said?"

"Ten if it's not too much trouble."

"I think I can do that." Howal handed Charyn the threat letter he had been using as a model for the paper.

"I'd appreciate that."

While Howal concentrated on the imaging, Charyn replaced all the messages and the golds in the hidden compartment.

Even after Howal finished imaging and turned the ten sheets over to Charyn, sheets cool and crisp to the touch, Charyn's thoughts remained on Ryel . . . and how he could reveal his uncle's treachery.

After some thought, he said, "Howal, would you draft a letter to Factor Elthyrd, requesting that he come to the chateau for a brief meeting on either Vendrei or Lundi, the time to be at his convenience?"

"Yes, sir."

Two quints later, just after Charyn had signed and sealed the letter to Elthyrd, Maertyl announced, "There's a Ferrand D'Delcoeur-Alte at the front entrance to see you, Your Grace."

"He's my cousin. You can show him in and up here."

Perhaps a fifth of a quint passed before Ferrand entered the study. "What's happened here?" His tone was between aggrieved and angry. "They wouldn't even let me beyond the foyer. I'm your cousin."

"It just might have to do with the three attempts on my life in the last week," replied Charyn dryly. The shooting was stretching things because Churwyl hadn't been aiming at Charyn, but it would help convey the seriousness of the situation.

Abruptly, Ferrand looked at Howal, then at Charyn.

"Howal is my personal secretary. He's also saved my life at least twice." Charyn gestured toward the chairs, then sat behind the desk.

"You *are* serious. How did all this happen?" Ferrand took the chair closest to the window, moving it closer to the desk.

"It's a continuation of the threats against Father. Apparently, nothing he did satisfied someone, and I'm not doing any better." Charyn managed a shrug. "You didn't come to the chateau in this weather to hear about my problems. What is it?"

Ferrand looked at Howal again.

Charyn ignored the glance and waited.

"It's Father. He's ill. Deathly ill. He's not expected to live out the month, certainly not the season."

"He's been in ill health lately, you'd said," temporized Charyn, thinking about all he had heard about his uncle's gambling and drinking.

"It's worse now. He can't get out of bed. He's still demanding wine and more wine, in the same Namer-damned way. He's never cared about anyone else. Just about himself. He set up his debts the same way. They were secured against the estates, and they're due and payable immediately upon his death."

"They can't be inconsiderable," offered Charyn.

"Ten thousand golds! Ten thousand! That's more than a year's worth of rents on the estates, and that doesn't take into account all the work that needs to be done . . . or the year's tariffs."

"It could take a while to pay those off."

"I won't have that time. The only way he could get that amount of golds was to stipulate that they had to be paid before I can succeed him. If I can't pay, the debt holders can force the sale of lands to come up with the golds. I'd likely lose enough land that I might not be a High Holder." Ferrand looked directly at Charyn. "I was hoping . . ."

Charyn smiled wryly. "Ten thousand golds? With what's happened here . . . You might recall someone burned over ten thousand golds' worth of wheat . . . and those golds were necessary to pay for running the estate at Tuuryl." Charyn didn't add that the landwarden had five thousand left in reserve and there were still ten silos there that had not been destroyed, but those had only been partly full. That still meant Charyn was going to have to find three thousand golds or so somewhere. "Then on Lundi, I got a dispatch that said the old palace in Solis, which has served as the residence and workplace of the regional governor, had been burned by the same people who are trying to kill me. That means I have to come up with golds for a governor's residence . . . not to mention that Father committed to building two more warships. They'll cost close to ten thousand golds, which we don't have. None of that includes a likely ten to fifteen thousand to rebuild the old palace."

"You're saying you won't help me."

"I'm saying that I don't happen to have a spare ten thousand golds at the moment, nor am I likely to in the next year. Depending on the circumstances, I still may be able to help, but not with ten thousand golds."

"I thought you were my friend." Ferrand's voice was cool.

"I still am. I need thirty thousand golds. Can you help me?"

Ferrand looked stunned.

"Are you my friend or not?" asked Charyn quietly, but before Ferrand could respond, he added, "Friends do what they can. Because we can't doesn't mean we don't care. There may be other things I can do. I don't know."

"But you're rex."

"And with being rex come certain limitations. Just as you will not be able to sell your holding house and remain a High Holder, I cannot sell the Chateau D'Rex. I could raise tariffs, but if I do without the agreement of the factors and the High Holders, I will likely face another revolt. If I sell land from the estates, then there will be less in the way of revenues and rents . . . and even more need to raise tariffs."

"But you're rex . . ." repeated Ferrand, almost as if he had not heard a word that Charyn had uttered.

"That hasn't exactly stopped four attempts on my life in the last month."

"That doesn't make sense."

"People who are angry often don't."

"You're not in much better shape than I am," declared Ferrand.

"No one's trying to kill you, either," pointed out Charyn.

"That's . . . a consolation, I guess." Ferrand's shoulders slumped. "You'll do what you can . . . then?"

"I will." I'll even pray to the Nameless that your father doesn't die any time soon. And that was a definite concession on Charyn's part, given his reservations about the existence of the Nameless.

He smiled and stood. "Give my best to your mother."

49

Vendrei morning dawned clear, and colder than ever. Charyn woke up disoriented for several moments before he realized he was in the regial bedchamber. Then after washing up and shaving with water that was far too cold, he had trouble finding warm garments because Delya had reorganized all his clothes when she had moved them. He ate alone, checked the new logbook at the duty desk, which showed no one seeking him, and made his way to his study.

Once there, he immediately read *Veritum*. The only news of great interest was a report that three more spice-trade vessels, one out of Westisle and two out of Solis, were long overdue and presumably lost to weather or privateers. Thankfully, there were no stories about Charyn or the chateau. One short story noted that the winter was already far colder than usual and that the River Aluse was frozen over from Rivages all the way to the north and as far south as Vaestora and might freeze all the way to L'Excelsis within a week.

That thought made Charyn shiver. The study was cool enough as it was, even with the windows largely covered by hangings.

He also needed to consider exactly how to approach Factor Elthyrd, who had responded on Jeudi afternoon that he would be pleased to meet with Charyn at the second glass of the afternoon on Vendrei. He had barely begun to consider that when Sturdyn announced the arrival of a courier from Marshal Vaelln.

Even if the courier had not announced that the dispatch was from Vaelln the green wax seal would have told Charyn that. He was opening the envelope even before the door had closed behind the departing trooper, hoping that Vaelln had more good news as he began to read.

> Your Grace—
> Word has just reached me that our flotilla stationed in the Abierto Isles was forced into an engagement with a larger Jariolan force on the third of Ianus. The Solidaran flotilla consisted of six warships, two of which were frigates, two of which were

third-rate ships of the line, and two of which were second-rate ships of the line. The Jariolan force consisted of eight ships, two of which were second-rate, four of which were third-rate, and two frigates.

Our force sank three of the Jariolan third-raters and both Jariolan frigates, but one of our frigates was lost with all hands, as was one of our second-rate ships of the line. The other Solidaran vessels were badly damaged and have returned to Westisle for repairs and refitting. Although the engagement resulted in a victory, it will be another three weeks before the replacement force can be readied and arrive near the isles, and it is likely greater losses of Solidaran merchant ships will occur during this time because there are Jariolan privateers in the area.

This is the second encounter between Solidaran and Jariolan warships, as such, and it would appear that such encounters will increase. For this reason, I wanted to inform you as quickly as possible.

Charyn lowered the dispatch. *Just what you need—a naval war with Jariola, even if no one is calling it that.* The Solidaran force had sunk five Jariolan ships and only lost two, but the immediate result was likely to be more merchant ship losses.

"We need to write a short response to Marshal Vaelln."

"Yes, sir."

After that, he had two petitions to read.

Charyn took a slow deep breath.

Shortly before second glass, after dispatching the message to Vaelln and drafting the responses to the petitions for Sanafryt to review, Charyn unlocked the hidden bookcase compartment and extracted the pouch with the golds and all the threatening notes, but not the blank paper that Howal had imaged. He put the papers into a neat stack, then stood and walked to the window, easing back the hangings and looking down at the rear courtyard. Despite the cold, it was swept clean. Charyn wasn't certain it had ever been that neat.

He smiled faintly, then moved back toward the desk as Sturdyn announced, "Factorius Elthyrd."

"Have him come in."

Charyn smiled warmly at Elthyrd and gestured to the chairs. "Thank you so much for coming." Then he seated himself.

Elthyrd settled into the middle chair. "You did request my presence."

"I did. I would have preferred to visit you, but with four attempts on my life this month, three last week, I'd rather not travel much for the moment."

"I read the article in the newssheets about the late Guard Captain Churwyl. I take it that there was more to that than was written."

"He attempted to knife me. When that failed, he lit a barrel of powder. Howal and I were most fortunate to suffer only bruises and the like. There is something strange and disturbing about all these attempts. You have great experience in the world and have seen far more than I. I would appreciate it greatly if you would read over each of the threatening missives that we—my father and I—have received in the past two months, beginning with the first one, which arrived several days after the shooting of a guard and Bhayrn's mount." Charyn handed the first threat to Elthyrd.

"Your father read this to me."

"I thought he had, but I wanted you to see it and read it again. When you're done, place it on the desk to your left, slightly to one side."

When the factor had done that, Charyn handed him the second one. "This is the one that was delivered to the landwarden at Tuuryl after fire and explosions destroyed twenty silos of grain at the estate there. Alucar estimated the loss at close to twelve thousand golds."

"Your father never mentioned this."

"I also have the landwarden's letter that forwarded the threat."

"I doubt I need to see that."

When Elthyrd finished reading the second threat and placed it on the desk, Charyn handed him the third. "This was left at the pulpit in Anomen D'Rex just before I offered my remembrance at Father's memorial service. It was in an envelope sealed with black wax and stamped with a blank seal."

Elthyrd frowned, but said nothing as he read the words before placing the third sheet beside the first two.

"This one I received a week ago on Vendrei, the day after someone shot at me when I was inspecting the rear courtyard." Charyn handed over the fourth threat. "It was also in an envelope sealed with black wax and a blank impression, with an indentation on one side of the seal."

Elthyrd read the fourth threat and put it on the desk.

Charyn handed him the fifth threat. "The last one was actually received in Solis by Regional Governor Voralch on the nineteenth of Ianus, the morning after someone used oils and explosives to destroy the old palace in Solis. It arrived here by urgent courier on Lundi."

After the factor read the last letter, he said dryly, "It would appear that someone is not fond of you and your father."

"That's clear enough." Charyn paused. "Did you notice anything . . . unusual about the letters?"

"They were all written in perfect standard merchant hand."

"Look at the paper, if you would."

Elthyrd studied each of the sheets, then said, "They're all on the same paper. It's a common paper, usually used by the smaller factors."

That was something Howal hadn't mentioned . . . or known. "But would a smaller factor have the resources to burn silos in Tuuryl and fire the old palace in Solis?"

"Only a comparative handful of factors could muster those resources. I couldn't, not without all Solidar finding out in days."

"Would any of the factors who are that wealthy want to kill me that badly?" Charyn laughed. "Well, some might, but would they consider taking that kind of chance?"

"You never know, but I'd think it highly unlikely. More like impossible."

"But everyone who knows about paper and writing merchant accounts could easily find out that this paper is used by factors and that standard hand is used almost exclusively by factors and merchants?"

Elthyrd nodded.

"All of this puzzles me," mused Charyn. "The threats seem to be from a factor, but most factors wouldn't have the resources to carry them out, and, from what you're telling me, the ones who do wouldn't be interested in taking the risk to apply this kind of pressure." He paused. "Or am I missing something?"

"What you say makes sense." Elthyrd smiled ironically. "Some people don't, especially people with great power who aren't often held accountable."

Charyn understood exactly what Elthyrd was implying. "The problem in dealing with such people is that they often have such power that they leave almost no proof linking them to their misdeeds. Others with less power will always defer to greater power, and attempting to bring them to account for what they have done could result in creating great unrest, especially if the factors thought I was being arbitrary or unjust."

"That proved an insurmountable problem for your father, I fear. As it would for anyone of a cautious nature."

"It's hard to know when caution is warranted, and when it is a barrier," replied Charyn. "I have done my best to deal with the problems of the factors, and I believe many of the factors are coming to understand that." He paused again. "Or am I mistaken or overly optimistic?"

"Perhaps a trace too optimistic. I have been endeavoring to point out to my colleagues that you have already attempted more than either your father or grandfather, and I believe that some are beginning to understand that."

"Do you have any other thoughts on . . . these?" Charyn gestured to the threatening missives.

"They're most suggestive, but . . ." Elthyrd shrugged. "Without at least a scrap of proof, it might be difficult to act against someone almost everyone suspected. And, if it happened to be someone no one suspected . . . that would be most difficult."

Charyn nodded. "Thank you. I appreciate your thoughts and your counsel. I am considering bringing the matter before both councils, possibly even before the next scheduled meeting."

"I would not mention it to either of the councils unless you have some proof. At least some of them, possibly more, will find anything inconclusive . . . not in your favor, if I might speak frankly."

"I respect that advice, as well. Thank you." Charyn smiled as he stood. "I will not keep you longer, and I do appreciate your kindness in coming, especially in this weather."

"Your Grace, I believe I understand, better than many, the difficult situation in which you find yourself. I can assure you that the factors are more than willing to look at approaches and leadership that represent an effort to be open and fair." Elthyrd rose. "It is known, if quietly, that you are a member of the exchange and that you visited often to learn its workings, and that you never acted beyond the station you assumed."

Once Elthyrd had left the study, Howal looked to Charyn. "Might I ask a question?"

"Go ahead."

"I could not help but hear what was said and what was not. I gained the feeling that both of you believe you know who the person behind all the attacks may be."

"So does Maitre Alastar," replied Charyn.

A look of surprise crossed Howal's face. "But . . ."

"It's not that simple." *Would that it were.* "There's the absolute lack of solid proof. There's also the fact that the rexes of Solidar have not exactly endeared themselves to the people of Solidar or to its factors and High Holders. I've done what I can with the factors, but two months is scarcely enough time to change perceptions formed over years."

"I can see that, sir."

"I'm going to have you undertake an exercise. Perhaps it will help in clarifying matters. I'm going to write something down. I want you to write it in perfect standard merchant hand on one of the sheets of paper you imaged the other day, using the same kind of ink as the other letters." Charyn went to his desk, where he sat down and wrote out two sentences. Then he stood and carried the single sheet to Howal, along with a sheet of the blank paper Howal had imaged earlier.

The imager took both, read the lines, and frowned.

"It sounds like what I've been getting, doesn't it?"

"Yes, sir . . . but . . ."

"Just write it as if you were making a perfect copy, the way you did with the one. I'll explain as we go." Charyn went back to his own desk, where he gathered the original threatening messages, as well as the bag holding the golds.

Almost a quint later, Howal walked back to Charyn's desk. "Here it is, sir."

"Thank you." Charyn looked at what Howal had written, then compared it to the other five threatening missives. "The lettering looks exactly the same as the others. Is it?"

"Yes, sir."

"How many people could have done the same? A score, a hundred? Possibly more? The ink is common, as is the paper."

"Across all Solidar? At least a hundred."

"Now, image an envelope out of the paper."

Howal did.

Charyn folded the single sheet and placed it in the envelope. "Can you image the black wax and the seal like this one?" He held up the envelope where he had slit the side rather than break the seal. "With the impression there on the edge of the blank seal?"

"I can."

"Please do."

When Howal had finished, Charyn said, "You see? Someone else could easily have used black wax and any circular piece of metal to seal the envelope. How could you prove who wrote or sent it? That's the problem of proof. We have five letters, and no way to tie them to anyone." He smiled as he picked up the sealed false threat letter. "For now, I'll keep this as a reminder of what I need to find."

He paused. "Could you image a stick of black wax?"

"Ah . . . yes, sir."

"I've never had any black sealing wax. It might come in useful."

After Howal had laid the stick of wax on the desk, Charyn left it there, then waited until

Howal returned to the conference table and resumed work on the final draft of one of the petition responses before quietly replacing the letters, including the false one, in the hidden bookcase compartment, along with the black wax.

Is there any other kind of proof you can find?

He needed to think about that . . . more than just a little.

50

Samedi turned colder and grayer, and from before dawn snow fell in fast
flurries followed by bitter winds, with more snow falling after the winds.
From the windows in the Chateau D'Rex, Charyn could see that there
was almost no one on the ring road.

While trying to ignore the whining and moaning of the intermittent
winds, Charyn buried himself in the Codex Legis, looking for something
that might help him deal with Ryel and the two councils, while Howal
and Alucar were working with Norstan in teaching him the new bookkeeping system for the chateau ledgers.

After more than a glass, Charyn came across one section that could
prove helpful:

> . . . the lands and property of any man found guilty of treason,
> before the High Justicer, become the property of the rex, for him
> to keep or dispose of, as he sees fit . . .

He kept looking. After several glasses' worth of search and study,
during which he was unable to discover any other provisions that appeared to be even marginally useful in dealing with Ryel and his current
situation, he finally set aside the Codex, stood, and walked to the window. The window hangings were cold to the touch, and when he pulled
them back, he immediately felt the cold that seemed to radiate from the
frosted glass. He scraped away the thin ice and frost from a section of
the pane and looked at the courtyard, its stones still swept. Letting the
hangings drop back into place, he stepped back.

What if Ryel isn't behind all this? But who else could it be? One of the
threats had mentioned the waste of high tariffs and had arrived only two
days after his meeting with the councils. That meant that the writer had
to be located in or near L'Excelsis. It also pointed to a council member
or someone close to him. But the threats from Solis and Tuuryl demon-
strated both knowledge of regial properties and the resources to arrange

significant destruction. What happened in Solis must have been arranged far in advance.

Charyn smiled sardonically. That also might provide a very good reason why there were no dates on any of them. Interestingly enough, the one from Solis, the most distant point, had one of the more general threats, at least in terms of how it was couched.

He was still pondering over the matter when Howal returned, closing the study door firmly but not noisily behind himself.

"How are matters coming with Norstan?"

"Slowly. He really didn't understand numbers."

"How could he not be able to count?"

"Oh, he can add and subtract, but he really didn't understand that the second column represents ten times the first, and that's why the columns have to be lined up, and why we use commas, for silvers, and decimal points for coppers. Once Alucar saw that, we explained it very simply. Then Norstan understood. I mean, he knew that ten coppers make a silver, and ten silvers a gold, but he'd never related that to the use of commas and decimal points. He also didn't think about writing the numbers clearly. There were a few other things, too. He also seems relieved that he won't have to keep the ledger for the stablemaster."

"It sounds like your morning was well spent. Have you talked to Dylert or Kaylet about how they're coming in cleaning up the Chateau Guard and the stables and barns?"

"Dylert has matters well organized. Kaylet's having to do a lot of teaching."

Somehow neither situation surprised Charyn.

"Oh . . . for some reason, there's not enough firewood to last out the winter. The head cook . . ."

"Hassala."

"She says she told Norstan back in Finitas. He remembers it, but thought he'd sent a message to the estate foresters. I drafted another message for him, and we sent it off."

"How much wood is there?"

"Enough for two weeks."

"We might have to thin some of the trees in the hunting park if it gets too bad," said Charyn. "There must be some that need pruning or others that are sickly."

"I'll mention that to Kaylet."

Charyn nodded.

The momentary silence was interrupted by a rapping on the study door, followed by Maertyl calling out, "There's a courier from Marshal Vaelln."

"Have him come in."

The courier was neither fresh-faced nor grizzled, but a lean trooper perhaps a year or two older than Howal, his face red from the cold. He bowed, then handed the envelope to the imager, who had stepped forward.

"Does the marshal request an immediate reply?" asked Charyn.

"No, sir. He said it was information you should know."

"Thank you. Stop by the kitchen and get something warm to drink before you leave the chateau."

"Thank you, Your Grace." The trooper bowed, then left the study.

Howal handed the envelope to Charyn.

"A message on Samedi that I should know about cannot possibly be good," opined Charyn sardonically as he took the smaller letter knife, the one Howal had imaged, and slit the envelope. After easing the single sheet of paper from the envelope, he began to read.

> Your Grace—
>
> We have just gotten word that two of our frigates patrolling off Stakanar were attacked by two Jariolan third-rate ships of the line on the thirty-first of Finitas. The frigates, having superior speed, and a favorable wind, managed to escape with minor damage. The presence of the Jariolan warships prevented them from intervening when a Jariolan privateer stopped and looted a Solidaran spice merchanter out of Kherseilles.
>
> I regret the result of the incident, but for the captains of the frigates to have engaged warships far superior in armament would only have lost both ships to no purpose. Because of the concerns voiced by many factors, I thought you should know about this immediately.

Wordlessly, Charyn handed the brief dispatch to Howal.

Howal read it, then returned it to Charyn, also without saying a word.

"There will be more dispatches like this," Charyn said quietly. "It may be years before we can stop the piracy, and the factors and those High

Holders who engage in trade may well lose patience with their rex and his deliberate plans." He laughed harshly. "Not that I have any other choice except to be deliberate."

"Don't you think many of them will understand? They may not like it, but they should appreciate that it takes time to build warships and train crews."

"I suppose I could commission privateers as well, but that would give the Oligarch greater excuse to use his warships against all Solidaran shipping. I'd prefer not to do that until later." Seeing Howal's quizzical look, Charyn went on, "I'm limited in what I can do. I cannot build ships faster. If I delay commissioning privateers, then when the outcry grows louder, I can do so. That will show action on my part, and it will also delay giving the Oligarch an earlier opportunity to prey on our ships even more widely than is presently happening." *At least, you hope that will be how it turns out . . . and that it won't be even worse.*

He just hoped there were no more dispatches from Vaelln—or anyone else—any time soon.

51

When Charyn woke on Solyai morning, the winds had died away, and the regial bedchamber was chill. Palenya was still sleeping beside him, and for a time he just watched her, thinking, *If only she were a little younger . . . and could have children.* The age difference wasn't impossible, but the fact that she both was not highborn and could not have children made any future with her—on any terms she would accept—absolutely impossible.

A rex had to have heirs, even if they were female, although that had occurred only once, and the regina and her husband had ruled together, if, it was said, uneasily. She had abdicated on her son's twenty-fifth birthday, five years after her husband's death, and most Solidaran histories said little about her reign, besides the fact that it was unexceptional.

Palenya slowly opened her eyes. "You're staring."

"I am. I enjoy looking at you."

"It's cold. All you can see is my eyes and nose."

"I still like looking at you. You have beautiful eyes and a good nose."

"It's a cold nose." Palenya offered a mournful expression.

"I'll put some wood on the coals in the hearth. Then I'll ring for breakfast." Charyn had to admit that he liked having the bellpulls in the regial rooms, rather than having to arrange for meals in his quarters in advance.

More than two quints passed before breakfast arrived, more than enough time for both of them to make themselves moderately presentable, and for the renewed fire to warm the sitting room. Once the servers had left, Charyn gestured to the small table, then seated himself as she sat down.

"I'm still glad you're here." He poured tea into her mug and then his. He did not say what else was on his mind—that their times together were numbered.

"I'm glad you are."

He raised his mug, as if in a toast. "To your being here."

She lifted hers. "To your wanting me here."

"How could I not?"

"Very easily . . . if you were most men."

"You flatter me . . . I think."

"A woman needs to keep a man a little off-balance at times." She lifted the mug and took a small swallow, then lowered it and said, "You know I have to play for your mother's gathering this afternoon?"

"You have mentioned it once or twice, I believe."

"I am a musician, and that's what I'm being paid for." After the briefest pause, Palenya added wryly, "Mostly, anyway. It is a good idea for a musician to be seen playing or teaching, if not both."

"Maybe we should play the duet together. For the gathering."

"I can't forbid you," she replied, "but I don't think it would do much for your regial image to be seen playing with a mere musician."

Not in any form of play. "We could play it together later, but before the gathering . . . and you could work with me some more on the nocturne. I haven't spent as much time on it as I would have liked." Charyn took a bite of the cheese and egg casserole, not hot, but still warm after its journey up from the kitchen.

"We had best do that well before the gathering."

"I think we can manage that. It's only eighth glass, and no one will be arriving until just before third glass." He looked at Palenya, who, for a moment, had looked distracted. "What were you just thinking?"

"About Aloryana, if you must know. I miss teaching her. She was always so interested, and she worked hard. You're like her in that respect. I wonder . . . Does the Collegium have any musicians?"

"I don't know. I should write Aloryana and ask." Charyn frowned. "I should have written her sooner. I also should ask her if there's a clavecin there somewhere. I didn't see one in the Maitre's dwelling. I could arrange to buy one and send it if they have a place for it." He managed to conceal a smile at what Palenya had just managed. *Let her think that you don't see it.* Besides, if Alastar would agree, Palenya would be far safer on Imagisle than anywhere else in Solidar that Charyn could think of.

"That would be very sweet of you."

"Aloryana more than deserves it." And so did Palenya. "I'll write her while you're entertaining the ladies of the gathering." With a smile, Charyn refilled his mug and took a swallow of the tea that was now only slightly more than lukewarm. He suspected that Palenya knew that he knew, but it was better—for now—that neither of them spoke of it.

He intended to enjoy what of the remainder of Solayi that he could, knowing that the future remained uncertain . . . and that he would not have Palenya's company for all that much longer, no matter how the events of the coming month played themselves out.

52

A light snow began to fall after sunset on Solayi, and kept falling through Lundi afternoon until it was more than knee-deep across L'Excelsis. From what Charyn could see from the upper windows of the Chateau D'Rex, the only places that were kept clear were the courtyards and the drives of the chateau itself. By midafternoon on Mardi, the ring road was again barely passible, and a few wagons and riders began appearing. Mardi night saw the last of the clouds vanish, leaving the air even colder, and Meredi dawned bright and bitter.

Despite the snow and cold, when Charyn, wearing a heavy woolen jacket, entered his study, a copy of Mardi's issue of *Veritum* lay on the corner of his desk. He picked it up and began to read as he stood there. One story reported that the River Aluse was now frozen over beginning a hundred milles north of L'Excelsis, so solid that wagons could be driven on the ice. The second story was headlined "More Ships Lost."

Fourteen merchant ships and three Solidaran Navy warships are known to have been sunk by Jariolan warships and privateers in the last two months of the previous year . . . Rex Charyn's efforts to build more Solidaran ships of the line represent a good first step in dealing with Jariola . . . the first question is why it took the new rex and his predecessor so long . . . second question is what else will the rex propose and how long will that take . . . only hope the beleaguered factors of Solidar aren't asking that question a year from now . . . Marshal Vaelln confirmed that the planned shipbuilding is on schedule . . .

Charyn shook his head as he set down the paper. It hadn't taken him that long to get the tariffs to pay for the additional ships. *And what about the poor beleaguered rex?* He turned to Howal. "Did you read *Veritum?*"

"Yes, sir. It's one of the coldest winters in years . . . and they're complaining that you're not doing enough to deal with the Jariolans."

"Have there been any letters from the Collegium?" Charyn was hoping for a response from Aloryana, since he'd dispatched his letter the first thing on Lundi morning, despite the snow.

"No, sir. There is one other matter. Norstan has informed me that with the snow so deep, we won't receive any wood from the regial wood-lots to the north until the middle of Fevier."

"You mentioned this the other day. Just how did it happen?"

"The firewood falls under the stablemaster because he is in charge of the stone barns . . ."

"Keithell, again? He didn't tell Norstan until it was too late or not at all?"

"Yes, sir."

"Can you make certain that word gets to everyone, quietly?"

Howal smiled. "I believe it has already. Hassala told me this morning. She mentioned that it was just another place where Keithell hadn't been doing his job."

"Did she say anything about Kaylet?"

"They all seem to like him and respect him, from what I've seen. He can be very funny, although you wouldn't see that. He has a way with all animals, but horses particularly."

"Why is everyone who's an imager so talented?" Charyn regretted the words as soon as he'd spoken, although Howal showed no reaction beyond a thoughtful expression.

"I'd have to disagree there, sir. We have more than a few imagers who cannot image very much, and who do not have great natural talents. Because there are so few of us, Maitre Alastar insists that everyone become good at something. At times, it takes many years. Some never become more than imager seconds."

"What you're saying is that those who are seen off Imagisle are the best."

"Yes, sir."

Even so . . . Charyn wanted to shake his head. He'd had his life saved by a young woman younger than himself, and then by two junior imagers not that much older than he was. The three junior maitres seemed to be more accomplished than most men years their senior. "You all seem rather accomplished."

"We're accomplished in a different fashion, sir. Might I point out that there is no one on Imagisle, except your sister and Maitre Malyna, who could play a clavecin with the skill you have shown. You also write well, and that is not a skill easily mastered."

"I'm not sure I'd like my uncertain skill with the clavecin bruited about." Charyn's lips curled wryly, but he couldn't really contest Howal's point.

Remembering something he'd almost forgotten he'd meant to do, he took a sheet of paper, and his pen, and began to write out the names of the High Holder members of the High Council and then the factors on the Solidaran Factors' Council, each name followed by the city or closest town to each. Then he drew a line under the last name and wrote two other names beneath the lines: "Solis" and "Tuuryl."

Charyn was still thinking if there might be something else that he should add when Sturdyn rapped on the study door.

"Guard Captain Dylert to see you, sir."

"Have him come in." Charyn gestured to the chairs in front of the desk, then waited for Dylert to seat himself.

"You had asked for my recommendations for the next guard captain and a guard undercaptain."

"I did."

"I would recommend Maertyl as the next guard captain, sir, with Fhaelln as the guard undercaptain."

"Why did you pick those two? Besides the obvious, that you feel they're the best?"

"Maertyl has been in charge of the armory when he hasn't been on duty up here, and the armory is in excellent condition. Everything was so well stored that even the explosion that Churwyl set off didn't affect anything. He has a natural command demeanor, and he has also been second-in-command of training the newer guards. He's respected . . ."

Charyn listened as Dylert outlined his reasons. He was especially attentive when the imager talked about Fhaelln, since he knew little about the man except his name. *And what does that say about you? That you still don't know enough about the people who protect and support you?*

". . . Fhaelln would not seem an obvious choice, but he is quiet and effective . . . notices details, and knows which are important and which are not . . ." When Dylert finished his assessment of Fhaelln, he paused, then said, "I would also recommend creating three lead-guard positions for older and more experienced guards. We talked about this earlier. There's no structure and no line of authority. Creating those positions would provide both."

"And that is as it should be," agreed Charyn. "You have names in mind?"

"I do, but I did not want to mention their names unless you approved the idea."

"They'd get higher pay for that responsibility."

"Yes, sir."

"We'll need some sort of written description of how the Chateau Guard will be organized, and the responsibilities of each of the officer and subofficer positions."

"I've been working on that, sir. With your approval, I'll finish the draft and submit it to you by tomorrow. With a recommended pay scale."

"Outstanding!" Charyn didn't have to counterfeit enthusiasm.

Dylert looked a little sheepish. "I hope you don't mind, but I talked over some of the structural and pay matters with Thelia and with Maitre Alastar."

"I'm glad you did. They both have more experience with those." From what Charyn had seen of the young imagers, his father could have learned a great deal more from the Maitre, and Charyn himself wasn't above or beneath benefiting any way he could from that knowledge and experience. There was a long moment of silence before Charyn spoke again. "There is another matter in which your wife and her contacts and family might be of great assistance. Just for information."

"Sir?"

"It would be of enormous value to me to know if any High Holders on the High Council or the factors on the Solidar Factors' Council have factorages or lands near Solis or Tuuryl." That really wasn't the question, but whether any of them did besides Ryel. "If your wife or others at the Collegium could shed any light on this in the next few weeks, it would be most helpful." Charyn extended the paper he had written out earlier. "Here are their names and where they're from."

"I don't know, sir. I mean, whether Thelia and her family might know."

"Anything she can discover will be helpful."

"Yes, sir."

Once Dylert had departed, Charyn turned back to Howal and asked with a grin, "I suppose you have a draft written plan for organizing the rest of the chateau?"

"I do have some thoughts along those lines, sir." Howal's expression was even more sheepish than Dylert's had been.

"Good. When might I see them?"

"By Vendrei?"

"When they're ready will be fine." Charyn could say that because he knew none of the imagers procrastinated, apparently with anything.

A quint or so later, Sturdyn again rapped on the door. "An imager courier for you, sir."

"Good!" At least, Charyn hoped it was good.

The red-faced courier, wearing a thick gray woolen overcoat, hurried into the study, looking at Charyn. "It's for you, sir."

"Thank you." As he took the envelope, he smiled, recognizing the handwriting, and added, "Very much."

"My pleasure, sir."

"If you can, stop by the kitchen and get something warm before you ride back."

"Thank you, Your Grace."

Charyn forced himself to wait until the courier left before slitting open the letter and beginning to read.

Dear Charyn—

Thank you so much for writing. I couldn't write back on Lundi because I had to talk to both Maitre Alyna and Maitre Alastar. They had to talk to some of the other senior maitres, but they all decided that a clavecin would be very welcome. There is a chamber in the administration building that could easily be turned into a music room, and it is large enough to seat perhaps twenty or so if I or others wished to do a chamber recital.

I do miss playing. I knew I would, but I hadn't realized how much I would. Thank you so much for thinking about it!

Usually, new imagers aren't allowed visitors for the first two months. While I don't think the maitres would hold you to that, I think it would be best if I abided by that rule. But the first of Maris isn't all that far away. I can't wait to tell you all that I've learned. I'm almost caught up to where Maitre Alyna says I should be in mathematics. I still have to get stronger before I'll be able to do shields and concealments the way Malyna and Lystara can do them. I don't know if I'll ever be as good as Lystara is, but Maitre Alyna says that there's no reason I shouldn't be a junior maitre by the time I'm Malyna's age . . .

Charyn was smiling when he lowered the letter. He could pay for the clavecin out of his own personal golds. That way, no one could possibly object, not legitimately. After a moment, he lifted the letter and re-read part of it. Concealments?

"Howal . . . you can do shields, obviously. What about concealments?"

"Yes, sir. Concealments are easier, sir, especially a blurring concealment."

"Blurring?"

"It's not really a true concealment, where people can't see you at all. With a blurring concealment, you sort of blend into whatever you're standing in front of. Those work better when no one is really looking."

"But you can do both?"

"Ah . . . yes, sir."

"That might explain a few things." Like why he hadn't been able to find Malyna that one time. "Thank you." He paused, then added, "Aloryana mentioned that she was learning the basics of shields and concealments."

"If she's already being taught those, she's very likely to become a maitre."

"Maitre Alastar thinks she has that potential." Charyn just hoped, for Aloryana's sake, that she did.

For the next glass, he worked on his reply. Aloryana deserved it, and with the snow, there wasn't that much else that was pressing—although he still needed to work out all the details for dealing with his uncle.

Finally, he read over what he had written.

Dear Aloryana—

I greatly enjoyed your letter, and I will try to be a better correspondent, at least until the proper time has passed, and we can come and visit you.

I do understand your feeling about not being able to play the clavecin. There are times when playing it, or learning to play a new piece—I'm working on a nocturne by Farray—removes me from all the daily duties and worries. Because you are not here, and Bhayrn has never cared that much for the clavecin, Musician Palenya has more free time. Once the Collegium has the clavecin, she can use the small coach to travel there and instruct you and a few others, if they are interested and Maitre Alastar approves. I will mention this to Maitre Alastar myself.

It may take a little while to locate a proper clavecin, and it may even have to be built, but you and the Collegium will have a good instrument, and, if the Maitre agrees, someone to instruct you and others . . .

And that will determine if Palenya might be able to become the Collegium's music master . . . Charyn wasn't about to say a word about any of that to anyone in the chateau, including Palenya, until she was providing instruction at the Collegium, and it was clear to all parties that it would work out.

Once he had signed and sealed the letter, he turned to Howal. "I'd like this sent to Aloryana, but hold it until I talk to Musician Palenya. After that I'll need to write a letter to Maitre Alastar as well. So we might as well send both at once."

"Yes, sir."

Charyn left the study and made his way down the grand staircase to the music room, noting how chill the chateau was. He found Palenya busy copying music. "Always working, I see."

"You do pay me for what musicians are supposed to do. Are you here to play the clavecin . . . or for some other reason?"

"Both, I suppose. I have another musical task for you. I need to purchase or commission the building of a clavecin for the Collegium, and that is something well beyond my knowledge. Among other things," Charyn added dryly.

Palenya smiled broadly. "Aloryana misses playing? I'd hoped she would."

"Once the roads are clearer, you can use the small coach to go wherever you need to in order to find or commission the clavecin."

"If you need one built . . ."

"It will take time. So it would be preferable to find one, but if you cannot . . ."

"You're leaving this in my hands?"

"I can't think of better hands. Oh, it must also be an instrument that you would enjoy playing."

That brought a frown.

"I'm going to ask Maitre Alastar if he would allow you occasionally to travel to Imagisle and continue instructing Aloryana, if you would be willing, and possibly a few other imager students, as well, also if you would be willing."

"Oh?"

"I can't think of a better teacher, and Bhayrn certainly doesn't want any more instruction, and there will still be plenty of time for you to teach me a few more pieces. Ones suitable to my level of ability, of course."

"I could manage that . . . for a while. I would like to continue teaching Aloryana."

Charyn nodded. "Now . . . for a quint or two, will you help me with the nocturne?" He tried to inject a mock-plaintive tone into his voice.

Palenya smiled at that, and followed him to the keyboard.

Two quints later, Charyn left Palenya and the music room and returned to his study. He immediately seated himself to write the letter to Alastar mentioning the clavecin and the possibility of Palenya instructing Aloryana and others. He also requested formally that the Maitre attend the coming meeting of the two councils on the eighteenth of Fevier.

When Howal left the study to arrange for dispatching the two letters, Charyn rose from the desk, stretched, and walked to the window. After pulling back the hangings and clearing away the frost from the glass, he looked down at the courtyard.

If only dealing with Ryel were as uncomplicated as the imagers have made improving the running of the chateau.

He let the hangings fall back into place.

53

Jeudi was at least as cold as Meredi had been, and the wind picked up as the day went on, then subsided toward dawn on Vendrei morning, leaving a cold hazy sky over L'Excelsis when Charyn entered his study. The lead story in the Jeudi edition of *Veritum* reported that the River Aluse had iced over all the way south of L'Excelsis to Caluse.

Although Maitre Alastar had responded that he would attend the council meeting and that Musician Palenya would be more than welcome to instruct at the Collegium, and that the Collegium would be able to pay her a modest stipend for each student taught, Charyn had so far received no response from Maitre Thelia—Dylert's wife—about the holdings of council members. Although Charyn hadn't expected an early reply, he had hoped for one. *Except you should have thought of that earlier.*

He also fretted, more than a little, about the fact that he had received no more threatening missives, and no more indications of attacks. The lack of such, when there had been four in less than four weeks, was worrisome, even if the weather had been so miserable that even Ryel might have had difficulty mounting another. The foul weather, Charyn supposed, was a blessing of sorts, but whether it came from the Nameless, the Namer, or chance was another question. At least, the cold and wind had put a damper on Bhayrn's desire to go riding. *If only for the moment.*

At ninth glass, Dylert arrived to talk over the timing for implementing the revised plan and structure for the Chateau Guard.

As the imager settled into the center chair, Charyn asked, "Has Maitre Thelia heard anything?"

"She said it would likely be next week, probably near Vendrei at the earliest."

"I do appreciate her doing this." Charyn nodded. "Now . . . for the guards. It seems to me that I ought to announce the plans and the new pay and ranks to all the guards at once. That might remove some of the past stench of secretiveness. What do you think?"

"We'll have to get word to everyone. It's late to let them all know for tomorrow, and Samedi isn't a good day to announce changes. Lundi might be best, but early in the afternoon."

"I also think you should remain, as an advisor, for a week or so after the change is announced."

"I think a day or two would be better. I could tell Maertyl and Fhaelln that I'll be back to see you on the following Vendrei, and that if they have any questions, or want to talk over anything, that would be the time."

Charyn thought for a moment, then nodded. "What about Kaylet . . . or Howal here? Has Maitre Alastar said anything to you? I'd like Howal to stay at least through the next council meeting."

"Maitre Alastar has said that what each of us is doing is different. Kaylet thinks he needs three more weeks. It's mostly training. You should talk to him personally."

"What else should I know? About the chateau guards?"

"Some should be riding or walking posts outside the chateau, and not just outside the courtyard gates . . ."

Charyn listened to Dylert's additional recommendations for almost two quints before the imager finished and departed.

Once the study door was shut, Charyn turned to Howal. "Has Maitre Alastar said anything to you recently?"

"No, sir. Not recently. When I came here, he did say that I'd likely be here longer than the others."

"Is that a problem for you?"

Howal shook his head. "Particularly not in the winter." He grinned. "I like working with the ledgers, especially. Sometimes, I get to help Maitre Thelia, when her daughter's not feeling well, but she's so good she doesn't need much help."

Charyn stifled a yawn. There wasn't any reason for him to be tired. Bored of being a prisoner in his own chateau, that was another question. "Send for Kaylet, but don't have him interrupt anything."

"Yes, sir."

Kaylet arrived less than a quint later.

"You asked for me, sir? If it's about the firewood, I've got three men pruning and cutting down damaged trees in the hunting park. Some of that will be seasoned because a few of the trees were mostly dead. Most will be green. It will burn hotter, but smokier. There's enough there for several weeks, depending on the weather."

"Thank you. That's very good to know, and I'm glad you've been able to take care of that." Charyn paused, then added, "I'd asked for you because I wanted to know how you are coming with the training and retraining."

"Well, I believe. The ostlers and stable boys are good people. They just needed more training. More than they should have, but they're all working hard. Except the one who left. He was the nephew of the former assistant stablemaster."

"And didn't do much work?"

"He didn't do anything. He didn't like it when he learned he had to."

Charyn smiled briefly. "Is there anyone who could be a good stablemaster?"

"I believe Aedryt could handle the job, if I could work with him for another few weeks."

"You can have all the time you need, provided Maitre Alastar agrees. Aedryt, you think?" Until he'd looked at the ledgers, Charyn hadn't the faintest idea who Aedryt even was, but he'd since learned that he had been the head ostler.

"Yes, sir."

"What about his assistant?"

"I'd recommend two assistants, one for the barns and all the wagons and coaches, and one for the horses and feed. Naelbarr would do well with the wagons, and Jorynt is already working with the feed and other supplies . . ."

Kaylet was more than willing to talk, with only a few questions from Charyn, and Charyn was also more than willing to listen, so much so that almost a glass passed before the imager who was clearly a very competent stablemaster left the study.

Howal grinned at Charyn. "Kaylet's very enthusiastic."

"I imagine the ostlers and stable boys could use some enthusiasm after Keithell." Charyn still worried about the fact that he hadn't noticed almost any of what had been going on. *You're going to have to pay much better attention.* "There hasn't been any of that in the kitchen, I trust?"

Howal shook his head. "Hassala's not only a good cook, but she's a good and fair person. Also, your mother keeps a close watch on what goes on inside the chateau proper."

That didn't surprise Charyn. "Speaking of which, I need to go talk to her. I won't be that long, but go do anything you want for a while."

"I may just read," replied Howal. "I borrowed one of the histories."

With a smile, Charyn slipped out of the study and made his way to the center foyer and then back toward what had been the guest quarters, where he opened the door, slightly ajar, and stepped inside.

Chelia was sitting at her desk, writing, but immediately set aside the pen and turned with a questioning expression.

"I didn't mean to interrupt you . . ." ventured Charyn.

"I'm writing Aloryana. It's likely more for my benefit than hers. I imagine she's doing quite nicely. By the way, it was thoughtful of you to think of sending a clavecin to the Collegium. Aloryana said it was sweet." Chelia smiled. "Prudent as well, if the instructionals work out."

"Palenya thinks she might have located a clavecin that I can purchase. She's looking at it this morning. Or she was, but she's not back yet." Although he could not have said why, Charyn decided not to mention that Maitre Alastar had agreed to pay Palenya for instructing students other than Aloryana. Charyn took one of the side chairs and set it so that he was facing his mother, then sat down. "She's very accomplished."

"She's done a great deal for you as well."

"I know." Before his mother could pursue that, he asked, "Do you know anything about the other members of the High Council besides Uncle Ryel?"

"Not much. I have heard that Fhaedyrk does have a large brewery and supplies lager to most of old Tilbor."

"Not anywhere else?"

"He's only able to do that because Tilbor is much colder and, in the colder months, he can cart the lager longer distances than brewers can here."

"What about Basalyt?"

"I've heard nothing, except that he is very traditional. His great-grandsire was apparently successful in getting possession of many of the lands of former nearby High Holders."

"And Khunthan?"

"He has a very large holding, but it's very isolated, your father said."

"Eshtora is a seaport, though."

Chelia shrugged. "I imagine his holding is away from the city. I don't know that, though. Your father didn't ever say much about any of the councilors."

"He didn't like to say much most of the time."

"At times, you got him to talk."

"Only in the last few months, and only when he was in the mood," Charyn replied.

"What are you going to do about the threats? They won't go away. Neither will the attacks."

Rather than answer his mother's question directly, Charyn asked, "Why does he hate us all so much?"

"Because of what his father did."

"What did he do?"

"Those are matters left largely unspoken, even to you. Let me assure you that our father was a man of great personal appeal and charm, and utterly depraved in almost every way possible."

"It has something to do with Grandmother, doesn't it?"

"Your grandmother was an extremely beautiful woman who was very ambitious and never loved your grandfather. Our father found her attractive. The results almost destroyed Solidar and embittered my brother. We will leave it at that, and I would appreciate your not telling either your brother or sister at the present time."

Charyn nodded, but studied his mother's face, seeing the tightness there. Finally, he said, "That's not all, is it?"

"No. We will leave it at that, Charyn, except to say that your uncle is no better than his father, far less charming, and far closer to the Namer."

To Charyn, Chelia's voice was colder and bitterer than the snow outside, and the way in which she spoke suggested even greater depravity than Charyn had imagined . . . and he hadn't thought he'd had many illusions about his uncle.

Her voice turned softer and warmer as she asked, "Is there anything else, dear?"

Charyn didn't want to say that there wasn't. "Does all that have to do with why Palenya is here?"

"Some of it. I wanted you to learn something about women. I don't have your invitation list for the Spring-Turn Ball."

Charyn understood that anything more even remotely connected to Ryel's depravity was not going to be talked about. "I'll get the names I'd personally like to see to you in the next day or so. I promise."

"How are you coming with the imagers?"

"Maitre Dylert and I have come up with a plan for making the chateau guards more effective . . ." He smiled as he began to explain the changes.

When he left his mother more than a quint later, Charyn headed down the grand staircase to the music room to see if Palenya had returned. She was standing beside the table desk when he entered the chamber.

"You're back, I see?"

"I've been back at the chateau for almost a glass. I've been talking to Kaylet about how to transport the clavecin."

"Was the one you looked at suitable?"

"It was a very good instrument." Palenya shook her head. "It's been neglected for several years. It belongs to the granddaughter of a musician. She got it from her father when he died. She's married to a cloth factor. He already had a clavecin built by Dhorek. The one he had is inlaid with mother-of-pearl. Her husband doesn't want two clavecins, and he told her she could keep the golds if she just sold it. They're both fools. The one they want to sell was a better instrument, but it looks plain by comparison. It needs work."

"How much will it cost?" Charyn wasn't that concerned, but he thought he should ask.

"It likely cost thirty golds when Dhorek first sold it. They were happy to sell it for ten. I gave them a gold to seal the bargain."

"How did you find out about it?"

"The way one always does. By going to the musicians' hall and asking who had a clavecin for sale."

Charyn wouldn't have thought of that, either. "What do you mean by 'it needs work'?"

"It's nothing I can't handle."

Charyn frowned.

Palenya offered a sigh that very much sounded like one of exasperation. "My father insisted that I be able to tune and repair a clavecin. He said it was important for a woman musician not to have to rely on men."

"Where . . . ?"

"At the Collegium. There's no point in working on it and then moving it. I already talked to Kaylet. There's a wagon in the back barn that will hold it until the Collegium can take it."

"If someone else did the repairs, what would it cost?"

"The work might cost eight silvers. I'll need to buy vulture quills to replace some of the plectra, and two jacks, maybe three, need to be replaced, and strings, more than a few. They sell those at the musicians' hall. It costs more there, but it will be quicker."

Charyn had only the vaguest idea of what she was talking about. "When do you need to pick it up?"

"Tomorrow. Kaylet said it wouldn't be a problem. He and Aedryt and two of the stable boys have it planned out."

"So you need nine more golds and how many silvers?" He frowned. "Do they know who you're representing?"

"I just said that I was representing my patron who wanted a second clavecin for his sister to practice on. I thought that was close enough to the truth. They had to know that my patron is wealthy. Free musicians don't show up in coaches drawn by matched pairs and hand over a gold as a seal."

"You'll need two golds more for the . . . quills and the strings?"

"I doubt if I'll need more than five silvers in addition to the golds. That might be too much, but it would be better to have ten just in case. Silvers, though, for the quills, jacks, and strings . . . and musicians' glue."

"You can do this?"

"I've already done some of that to your clavecin. I had to revoice it completely in Erntyn. I'll have to do that for the one you're buying as well."

"You amaze me. Again."

She smiled.

With the warmth of her expression, Charyn forgot, for the moment, that he needed to compose a letter to Maitre Alastar to let him know about the clavecin.

54

By two quints past ninth glass on Samedi morning, Charyn was almost continuously looking out the study window for any sign of Palenya . . . and the clavecin. As soon as he saw the wagon start up the drive, he pulled on a heavy winter jacket and hurried down to the rear courtyard. There, he stood on the small landing outside the rear door and watched as Kaylet deftly maneuvered the wagon into the coach barn.

Is there anything they don't do well?

In the comparatively short time that it took to move the wagon into the barn, Charyn could feel his ears beginning to go numb. Once the horses were unhitched, he crossed the courtyard to where Palenya stood, waiting for him. So well covered was she with her scarf that only her eyes were visible.

"Did everything go as you planned?"

"It did. Did you expect it wouldn't?"

"I was worried. You seemed to be taking a long time."

"That's because I had Kaylet stop at the musicians' hall so I could get what I needed. It was only three blocks out of the way, and it seemed stupid to have to make a second trip in this kind of weather."

"Only three blocks?" asked Charyn wryly.

"Well . . . three . . . and another half score."

Charyn shook his head. "I'd like to see the clavecin."

"You should, but don't be surprised. I told you it needed work." Palenya turned and walked through the barn doors that one of the stable boys was beginning to close.

It was warmer inside the coach barn, but not all that much. Palenya climbed up into the wagon bed, and Charyn followed.

Slowly, she eased back the old blankets that had covered the clavecin. "The keyboard is in good shape, but it needs to be cleaned. The entire soundboard needs restringing and most of the plectra need replacing. So I bought enough quills to replace them all. That will make getting an even sound volume easier. The wood on the spine is in good shape. The same for the bentside and the cheek, but the tail of the cabinet is badly scratched. I'll have to smooth that down, but trying to match the finish . . ."

"I'd wager that for just the finish on the wood," suggested Charyn, "one of the maitres, possibly Maitre Alyna, could image a match, especially if you told her what was in most finishes. I don't know that I trust imaging for the inside, though."

"Do you think . . . ?"

"Howal has been able to match . . . the finish on the hilt of my letter knife." Charyn had almost mentioned inks, and that would have been a very bad slip. "This sounds like you'll have to practically rebuild the inside."

"Not really. Most of what I'll have to do isn't that much more than I did for the clavecin in the chateau music room. It hadn't really been worked on for quite a while." She smiled mischievously. "That's one reason why you all sounded so much better after I came. Playing a well-tuned clavecin does make a difference."

"The difference didn't just come from a better-tuned instrument," replied Charyn as he studied the clavecin, starting with the goldenwood cabinet and taking in the keyboard with its double row of keys, as well as the well-turned legs. "Do I want to look inside?"

"I'd rather you didn't. It's possible that the moving might have loosened or frayed the strings. I'd prefer not to open it until it's in place."

"Then we should head back to the chateau proper."

Palenya jumped down from the wagon bed before Charyn could even offer a hand, and he had to hurry to catch up to her.

"If I weren't going to have to do all the work on the inside, I'd worry about leaving it in the cold, but since we'll have to move it again in the cold, it's better that it stays here. That way it doesn't get warmed up, then chilled, then warmed up again. Shifts from hot to cold and back again, or from moist air to dry and back over short periods of time aren't good for any instrument."

As they entered the rear foyer of the chateau, Bhayrn approached, also wearing a heavy winter coat of dark teal wool. He looked to Charyn. "You won't be using the plain coach this afternoon, will you? I'd like to go to Kharlyn's. I can stable the horses there until I return this evening."

"Go ahead, but make sure the guard going with you is scheduled for duty."

Bhayrn frowned, but nodded.

"You can check with the duty desk. In the alcove off the front entrance," Charyn added.

Bhayrn sighed, then turned and headed toward the front of the chateau.

Palenya raised eyebrows, but said nothing, then began to unwind the scarf that had protected her from the intense cold.

The two walked to the music room, where Palenya took off her gloves and heavy woolen coat, revealing that she had worn a woolen jacket underneath.

"You were prepared for the cold." Charyn tried not to wince at the twinges that radiated from his ears, apparently from thawing out from the chill outside.

"Better than you." Palenya smiled.

"I hadn't thought my ears would get so cold so quickly."

"I saw how cold the guards were, and riding on an open wagon . . ." She shook her head. Then, from inside her jacket, she extracted the cloth bag that Charyn had given her earlier and extended it. "There's only a gold and four silvers left. After looking at the instrument, I realized I had to buy more than I'd thought. I also bought some extra quills, strings, and a spare jack, just in case. They'll be used, sooner or later."

Charyn handed the bag back. "What's left is yours. Call it repayment for doing all sorts of things I couldn't in obtaining the clavecin. I had no idea getting a clavecin was going to take all . . . everything. There's much . . . more . . ."

"To being a musician than you realized?" Palenya slipped the bag back inside her jacket. "Thank you."

"You're more than welcome." He paused, then asked, "How good will that clavecin be when you've finished with it?"

"The soundboard and the inside workings are as good as the one here. It should produce a sound that's comparable, but I won't know for sure until I'm finished. It doesn't have the elaborate finish that yours does, nor all the gilt, but it looks to be as good a basic instrument. It should be, since it was made by Dhorek."

"That's very good." Charyn nodded. "You're pleased to have found it, aren't you?"

"I am. They were both fools. Now the clavecin will be played by someone who will enjoy it."

"I'm not certain that all students always enjoy playing," said Charyn dryly.

"But Aloryana does. So does Maitre Malyna, whether she will admit it or not."

"Speaking of playing . . . I'd like to play the duet with you later, perhaps midafternoon, and work on the nocturne . . . and we could have dinner. But I need to write a letter to Maitre Alastar first so that I can send it off. And I need to go over some changes in the stablemaster's plans and the Chateau Guards plan that Dylert gave me . . ."

"I would like that . . . if you would."

"Of course I would. What ever . . ." He broke off his words as he saw her smile. "You . . ."

He was still shaking his head as he left Palenya in the music room and headed up to the study, marveling at all she knew about clavecins, so many aspects of the instrument that he'd never even realized. *Like so many other things you hadn't even considered a year ago.*

The first thing he intended was to write the letter to Maitre Alastar telling him that the clavecin was in hand. He wanted to make it clear that it would require considerable work by Musician Palenya before it would be ready to play. Then would come writing out the list of names of potentially suitable High Holders' daughters to appease his mother. The name that easily came to mind was that of Alyncya D'Shendael, but he'd list the others, if only for political reasons, since the last thing he could afford was any unnecessary or perceived slight to any High Holder. Then would come poring over the plans from Dylert and Kaylet.

He took a deep breath.

55

Samedi and Solayi were cold and windy, with scattered snow, not enough to block the roads and streets, although those streets were largely deserted, unsurprisingly, given the biting winds. When Charyn entered the study on Lundi morning, the chamber was cold enough that he thought he ought to have been able to see his breath. He did not. He did detect a faint floral and smoky scent.

"It was colder earlier, sir," announced Howal, "but I had Norstan bring up some braziers."

Charyn frowned involuntarily. "I don't recall braziers . . ."

Howal offered a sheepish grin. "I . . . found several. There were cuttings from the gardens in the wood barn, and several barrels of dried rose petals."

Charyn looked around for the braziers.

"I had them removed. Even under the best of circumstances, it's not good to leave them in a closed room for long. They did take off the worst of the chill."

"Thank you." Charyn didn't even bother with going to the window. He knew that the hazy white sun just made everything look even colder, and pulling open the window hangings would just make the study more frigid.

He began to think about how to confront Ryel in a way that would make him reveal what he had done, but he realized that Ryel would admit nothing unless he saw that he was doomed, in which case, he might reveal matters in a way to attempt to undermine Charyn, as a last attempt to destroy the regial family. *You can't give him any openings.* And that would be difficult.

Just after seventh glass, while Charyn was still thinking, Sturdyn announced, "An imager courier, sir."

"Have him come in." Charyn noted that the only part of the courier's face that was reddened was around his eyes, suggesting that the gray scarf around his neck had been wound around not only his neck, but all of his face but his eyes. "It's really bitter out there, isn't it?"

"Yes, sir. This is from Maitre Alastar." The man handed the sealed envelope to Charyn.

"Thank you. Before you leave, go down to the kitchen and get warmed up."

"Yes, sir. Thank you, sir."

Charyn was already opening the envelope when the courier left.

Rex Charyn—

The Collegium is most grateful for your kind offer and your generosity in presenting a clavecin for the use of imagers and students. The changes to the new music room in the administration building will be completed by the evening of Mardi, the fourth of Fevier, allowing arrival of the clavecin on Meredi or thereafter.

Both Aloryana and Maitre Malyna are especially looking forward to its appearance.

You and your mother should be pleased to learn that Aloryana is already making great progress in both her studies and in her imaging, and Lystara is very much enjoying her company.

Charyn smiled at the last words.

"Sir?"

"The Maitre will be most pleased to have a clavecin at the Collegium, and Musician Palenya and Maitre Kaylet can deliver it any time from Meredi onward, depending on the weather."

Before that long, Bhayrn slipped into the study, almost ahead of Sturdyn's announcement of "Lord Bhayrn." He stood before the desk, not quite glowering.

"How are you doing?" asked Charyn.

"I'm bored enough with whist and other plaque games that I've started counting the marble tiles in the grand foyer. You at least have things to do to keep you busy."

"Why don't you take the plain coach and go visit one of your friends. No one is going to find fault with you for taking a coach in this weather. But make sure that the horses, driver, and guards have shelter wherever you go. If that's not possible, send them back here and have them return for you later." Charyn knew he was repeating himself, given that he had reminded Bhayrn before, but it was cold, and he wanted to make certain his brother understood his concerns.

Bhayrn opened his mouth, shut it, and frowned. Finally, he nodded. "Thank you. I think I will."

"Try not to go too far in this cold."

"I wouldn't think of it." With that, Bhayrn turned and strode out of the study.

After watching his brother leave, Charyn resumed his study of the Chateau Guard reorganization plan. Even though he and Dylert had worked on it together, he wanted to make certain he could describe it well enough without needing notes. He knew he had to give the impression of being the rex while improving the lot of the guards.

A quint before the first glass of the afternoon, Dylert arrived in the study. "All the guards except the ones at the gates and the palace doors will be in the grand ballroom when the chimes strike. Oh . . . and the two with your brother."

"What have you told them?"

"Just that you're going to announce the improvements to the Chateau Guard."

"But Maertyl and Faelln know?" Charyn knew that Dylert had talked to each, but he still wanted confirmation.

"They know. Each said the other should be guard captain, but you'll be able to tell that they're both pleased. They get along. That was another reason I suggested those two."

Charyn nodded. *The last thing we need is dissension among the guards.*

Shortly before first glass, Dylert and Charyn left the study and walked along the north corridor, then turned and made their way to the ballroom.

"The rex!" Norstan announced from the door as Dylert and Charyn entered.

The two then made their way to the dais and up the short side steps before turning and standing facing the assembled guards.

Charyn waited several moments before saying a word. "What has happened in the last few months showed several things. First, it showed that those of you who remain are loyal and hardworking. It also showed that many of you are not paid enough and have not been paid according to your abilities and your time as a guard. And finally, it showed that there was no clear line of command from me to the guard captain to you. Acting guard commander Dylert and I have worked out a better organization and pay structure for the guard. In addition, there will be a new guard captain and the new position of guard undercaptain. There will also be three new lead guards, each in charge of a section of guards." Charyn paused for several moments to let the guards think about what he had just said.

"Your new guard captain is Maertyl. Your undercaptain is Faelln. The three lead guards are Reynalt, Charseyt, and Woelt." From what Charyn could tell, the murmurs seemed to be generally of approval, and he didn't see any unhappy faces. "The new pay rates will mean everyone will get some sort of increase. It won't be much for those of you who are new, and it will be significant for those of you who have been guards for more than ten years." Charyn turned to Dylert. "Would you like to add anything?"

"There isn't much I can add," said Dylert with a smile. "Except for one thing. The whole idea of improving matters for you came from Rex Charyn. I and some others helped with the details, but the idea was his."

"He helped a great deal," said Charyn quickly and loudly, adding, "There aren't any other changes. I'd like to see the guard captain and undercaptain right here."

Maertyl and Faelln immediately came up onto the dais.

Maertyl grinned as he faced the guards. "My first order as guard captain is simple. Those on duty, back to your posts. Those of you off-duty may go."

Charyn saw more than a few smiles among the departing guards. He just watched as the guards left. When the ballroom was empty, he turned back to the other three.

"Your Grace," offered Maertyl, "I wish to thank you for your confidence in me."

"It wasn't just my confidence," replied Charyn. "It was also Maitre Dylert's recommendation."

Maertyl turned to Dylert. "Then I thank you as well." He turned to Charyn, then swallowed before he spoke. "Your Grace, I've been a chateau guard for more than ten years. This is the first time a rex has taken the time to address us all, or even a few of us. It's the first time anyone has said words about the time we've served. And it will be the first increase in pay many have ever seen."

"It's long overdue, and if times weren't so bad, the pay increases would have been more."

"It's probably better that times are hard," said Faelln. "We all know times are hard. Any time that a rex gets attacked so often, times are bad."

To that, Maertyl nodded. "Getting a small increase in bad times means more than a big increase in prosperous times."

"There is one other matter," said Charyn. "I'll meet with the guard captain or the undercaptain first thing in the morning most mornings. I'm sure those meetings will be brief, but necessary." He smiled sheepishly. "I might not be too regular on Solayi mornings."

Maertyl chuckled; Faelln grinned.

"Is there anything else either of you wants to tell me or thinks I should know?"

"Not at the moment, sir," replied Maertyl.

Fhaelln shook his head.

"Then I'll see one of you in the morning."

"Yes, sir."

As Charyn and Dylert left the ballroom, Charyn said, "You did say that you'd be here for a day or so."

"I did."

"Good. I imagine you'll be glad to get back to the Collegium, but I do appreciate all that you've done. It had to be done, and it's not something I could have done nearly as well."

"Maitre Alastar said that for it to work someone else had to be the one working with the guards. You can't be too familiar."

Charyn understood what Dylert wasn't saying—that Charyn had to be both firm and fair, while still showing that he cared about the men.

56

Meredi morning Charyn was up earlier than usual, and he dressed in heavier woolens for the day, because he wanted to be there when Palenya and Kaylet left the chateau with the clavecin. Neither his mother nor Bhayrn was in the breakfast room, nor did either arrive before he finished and stopped by Norstan's study.

The seneschal stood as Charyn stepped into the small space. "Sir?"

"I don't suppose anyone wishes to see me?"

"There are the choristers, but I've told them you will let them know when it is convenient. Factor Roblen asked for an appointment. He's a wool factor."

Charyn didn't mention that he knew Roblen, even as he wondered why the factor wanted to see him. *Certainly not about cloth or tailoring.* At least, he hoped not. "That might be interesting. Arrange a time for next week."

"Also, you did receive a letter from Ferron D'Fhernon-Alte. It just arrived." Norstan bent over the desk for a moment, then picked up an envelope, which he handed to Charyn.

Charyn took it, and slipped it into his jacket. "Thank you."

From Norstan's study, Charyn headed toward the duty desk in the alcove off the main entry, judging that Dylert might be there. He did want to see the imager maitre off, and wish him well in front of the chateau guards on duty.

Dylert was in fact standing just outside the alcove, wearing his imager grays, as he had been from right after the time he'd announced his replacement, but in addition to the gray visor cap and the heavy gray riding jacket, he had a thick gray scarf loosely around his neck. He smiled as he saw Charyn walking toward the front entry.

"I do hope you're leaving by the front," Charyn said.

"Maertyl wouldn't have it any other way."

"You look prepared for the weather."

"I hope so."

"As I've said before, I very much appreciate all you've done."

Dylert smiled, not quite sheepishly. "I appreciate being given the opportunity to do it for you, sir. I learned quite a bit along the way."

Charyn laughed softly. "So did I." After a moment of silence, he added, "You better get on your way, or I'll be tempted to keep you here." *As if you really could, but what else can you say?* "And Thelia would not be happy with me for that."

Dylert grinned. "No, sir." After inclining his head to Charyn, he turned and walked out through the doors, one of which was held by Maertyl.

As Dylert stepped out the front entry, a score of chateau guards appeared, forming up into two files, one on each side of the center of the steps.

"Honor! Arms!" snapped Faelln from the bottom of the white stone steps.

Twenty rifles went to presentation, and remained there as Dylert walked down the steps toward his mount, held by Woelt, one of the three recently named lead guards. The imager mounted, then raised his arm in salutation, and then urged his mount down the drive.

When Dylert reached the ring road, Faelln called out, "Order arms," followed several moments by, "Dismissed to duties."

Maertyl joined Charyn. "I can see why you called on the imagers, sir. They're good. They're also tough. He started a morning exercise program—in the covered courtyard. He led everyone. He had a lot of the men gasping. It didn't even seem to make him breathe hard. A couple of times, the other imager joined him, and he led the exercises while Maitre Dylert went around making sure everyone did them right."

"You're keeping that up, I trust?"

"Yes, sir. One session for the day guards, one in the afternoon for the night guards."

"Good." Dylert had mentioned the exercise program to Charyn, almost in passing, but had said nothing about his leading it.

After leaving Maertyl, Charyn hurried to the rear courtyard. He saw Palenya, well wrapped in her heavy scarf, leaving the barn as one of the stable boys began to open the doors. Charyn immediately crossed the courtyard to where she waited while the horses were hitched.

"Are you sure you have all the tools you'll need?"

"They're already in the wagon." Palenya gestured.

"I'll send the coach for you at fifth glass."

"I won't be done by then."

"When would you like the coach, then?"

"Fifth glass," she replied, with a glint in her eyes that suggested her well-covered mouth was smiling. "I'll have to go back tomorrow, and possibly on Vendrei."

"You're rebuilding that clavecin, aren't you?"

"Oh, no. Just replacing the strings and the broken parts, and revoicing all the plectra. What any good musician would do."

"Any really good musician."

"You're going to freeze out here. That jacket's not heavy enough, and you don't have a cap or a scarf. I don't want to be responsible for making the rex of Solidar sick."

"I'm the only one responsible for that. Besides," said Charyn, pointing toward the barn, "Kaylet and the ostlers have the horses hitched, and he's bringing the wagon out. I'll see you tonight." He stepped back and watched as Palenya climbed up into the seat beside Kaylet, and then as the team and wagon slowly headed down the drive.

Charyn turned and made his way back into the chateau. His ears were burning by the time he reached the grand staircase and started up. He hadn't realized that they had gotten that cold. When he reached the top, he found Chelia standing there, clearly waiting for him.

"Mother . . ."

"Thank you for the list of young ladies. I trust you will not mind if I also add a few other names that have come to my attention."

"Of course not. I would not wish to overlook anyone." *Or to give any High Holder offense, especially now.*

"I thought you might feel that way. How is Palenya faring?"

"She and Kaylet just left to take the clavecin to the Collegium. From what she said, it will take her days to put the clavecin to rights."

"It took longer than that for her to get the one in the music room to sound right. Your father didn't want any musicians in the chateau that he couldn't control. He didn't have much of an ear for music, although he never admitted it."

Charyn almost said he hadn't recalled that it had taken that long, but managed to reply, "The one she found is a good instrument, but without the elaborate finish of ours."

"Do you think what you have in mind will work out?"

"We'll have to see. There's no harm done if it doesn't."

"She does like you, Charyn. I hope you understand that."

"She's also said that it can't possibly work out. I just wish . . ." He shook his head. "She's so much . . . more than . . ."

"Than some High Holders' daughters?" Chelia laughed gently. "You haven't met the right ones. Remember, Malyna is a High Holder's daughter. So is Maitre Alyna. And yes, Palenya is special. It took me more than a year to find her. She has been good to you and good for you. That's why, whatever happens, you will treat her very well. Very well."

"But . . . why . . . ?"

"I didn't want you ending up like all the other men in my life. That's why." Chelia smiled pleasantly. "I do like some of the names you gave me. Very much. I won't keep you, dear." With another smile, she turned and headed down the grand staircase.

For several moments, Charyn just stood there. *All the other men . . . ?* His uncle, of course, but . . . He swallowed. Finally, he resumed walking toward his study, still thinking over what his mother had said.

Once he was settled at his desk, he retrieved the letter from his jacket and slit the envelope with the miniature letter knife that Howal had imaged.

Your Grace—

I would like to offer my deepest condolences, belated as they may be, over the untimely and truly unfortunate death of your father following the Year-Turn Ball. In this time of unrest and disruption, he attempted to guide Solidar on a middle course, one that took into account the more pressing needs of both High Holders and factors, while not requiring massive increases in tariffs on either group. Such moderation should have been commended by all responsible individuals, rather than have become a cause for a violent act that will benefit neither group in the end, and possibly only one individual, whoever he may be, and only in the immediate times, certainly not in the years to come.

I would hope that you would continue the moderate stance that you have thus far presented, despite what must be many challenges and possible dangers from those of intemperate mind and possibly a Namer-like penchant for unseemly personal notoriety, or contrariwise, a secretiveness that may never uncover his identity, leaving only the evil of his deed . . .

Charyn frowned. *What in Terahnar does he want?*

. . . The ill-gotten fame of Naming that some men lust after while denying that they so do will overshadow any good that they may have accomplished and,

without a strong rex in L'Excelsis, will blight all Solidar. May you continue a course of strong moderation in these troubled times, and know that those of our holding stand behind you in such an endeavor.

I also wish to convey my profound appreciation to you and your family for allowing me to attend the Year-Turn Ball and for allowing me to make the acquaintance, however fleeting, of the most charming Malyna D'Zaerlyn . . .

Charyn somehow managed not to burst out into raucous laughter. *Smitten by Malyna.* After a moment, he had to admit that he'd certainly been intrigued to begin with. After he swallowed his laughter, he kept reading.

. . . whose whereabouts, despite my most heartfelt efforts, have eluded me. I was hoping that you might look favorably upon me and provide some assistance in this matter, since I was informed by your lovely sister Aloryana, and I earnestly hope that such information is accurate, that your attentions and affections were not devoted to Lady Malyna. If I have erred in this, please understand that I would not in the slightest . . .

Charyn shook his head. For the courage alone—and the desperation—it must have taken to write such a missive, young Ferron deserved an answer. As he set down Ferron's letter, he couldn't help thinking that the letter also showed what Palenya had pointed out when he'd told her that Aloryana was an imager—just how invisible most women in Solidar were, even the daughters of High Holders. It also pointed out that Ferron and his family were not reading the newssheets, which had mentioned Malyna, and that showed how out of touch some of the High Holders indeed were.

After finishing the letter, he immediately began his reply to the unfortunately smitten heir.

My dear Ferron—

My family and I thank you for your thoughtful and heartfelt letter of condolence, and we appreciate greatly those thoughts you expressed so carefully and warmly, as well as your thoughts for a moderate course in the governing of Solidar. Certainly, that is what I have endeavored to provide in the comparatively few weeks that I have been rex . . . and what I will continue to work toward, even given the clear presence of the Namer in the hearts and minds of some men.

Malyna D'Zaerlyn, whom my sister likely mentioned is a distant relative, is

no longer guesting at the Chateau D'Rex. I must confess to a certain deception.
Because Malyna never had the opportunity to attend a Year-Turn Ball, as a favor,
my father allowed her to do so in disguise, if you will, since she is most properly
Malyna D'Imagisle, and a Maitre D'Aspect at the Collegium Imago. For your
information, she did tell me that she found you both charming and most polite . . .

I have not informed anyone else of your letter, and this letter will be sealed
and sent without another person seeing either your letter or mine . . .

Charyn wasn't totally pleased at continuing the deception about why
Malyna had been there, but it was better left that way . . . at least until
he was absolutely certain that the problems with Ryel had been fully resolved. *Laid to rest, if you will.*

When he finished the letter, he signed and sealed it, and gave it to
Howal to have sent. He really didn't want any word of Ferron's plea to be
circulated anywhere that Ferron himself did not choose.

Less than a glass later, just after the wind outside the study began to
moan, he received another dispatch from Marshal Vaelln. Even before
the courier left and Charyn opened it, its thickness suggested that the
information within was anything but something he wanted to read.
Nonetheless, he did.

Your Grace—

Just this morning I have received at headquarters reports of
three additional naval incidents. The first occurred on the
sixth of Ianus, north of the Strait of Anghyl, off the west coast
of Ferrum. A Solidaran second-rate ship—the Chayar—was escorting three Solidaran merchanters away from Ferial when
she was attacked by a two Jariolan second-raters and a frigate.
The captain had position and dispatched the frigate before the
Jariolan heavies could close. He then demasted one second-
rater, and sank her, but took heavy damage. Apparently, he
knew the Chayar would not survive, but he managed enough
sail to ram the last Jariolan, which appeared to be sinking,
along with the Chayar, when the three merchanters fled. They
reported this when they ported in Kherseilles. We have no
reason to believe otherwise.

The second encounter took place on the ninth of Ianus, off-
shore from Caena. Two Jariolan frigates were bearing down

on a Solidaran spice merchant, when the *Aegis*, one of our older third-raters, intervened. She drove off one privateer and sunk the other, but suffered enough damage that she had to return to Solis for refitting and repair.

The last conflict was off Tobiara, the second-largest of the Abierto Isles, on the twelfth of Ianus. A Jariolan flotilla attacked and then boarded four Solidaran merchanters when they refused to heave to and attempted to escape. The merchanters were escaping from two frigates when they were trapped by three other ships of the line, consisting of two second-raters and a third-rater. The Jariolans sacked three ships and then sank them, and dumped most of the crew onto the fourth ship, except for a score of seamen they declared were Jariolan deserters. The Jariolans claimed the sackings and sinkings were reparations for the practice of Solidar factors using Jariolan deserters to crew their ships. Marshal Tynan enclosed a letter of protest from the shipowners affected. They are demanding greater protection around the Abierto Isles . . .

Charyn continued on to the end of the long dispatch. Although the Solidaran Navy was doing well against the Jariolans, it was more than clear that Solidar needed more ships sooner than it was possible to build them, either that or settle in for a long and sporadic naval conflict.

Do you have any choice? Even if you deal with Ryel, will the rest of the factors and High Holders follow your lead?

Notwithstanding Ferron's letter, Charyn had strong doubts about whether they would.

A second question came to mind, one that he'd entertained more than once. *Should you call a special meeting of the councils, earlier than the scheduled date?* Tempting as that was, as it had been the first time he'd thought of it, he shook his head. *You don't want anyone thinking there's something out of the ordinary about to happen.* Matters were tenuous enough as they were.

57

Nothing had changed much by Vendrei afternoon. On Jeudi, there had been light snow, on and off, and the air was slightly warmer, "slightly" meaning that it took a good quint outside before the cold seeped into the bones instead of mere moments. Palenya was still working on the clavecin at the Collegium, although she had assured Charyn that her work would be done by Vendrei evening. And Chelia had added a few more names to the personal invitation list for the Spring-Turn Ball, some of whom were totally unfamiliar to him.

Given that little had happened, except for the large story in *Veritum* detailing the continuing losses of Solidaran merchant ships to the Jariolans, Charyn was surprised when Moencriff, who had replaced Maertyl as one of the study guards, announced, "Maitre Kaylet to see you, sir."

"Have him come in."

Kaylet entered, wearing heavy imager grays and holding an envelope. "Maitre Thelia asked me to deliver this to you personally."

"Thank you." Charyn stood and took the envelope, then asked, "Since you're here, how are you coming with the stables and barns, and all the ostlers and others?"

"Right now, Aedryt and the others could handle things better than they were before. I'd feel much more comfortable being here another week or so."

"I'll leave that to your judgment." Charyn smiled. "I've also noticed that the courtyard, the stables, and everything to the rear of the chateau looks to be in much better condition. Personally, I also appreciate your coming up with all the replacement firewood."

"Some of the trees in the hunting park should have been trimmed years ago. Most needed pruning. Johran and I have worked out a plan for dealing with that in the future. He's the one that Aedryt and I decided would do the best job of taking over the maintenance of the hunting park. No one really had the responsibility for that."

Charyn nodded, although he had long since gotten the impression that there had been a number of areas where that had been the case. *You're going to have to take a much more active look at everything . . . unless you want matters to return to the way they were.*

"Is there anything else, sir?"

"I'm sorry, Kaylet. My thoughts wandered. No. Thank you again."

"My pleasure, sir. I've learned a lot."

"So has everyone you've worked with."

After Kaylet had departed, Charyn broke the plain seal and took out the single folded sheet of paper. It contained nine names, with notations after each, nothing else. The writing was in standard merchant hand, although, somehow, it looked just a shade different from that used with the threatening letters. The way the information was presented suggested that Thelia didn't want it obviously traced back to the Collegium.

Why? Because if any paper with that information was linked to the imagers, it might reveal how much they knew and could find out?

Charyn studied the listing carefully:

High Holder Basalyt	Four estates between Kephria and Loha
High Holder Fhaedyrk	Estate north of Tilbora
	Breweries in Midcote, Tilbora, and Nacliano
High Holder Khunthan	Estate northeast of Eshtora
	Part owner of Khellan Trading, 15 ships [Eshtora, Ouestan, Kherseilles]
High Holder Ryel	Estates in Tuuryl, Laaryn, Tacqueville, and Rivages
	Owner Solisan Traders [Solis], 21 ships, purchased
	interest of High Holder Oskaryn after Oskaryn's death
	Warehouses in Solis and Kephria
Factorius Elthyrd	Timber factorages in L'Excelsis and Asseroiles
	Canvas/Rope factorages in L'Excelsis and Solis
Factorius Harll	Brick Kilns [Montagne]
	Quarries [Mont D'Point, Mont D'Fleuve, Epignard]
Factorius Hisario	Family shipping [10 ships] Westisle
	Warehouses [Westisle, Liantiago, Kherseilles]
Factorius Jhaliost	Salt Mine [Khelgror]
	Coal Mine [Ghoran]
	Coke Works [Kherseilles]
Factorius Thalmyn	Fishing fleet [18 boats, Tilbora]

NOTE: The largest of merchant fleets owned by a High Holder are the twenty-eight "Diamond" ships of High Holder Ghasphar, out of Estisle

The only councilor's name missing was that of High Holder Oskaryn, and he couldn't have been involved, not when he'd died the same night as Charyn's father, but the fact that he'd been involved with Ryel seemed more than a little strange.

There was *something* . . . something about the list. Except it wasn't the list. He looked over the list again, but he just couldn't think what it might be that he was missing. Finally, he refolded the paper and slipped it into his jacket. "I'll be back in a bit."

"I'll be here," replied Howal. "I'm still trying to make Norstan's ledgers simpler."

Charyn walked from the study to the south side of the upper level and to Chelia's "new" sitting room, which now contained the same furnishings as her previous sitting room.

Chelia looked up from her desk and a stack of papers, possibly the personal invitations for the Spring-Turn Ball. "What is it, dear?"

Charyn didn't answer immediately, but lifted a side chair and moved it closer to the desk before sitting down. "Where did your brother's wife come from?"

"That's a rather blunt question, as if she came from nothing. She didn't. She is Oskaryn's much younger sister. The late High Holder Oskaryn, that is."

"The one who was shot on Year-Turn Eve?"

Chelia nodded.

"Did you know that he and Uncle Ryel owned a shipping business and that Ryel bought his interest right after his death."

"That's not surprising. Brother dear's interest in Solisan was Doryana's dowry. Oskaryn's father never had much besides his estates and the shipping. His son probably had to sell, and at a loss."

Charyn nodded, but his thoughts were racing. *Ryel gets Oskaryn shot, diverts attention from himself, and then buys his interest . . .* But that still left questions. "Then, with Uncle Ryel marrying Doryana, did he spend any time in Solis?"

"Far too much, to hear him talk. Father put him in charge of the warehousing there almost right after their wedding. I'm not so sure that Doryana really didn't do a great deal of the work. He couldn't wait to get back to Rivages when Father died. Neither could Doryana. Do you think this bears on the rest of it?"

Of course, it does! At that moment, Charyn recalled exactly what he'd been trying to remember—what his uncle had said at the Year-Turn Ball, that almost no High Holders were involved in shipping. How had he known that? Because of his years in shipping, and that meant he could position the "factors" as the ones behind the assassination and attempts on Charyn.

"Dear . . . you look so pensive."

"Oh . . . I was just thinking. You once said that Uncle Ryel didn't like dirty coins because of his early years. Did you mean the shipping?"

"Yes. And you think that means something?"

"I'm sure that it does." Charyn shrugged. "It's just that there's no way to prove it."

"There never was any way with him . . . even in the most despicable acts. He always had someone to vouch for his presence elsewhere. Or people disappeared without a trace. Or wouldn't speak."

"What? He had his own private army?"

"Oh, no. He would have regarded that as wasteful."

Charyn counterfeited a deep frown.

"I always thought he had his own assassins' guild. Not that I ever saw anything that ever pointed to it. There were just too many people who always died when it benefited him . . . or disappeared when they might have made life difficult. Brother dear has never liked those who might have . . . caused complications."

"Is there anything else?"

"Should there be, dear?"

"Probably, but I don't know enough to ask what it might be."

"I'm sure you'll think of something."

"Are those invitations?" Charyn gestured.

"They are. They will keep your post riders busy for a few days."

Looking at the stack as he stood, Charyn didn't doubt her words in the slightest. He was still thinking about Ryel when he returned to the study.

And he was still worrying about his uncle and the forthcoming meeting of the councils when he heard a coach enter the rear courtyard. Knowing that could only mean that Palenya had returned, he hurried from the study and down the grand staircase and from there to the rear foyer, where he waited until she trudged up the steps and into the chateau, carrying a large and obviously heavy satchel.

"It's done."

"Does it play as well as you hoped?"

"A little better, I think. I try not to expect too much. Aloryana was the first one, besides me, to play it. She looked so pleased."

"Good." Charyn reached for the satchel, and took it from her. It was even heavier than it looked. "All your tools?"

She nodded.

"You look exhausted."

"I am."

"Why don't you just rest or take a nap? I'll arrange for a late dinner . . . if you'd like that."

"I would, if you . . ."

"I do. I definitely do." He took her arm and began to walk with her toward her quarters. He couldn't help marveling at the weight of her tools.

After settling Palenya in her room, on the lower level, he returned to the study.

"She's repaired the clavecin at the Collegium," Charyn told Howal. "Aloryana seems to be pleased. I hope the Maitre is as pleased as his letters indicated." He walked to the window and looked out. Nothing had changed.

Then he settled behind the desk and tried to think about the implications of the information provided by Thelia and whoever her sources might have been. All of it was like everything else, indicative, but not really proof. *How many indications do you have to have before it's proof?* Sanafryt would have been the first to have told him that proof was proof, and indications counted for little in law. *Which is why Ryel has gotten away with it . . . and with probably more than you'll ever know. Most likely many feel exactly as you do . . . but are they enough?*

If he couldn't get better proof, Charyn knew, he'd have to gamble with what he had because, sooner or later, one of the assassination attempts would be successful . . . unless he remained holed up in the chateau with an imager nearby for the rest of his life—or Ryel's.

Finally, he went to the kitchen and arranged for dinner at two quints past sixth, and then went to Palenya's room. She wasn't there, but he found her in the music room, just sitting at the small table desk.

"I've been looking for you."

"I couldn't sleep. So I washed up and changed and came here. I'll miss it. It's so beautiful and peaceful here in the music room."

"You're not going anywhere yet."

"Let's not spoil dinner." She smiled. "What are we having?"

"Fowl in a cream sauce over noodles. The only thing special about dinner is you."

"Just be that sweet to whoever you marry, and you'll be happy."

"You make that easy for me."

"The right lady will do that. If she doesn't, don't marry her."

Charyn took her hand, and she stood. He didn't say anything as they walked up the grand staircase. They arrived in the regial sitting room to a table fully set, with hot breads under cloth already in place, and two full pitchers of wine, white for him and red for her.

"Not special?" Palenya raised her eyebrows.

"Not as special as you."

"Charyn . . ." She shook her head.

He smiled as they sat down, and Delya and another server appeared with covered dishes. Charyn immediately poured the wine

"You need to eat," he said. "You've been working hard for days. I'd also wager that clavecin sounds better than the one in the music room."

"No. It's almost as good, but the one downstairs is one of the best."

"Only because you worked on it. Don't argue. Have some of the chicken."

"I am hungry."

"How could you not be? You haven't had anything to eat since this morning."

Palenya took a small swallow of the wine, then a mouthful of the fowl, then a second.

Charyn smiled, then had some of the fowl and noodles. The cream sauce was good, and best of all, still warm. He broke off a chunk of the dark bread and then eased the basket toward her. "The bread's still warm."

She finished the mouthful she was eating before replying. "Thank you." Then she had another sip of wine. "This is good."

"You're welcome. Only the best for you."

"More flattery . . . but you're being very sweet."

Because Charyn wasn't quite certain what else to say that wouldn't repeat what he'd already said or would have been something about papers, petitions, or the threats that still hung over him and his family, he said nothing for a time, enjoying both the food and looking at Palenya.

"You're quiet," she finally said. "Attentive, but quiet."

"I was just enjoying being with you . . . and the food."

"You do flatter me." She paused, then said, "You really do need to start looking for a wife, Charyn."

"I'm not all that interested. You're far more intriguing than most of the High Holders' daughters."

"I can see that you mean it. I'm incredibly flattered, but you're the ruler of Solidar. Rulers need heirs—blood heirs. You owe it to everyone. Rulers without heirs leave chaos behind."

Charyn knew what she wasn't saying, that Solidar had already suffered enough chaos and bloodshed and didn't need any more.

"Also, I'm older than you. Enough that I'll get fat and gray while you're still young and handsome."

"I'm not all that handsome, and you'll never be fat and ugly . . . and you're a wonderful musician."

"No. I'm a very good musician, not a wonderful musician . . ."

In the end, much, much later, Charyn just held her as they drifted off to sleep, his thoughts on how he'd never find anyone to compare to her . . .

58

Samedi and Solayi passed slowly for Charyn, not unpleasurably, because he spent more time than he had in recent weeks with Palenya, including several glasses of intensive practice on the clavecin learning to play—correctly—several of the more intricate passages in the Farray nocturne. He still couldn't believe that it only had a number, and not a real name—just Nocturne Number Three.

Lundi morning was gray and cold, but not quite so cold as the previous week, under high gray clouds, when Charyn met with Maertyl at the duty desk, as he had done every day except Solayi since Dylert had left. "Have any of the guards noticed anything unusual?"

"No, sir. It's been very quiet."

Although Charyn nodded, that bothered him, because he had the feeling that something was bound to happen sometime soon. It had just been too long since the last attempt. "Thank you."

"You're worried, sir?"

"We haven't discovered who's behind it all. I don't see them stopping now."

"I'd thought that, too, sir. Fhaelln and I both think they might try again. We've told all the guards to watch for anything that seems out of sorts."

"I appreciate that. Oh, there will be a Factor Roblen coming to see me."

"Yes, sir. Thank you."

As Charyn made his way to the study, he tried to think of how Ryel's next attempt might be made. It was unlikely to come through treachery at the chateau, not after all the changes that had been made and the death of everyone who had attempted such treachery, but, given Ryel, there would be some form of deception. *As if knowing that helps very much.*

At just before eighth glass, Factor Roblen appeared, a youngish factor, by that meaning he looked merely some five years older than Charyn, with bright green eyes, broad shoulders, and thin brown hair. "Thank you so much for seeing me, Your Grace."

Charyn gestured to the chairs and seated himself, waiting until

Roblen sat down before asking, "Why did you wish to see me? I assume it's not about cloth or tailoring."

"No, sir. I thought I should, Your Grace." The factor looked down nervously, then seemed to force himself to face Charyn. "You see . . . things have happened in my life, and I learned what I thought was not always the way I had thought. I keep reading in the newssheets . . . well . . . that factors are upset with you because you aren't doing enough to stop the Jariolan raiders. The piracy hurts us. I lost my part of a cargo of woolens going to Ferrum last month . . ."

"The piracy and privateering hurt us all," Charyn replied.

"Yes, Your Grace, it does. We do need more warships, it seems to me. But it also seems to me that we have to pay for them. I can't say I'm pleased that it's necessary. No factor in his right mind would be pleased with higher tariffs. The thing is . . . well . . . I mean . . . so long as the tariff increases are fair, and we all pay, and that includes High Holders . . . well . . . it seems right to me." Roblen paused, then swallowed. "I mean . . . that's really all I came to say."

"You're a brave man, Factor, and more fair-minded than many. I can tell you, if you haven't heard, that I have made arrangements to build more warships. There will be a small increase in tariffs for both High Holders and large factors, and a smaller increase for smaller factors."

"Might I ask?"

"Ten additional golds for the High Holders and large factors. Five more golds for factors who pay less than fifty golds a year in tariffs, and a one-part-in-ten increase for those who owe less than twenty-five golds."

"That is more than many will like, but . . . I cannot say it is not fair."

"Both the High Council and the Factors' Council of Solidar have agreed to those terms, and I have pledged not to further increase tariffs unless great straits face Solidar, and only then after meeting with the councils."

"You . . . have thought this through."

"I've tried."

"I can say no more, Your Grace . . . I . . . do appreciate your seeing me."

Charyn stood. "No more than I appreciate your seeing me and offering your honest thoughts. I thank you and wish you well . . . and hope the efforts Marshal Vaelln has undertaken will keep your future cargoes safe."

Roblen stood, then bowed deeply before leaving.

At least there's one. Charyn could only hope there were more like

Roblen, even as he wondered what the event Roblen had alluded to had been, the one that suggested that what people thought was not always so.

He walked to the window and looked out, still thinking.

At two quints past ninth glass, an imager courier delivered two envelopes. After he left, Charyn looked at the two, each one addressed to him. He recognized the handwriting on the second—that of Aloryana—and immediately decided to open the first, since it was most likely from Maitre Alastar. Setting Aloryana's letter aside on the desk, he used the miniature letter knife to slit open the envelope.

As he had suspected, it was from the Maitre, a short missive thanking Charyn for the gift of the "excellent and well-tempered clavecin," praising Palenya for her skill and diligence, and asking if she would be available for instructionals in the afternoons on every Lundi and Meredi.

Charyn nodded. That seemed perfectly possible, but he would still ask Palenya if that arrangement would be agreeable to her. He replaced Alastar's missive in its envelope and opened the second, which was, indeed, from Aloryana.

Dear Charyn—

Thank you so very, VERY much. The clavecin is wonderful. It sounds just as good as the one in the Chateau music room. Palenya let me be the first to play it after she finished. It felt so good to play again. I know it's only been weeks, but it seemed like it was so long ago. Palenya worked so hard to rebuild it, and Maitre Alyna helped image the finish in the places where it was scarred. It looks like it was just new. Even Malyna was impressed with it. She says it's better than the one at her father's holding . . .

Charyn was smiling for a good half quint after he finished reading Aloryana's letter. In time, he turned to Howal. "How would you like to take a drive? I'd like to visit Factor Paersyt and see how he's coming with his engine."

"Do I have a choice?" asked Howal with an amused smile.

"If you really think I shouldn't go, I won't, but I haven't gone anywhere in weeks, and I doubt anyone would anticipate my going to see Paersyt."

"You're probably right about that, sir, but I would suggest that you make the visit short."

"In the event that someone is watching? So that they can't gather a larger group of men or some destructive force like a cannon that can overwhelm your shields?"

"Yes, sir."

"Then we'll make the visit short."

Two quints later, the two were in the plain coach, with a driver and a single guard, both wearing heavy but nondescript brown coats.

Charyn watched from one side of the coach, and Howal from the other as the coach turned from the drive onto the ring road, and started south to the Avenue D'Commercia. From there, the driver followed it to the West River Road and continued southwest. Before long, Charyn could make out the brown stone building with its single pier projecting out over the ice of the river. A thin line of white smoke rose from the main factorage chimney.

As soon as the coach pulled up as close to the main door as practicable, Howal stepped out, looking around, followed by Charyn. Both moved to the solid and aged oak door.

Charyn was about to lift the heavy brass knocker, when the door opened, and the graying and wiry Paersyt stood there in a heavy brown leather apron over a worn woolen shirt and trousers.

"I thought it might be you, Your Grace. I couldn't think of anyone else who would be here to see me in this weather." He stepped back into the factorage.

Howal led the way, and Charyn closed the door after he entered. Even though he had been there before, he was still surprised by how large the factorage appeared on the inside.

"I thought I would see how you're coming on your engine," Charyn said blandly.

"I do have a small working model almost completed." The factor led the way to a workbench beside the forge set on the left side of the huge stone-floored hearth. The workbench was smoothly finished and spotless—as it had been before.

"This one doesn't look that different from the one you showed me before," observed Charyn.

"Not at first glance, but let me show you the differences. I told you about the problem with the seals on the second one. This is the third. I had to make a shorter and slightly wider cylinder in order to make it more effective at moving back and forth more quickly without losing power . . ."

As Paersyt explained, Charyn began to understand more of what the factor had in mind.

"... thought that the most useful application would be to power a boat. Once I showed how well it worked on a rivercraft, traders might be interested in a larger version for a seagoing vessel. The crankshaft here can be attached to a set of gears that turn this water screw."

"Water screw?"

"People used to use a different kind of water screw to hand-pump water from a lower level to a higher one. The Naedarans used a version to dewater their lead mines, but they're limited in how high a single one can lift water . . ."

Charyn tried not to frown. He'd never known that the ancient Naedarans even had had lead mines.

"I thought that if I turned the screw in the other direction and removed the casing and just used three angled blades, my water screw would push the water away. I used wooden blades to begin with until I found the right shape and angles."

"Does it work?" asked Charyn quietly.

"It does, but . . ." Paersyt sighed. "It's still not as effective as I'd like. I mean, the engine works, and the gears turn the water screw fast enough, but I think I need a bigger screw that turns more slowly . . . There's a trade-off between blade size and speed, but . . ." The factor shook his head.

"Can you keep working on what I gave you?"

"Yes, Your Grace . . . for another month or so."

"Let me know about your progress then. I'd like to see you get to where you can build an engine big enough to move a sizable boat."

"Yes, sir."

"Now . . . if you will pardon us." Charyn stepped back.

Paersyt only offered a pleasant expression short of a smile as the two left the factorage.

Once Howal and Charyn were in the coach headed back to the chateau, Charyn turned to Howal. "What do you think?"

"He's not after your coin."

"But?"

"It will cost golds for any factor to purchase one of those engines."

"I've thought of that, but they have to pay rowers, or sailors, or feed oxen. As I understand it, once the engine works, you only pay for wood or coal to heat the firebox. Animals and men get tired, and the wind doesn't always blow." Charyn shrugged. "If he can make this engine work, and make bigger ones, it just might give our traders and warships an advantage."

"You think so?"

"I'm already spending tens of thousands of golds on shipbuilding. Even if it costs a thousand to get a larger working engine . . . and it works, in time, it should be cheaper. Even if it's not, to have something that can move a ship when there's no wind would give our ships a great advantage."

"But factors want things cheaply."

"They don't have to buy the engines . . ." *If Paersyt can even make them.* "They'd be more useful for warships, I think." Charyn couldn't help but smile wryly. He was planning as if he'd be rex for years when it still wasn't certain he'd last weeks.

They arrived back at the chateau slightly past the first glass of the afternoon, and slightly before second glass, Sturdyn announced that a Ferrand D'Delcoeur was in the foyer with an urgent need to see the rex.

Charyn feared he knew why. "Have him come up."

Ferrand arrived in the study in what seemed moments, still red-faced and slightly disheveled. Charyn gestured him to the chairs, asking, "I take it matters aren't going well."

"No, Charyn, they're not. Father died late last night. Word hasn't gotten around yet, but I can't believe that it will be long. Over ten thousand golds owed. What am I going to do?"

"Who holds the loans?"

"Most of them are held by the Banque D'Aluse. I'd say over eight thousand. The rest are older. They're owed to the Banque D'Excelsis."

"Because Factor Estafen wouldn't lend any more, and Weezyr would?"

"How . . . ?"

"I've met them both. Shall we say that one is somewhat more honorable."

"But what am I going to do?"

"Deal with Estafen first . . . and immediately. Tell him the truth . . . and the fact that you will pay off the loans with a premium . . . if he gives you time. Then go to Weezyr and offer the same terms. Can you raise any golds?"

"Given a week or two . . . a thousand at most."

"Tell Estafen you've met with me, and I suggested those terms. If he wants some token of good faith, offer him five hundred as soon as you can raise it. Then see if Weezyr will agree. He'll want a larger amount."

"I don't have it."

"Come back and see me once you arrange the best terms you can."

"You seem to think they'll accept some terms."

"They will accept some terms. The only question is whether the terms are affordable. No matter what Weezyr has said, I doubt he wants to take on waiting on the sale of lands . . . or having to sell them himself."

"You said you'd help me."

"I am. The last thing either one of us wants or needs is for Weezyr to know I'll support you, even in the slightest. You want to give the impression that you can raise the amount owed, in time, as well as pay more than interest. If he wants to know . . . tell him you have some sources, but that you won't have their support if you tell who they are."

Charyn had to go over the strategy in different words three times or more before Ferrand finally left the study. Once the study door closed, he took a long and deep breath.

"He's in great trouble," observed Howal.

"His father left him in that position. It sometimes happens. Sometimes, it's avoidable. Sometimes, it's not." With the last words, he was thinking of his own father. Although Charyn wasn't certain, he thought that Lorien had been faced with a situation not entirely of his own making. Charyn couldn't help but wonder just how long Ryel had been working to undermine the regial family.

"Your Grace," called out Sturdyn, "there's a dispatch pouch from Solis. Would you like me to bring it in?"

"If you would." *Another announcement of less than good news.* Since whatever it was had come by dispatch pouch, it had to have been sent by either navy marshal Tynan or by Governor Voralch. Tynan most likely would have sent anything to Vaelln first; so the message had to have come from Voralch.

Howal took the dispatch pouch.

"Go ahead and open the pouch. Whatever's inside will be sealed as well."

The imager broke the seal on the pouch and extracted a small oblong wrapped in oilskin. After unwrapping the oilskin, he handed the oblong, with a piece of thin leather around it, to Charyn, who peeled the leather off the envelope and noted the green seal of the regional gov-

ernor. Without a word, he broke the seal and took out the letter. He
began to read.

> Your Grace—
>
> I have received the most recent dispatch, the one signed
> jointly by yourself and Minister Aevidyr. While I understand
> the financial position facing the rex, especially with regard to
> the unrest created by factors displeased by the attacks on their
> merchant vessels, I must stress that my physical position is
> simply untenable at this point. Without a permanent resi-
> dence suitable for the conduct of my position as Regional
> Governor, I will not be able to long function in the fashion
> required. Because I would not wish you to be surprised, I
> thought you should be informed of my situation immediately.
>
> From the inquiries that I have made, there is no structure
> suitable for both the personal and functional demands of the
> position as regional governor for less than 2,000 golds . . .

"Another form of blackmail," murmured Charyn, largely to himself.
Before even finishing the letter, he looked up. "Howal, would you have
someone summon Minister Aevidyr?"

"Yes, sir."

Charyn had long since finished the letter by the time Aevidyr entered
the study and was considering his options. He gestured for the minister
to sit down and then handed him Voralch's missive. "Read it."

Aevidyr nodded, took the sheet, and read. When he finished he looked
up. "I cannot say that this is unexpected."

"Why not? Did he send you any other correspondence before
this?"

"No, sir. It is just that . . . well . . . Governor Voralch has always felt
that, since Solis is the ancestral home of the regial family—"

"That's bulldung. It was the center of government for only a few generations. The regial family has been here far longer, and the true ancestral
home is buried under lava in Extela."

"The governor, nonetheless, has expressed that sentiment, and apparently believes it to be so."

"Perhaps you should take a trip to Solis and see what you can find
for a residence."

"You are jesting, are you not, Your Grace?" Aevidyr could not quite hide his appalled expression.

"Am I?" Charyn waited a moment before adding, "Perhaps I am. But I think that the regional governor needs to be summoned here to explain a number of matters."

"Sir?"

"Draft a message for me to sign requiring his immediate departure from Solis and return to L'Excelsis posthaste. I will be very disappointed if he discovers my requirement before he receives that letter."

"Yes, sir."

Charyn could tell that Aevidyr was anything but pleased, but he just gestured for the minister to leave.

After a time, he turned to Howal. "Draft a letter to Marshal Vaelln telling him that I have required Regional Governor Voralch to return to L'Excelsis to explain certain matters, and that I would like him to take the necessary steps so that Sea Marshal Tynan can assure that Voralch does indeed return to L'Excelsis without any delay."

Howal nodded. "I'll have it in less than a quint."

"Thank you."

Charyn glanced toward the window, then shook his head. There was little point in looking out at the snow and gray stones. He just wondered what else might go wrong before the day ended. He didn't want to think, for the moment, about the rest of the week, although he knew he would.

59

Mardi came and went without much change, including the weather, which remained cold and dry, and the snow piled around L'Excelsis remained, although it became sootier and dirtier with each passing day. When Charyn read the latest edition of *Veritum* on Meredi morning, he noted, in particular, the lengthy article about the continued losses of merchant shipping, with a few comments about how the rex seemed unable to do much about the problem.

He set down the newssheet and shook his head before addressing two more petitions sent to him by Sanafryt. The first dealt with the denial of a small holder's request that the Minister of Administration failed to repair a post-road bridge outside of Laaryn because the path underneath had been destroyed by a flood and the small holder had been fined for using a post road to move his sheep from one pasture to another. The petition also asked for redress of the ill created by the fine.

The second petition requested a reduction in tariffs because lands formerly used for crops and pasture had been flooded by the runoff from an abandoned copper mine and the ground rendered permanently fallow.

Much as Charyn tried to concentrate on the first petition, his thoughts kept going back to Ryel. So he was almost relieved when, just after ninth glass, Moencriff announced, "Army courier with a dispatch from Marshal Vaelln."

Charyn nodded. It was about time the marshal replied to his instructions for dealing with Voralch. "Have him come in."

The study door opened, and the courier stepped inside, then stopped for a long moment, seeming to adjust the courier pouch as Howal moved toward the ranker in the heavy gray-green winter riding jacket to accept it.

"Howal! He's no courier!" Charyn bolted to his feet, shoving the chair back and drawing his pistol, too slowly, as he saw the green-clad false courier hurl the dispatch pouch toward him, then jerk the door open and begin to bolt.

WHUUMPP!!

Charyn found himself flung back into the bookcase, his ears ringing and gasping for breath. He looked to where the courier had been, gaping at what he saw—a crumpled and blackened pile of cloth, flesh, and other unrecognizable items, topped with a scattering of small iron shards. He didn't glimpse much blood. He turned just in time to see Howal stagger and begin to crumple.

Pistol still in hand, Charyn jumped toward the imager, catching him one-armed, and almost falling himself before managing to ease the unconscious figure to the carpet, not quite so gently as he would have liked.

"Sir! Sir!" Moencriff's voice seemed to come from a great distance, yet with a ringing echo behind it, as happened when Charyn had been firing his pistol in the covered outside courtyard.

"Send for Maitre Kaylet! Now!" Charyn slipped the pistol back into his jacket, then turned Howal over. He could see that the imager was still breathing, and nothing looked obviously broken. Nor was he bleeding from anywhere that Charyn could see.

Still dazed from what had happened so quickly, he remained kneeling beside the injured imager. He also realized that his shoulders and lower back hurt.

Moencriff reappeared in the door. "They're on their way, sir." Then another guard appeared beside Moencriff in the door, and Charyn realized, belatedly, that it was Maertyl.

Moencriff looked down, then looked away, as he seemed to be trying not to gag or retch at what lay just inside the study door, a door which appeared to be cracked in a number of places, as well as smeared with various substances.

"Oh . . ."

At the sound from Howal, Charyn looked down again and saw that the imager's eyelids were moving.

"Don't move yet," he said. "You need to lie there for a few moments."

Howal slowly opened his eyes. "You . . . all right?"

"I seem to be. How do you feel?"

"Sore . . . all over. What about . . ."

"Your shields kept the explosion around him. There's not much recognizable."

At that moment, Kaylet burst past Maertyl and into the study, stopping only when he stood over Howal and Charyn.

"He's going to be all right . . . I think," Charyn said. "I told him not to try to sit up until he felt better."

"I feel . . . like I could sit up. It's cold down here."

Both Charyn and Kaylet slowly helped Howal into a sitting position. Then Charyn gingerly stood, abruptly realizing that his legs were shaking. He took two wobbly steps to where he could put his right hand on the conference table to steady himself.

"Are you all right, sir?" asked Maertyl.

"I think Howal and I both need hot cider or something like it." Charyn eased himself around the table and into the chair at the end.

"Yes, sir." Moencriff ducked back from the doorway.

Kaylet helped Howal into the adjacent chair, then said, "You don't seem to have any bumps or bruises."

"His shields held long enough, I think," replied Charyn. "I managed to get there in time to break his fall." He motioned for Maertyl to come over.

"What happened?" asked Kaylet in a voice just short of a command.

"Moencriff announced a courier from Marshal Vaelln," said Charyn. "The courier came inside and stopped and did something with the dispatch pouch. I realized he wasn't a real courier and called out a warning to Howal . . ." Charyn finished with a quick description of what had happened after that.

"Your Grace, might I ask how you knew the man wasn't a courier?" asked Maertyl.

"I can't tell you. There was just something not right about his uniform, and about the way he looked at me. I might have been wrong, but that's why I yelled to Howal."

"I'm very glad you did," said Howal slowly. "We both would have been killed if I hadn't thrown shields around him. They weren't very good shields."

"They were good enough," Charyn pointed out. "I still don't understand how he set off the explosives in the pouch."

"He must have used a pressure striker," replied Kaylet. "You squeeze it and it sends sparks down a tube to a special powder. They're used on ships sometimes when it's really wet."

Pressure striker? Charyn was still thinking about that when Moencriff reappeared. "There's some hot mulled wine coming. It's ready. The cider is cold."

"Thank you. That will do." Charyn turned back to Howal. "Are you feeling better?"

"I'm supposed to be the one asking you," replied the imager ruefully.

Charyn stiffened. "Maertyl, there will likely be a message coming. Someone, somewhere will deliver a message. Most likely it will be a public messenger, or someone innocent, but let all the guards know immediately. Hold anyone who delivers a message. Anyone! It might be that they can tell us something about who hired them. Don't open the message!"

"Yes, sir." Maertyl left the study not quite at a run.

Before long, the hot mulled wine arrived, along with Chelia, who took one long and searching look to see that Charyn was fine, and then vanished. As a result, Charyn suspected, shortly after that, two junior ostlers arrived and carted off the remains of the unfortunately false courier, and after that, two scullery maids arrived, and they scrubbed away the last remnants of the near-disaster.

While the maids were finishing, Maertyl returned. "Sir, all the guards have been told what to do if they're approached."

"Good."

"You should also know that we've stabled and unsaddled the dead man's horse. It's marked with an army brand and all the tack looks to be army."

"Keep the mount for now. I'll send a message to Marshal Vaelln about someone stealing an army mount and using it to impersonate a courier." Charyn wanted to see the marshal's response. He also wondered if someone had ambushed or otherwise replaced a real courier who might have been bringing Vaelln's reply to Charyn's orders dealing with Voralch.

After Maertyl departed, Charyn quickly wrote the message to Vaelln and had Howal arrange to have it sent.

By first glass, only the cracks and scars in the door gave any hint of what had occurred, and Charyn was back sitting behind his desk, still sipping the vaguely warm mulled wine. Howal was doing the same where he sat at the conference table.

As Charyn thought over the morning's attack, he realized something else, something obvious in hindsight. Whoever planned it knew that couriers from Vaelln were allowed into the study, and that was not known to someone unfamiliar to the chateau.

Then, just before second glass, Faelln appeared with a street urchin, wrapped in rags. A second chateau guard carried an envelope.

"Just put the envelope on the corner of the desk," Charyn said, reaching for his letter knife. "I'll read it, and then we'll see what to do with you, young fellow."

The ragged youth glared at Faelln. "I didn't do nothing wrong. I didn't."

"No, you didn't," said Charyn, his voice far more calm than he felt. "But the man who hired you to deliver the message did. We'll get to that shortly." He picked up the letter, with "Rex Charyn" written in standard merchant hand on the outside, and a blank seal impressed on the black wax. He studied it. The seal had the same indentation at the edge. He was careful to slit the envelope so as not to disturb the seal.

The message didn't surprise him:

> You have continually failed to address the problems of the factors.
> If you do not, the attacks will continue until you do or you perish.

Charyn nodded. *If the attack had been successful, there would have been a different message, one addressed to Bhayrn.* Most likely both had been written, and then Ryel or his agent had watched the chateau, knowing there would have been a great uproar if Charyn had been killed or severely wounded. He replaced the message in the envelope, most carefully, and turned to the youth.

"How much did he pay you?"

"Not a copper . . . not a copper."

Faelln glared at the youth in the ragged clothes. "Just hand it over, all if it. Before we shake it out of you."

The boy seemed to wilt. Slowly he rummaged in his ragged garments before coming up with a silver.

"What about the rest?" asked Charyn coldly.

After a moment, a second silver appeared beside the first.

Charyn took the silvers and studied them. Each had a mint mark, one a curled "N" and the other a blocky "T," neither the stylized "L" that graced the golds minted by Lythoryn. *But Lythoryn does mint silvers.* Charyn smiled sardonically.

"I earned them, I did," the youth protested.

"You did indeed." Charyn turned to Howal. "Would you please go down to Norstan and tell him I need some silvers." As the boy turned his head, Charyn mouthed "four" to Howal before saying, "Two silvers. I'm keeping these for proof, but our young friend deserves his pay. That is, if he's willing to tell us about the fellow who told him to deliver the envelope."

Howal nodded and slipped out of the study.

"You'd better tell all of it," added Faelln.

The youth looked from Faelln to Charyn and back again. Then he swallowed. "He was tall, taller'n me, by a good two heads. Not so tall as you," he said to Faelln.

"What was he wearing?"

"A big brown coat, and boots, and a gray scarf wrapped all around his face. Only could see his eyes."

"Did he have a beard?" pressed Faelln.

"I couldn't tell. He had the scarf wrapped over everything, excepting his head. He wore a black cap . . . came down over the scarf."

"What about his hands?" asked Charyn.

"He had on gloves. Black gloves, leather, the kind the swells wear . . ."

"Were his hands large or small?"

The youth looked at Charyn helplessly.

Charyn kept looking at him. Hard.

"I couldn't say, sir . . . bigger'n mine, not real big like a docker's."

"Boots—what about them? What color?"

"Black. They were black. Saw them good. With heels. Not low, not real high."

"What about his voice?"

"He was sorta hoarse. Gave me the shakes. The kind that you don't want talking to you."

"Was it a big low voice?" asked Charyn.

"He didn't talk rumbly or squeaky. He didn't talk all that much. Just told me he'd be watching, and he'd cut the silvers outa me if I didn't deliver the paper."

Although Charyn and Faelln questioned the youth about everything they could think of for another quint, a good half quint after Howal had returned and surreptitiously handed four silvers to Charyn, in the end they learned nothing else about the man who had paid the boy to deliver the message.

Finally, Charyn stood and addressed Faelln. "Keep him until it's dark. Then take him out the rear entrance and through the barns and let him go there."

"What about my silvers?"

Even though the boy's voice quavered, Charyn admired his pluck. He took the four silvers from his pocket and handed them to the youth. "There's a bit extra there for your time, and your answers."

"I'll make sure it's well after dark, sir," Faelln said.

"Good."

Once the two had left, Howal looked to Charyn. "You think someone might try to grab him and find out what he saw?"

"That's possible. It's also possible that some of the other urchins might decide he should share. I'm thinking he's scared enough that he'll hide for a while. I don't think whoever paid him knew him in the slightest. That would be too dangerous. They also paid him in advance, and that meant they didn't want to be around when he was caught."

"You think they planned that he'd be caught?"

"That's why he got two silvers. No one else would pay more than a few coppers for a boy to run a message. They expected the guards would hold him, especially if the explosion had done what it was intended to do. It's another form of message."

"That they'll spend whatever is necessary to destroy you?"

"Doesn't it seem that way to you?"

"I'd have to admit that it does, but this seems to go beyond just being angry at you, sir. It's almost like it's personal."

Charyn laughed. "When someone is trying to kill you, it gets to feeling very personal. But I understand what you mean." That was just another aspect of the attacks that reinforced his more-than-suspicions about Ryel, as did the two silvers.

Thinking of the silvers reminded him of something else he'd forgotten to do. "Moencriff!"

The guard opened the study door. "Yes, sir?"

"Would you have someone send for Minister Alucar?"

"Yes, sir."

When Alucar arrived in the study, Charyn had gone back to reading the second petition and thinking about it. He didn't bother with gesturing the minister toward the chairs. "Alucar, I have a strange request. I need two newly minted silvers with a mint mark by Lythoryn."

The Finance Minister frowned.

"It's necessary," said Charyn, knowing he was explaining nothing. "Sometime in the next day or so."

"Yes, sir."

"That's all." Charyn smiled pleasantly, ignoring the puzzled expression on Alucar's face and returning to the petition, one he knew he could at least grant. While he might not be able to change the law dealing with foul substances in the water, he could certainly reduce the tariffs on a small holder who suffered because of them.

Late in the afternoon, just before fifth glass, Subcommander Luerryn arrived at the chateau and was promptly shown in to meet with Charyn.

As soon as he was seated in the middle chair across from Charyn, Luerryn began. "Marshal Vaelln sent me, Your Grace, as soon as he got your message about events here at the chateau earlier today. That is, as soon as he made inquiries and had more information."

"And?"

"Begging your pardon, sir, I did take the liberty of inspecting the mount that the impostor used before I came up to report to you. The horse was stolen from a courier two weeks ago, along the Great Highway near Tuuryl, along with his spare uniform and boots."

"How did that happen?"

"We don't know. The courier was found dead in an adjoining stream a week ago. He was still in uniform. He'd been dead for some time. Couriers aren't supposed to stop for anything. Some don't understand why. Then something like that happens, and they understand, for a time. The marshal greatly regrets that any lapse on the part of the dead courier caused you such inconvenience." Luerryn waited, then said, "Could you determine anything about the impostor that I could tell the marshal?"

"Very little. He was caught too close to the bomb he wanted to throw at me when it went off."

"It appears as though you were fortunate, Your Grace."

"Fortunate enough considering." After the slightest hesitation, Charyn went on, "I haven't had a response to my previous message to the marshal."

Luerryn extended an envelope. "My apologies, Your Grace. The courier was about to depart when your latest message arrived, and the marshal thought you might be wary of another army courier So he sent me to tell you about the missing horse, and to see if you had found the mount of the impostor. And to deliver the message."

Charyn took the sealed envelope. "Thank you. I do appreciate your coming to inform me personally."

Luerryn inclined his head. "It was my pleasure, Your Grace."

"Scarcely that, in this weather. But I do appreciate the information." Charyn stood.

"The marshal wanted you to know," said Luerryn as he immediately rose, then inclined his head, before turning and leaving the study.

Charyn opened the envelope. The message from Vaelln was brief . . . and abrupt.

Your Grace—

In accord with your request, I have sent orders to Sea Marshal Tynan to arrange a secure escort for Regional Governor Voralch back to L'Excelsis. I have ordered that the Governor be delivered directly to you as soon as possible.

Charyn nodded. Vaelln wasn't pleased with the order, but he and his officers and men would comply. He thought about sending another message asking how the inventory of materials recovered from the ruined palace had gone, then shook his head. That could wait . . . for a time.

60

Just before dinner, Charyn walked into the family parlor. Although he wasn't surprised to arrive before Bhayrn, he was there before his mother, for once, and that was unusual. Even more unusual was the fact that his brother and mother arrived together.

"Good evening," he offered.

"Good evening," replied Bhayrn cheerfully. "I'm glad to see that you aren't noticeably battered and bruised."

"No. A few sore places on my back where I hit the bookcase. Howal's the one sore all over, I think."

"Maertyl said that someone disguised themselves as an army courier . . ."

"Complete with uniform and the proper mount—stolen two weeks ago, according to Marshal Vaelln. There was also another threatening and warning letter."

"Oh?" Chelia's single word did not hold any suggestion of surprise.

"Much the same as before," replied Charyn. "Something to the effect that I have failed to address the problems of the factors and warning me that the attacks will continue until I do or until they succeed. He is persistent, whoever he is. I'll grant that."

"How can you do any more?" asked Bhayrn. "Even I know warships don't grow on trees and that it costs golds to build them."

"I don't think he's giving much consideration to that. Angry men don't often listen to logic." Charyn gestured toward the dining room door. "Shall we? I'm rather hungry."

"Of course," replied Bhayrn.

Once the three were seated, and Chelia had said the gratitude, and Charyn had poured the wine, Bhayrn said, "Why are they persisting?"

"Perhaps because we don't know who they are, and until I can stop whoever it is," replied Charyn, "the attacks are likely to continue."

"It has to be a factor, maybe even a group of them," asserted Bhayrn. "Who else could it be?"

As his brother spoke, Charyn watched Chelia, but their mother just nodded faintly, without saying a word.

"With all the effort the attacks have taken," Charyn replied, "it would appear that whoever is behind them has to be wealthy and powerful. It can't be some petty factor or an angry impoverished High Holder. It has to be a wealthy factor, or even possibly a wealthy High Holder."

"I suppose," returned Bhayrn dubiously, "but the notes I saw kept talking about the factors, and you just said that the latest one did as well. That suggests a wealthy factor."

"All of which means, if he is wealthy, that I can't very well punish all the less well-off factors."

"That would seem to present a problem," said Bhayrn blandly. "You'll have to find a way around that. That is, if you can't immediately discover who the wretch is." He paused. "I'd like to use the plain coach tomorrow. If that's agreeable."

"It is. I have no plans. Just give consideration to the horses, the driver, and the guards . . . as you always do."

"I can do that." Bhayrn smiled, then took a careful sip of the red wine Charyn had poured for him. "Ah . . . the Mantes red. Thank you. It's a good robust wine for winter, even if it's not traditional for pork."

"It is a good wine," agreed Chelia, "although I prefer the Cloisonyt white with the pork, especially with the cream sauce. The red is a trace heavy for me."

Charyn nodded, sipped his wine, cut a slice of pork, and then ate it, knowing the rest of the dinner conversation would be pleasant.

After dinner, Charyn walked Chelia up the stairs to her sitting room and invited himself in, closing the door firmly behind them.

Even before he settled into a chair facing his mother, he asked, "Why is Bhayrn being so civil? Not that I mind it in the slightest, but he was more polite tonight than he's been in weeks."

"It might be because I pointed out that he was likely to feel extraordinarily guilty if one of these attempts at killing you succeeds, not to mention the fact that, if it does, he'll be the next target."

Charyn nodded.

"That nod suggests you agree," said Chelia sardonically.

"Unhappily, it makes a great deal of sense, especially if the man behind happens to be the one I think it is. There is, unfortunately, the small matter of proving that . . . or even coming close."

"Coming close, after all the attempts, might well be sufficient, dear."

"Why do you think that?" asked Charyn, genuinely curious.

"Because you've been incredibly calm amid all of the attempts. You've worked out a compromise on tariffs, and . . . well . . . I hate to say it, but you seem more levelheaded and less prone to rage than your immediate predecessors."

In short, the High Holders and factors just might lean to your side rather than chance yet another rex. Charyn managed a frown. "There still has to be some proof. Plausible proof."

"Of course there does." Chelia smiled. "I thought the white Cloisonyt was the better vintage for the pork, although the red is more suited to a winter evening."

"I've always been partial to whites, just as Bhayrn has been to reds." Charyn returned his mother's smile, knowing that anything else he said verging on the day's events would be deflected by yet another observation about wine, food, weather, or possibly speculative comments about how Aloryana was doing at the Collegium.

At the moment, that was fine with him. He really didn't want to think more about the past day.

61

Jeudi passed without incident, for which Charyn was most grateful, and there wasn't even a story in *Tableta* about the explosion in the chateau, most likely because the newssheet learned about it too late to print. That newssheet silence did not extend to Vendrei, because almost the entire front page of *Veritum* consisted of a story focused on the events at the Chateau D'Rex and affecting Charyn, a story that Charyn immediately read, slowly and carefully, once he reached his study.

On Meredi an explosion occurred in the Chateau D'Rex. It was the second explosion within the Chateau in the past month. A former worker at the Chateau reported that the first explosion was created by a disgruntled officer in the Chateau Guard. While the explosion killed the officer, it caused only minor injuries to the rex . . .

Which former worker? Keithell or his assistant?

. . . no indications that the second explosion caused any injuries, but a senior Army officer visited the rex later on Meredi afternoon. The Chateau seneschal offered no comments except to insist that the rex was in good health and continuing his daily work . . .

The fact that explosions have occurred suggests unhappiness on the part of some individuals, possibly factors, because of the inability of the rex to move more quickly in dealing with the losses of Solidaran merchant ships and the continuing threat posed by Jariolan privateers and warships . . . at least one regional governor has quietly expressed dissatisfaction with the rex . . .

Voralch or Warheon? Both?

. . . spice trade is so affected by the Jariolan threat that various factors councils are pushing the rex to increase tariffs on High Holders so that factors don't have to pay as much to protect their ships and cargoes. For all the High Holder dissatisfaction with the rex, after two failed revolutions . . . seems unlikely that High Holders would attempt a third with all that they might lose . . . can be said that whoever is behind the unwise attempts on Rex Charyn and the regial family should cease such counterproductive efforts. Some have even speculated that whoever is behind them is most likely deeply involved in trade with Otelyrn and the Abierto Isles . . . One can only hope that, after his meeting with the joint councils next week, Rex Charyn will have a clearer plan for dealing with the crisis. If not, matters could worsen . . .

Charyn shook his head and set down the newssheet, thinking. He couldn't help but feel that Ryel believed he would succeed, even if the attacks failed. And that made an unfortunate kind of sense, because Ryel had planned the attacks on several different levels. If he didn't kill Charyn, he would either force Charyn to act against factors or succeed in portraying the factors as selfish and greedy and thus strengthen the position of the High Holders. Worse, if the attacks continued, Charyn's failure to stop them would portray Charyn as bumbling and ineffectual. And all that, too, was another indication—once more totally without physical proof—that Ryel had to be behind it all.

Charyn paused. Had Ryel also been behind the fire destroying the factors' exchange in Solis? *But why would he have been?* Just to create unhappiness with the factors so that they'd be harder for Charyn to deal with? That was a possibility, but another thing Charyn might never discover.

All the items of physical proof he had, the letters, the golds, and the two "replacement" silvers Alucar had procured for him, were indicative, but far from conclusive. Even if Cauthyrn and Churwyl had survived, they could only have said that someone had hired them, but not who. The street urchin who had delivered the last warning had given a description that suggested a woman, but could have been either man or woman.

There was no help for it. He couldn't afford to wait longer, not the way things were going. He took out paper and pen and began to write. Even knowing what he wanted to put in ink, it took Charyn almost a glass to word the letter to Marshal Vaelln to convey the impression he wanted. Even so, he read it again, slowly, word for word.

Marshal Vaelln—

As you doubtless know and may have read in the newssheets, both the High
Holders and factors, particularly those involved in shipping and especially in the
spice trade dealing with the Abierto Isles and Otelyrn, have expressed growing
concern about the ongoing losses of Solidaran merchant vessels. You have been most
persuasive in educating me as to the realities of the situation, and the members of
both the High Council and Solidaran Factors' Council respect your knowledge and
your integrity. For this reason, and in view of the most recent articles in the
newssheets, I am requesting that you brief the joint councils at their monthly
meeting at the Chateau D'Rex, next Meredi, the eighteenth of Fevier at the first
glass of the afternoon.

   I would also request that you bring a full mounted squad and arrive a glass
before the meeting, in the event, however unlikely it might prove to be, that the
meeting might provoke yet another attack on the regial family, or members of the
councils. The presence of Army troopers should also serve as a deterrent to other
possible unpleasant events.

After reviewing the letter once more, Charyn signed and sealed it,
then had Howal make a copy and arrange for its delivery to the marshal.

   When Howal returned, Charyn was writing out a listing of all the
items of indication or evidence, but he set that sheet aside as he saw that
Howal remained standing. "You had a question, Howal?"

   "Yes, sir. I did. How much longer do you believe that you will be
needing my services?"

   "Is that your question or Maitre Alastar's?" Charyn smiled pleasantly.

   "Mine, sir. Although I believe Maitre Alastar would also like to know.
You seem to have dispatched and otherwise handled a rather large amount
of correspondence, petitions, and opinions, to the point that your actual
need for a private secretary . . ."

   "Is much diminished?" Charyn nodded. "That's true. And you have
helped immeasurably. Without all your assistance I would still be struggling through petitions and reviewing justicer opinions. Without your
shields, I would be dead, at least on two occasions. What you have tactfully refrained from observing is that the attacks upon my person have
continued . . . and it would appear that they will continue for the foreseeable future, since there is almost no evidence of a physical nature and
no one who can say who is behind such acts. Is that not so?"

   "It would appear that way, sir."

"It does. I had originally asked Maitre Alastar for your services until next Meredi's meetings with the two councils. There will almost certainly be a need for certain reports after the meeting. There always has been. I don't see that changing. Your help with those would be most appreciated. After that . . . I trust you will not be unduly disappointed to return to the Collegium." Charyn kept his tone of voice light and humorous.

"Even though the attacks . . ."

"I cannot ask the Collegium to safeguard me and to keep risking your life because angry individuals are unhappy with me as rex. After the changes that Maitre Dylert implemented with the Chateau Guard, and the ones Maitre Kaylet and you are completing with the rest of the chateau functions, I think I will be reasonably safe, given certain personal precautions. As we have seen, the assassin master is already having a more and more difficult time in getting to me personally. We will make it more so."

"Sir . . . are you certain . . . ?"

"If some great change occurs between now and next week's meeting, I do reserve the right to ask you to stay longer, but . . . as matters stand, I believe I've taken excessive advantage of you already. And of the Collegium." Charyn offered a wry smile.

"The time I've spent here has been valuable to me as well."

"In learning how many mistakes a young ruler can make, perhaps?"

"You seem to have avoided many, from what I've observed."

"Whether I've avoided enough remains to be seen."

"Maitre Alastar says that you can only avoid mistakes through experience, but you only get experience through making mistakes."

Charyn couldn't help smiling and shaking his head. The aphorism sounded all too like the Maitre.

By third glass, Charyn had thought and prepared all that he could, or all that he thought he could, although he'd likely wake up in the middle of the night thinking about something he'd forgotten. He dismissed Howal for the day, promising not to leave the chateau, and made his way down to the music room.

Palenya was, once more, copying music.

"Don't you ever rest?" he asked cheerfully.

"Not when I'm being paid." She offered an embarrassed smile. "I'm making copies of some of your music to give to the Collegium. You don't mind, do you?"

"No. I wish I'd thought of that. It's a good idea."

"You can't think of everything."

"No, I can't, and I haven't." *Unfortunately.*

"You look worried," said Palenya.

"I am. Did you read *Veritum?*"

"I heard that the newssheets are saying you're not doing enough. What else can you do?"

"Not much. Not that Solidar can afford without higher tariffs, and I've arranged for those. As much as was possible. That's why I'm here."

Her brows knit into a puzzled frown. "Oh?"

"Since I've done all I can do for the moment, I thought I'd take a break and work on Nocturne Number Three . . . and then persuade you to play the duet with me. That way, maybe my thoughts will be clearer when I go back to the study and look at more papers and petitions."

There really weren't any more petitions to address, but Charyn didn't want to admit that he'd likely just sit behind his desk and stew. Besides, he liked being with Palenya, and she'd made it all too clear that such times were numbered and not likely to last.

That's all too true, one way or the other.

62

Samedi morning at eighth glass found Charyn standing at the study window, looking down at the courtyard where two days before, there had been all manner of tack stacked in neat piles, the result of Kaylet's decision to totally clean and reorganize the tack rooms, after discovering that there was an older chamber in the back of the stable, the entrance to which had been covered by a hayrack. Inside the old chamber had been moldering and discarded saddles, bridles, traces, and chains, but in addition, a number of items that, once cleaned, were completely usable.

Kaylet had also presented Charyn and Norstan with newly drawn plans for every chamber in the barns, stables, and sheds to the rear of the courtyard. Charyn had checked the archives, and discovered that no current plans existed. In fact, he wasn't certain there had ever been plans, although there must have been.

At ninth glass, Sturdyn rapped on the door. "Maitre Kaylet and Stablemaster Aedryt are ready for you to inspect the changes to the stable and the barns."

Charyn pulled on his heavy riding jacket and, with Howal beside him, headed down the grand staircase, and then to the rear foyer and out into the rear courtyard.

Kaylet and Aedryt stood waiting in front of the main stable doors.

"Good morning, Your Grace," offered Aedryt.

"Good morning," replied Charyn cheerfully, taking a moment to study the new stablemaster, a stocky man with black hair and a short well-trimmed black beard who looked some ten years older than Charyn. "Are you pleased with the changes, Aedryt?"

"Yes, sir. Very much, sir."

"Many of the changes were his idea," added Kaylet.

"Much of the work could not have been done without Maitre Kaylet," Aedryt said quickly. "We should start with the main stable." He gestured to the doors.

"Lead on," said Charyn.

Once inside the stable, Charyn could immediately see that each stall had been scrubbed clean, and the wood re-smoothed. The stone flooring had been scraped and scrubbed as well, and the only noticeable smell was that of hay.

"I thought you'd like to see the new study for the stablemaster," Kaylet said, leading Charyn toward the west end of the stable. Where the old and battered hayrack had stood, on one side was a wooden rack for barrels, and on the other an open door.

Charyn looked inside. The old chamber had been cleaned and the walls refinished—through a certain amount of imaging, Charyn was certain—and turned into a study for Aedryt, with a small table desk and file chests for the ledgers to keep track of all the supplies used by the activities under the stablemaster and with two locked cabinets against the south wall.

"Those are for the more valuable supplies, sir," explained Aedryt as he pointed to the cabinets.

From the main stable, Aedryt led the way to the coach barn, explaining as he went, "We rearranged the main coach barn so that we could hitch to either coach without moving the other, and we rebuilt the tack room on the north corner so that it's easier to get to the harnesses . . ."

Charyn just listened, but he studied each and every aspect of the main barn, and the smaller barn that held the carts, the chaise, and two wagons, as well as the changes to the grain bins and the haylofts.

By the time the group returned to the rear courtyard more than a glass later, Charyn was almost overwhelmed by what Kaylet—and Aedryt—had accomplished in little more than a month, and he turned to the pair. "I cannot overstate how much I appreciate all you have done. Everything appears almost new-built, and it's clear that great effort and much thought have gone into this . . . transformation."

Aedryt inclined his head. "Thank you, Your Grace. I'm happy you're pleased. The men and boys all find it a much better place now."

"I can certainly see why." Charyn paused. "It seems to me that you deserve at least a token of appreciation."

"Your Grace, everyone pitched in."

Charyn smiled. "Then everyone deserves a small token of appreciation. There will be an extra silver for everyone . . . and a bit more for you, Aedryt. I'd like it to be more, but . . . as you must know, times are hard."

Aedryt actually swallowed, Charyn noticed, before he said, "We didn't do it . . . in hopes . . ."

"I know. The care everyone took shows. But my appreciation doesn't buy shoes or the like."

"Thank you, sir." Aedryt inclined his head.

"You all deserve it, you especially for taking charge and getting it done." *Without beatings and theft.* Charyn nodded in return, then turned and headed for the rear entrance to the chateau. Although the day was warmer than those of the past week, he still found himself shivering as he stepped into the rear foyer.

"That was quite something," he finally said to Howal as they climbed the grand staircase.

"It was. Kaylet and Aedryt worked hard." Howal lowered his voice as he continued, "You know that no one in the chateau can remember the last time your father showed appreciation for anything?"

Charyn couldn't say he was surprised, except that Howal knew that. "You've been talking to everyone, haven't you?"

Howal chuckled. "Not so much lately. I heard more when no one knew I was an imager."

"What else have you heard that I don't want to hear and that I likely should?"

"I think you know all that you need to know."

"That's not exactly an answer."

"You know that you can't trust Aevidyr or Sanafryt to do anything but what is in their own interest . . . or that Alucar is good with numbers and is honest, but doesn't like to offer unpleasant news to you. If you rely on what others tell you, you become their captive. Listen, but don't rely on it unless you know it yourself or can find out."

"That's still not an answer."

"It's the only one that's in your own interest."

"That sounds more like Maitre Alastar."

"That's because he advised me to tell you that."

Charyn laughed softly.

When they reached the study, Charyn made his way to the desk and began to write out the authorization for the extra pay to be handed out by Aedryt.

By the first glass of the afternoon, Charyn had sent Howal back to Imagisle for the rest of the weekend. Then, with nothing immediate to do, and no desire to brave the cold, or another possible attempt on his life, he retreated to his sitting room with a history of Solidar. A quint or so after second glass, he stopped and massaged his forehead. He had just reread a passage that had struck him as strange. He read it for a third time.

> By the time of the first Rex Regis, the decline of the scholariums across the continent of Lydar had become precipitous, largely caused by a distrust of the secretiveness of the scholars and of their dubious connections with those in power, as in the covert alliance between the scholars of Tilbor and the Tilboran hill holders, an alliance destroyed by the success of Rex Regis . . . It can be argued that the rise of the Collegium Imago sealed the fate of the last of the scholariums, in large part because the rigid discipline, the high personal ethics, and the isolation of the imagers from the day-to-day power struggles of the elites contrasted all too favorably with the apparent pettiness, secrecy, and seeming grasping for gold and favors on the part of the scholars . . .

Seeming . . . apparent . . . ? Charyn frowned, sitting in his armchair and continuing to ponder what the author had written. Yes, the imagers did have high personal standards, and they were clearly well disciplined . . . but did they really refrain from getting involved in power struggles? Or was the key phrase "day-to-day" power struggles?

At that moment, there was a knock on the sitting room door.

"Yes?"

"Are you occupied?"

Charyn recognized his mother's voice. "No. I'm just reading. You can come in."

The door opened, and Chelia stepped inside. "If you have a moment, dear?"

"I do . . . at least for the next three glasses."

"You're having dinner here with Palenya?"

"You must already know that." Charyn's words were wry.

"Are you being fair to her?" Chelia eased into the other armchair, turning slightly so that she could face her son.

"She's made it very clear that she will be gone before long, one way or the other. I've arranged for her to teach other students at—"

"I know. Aloryana wrote me about it."

"Palenya's very quietly clever. She's the one who planted the entire idea about the clavecin and teaching imager students. Did you give her the idea?"

"I only said that it was a shame Aloryana couldn't continue improving her skills on the clavecin."

"I should leave governing to you and her." Charyn's voice was not quite bitter. "I'd do better."

"You've done quite well so far under the circumstances."

"With other people's ideas."

Chelia sniffed. "There are ideas everywhere. What counts is knowing which ones are good and making them work."

"Why did you stop by? Just to suggest that I let Palenya go and get on with finding a suitable wife?"

"A suitable wife, as you put it, would be most unsuited to you. Were Palenya younger and able to have children we could have trumped up a way to make it work. She isn't, and she knows it. Whether you want to recognize it or not, I like her a great deal."

Charyn didn't know what to say.

"It took me a long time to find her. And no, I don't think you should hurry to find a wife. That would be a disaster, because you might actually make it work with the wrong woman, and that would ruin everything."

"The wrong woman? Who would be the wrong woman?"

"Any woman who flattered your considerable ego. A ruler needs a solid ego, but he also needs someone who loves him who won't flatter that ego, but who is gentle about it without yielding." Before Charyn could respond, she held up a hand, almost imperiously. "We can talk more about this later. None of it will matter unless you can deal with your most pressing problem."

"How do you propose I do that?"

"I'm not the rex, dear. I'm only your mother. I'll only say that there are times to be kind, and times to be quietly and coldly ruthless. This is one of those times. You know that as well as I do." Chelia smiled and rose from the armchair. "That is a very good history, by the way. I'm glad you're reading it and not the Sanclere."

Charyn just sat in the armchair for a long time after she left.

63

Solayi might have dawned cloudy, but it was sunny and bright by the time Charyn finally woke . . . and discovered that Palenya had left sometime earlier. Possibly a great deal earlier, since it was well past eighth glass when he opened his eyes and almost ninth glass by the time he made his way down to the family breakfast room, where he found Bhayrn sulking over a mug of hot cider and a mostly eaten breakfast of flatcakes and ham strips.

Charyn sat across from his brother and took a cautious sip from the mug of hot tea that appeared, before taking a fuller swallow to ease the dryness in his throat. He looked to the server, trying to remember her name, and finally recalling it. "Therosa . . . eggs with the flatcakes, please, and some berry syrup, if there is any." He managed a pleasant smile, despite the nagging headache with which he had awakened, although he hadn't recalled drinking that much wine the night before.

He took another swallow of the tea.

"You must have had a pleasant night," growled Bhayrn. "It's been a while since I've seen you at breakfast."

"I slept late." Charyn had the definite sense that his brother was angry. "It does happen on Solayi."

"Worn out from inspecting the stables and barns? Or from playing duets, and other duets, with Palenya?"

"I enjoy playing the clavecin with her."

"And a few other things." Bhayrn snorted. "I heard you promised a silver to every stable boy and ostler. There must be thirty of them. Three golds! For what? Finally doing their tasks right?"

"Did you see what they did? How much better and clearer the court-yard is. They reorganized the stables and barns . . ." Charyn broke off, seeing that Bhayrn wasn't really listening. "What is it?"

"I hate doing nothing. I hate being gaoled in the chateau. All because you and father feel like you have to listen to the High Holders and factors. Why didn't you just order the army to shoot every single one of them who gave you trouble? That would have solved the problem without half the difficulty."

"Would it have built ships to stop the Jariolan piracy? When none of them would have paid their tariffs? And without tariffs, how would I pay the army?"

"You have answers for everything—except you can't stop someone from trying to kill us all." Bhayrn did not meet Charyn's eyes. "I'm sick and tired of it all. The weather's sowshit. Aloryana's gone, and there's no one even to play placques with."

"You could play with Mother."

"No, I can't. That wouldn't work."

Because you have to win, and you can't win without cheating, and you can't cheat against Mother because she'd notice. Charyn wasn't about to voice that thought. "Some times are like that. It will get better."

"When?"

"Before long."

"It's been too long already."

"It's been less than eight weeks since . . . the Year-Turn Ball. That's not a lot of time to change things."

"That's easy for you to say." Bhayrn rose abruptly, then bolted from the breakfast room.

Several moments later, as if she had been waiting for a lull, the server returned with a platter holding Charyn's breakfast and a small pitcher of syrup. "Your breakfast, Your Grace."

"Thank you very much, Therosa." Charyn managed a smile.

He ate slowly, almost methodically. Whether it was the tea, the food, or the quiet, by the time he finished, Charyn found that his headache had retreated and had almost disappeared. *Almost.*

After leaving the breakfast room, drawn by the sound of Palenya's playing, Charyn made his way to the music room, where he slipped in and stood beside a bookcase that mostly shielded him, listening as she played for almost a glass before stopping. Only then did he move toward the clavecin.

She looked up from where she sat on the bench, a slight smile suggesting that she had known he was there all along.

"I always enjoy your playing."

"I like playing, as much for myself as for others."

"You should. You play well."

"You didn't come to flatter me."

"Why did you leave this morning?"

"It seemed for the best. You were restless, and I didn't want to wake you."

"You're all right, aren't you . . . I mean . . ."

"I'm fine. That was last week."

"Can we talk?"

"We are, but . . . the chairs might be more comfortable."

"What about the settee?" asked Charyn lightly. "Chairs seem . . . so formal."

He was rewarded with a brief smile as Palenya stood and walked to the settee, easing onto one end and turning. Charyn sat at the other end, facing her. Their trousered knees did not quite touch.

"What were you playing at the end? I liked it very much."

She lowered her eyes for just a moment, then met his once more. "It was something I wrote. More of a ballade for clavecin."

"Have you written many of your own compositions? For clavecin or for more instruments?"

"I have written a few . . . just for clavecin. No one wants music written by a woman."

"That's stupid."

"Would you have thought that a year ago?" Palenya's voice was gentle, firm, and not challenging.

Just what Mother said I needed. Charyn flushed.

"You see?"

"That was then. I've learned a little since then. I understand patrons can commission works."

"Yes, that is so." Palenya's voice was wary, the first time Charyn had heard that tone in months.

"Then I have a request . . . a commission."

"Oh?"

"I'd like you to write something for me. I'd like a nocturne, and I want it to have a title, not just a number." Charyn waited, but Palenya was silent. He finally went on. "I'd like it to be called 'Nocturne for a Rex.' You can write it however you see fit."

Palenya swallowed. "That's . . . frightening. Like . . ."

"I don't want it as a memorial . . . more like the nostalgia of first love . . . if you can do that."

She just sat there, her eyes bright, even in the dim light, before she finally nodded.

Charyn waited. He had learned that, too.

64

Charyn did wake early on Lundi, early enough that Palenya was still there, early enough that he could spend some time looking at her before she became aware that he was. As was sometimes the case, she even offered a sleepy smile, one that Charyn always relished. Too soon, she slipped away, and he washed up, shaved, and dressed.

By the time, he reached the study, after breakfast and checking with both Norstan and Maertyl, where he looked out the window, he could see that, early as it was, the sun was warm and bright enough that its light had begun to melt some of the snow at the edges of walks and paved roads and streets.

An omen from the Nameless . . . or a deception from the Namer just before more snow and ice? Charyn had little faith in omens. In the end, after he had done all he could, what would be would be.

Outside of Factor Roblen, it appeared few, either High Holders or factors, wished to see him, and even the number of petitions had dwindled.

Just after ninth glass, another courier from Marshal Vaelln delivered a dispatch, but the sealed courier pouch was brought up to Charyn by one of the chateau guards, while Howal broke the outer seal and carried the envelope to Charyn.

Charyn read it slowly and carefully.

> The most recent encounter about which I have been thus far informed between Jariolan forces and ours occurred east of the Abierto Isles on the sixteenth of Ianus. The Solidaran flotilla patrolling the isles came across a privateer and two Jariolan warships just as they were concluding the process of plundering two Solidar merchant ships. The flotilla sank both Jariolan vessels without significant damage to our ships, but in the conflict the Jariolans sank both merchanters. The ships of the flotilla did manage to rescue over thirty of the merchant crew. No rescue of the Jariolan crews was attempted.

Charyn winced, but he understood the reasoning of the Solidaran Navy captains, that anyone who sank a merchant ship because they were losing a battle didn't deserve saving. He continued to read.

> The second southern flotilla, posted off the east coast of Ote-lyrn, was successful in shielding eight merchanters bound to Solis, after sinking one Jariolan privateer. Because of the presence of three Jariolan warships that shadowed the convoy, the flotilla was obliged to continue accompanying the merchanters for nearly a week, ending on the twenty-third of Ianus, which likely and regretfully removed some degree of protection for other Solidaran merchant ships engaged in the spice trade.

He set down the message, not really looking anywhere. *Another trade-off.* But wasn't everything associated with being rex turning into a trade-off of one sort or another? *And if what you have in mind works, you're going make another trade-off.* As if he could see any other choice.

"Sir?" asked Howal respectfully.

Charyn picked up the dispatch and held it up for Howal. "Mostly good news from Vaelln, but not enough to keep some factors from complaining that I'm not doing enough."

Howal took the letter and read it quickly, returning it to Charyn. "This doesn't sound so bad as you make it out to be."

"Right now, their merchant ships are free to trade. Ours are the ones running the risks. If I commission privateers the way the Oligarch has, and turn them loose on Jariolan merchants, that will turn matters into a complete state of war. It will also largely stop our warships from protecting merchanters. So we'll lose both more merchant ships and more warships at a time when we have fewer warships. Right now, we're destroying more of their warships than they are ours. If we keep that up, and build more ships, we'll end up in a much stronger position."

Howal did not reply for several moments. Then he said, "Why haven't you told more people that?"

"And let the Jariolans know that our strategy is working better than theirs so that they can change what they're doing?" Charyn paused. "I do intend to let the councils know that we are destroying more of the Jariolan ships than they're taking in return."

"But not the rest of it?"

"I'd rather not. Not yet. They'd take that as a promise, and things can always change."

Howal nodded. "Thank you, sir."

Charyn had the feeling that what he had said had not displeased Howal, but he had no idea whether the imager agreed with his strategy. Unhappily, that strategy was the best one he'd been able to come up with.

A quint or so later, Aevidyr arrived in the study.

"Your Grace . . . there is a matter of which I believe you should be aware."

Charyn motioned for him to take a seat. "What might that be?"

"You may have noticed that the River Aluse is now frozen over all the way from the Montagnes D'Glace to well south of Caluse."

"I have."

"When the river freezes that solid and as early as it has, there are always floods in the spring, often very high waters."

For several moments, Charyn couldn't see why Aevidyr was warning him of floods in the spring. Then he remembered. "You sent me a proposal about repairing the river walls on the west side of the river near the barge piers . . . rather you sent it to my father."

Aevidyr frowned. "You read it?"

"Alucar mentioned that it might be a problem. So I found the proposal and read it. It seems like a good proposal. The problem isn't the proposal. It's the cost."

"It will cost the factors and crafters along the river more than what repairs would cost," Aevidyr pointed out.

"The factors pay tariffs. Most of the crafters don't." Even as he spoke, Charyn couldn't help but wonder why Aevidyr was so worried. The Minister of Finance had never worried about factors and crafters before.

"That is true. But many use the barge piers."

"I'm afraid I don't see exactly," replied Charyn. "The barge piers . . ." He stopped, trying to recall what he remembered about the barge piers . . . that they were level with the top of the river walls . . . and anchored to them. "How strong are the walls to which the piers are anchored?"

"Ah . . . that is the problem. Most of the golds for repairs would go to strengthening the walls because they have become weak . . ."

"That's where most of the grain and produce from the north is unloaded, isn't it?"

"Yes, sir. And other goods as well."

All the goods and grains from all the High Holders to the north of L'Excelsis. Charyn thought he understood very well why Aevidyr wanted the river walls repaired. "Aren't there other piers along the river?" he asked guilelessly—at least he hoped he sounded guileless.

"Yes, sir, but the others are not open to except to factors who own them, not without high fees."

"I see." Charyn nodded. "You make a very good point. A very good point. The only problem is that the treasury doesn't have four thousand golds to spare at this moment. Both the factors and the High Holders have refused to consider any significant increases in tariffs. Now . . . if the spring floods are as bad as you say they will be . . . they might reconsider." He smiled sadly. "Then again, they might not, if they felt such a flood might not come again for years." He paused again. "Also, I don't see how we could make repairs at present. The ground is frozen solid—"

"Oh, no, Your Grace, I am well aware of that difficulty. I just wanted you to be aware of the possibility . . ."

"And you wanted to make certain I knew you had warned my father in advance of what may happen?"

"Yes, sir."

"Thank you. I do appreciate your diligence, and after we know more about the tariff revenues for next year, we will confer and see what might be done."

"Thank you, sir."

Charyn stood, as did Aevidyr, who inclined his head before turning and departing. *He's definitely worried.* The fact that Aevidyr was worried hinted that he felt he might have to deal with Charyn for a while, and that was a good sign. But when ministers worried, Charyn suspected that was never a good sign. *What does he know that you don't?*

That was the sort of question that there was little use in asking, because, as Charyn had become well aware, there was all too much he didn't know.

When Charyn heard the coach enter the rear courtyard just before fifth glass, he smiled and hurried down from the study so that he'd be there waiting in the rear foyer when Palenya entered the chateau.

She walked in swiftly, unwrapping the voluminous scarf as she did, then stopped as she saw Charyn. "I didn't expect you."

"How could I not be here? How did the instructionals go."

Palenya smiled. "They went very well. Maitre Alyna observed, and she told me she was very pleased. I will have five students each afternoon on Lundi and Meredi. That is besides Aloryana. Some of them even know how to play simple tunes."

"You like the idea of teaching all of them . . . even those who know little?"

"All of them want to learn. Some will discover it is not for them, but what is a musician for except to make beautiful music and teach others to do the same." Palenya shrugged, although the gesture was anything but fatalistic. "We should go to the music room. I need to look over some of the music." She turned and began to walk.

Charyn walked beside her. "That's why you were copying all that music—to allow others to learn it and play it."

"That was one reason."

"And the other?"

"I cannot accept your silvers and spend time doing nothing."

Charyn almost said that they didn't do that much, at times, when they were together, before he realized, fully, that Palenya was also paid to teach him more than music and to be his companion. "You've been here to teach me. I never would have learned to play, truly play the clavecin, without you."

Her step faltered, if but for a moment. "I always said you could be a good musician."

"You were honest. You've always been honest. You never said I would be a great musician."

"You could make your living as a musician, if you were willing to work hard all the time at playing and at learning more about the structure of music." She opened the door to the music room.

Charyn followed her in and closed the door behind them.

She turned. "I'm not what you think I am."

Charyn stopped dead in his boots. "What do you think I think you are?"

"More perfect than I am. You're kind, but you have absolute power over me. I still worry about my littlest flaw displeasing you." Her face was flushed, not entirely from the cold, Charyn suspected. "I'm a sharp-tempered barren widow who is a very good but not excellent musician. I have a weakness for wanting the better things in life, and I like being admired and wanted. I should have left soon after Aloryana did. That would have been for the best."

"No," he said. "No, it wouldn't. I needed you, and you've helped me so much."

She smiled, sadly. "You said it perfectly. You needed me. Before long, you won't. You may not have realized that yet, but you won't."

"I won't hold you, not against your will. But it's not time for you to go." *Not yet.* "A little while longer."

"Is that a promise? You keep your promises, I've noticed."

"It's a promise."

She bent forward and kissed his cheek. "Thank you."

Charyn felt himself flushing. "You deserve more."

"We don't always get that, my dear rex. But could I trouble you to go over the sheet music with me, so that you know what I have copied of yours, and what copies of mine are now yours?"

He smiled. "I can do that."

65

As was usually the case in winter, the comparative warmth did not last, and while Mardi morning was still sunny, the sun seemed to give less warmth, the wind had picked up, out of the north, and the air was bitter. The remaining water from what little snow had melted had frozen, creating spots of ice in the low places in the roads.

The first thing Charyn did when he reached his study, after meeting with Norstan and Faelln, was to write out the order of items he intended to present at the joint council meeting on Meredi. Although he had them in his head, the entire proceeding was going to be nerve-racking, and he wanted the order on paper as well.

He was writing the last few words when Howal entered the study. "Good morning."

"Good morning, sir. I was talking to Kaylet. He'd like to meet with you at eighth glass, if that's convenient."

"That's more than convenient. Between the weather and the uncertainty, not many want to meet with me at the moment."

"That is changing, sir."

"I would hope so, but that remains to be seen." *At least until tomorrow.* "Go tell Kaylet that I'll see him at eighth glass."

"Yes, sir."

Charyn looked at the sheet he had written, then folded it in half and tucked it into the leather folder he was readying.

Kaylet arrived promptly at eighth glass, but then, all the imagers were punctual, organized, and disciplined, qualities that Charyn knew he needed to keep fostering among the chateau staff.

As the imager sat down in the middle chair, Charyn said, "You asked to see me?"

"Yes, sir. I think I've done what I can do here. I've turned everything over to Aedryt, except for a few things I'd like to repair and replace over the next few days."

"Staying in the background, so to speak?"

"Yes, sir."

"What do you recommend that I look out for?"

Kaylet frowned. "That's not an easy question to answer. Being a good stablemaster requires attention to many small details. There is no one thing . . ."

"I think what you're saying," replied Charyn dryly, "is that I need to wander through the stables and barns and just look—frequently. Especially at the little items, because those slip first. Is that it?"

Kaylet offered what might have been a sheepish smile. "That is much like what the Collegium stablemaster said to me years ago. As you discovered yourself, the ledgers will also tell you if there are problems."

"They just won't tell me what the causes of those problems are."

In the end, Kaylet and Charyn talked for close to another quint, mostly about the strengths and weaknesses of the more experienced ostlers and others.

When Kaylet had left, Charyn turned to Howal. "He's very good."

"He is. Before he came to the Collegium he was an acrobat and worked with animals. He understands them better than people, and he understands people very well."

Before all that long, Moencriff rapped on the door. "Two dispatches for you, Your Grace."

"I'll get them," Howal said, rising from the conference table and moving to the study door, which he opened, taking the two envelopes from the guard and bringing them to Charyn.

Charyn frowned. One of the envelopes merely bore his name and a green seal, meaning it was likely from a regional governor. The other bore Vaelln's seal and was much thicker. He slit open the envelope with the green seal, extracted the single sheet, and began to read.

Your Grace—

Because of events of a personal nature well beyond my control, it is with sadness and with deep regret that I must resign from the position of Regional Governor of Khel.

My time as Regional Governor has been fulfilling and rewarding, if occasionally marked with challenges, and I thank you and your father for the opportunity to serve you and the people of Khel . . .

Not to mention, most likely, the opportunity to enrich yourself, thought Charyn, his lips curling, as he thought of Warheon's effort to change water-rights precedence to benefit High Holders, for which, he wouldn't have been surprised, Warheon might well have received favors or golds, at least if Charyn hadn't precluded the effort by making the law standard across all Solidar.

> . . . had thought to remain at my post until the first of Avryl to allow you time
> to select a replacement, but, as always, I serve at the pleasure of the rex. With my
> gratitude and I appreciation, I remain, sincerely yours,

Warheon's signature and seal were below the short body of the letter.

Why now? Why would he resign now? Just because I overturned some of his rotten decisions? That didn't make sense to Charyn. His own position as rex was, for the moment, unsteady, and everyone knew it. So what did Warheon have to gain by resigning? Except the resignation wasn't truly effective for another month and a half.

Was it timed so that he could leave if nothing changed, or remain if something happened to Charyn, claiming that he would not leave a new rex without a regional governor?

Most likely. Charyn shook his head, then replaced the letter in its envelope and set it down on the desk, turning to the dispatch from Vaelln. He opened it to find little more than a note saying that Vaelln was enclosing a report from Sea Marshal Tynan that Vaelln thought Charyn would find of interest.

> Marshal Vaelln—
>
> You requested a report on the degree to which materials and valuables were recovered and salvaged from the ruins of the palace of the Lords of Telaryn. Even before receiving your orders, I took the liberty of securing the grounds and what remained of the structures, despite some initial disagreements with Regional Governor Voralch. As complete an inventory of recovered property and items as my men could develop is attached. While it was not possible to determine what artifacts and items of value were removed from the ruins prior to my men securing the site, it is probable that many items were looted at some point, possibly even before the fire reached all areas of the palace.
>
> The deeper storerooms were largely undamaged . . . and a great many artifacts, statutes, and even a considerable amount

of antique silver cutlery were recovered and placed in the Naval strong rooms. As you can see from the inventory, the total value of the smaller items recovered is estimated in excess of eight thousand golds . . . no feasible way of determining the value of the usable building materials remaining in the ruins, but suggest that it exceeds a thousand golds.

Charyn scanned the four pages of small lettered items with estimated values, trying not to shake his head as he did. From what he could see, if the descriptions were accurate, the valuation placed on the items was likely low. *And Voralch never mentioned any of this?*

Once Charyn finished studying the report and the inventory, he immediately drafted, and then rewrote, a letter to Vaelln, congratulating both the marshal and the sea marshal on their efforts, and expressing his deep appreciation for their efforts in saving as much as they had of the regial heritage and history. His letter also requested Marshal Tynan's recommendations as to what items should be retained for their heritage and eventually brought to L'Excelsis and what items should be sold to raise funds to defer the future costs of reconstructing at least the palace proper of the complex.

He and Howal had no sooner finished that letter and readied it for sending than yet another dispatch arrived, this one from Regional Governor Paetrark of Antiago. Charyn almost hesitated to open it, but did, reading it with a dismay that increased with each line.

Almost all of Antiago has been besieged by continuing rains and storms. Longtime residents do not recall the winter rains ever being this severe. As I write, almost a third of Liantiago suffers from standing water, in some places almost three yards deep. A section of the harbor wall close to half a mille long has collapsed. The combination of heavy rains, high tides, and strong winds has eroded two-fifths of the harbor breakwater at Westisle.

I have received reports of great damages from Barna and Suemyron as well. In a number of locales, whole hillsides have collapsed. One village lost nearly fifty homes and nearly a hundred inhabitants were buried by the mud. Lightning from thunderstorms also ignited hundreds of hectares of oil tree plantations,

largely on the hills bordering the post road from Barna to Liantiago. The losses are likely to result in shortage of lamp oil for
some time to come . . .

. . . also request an additional thousand golds to pay for repairs to governor's residence and outbuildings . . .

When Charyn finished reading Paetrark's letter, he could only hope
that no more dispatches like the ones he'd received that day were on the
way, especially not when he had to meet with the two councils the next
afternoon.

66

Meredi dawned windy and cold, but not quite so cold as the coldest days of Ianus, reflected Charyn as he dressed with care for the day, and for the meeting with the two councils that he hoped would resolve matters with his uncle . . . and put an end to the threats and uncertainty that they and the various attempts on his life had caused. He actually looked at himself in the wall mirror in the oversized dressing room that adjoined his sleeping chamber, making certain that the greens he wore—the same as army officers, except for the lack of insignia—were crisp and without stains, and that his boots were polished.

He still looked too young, but there wasn't much he could do about that, and trying to grow a beard or mustache would have looked ridiculous. Palenya had told him that more than once.

After a quick breakfast, he met first with Kaylet, asking that the plain coach be held in readiness by second glass, and then with Maertyl and Faelln, informing them of their duties during the time that all the council members would be at the chateau, and the fact that they should anticipate a squad of army soldiers accompanying Marshal Vaelln.

At that, Maertyl frowned. "Sir . . . he's never brought troopers before."

"I know, but I've never been attacked so many times before, and with all the councilors here, I thought it wouldn't hurt to have some armed soldiers for support as well."

"Do you expect another attack?" asked Faelln.

"I don't, but I didn't expect all of those that have happened already." Charyn kept his tone dry and ironic. "A glass before noon, I'd like both Sturdyn and Moencriff posted outside the study door."

Maertyl nodded, but asked, "What about inside?"

"I think that Maitre Alastar will be able to assist with that. Also, Howal will be nearby."

Both the guard captain and undercaptain nodded.

"Keep a good eye on the coaches and men who serve the High Holders," Charyn concluded before turning and heading for the grand staircase.

Upon reaching his study, he immediately picked up the copy of *Veritum*, scanning the main story on the front page:

> . . . merchant ship losses continue . . . successful arrival of eight ships from Otelyrn because of Naval warship escorts . . . still continuing losses of ships and cargoes has some factors upset that the rex has not done more . . . feeling by some that the attempts upon the life of young Rex Charyn are a result of factor unhappiness . . . Certain persons have revealed that there may have been even more attempts than have become public.

And by whom were those attempts revealed? Charyn had few doubts about that, although that would have been through intermediaries or anonymous letters.

By two quints before ninth glass, Charyn had all the threat letters, except one, which was inside his jacket, in the leather folder on his desk, beside which was the pouch containing the golds and the two silvers. There was also the stick of black wax, wrapped in cloth, in his jacket pocket.

"Howal . . . when Marshal Vaelln arrives, I'd like you to repair to the music room and await the High Holders there."

"Yes, sir. Will you be—"

"I would hope so. Moencriff will be joining Sturdyn outside the study just before noon, and there will be extra guards at the front entrance to the chateau. Then, once you escort the factors in, I'd like you to step back to the corner there and conceal yourself when no one is looking. Can you remain concealed while the councils meet?"

"Yes, sir."

"No matter what happens, unless my life is threatened, please remain concealed."

The imager nodded.

At two quints before noon, Sturdyn announced, "Marshal Vaelln," then opened the study door.

Charyn immediately stood, as did Howal, who quietly moved to the door and then departed.

Vaelln strode briskly into the study, stopping short of the desk. "Your Grace, I am here with the squad of troopers you requested. They are in the rear courtyard. I thought that positioning might be best."

"It will be, for now. Once all the councilors have arrived, I would suggest half of them move to the area around the front entry. I would also like your men to make certain no one leaves except by your permission."

"Your Grace?"

"I can see you would like to know why I made the order? I did order it, Marshal, although you are kind to suggest it was a request." Charyn gestured to the chairs before the desk and seated himself. "The reason is simple. I have some evidence to present to the councils, after you report on the status of naval evolutions in dealing with the Jariolans. That evidence might well reveal who is behind the assassination of my father and the attempts on my life. It may be necessary to take someone into custody, and since treason is a crime against not only the rex, but all Solidar, I believe that custodial duty lies in your purview."

"The evidence *may* reveal." Vaelln sat forward in the middle chair.

"I have reason to believe that revealing that evidence will result in uncovering more evidence. If not, I may have subjected your men to a long and cold ride for nothing. Your presence is necessary in any event, because the councils will trust your words far more than mine in naval matters."

Vaelln nodded slowly. "I see."

Charyn hoped he didn't see everything, but there was no help for that. "Once you have given the necessary orders to your men, please return here. Maitre Alastar will be here shortly."

"Yes, Your Grace."

As Vaelln stood, so did Charyn, but he did not sit back down at his desk. Instead, he walked to the window so that he could watch some of what Vaelln did, not that he expected any problems. *Not yet.*

At a quint before noon, Sturdyn announced, "Moencriff has joined me, sir, as ordered."

"Thank you."

Before long, Vaelln returned. "My men are briefed and in position, Your Grace."

Although Charyn had turned from the window at Vaelln's entrance, he did not seat himself or motion to the chairs. "Thank you. As I mentioned in my letter, you are to describe the situation with regard to the Jariolans. I want you to be as honest and forthright as you can be."

"Yes, sir."

"Is it your opinion that, if we continue on our present course, we will eventually win and remove the Jariolan threat?"

"Yes. It will take several years, but we have seen no sight of new Jariolan ships of the line during the time that we have commissioned six."

"If you would make that point, Marshal . . ."

Vaelln nodded.

Before long, Sturdyn announced, "Maitre Alastar."

While Charyn had expected the Maitre early, he had not expected him quite so early. "Have him come in."

"Good day," offered Alastar, nodding to Charyn and then to Vaelln. "I thought you might be here, Marshal."

"He'll be briefing the councils on the situation with the Jariolans. After that, I'll be presenting some materials dealing with the assassination of my father and the subsequent attacks, including the letters I received in conjunction with those attacks."

Alastar nodded. "I look forward to seeing those."

"I thought both you and the marshal should see them and hear other indications as well. It's taken a great deal of time and effort to gather all of the evidence."

Vaelln frowned momentarily, but said nothing.

Sturdyn rapped on the door just after the chimes began to ring out the glass. "The members of the councils are all present, Your Grace."

"As before, Howal will escort the factors, Norstan the High Holders."

"Yes, sir," replied Sturdyn.

Charyn carried the chair before the goldenwood desk and closest to the window over to a position next to but not actually at the conference table. "As you suggested the last time, Maitre." He then moved a second chair and placed it beside the first. "For Marshal Vaelln." He half-turned. "I'd like you here for the entire meeting."

Vaelln nodded.

Charyn then took a position standing behind the chair at the head of the table, his back to the north windows as he stood behind the chair. "I'll be announcing the marshal first, and then I'll be bringing the council members up to date on all the attacks on the regial family and upon me." He glanced at the table, where the folder holding the original threat letters lay before his place, with the cloth bag containing the golds and silvers beside the folder.

"You think that is wise?" Alastar's tone was even.

"I think it would be less wise not to bring up the matter. After all,

I do have a few concerns after all the attempts on my life, and there are some facts which you, Marshal Vaelln, and the members of the councils should be aware of. Some you already know. Some you do not."

Within a few moments, the door to the study opened. As before, Elthyrd led the factors. Thalmyn came next, then Harll, Jhaliost, and Hisario, standing behind their chairs on the left side of the table. After a good tenth of a quint, a delay Charyn suspected had been created by Ryel, the four High Holders appeared, Ryel being the last, but once more he smiled warmly as he nodded to Charyn before standing behind the chair at the far end of the table. He laid a leather folder on the wooden surface. Charyn refrained from nodding. That would help. The other three High Holders took exactly the same positions they had at the last meeting, with Basalyt closest to Charyn on the right side of the table, Fhaedyrk next, and then Khunthan.

"Welcome to the chateau on this cold Fevier day." Charyn motioned everyone to seat themselves, then seated himself. "Given the weather, I do appreciate all of you coming. I do have some information for all of you regarding the situation with Jariola, but I think it is better that you all should hear that from Marshal Vaelln himself."

Vaelln stood and surveyed those at the table, then nodded to Charyn. "Thank you, Rex Charyn. As most of you should have heard, we have had a number of engagements with the Jariolans over the last month. These engagements have made several matters much clearer. For example, in any engagement of warships of the same rate, our forces have prevailed. On three occasions, our ships have defeated and destroyed Jariolan vessels of a higher rating. Thanks to the foresight of Rex Lorien, Rex Charyn, and the councils, our shipbuilding is proceeding well, and we appear to be producing ships more quickly than the Jariolans. If this continues, and I have every reason to believe that it will, within the next year or so, Solidaran ships will begin to control the oceans of Terahnar . . ."

Vaelln described the reasons for his conclusions for not quite a quint before stopping.

"What about the Ferrans?" asked Hisario immediately.

"In the last two months, they have avoided becoming involved, and there are no reports of their warships aiding the Jariolans or attacking our warships or merchant ships. As we become stronger, they are even less likely to be considered an enemy."

"Will you be forming another flotilla to protect Solidaran ships trading with the lands of Otelyrn?" asked Khunthan.

"That is our plan. We believe we can have another flotilla on station there in late Maris . . ."

The questions only lasted half a quint, at which time Vaelln turned to Charyn.

"If you would remain, Marshal," said Charyn. "You also should hear what I have to say, because it impinges on your duty and responsibilities." He squared himself in his chair. "As all of you know, my father was assassinated here in the chateau, by traitor guards hired by a traitor guard captain, although that did not become clear until later. Before my father was killed, he received a threatening letter. Since then, I have received five more. Of the six, one was left at the family estate at Tuuryl after silos containing twelve thousand golds' worth of grain suffered explosions and were burned, and one was left for the regional governor of Telaryn after arsonists burned the ancient palace there. One was left in the pulpit at the Anomen D'Rex when I delivered the memorial for my father. Two were delivered here to the chateau by public messenger, and the last was handed to a chateau guard at his post by a beggar boy who received it from someone so heavily cloaked and muffled that the child could not even tell if the figure was man or woman, only that he received two silvers for carrying the envelope to a guard . . .

"I have here, with me, these various threatening letters that my father received, and then those that I have received following his assassination. When you examine them you will notice that they all have been written on the same kind of paper, with the same ink, and in the same script. It's what is called standard merchant hand, and it is used for all merchanting and factoring documents."

"That means nothing," declared Hisario. "Standard merchant hand is so alike that it's practical impossibility to tell who wrote it."

"I wasn't casting blame on factors," replied Charyn as he handed the stack of letters to Elthyrd, the factor sitting closest to him. "I rather admire the man who thought up the idea of using merchant hand. It's the use of the obvious to conceal his identity. The paper is the kind never used by High Holders, nor by the wealthiest of factors, for their personal correspondence. And the letters all use references that suggest that the writer is a factor or merchant. I'd like each of you to look at each document."

"What will that accomplish?" demanded Khunthan.

"Since I've been the target of five assassination attempts, don't you think it would be useful for all of you to see just how clever the man behind this is?"

"He can't be that clever," said Ryel, "if you're still alive after five attempts."

"He's been clever enough to leave very little evidence," replied Charyn. "Please examine the letters."

Then he waited until everyone at the conference table, as well as Vaelln and Alastar, had seen them. He gathered the letters and replaced them in the leather folder, remaining on his feet.

"Then there is the matter of the golds, and the two silvers."

"Golds?" asked Jhaliost. "What—"

"I'm getting there," replied Charyn. "The imagers posted here at the chateau and I recovered the actual golds paid to the late guard captain Churwyl and to a guard named Cauthyrn. I've kept the golds in the same bag in which Churwyl received his fee for killing me. I'd like you all to notice that all the golds are fresh-minted, and that they all bear the same mint mark. Interestingly enough, the silvers also bear the same mint mark."

"That is supposed to prove something?" asked Basalyt. "Mint marks?"

Charyn noticed that Elthyrd had nodded slightly, as had Hisario, and even Fhaedyrk.

"I'd just like you all to verify that the golds and silvers are fresh-minted and from the same mint. Then we'll proceed."

Once again, Charyn waited until the golds and silvers were back in his hands, and he replaced them in the pouch, which he set beside his folder. He could feel the letter inside his jacket as he began to speak again from where he stood beside his chair. "The man behind all these letters wanted me to believe that a factor or several factors were behind the assassination of my father and the attempts against me. Two were designed to fail, the first one, where it appeared my brother was the target, and a later one here at the chateau when someone fired at me when I was outside in the rear courtyard. The idea behind these efforts was twofold—either to be effective in eliminating much if not all of the regial family or to provoke me into taking direct and severe action against the factors of Solidar."

"That seems rather extreme, and also based on very little evidence." Ryel's voice was almost genial.

"That depends on what one calls evidence," replied Charyn, his tone cheerful. "It might be considered a form of evidence that every story in the newssheets has stated that the individuals most upset by the loss of ships were factors. Yet three of the largest fleets of merchant ships are owned largely or in part by High Holders."

"Oh . . . and who might those be?" asked Hisario.

"The Diamond ships of High Holder Ghasphar, Khellan Trading, owned in part by High Holder Khunthan, and Solisan Traders, owned by High Holder Ryel."

"Owning ships is a crime, now?" asked Ryel.

"By itself, no. It's just part of a larger pattern. I'll get to that. Let's get back to the attempted assassinations. The last attempt, which took place exactly a week ago, happened when a uniformed army courier threw an explosive courier pouch at me when supposedly delivering a message from Marshal Vaelln. Whoever planned it knew that couriers from Vaelln were allowed into the study, and that fact was not known to someone unfamiliar to the chateau. That effectively rules out almost all factors. That means that the man behind this had to be very familiar with the chateau, and its operations. Then, less than a glass later, an urchin delivered another threatening and warning letter, identically written. The other thing is that the boy who delivered the message was paid in silver. Two silvers, as I mentioned, the same two silvers that are in that pouch. The idea behind that, I'm sure, was to make the point that the man seeking my death would pay any price to anyone. But . . . I find it hard to believe that a factor would overpay an urchin by such a huge amount." Charyn inclined his head to Elthyrd: "Begging your pardon, Factors."

Elthyrd smiled dryly.

"Whoever it was, as you just said," offered Ryel, "was making a point."

"He was. But he wasn't making it the way a factor would. Then there are all those golds and those silvers. They were paid in connection with all the assassination attempts, and they all came from the same mint in Asseroiles. Most likely, again, because it is the closest mint to the man behind this. Also, golds and silvers change hands quickly among factors. Factor Elthyrd, just how likely is it that any factor would count out ten golds and come up with ten newly minted pieces with the same mint mark? Or that the two silvers paid an urchin also had that mint mark?"

"Extremely unlikely," Elthyrd admitted.

This time Thalmyn nodded.

"This is preposterous," said Ryel, his voice still well-modulated. "It's all speculation."

"Not exactly," replied Charyn. "It's a significant collection of indications of who the guilty man has to be. You forget one thing. Factors are governed far more by profit than rage. When the attempts continued with less and less success, any rational factor would have cut his losses."

"You have the nerve to suggest that a High Holder is behind these deplorable acts?" Ryel snorted dismissively.

"Oh . . . I can do more than that." Charyn strode down the side of the table, reached out and seized Ryel's leather folder, and, as he did, slipped the letter he had been carrying under the folder, so that when he opened the folder, the letter dropped to the table with several other sheets of paper.

"That!" snapped Charyn, "is exactly what I thought. All of you notice. That looks exactly like every other one of those threatening letters received by the regial family."

Ryel's mouth dropped open. "You—"

"I did nothing. I merely uncovered what you have had in mind all along. You have been plotting not for months, but for years." Charyn snatched up the sealed letter and walked back to the head of the table, where he handed it to Elthyrd. "I'd like you to open it, but leave the seal untouched."

Elthyrd held the letter, his eyebrows raised. "You think it matches?"

"It looks to be identical, as does the paper, but until we put them side by side, we won't know."

"This is absurd!" Ryel started to stand.

"Sit down!" snapped Charyn, remaining standing.

Ryel opened his mouth, but did not speak as Alastar stood.

"I suggest you reseat yourself," the Maitre said. "That would be the wisest course." His voice was cold.

Ryel glanced from Alastar to Charyn and back again. "Really . . . will this charade accomplish anything?"

Charyn waited, thinking Alastar might speak.

The Maitre did, in fact. "It is most likely to make many things that have remained hidden far more clear than you would wish."

Ryel sank into his chair, and the other three High Holders exchanged quick glances.

Elthyrd produced a belt knife and slit the side of the envelope, then eased out the single sheet of paper and unfolded it. He read it silently, with Charyn looking down over his shoulder.

The words were clear to Charyn.

> You have been warned for the last time. If you fail to act more
> decisively than the preceding rex, you won't be ruler of Solidar nearly
> so long as your immediate predecessor.

Elthyrd glanced up, turning his head toward Charyn.

"The others should see it, all of those besides Ryel. He can see it last. Leave the envelope here."

Elthyrd passed the letter to Thalmyn, who read it in turn, followed by the other three factors on that side of the table, and then by the three High Holders on the other side. After Basalyt had read the letter, Charyn took it from the High Holder and carried it back to the foot of the table where Ryel sat. He placed the letter on the wood, but only straightened slightly.

Ryel glanced at the letter. "This is a farce." Then he looked at Charyn.

Charyn shook his head. "I wish it were. I truly do." And, as he retrieved the letter, he meant those words and what lay behind them. He straightened and turned to Vaelln. "I believe the handling of treachery and assassins falls under your purview, Marshal. You will keep the High Holder under lock and key until he comes before the High Justicer. Before you imprison him, search him carefully." Charyn shifted his eyes back to Ryel. "Once you are convicted, and you will be, given this evidence, and all those who will testify against you now that your power over them has been removed, your holding will fall forfeit, as it should once you are convicted before a High Justicer."

Ryel paled. "You would, wouldn't you?" He stood slowly, deliberately.

"After all you have done . . . yes. Assassination and murder have their price, too, and you're going to pay the assassin's price." Charyn's eyes fixed on his uncle, unwavering.

Ryel could only meet that gaze for a moment before looking away. Then he cleared his throat, coughed, and took a kerchief from his pocket, wiping his mouth, and then swallowing. He looked at Charyn. "You are much too clever, Charyn, unlike your father. That will be your downfall."

Charyn nodded politely. "Cleverness may run in the blood, Uncle, but I learned much of what I have done from watching how you acted."

Ryel swallowed again as Vaelln stood and walked toward him. Charyn stepped back, his eyes remaining on his uncle as Vaelln gestured toward the study door.

Once Vaelln had escorted Ryel out of the study, where Sturdyn joined the marshal to accompany Ryel down the grand staircase, Charyn turned to the remaining members of both councils.

For a long moment, he said nothing. When he began, his voice was pleasant, but firm. "I am not fond of treachery. I am even less fond of a man, particularly a relative, who uses his wealth and power to blame an entire group of people and who attempts to kill an entire regial family, not to mention those who carried out his orders. No man should be able to do that." He paused. "Because my uncle is a brilliant and cunning man, it has taken months to gather the evidence to prove his wrongdoing. And now that he is in custody, I have no doubt that more evidence will appear in great measure. Unlike some, I can be patient, when necessary. When required." He paused again. "This council also needs to be patient. We can surmount the difficulties posed by the Jariolans. What Marshal Vaelln has told you confirms that by holding fast to our course, we will triumph. The question is whether you are dedicated enough to the preservation of Solidar and to more than your own personal interests to join with me holding to that course. I am not asking for great sacrifices. That would serve no one. I am suggesting that supporting this course would be in all our interests."

Charyn looked at each High Holder, beginning with Basalyt, then Khunthan, followed by Fhaedyrk and then the factors, in turn. Each nodded.

Then he turned to Elthyrd. "This joint council will meet permanently every month, more often if necessary. The factors have asked for a voice. They have it in you. In return, you need to explain to the factors of Solidar the realities of what this council and the rex can do . . . and what we cannot."

Looks passed between the factors. After a time, Elthyrd nodded.

Charyn looked back to Fhaedyrk, then Khunthan, and finally Basalyt. Basalyt and Khunthan both looked to Fhaedyrk.

Fhaedyrk smiled, faintly. "You make a very convincing case. Are you also suggesting that the members of this joint council will have a stronger voice in how Solidar is governed?"

"I am. That will require that you all will have to work out common interests." Charyn turned to Alastar. "Those interests must include those I see as rex and those you see as those of the Collegium."

Alastar nodded solemnly.

At that moment, there was an urgent pounding on the door, which opened to allow Vaelln to step inside. The marshal's face was grim.

"Yes, Marshal?" Charyn had a very good idea what Vaelln was about to say.

"Your Grace, High Holder Ryel is dead. He collapsed in the front entry hall in front of a number of soldiers and guards. He apparently took poison shortly before he was leaving the study. It must have been in that handkerchief."

For several moments, there was silence.

Then Charyn spoke. "Under the circumstances, that is not entirely surprising. I would note that one of the assassins of my father took poison before he could be questioned."

Fhaedyrk, Khunthan, and Basalyt all exchanged glances.

Khunthan cleared his throat, then said, "None of us were aware of any of this."

"I believe that," replied Charyn. "Unhappily, I also have reason to believe that the late High Holder Oskaryn would have learned shortly that Ryel was behind it, and that is why Ryel had him killed."

"How would Oskaryn—"

"The standard merchant hand. They were partners in Solisan Traders, and Ryel operated the trading in Solis until his father died. He bought out that interest from Oskaryn the younger." Charyn could see a knowing nod from Hisario, as well as from Fhaedyrk.

"The High Council is somewhat depleted," Fhaedyrk said quietly.

"Which of you will act as Chief Councilor?" asked Charyn.

Both Basalyt and Khunthan looked to Fhaedyrk, who offered a rueful smile. "It appears I will."

"Please inform me as soon as you know who the two new councilors will be."

"We can do that."

Charyn then looked to Elthyrd. "Are there any other matters . . . ?"

"Nothing that cannot wait until the next meeting. The eighteenth of Maris?"

Charyn nodded. "I will see you all then."

When the last of the councilors was leaving the study, Charyn said, "You can release the shields, Howal."

As Howal appeared, Vaelln looked to Charyn questioningly.

"I didn't know how Ryel might react. That's why I asked Howal to remain there."

Vaelln looked to Alastar.

"It wasn't my idea," replied the Maitre. "I did notice someone was there, but, if Rex Charyn had a reason for it, and it didn't hurt anyone, what was the harm?" He turned to Charyn.

"You seemed unsurprised that he took poison."

"I thought it likely. He knew that a man's lands can be taken once he is convicted of treason. He also knew that I'd stoop to anything to make certain he was convicted. Once it became clear that there was enough evidence that no one was going to object, or not in public, he realized that he would likely be searched before being physically imprisoned, and that he needed to act. From what I can see, the poison he took was exactly the same as that taken by one of the chateau guards to avoid being questioned. In a way, that's another sort of proof."

"But how could you have possibly known that he had it on him?" asked Vaelln.

"Ryel has been prepared for every possibility all along. His agents had poison. He might have thought it unlikely that I'd confront him here, but he had to know it was possible. And he definitely had to know that being convicted of treason would allow me to strip the High Holding. Speaking of which, we need to get to the Chateau D'Council before Lady Ryel discovers what has happened and destroys the evidence there. "

Alastar raised his eyebrows.

"I have reason to believe that Lady Ryel has great knowledge and skill with standard merchant hand. We need to gather that evidence before it vanishes." Charyn gestured. "If you'd ready your squad, Marshal. Go ahead. We'll be right behind you. I have a coach in readiness."

"Yes, sir."

Once Vaelln had departed, and Charyn and Alastar walked down the north corridor toward the grand staircase, Alastar asked, "How did you know he had that last letter with him?"

"When your imagers and I restructured the entire chateau staff, especially the guards, it was more than likely that he had no way to deliver a message directly, and with the number of men who died, he was also most likely having trouble finding others to do it."

"Did he even write that last letter?" Alastar's voice was even.

"Does it matter?" replied Charyn. "It expressed exactly what he felt and what he intended to do . . . and continue doing."

"So it did," replied Alastar dryly.

67

Almost three quints passed before the plain coach, carrying Charyn and Alastar and escorted by Marshal Vaelln and his squad of armed troopers, approached the iron gates of the Chateau D'Council, guarded by two men in maroon livery. The Council guards took a single look at the army troopers and opened the gates.

When the coach came to a halt at the entry portico, Charyn could see two more armed guards, uniformed in the black and silver of Ryel, flanking the bronzed doors of the main entryway. Both surrendered their weapons immediately.

Only after that did Charyn follow the white-and-silver-haired Alastar from the coach up the steps to the portico and past a footman in black into the circular high-ceilinged entry hall beyond the bronzed double doors, where Vaelln waited with four troopers. In Charyn's left hand was a small leather kit bag, perhaps optimistically there to hold whatever he found.

"The main study—the receiving study—is to the left," offered Alastar in a low voice.

At that moment, a woman in shimmering black trousers and a silver jacket came down the steps from the upper level. "What are you doing here, might I ask?" Her voice was every bit as imperious as Charyn remembered.

He stepped forward. "Just investigating high treason, Aunt Doryana." He gestured. "Restrain Lady Ryel."

Two troopers dashed up the steps and took Doryana by the arms.

"You can't do this! This is High Council property."

"High Holder Ryel was charged with high treason," Charyn said. "He took poison in plain sight, rather than face the High Justicer."

For a moment, Doryana was silent. "Lies! All lies!"

"That's what we're here to discover." Charyn looked to Vaelln. "Just keep her here while we search the studies."

Charyn led the way down the corridor and into the receiving study, an imposing chamber with floor-to-ceiling windows looking out on the front entry drive and gardens, and floored in black marble, except for the carpeted area on which rested a circular ebony conference table. Five wooden armchairs were positioned around the table. Just out from the south wall was a wide desk with drawers, rather than a table desk, and to one side was an ebony stand holding three file chests.

"Do you really think you'll find anything?" murmured Alastar.

"It's more likely we'll find evidence in her study, but it's always possible here."

Charyn opened the top desk drawer. All it held were pens, none with a point broad enough for standard merchant hand, and two bottles of ink, neither of which was the common iron-gall black. The second drawer held stationery in angled slots.

In the end, Charyn found nothing of interest in the desk—except that hidden behind a false panel in one bottom drawer was a small strongbox.

"Can you image away the lock?" asked Charyn.

"Mint marks?" asked Alastar dryly.

"It is a thought," replied Charyn sardonically.

Moments later, Alastar had the lock in his hands.

Charyn opened the small strongbox, which looked to hold perhaps a hundred golds. He picked up one. It had the curled "L" mint mark. So did the second. In fact, all one hundred and eleven golds did. When he finished, he looked to Alastar. "It's at least a stronger indication."

"You may not find much more."

Alastar was correct in that.

Charyn had been hoping there might be something in the file chests. There was not.

Next came Doryana's study, back behind the family parlor. The table desk revealed nothing. Neither did the first file chest. The second, however, contained ledgers, as well as a partial sheaf of paper of the type used by the writer of the threats and two bottles of iron-gall ink, one only half full, plus several pens cut in a fashion that looked to match the width of the lettering on the threats. Charyn studied the ledgers, all of which dated back more than ten years. *To when Doryana had likely been doing the bookkeeping for Solisan Trading.* The lettering was in merchant standard hand and looked to be a perfect match to the threat letters, not that such meant much.

Charyn stepped back from the desk and studied the room, his eyes lighting upon the half bookcase set under the moderately high window.

He bent down and began to examine the sides of the bookcase, both somewhat thicker than they needed to be. It took some time, but he managed to open both panels. In one side was a leather pouch with fifty golds, all with Lythoryn's mint mark, once he'd counted and studied them. In the other was a small cloth bag, and inside that was a blank seal ring with a raised edge, which he had no doubt would match the indentation on all of the black wax seals, as well as two sticks of black sealing wax, one of which was half used.

As he showed them to Alastar, he said, "The seal matches . . . and the golds."

"It's not a lot."

"It's enough," declared Charyn. *As much as I need, in any case.* He straightened and slipped the items into the small kit bag.

Doryana was still in the main foyer, as if she had any choice. She did not speak, but glared at Charyn.

"I found the blank seal ring that matches the seals on the warning and threat letters." He smiled pleasantly.

"I know who is behind all of this." Doryana's voice was trembling, not with fear, but rage. "You don't know enough, and you don't have the intelligence to set up an innocent High Holder. Your mother has made you her puppet. She always hated Ryel. She wanted him dead a long time ago." Doryana's eyes fixed on Charyn. "You're a dumb marionette, dangled by her strings."

"I was the one who was behind it all," interjected Charyn firmly. "Ryel was my uncle, but he was behind the High Holder revolt, and he was the one who arranged my father's assassination. There was uncontestable proof of his wrongdoing . . ."

"It was all created. Ryel never would have been stupid enough . . ."

Charyn smiled. Coldly. "Never would have been stupid enough to have proof on him? Your words suggest that he was guilty, but that you and he believed there would never be proof of what he did. And that his power was so great that no one would ever talk. They will now. And your words and belief also constitute another kind of proof." He paused. "You wrote all of the invoices and bills of lading for Solisan Trading, didn't you?" Charyn paused, then added, "In perfect standard merchant hand, I trust."

Doryana's face hardened. "You are despicable. Both you and your mother. I suppose you'll destroy the holding, too."

"That's up to you," replied Charyn.

Doryana's eyes narrowed.

"I already found enough, both in the letter he carried, and in Ryel's study, to show his guilt, and there was more than enough in yours to prove your part in his schemes. All that shows clearly that the two of you not only masterminded my father's death, and intended mine, but also Bhayrn's, which would have resulted in the Chateau D'Rex going to young High Holder Regial, since as an imager, Aloryana could not even be the consort of a rex. Regial is your husband's nephew, even if that is not widely known, and, most conveniently, just the right age to marry your granddaughter Iryella."

At that, Lady Ryel smiled. "That's just speculation."

"I think not. The proof is there. Ledgers with writing that matches the writing on all the threat notes. Matching ink. The black wax. Also the blank seal ring with the tiny raised section in the corner." All of that was indeed there, although it would have been, even if Charyn had needed to plant it, although he had doubted that would be necessary in the slightest. "And now that Ryel is dead, the men who did his dirty work under pain of death or worse will talk. Of course, if you were to name Lady Chelia as guardian for Karyel—he is your oldest grandchild, I believe—in your will, then I suppose I would be forced to spare the High Holding. Otherwise, well, I do have the right to seize lands from High Holders or their heirs or guardians who are proved guilty of treason before the High Justicer. Killing one rex and plotting to kill another, while arranging four attempts on his life, certainly can't be anything but treason."

"My will . . . ?"

"Or a letter stating your intent that Chelia should become Karyel's guardian in the event of your death." Charyn paused. "In any case, you will be put before the High Justicer and doubtless convicted of treason. With both the High Holder and his lady guilty of treason, and no responsible heir of age, I will have no choice but to take the lands. If you go to trial."

"You wouldn't . . ."

"I wouldn't, unless I have to. I'm leaving the choice entirely up to you. And I'm being incredibly merciful, considering what you and Ryel have done."

He turned to Marshal Vaelln. "Have your men escort her to her chambers. Give her a few moments to gather her things. Have your men wait outside her door. Then you can take her into custody. Once imprisoned, she is not to leave the cell until she faces the High Justicer."

Doryana's shoulders slumped as she walked to the staircase, followed by two armed troopers, and the marshal.

"How did you know?" asked Alastar blandly.

"There had to be a reason why my mother hated her brother. There had to be a reason why the Maitre of the Collegium offered hints and inferences, but no proof. Also, one of the biggest clues was right in front of me from the beginning, and I never saw it until recently."

Alastar frowned.

"The golds. Uncle *hated* dirty coins. When I was a tiny boy, he gave me new-minted shiny golds." Charyn smiled wryly. "Beyond that, the biggest reason why it had to be a High Holder was that the attacks continued even after all the factors agreed to the slight increase in tariffs. Factors, even the angriest, prefer to win in terms of the counting-house. I saw that in my times at the exchange."

At Alastar's blank look, Charyn realized that there were some things that the knowledgeable Maitre didn't know. He laughed softly, and said, "I actually have a factor's account at the L'Excelsis Factors' Exchange."

"I think the joint council may be in for more surprises than they expected from you."

"I'll try to keep them from being unpleasant."

A quint passed, and Charyn heard nothing. After another half quint, he walked to the base of the ornate black marble staircase and called, "Marshal! Perhaps you should check on my aunt."

Before long, the marshal descended the black marble staircase. He stopped before Charyn, looking coldly at the rex. "She hung herself, but I think she took poison as well. Her body was contorted and damp."

Charyn returned the look with one even more frigid. "Don't ever look at me again that way, Marshal. Doryana and Ryel were behind the last High Holders' revolt as well as behind this. They would have broken Solidar into pieces in their efforts to control everything and to destroy my mother, myself, and the rest of the family. I did what was necessary when no one else would or could."

Vaelln stiffened.

"Isn't that what a rex is for, Marshal? To do what he must for his land?" Charyn's voice was pleasant, not that he felt that way. "I won't speak of this again. I trust you won't, either. You're a good man and a good marshal, and I couldn't have done what needed to be done without your help and that of Maitre Alastar."

Vaelln looked to Alastar.

The Maitre nodded. "He's right, Vaelln. In everything he said. It's best to leave it at that."

Vaelln's face lost some of its stiffness.

That was likely the best Charyn could hope for. "We'll need to collect the letter Aunt Doryana wrote, as well as Karyel and Iryella, and allow the staff to deal with the memorial arrangements, modest as they must be."

He turned and started for the staircase. Alastar accompanied him. Vaelln did not.

Charyn wanted to ask Alastar if he'd overreacted with Vaelln, but decided against it. *That would be looking for approval.*

The trooper at the door to Doryana's rooms just said, "In the dressing room, sir."

Charyn stopped by the table desk in the sitting room. There was indeed a letter there, very simply stating that in the event of her untimely death, Doryana's wish was that the guardianship of her grandchildren be exercised by Chelia D'Lorien, widow of Rex Lorien.

Charyn took the letter, and then he and Alastar went into the dressing room.

Doryana had simply used a chair to tie a long silk sash around the heavy cornice of the tall and massive wardrobe in her dressing chamber. Then she'd fastened it around her neck and kicked the chair out from under herself. The wardrobe hadn't even moved. Doryana's contorted face was tinted grayish blue. The sight wasn't pleasant, but it was far less gruesome than the remains of the courier trapped with his explosives inside Howal's shields.

"You thought she would," offered Alastar.

"I forced her to. The last thing she would have wanted was confirmed public disgrace. Without a trial, that won't happen."

"A trial would have made your position seem fairer."

"For a short time, perhaps. But then I would have been seen as vindictive if I seized the holding, and weak if I'd returned it to Karyel."

"You think so?"

"Do you think otherwise after all that's happened in the past two months?" Charyn shook his head. "We need to tell her grandchildren."

"You're going to tell them?"

"Who else?"

Less than a quint later Charyn stood in the receiving study as Alastar ushered in Karyel and Iryella. From what Charyn recalled, Karyel was fourteen, Iryella twelve. Karyel didn't look that much like his grandfather, although he did have sandy blond hair, but his eyes were brown and his face narrower. Iryella looked much the way Charyn thought his mother might have as a girl, with bright blond hair and wide-spaced deep blue eyes.

"This is Rex Charyn," Alastar said, stepping back as the two young people stopped short of Charyn. "He has some things to tell you both."

"Karyel, Iryella . . . something's happened to your grandmother."

"Did you kill her?" demanded the youth. "She said you hated her and Grandfather."

"No. She killed herself rather than face trial for helping to kill my father and trying to kill me. Your grandfather did the same earlier today."

"You killed them."

"I did not," replied Charyn, "but I might as well have because they were guilty, and they knew it. They didn't want to face the disgrace of a trial before the High Justicer." Later they could find out all the reasons.

"You admit it?"

"My father was killed by the orders of your grandfather. Five times people have tried to kill me by his orders. That's murder and treason." Charyn kept his voice absolutely firm, but not cold.

Karyel looked shocked. "They wouldn't do that."

"They did. There's proof of that."

Karyel looked sideways to Alastar.

"There is, unhappily," said the Maitre.

Karyel stood there.

"What will happen to us?" asked Iryella.

"Your grandmother asked that your great-aunt, my mother, be your guardian. Karyel, when you are older, you will hold the lands of your grandfather. You are already High Holder Ryel, but right now you can only run those lands through Lady Chelia. For the moment, you will accompany us to the Chateau D'Rex where you will live for a time."

"Can we go back to Rivages?" asked Iryella.

"Not right now. That will be up to Lady Chelia, but I'm certain that it will not be that long before you can return there."

"And I'll be High Holder?" asked Karyel.

"Yes, but for the next few years, anything you do must be approved by Lady Chelia," said Charyn. "You'll be coming to the chateau with Maitre Alastar and me now. We'll send for your things." He had the feeling that Karyel was all too like his grandfather, but time would tell, and perhaps his mother could change some of that. *Perhaps.*

68

The coach ride back to the Chateau D'Rex was largely silent, and as soon as everyone was out of the coach in the rear courtyard, Charyn sent the driver and a guard back to the Collegium to pick up Palenya. Then, leaving his charges with Howal in the study, he walked back down to see Alastar off.

The Maitre was in the rear courtyard about to mount when Charyn appeared.

"I'm sorry that I've taken most of your day," Charyn offered.

"I cannot say I regret it," replied Alastar. "You appear to have matters under control."

"We'll see." Charyn smiled pleasantly. "You helped me, quietly, but you still owe this family."

Alastar offered a faint smile. "What else do you need?"

"I *need* nothing at present. I want a favor."

Alastar frowned.

"I want you to appoint Palenya as master musician of the Collegium Imago. Permanently. With suitable quarters."

Alastar's frown vanished, and he smiled. "Maitre Alyna would be pleased with that. At any time following next Lundi she would be more than welcome to move to quarters at the Collegium."

"I see you anticipated me."

Alastar shook his head. "Alyna did. She and Palenya have talked quite a bit over the last week."

"Thank you." Even as he spoke the words, Charyn could feel a cold sense of gloom creeping over him, a feeling that remained with him as he headed back upstairs to Chelia's sitting room.

As he stepped into the chamber, Chelia looked up from where she sat at the desk. "You didn't tell me."

"No, I didn't. I had to get to the Chateau D'Council before Doryana heard and destroyed the evidence that she and Uncle Ryel were behind the assassination and all the attacks."

"I take it you were successful. Where is Doryana dear?"

"Dead. She went to gather a few things and took poison, and then hanged herself."

"She always did have a tendency to overdo things."

"Her death has left you with a slight problem," Charyn said quietly.

"Me?" Chelia raised her eyebrows.

"Doryana left a letter naming you as Karyel and Iryella's guardian."

"I doubt she did that of her own free will."

"You know that Uncle poisoned himself to avoid going before a High Justicer. If he had, I could have seized his holding. The lands then went to Doryana, as guardian of Karyel. She was part of the plot. She was the one who actually wrote the threatening notes. She has a very precise script, even in standard merchant hand. The seal ring hidden in her bookcase matches the seal on many of the envelopes containing the threats." Charyn shrugged. "I did point out to her that if a High Justicer found her guilty of complicity in treason I could and would seize the holding."

"You still could have returned it to the heirs after her death," said Chelia.

"I could, but that would have put a blot on the holding. Also, everyone would remember that I seized the lands, and not that I returned them. Also, if I didn't seize them, then everyone would think I was weak. This way . . . I have no choice but to allow the lands to succeed to Karyel. When he is of age."

"My father would be proud of you."

Charyn winced.

"So am I," Chelia went on. "For different reasons. You suggested me as guardian, didn't you?"

"I thought you'd be fair. I also thought that, if anyone could, you might be able to change Karyel for the better. He's more arrogant than I ever was."

"You're not asking much," she said sardonically.

Charyn forced a grin. "It will give you something meaningful to do, and it's something I would end up handing over to you if I'd been named as guardian, because you'd do it better."

"I never thought I'd go back to Rivages," she mused. "Now, after winter, I suppose I must."

"I hope that won't be too much of a travail." Charyn hadn't thought of that.

"I will make many changes."

"Whatever you see fit to do."

"And I will insist on handling the regial balls until you find some-one who is suitable to you personally to marry."

"I wouldn't have it any other way." Charyn frowned. "There is one thing that bothers me. Ryel wanted us all dead. The one thing that doesn't fit is that Churwyl could easily have killed Bhayrn. That would have made it easier for High Holder Regial to succeed as rex. But Ryel obviously instructed Churwyl not to kill Bhayrn."

"You're missing one thing, dear," said Chelia. "Brother dear was more devious than that. He didn't want Bhayrn dead. Not immediately. He wanted Bhayrn to succeed you because Bhayrn would need a regent, and no woman can act as a regent, and as head of the High Council . . ."

Charyn nodded, but he also realized that, because Bhayrn acted before he thought, before long, no one would be that displeased if some accident befell Bhayrn, and no one would likely have ever connected Ryel to the attacks because he would have been an excellent regent for Bhayrn . . . until . . .

Chelia's face became more serious. "Palenya?"

"I've talked to Maitre Alastar. He and Maitre Alyna will be offering her a position as master musician to the Collegium, along with suitable quarters. I'd thought to supplement that with a stipend, the way chateau guards are when they've served faithfully. I haven't told her yet, obviously."

"Don't drag it out, dear. It won't be fair to her nor good for you."

Charyn knew that, but he didn't want to talk about it at the moment. "I need to take you to see Karyel and Iryella. They're in my study with Howal."

"Of course." Chelia immediately rose.

Charyn realized, belatedly, that he had been standing the entire time since entering the sitting room. He moved to the door and held it for his mother.

Once they were in the corridor, she asked, "What do they know?"

"I told them that both their grandparents arranged Father's assassination and the attacks on me and the regial family, and that when proof appeared, they took their lives to avoid public disgrace."

"That was all?"

"I did say that there was a great deal of proof. Other than that . . . no."

"Don't tell Bhayrn any more than that, either."

"I hadn't planned on it."

"Good."

Moencriff opened the study door when Charyn and Chelia approached, then closed it behind them.

Both Karyel and Iryella were seated at the conference table, but immediately stood when they saw Charyn. Both appeared very subdued.

"This is the Lady Chelia . . . and my mother," Charyn said. "She is your guardian, under the protection of the rex." He added the last words just to emphasize Chelia's authority.

"You both have been through a great deal," Chelia offered warmly. "We need to get you settled here—at least until the weather is warm enough that we can safely return to Rivages. I thought we'd begin by deciding which rooms would be suitable for each of you, and then, if you're feeling better, I'll show you the chateau so that you can get to know your way around."

She smiled. "Shall we go?"

From where he stood beside his desk, Charyn watched as Iryella immediately moved toward Chelia, followed more slowly by Karyel.

Once the door closed, Howal moved toward Charyn. "I didn't have a chance to tell you, sir. You got a dispatch directly from Sea Marshal Tynan. It's on the corner of the desk. Also, all of the materials you used at the meeting are in your second drawer. I didn't want to leave them out."

"Thank you." A direct dispatch meant trouble. *What else?* Charyn picked up the envelope, opened it, extracted the dispatch, and began to read.

> Your Grace—
> In view of your immediate and pressing interest in Regional Governor Voralch, I am sending this directly to you with a copy to Marshal Vaelln.
>
> As soon as we received orders to place the governor in custody, I immediately sent a detachment of naval marines, under the command of Major Helsior, to the temporary residence of the governor. The major learned that Voralch had departed the previous day. Further inquiries revealed that he sailed aboard an Abiertan vessel—*Maid of the Isles*—the very day he left the residence. He also took with him the majority of the golds previously held in the Regional Governor's account at the Banque D'Solis, which he had withdrawn under the pretext of needing to make a deposit on a new governor's residence.

Several crates belonging to him were also reported as being
loaded onto the Abiertan vessel. It is probable that they contained valuables taken from the ancient palace . . .

Charyn shook his head. He wordlessly handed the dispatch to Howal.
You should have relieved him immediately. Another lesson learned too late.

As he stood and walked to the window, where he pulled back the
hangings and looked out into the courtyard, he supposed that ruling would
always be a balance between patience and decisive swift action—and
gaining the wisdom to know what problem required which approach.

Abruptly, he turned. "I'll be back in a bit. I need to go to the kitchen
and make some arrangements." Then he stopped. "There's no reason for
you to stay around here, Howal. Go get some rest or food. Or take a
mount and go back to the Collegium for the night."

"I'd feel better staying at the chateau, but it has been a long day."

Charyn grinned. "Go. I'll see you in the morning."

Howal grinned back.

Charyn waited for him to leave, then told Moencriff, "I'll be back
before long."

"Yes, sir."

When he returned from the kitchen and talking to Hassala, he had
no more entered the study than Bhayrn appeared, moving inside even
as Moencriff announced him.

"Your guard wouldn't let me wait in the study for you."

"That might be because they have orders not to let anyone in the study
when I'm not there," replied Charyn. "What do you have in mind?"

"How could you even think of letting Mother foster those brats? How?
After what their grandfather did?"

"That's exactly why she is. Do you want one of Ryel's sisters or
daughters doing it . . . with how they must hate us?"

"I still don't see why you didn't seize their holding and be done
with it."

"Because I can't under the law. They have to be convicted of treason
or high crimes. Why on Terahnar do you think they both killed themselves?"

Bhayrn was silent for a moment. "They can get away with that?"

"If you call killing yourself getting away with something, yes, they
can. If you read the histories, it's happened more than once."

"But in the High Holder revolt . . ."

"If both father and heir take up arms in revolt, that's considered equivalent to conviction before a High Justicer. But it has to be both. That's why Father's brother's son is still High Holder Regial."

"Oh . . . sometimes the laws are stupid. You should change them."

"I have changed a few already. There will be more. Is there anything else?"

"By next week, can I go riding . . . ?"

"By all means, if you wish to freeze, but I'd suggest the coach."

"Most humorous . . ."

After Bhayrn left, Charyn moved to the window where he could watch for the coach returning Palenya while he thought over the day, wondering what he might have missed that he should have done.

There's bound to be something.

CODA

Mardi morning Charyn woke early, well before Palenya. In the grayness before true dawn, knowing that she would be gone before long, he let his eyes run across her face, taking in the fine, but disarrayed dark hair, even the tiny lines running from the corners of her eyes, her thin but well-formed lips, and the angle of her high cheekbones. He had insisted on spending the majority of the last five days, and all the nights, with her, including long glasses trying to perfect his playing of Farray's Nocturne Number Three, but now he had little more than a glass before she would be gone.

He'd done what he could, including the account at the Banque D'Excelsis and the healthy monthly stipend, little as it was compared to what she had given him. Pushing that thought away, he concentrated on her. He tried not to move at all, but successful as he was, she slowly opened her eyes and smiled.

"You are sweet," she murmured.

"For a rex," he countered.

"For a man." She leaned forward and kissed him gently. "You will find someone who is right for you. Just do not settle . . ."

"For anyone less than you?" Charyn forced a smile.

"Certainly not. I'm not that special."

Charyn wasn't going to argue that point. He already knew she was wrong. She was special . . . even if she was right about what he needed in his choice of a wife.

She eased back from him. "I need to dress."

"We need to dress. I will see you off." He'd wanted a last breakfast with her, but she had demurred, and he had acceded to her wish to leave quietly and early, just as she had arrived more than a half year ago.

Because he kept looking at her as she dressed, he had to hurry to finish getting his clothes on, wash and shave quickly. With a smile on her face, she waited for him to pull on one of his regial green jackets. Then they walked from his quarters.

She turned her head. "You will redecorate the bedchamber."

"I will. I promised."

"Thank you."

The upper corridor was silent in the dim light cast by a single lit lamp on a wall sconce, and their steps echoed through the space above and below the grand stairway as they descended to the main level.

A chateau guard stepped forward, bowing to Palenya. "Musician Palenya, the coach is ready at the foot of the main steps."

"Thank you," she replied softly, but firmly, before turning to Charyn with an amused and warm smile.

"There is no way I could let you leave by the rear courtyard. You may be leaving the Chateau D'Rex, but you're going to be the music master for the two most powerful people in Solidar. That should be recognized, at least by me." He offered his arm, and they walked out through the door held by the guard, and then past a pair of chateau guards in dress uniforms, who presented arms as they passed and started down the white stone steps, unmarked, as they had been for generations, by the footsteps of the past.

When they reached the coach, Charyn opened the door, then lifted her gloved hand and kissed it before releasing it. He could barely see as she bent forward and kissed him on the cheek, but he felt the dampness on her face for a brief instant before she straightened, then turned and entered the coach.

Watching the coach as it headed down the drive toward the ring road, carrying Palenya to the Collegium, Charyn realized, not for the first time, that regardless of the depth of passion and desire, and the power of position, trying to attain some dreams could only destroy the dreamer . . . *And Solidar.*

As the coach vanished from his sight, he slowly turned and walked up the white stone steps.